17⁹⁵

THE YEAR'S BEST

Fantasy & Horror

THE YEAR'S BEST

Fantasy & Horror

THIRTEENTH ANNUAL COLLECTION

Edited by

Ellen Datlow & Terri Windling

St. Martin's Griffin ❦ New York

Contents

Acknowledgments

It takes a large team of people to put together a book as extensive as this one. Many people contributed books and music for review; many magazines and web sites were consulted; many librarians provided assistance in Tucson and Devon; and I'm grateful to them all. The fantasy half of the book would be a much poorer thing without the crack Tucson team: assistant editors Richard and Mardelle Kunz, and library scout Bill Murphy. My heartfelt thanks to them, as well as to my partner-in-crime, Ellen Datlow, our inimitable cover artist, Thomas Canty, our patient St. Martin's Press editor, Gordon Van Gelder, and his assistant, Bryan Cholfin, and our hardworking series creator/packager, Jim Frenkel, along with his assistants, Kristopher O'Higgins and Seth Johnson. The following folks also contributed to this volume in various ways: Charles de Lint, Harlan Ellison, Robert Gould, Tom Harlan, Ellen Kushner, Joe Monti, Patrick Nielsen Hayden, Andy Heidel, Delia Sherman, Ellen Steiber, Jim Thomas, Meredyth Inman, Steve Pasechnick, and Jane Yolen. More information (including submission guidelines for future volumes) can be found on the Endicott Studio of Mythic Arts web site: www.endicott-studio.com.   —T.W.

Producing an annual series like *The Year's Best Fantasy and Horror* requires the cooperation of a number of people. I'd like to thank the publishers, editors, writers, and readers who send material and make suggestions every year. This year I'd particularly like to thank Linda Marotta, Jenna Felice, Bill Congreve, and F. Gwynplaine MacIntyre for their input. Special thanks to Kelly Link for her help.

   Thanks go to Jim Frenkel, our packager, and his assistants, Kristopher O'Higgins and Seth Johnson; to our in-house editor, Gordon Van

Gelder, and his assistant, Bryan Cholfin; and to Tom Canty, for his imaginative and elegant cover art and design.

Finally, thanks to my co-editor and friend, Terri Windling, for her graceful and complementary participation in our annual marathon.

I'd like to acknowledge the following magazines and catalogs for invaluable information and descriptions of material I was unable to get hold of: *Locus, Science Fiction Chronicle, Publishers Weekly, The Washington Post Book World, The New York Times Book Review*, the DreamHaven catalog, *Necrofile, Hellnotes*, the DarkEcho Newsletter, *The Heliocentric Network,* and *Gila Queen's Guide to Markets*.   —E. D.

Thanks to our editorial team, Datlow/Windling, for a great job of selecting the very best short works of the year and writing fine, comprehensive, yet concise summations; thanks, too, are due to Ed Bryant and Seth Johnson for their insightful columns. Big, big thanks to Kristopher O'Higgins, who has done an extraordinary job with permissions this year, even while being hit with several waves of "last-minute" additions; and thanks to our interns, Emily Netzel, Tracy Berg, Lauren DeAre, and Sean Hobbs, for their help. Thanks also to Melanie Orpen and Holly Laux O'Higgins, Insty-Prints on Park, and the many others who helped in various ways too numerous to mention.   —J. F.

Summation 1999: Fantasy

Terri Windling

Welcome to the thirteenth edition of *The Year's Best Fantasy and Horror*. This anthology series was created to be an annual celebration of the best in nonrealist literature—ranging from magic realism (à la Márquez) to imaginary world fiction (à la Tolkien), as well as from dark stories of supernatural magic to those of psychological horror. By combining works from the genres of "fantasy" and "horror," along with magical tales from "mainstream fiction," Ellen and I seek to ignore the limiting boundaries that strict genre categorization places upon contemporary writers. Thus all nonrealist writing rooted in myth, magic, and surrealism is eligible for inclusion in this collection, which contains selections from sources as diverse as *The Magazine of Fantasy & Science Fiction* and *The New Yorker*. This fantasy/horror/mainstream combination reflects the wide spectrum of magical fiction published each year in English-language publications—and we are firm believers in the idea that the three fields are greatly enriched when their stories are viewed side by side. But for those readers who maintain a diehard preference for fantasy over horror, or vice versa, please note that the fantasy stories carry my initials after their introductions, horror tales carry Ellen Datlow's, and stories in the shadow realm between carry both our initials (with the acquiring editor listed first).

This introductory summation, for those new to the series, provides an overview of fantasy publishing in the year just past, with lists of recommended novels, nonfiction, children's books, art books, etc. Usually at this point I wax on a bit about what a great year it was in the fantasy field, for we've been blessed by many such lately. But 1999,

I'm sorry to report from the trenches, was not a banner year. Short fiction was as strong as ever (as you'll see from the stories in this book), but novel-length fiction was disappointing. There *was* a handful of excellent books (such as *Minions of the Moon* by Richard Bowes, in genre, and *Prince* by Ib Michael, in mainstream fiction), but nothing close to the glorious abundance of extraordinary novels that have appeared in the last few years. I've been pondering the question of why this should be so, as well as talking to editors and publishers, and the explanation is a simple one. I don't believe we're witnessing a sudden decline of interest in magical fiction; rather, 1999's lackluster offerings are a direct result of the particularly sterling year we had in 1998. Many of the fantasy field's top authors gave us their best efforts in 1998 (Guy Gavriel Kay, George R. R. Martin, Patricia A. McKillip, Sean Stewart, Sean Russell, and Jane Yolen, to name just a few of them), and were absent from the publishing lists while working on their next books. These writers, as well as the field at large, seemed to be catching their breaths in 1999, making it a good year to check out some of the newer talent, such as Elizabeth Haydon, Thomas Harlan, China Miéville, Judy Budnitz, and Valery Leith.

The slimmer than usual offering of quality fantasy fiction for adult readers contrasts with a bumper crop of thoroughly enchanting novels in the children's book field. Love Harry Potter or hate him, there's no denying that he's had a massive impact on the New York publishing industry. It's still too soon to tell whether a significant portion of Harry Potter fans will move on to other fantasy books (as readers did in the wake of Tolkien's bestsellerdom in the 1970s), but my best guess is that a number of them will, now that the word "fantasy" has lost its faint whiff of disrepute in the children's book field. (This, despite the fact that so much classic children's fiction—Carroll, Nesbit, Eager, Baum, Lewis, Tolkien, etc.—is indisputably fantastic in both senses of the word.) Already we're seeing a surge in the amount of children's fantasy being published, with bigger advertising budgets and expectations. According to editors at several publishing houses, this is a trend that's only just beginning—and one that bodes well for the larger fantasy genre, considering that several of the field's best writers once came to us from children's books. We have not only J. K. Rowling to thank for this, but also the brilliant Philip Pullman, whose best-selling books *The Golden Compass* and *The Subtle Knife* are complex, hard-hitting, and literary enough to gladden any discerning reader's heart—and to ensure that "children's fantasy" isn't limited to light, humorous books of the Potter sort. (The most interesting article on the Potter phenomenon I read this past year, by the way, is "Harry Potter's Girl Trouble," about the dubious role of female characters in Rowling's series. This insightful piece by Christine Schoefer can be found in the archives of *Salon* magazine, www.salon.com).

While Rowling and Potter will probably be the dominant influences in magical children's fiction for some time to come, in adult fiction (both in the genre and the mainstream) Gabriel García Márquez continues to be a strong inspiration for young writers from Latin and non-Latin cultures alike, as do, to a lesser extent, other magic realist/surrealist authors like Jorge Luis Borges, Italo Calvino, Isaac Bashevis Singer, Ben Okri, and Angela Carter. Judging from the books that have crossed my desk in the last thirteen years, I believe it is impossible to overstate the impact Márquez has had on late–twentieth century fiction the world over. In our country, *One Hundred Years of Solitude* is a book that, more than any other, gives young writers the permission and the courage to stray from the path of strict realism (and Gordon Lish–style minimalism) to which creative writing graduate programs all over the country seem so determined to steer them. In the fantasy genre, a particularly Márquezean way of explicating the modern world through quiet moments of transcendent enchantment can be found in the works of quite a number of our top writers (Crowley, Fowler, Carroll, Goldstein, etc.), while Angela Carter's sensuous, folkloric work has inspired a modern renaissance in adult fairy-tale fiction. At the same time, literary Tolkienesque fantasy (aka imaginary world or traditional fantasy) has not disappeared—1998 marked a strong resurgence of the form. The year 1999, it must be noted, only brought us a very few good novels of the type, but this spike downward seems to be temporary, as I've already received several good Tolkienesque novels to review for the year 2000.

On the whole, the lines drawn (by publishers, bookstore managers, and critics) between mainstream fiction and genre fiction continue to get blurrier every year, and I long for a day when all these books sit side by side on a shelf marked Fiction. Modern bookselling being what it is, however, books are still organized and sold by category labels, leading a group of writers from the fantasy and science fiction genres to come up with a label of their own: interstitial fiction. Here's a brief excerpt from the somewhat (but not entirely) tongue-in-cheek *Interstitial Arts Manifesto*:

> Perhaps you've had this experience. You read a book, go to a gallery opening, attend a concert. You come out exhilarated, excited, enthralled. "It was great!" you tell your friends. "I loved it!" "So, what is it?" they ask. "It was . . ." You think for a moment. "Sort of . . ." You wave your hands helplessly in the air. "Different," you conclude weakly. Pressed, you can

find analogies. A book is a "magic realist Victorian biography in the guise of a mystery novel." A painting is "symbolist Renaissance surrealism." Music performed on sitar and didgeridoo is "Afro-Celtic-punk." What all these different art forms have in common is their resistance to easy definition, to niche-labeling by either marketers or critics. It is art that is hard to pigeonhole, hard to describe in one simple sentence, art that lies in the interstices, between the cracks of recognized genres. It is Interstitial Art. Our society likes to divide its arts into tidy categories. When we walk into a bookstore, we rarely see all the newly written novels sitting side-by-side. Instead, they are divided into categories, subcategories, and genres. There's a special section for novels containing crimes and mysteries; a special section for books by women, by gay and by black authors . . . science fiction and fantasy have their own little ghetto segregated from "literature." If Jane Austen were writing today, no doubt her work would be shelved under romance. Of course, labels can be useful. Such labels enable merchants and marketers to treat creation as Product, to be sold and marketed in mass quantities. For consumers, labels mean we have to spend less of our precious time distinguishing one created work from another. Genre label equals recognizable product, with clearly defined parameters and narrowly allowable variations within each one. For artists working in forms that fall between the genre cracks, too often these labels are arbitrary and ill-fitting. As Interstitial Artists, we believe that fine art can be made within any genre, and from even the most unlikely of materials (and their combinations), provided it is done with skill and style. A Mexican-American woman writes her autobiography as a magic realist tale that includes both poems and recipes (*House of Houses* by Pat Mora). An American jazz composer finds classical Indian musicians who will play his tunes and improvise their own (*Antigravity* by Warren Senders). Tibetan religious chants join with Native American flute (*Winds of Devotion* by Nawang Khechog and R. Carlos Nakai). A British-Portuguese painter draws on traditional fairy-tale images to create a perverse, sensual, feminist dialogue (Paula Rego). A comic book weaves together myth and gender, history, literature, and complex illustration (Neil Gaiman's *The Sandman*). A "folksinger" incorporates Sufi prayer and Scottish pipes in a meditation on mortality (Loreena McKennitt). How do you label it all? What do you call it? We call it Interstitial Art: a label for art that can't be labeled, a definition for work that can't be defined.

For more on this topic (and the related Young Trollopes movement) look on the Web at www.endicott-studio.com/ia.html. For other good discussions and observations on the state of the contemporary fantasy and horror fields, I recommend the archives of the *Event Horizon* web site, www.eventhorizon.com, *The New York Review of Science Fiction,* and the author interviews conducted by Charles N. Brown in *Locus* magazine.

Having taken a general look at the state of fantasy publishing in 1999, let's turn to the books that were published last year and some recommended titles broken down by type (those pesky labels again). As usual, I won't claim to have read *every* magical, mythical, or surrealist work published in this country and abroad in 1999, but I made a darn good stab at it. Here are the best books I found among the five-hundred-odd books we received for review (gathered by my hard-working assistant editors, Richard and Mardelle Kunz). We think there were some real gems among them, and we hope that you'll agree.

Top Twenty

Each year in this spot we list twenty novels that no fan of magical literature should miss—books chosen not only for their excellence of craft and overall entertainment value, but also those that give an indication of the direction in which the fantasy field is heading. In 1999 the strongest area of fantasy fiction was, hands down, in Young Adult books. In recognition of the strong contribution made by YA writers to our field in 1999, you'll find seven of the best YA fantasy titles listed among this year's Top Twenty, recommended to readers of all ages.

Skellig by David Almond (Delacorte): Don't be mislead by the slim size of Almond's novel, or its YA label—this is a book that deals, in deceptively straightforward prose, with the grand themes of life and literature: birth, death, hope, despair, mystery, tragedy, and redemption. (Artistic influences here, the author said in one interview, are the works of Italo Calvino, Gabriel García Márquez, and Raymond Carver—quite a trio to inspire a children's book.) It's the story of a boy who finds a broken man with tattered wings huddled in the garden shed. Michael shares this strange and troubling secret only with his new friend, Mina, while his sister lies in the hospital and life crumbles around his family. *Skellig*, which won England's Whitbread Award, is a rare and beautiful book, full of art, owls, natural history, and the poetry of William Blake.

Tamsin by Peter S. Beagle (Roc): One of our field's best writers turns his hand to YA fiction in this suspenseful tale of ghosts, faeries, and medieval history, set on a ramshackle English farm. Jenny is a New York City girl who bitterly resents being stuck in rural Dorset when her mother remarries, until she comes into contact with the magical spirits who haunt the place—including a troublesome boggart, a shifty pooka, and the three-hundred-year-old ghost of Tamsin Willoughby. Beagle does a fine job of bringing modern and Jacobean characters together, mixed with large dollops of British folklore, in a tale that hinges on the bloody history of the Monmouth rebellion in Dorset, in the time of King James II.

The Folk Keeper by Franny Billingsley (Atheneum): This atmospheric YA novel is told through the voice of young Corin Stonewall, a fiercely independent orphan who has cut off her long, uncanny silver hair and disguised herself as a boy in order to become a keeper of the "Folk" (dangerous subterranean creatures who will despoil the land and livestock if not kept regularly appeased). A dying man's bequest takes Corin away from her underground world to the halls of a vast seaside estate. Here she comes face to face with a past full of secrets, tragedy, and magic. The narrative voice here is an uncommon one, and the imaginary world convincing, even though we see only a corner of it. Billingsley uses standard folklore ingredients, including a wealth of selkie (seal-people) legends, but she cooks them up into a highly original, memorable story.

The Rainy Season by James P. Blaylock (Ace): Blaylock's chilling ghost tale is set in the author's usual territory of southern California, combining modern and nineteenth-century characters in a taut psychological drama. Phil Ainsworth, photographer and widower, is the sole guardian of a young orphaned niece, who comes to live with him in the rambling old house he inherited from his mother. An unusually heavy rainy season fills a long-dry well on the property, setting the story in motion—for it's a well in which a child was ritually drowned one hundred years ago, giving it magical properties that others (including ghosts from the past) are eager to exploit. Unlike so many supernatural stories, which get bogged down by their special effects, Blaylock uses the magical elements to explore characters and their relationships. *The Rainy Season* is yet another gem from the man *Library Journal* correctly called "one of the most distinctive contributors to American magic realism."

Minions of the Moon by Richard Bowes (Tor): Kevin Grierson is a man with a Shadow. This reckless, destructive part of himself dominated his troubled youth (hustling on the streets of Boston) and his subsequent years in New York City (addicted to drugs, drink, power, anything that would bring another rush). Kevin's Shadow isn't just a metaphor, however, it's a doppelganger with a life of its own. In order to confront it, he must also confront the dark years of the past and his brutal life story. This is a novel about coming of age the hard way, and the things we do to survive. *Minions of the Moon* shows this World Fantasy Award–winning author at the top of his form, recommended for fans of dark fantasy of the Neil Gaiman or Jonathan Carroll sort.

Enchantment by Orson Scott Card (Del Rey): The latest novel from this multi-award-winning author is a unique adult retelling of the Sleeping Beauty legend, set in a Carpathian forest and linking the ninth and twentieth centuries. When Ivan Petrovich Smetski was ten years old, his Jewish family left Russia for the United States. Now a grown man, he is haunted by vivid memories of the old country, particularly one from his last days there, when he stumbled into a clearing in a forest where a woman lay fast asleep. Ivan returns to Russia eventually and finds the clearing once more. This time he kisses his princess awake and follows her back into time. *Enchantment* is a bewitching book from a writer who can spin even lesser materials into gold. Here he has all of Russian folklore and history to work with, and the result is pure magic.

The Marriage of Sticks by Jonathan Carroll (Tor): This is a controversial book. For some Carroll fans, it's the best one yet; for others (and I'm among them), the ending disappoints. Nonetheless, Carroll is one of the most consistently original authors in the dark fantasy field. His skill at character study alone makes this a Top Twenty book (not to mention his habit of tossing off breathtakingly insightful metaphors every other page), whatever your opinion of the plot. *The Marriage of Sticks* is the story of a self-possessed antiques dealer and her passionate affair with a dazzling married man—an affair which is going a shade too smoothly for the protagonist's comfort. She seems to suspect, as Carroll's readers certainly do, that the author will pull the rug out from under her soon—and he does, introducing one sinister element after another until her life has become completely surreal. Then Carroll pulls out all the stops.

The King of Shadows by Susan Cooper (McElderry Books): This is a darn near perfect book, so you'll have to forgive me if I gush a bit. Cooper, of course, is the Newbery Award–winning author of the "Dark is Rising" series—but don't expect epic fantasy here. *The King of Shadows* is a smaller tale, a beautifully crafted YA time-travel novel about a young American actor who travels to England (with a boys' theater troupe) and finds himself transported back to Shakespeare's time. This book works on three levels at once: as a fantasy tale, as an impeccably researched historical novel about life at the old Globe Theater, and as a deeply moving psychological story exploring the nature of death, loss, eternity, and art. If you can finish the last page with a dry eye, you're a better man than I.

The Birchbark House by Louise Erdrich (Hyperion Press): The winner of last year's World Fantasy Award (for *The Antelope Wife*) is back with another warm-hearted tale infused with Native American myth and history, this time written for young readers, but ageless in its appeal. Little Frog is the sole survivor of her tribe's disastrous first contact with

Europeans. Taken in by an Ojibway family on Madeline Island in Lake Superior, Little Frog (and the reader) are gently drawn into Ojibway culture over the course of four seasons. This evocative nineteenth-century story grew out of Erdrich's research into family history (she's Chippewa/Turtle Mountain Band Ojibway), and stories told by Ojibway elders about the spiritual history of Madeline Island. The book is illustrated with delicate black and white drawings by the author.

Memoranda by Jeffrey Ford (Avon): This is the sequel to Ford's World Fantasy Award–winning novel *Physiognomy*, a sardonic, densely allegorical, dark fantasy of ideas. The protagonist is Cley, the physiognomist of the previous book, who has turned his back on his former calling. The Well-Built City has fallen. Cley's allies are building a new society in the ruins. But the tyrannical Drachton Below has unleashed a plague of never-ending sleep, and Cley must find the antidote, journeying into the landscape and "memory palace" of Drachton Below's mind. Ford's story (the middle volume of a trilogy) is told in hypnotically beautiful prose, making fascinating use of Renaissance ideas about the nature of memory.

The White Bone by Barbara Gowdy (Holt): This is a major new work from an acclaimed Canadian writer (*Mister Sandman*, etc.), a literary novel told from the point of view of African elephants facing extinction. It's the story of an elephant named Young Mud, adopted into the She-S clan when her own is decimated by ivory hunters and drought in the sub-Sahara. When this clan, too, is nearly wiped out, the survivors set off on a cross-continental quest to find the legendary White Bone, in hope that this will lead them to the Safe Place (away from us humans). Much more than just "the *Watership Down* of elephants," this is a mystical tale of epic proportions that brings the African landscape vividly to life. *The White Bone* is a remarkable achievement, a rousing good read, and a painful one. The book's nomination for several major awards comes as no surprise.

Black Light by Elizabeth Hand (HarperCollins): Hand's sixth novel is related to *Waking the Moon* (and other "Kamensic" stories), a modern mythic tale that falls in the shadow realm between fantasy and horror. Seventeen-year-old Charlotte Moylan is the precocious daughter of actors who were once involved with the film director Axel Kern, a Warhol-like figure who lords it over the seedier side of the New York art world. Charlotte has been raised in Kamensic Village, an upstate town with more than its share of dark pagan mysteries. Kern maintains a mansion there but hasn't set foot in it for years. Now he's coming back to throw the mother of all Halloween parties, to which the Moylans are invited. Thus the stage is set for a sensual, diabolical novel chock full of Hand's usual preoccupations: old gods (in this case, Dionysis and Ariadne), pagan rites in the contemporary world, artists and their acolytes, sinister secret societies, witches, warlocks, and mystics. *Black Light* is ingeniously plotted, suspenseful, and skillfully written.

A Red Heart of Memories by Nina Kiriki Hoffman (Ace): For fans of contemporary fantasy (of the Charles de Lint or Alice Hoffman variety), here's a book by a different Hoffman (no relation) that I strongly recommend. Set in the Pacific Northwest, it's an entertaining, insightful tale about modern magic—not only magic of the supernatural sort, but the quieter magic of love and friendship that can transform desperate lives. The story is about young Matt, a homeless waif for whom all objects have spirit—she talks to tables, shoes, parking meters and, what's more, they respond to her. Edmund, a witch, is a mystery—he appeared one day in a crumbling stone wall. When the two pair up to seek Edmund's missing past, adventure and peril are in store. If Nina Hoffman isn't yet as well known as Alice Hoffman or de Lint, novels like this one indicate that it's only a matter of time.

Confessions of an Ugly Stepsister by Gregory Maguire (Regan Books/HarperCollins): This new novel by the author of *Wicked* is a sophisticated adult fairy tale that you'll find over on the mainstream shelves. It's a clever resetting of the Cinderella story in a market town in seventeenth-century Holland. Maguire tells most of the tale through the eyes of Iris, a plain, intelligent child whose mother marries a tulip merchant possessed of a strange and beautiful daughter. (The other stepsister is the oxlike, gentle Ruth, apparently retarded.) Maguire beautifully evokes the world of Dutch burghers, painters, and tulip speculators as he explores the nature of beauty, art, and the stories we tell about our lives.

The Prince by Ib Michael, translated from the Danish by Barbara Haveland (FS&G): This engaging work of Scandinavian magic realism was my favorite novel of 1999, set in a fishing village on the coast of Denmark in 1912. Malte, the main protagonist (in a rich extended cast), is an adolescent boy who spends his summers at the Sea View guest house—abandoned by his self-absorbed mother as she pursues a series of wealthy escorts. One day a coffin washes ashore, with a perfectly preserved dead sailor inside. This sets off a long chain of events involving a mysterious shape-shifting spirit, an elf in amber, a lighthouse keeper, a mute girl, a parlor maid and her false lover, an Inuit child, and an old woman in a tower by the sea. Part fairy tale, part historical novel of the Louis de Bernieres variety, it's a splendid book, laced with wit, compassion, and Rilke's poetry.

Spinners by Donna Jo Napoli and Richard Tchen (Dutton): Napoli (author of *Zel, Sirena,* etc.) is one of the best writers working with fairy-tale material today, creating psychologically complex novels that are published as YA fiction, but read and beloved by adult readers, too. Her latest is a collaboration with Richard Tchen, focusing on "Rumplestilt-skin" this time. It's the story of a girl with astonishing weaving skills, of a troubled father, and of a cruel and greedy king—ordinary components of the tale turned extraordinary by this talented team. If you enjoy the novels of Robin McKinley, Patricia A. McKillip, and Jane Yolen, I recommend *Spinners* highly.

The Stars Compel by Michaela Roessner (Tor): Roessner's latest is the sequel to her sparkling Renaissance fantasy *The Stars Dispose,* and is every bit as good as that volume—a delicious feast of magic, may-hem, and food, set in sixteenth-century Italy. It's the story of Tommaso Arista, son of two famous chefs in a magical Florence in which cooking is inextricably bound with politics and sorcery. It's also the tale of his employer, friend, and confidante, Catherine de Médicis, as she maneu-vers through the schemes of popes and princes and puts her own mark on society. This one's a delight, pure fun, and comes complete with recipes.

The Ground Beneath Her Feet by Salman Rushdie (Holt): Another tour de force from Rushdie (does he write any other kind of fiction these days?), as he wings his way through several continents and forty-odd years of pop music. The Orpheus myth is at the center of this extravagant book about the undying love between a supernaturally gifted Indian musician and a strong-willed half-Indian diva (as seen through the eyes of another one of her lovers, a world-renowned photographer). Set in a universe parallel to our own, Rushdie plays fast and loose with history, celebrity iconography, and popular culture in a book in which the lan-guage is as intoxicating as the breathless, globe-trotting plot. Rushdie has become a writer so good that it's almost frightening.

A Series of Unfortunate Events, Book 1: The Bad Beginning by Lemony Snicket, illustrated by Brett Helquist (HarperCollins): "Dear Reader," cautions the author on the back of this little novel, "I'm sorry to say that the book you are holding in your hands is extremely un-pleasant. It tells an unhappy tale about three very unlucky children. Even though they are charming and clever, the Baudelaire siblings lead lives filled with misery and woe. In this short book alone, the three youngsters encounter a greedy and repulsive villain, itchy clothing, a disastrous fire, a plot to steal their fortune, and cold porridge for breakfast." Well, there's nothing like truth in advertising. It *is* an exceedingly unpleasant book, and wickedly funny.

The Intuitionist by Colson Whitehead (Anchor): Whitehead's interstitial novel could be called mystery, science fiction, fantasy, alternate history, or all of the above. It takes place in an unnamed, high-rise city much like Manhattan (with nineteenth century, twentieth century, and near-future elements), and is the story of Lila Mae Watson, the city's first black, female elevator inspector. When an elevator comes crashing down soon after Watson inspected and certified it, she smells a rat somewhere in the old boys' network of the Department of Elevator Inspectors. Seeking to clear her name, and to uncover the truth behind this tragedy, Watson is drawn into an underworld of increasingly shady characters, and learns about the lost writings of James Fulton, the Intuitionist—whose perfect Black Box would make all other elevators obsolete. In the guise of a stylish noir thriller, Whitehead skewers race and gender issues, riffs on history past and the future, and all the while tells a damn good tale. Highly recommended.

First Novels

In 1999, three writers made particularly strong debuts: Thomas Harlan, Elizabeth Haydon, and Judy Budnitz. *The Shadow of Ararat* by Thomas Harlan (Tor) is a sweeping, epic-length novel set in an alternate version of the seventh-century, in which the Roman Empire still stands. Brimming with myth, magic, well-researched historical speculation, cleverly plotted military strategies, and a far-flung cast of vivid characters, this is Must Reading for anyone who likes muscular adventure fantasy written with intelligence and panache. *Rhapsody* by Elizabeth Haydon (Tor) is a superior quest-type fantasy about an excourtesan and her companions on the run from magical forces. This, too, is a page-turner—but it's also beautifully crafted and ingeniously conceived, distinguished by the author's skillful use of elements drawn from Norse, Celtic, and other animist mythologies. *If I Told You Once* by Judy Budnitz (Picador) is a family saga with a folkloric tone, similar to Budnitz's short story "Hershel" (about a village baby-maker) reprinted in last year's volume of *The Year's Best Fantasy and Horror*. There are flourishes reminiscent of Angela Carter and Isaac Bashevis Singer in this unusual magic realist tale, which follows four generations of women from Eastern Europe to America.

Other noteworthy debuts: *The Angle Quickest for Flight* by Steven Kotler (Four Walls Eight Windows Press) is a contemporary quest novel about the search for an ancient manuscript (believed to contain Jesus's own words) by a runaway boy in Santa Fe, a semi-retired smuggler, a sinister Catholic mystic, and an albino Rastafarian rock climber. It's an uneven book with distinct first-novel flaws, but also erudite and uncommon. *The Gumshoe, the Witch and the Virtual Corpse* by Keith Hartman (Meisha Merlin Publishing) is another problematic small press book, but worth taking a look at. This murder mystery is set in an alternate version of our own world where pagan magic is real and its practitioners are in conflict with Christian and other religious groups. *In the Forests of the Night* by Amelia Atwater-Rhodes (Delacorte) is the tale of a teenage vampire on the streets of New York City. The book is fast-paced and enjoyable, if not particularly original, and most notable for the well-advertised fact that the author is fourteen years old.

Contemporary and Urban Fantasy

1999 was a good year for contemporary and urban fantasy—a category consisting of contemporary tales in real-world settings infused with magic (sometimes differing from mainstream "magic realism" only by the fantasy label on the cover). James P. Blaylock, Richard Bowes, Jonathan Carroll, and Elizabeth Hand published good novels of this sort (listed in the Top Twenty). Here are four more books that I strongly recommend, by three of the fantasy field's best authors and one talented newcomer: *Dark Cities Underground* by Lisa Goldstein (Tor) is an intriguing book that ought to be longer, packed so full of characters (human and inhuman), ideas, and convoluted plot twists that at 252 pages it whizzes by with the speed of the subway trains at its heart. Jeremy Jones is running from disturbing memories of his childhood, as well as from the fame of his mother's children's books (set in a land called Neverwas), tales secretly drawn from young Jeremy's own experiences in a magical world below his childhood home. Goldstein's reluctant protagonist is soon pulled back into the "dark cities underground" controlled by the mysterious Shadow Committee—a realm linked not only by subway systems around the world but also by generations of children's fiction from *Alice in Wonderland* to *The Lord of the Rings*. *Dark Sister* by Graham Joyce (Tor) is the overdue U.S. publication of a novel that won the British Fantasy Award in 1993, about a couple who uncover a diary full of Wiccan spells and herb lore while renovating a Victorian townhouse. An ancient spirit (the diarist's "dark sister") is subsequently released in a deft and highly suspenseful tale in which the magical elements are used to chronicle the breakdown of a marriage. *Kaspian Lost* by Richard Grant (Avon) is a sequel to a previous novel (*In the Land of Winter*) but can easily stand alone. It's the story of fifteen-year-old Kaspian Aaby, the embittered son of a religious zealot, who strays away from a camp for troubled teens into a strange Otherworld (full of sinister leprechauns) and then reappears, inexplicably, four days later and sixty miles away. The magical elements here are stranger, and not as well integrated, as in the previous novel, but the portrait of adolescent Kaspian and his battle with the whole exasperating adult world is truly first rate. *King Rat* by English newcomer China Miéville is a book we listed as one of the best first novels of 1998 (in its initial U.K. edition). This year Miéville's quirky book is available in a U.S. edition, so I'm happy to recommend this innovative hip-hop/noir/urban fantasy version of the "Pied Piper of Hamelin" to anyone who might have missed it.

Imaginary World Novels

Last year, we were spoiled by a bumper crop of fine Imaginary World novels. This year, by comparison, it has been slim pickings. Nonetheless, there were a *few* good books, most particularly Elizabeth Haydon's *Rhapsody* (listed under First Novels), as well as books by Franny Billingsley, Jeffrey Ford, and Donna Jo Napoli (listed in the Top Twenty). In addition, here are three reprints that should be on every fantasy lover's shelf, two by an early master of the field and one by a modern master: *The King of Elfland's Daughter* and *The Charwoman's Shadow* by Lord Dunsany (Del Rey) have been released in handsome trade paperback editions with new introductions by Neil Gaiman and Peter Beagle. These Irish novels date from the 1920s and yet remain utterly fresh, demonstrating why Dunsany has strongly influenced generations of fantasists ever since. Patricia A. McKillip's "Riddlemaster" trilogy dates back only to the 1970s, and yet it too is a fantasy classic—for it was written in the early years of the post-Tolkien fantasy publishing genre and cast, like Dunsany's books, an enchanted spell on a generation of subsequent young writers. The new Ace edition combines *The Riddlemaster of Hed, Heir of Sea and Fire*, and *Harpist in the Wind* in one attractive omnibus volume, titled *Riddlemaster*. I highly recommend this lyrical tale of riddles, harpists, wizards, and wolves if you've somehow missed it.

If you're looking for adventure fantasy that won't insult your intelligence, I can recommend the following: *Dragonshadow* by Barbara Hambly (Del Rey) is the sequel to *Dragonsbane*, one of Hambly's early books, but can easily be read alone. This talented author subverts the usual fantasy plot by giving us a heroine who is married, middle-aged, and still fighting to save the Winterlands from dragons and worse. Hambly's in top form here in a book combining skillful character studies with a rousing good plot. *Mad Ship* by Robin Hobb (Bantam) is the middle book of a trilogy that began with *Ship of Magic*. It's a well-crafted series about sentient ships, intrigue, and magic on the high seas, aptly dubbed "Patrick O'Brian for fantasy readers." *Heir to the Shadows* by Anne Bishop (Roc) is dark, erotic, passionate, violent, and definitely not for the faint of heart. It's the second book in Bishop's lush, unusual "Black Jewels" trilogy. *Traitor's Moon* by Lynn Flewelling (Bantam) is the third book in the "Nightrunner" series, a page-turner distinguished by Flewelling's careful world-building and well-drawn characters. *Aramaya* by Jane Routley (Avon) follows her previous books, *Mage Heart* and *Fire Angels*, in an engaging series about the struggles of a young mage in a magical world. There's nothing startlingly new here, but Routley brings fresh life to her tale with vivid descriptions and a gift for well-structured plots. *Company of Glass* by Valery Leith (Bantam) is the first book of the "Everien" trilogy, set in an intriguing landscape where reality slips and shifts underfoot. Though in many ways a standard swords-and-sorcery tale, the book is vigorous and well written.

Other entertaining page-turners, noted briefly: *A Cavern of Black Ice* by J. V. Jones (Warner), *Lord of the Fire Lands* (sequel to *The Gilded Chain*) by Dave Duncan (Avon), *The Changeling War* by Peter Garrison (Ace), and *Dragon and Phoenix* (sequel to *The Last Dragonlord*) by Joanne Bertin (Tor). Notable reprints include *The Great Book of Amber* by Roger Zelazny (Avon), containing the complete "Amber Chronicles, Books 1–10" in a handsome package; *The Book of Jhereg* by Steven Brust (Ace), containing the first three Vlad Taltos adventures; and *Watchtower* by Elizabeth A. Lynn (Ace), a groundbreaking novel that won the 1980 World Fantasy Award.

Historical Fantasy and Alternate History

1999 was a good year for magical books based on real or alternate history, including the Beagle, Cooper, Erdrich, Roessner, and Whitehead novels in the Top Twenty list. Here's the best of the rest: *The Messenger* by Mayra Montero, translated from the Spanish by Edith Grossman (HarperCollins), is the splendid new novel from a top Cuban writer. In 1920, a bomb exploded in a Cuban opera house while the great Enrico Caruso was performing in *Aida*; fearing a plot by the Sicilian Mafia, Caruso fled into the streets of Havana and disappeared. Montero takes these true historical facts and weaves them into a magical novel speculating on what may have occurred during the period of Caruso's disappearance, creating a darkly atmospheric tale of love and adventure involving opera, Chinese folklore, and the mystical, secretive Afro-Caribbean religion of Santeria. At 218 pages, Montero's novel is a short one but packs a punch. *Benjamin's Gift* by Michael Golding (Warner) is a winsome novel about an obscenely wealthy man in early twentieth-century Manhattan, the orphan boy he adopts (born with the ability to teleport), and the jazz-playing housekeeper they both love. The tale follows its three protagonists from the 1920s to the 1960s, watching them change, and the world change around them, as Benjamin comes to terms with his strange gift. *Ahab's Wife* by Sena Jeter Naslund (Morrow) is a beautiful novel looking at the mores of early nineteenth-century America through the eyes of the wife of the seafaring hero of Melville's *Moby-Dick*. Naslund has created an extraordinary tale, adventurous, vigorous, and thought-provoking. *Nevermore* by Harold Schechter (Pocket) is an odd but engaging alternate history novel in which Davy Crockett and Edgar Allan Poe team up to fight crime, a fantasy spun on the slim fact that these two American heroes did indeed once meet. *The Crook Factory* by Dan Simmons (Avon) imagines Ernest Hemingway as the leader of an anti-submarine squad during World War II. This alternate history/espionage novel is suspenseful and skillfully written. *The Phantom of Manhattan* by Frederick Forsyth (St. Martin's Press/Dunne) is a book to avoid. Thriller writer Forsyth has taken up the characters of Gaston Lereux's *The Phantom of the Opera* and set them in early twentieth-century New York—a concoction which, although praised by some reviewers, is sadly ill-conceived.

A Calculus of Angels by J. Gregory Keyes (Del Rey), the sequel to *Newton's Cannon*, is an entertaining alternate history tale about Sir Isaac Newton and his young apprentice Ben Franklin, set in a version of the eighteenth century (after an asteroid has destroyed much of Europe) where alchemy works. *Saint Fire* by Tanith Lee (Overlook), book two in the "Secret Books of Venus" quartet, is set in a lush, darkly sensuous version of eighteenth-century Venice. Each book in the quartet is inspired by one of the four elements of alchemy. Here, Lee conjures fire with a magical version of the Joan of Arc legend. *The Master of All Desires* by Judith Merkle Riley (Viking) is an enjoyable page-turner set in mid-sixteenth-century France, about Catherine de Médicis, Nostradamus, and the Undying Head of Menander the Magus. *The Shadow of Albion* by Andre Norton and Rosemary Edghill (Tor) is a frothy confection mixing the tropes of fantasy with those of Regency romance—a lightweight but congenial tale. *Against the Tide of Years* by S. M. Stirling (Penguin) is the sequel to *Island in the Sea of Time*, an inventive time-travel story about contemporary folk from Nantucket Island who are stranded in the Bronze Age past. Also of note: Del Rey has just reprinted one of the best alternate history novels of the past twenty years: *The Drawing of the Dark* by Tim Powers, about the Fisher King, an Irish mercenary, and the art of brewing beer in sixteenth-century Vienna.

Mythic Fiction

This category includes novels inspired by myths, ancient epics, fairy tales, folklore, and folk ballads. Orson Scott Card's version of Sleeping Beauty, Gregory Maquire's recasting of Cinderella, Napoli & Tchen's Rumplestiltskin, Louise Erdrich's weaving of Native American myth and history, Salman Rushdie's virtuoso riff on Orpheus, and Franny Billingsley's exploration of selkie tales are all excellent works of mythic fiction listed in the Top Twenty above, but here's a book I'd recommend every bit as highly: *Sister of My Heart* by Chitra Banerjee Divakaruni (Doubleday). Divakaruni's second novel contains no overt magic or fantasy (unlike her first, *The Mistress of Spices*) but it's saturated with the Indian fairy tales beloved by its two protagonists, who are cousins, "sisters of the heart," growing up in a strict traditional household in modern Bombay. There's deep magic at the core of this book, and I can't recommend it too strongly.

Other recommendations: *Enchanted Night* by Steven Millhauser (Crown) is a 110-page novella published in a slim hardcover edition. Despite its brevity, this gorgeous tale—told as a series of luminous vignettes—uses myths, dreams, and the Pied Piper of Hamlin theme to tell the story of one enchanted night in a small Connecticut town. *Kafka's Curse* by Achmat Dangor (Pantheon) is a poetic, passionate book about life in post-apartheid South Africa, mixing magic realism and fairy-tale imagery with the gripping story of an extended, mixed-race family as they deal with lives, and a country, in the process of transformation. It's a wonderful, magical book (although I could have wished for a stronger ending), reminiscent of Gabriel García Márquez, laced throughout with an Arabian fairy tale about a gardener who loves a princess and is turned into a tree for his presumption. Highly recommended. Lovers turning to trees is the mythic theme running through another lovely book, *In the Shadow of the Amates* by Anne James Valadés (Ash-Tree Press). This heartrending novel begins in a small Mexican village during the Mexican Revolution, intertwining a multi-generation saga with the legend of Amacuepantle. *Madame Fate* by Marcia Douglas (Soho Press) tells the story of Jamaica from God's creation of the island to the present, as seen through the eyes of generations of women with a magical connection to the land and its spirits. It's a tale of shape-shifters, animism, and herbalism ("Madame Fate" is a plant said to cure all ills), weak on plot, strong on folklore, told through a collage of prose and verse. *The Frog Prince* by Stephen Mitchell (Harmony) carries the worrisome subtitle: "A Fairy Tale for Consenting Adults." Alas, this adult retelling of the "Frog Prince" fairy tale is more a meditation on the nature of love than a novel. Set in a magical sixteenth-century Europe, yet containing large dollops of Taoist philosophy, Mitchell's confection has its moments but doesn't manage to sustain them. If you're a diehard fairy tale fan, you'll want to take a look, but wait for the paperback edition. A better book for fairy tale aficionados is *The Wild Swans* by Peg Kerr (Warner), told in the form of parallel stories about two young people at odds with their families: a young woman in Puritan New England whose brothers have been turned into swans, and a young gay man in contemporary New York, living in the shadow of AIDS.

Thunderwoman by Nancy Wood (Dutton), a celebrated poet and folklorist, uses the language of myth to tell the story of how the Pueblo tribes of New Mexico survived cultural genocide at the hands of Spanish invaders. *Gardens in the Dunes* by Native American author Leslie Marmon Silko (Simon & Schuster) is a panoramic, richly mythic novel about the clash between Native American and Anglo cultures in the nineteenth century, ranging from the Arizona/Mexico border region to Brazil and Europe, exploring indigenous earth-based religions, Celtic magic, botany, medicine, women's emancipation, and a host of other topics along the way. Although a bit overlong in some places, a bit didactic in others, it's nonetheless a remarkable book—and more accessible than Silko's *Almanac of the Dead*. Another good novel about the American West—and the conflicts between peoples of different colors, backgrounds, and agendas to be found there in the nineteenth century—is *Liar's Moon* by Philip Kimball (Holt), a multivoice narrative wrapped around the central story of two lost children, one black, one white, raised by coyotes. The book doesn't entirely hang together, and some narrative voices work better than others, but it's definitely worth a look.

The Leper's Companions by Julia Blackburn (Pantheon) is another novel that is problematic, but it's so richly imagistic that I recommend seeking it out nonetheless. Published as a mainstream novel (with magical cover art by Thomas Woodruff), Blackburn's tale is pure fantasy: the story of a modern woman who strays into a fifteenth-century world populated by spirits, mermaids, wild men in the forest, mystics, and saints. A rather grim pilgrimage to the Holy Land becomes a metaphor for personal rebirth. Personally, I found Blackburn's novel more symbolic than satisfying, but other readers of my acquaintance have truly loved it—so give it a try, too. *Medusa: The Fourth Kingdom* by Marina Minghelli, translated from the Italian by Beverly Allen (City Lights), is an interesting work of postmodern metafiction exploring the Medusa legend through the journal of a young Italian woman embroiled in a troubled love affair. Minghelli shines her fiercely intelligent, if idiosyncratic, vision on classical myth, history, literary theory, and psychology in a fashion that is highly experimental, yes, but really works. If you like the fiction of Jeanette Winterson, give this one a try, too. *Leaving Eden* by Ann Chamberlin (Forge) is mythic fiction about Adam, Eve, and Adam's first wife Lilith, narrated by Adam and Lilith's daughter. This sweeping, romantic, thought-provoking saga by a top historical writer conjures a time of change from goddess-centered religions to a new patriarchal system. Occasionally didactic, overall it's an enjoyable story based on a combination of scholarship and speculation. *The Feast* by Randy Lee Eickhoff (Forge) is a rousing mythic saga by an accomplished Celtic historian. Sequel to *The Raid* (which was based on the "Tain"), this one chronicles the further adventures of the young Irish hero Cuchulainn based on material from the lesser-known Irish epic "Fled Bricrend."

Fans of Arthurian fiction have several volumes to choose among. My own first choice would be *Guenevere: Queen of the Summer Country* by Rosalind Miles (Crown), an epic tale of Camelot as seen through the eyes of its queen. This is a fat, satisfying, romantic, feminist look at the Matter of Britain by a best-selling historical writer (*I, Elizabeth* and *Return to Eden*) who is also a lauded women's study scholar (*The Women's History of the World*). If the New Agey orientation of *The Mists of Avalon* put you off, here's one based on impeccable scholarship. A close runner-up for first choice is *The Serpent and the Grail* by A. A. Attanasio (HarperPrism), book four in this author's marvelous series about the boy-king Arthur. *The Sorcerer: Metamorphosis* by Jack Whyte (Forge) is book six in the "Camulod Chronicles" by this best-selling Canadian author, a violent and gripping tale of Merlyn and his young warrior protègè. Diane Paxson's *The Hallowed Isle: The Book of the Spear* (Avon/Eos) is book two in a projected four-book series, swords and sorcery with a mystical bent, set among the tribal cultures of sixteenth-century Britain. *The Lovers* by Kate Hawk (Avon/Eos) is a new retelling of the tragic tale of Trystan and Yseult, from the point of view of a young servant who becomes Trystan's companion-at-arms. *Avalon: The Return of King Arthur* by Steven R. Lawhead (Avon/Eos) is an odd, near-future Arthur-come-again novel by the author of the Pendragon Cycle. In this version of the mythos, Arthur returns to a troubled Britain as a young Scotsman related to the royal family, in line for the throne.

Other notable mythic and fairy-tale works: *The Life of High Countess Gritta von Ratsinourhouse* by Bettine von Arnim and Gisela von Arnim Grimm, introduced and translated from the German by Lisa Ohm (University of Nebraska Press), is the first U.S. publication of this lost masterpiece of German magical fiction, an arch fairy tale written by a mother-and-daughter team in the 1840s. This story of twelve young girls who run away from a dreadful convent and make new lives on a magical island populated by elves and dancing rats is a thinly veiled commentary on German society and the lives of nineteenth-century women. (Here's an interesting factoid: Gisela von Arnim Grimm was married to Herman Grimm, son of fairy tale collector Wilhelm.) *The Complete Fairy Tales* by George MacDonald (Penguin) is an attractive trade paperback edition containing eleven short fairy tales and one essay ("The Fantastic Imagination") by this much-loved nineteenth-century Scottish writer, about whom C. S. Lewis once said: "I have never concealed the fact that I regarded him as my master."

Humorous Fantasy

For fans of funny fantasy I recommend *Deep Secret* by Diana Wynne Jones (Tor), an irrepressible novel that falls halfway between fantasy and science fiction. Jones sets her tale at PhantasmaCon, an English fantasy convention held at a hotel that just happens to be built on a multidimensional gateway. This year, the convention is the gathering place for candidates who hope to join the Magids: magicians whose job is to maintain the balance of good and evil throughout the universe. *Lord Demon* by Roger Zelazny and Jane Lindskold (Avon/Eos) is an offbeat novel about demon refugees from a cosmic war against the gods. Moving between comedy and tragedy, it's a tale of Chinese sorcerers, kite makers, feng shui masters, and magical little Pekingese dogs. (Lindskold, who often collaborated with Zelazny during his lifetime, finished this manuscript after his death.) On the mainstream shelves, try *The Lust Lizard of Melancholy Cove* by Christopher Moore (Avon/Eos). This is another loony-tunes adventure from the author of *Island of the Sequined Love Nun*, about the inhabitants of a small California town and a blues-loving sea monster that arises off its coast. *Messiah* by Romanian-American author Andrei Codrescu (Simon & Schuster) is a sly, good-natured millennial spoof about two unlikely heroines—a punky private detective in New Orleans and a refugee from Sarajevo—who take on the televangelist industry, the Internet, and avert the apocalypse.

For YA funny fantasy, see the Lemony Snicket book in the Top Twenty, as well as *Which Witch?* by Eva Ibbotson (Dutton), about a wizard who throws a spell-casting contest in order to find a wife.

Fantasy in the Mainstream

Magical books on the mainstream shelves are harder to spot than those grouped under a fantasy label, so each year we make a special effort to point the way to books you might otherwise overlook. This year, the very best of these were the Gowdy, Maguire, Michael, Rushdie, and Whitehead books listed in the Top Twenty; the Montero, Golding, and Naslund books listed under Historical Fantasy; and the Divakaruni, Millhauser, and Dangor books listed under Mythic Fiction. Here are a number of others that fantasy readers may find of interest: *Thine Is the Kingdom* by Abilio Estévez, translated by David Frye (Arcade) is an extraordinary new novel from Cuba: a brash, ebullient work of magic realism set on "the Island," an enclave at the center of pre-Castro Havana. Estévez is wildly, relentlessly inventive, telling his tale through multiple narrative voices and a cast of thousands. This clever, language-rich book is clearly influenced by Gabriel García Márquez (as well as by Dostoyevsky, Joyce, and others). Estévez's English-language debut is not a quick or easy read, but it's a rewarding one, on the cutting edge of Latin-American fiction. *The Lazarus Rumba* by Ernesto Mestre (Picador) is another book with a strong Márquezean influence, this one by a young Cuban-born writer living in the U.S. Less dazzling than the Estévez book, but in some ways more thoughtful and appealing, it's the story of post-Revolution Cuba seen through the eyes of three generations of the Lucientes family. Spiritual, political, and deeply moving, this novel marks a strong debut. *Gods Go Begging* by Alfredo Vea, Jr. (Dutton) is the third novel from this Yaqui/Mexican/American author who is, in my opinion, one of the finest writers in America today. This book draws on the author's experiences as a soldier in Vietnam, looking at the war through the eyes of a Latino soldier—a tale divided between the soldier's past in Vietnam and his present as a public defender involved in a double-murder trial in San Francisco. The magic realist elements are less pervasive than in Vea's previous works (*La Maravilla* and *The Silver Cloud Café*), but they simmer quietly under the plot of this hard-hitting, brilliant book. For fans of magic realism Latin-American-style, I also recommend *Loving You Was My Undoing* by Javier Gonzalez-Rubio, translated from the Spanish by Yareli Arizmendi and Stephen Lytle (Holt), a tragic romance of the *Wuthering Heights* variety, laced with mysticism and set during the Mexican Revolution.

Moonlight on the Avenue of Faith by Gina B. Nahai (Harcourt Brace) is a spiced and scented work of Middle Eastern magic realism, the exotic coming-of-age story of Roxanna, born in a Tehran ghetto in the 1930s, whose mother grows wings one night and disappears. This "bad luck" child's search for her mother, and then her own identity and freedom, ranges from Iran to Turkey to Los Angeles. It's an enchanted and impassioned look into the lives of Iranian-Jewish women. *The River Midnight* by Lilian Nattel (Scribner) could be called Yiddish magic realism, an atmospheric novel looking at the lives of four women in a Polish village at the turn of the last century. Canadian author Nattel mixes humor, folklore, and the magic of women's friendships into a truly memorable story. *Four Mothers* by Shifra Horn, translated by Dalya Bilu (St. Martin's Press) is yet another new novel (an English translation of an Israeli bestseller) that uses magic realism, folklore, and fables to depict the lives of Jewish women—in this case, five generations of women in a Jerusalem family plagued by a curse.

Broke Heart Blues by Joyce Carol Oates (Dutton) is an interstitial work that defies easy characterization. On one hand, it's a murder mystery; on another, it's a meditation on American celebrity and the way lives can be turned into myth, told through the story of John Paul Reddy, a supernaturally charismatic high school "bad boy" in suburban Buffalo in the 1960s. Label it mystery, fantasy, horror, or mainstream fiction; whatever you call it, it's yet another gem from Ms. Oates. *Mosquito* by Gayl Jones (Beacon Press) is an ambitious, rambling narrative (more a jazz riff than a novel, despite its length) by a well-known African-American writer, following the adventures of a sassy truck driver as she journeys through the American Southwest and becomes involved with Hispanic refuges, Native Americans, and other "second class" people. Jones manages to pull in Trickster folklore, Buddhist mysticism, Shakespeare, Mexican colonial history—everything but the kitchen sink. Readers either love or hate this book; you'll know on which end of the spectrum you stand within a very few pages. *The Eternal Footman* by James Morrow (Harcourt Brace) is the final volume of a trio of books (following *Towing Jehovah* and *Blameless in Abaddon*) that have raised comparisons with the works of Barth and Vonnegut. Morrow's latest (like the others) is insightful, sharply satiric, and ultimately redemptive—set in a world in which God is dead . . . indisputably dead, His holy skull staring down from the heavens. I highly recommend it. Simon Louvish is another author often compared to Vonnegut. His new novel *The Days of Miracles and Wonders* (Interlink) is a big, sprawling satirical novel that roams from Scotland to the Middle East, mixing medieval heroes with modern characters in order to tickle the underbelly of world politics, history, and religion. *A Corner of the Veil* by Laurence Cosse, translated from the French by Linda Asher (Simon & Schuster) was a bestseller in its original French edition, winning several literary prizes. This book (which makes an interesting pairing with Morrow's *The Eternal Footman*) is a smart, funny novel about six pages that turn up on the desk of the editor of a Catholic magazine which utterly prove the existence of God—and the havoc which this discovery unleashes around the world.

The 27th Kingdom by Alice Thomas Ellis (Moyer), the latest from the author of *Fairy Tale*, is a supernatural black comedy of manners set in an eccentric boarding house in London in the 1950s. It's light, droll, and very English. *All Quiet on the Orient Express* by Magnus Mills (Arcade), the second novel by a lauded new British writer (his previous novel was shortlisted for the Booker Prize) is a much darker look at English society. This novel is an allegorical tale about a man camping in the Lake District who gets drawn into the Kafka-esque lives of the inhabitants of a mysterious town. *Crowe's Requiem* by Mike McCormack (Henry Holt) is a mordant tale of Irish magic realism about a lonely boy in a rural village who refuses to speak as he grows up, and his subsequent tragi-comic life at university in the city. *A Witness to Life* by Terence M. Green (Forge) is a lovely, semi-autobiographical story of an extended family in Canada. The fantasy element here is that the tale is narrated by a dead man who watches over his family in the form of a black starling sitting on the phone wires. *The Handyman* by Carolyn See (Random House) is a book whose critical acclaim has me puzzled. It's the story of a failed-painter-turned-handyman who becomes involved in a variety of desperate lives and ends up fixing more than roofs and drains—becoming, in the end, a cult artist-messiah in the twenty-first century. You may want to take a look for yourself, but it didn't work for me. *Ferney* by James Long (Bantam) is a highly touted mystery/romance/reincarnation story (in the Jack Finney tradition) set in a crumbling cottage in England—a quick read, light, enjoyable, and somewhat forgettable. *The Haunted Major* (Ecco Press) is the reprint of a 1902 novel by the Scots writer Robert Marshall, an offbeat, supernatural, Wodehousean tale about the game of golf.

There were several novels in 1999 using magical, mythic, or folkloric motifs to tell coming-of-age stories, usually involving coming to terms with parents who were mad, bad, or dangerous to know. Other writers have done this beautifully in the past (Seamus Deane's *Reading in the Dark*, Heinz Insu Fenkl's *Memories of My Ghost Brother*, Will Shetterly's *Dogland*, and Susan Palwick's *Flying in Place* come immediately to mind). The following books, by contrast, all seem to fall a little flat—but each has moments of interest. *The Professor of Light* by Marina Budhos (Putnam) is one of the best of the lot, concerning a young American girl (with a Jewish mother and a Guyanese father) who spends each summer with relatives in England. Budhos knits Guyanese folklore and physics into the tale of a charismatic father's delicate descent into madness. This first novel suffers from art-novelitis (inattention to pacing, structure and plot), but less so than the others, and it carries you along. *Last Things* by Jenny Offill (FS&G) is another first novel about a mentally ill, science-obsessed parent—in this case it's the mother, an ornithologist, for whom the boundary between reality and myth is growing daily thinner. Offill's book received wonderful reviews, but I found it too self-consciously stylistic to be effective or truly engaging. *Homework* by Suneeta Peres da Costa (Bloomsbury), by a young Asian-Australian writer, is another first novel published with much hoo-ha and fanfare. The central conceit is endearing: Mina, the protagonist, is born with antennae on her head that betray her every passing emotion. But there's no plot to speak of and little in the way of character development here. I'd say, ignore the reviews and give this one a miss. *Geographies of Home* by Loida Maritza Pérez (Viking) could be considered a Dominican-American version of Dorothy Allison's *Bastard Out of Carolina*. Pérez does a lovely job of conjuring the life of a large and troubled family of Dominican immigrants in New York, and the story has some terrific supernatural touches . . . but it lacks the flashes of warmth that made the brutality of *Bastard Out of Carolina* bearable. Here, everyone is so relentlessly awful that it's difficult to maintain one's interest in them. There's some genuine magic in the muddle of this painful story, but I'd recommend waiting to see what Perez comes up with next. *The Cornflake House* by Deborah Gregory (St. Martin's Press) reverses the usual scenario and tells its story from a mother's point of view—in this case, a free-spirited hippie mother of seven, with a gift for clairvoyance, relating her saga of woe from jail. I found this first novel slight and the narrator annoying, but it has its moments. Art-novelitis is a problem in the otherwise intriguing *One Hundred and One Ways* by Mako Yoshikawa (Bantam), which tells the story of three generations of Japanese women in the voice of a Japanese-American college student (the granddaughter of a famous geisha). Despite the usual problems with plot and pacing that seem to plague young mainstream writers these days, Yoshikawa's tale of a young woman torn between two worlds (literally haunted by the ghost of her dead lover) is a sensuous, poetic, introspective tale, and definitely worth a look. *Big Fish: A Novel of Mythic Proportions* by Daniel Wallace (Algonquin) is the least exotic but the most successful of these coming-to-terms-with-one's-family books. It's the story of a man trying to understand his elusive father as the father lies on his deathbed. It's a humorous but poignant little story, punctuated with tall tales, Southern folklore, and Greek myths.

For fans of surrealist fiction there are several good books to chose from. The best of them is *The Divinity Student* by Michael Cisco (Buzzcity Press). After a near-death experience, an unnamed divinity student is sent away from the seminary to take up employment as a "word finder" in a strange, distant desert city. He soon becomes involved in reconstructing the "Lost Catalog of Unknown Words," stealing secret words from the corpses of dead scholars. If you have a taste for dark surrealism and a love of language, this one is a treat. *The Artist of the Missing* by Paul LaFarge (FS&G) is beautifully descriptive, haunting, but has little in the way of coherent plot. It concerns a young artist who travels to a nameless city to explore the mystery of his parents' disappearance. The young man subsequently becomes involved in other, increasingly bizarre disappearances in LaFarge's pyschological, political, and artistic fable. *Orlanda* by Jacqueline Harpman, translated from the French by Ros Schwartz (Seven Stories) is a postmodern, surreal mystery novel about female identity and sexuality which recasts Virginia Woolf's *Orlando* in contemporary Belgium. The protagonist is a professor of literature who discovers that a repressed part of her psyche has taken on a life of its own, inhabiting the body of a twenty-year-old rock journalist. This witty novel was the winner of the 1996 Prix Medicis; *Booklist* aptly dubbed it "Kafka with a dash of Ursula K. Le Guin."

Oddities

The Best Peculiar Book award for 1999 goes to *A Hive for the Honeybee* by Soinbhe Lally (Arthur A. Levine/Scholastic), a curious little fable about a worker bee and two rebel drones, written by an Irish writer and nominated for a literary prize in that country. Lally mixes wonderful bee lore with (occasionally heavy-handed) philosophy. Even when the story doesn't quite work, it's endearing—and the entire package is a delight, from the honeycomb-patterned book covers to the charming art by Patience Brewster.

Runners up: *Seven Dreams of Elmira* by Patrick Chamoiseau, translated from the French by Mark Polizzotti (Zoland) is the story of a beautiful spirit named Elmira who appears to the workers of an antiquated rum distillery on the West Indian island of Martinique. The narrator is an old rum worker who is more than one hundred years old; the book is made up of interviews with the rum workers relating their visions of Elmira, along with photographs of Martinique, the distillery, and the workers. This is a beautiful, dreamlike little book, full of folk-lore and gentle humor, by an author who has been called the Gabriel García Márquez of the Antilles. *The Tale of the Unknown Island* by José Saramago, translated from the Portuguese by Margaret Jull Costa (Harcourt Brace) is another quirky little publication—an illustrated book (part fairy tale, part philosophical/political fable) about a man with a dream, a king's cleaning woman, and a boat sailing off toward an island that may or may not exist. Saramago was the 1998 winner of the Nobel Prize for Literature. *The Museum at Purgatory* by Nick Bantock (HarperCollins) is the latest from this master of the peculiar, consisting of a surreal art catalog and the story of a mysterious art curator who is on an afterlife journey, heading either to Heaven or Hell.

Animal Tales

The best animal story of 1999 was Barbara Gowdy's African elephant saga, *The White Bone*, listed among the Top Twenty novels. Here are some others you may enjoy, filled with fantastical felines and a couple of clever mutts.

The Golden Cat by Gabriel King (Del Rey) continues the story begun by the talented team of Jane Johnson and M. John Harrison (under the King pseudonym) in their previous novel, *The Wild Road*. This is a charming and truly magical story about English cats who travel the "wild roads"—secret intercontinental pathways—in an ongoing battle between good and evil. In this new volume, the golden kittens of the king and queen have been villainously catnapped, and an expedition must be mounted to find them. *To Visit the Queen* by Diane Duane (Warner) is the second book in a less successful cat saga. Following *The Book of Night with Moon*, this is the story of cats who guard the gates between worlds and foil plots to destroy civilization as we know it. Duane is a good writer, but in this series she's just not at her best. *Cat in a Jeweled Jumpsuit* by Carole Nelson Douglas (Forge) is book eleven in Douglas's wacky "Midnight Louie" series about a wise-ass feline detective. This one is set in Las Vegas and involves the ghost of Elvis—need I say more? *The Lighthouse, the Cat, and the Sea* by Leigh W. Rutledge (Dutton) is a best-selling little book that tells the story of the highly adventurous life of a cat named Mrs. Moore, from her beginnings as a kitten stowaway on a schooner sailing through the tropics to her subsequent life with a lighthouse keeper in Key West. *Jane on Her Own* by Ursula K. Le Guin (Orchard) is book four in the author's "Catwings" series for young readers. It's about, well, cats with wings. The illustrations by S. D. Schindler are truly delightful. *Ghost Cats* by

Susan Shreve (Arthur A. Levine/Scholastic) is a sweet little tale for young readers about a troubled young boy in Boston and the phantom cats who haunt him. Cat fanciers will also want to take a look at the anthology *Catfantastic Vol. V*, edited by Andre Norton (that famous cat lover) and Martin H. Greenberg (DAW). It contains a range of middling-to-good stories, and sports a witty Renaissance-style cover by Mark Hess. Speaking of cat art, don't miss *Pre-Raphaelite Cats* by Susan Herbert (Thames & Hudson), famous Pre-Raphaelite paintings recast with feline stunners instead of human ones. (Someone was bound to do it, weren't they?)

Dog Eat Dog by Jerry Jay Carroll (Ace) is the follow-up to Carroll's surprisingly good novel *Top Dog*, about an amoral corporate raider who finds himself in a canine body. In this volume, back in his own body but surrounded by dozens of homeless pooches, Carroll's hero finds himself menaced once again by his enemies from the previous book. This volume has some amusing moments but, sadly, it's not as fresh as *Top Dog*, which didn't really need a sequel. *Timbuktu* by Paul Aster (Henry Holt) is the first-person narrative of a dog named Mr. Bones, companion to the homeless "poet-saint" Willy G. Christmas, on a quest from Brooklyn to Baltimore to find Willy's high school mentor in the hope that she will become the literary executor of the poet's opus (seventy-four notebooks stashed away in a bus-terminal locker) when Willy, in failing health, crosses over to the otherworld of Timbuktu.

Also Noted

In the field of science fiction, there were a few books with magical elements published last year which fantasy readers might also enjoy: *Land of the Golden Clouds* by Archie Weller (Allen & Unwin) is a science fiction novel from Australia with strong fantasy and mythological underpinnings. Set three thousand years after a nuclear holocaust, it's a sweeping, though somewhat episodic story about a future Dark Age, where tribal cultures struggle to survive on an irradiated continent and can recall the past only with the language of myth. Weller makes good use of aboriginal languages and folklore to create his intriguing future world. *Obernewtyn* by Isobelle Carmody (Tor) is another post-apocalypse tale from a talented Australian writer. If you love the early works of Andre Norton, try this captivating story of an orphaned child with exceptional abilities. *The Stone War* by Madeleine E. Robins (Tor) is a science fiction/horror/disaster novel with ingenious fantasy elements, set in the ruins of a magical version of Manhattan. It's a brutal, breathtaking novel in which the author's love for the city shines from every page.

The following fantasy novels hit the bestseller lists in 1999. Beloved by large numbers of readers across the country, they deserve a mention: *Angel Fire East* by Terry Brooks (Ballantine), *Servant of the Dragon* by David Drake (Tor), *Brotherhood of the Wolf* by David Farland (Tor), *Krondor the Betrayal* by Raymond E. Feist (Avon), *Soul of the Fire* by Terry Goodkind (Tor), *The Path of Daggers* by Robert Jordan (Tor), *The Black Swan* by Mercedes Lackey (DAW), *Owlknight* by Mercedes Lackey and Larry Dixon (DAW), and *The Demon Apostle* by R. A. Salvatore (Del Rey).

Children's Fantasy

The most notable books in YA fantasy, of course, are the two new Harry Potter volumes: *Harry Potter and the Chamber of Secrets* and *Harry Potter and the Prisoner of Azkaban* by J. K. Rowling (Arthur A. Levine/ Scholastic). Yes, Rowling may be turning them out a bit too quickly. (*Secrets* doesn't quite live up to the first Potter book, although the series picked up steam again with *Azkaban*.) And yes, there are better YA fantasists out there (Jones, Cooper, Pullman, Yolen, Barron) who, in a better universe, would also receive Rowling's level of fame, wealth, and adulation. But the Potter books are fun, and no eight-year-old diehard fan is going to quibble about the quality of the prose from one book to another. The Potter books are lightweight, to be sure, but they're clever and clearly doing their job: persuading a generation of kids that the world can be a magical place.

In addition to the Almond, Beagle, Billingsley, Cooper, Erdrich, Napoli, and Snicket books listed previously (in the Top Twenty), and those ubiquitous Potters, here are some other children's fantasy novels you may enjoy: *The Mirror of Merlin* by T. A. Barron (Philomel) is book four in Barron's mystical, utterly gorgeous "Lost Years of Merlin" series exploring the youth of this legendary magician from the Arthurian mythos. *Downsiders* by Neal Shusterman (Simon & Schuster) is yet another "there's a society of people living under the city" book (*Downtown, Neverwhere, King Rat, Dark Cities Underground*, etc.), but don't let that deter you. Shusterman's tale of the forbidden friendship between a "Topsider" girl and a "Downsider" boy in New York City is witty, wise, and chock full of urban folklore and Manhattan history. *Midnight Magic* by Avi (Scholastic, packaged with gorgeous cover art by Laurel Long) is a medieval mystery novel—entertaining and ghostly. Set in xlii ·•· Terri Windling

the fifteenth-century kingdom of Pergamontio, it's the story of the clever young servant of a magician who doesn't believe in magic. *First Test* by Tamora Pierce (Random House) is the first in a new sequence of books set in Pierce's imaginary kingdom of Tortall, revisiting ten-year-old Keladry (from "The Lioness Quartet") as she trains to be a knight. *The Coyote Bead* by Gerald Hausman (Hampton Roads) is a haunting novel based on Navajo legends, set in the American Southwest; *The Banished* by Betty Levin (Greenwillow) roams through lands much farther north, telling the story of a young girl, polar bears, and the tribal "Furfolk." Random House has begun a new series of books, each by a different fantasy author, based on *The Voyage of the Bassett* art book by James C. Christensen about a magical ship that sails through the lands of myth. Book I is *Islands of the Sky*, a Greek adventure by Tanith Lee; Book II is *The Raven Queen*, a Celtic faery story by Ellen Steiber and yours truly; and I hear that Sherwood Smith and Will Shetterly are doing the next ones.

The Adventures of Blue Avenger by Norma Howe (Holt) is a funny, romantic, and wonderfully manic novel in which a teenage boy endeavors: a) to become a comic book hero and b) to solve the mysteries of the universe. *Hidden Talents* by David Lubar (Tor) is a strong debut novel about a group of five misfits with strange "hidden talents" at the Edgeview Alternative School for delinquent children. *Violet & Claire* by Francesca Lia Block (HarperCollins) starts off with a good premise: the friendship between two high school girls, one who dresses entirely in black and wants to be a screenwriter, the other who wears fluttery fairy wings and wants to be a poet. Unfortunately, the book falls apart as the two friends are drawn into the black heart of Hollywood—the jaded vision of L.A. depicted by Block is just so trendier-than-thou that it's hard to take it seriously. (For a much better book with the theme of teenage girlfriends, try *Local Girls* by Alice Hoffman (Putnam), fifteen interconnected stories about a young girl in a troubled Long Island family and her best friend.) Block has been a fine writer in the past, but her decadent-L.A. shtick is in danger of becoming a parody of itself.

For younger readers, I recommend *The Wizard's Map* and *The Pictish Child*, the first two books in the new "Tartan Magic" series by Jane Yolen (Harcourt Brace). These are fun, atmospheric tales about three American children visiting relatives in Scotland who are pulled into adventures involving time-travel, wizards, and witches. *The Lost Flower Children* by Janet Taylor Lisle (Philomel) is a gentle, wistful story about finding fairies at the bottom of the garden. *The Firework-Maker's Daughter* by Philip Pullman (Arthur A. Levine/Scholastic) is a magical fable about a rebellious girl who wants to become a master firework-maker; this book is short and rather lightweight compared to Pullman's utterly brilliant novels for older children (*The Golden Compass*, etc.), but skillfully rendered nonetheless. Notable reprints: E. Nesbit's classic children's fantasy *Five Children and It* has been reprinted in a splendid new edition with illustrations by Paul O. Zelinsky, in Peter Glassman's "Books of Wonder" series (Morrow). Houghton Mifflin has released a fiftieth anniversary edition of *Farmer Giles of Ham*, a short dragon story by J. R. R. Tolkien, containing pleasant if unexceptional black-and-white art by Pauline Baynes. Also from Houghton Mifflin: *The Father Christmas Letters*, an edition containing the letters Tolkien wrote, illustrated, and sent to his children in the guise of Father Christmas each December beginning in the 1920s, describing life among reindeer and polar bears at the North Pole. The letters have a certain whimsical charm, but will be of interest mainly to Tolkien collectors. Alan Garner's stunning Welsh fantasy novel *The Owl Service* has been reprinted in a handsome new edition (Voyager), as has Diana Wynne Jones's sprightly, pre–Harry Potter tale *The Magicians of Caprona* (Beech Tree/Morrow). *The Hounds of the Morrigan* by Pat O'Shea is fine Celtic fantasy full of Irish gods, spirits, and fairies, nicely repackaged (Holiday House). *The Random House Book of Greek Myths* by Joan D. Vinge, with full-color illustrations by Oren Sherman, is the first big, lushly illustrated Greek myths book since the D'Aulaires's more than thirty years ago. This book of retellings has all of the major and many minor myths told in the crisp, evocative style of award-winner Vinge, with colorful renderings by a talented poster artist. And for Oz fans, there are several good reprints to chose from: *The Tin Woodman of Oz* and *The Magic of Oz* by L. Frank Baum, meticulously reproduced editions with the original John R. Neill illustrations, from the "Books of Wonder" series (Morrow); *The Wonderful Wizard of Oz: The Kansas Centennial Edition* by L. Frank Baum, with wood-engravings by Michael McCurdy and an introduction by Ray Bradbury (University of Kansas Press); and *The Scarecrow of Oz* by L. Frank Baum, a paperback facsimile of the 1915 edition, with John R. Neill illustrations in both black-and-white and color (Dover).

Single-Author Story Collections

Elementals by A. S. Byatt, which was far and away the best story collection of 1998 (in its original U.K. edition) is now available in the U.S. in a volume from Random House. The book contains Byatt's brilliant adult fairy tale "Cold" and other magical works. *Moonlight and Vines* is a new collection from Canadian mythic fiction writer Charles de Lint

(Tor), containing interconnected stories set on the streets of Newford, a contemporary city located somewhere in North America where myths, legends, and wonders intersect with modern life. Most of these tales are reprints, but they've not been collected in one volume before. *A Vaudeville of Devils* by Robert Girardi (Delacorte) contains seven supernatural stories (by the author of *Vaporetto 13* and other literary ghost novels) that are richly imaginative, erotic, and sinister, set in various centuries and locations around the globe. *A Citizen of the World* by MacLin Bocock (Zoland Books) is another collection of fine stories with far-flung settings, some of which have magical and fabulist elements. This edition contains an introduction by Alice Hoffman. *The Oracle Lips* by Storm Constantine (Stark House) is a collection of fantasy, horror, and science fiction tales from this stylish, iconoclastic British author. This edition contains eighteen reprints, four originals, one poem, and an introduction by Michael Moorcock. *Reave the Just and Other Tales* by Stephen R. Donaldson (Bantam) is a collection of eight tales, three of them original to the volume. ("The Killing Stroke," a story about martial arts, is particularly recommended.) *Refugees from an Imaginary Country* by Darrell Schweitzer (Owlswick Press) is a reprint collection of atmospheric, dark fantasy tales, illustrated by Stephen E. Fabian. *Dragon's Fin Soup* by S. P. Somtow (Alexander Publishing) contains eight modern Siamese fables by this highly talented Thai-American writer. *The Square Moon* by Ghadah Samman, translated from the Arabic by Issa J. Boullata (The University of Arkansas Press) contains contemporary gothic tales by a celebrated Lebanese writer now living in Paris. *Ghost Dancing* by Anna Linzer (Picador) is a collection of eleven wry stories about Jimmy One Rock, his wife Mary, and their assorted relatives and neighbors, penned by a Lenape writer from the Suquamish reservation in Washington. *Men on the Moon* by Simon J. Ortiz (University of Arizona Press/Sun Tracks Vol. 37) collects the short fiction of this underrated Native author from the Acoma Pueblo in New Mexico. Ranging from humorous to tragic, with some mythic elements, these stories explore the spiritual conflict between Native and Anglo cultures. (I particularly recommend Ortiz's tale "What Indians Do.")

B. Horror by Wendell Mayo (Livingstone Press) is an offbeat mainstream collection of stories making unusual use of horror movie imagery. (The poignant title tale, "B. Horror," is particularly recommended.) *The South & Bene* by Adelaida García Morales, translated from the Spanish by Thomas G. Deveny (University of Nebraska Press) contains two novellas by this contemporary Spanish writer, the second of which is gothic and disturbing. *Haunted Traveller: An Imaginary Memoir* by Barry Yourgrau (Arcade) is a collection of linked short-

short stories forming an imaginary travel memoir through a Borgesian, surrealistic landscape. *Nude in Tub: Stories of Quillifarkeag, Maine* by G. K. Wuori (Workman) is a collection of eighteen loosely connected stories set in a Maine border town, several with surreal elements. Wuori has a great prose style, but most of his stories have little in the way of plot. These are brief snapshots of north coast life, rather than fully satisfying tales. *The Woman Who Cut Off Her Leg at the Maidstone Club and Other Stories* by Julia Slavin (Henry Holt) is a volume of strange stories about suburban life: some of them surrealistic, some of them witty, some grotesque, and some just slight.

Two Young Adult fantasy collections are recommended to adult readers: *Believing Is Seeing* by Diana Wynne Jones (Greenwillow), containing six terrific reprint tales and one lightweight original; and *Odder Than Ever* by Bruce Coville (Harcourt Brace), another strong collection mixing reprint and original material, all vintage Coville. ("The Stinky Princess" is particularly recommended.) Small press volumes published in 1999 include *Leaving the Autoroute* by Bill Lewis (Lazerwolf Press), *Women's Work* by L. A. Taylor (Allau Press), *The Hoegbotton Guide to the Early History of Ambergris by Duncan Shriek* by Jeff VanderMeer (Necropolitan Press), *Shadow Bones* by David Memmott (Wordcraft), and *What Ho, Magic!* by Tanya Huff (Meisha Merlin Publishing). Notable reprint collections: *The Fantasies of Robert A. Heinlein* (Tor), a fat volume of stories, many of them first published in the pulp magazine *Unknown Worlds*; and *The World and Other Places* by Jeanette Winterson (Knopf), a small volume reprinting works dating back to 1986 (some of them magical or surrealist) by this award-winning British author.

Anthologies

1999 was, frankly, another lackluster year for fantasy anthologies. Among the few collections of original tales were *Merlin* edited by Martin H. Greenberg (DAW), an Arthurian anthology with notable contributions by Charles de Lint and Jane Yolen (the latter reprinted in this volume); *A Dangerous Magic* edited by Denise Little (DAW), a collection of romantic fantasies with a noteworthy tale from John DeChancie; *Flights of Fantasy* edited by Mercedes Lackey (DAW), stories about "fantastic flying creatures"; *Sword and Sorceress Vol. XVI* edited by Marion Zimmer Bradley (DAW), with a nice contribution by newcomer Carol E. Leever; *Catfantastic V* edited by Andre Norton and Martin H. Greenberg (DAW), with a clever tale by India Edghill; and *Silver Birch, Blood Moon* edited by myself and Ellen Datlow (Avon), containing original adult fairy tales by Tanith Lee, Neil Gaiman, Robin McKinley, Patricia A. McKillip, Wendy Wheeler, and others (the last two reprinted in this volume). *Time Out Book of Paris Short Stories* edited by Nicholas Royle (Penguin) contains a few good fantasy pieces among its mainstream contributions; stories by Kim Newman, Christopher Kenworthy, and Erica Wagner are particularly recommended. For dark fantasy fans, *The Last Continent* edited by John Pelan (Shadowlands Press) is a small-press collection of original "tales of Zothique," based on the works of Clark Ashton Smith.

As for reprint collections, if there were any good volumes devoted to fantasy out there, I sure couldn't find them. The only good reprint anthologies to cross my desk were mixed-genre volumes, or those devoted to gothic tales. Even *The Dedalus Book of Spanish Fantasy* edited and translated by Margaret Jull Costa and Annella McDermott (Dedalus) is really a collection of gothic and horror stories, although interesting. *Crossing the Border* edited by Lisa Tuttle (Indigo), billed as "tales of erotic ambiguity," is a fine literary collection of erotic tales, some with dark fantasy or horror elements, by authors ranging from Angela Carter and Joyce Carol Oates to Neil Gaiman, Geoff Ryman, and Graham Joyce. *The Best from Fantasy and Science Fiction* edited by Edward L. Ferman and Gordon Van Gelder (Tor), contains a wide range of good stories, many of them award winners or nominees, including fantasy and dark fantasy by Elizabeth Hand, John Crowley, and Rachel Pollack. *The Mammoth Book of Lesbian Short Stories* edited by Emma Donoghue (Carroll & Graf) contains some nonrealist stories by the likes of Tanith Lee, Elizabeth A. Lynn, Christine Crow, and Sara Maitland. *Night Shade* edited by Victoria A. Brownworth and Judith M. Redding (Seal Press) is a reprint collection of gothic tales by women; while the closely named *Nightshades* edited by Robert Phillips (Carroll & Graf), is a solid collection of "literary ghost stories" ranging from Henry James and Shirley Jackson to Gabriel García Márquez and Joyce Carol Oates.

Poetry

Girls on the Run by John Ashbery (FS&G) is the latest from this Pulitzer Prize–winning poet. The book consists of a single poem based on a band of little girls called the "Vivians" created (in an illustrated novel) by outsider artist Henry Darger (1892–1972). It's a surreal, strange, subversive work, and I can't describe it better than David Kirby (writing in *The New York Times*): "If Andy Warhol and T. S. Eliot had played with Barbies together, the result might have been something like the adventures of [the Vivians]."

Beauty Is the Beast is the latest chapbook from Kentish poet and performance artist Bill Lewis. (Lazerwolf Press, 66 Glencoe Road, Chatham, Kent, U.K.) As always, Lewis's work is wound through with myths, fairy tales, gypsy lore, and dreams. *Sixty Odd* is a strong but primarily realist collection from Ursula K. Le Guin (Shambhala). *In the Bear's House* combines poetry and prose, some of it mythic in flavor, by the excellent Native American author N. Scott Momaday (St. Martin's Press).

Magazines

The best market for writers of short fantasy fiction continues to be the big three genre magazines: *F&SF* edited by Gordon Van Gelder; *Asimov's* edited by Gardner Dozois; and *Realms of Fantasy* edited by Shawna McCarthy. The number of "Year's Best" selections and honorable mentions from these magazines spiked sharply upward this year. In particular, *F&SF* is publishing some first-rate work with Van Gelder at its helm. *Omni* continues to be sorely missed for its consistently high quality fiction that blurred the borders between fantasy, science fiction, and the mainstream. Ellen Datlow (former fiction editor of *Omni*) picked up some of the slack at her own website, *Event Horizon* (which supplied two excellent stories for this volume)—but now *Event Horizon*, too, has disappeared (officially it's "on hiatus"), and Ellen has moved on to *SCIFI.COM* (www.scifi.com), where she's the new fiction editor. The fantasy genre's semipro and little magazines continue to be as discouraging as ever, ranging from mediocre to downright awful, with one sterling exception: *Century* is back! This elegant little magazine of science fiction, fantasy, and interstitial fiction (edited by Robert K. J. Killheffer and Jenna A. Felice) is finally back on a quarterly schedule as of their recent Winter 2000 issue, and I urge you to support this much-needed outlet for literary and unusual works. (For more information, write: Century Publishing, P.O. Box 150510, Brooklyn, NY, 11215–0510. Web address: www.centurymag.com.)

On the mainstream shelves, small literary journals continue to be a good source for magical stories and poetry. This year we've reprinted material from *Calyx, Pleiades, Descant, The Hudson Review, The Iowa Review,* and *Columbia.* The latter journal dedicated a portion of the Winter 1999 issue to "Reinventions: a new look at fairy tales, legends, parables, and fables," which included short fiction by Jeanette Winterson, an interview with Rick Moody, and an essay by Neil Gaiman. A small quarterly out of Los Angeles, *Lynx Eye* (edited by Pam McCully and Kathryn Morrison) also deserves a mention. Although not as polished as *Century*, this journal (mixing realist and magical stories) is far more ambitious than most that cross my desk and has contained some memorable fiction, including the Mary Sharratt story we're reprinting in this volume. (For more information, write: *Lynx Eye*, 1880 Hill Drive, Los Angeles, CA, 90041.)

On the Web, there's no single source for fine fantasy fiction (now that *Event Horizon* is suspended), but here are several good sites for news, reviews, essays, and useful links: *Folk Tales* edited by Cat Eldridge (www.folk-tales.com); *Rambles* (www.rambles.net); Rodger Turner's *SF Site* (www.sfsite.com); and *Phantastes*, edited by Staci Ann Dumoski (www.phantastes.com). For magical art from Beardsley to Rackham to Waterhouse, try Julia Kerr's *ArtMagick* site (www.artmagick.com). For fairy tale information, book recommendations, essays, and art, try the *SurLaLune Fairy Tale Pages*, edited by Heidi Anne Heiner (www.members.aol.com/surlalune/frytales/index.htm), Christine Daae's *Introduction to Fairy Tales* (www.darkgoddess.com/fairy), and *The Endicott Studio of Mythic Arts* (www.endicott-studio.com).

Art

For me, the most important art news of 1999 is the fact that *The Golden Book of Fairy Tales*, translated by Marie Ponsot (Golden Books), is finally back in print after too many years of obscurity, featuring the distinctive fairy tale art of French illustrator Adrienne Segur—a woman whose work has profoundly influenced several of us in the fantasy field. It's a gorgeous volume, reproduced in a format similar to the battered 1950s edition I've been hauling around for decades now. But for those of you who aren't diehard Segur fans, here's what else the year had to offer: *Maxfield Parrish, 1870–1966*, with text by Sylvia Yount (Abrams) is an important new art book dedicated to this great American illustrator. Yount's excellent text carefully builds the case for placing Parrish in a more prominent place in American art history. *The Genres and Genders of Surrealism* by Annette Shandler Levitt (St. Martin's Press) offers a fresh look at this imaginative group of artists, writers, and filmmakers, including the all too often overlooked women in the movement. *Surreal Lives* by Ruth Brandon (Grove/Atlantic) is a lively biographical work following these artists from Europe in the 1920s and 1930s to New York in the 1940s. *The Essential René Magritte* by Todd Alden (Andrews McMeel) is a welcome new addition to Magritte scholarship. *The Collected Writings of Salvador Dali* edited by Haim Finkelstein (Cambridge University Press), containing writings from the 1920s to 1970s, shows the artist to be just as mad (and occasionally brilliant) as we'd expect. *Barry Windsor-Smith: Opus* by Barry Windsor-Smith (Fantagraphic Books) is an art-packed volume in which this innovative and idiosyncratic artist offers us a retrospective of his own life's work, combined with a highly personal, hallucinatory text. It's a strange but courageous book. Here's a fascinating book you might not have run across: *Goddess Embroideries of the Balkan Lands and the Greek Islands* by Mary B. Kelly (StudioBooks). This volume not only collects wideranging examples of this beautiful art form, but also talks about the meanings of the various symbols, the rituals in which they were used, and the remnants of those rituals still evident in art and folk customs today.

Fans of "fantasy art" of the bronzed barbarian variety have two new books to chose from: *Legends: Selected Paintings & Drawings by the Grand Master of Fantastic Art: Frank Frazetta*, with text by Arnie and Cathy Fenner (Underwood Books), and *Dreams: The Art of Boris Vallejo*, with text by Nigel Suckling (Avalon). You'll find heroic-school fantasy illustration mixed in among the science fiction art in the following volumes: *Spectrum 6: The Best in Contemporary Fantastic Art*, edited by Arnie and Cathy Fenner (Underwood Books), a collection of science fiction/fantasy art selected by jury from works submitted by art directors and the artists themselves. Painterly works by Kinuko Craft, Jeffrey Jones, Phil Hale, Dave McKean, and Charles Vess stand out among the swords and spaceships. *Fantasy Art Masters: The Best Fantasy and Science Fiction Artists Show How They Work* by Dick Jude (Watson-Guptill) is not a bad volume of science fiction illustration if that's what you're in the market for—but the name is strangely misleading. Alan Lee is the only artist who can possibly qualify for master status here, and the book seems to be focused on American and English commercial art. Er, what happened to the rest of the world?

Picture Books

Children's picture books provide a good showcase for magical storytelling and art. Here's a baker's dozen of the best to cross my desk this year (in alphabetical order by title):

Alice in Wonderland by Lewis Carroll, illustrated by Lizbeth Zwerger (North South): a wonderful new vision of a classic tale featuring spare and exquisite watercolors by the peerless Ms. Zwerger, a young Austrian artist who won a well-deserved Hans Christian Andersen Medal in 1990. (There are two other new Alice editions worth taking a look at as well: *Alice's Adventures in Wonderland* illustrated by Helen Oxenbury, with its charming modern Alice (Candlewick Press) and a boxed-set edition of *Alice's Adventures Underground* and *Through the Looking Glass* featuring the handsome original illustrations by Sir John Tenniel (Harcourt Brace).)

The Fairies' Ring by Jane Yolen, illustrated by Stephen MacKey (Dutton): a beautifully designed edition containing fairy stories from around the world, retold in Yolen's lyrical prose, as well as fairy poetry and MacKey's dreamy, romantic art. It's a gem.

The Gargoyle on the Roof by Jack Prelutsky and Peter Sís (Greenwillow): a mischievous book about gargoyles, werewolves, griffins, gremlins, and other magical creatures featuring Prelutsky's loony poetry and Sís's ebullient art.

The Goblin Baby, written and illustrated by Lauren Mills (Dial): this one works with the "changeling" theme from folklore, involving goblins, gnomes, and fairies in the garden. Mills's art is a treat.

Jack and the Beanstalk, retold by Ann Keay Beneduce and illustrated by Gennady Spirin (Putnam): the familiar tale is competently retold, but buy this volume for the art—utterly gorgeous watercolors by a Russian master of the form.

The Magic Tree, story by T. Obinkaram Echewa, illustrations by E. B. Lewis (Morrow): this is a fine retelling of an African folk tale by Nigerian writer Echewa, accompanied by beautiful watercolor paintings, skillfully rendered.

The Perfume of Memory, story by Michelle Nikly, illustrations by Jean Claverie (Arthur A. Levine/Scholastic): a fabulous original fairy tale inspired by the author's childhood in Algeria, Tunisia, and Morocco, with equally good watercolor illustrations by an award-winning French illustrator.

Shibumi and the Kitemaker by Mercer Mayer (Cavendish): the lovely story of a princess, a kite-maker, and a young samurai in an ancient, Japan-like kingdom. Mayer brings Asian art influences into his usual distinctive style, and the result is enchanting.

Puss in Boots by Charles Perrault, translated by Anthea Bell, illustrated by Giuliano Lunelli (North South): Bell's rendering of the tale is excellent, as her translations always are, but this is another edition to buy for the art—which is sly, highly original, and wickedly good.

Sleeping Boy by Sonia Craddock, illustrated by Leonid Gore (Atheneum): this is the most unusual book of the lot, a reworking of the Sleeping Beauty theme told through a series of collagelike pictures, set in Berlin from the turn of the century to the dismantling of the Berlin Wall.

The Tale I Told Sasha by Nancy Willard, illustrated by David Christiana (Little, Brown): two major talents team up here to create a whimsical, captivating tale about a land of lost treasures. Willard's deceptively simple prose is lovely, and the art is first rate.

Watakame's Journey: The Story of the Great Flood and the New World by Hallie N. Love and Bonnie Larson, illustrated by Huichol artists (Clear Light Publishers): here's another unusual one, particularly recommended for fans of folklore and myth. A traditional legend of the Huichol Indian people of Mexico is accompanied by the brightly colored, intricate "string art" pictures for which this culture is famed, filled with shamanic and folkloric symbolism. It's an amazing volume.

Wind Child by Shirley Rousseau Murphy, illustrated by Leo and Diane Dillon (HarperCollins): yet another gem from the Dillons, this one contains a bewitching original fairy tale by Murphy, embellished by the stunning art of this husband and wife design team.

The best of the rest, noted briefly: *Trickster and the Fainting Birds: Seven Algonquin Tales* retold by Howard Norman, illustrated with charming paintings by Tom Pohrt (Harcourt Brace/Gulliver Books); *Westlandia* by Paul Fleischman, about a boy who creates an imaginary country in his backyard, with delightfully quirky illustrations by Kevin Hawkes (Candlewick Press); *The Bone Keeper* by Megan McDonald, an eerie, deeply mythic desert tale illustrated by G. Brian Karas (DK Publishing); *The Crystal Mountain* by Ruth Sanderson, an original fairy tale about a magical tapestry and some thieving fairies, with lushly detailed art (Little, Brown); *In the Moonlight Mist: A Korean Tale* retold by Daniel San Souci, distinguished by the lyrical art from Eujin Kim Neilan (Boyd Mills Press); *The Lost Boy and the Monster*, a Native American tale written by Craig Kee Strete, with gorgeously weird paintings by Steve Johnson and Lou Fancher (Putnam); *Under the Lemon Moon*, a tender Mexican tale by Edith Hope Fine, with simple, effective pictures by Rene King Moreno (Lee & Low Books); *The Acrobat and the Angel* by Mark Shannon, illustrated by David Shannon, a retelling of the spiritual French medieval folk tale of the "Acrobat of God" (Putnam); *Blue Willow* by Pam Conrad, illustrated by S. Saelig Gallagher, a gentle Chinese love story based on the "blue willow" china pattern (Putnam); *Dog Tales* by Jennifer Rae, illustrated by Rose Cowles, clever fractured fairy tales about dogs and cats (Tricycle Press); *Turtle Songs: A Tale for Mothers and Daughters* by Margaret Olivia Wolfson, illustrated by Karla Sachi, a sweet Fijian folk tale about a brave princess, her daughter, and giant sea turtles (Beyond Words); and *Animalia: Thirteen Small Tales* by Barbara Berger, a reprint edition (first published in 1982) of short-short stories inspired by world folk tales and religious parables, with intricate illustrations resembling an illuminated manuscript (Tricycle Press).

Nonfiction

Nonfiction works of interest to fantasy readers and writers in 1999: *No Go the Bogeyman* by Marina Warner (FS&G) is the American edition of an English book we recommended highly last year, a study of ogres, giants, bogeyman (and other figures of masculine terror) in myth, folklore, and popular culture, by a dazzlingly erudite writer. *Myth & the Body* by Stanley Keleman (Center Press) is based on topics explored by Keleman and Joseph Campbell during fourteen annual seminars on the subject. It's an interesting read, bursting with ideas from two highly original thinkers. *When Dreams Come True: Classical Fairy Tales and Their Tradition* by Jack Zipes (Routledge) is an examination of fairy tales and their tellers from the sixteenth century to the twentieth by one of the leading scholars in the field. *The Witch Must Die: How Fairy Tales Shape Our Lives* by Sheldon Cashdan (Basic Books) is a sound, clear-eyed look at the history of fairy tales from a psychologist/historian who avoids the pitfalls of assigning modern psychoanalytic interpretations (à la Bettelheim) to tales rooted in older cultures. *Fabulous Identities* by Patricia Hannon (Rodopi) is a 1998 book I missed last year, an excellent study looking at the women fairy tale writers in the aristocratic salons of seventeenth-century France. *In the Shadow of the Dreamchild: A New Understanding of Lewis Carroll* by Karoline Leach (Peter Owen/Dufour Editions) is a controversial and interesting new study in which Leach argues that Carroll's famous obsession with little girls is a literary myth, and that the Alice books were not written for Alice Liddell but for another member of the Liddell family. Leach supports her arguments with previously unpublished material from the Liddell family archives, along with Carroll's letters and unpublished diaries. *The Culture of Christina Rossetti: Female Poetics and Victorian Contexts* edited by Mary Arseneau, Anthony H. Harrison, and Lorraine J. Kooistra (Ohio University Press) contains essays on Rossetti's great fairy poem "Goblin Market," her relationship to the Pre-Raphaelite movement, and other subjects. *100 Years of Oz* by John Fricke (Stewart, Tabori & Chang) is an illustrated edition of Oz history, imagery, and memorabilia drawn from the Oz collection of Willard Carroll.

Fantasy reference volumes: *The Ultimate Fantasy Encyclopedia* by David Pringle (Peter Mayer Publishers) is an illustrated book devoting many pages to film, television shows, and fantasy gaming, but it also contains a survey of fantasy fiction, lists famous fantasy characters, and describes classic imaginary worlds. Pringle does a good job within the limited parameters of the book, clearly meant to be an entertaining guide to fantasy in pop culture, and not a reference volume for the serious reader. (Readers looking for the latter should seek out Pringle's *St. James Guide to Fantasy Writers*, as well as John Clute and John Grant's *The Encyclopedia of Fantasy*.) *Fluent in Fantasy: A Guide to Reading Interests* by Diana Tixier Herald (Libraries Unlimited, Inc.), published as part of the "Genreflecting Advisory Series," is a book aimed at librarians, giving lists of recommended reading, a short history of the genre, definitions of fantasy terms, and a limited listing of authors. Herald's choices here are a bit idiosyncratic (as any such book limited to 250 pages is bound to be), but it's a good guide for libraries (and new readers) building a fantasy collection. *Myth and the Movies* by Stuart Voytilla and Christopher Vogler (Michael Weiss Publications) is an interesting volume looking at fifty popular films through a Joseph Campbell lens. *Fantasy and Horror: A Critical and Historical Guide to Literature, Illustration, Film, TV, Radio, and the Internet* edited by Neil Barron (Scarecrow Press) is a book we haven't yet received for review, so I'll just note its existence here.

The American Writer: Shaping a Nation's Mind by Jack Cady (St. Martin's Press), is "an open letter to young writers" by this World Fantasy Award–winning author. It's a passionate discourse on American history with letters delivered in Cady's blunt, plain-spoken prose. I highly recommend it. *Writing and Fantasy* edited by Ceri Sullivan and Barbara White (Addison Wesley/Longman) is a book with a misleading title—sounding, as it does, like a guide to writing genre fiction. This is actually an academic collection of short essays on subjects ranging from fairy mistresses in medieval literature and sexual fantasy in the English Renaissance to the "fantasies" of travel, credit, and female criminality. *The King of the Ants* by Zbigniew Herbert, translated from the Polish by John and Bogdana Carpenter (Ecco), is a slim volume of musings that are part essay, part fiction, and part philosophical meditations on classical myth.

Mythology and Folklore

1999 was a great year for books on myth and folklore, definitely putting a dent in my book-buying budget. Here's the best of what I've found: *The Hero with an African Face: Mythic Wisdom of Traditional Africa* by Clyde W. Ford (Bantam) is a terrific book in the Joseph Campbell tradition, not only exploring the many facets of African folklore and myth, but also looking at the relevance of these stories in modern life. I highly recommend this one. Other good books on African lore: *A Dictionary of African Mythology: The Mythmaker as Storyteller* by the always excellent Harold Scheub (Getty), and *Children of Wax: African Folk Tales* by Alexander McCall Smith (Interlink), collecting stories from the Ndebele people of Zimbabwe. Also check out *African American Folktales: Stories from Black Traditions in the New World* edited by Roger D. Abrahams (Pantheon Fairy Tale and Folklore Library). Another favorite of the year is *Magnificent Corpses: Searching Through Europe for St. Peter's Head, St. Chiara's Heart, St. Stephen's Hand, and Other Saints' Relics* by Anneli S. Rufus (Marlow & Co./Avalon Publishing). This is a fascinating volume full of macabre stories and mystical Catholic lore, presented in a travel book format, marred only by its breathless prose style. *Ghosts in the Middle Ages: The Living and the Dead in Medieval Society* by Jean-Claude Schmitt (University of Chicago Press) is a wide-ranging and entertaining look at ideas about death and the afterlife in medieval culture.

The Grail: The Celtic Origins of the Sacred Icon by Jean Markale (Inner Traditions) is a provocative new study by one of the great French scholars of Celtic myth. Also check out: *Celtic Legends of the Beyond: A Celtic Book of the Dead* by Anatole Le Braz, translated from the French by Derek Bryce (Samuel Weiser), and *The Chronicles of the Celts: A Survey of Tales from Ireland, Scotland, Wales, Cornwall, The Isle of Mann, and Brittany* by Peter Berresford Ellis (Carroll & Graf). *The Key to the Kalevala* by Pekka Ervast, translated by Tapio Joensuu (Blue Dolphin Publishing) is an English edition of a classic text by a famous Finnish mystic and theosophist, first published in 1916. Ervast's influential interpretation of the Kalevala (the national epic of Finland) is idiosyncratic, shamanic, poetic, and mind-expanding. *Ancient Goddesses*, edited by Lucy Goodison and Christine Morris (University of Wisconsin Press), is a welcome volume indeed. Recent books and ideas about ancient goddess religions have been so permeated with fuzzy New Age theories that the whole area of goddess mythology scholarship has hung under a cloud of disrepute. In this well-researched, informative collection of essays (written for the lay reader), top feminist archaeologists and scholars take a hard look at the subject.

Women of Mythology by Kay Retzlaff (Metro Books) is a glossy, illustrated coffee-table book looking at women in myth, legend, and folklore around the world. *Ancient Land, Sacred Whale: The Inuit Hunt, Its Rituals and Poetry* by Tom Lowenstein (Havrill Press) is a brilliant mythic study of the Inuit people, beautifully written. *Over the Lip of the World: Among the Storytellers of Madagascar* by Colleen J. McElroy (University of Washington Press) is a mythic journey through a little-known part of the world, highly recommended. *Jamaican Culture and International Folklore, Superstitions, Beliefs, Dreams, Proverbs and Remedies* by Claudette Copney (Pentland Press) is a good reference volume, full of interesting lore. Some other useful reference volumes: *The Encyclopedia of Eastern Mythology* by Rachel Storm (Lorenz Books); *Chinese Mythology: An Introduction* by Anne M. Birrell (John Hopkins University Press); and *Zoo of the Gods: The World of Animals in Myth & Legend*, a slim trade paperback edition by Anthony S. Mercatante (Seastone). *A Field Guide to Demons, Fairies, Fallen Angels, and Other Subversive Spirits* by Carol K. Mack and Dinah Mack (Owl Books) is a well-researched look at demon legends and lore worldwide. *Sirens: Symbols of Seduction* by Meri Lao (Inner Traditions) looks at mermaids and sirens in myth, literature, and art. Some good new folk tale collections: *Grey Heroes: Elder Tales from Around the World* edited by Jane Yolen (Penguin); *Folktales of India* by Brenda Beck (University of Chicago Press); *The Clever Sheikh of the Butana and Other Stories*, Sudanese folk tales retold by Ali Lutfi Abdallah (Interlink), and *California Indian Folklore* by Frank F. Latta (Brewers Historical Publications), an important volume of tales collected from Yokut elders early in the twentieth century. And here's an oddity: *Wilson's Grimm* (Cottage Classics, San Francisco), containing seven German fairy tales with peculiar (and thoroughly adult) illustrations by the underground comics artist S. Clay Wilson.

Recommended folklore collections for children: *Not One Damsel in Distress: World Folktales for Strong Girls*, collected and told by Jane Yolen, illustrated by Susan Guevara (Harcourt Brace); *Dogs of Myth*, tales from around the world collected by Gerald and Loretta Hausman, illustrated by Barry Moser (Simon & Schuster); *The Element Illustrated Encyclopedia of Animals in Nature, Myth and Spirit* by Fran Pickering (Element); *The Barefoot Book of Giants, Ghosts and Goblins* by John Matthews, illustrated by Giovanni Manni (Barefoot Books); *The Troll With No Heart in His Body and Other Tales of Trolls*, from Norway by Lise Lunge-Larsen (Houghton Mifflin); *Italian Fairy Tales* by Lilia E. Romano (Hippocrene/World Folklore Library); *And It Is Still That Way*, legends told by Navajo, Hopi, Apache, Tohono O'odham, Pima, and other Native American children in Arizona, collected by Byrd Baylor (Cinco Puntos Press, Texas); and *Turtle Island: Tales of the Algonquian Nations*, retold by Jane Louise Curry (McElderry Books). I also recommend *Witches and Witch-hunts* by Milton Meltzer (Blue Sky/Scholastic), an excellent, timely book for young people on the subject of witches, witch-hunts, prejudice, and discrimination throughout Western history. (This one ought to go out en masse to all the anti–Harry Potter parents.)

For fans of faery lore and art, there are several new books to chose from: *Strange and Secret Peoples: Fairies and Victorian Consciousness* is an extensive, fascinating survey of this subject by Carole G. Silver (Oxford University Press). *The Faeryland Companion* by Beatrice Phillpots (Barnes & Noble Books) is a terrific edition with an informative text and a wide range of illustrations from the Victorian "fairy painters" through mid-century artists like Cicely Barker to modern painters like Brian Froud and Alan Lee—but (annoyingly) it's only available through Barnes & Noble bookstores. *Faeries: Doorways to the Enchanted Realm* by Lori Eisenkraft-Palazzola (Smithmark) is a coffee-table book of classic faery art from the turn of the last century: Richard Doyle, Arthur Rackham, Warwick Gobel, etc. More a gift book than a reference volume, this edition has no text to speak of, but the art is handsomely reproduced. *Fairies* by Suza Scalora (HarperCollins) is an unusual art book of contemporary faery photographs, by a photographer who (according to the tongue-in-cheek text) has tracked these elusive creatures around the world. Urban fantasy fans should check this one out. For children: *Talking to Fairies* by Sheila Jeffries (Element) is a well-researched, informative little book on fairy lore and customs—I highly recommend it for young fairy fans of your acquaintance. *How to See Fairies* (Smithmark) is more of a gimmick edition: a gift box containing a little volume of illustrations by Charles van Sandwyk, a blank fairy journal, a poster, and notecards. Nonetheless, little girls will probably love it. I should also mention my own new children's faery book, if only so that you don't miss the exquisite art by doll-artist Wendy Froud. *A Midsummer Night's Faery Tale* (Simon & Schuster) features an original fairy tale illustrated by Froud's enchanting three-dimensional faeries (photographed in a woodland setting), reminiscent of the creatures she created (with her husband Brian Froud) for the films *Labyrinth* and *The Dark Crystal*.

Music

Traditional music is of interest to many fantasy lovers because it draws on some of the same cultural roots as folk tales and other folk arts. Contemporary "world music" can be compared to contemporary fantasy fiction (by writers like Charles de Lint or Emma Bull), for artists in both fields are updating old folk themes for a modern age. There is such a wealth of traditional material available these days that we have room to mention only a handful of favorites from 1999 here, with priority given to those that include magical, mystical, or storytelling elements. For further recommendations, check out the *Folk Tales* and *Rambles* review web sites (the URLs are listed under "Magazines").

The real buzz in world music these days, at least here in North America, is all the terrific music coming out of Scandinavian countries, brought to this side of the Atlantic almost single-handedly by the Minneapolis label Northside. Here are just a few of the 1999 Northside releases you should give a listen to: Top of the list is *Wizard Women of the North*, a survey of leading women vocalists and musicians who are "taking the music of their foremothers and making it relevant today." It's wild and gorgeous. *Nordic Roots 2* is a sampler CD and makes a good introduction to this kind of music. *R7* by Rosenberg 7, recorded in Sweden, is another favorite: a stirring mix of four female voices, fiddle, viola, and cello. *Vengeance* is the latest from the amazing Swedish band Garmarna, full of raucous vitality. Yet another good Swedish CD is *Lavalek*, from the band Groupa. *The Stone Chair* by Bukkene Bruse mixes ancient and modern instruments, playing the traditional music of Norway. Sorten Muld is a Danish singer of traditional ballads (with titles like "The Man and the Elf-girl") who also blends the old with the new in odd and interesting ways; check out her new one, *Mark II*. *Gierran* by Wimme is even stranger, and completely hypnotic: a CD of traditional Finnish shamanistic chants (called "yoik"—songs about reindeers, magical journeys, and the like) recorded in a fusion of old and new instrumentation.

If you like innovative music that combines the old and the new, here are some great releases with a tribal/techno/trance/dance beat: *The Best of Agricantus* by Agricantus is an infectious CD by an Italian band working with Celtic, African, and Middle Eastern rhythms. The Blue Chip Orchestra (Hearts of Space) is a band out of Austria inspired by Native American music—dubious as this may sound, their CD *Red Sky Beat* is actually good. *Vol. 2: Release* (Real World/Virgin), the new release by Afro Celt Sound System, is every bit as good as this groundbreaking band's previous work. *Prayer* by Uttara-Kuru fuses world rhythms with haunting Japanese folk songs, while Dagda trances out on the music of the British Isles on their aptly named CD *Celtic Trance* (PARAS/Owl). For traditional Celtic music played in lively untraditional ways, the three top releases of the year in my opinion are: *Tóg É Go Bog É* from the Irish band Kila (Green Linnet), *In My Hands* by Cape Breton fiddle player Natalie McMaster (Rounder), and *Crossing the Bridge* by Irish fiddle virtuoso Eileen Ivers (Sony Classical). Some other good ones are: *Rising* by Tarras, a talented new band from the English-Scots border region (Rounder); *Tierre de Nadie* by Helvia (Higher Octave), the Celtic music of Spain, a hot release over there right now; *Xieme* from the French-Canadian band La Bottine Souriante (Mille-Pattes); *Turn* by Great Big Sea from Newfoundland (Wea); and *At*

Home, the latest from Ireland's fabulous all-women band Cherish the Ladies (RCA). For good old Celtic rock-and-roll, try SixMileBridge's *No Reason* (Loose Goose). If you're looking for ballads with a bit of storytelling to them, your first stop should be *Celtic Voices* (Green Linnet), a compilation CD with Loreena McKennitt, Kíla, Tarras, Altan, and other first-rate performers. Maddy Prior's latest is well worth checking out even if, like me, you haven't loved her recent work: *Ravenchild* (Park Records) is a bit uneven but worth the price for a whole cycle of songs inspired by raven mythology—Prior ought to be doing more of this kind of thing. The latest CD by the other half of Silly Sisters, June Tabor's *A Quiet Eye* (Green Linnet) is divine, as usual. Boy, can this woman sing. Niamh Parson's *Blackbird and Thrushes* is quietly beautiful, with a power that sneaks up on you. *In the Greenwood* (Prairie Druid) is a very nice CD (a debut, I think) from Paddy Tutty—a Canadian singer/musician from Canada (female, despite the name). I also recommend *Trespass* by British folksinger Pete Morton (Harbourtown) for pleasing, unflashy ballad renditions. Sheela Na Gig's *Live by the Aire* (Arktos) mixes old ballads with a range of world rhythms; *Full Throated Abandon* by Tanglefoot (Borealis) specializes in long story ballads; and *The Dragon by Elvendrums* (American Entertainment) is a quirky CD made by four drummers using percussion as the backdrop for stories and ballads. A few final recommendations: *Inner Voices* by R. Carlos Nakai (Canyon) and *Inside Monument Valley* by Paul Horn and Nakai (Canyon) are hauntingly beautiful CDs of Native American flute music; *Sacred Voices* by December Wind (Canyon) features new music infused with traditional aspects of Akwesasne Mohawk culture; and *One Truth* by Omar Faruk Tekbilek (World Class) presents mystical Sufi song-poems from the Middle East.

Celtic Solstice by folk/jazz/New Age musician Paul Winter, is a rather lovely CD in which he gathers top Irish and American musicans to play together in the world's largest Gothic cathedral, St. John the Divine in New York City. And finally, the fantasy field's own Ellen Kushner is the maestro behind a CD related to her nationally syndicated "Sound & Spirit" radio program: *Welcoming Children into the World* (Ryko), a survey of music from around the world exploring the ways different cultures celebrate the birthing process. Ranging from chants of the Baka Forest People to Navajo lullabyes, it's a delight.

Recommendations from Charles de Lint: "Without question, the disc of the year for me was *Otherworld* by Lúnansa (Green Linnet). It's acoustic, traditional, yet still manages to be innovative, and the music and playing really does sound as thought it came right out of the otherworld—evocative and sinewy, and not at all like that twee wave of mushy New Age CDs with 'Celtic' in the title where often the only Celtic element is a bad version of an O'Carolan tune. And speaking of Turlogh O'Carolan, what's often forgotten is that much of his inspiration came from classical composers and musicians. For a wonderful collection of rarer O'Carolan pieces that show this, the music played with great heart and integrity, give a listen to *O'Carolan's Dream* by Garry Ó'Briain (Gael Linn). If Lúnansa is the music of a revel in the fields, then Ó'Briain's CD is what they're playing in the fairy court, under the hill. Other great Celtic releases of the year featuring some lively tune sets and occasional vocals include *Midsummer's Night* by Dervish (Whirling Music), *From the Inside Out* by Loretto Reid Band (Reta Ceol), *Debatable Lands* by Kathryn Tickell (Park Records), *Come to Dance* by John Whelan (Narada), and *Buzzin' by Bumblebees* (Beehave Records). If the ancient goddesses could still be heard today, they'd probably have made these CDs: *Live in Paris and Toronto* by Loreena McKennitt (Quinlan Road) and *Sleepless* by Kate Rusby (Pure Records). But faerie folk living on the city streets probably sound more like *à ma zone* by Zap Mama (Virgin) with its mix of hiphop beats, rap, and pure vocal gymnastics, or the harder rocking R&B of *street faerië* by Cree Summer (Work). And the hill faeries down the holler are undoubtably listening to the acoustic bluegrass flavorings of *The Mountain* by Steve Earle and the Del McCoury Band (E-Squared), and more electric and eclectic story songs of Fred Eaglesmith on *50-Odd Dollars* (Razor & Tie)."

Literary Conventions and Awards

The World Fantasy Convention, an annual gathering of writers, artists, publishers, and readers in the fantasy and horror fields, was held in Providence, Rhode Island, Nov. 4–7. The Guests of Honor were writers Charles de Lint, Patricia A. McKillip, and Robert Silverberg, with special guest Samuel R. Delany, and artists Leo and Diane Dillon. The following World Fantasy Awards (for works published in 1998) were presented at the convention: Best Novel: *The Antelope Wife*, mythic fiction by Louise Erdrich. Best Novella: "The Summer Isles," alternate-history fiction by Ian R. Macleod. Best Short Fiction: "The Specialist's Hat," an eerie tale on the border between fantasy and horror, by Kelly Link. Best Anthology: *Dreaming Down-Under*, a multigenre anthology of Australian fiction edited by Jack Dann and Janeen Webb. Best Story Collection: *Black Glass*, a multigenre volume of tales by Karen Joy Fowler. Best Artist: Charles Vess, illustrator/co-creator of the graphic novel *Stardust* and other works. Special Award/Professional: Jim

Turner, editor of Golden Gryphon Books. Special Award/Non-Professional: Richard Chizmar of the small press Cemetery Dance. Life Achievement Award: horror writer Hugh B. Cave. The judges for the 1999 awards were Gregory Frost, Don Hutchison, Michael Kandel, Rebecca Ore, and Al Sarrantonio.

The Mythopoeic Award was presented at Mythcon, an annual convention for academics, writers, and readers of fantasy literature. Mythcon was held July 30–August 2 in Milwaukee, Wisconsin, where the Guests of Honor were writer Douglas A. Anderson and scholars Gary and Sylvia Hunnewell. Winners of the Mythopoeic Award were as follows. Adult Literature: *Stardust*, an illustrated "faerie novel" by Neil Gaiman and Charles Vess. Children's Literature: *Dark Lord of Derkholm*, humorous fantasy by Dianna Wynne Jones. Scholarship Award for Myth & Fantasy Studies: *A Century of Welsh Myth in Children's Literature* by Donna R. White. Scholarship Award for Inklings Studies: *C. S. Lewis: A Companion and Guide* by Walter Hooper.

WisCon, a convention for writers, artists, publishers, readers, and academics interested in feminism and gender issues in speculative fiction is held each year over Memorial Day weekend in Madison, Wisconsin. Mary Doria Russell and I were the 1999 guests of honor. The James Tiptree, Jr. Memorial Award, for works exploring issues of gender, was presented to Suzy McKee Charnas for *The Conqueror's Child*. The judges for awards were: Bill Clemente, L. Timmel Duchamp, Kelly Link, and Diane Martin.

The winner of the 2000 William L. Crawford Award for best first fantasy novel is Anne Bishop for the "Black Jewels Trilogy," *Daughter of the Blood, Heir to the Shadows*, and *Queen of Darkness*. Second place went to Elizabeth Haydon for *Rhapsody*. Judges for the award were Stefan Dziemianowicz, Diana Francis, Larry Segriff, Pat York, and Kathleen M. Massie-Ferch. The award was presented at the International Conference on the Fantastic in the Arts, March 25, 2000, in Ft. Lauderdale, FL.

That's an overview of the year in fantasy, now on to the stories themselves. As usual, there were stories we were unable to include in this volume but which should be considered among the year's best:

Robert Antoni's erotic fable "My Grandmother's Tale of How Crab-o Lost His Head," in *The Paris Review*, #152.

Jeffery M. Brockman's bizarre tale "A Misery of Shoes" in *Chelsea* 66.

Orson Scott Card's ghostly story "Vessel," in *F&SF*, Dec.

Bruce Colville's fractured fairy tale "The Stinky Princess" in his collection *Odder Than Ever*.

Charles de Lint's long Newford tale "The Buffalo Man," published as a chapbook by Subterranean Press.

Tim Nickels's contemporary mermaid tale, "The Hungry Shine," in *Timeout: Net Books*.

Viktor Pelevin's riff on myths in modern Russia, "The Greek Version," in *Agni 50*.

Robert Silverberg's Roma Eterna novelette, "A Hero of the Empire," in *F&SF* Oct./Nov.

Jeff VanderMeer's surreal novella "The Transformation of Martin Lake" in *Palace Corbie Eight*.

I hope you will enjoy the stories and poetry chosen for this volume as much as I did. Many thanks to the authors, agents, and publishers who allowed us to reprint them here.

—T.W.
Devon, U.K. and Tucson, U.S.
1999–2000

Summation 1999: Horror

Ellen Datlow

Book and Magazine Publishing News

If you thought things couldn't get worse after last year's consolidations in trade book publishing, you were wrong. About the only good news was that the Bertelsmann/Ingram deal fell through after rumors surfaced in June that the Federal Trade Commission staff would recommend that the Commission block the deal. Various independent bookselling and writers' groups fought against the merger; Barnes & Noble had announced its intention to purchase Ingram in November 1998, but in June 1999 the deal was called off because of opposition from antitrust regulators. In Bantam Dell's consolidation and restructuring, four Dell executives were let go. Carole Baron, Thomas Harris's editor, was one of them but was quickly appointed president of Dutton and took over that position just after Labor Day.

Only months after publishing director John Silbersack split off from HarperPrism to create HarperEntertainment, slashing the Prism list from seventy to eighty titles per year to twenty-four to thirty-six books per year, News Corporation Ltd., the parent company of HarperCollins, bought Avon Books from The Hearst Corporation. The transaction, according to the *New York Times*, is estimated at less than $180 million. The merger united two of the country's largest children's publishers, and the addition of Avon was intended to give a boost to HC's mass-market paperback efforts. In late September HarperCollins reorganized the combined operations, eliminating 74 positions, including John Silbersack and John Douglas at HarperCollins and Lou Aronica of Avon, and a number of William Morrow editors. It also eliminated the Rob Weisbach, Spike, Bard, Twilight, and other imprints, reducing the number of adult imprints from twenty-four to sixteen and the number of children's imprints from seventeen to eight.

HarperCollins acquired The Ecco Press for an undisclosed price. The small literary press has published titles by Joyce Carol Oates and Paul Bowles, and reprinted the classic serial killer novel, *The Bad Seed* by William March. Ecco Press has been publishing about sixty titles a year and has a backlist of seven hundred books. Publisher and co-founder Daniel Halpern was named VP and editorial director of Ecco and serves as executive editor of HC's adult trade division.

Carol Publishing laid off all its production and editorial staff and put all its new books on hold after its planned sale to the LPC Group, which reached a preliminary agreement to acquire Carol in April, apparently failed.

Robert Reginald's Borgo Press closed down after twenty-four years of publishing hundreds of bibliographical, biographical, and critical works on science fiction, fantasy, and horror.

EMR Publishing, comprised of Alfred Krever and Arthur Bryon Cover, started an ambitious publishing program intended to reprint books that are either out of print or were never published in the U.S., in sturdy, attractive trade paperback editions. Three titles were published in 1999: collections by S. P. Somtow (with an erroneous 1998 copyright), David J. Schow, and Dennis Etchison, all with attractive cover art by Lydia Marano. Soon after, the company reorganized into Babbage Press, founded by Cover, Lydia Marano, and Kristina Etchison. The first book published under the Babbage Press imprint was the revised and updated edition of John Shirley's 1985 novel *Eclipse*.

Hasbro acquired Wizards of the Coast for $325 million. Although best known for its card and role-playing games, the company also publishes approximately fifty fantasy and science fiction books annually. Wizards also distributes the best-selling Pokémon titles in the U.S. In 1997 WOTC bought TSR, taking over *Amazing Stories* from TSR. It remains to be seen whether the sale to Hasbro will affect that magazine.

Del Rey launched "Impact," a trade paperback line of classic fantasy and science fiction reprints, with Lord Dunsany's *The King of Elfland's Daughter* and *The Charwoman's Shadow* and Walter Tevis's *The Man Who Fell to Earth*. Most of the books are introduced by prominent writers in the field of fantastic literature.

The House voted down The Children's Defense Act of 1999 (H.R. 2036), a proposal calling for curtailing minors' access to pictures, drawings, video games, movies, books, recordings, or other materials containing "explicit sexual material or explicit violent material." Lawmakers felt the restrictions would have violated the Constitution's free speech guarantee. The bill prohibited "verbal descriptions or narrative accounts of explicit sexual or violent material" and applied to books, pamphlets, magazines, any printed matter, and photographs as well as recorded lyrics, video games, and movies. H.R. 2036, introduced by Rep. Henry Hyde (R-IL) would have made it a federal felony, punishable by up to five years in jail, to sell, show, or lend a wide range of materials to anyone under age seventeen. Hyde said the laws were designed to "slow the flood of toxic waste into our kids' minds."

For the first time in American publishing history a publisher was held liable for crimes committed by a reader. Paladin Press, publisher of the murder how-to manual, *Hit Man*, agreed to pay a reported $5 million to end a six-year-old suit in which the house was charged with aiding and abetting murder. The press also agreed to cease publication of the book. The publisher blamed its insurance company for declining to risk a jury trial. Legal experts fear that Paladin's decision to settle the case will lead to more lawsuits citing books with similar information.

HorrorNet, run by Matt Schwartz, but moribund for several months during and after Schwartz's illness, was closed down and bought by Vincent Harper, who plans to reopen it in 2000. FrightNet, edited by Ivan S. Graves, was shut down in August after thirteen issues. Graves announced that "time" was the major contributor to its demise. *Event Horizon: Science Fiction, Fantasy and Horror*, edited by Ellen Datlow, suspended publication in December after one year. One story it published won the World Fantasy Award. Datlow went on to become Fiction Editor of SCIFI.COM, the Sci Fi Channel's web site, which launches its new fiction area in spring 2000.

TransVersions, a Canadian cross-genre magazine currently edited by Dale L. Sproule, will be edited by Marcel Gagné and Sally Tomosevic as of its twelfth issue.

There is evidence to support cautious optimism concerning the health of our field. Despite the ongoing refusal by the majority of mainstream publishers to admit in their packaging and promotion that some of their books are horror, Don D'Auria of Leisure Books continued to develop and expand his varied list into a successful mass-market horror program.

Peter Crowther and Simon Conway founded a specialty press called PS Publishing to publish a series of novella-length chapbooks of original horror, fantasy, science fiction, and crime/suspense. The first titles, published in 1999, were by Graham Joyce, James Lovegrove, Kim Newman, and Michael Marshall Smith.

The 1999 Bram Stoker Awards weekend took place in Los Angeles, California, June 4–6. The Stoker Awards for Superior Achievement were given out Saturday night, June 5, 1999 to: Stephen King for the novel *Bag of Bones*; Michael Marano for First Novel *Dawn Song*; Peter Straub for "Mr. Clubb and Mr. Cuff" in the Long Fiction category; Bruce Holland Rogers for "The Dead Boy at Your Window" in the Short Fiction category; John Shirley for his collection *Black Butterflies*; Stefan Dziemianowicz, Martin Greenberg, and Robert Weinberg for *Horrors! 365 Scary Stories* in the Anthology category; Paula Guran for Darkecho Newsletter in the Nonfiction category; no award in the category of Illustrative Narrative; a tie of *Gods and Monsters* by Bill Condon and *Dark City* by Alex Proyas, Lem Dobbs, and David S. Goyer for Screenplay; Nancy Etchemendy for *Bigger Than Death* in the Work for Young Readers category; and no award in the Other Media category.

The Aurealis Awards were also announced: *Foreign Devils* by Christine Harris for Horror Novel; "Atrax" by Sean Williams and Simon Brown for Horror Short Story; *Aramaya* by Jane Routley for Fantasy Novel; and "Whispers of the Mist Children" by Trudi Canavan for Fantasy Short Story.

The British Fantasy Awards were announced at FantasyCon 23, on Sunday, September 19, 1999. Winners were: Karl Edward Wagner Award (British Fantasy Special Award): Diana Wynne Jones; August Derleth Fantasy Award for Best Novel: *Bag of Bones* by Stephen King; BFA for Best Anthology: *Dark Terrors 4* edited by Stephen Jones and David Sutton; BFA for Best Collection: *Ghosts and Grisly Things* by Ramsey Campbell; and BFA for Best Short Fiction: "The Song My Sister Sang" by Stephen Laws (from *Scaremongers 2: Redbrick Eden* edited by Steve Saville); BFA for Best Artist: Bob Covington; and BFA for Best Small Press: *The Third Alternative*, edited by Andy Cox.

Novels

Instruments of the Night by Thomas H. Cook (Bantam) is a riveting thriller about a writer who has sublimated a childhood trauma and his complicity in it into a popular series of historical crime novels. His books are growing darker over the years. While he's vacationing at an artists' community, the estate's owner asks him to research the mysterious murder of her best friend years before, and he's grateful for the distraction. As he investigates, his past haunts him as memories surface from his subconscious. Psychologically rich, horrifying in its believable depiction of corruption of the innocent, and ultimately poignant.

White Bird in a Blizzard by Laura Kasischke (Hyperion) may not at first seem dark enough for some horror readers, but for those with open minds and a love of good writing, puzzles, and unexpected darkness welling up from apparent normality, this novel will intrigue. One day in the mid 1980s, an increasingly withdrawn and dissatisfied housewife abandons her bland husband and their teenage daughter. The story is told from the point of view of the daughter, who initially seems unaffected by her mother's disappearance. But over the three-year period during which the novel takes place, the reader begins to see how profoundly the mother affected her both before and after she disappeared. As the girl grapples with her emerging sexuality and her womanly power, she dreams unsettling dreams about her mother. And gradually, the true picture comes into focus in a powerful surge of suspense.

A Prayer for the Dying by Stewart O'Nan (Henry Holt) is a short, heartwrenching horror novel about a deeply religious Civil War veteran who is constable, preacher, and undertaker for a small town. A tramp's mysterious death and the appearance of a raving woman from a secretive religious enclave set into motion a series of horrific events that challenge the constable's faith. He is caught between two deadly threats: a diphtheria epidemic and out of control brushfires circling his town—either of which could destroy his family and his community. One of the best novels of the year.

Every Dead Thing by John Connolly (Simon & Schuster) is a refreshing, hard-hitting, and grisly debut by a Dublin journalist who brilliantly captures two quintessential American cities—New York and New Orleans. Former policeman Charlie (Bird) Parker is haunted by the sadistic murders of his wife and young daughter. Working as an unlicensed detective, Bird is unexpectedly drawn into New York mob rivalries and a series of thirty-year-old murders by what seems to be a routine missing persons case. Complicating things, he begins having visions of a young woman murdered in a manner similar to his family, years earlier in the bayous of Louisiana. Bird's journey south takes him down an increasingly intricate and twisted path of secrets, discoveries, and betrayals. Connolly develops believable, flawed characters who conduct relationships that make sense, and he holds the reader in his hand all the way.

Hannibal by Thomas Harris (Delacorte Press) is every bit as inventive, grisly, and suspenseful as *Red Dragon* and *The Silence of the Lambs*. But *Hannibal* is given an additional dimension by its depiction of the continuing pas de deux between serial cannibal, Hannibal Lecter, and FBI agent Clarice Starling that began in *The Silence of the Lambs*. Since escaping from custody seven years earlier, Lecter has been living a life of comfort, culture, and satisfaction in Florence, Italy. During that same period, Starling's career trajectory has been in a downward spiral since capturing the serial killer dubbed Buffalo Bill, as she deals with FBI bureaucracy and politics, and resentment of her early success. In the meantime, a surviving victim of Lecter's plots a gruesome revenge for the doctor.

Although these three form the nexus of *Hannibal*, there are other, equally fascinating characters who play important roles in the plot. But the novel, as fitting its title, becomes Hannibal's story—gradually shifting focus from Clarice. Harris does well to make the mysterious Dr. Lecter's perversions/interest in Starling more comprehensible by giving him a believable past. Lecter's life beyond his murderous impulses keeps the book lively and the reader on her toes. And the ending is perfectly if perversely apt. This does not mean the book is perfect—the shifting point of view with Harris addressing the reader directly is off-putting. I also find that the *very* last scene makes the ending more literal than necessary, damaging the delicate psychological and moral balance Harris so carefully constructed.

L.A. Requiem by Robert Crais (Doubleday) is the eighth title in this entertaining series about an L.A. private eye with the unlikely name of Elvis Cole. Just as Cole's lover and her young son move cross-country as a commitment to their relationship, Cole's partner and friend Joe Pike asks Elvis to help find a missing ex-lover. When the woman is found dead, her powerful father hires Pike and Cole to monitor the police investigation. Joe Pike has been a shadow figure in each of the previous Cole novels—tough and silent, he keeps to himself except when his partner needs help. Here, the reader learns a great deal of Pike's backstory as his past as an L.A. cop comes back to bite him. Crais does an excellent job developing his characters, providing the reader with insights into them over time, and giving the characters themselves realistic problems to deal with. *L.A. Requiem* is a suspenseful and colorful addition to the series.

The Extremes by Christopher Priest (St. Martin's Press) is a futuristic suspense novel about an FBI agent whose husband, also an agent, died in a Texan killing spree the same day as another spree took place in England. She goes to the town of Bulverton, England in an attempt to make some kind of sense of her husband's death—and to explore the meaning of the coincidental events. She visits the local ExEx (Extreme Experience) parlor, where anyone can enter virtual realities based on hundreds of scenarios involving sex and/or violence, including spree killings like the one that killed her husband. She is warned by GunHo (the company that produces the scenarios) representatives to leave because her investigations may contaminate the ExEx project they are creating using memories of the survivors. As she gets sucked into playing various mass murder scenarios in an attempt to affect the events within them, her reality starts shifting. The ambiguity of this ambitious and chilling novel's ending is perfectly appropriate. A fascinating precursor to the Cronenberg movie *eXistenZ*, which came out soon after the book was published in the U.K. and for which, (all too logically) Priest was hired under a pseudonym to write the novelization.

Mr. X by Peter Straub (Random House) is a feat of complexity as Straub deftly intertwines the experiences of two families in a southern Illinois town. Each birthday, Ned Dunstan has experienced convulsions during which he sees horrific visions of slaughter perpetuated by a mysterious man Ned thinks of as Mr. X. Ned has grown up fatherless and in foster homes, left there by his eccentric jazz singer mother throughout most of his childhood. He knows Star loves him but only begins to understand her seeming abandonment of him when he visits her on her deathbed. Before she dies, Star whispers two names, leading Ned on a quest for his true father. As Ned nears his thirty-fifth birthday, he is forced to accept his family's powerful genetic legacy—and the possibility that the mischievous doppelganger shadowing him might be his brother. The story is told from the shifting viewpoints of Ned and Mr. X, a man who follows the beliefs of a cult relating to H. P. Lovecraft and who is hunting Ned. Straub is one of the finest stylists writing in horror today, and has an imagination that continually creates colorful and memorable characters and strange magical places. This is a terrific multilayered novel with both supernatural and psychological horror elements.

King Rat by China Miéville (Macmillan/Tor) is about a young man whose life is turned upside down when he's framed for the murder of his father. A mysterious man/creature calling himself King Rat effortlessly helps our bewildered protagonist to escape jail, leading him through the sewers of underground London. King Rat informs him that his mother was a rat and that he, King Rat is his uncle. This strange creature seeks revenge against the piper of Hamelin, who killed his minions and stole his power five hundred years earlier. In the meantime, something vicious and powerful is murdering Londoners, and the cops who arrested him for his father's death believe it's our hero. Music and politics both play crucial (but not intrusive) roles in this beautifully written first novel, a dark fairy tale that is a welcome addition to the tradition of alternate Londons such as those conceived of by Michael Moorcock, Christopher Fowler, Neil Gaiman, Iain Sinclair, and Peter Ackroyd.

Heartwood by James Lee Burke (Doubleday) is the author's second novel about Deaf Smith, Texas, and Billy Bob Holland, the defense lawyer and former Texas Ranger who lives there. Literally haunted by the best friend he accidentally killed years earlier, Billy Bob gets drawn into the circle of the wealthy and arrogant Dietrich family. Billy Bob feels compelled to defend an unlucky local accused by the Dietrich family of theft. Unfortunately his loyalties, not to mention his emotions, are torn every time he encounters his first love, now Earl Dietrich's wife. Not unexpectedly, he uncovers greed and ruthlessness among the rich, and corruption in a justice system stacked against the poor. But Burke's true talent is multidimensional characterization. Billy Bob may be the protagonist of this complicated novel, but he's deeply flawed, continually struggling against his uncontrollable violent streak and his guilt for past sins.

Motherless Brooklyn by Jonathan Lethem (Doubleday) has for its protagonist and narrator, Lionel Essrog, a victim of Tourette's Syndrome. This means he twitches, tics, mumbles, and often yells curses uncontrollably. Lionel is one of Frank Minna's "boys." Minna is a local neighborhood tough who mentors Lionel and three other orphans living at St. Vincent's Home for Boys in the early 1970s, giving them something more interesting to do than just hang out after school—little "moving" jobs that none of the boys question. Once they leave the home, the four work for Minna's shady detective agency under the guise of a limousine service, loyal but ignorant of most of Minna's activities until the night Frank Minna is knifed to death and they are suddenly without a rudder. The unlikely Lionel, who because of his affliction is assumed to be stupid, sets out to find out who murdered Minna and why. This is Lethem's second unconventional foray into detective fiction; his first novel, *Gun, With Occasional Music* featured an evolved kangaroo as the villain. In *Motherless Brooklyn*, the author injects humor and irony into what could be a standard crime fiction plot. But what raises this novel exponentially out of any genre is his brilliant creation, Lionel, with his trials and tribulations.

The Marriage of Sticks by Jonathan Carroll (Tor) is a return to what Carroll does best: create marvelous characters then systematically dismantle their reality little by little, forcing them to come to terms with the mysteries hovering around them. Carroll's work always has the underpinnings of horror; his characters are forced to face the dark just under the surface of their seemingly cheery lives. This novel is no exception. The ostensibly charmed life of a lovely, rare-book dealer is completely altered by her high school reunion in Crane's View, New York (where Carroll's previous novel, the mystery *Kissing the Beehive*, takes place). Hoping to rekindle her high school romance with its bad boy, she is shocked to discover that he died a few years earlier. Upon her return to New York City she meets two fascinating people, a wealthy, elderly woman who knew just about *everybody* in her youth and a married man who knew her boyfriend. Carroll's panoply of images leaves imprints in the reader's mind: A woman in a stadium surrounded by every person she has ever encountered during each of her past lives; a lone woman in a wheelchair by the side of a teeming highway. But the author's depiction of his protagonist as a kind of psychic vampire destroying those around her is perplexing because this supposed character trait is never sufficiently rendered. As a result, the reader is left with a sense of auctorial intrusion rather than a natural perception of his protagonist's character.

The Intuitionist by Colson Whitehead (Anchor Books) is an ingenious mystery/alternative history that takes place in an unnamed big city modeled on New York in the 1940s. Two factions of elevator technicians are feuding: the empiricists and the intuitionists. Intuitionist Lila Mae Watson, whose work is under the strictest scrutiny because she is the first "colored" inspector in the city, and a female to boot, is under suspicion for an accident in one of her buildings. In order to clear herself, she accepts the assignment to search for the rumored lost notebooks of the founder of the intuitionist movement. The internal contradictions might make it unclear exactly *when* this story takes place but there's no doubt as to the racism permeating the world. The mystery is secondary to the author's fascinating riff on the zen of elevator maintenance plus his overt and covert attack on racism. But this makes the book no less enjoyable.

Collectors by Paul Griner (Random House) is an absorbing and sinister short novel about the peculiar mating dance between a sociopath and a troubled neurotic with a suspicious past. A talented advertising art director meets an attractive young man at her cousin's wedding and responds to his advances despite her misgivings. A beautifully written, unnerving tale that unfolds with a stark inevitability.

The Boy by Naeem Murr (Mariner Books) is a powerful debut novel about a human monster—a beautiful boy who insinuates himself into the lives of those around him, destroying them. One foster father, whose family has been victimized by the boy's maliciousness, is searching for the boy (who goes under different names), tracking him to a group home, then to the streets where he sells his body. Murr weaves a masterful web of interrelationships and creates a fascinatingly ambiguous character in this beautifully written and ultimately terrifying novel.

Black Light by Elizabeth Hand (HarperPrism) is a wonderful dark fantasy, related to the author's *Waking the Moon*. Charlotte Moylan (known as "Lit") is a typical seventeen year old living in the very untypical town of Kamensic, in upstate New York. Her actor parents and their friends are quirky and a little peculiar (not that Lit notices). The town is preparing for a huge Halloween bash being thrown by the charismatic film director Alex Kern who years before consorted with Andy Warhol and his entourage. As guests gather and the town prepares, Lit sees startling visions of ancient creatures that seem to be trying to communicate with her. And she is attracting the attention of Kern and others who see her as a powerful tool to create a New World order.

More Novels

Fountain Society by Wes Craven (Simon & Schuster); *Grimoire* by Kim Wilkins (Random House, Australia); *A Darker Place* by Laurie R. King (Bantam); *Ashes to Ashes* by Tami Hoag (Bantam); *Starr Bright Will Be With You Soon* by Rosamond Smith (Dutton); *The Breaker* by Minette Walters (Putnam); *Vittorio the Vampire* by Anne Rice (Knopf); *Skeptic* by Holden Scott (St. Martin's Press); *Sisters of the Night: Soul of an Angel* by Chelsea Quinn Yarbro (Avon); *Brass* by Robert J. Conley (Leisure); *Hexes* by Tom Piccirilli (Leisure); *Minions of the Moon* by Richard Bowes (Tor); *The Fall* by Simon Clark (Hodder & Stoughton, U.K.); *Mesmer* by Tim Lebbon (Tanjen); *Toyer* by Gardner McKay (Little, Brown); *Seize the Night* by Dean Koontz (Bantam); *Among the Missing* by Richard Laymon (Headline, U.K.); *The Homunculus* by Martin Wilson (Christoffel Press, U.K.—1998); *The Blue Hour* by T. Jefferson Parker (Little, Brown); *The Sub* by Thomas M. Disch (Knopf); *The Haunt* by J. N. Williamson (Leisure); *Bite* by Richard Laymon (Leisure); *Rats* by Paul Zindel (Hyperion); *Nightmare's Disciple* by Joseph Pulver, Sr. (Chaosium); *The Right Hand of Evil* by John Saul (Ballantine); *The Willow Tree* by Hubert Selby, Jr. (Bloomsbury, U.K.); *Dragonfly* by Frederic S. Durbin (Arkham House); *Solar Eclipse* by John Farris (Forge); *Cruddy* by Lynda Barry (Simon & Schuster); *The Rainy Season* by James P. Blaylock (Ace); *Night of the Wolf* by Alice Borchardt (Del Rey); *The Grigori Trilogy #2, Scenting Hallowed Blood* by Storm Constantine (Meisha Merlin); *The Repository* by Adam Niswander (Meisha Merlin); *Laws of Blood: The Hunt* by Susan Sizemore (Ace); *Regeneration* by Max Allan Collins and Barbara Collins (Leisure); *Incubus* by Ann Arensberg (Knopf); *Sips of Blood* by Mary Ann Mitchell (Leisure); *Waiting* by Frank M. Robinson (Forge); *Strangewood* by Christopher Golden (Signet); *Black Oak: Winter Knight* by Charles Grant (Roc); *The Promise* by Donna Boyd (Avon); *Bourland*

by James P. Roberts (Battered Silicon Dispatch Box); *The Guardian* by
Beecher Smith (Hot Biscuit Productions); *Snowman* by Graham Mas-
terton (Severn House); *Wild Horses* by Brian Hodge (Morrow); *Riders
in the Sky* by Charles Grant (Forge); *Welcome Back to the Night* by
Elizabeth Massie (Leisure); *Darker than Night* by Owl Goingback (Signet); *The Boy in the Lake* by Eric Swanson (St. Martin's Press); *Last
Things* by Jenny Offill (FS&G); *Hunting Down Amanda* by Andrew
Klavan (Morrow); *The Second Angel* by Philip Kerr (Holt); *The Great
Bagarozy* by Helmut Krausser (Dedalus, U.K.); *The Heart of a Witch*
by Judith Hawkes (Penguin/Signet); *The House* by Bentley Little (Pen-
guin/Signet); *Laws of the Blood: The Hunt* by Susan Sizemore (Ace);
Lords of Light by Steven Spruill (NEL, U.K.); *Midwinter of the Spirit*
by Phil Rickman (Macmillan, U.K.); *Seven Deadly Sins* by Michael
Bishop (pseudonymous author, not the well-known SF/F author)
(Checkmate); *Cleopatra's Needle* by Steven Siebert (Tor/Forge); *Others*
by James Herbert (Macmillan, U.K./Tor); *Satan Wants Me* by Robert
Irwin (Dedalus, U.K.); *Graveyard Dust* by Barbara Hambly (Bantam);
The Visionary by Don Passman (Warner); *News From the Edge: Vam-
pires of Vermont* by Mark Sumner (Ace); *The Green Mile: The Screen-
play* by Frank Darabont (Scribner); *The Reckoning* by Thomas F.
Monteleone (Forge); *The Crow: Temple of Night* by S. P. Somtow
(HarperEntertainment); *Demonesque* by Steven Lee Climer (Dark Tales
Publications on-demand book); *Skinners* by John Gordon (Scholastic/
Point, U.K.); *Man of the Hour* by Peter Blauner (Little, Brown): *Perl-
man's Ordeal* by Brooks Hansen (FS&G); *Something Dangerous* by
Patrick Redmond (Hyperion); *Boy in the Water* by Stephen Dobyns
(Metropolitan Books/Holt); *The Summer of 39* by Miranda Seymour
(W. W. Norton); *Body Politic* by Paul Johnston (St. Martin's Press);
Monster by Jonathan Kellerman (Random House); *A Red Heart of Mem-
ories* by Nina Kiriki Hoffman (Ace); and *Saint Fire* by Tanith Lee
(Overlook Press).

Anthologies

Whitley Strieber's Aliens edited by Whitley Strieber (Pocket Books) is
the HWA official anthology, intended to showcase work by members
of the Horror Writers Association. Although aliens are generally considered science fictional rather than horror, there's nothing that prevents
the use of aliens to create horrific fiction. So what is most surprising
about this anthology is that although it includes some fine stories, relatively few of them are horror.

In contrast, *Alien Abductions* edited by Martin H. Greenberg and

John Helfers (DAW) has a higher percentage of truly scary stories and novellas in it, notably by Peter Crowther and Nina Kiriki Hoffman. There's also a remarkable (but not horrific) story by Gary A. Braunbeck.

California Sorcery edited by William F. Nolan and William Schafer (Cemetery Dance Publications) is meant to honor a group of writers living in L.A. who were most active in the early 1950s to 1960s (although some continue to write fiction and/or screenplays). This prolific and creative group revolved around the tragic Charles Beaumont and included Ray Bradbury, Richard Matheson, William F. Nolan, and Harlan Ellison, among others. The twelve stories in the book, all but three previously unpublished, demonstrate the range of writing in the group— from science fiction by Nolan and dark mainstream by Matheson and Bradbury to a ghost story by Beaumont, erotica by Ray Russell, and a story by George Clayton Johnson that would have made a perfect *Twilight Zone* episode. Some of the stories feel like flashbacks to earlier decades—which is not to say they're dated, but that they lack a contemporary feel to them. An informative group profile by Chris Conlon rounds out this attractive, important tribute to our horror/suspense roots.

Dark Detectives, edited by Stephen Jones (Fedogan & Bremer), is one of the best anthologies of the year, with psychic detective stories by diverse hands, including Kim Newman's fine interstitial novel *Seven Stars*. With cover art by Les Edwards, excellent interior illustrations by Randy Broeckner, and an informative history of supernatural sleuths by Jones from Poe's C. Auguste Dupin to those more recent. A limited hardcover edition of one hundred copies was published in addition to a trade hardcover edition.

999, edited by Al Sarrantonio (Avon), was the most hyped book of the year. The editor and publisher proclaimed it the *Dark Forces* of the new millennium. The editor's brief: "to prove once and for all that the horror and suspense genre is a serious literary one" implies either that the anthology it attempts to emulate didn't do the trick or, that his anthology is more literary than *DF*. In either case, he's dead wrong. There is nothing in *999* that couldn't have been published in any other horror anthology. As with even the best original anthologies, there are some excellent stories and some mediocre ones. The ballyhooed William Peter Blatty piece reads like a trunk screenplay. That said, the book does contain some excellent work, including stories by Neil Gaiman and Gene Wolfe reprinted herein. But was it worth the reported $300,000 advance paid by the publisher?

Another eagerly anticipated original anthology was *Subterranean Gallery*, edited by Richard Chizmar and William Schafer (Subterranean

Press). The anthology has an excellent lineup of mostly psychological stories (four reprints), and a few of them are quite good, particularly those by Gary A. Braunbeck and Tia V. Travis. Disappointingly, there are no author bios and no introduction to the volume.

Northern Frights 5 edited by Don Hutchison (Mosaic Press) is an excellent entry in this predictably fine anthology series from Canada. There were terrific stories by Susan MacGregor, James Powell, and Gemma Files, the last reprinted herein.

Night Shades: Gothic Tales by Women edited by Victoria A. Brownworth and Judith M. Redding (Seal Press) contains mostly original stories by contemporary women writers. While some of the stories are effective, there's very little horror and even less edge.

White of the Moon: New Tales of Madness and Dread edited by Stephen Jones (Pumpkin Books—available from Firebird Distributors in the U.S.) is a nicely varied companion volume to *Dark of the Night*, Jones's earlier non-theme anthology, with some excellent stories, including one by Kim Newman reprinted herein.

Palace Corbie Eight edited by Wayne Edwards (Merrimack Books) is the last volume of this notable cross-genre anthology series that began as a magazine and mutated into an annual. There is some good horror in the book, particularly the story by Douglas Clegg.

The Asylum: Volume 1, The Psycho Ward edited by Victor Heck (Dark Tales Publications) takes its title too literally and its theme too seriously. Most of the stories take place in a psycho ward or end up there. The strongest are by Douglas Clegg, Sephera Giron, and J. F. Gonzalez. If crazed serial killers and other assorted bogeymen and women are your cup of tea, this might be for you.

Bedtime Stories to Darken Your Dreams, edited by Bruce Holland Rogers (IFD Publishing), is designed and illustrated by Alan M. Clark, and as such makes a spectacular package for older children and young adults. It features a mixture of reprints and originals by writers such as Jane Yolen, Gary Braunbeck, Melanie Tem, Elizabeth Engstrom, and Steve Rasnic Tem.

Cemetery Sonata, edited by June Hubbard (Chameleon Publishing), is a trade paperback of mostly original stories about death by predominantly new writers. The production values are dreadful, with no design sense in evidence (the text is double-spaced and unjustified). Some good stories but not worth the hefty price.

Dead Promises, edited by June Hubbard (Chameleon Publishing), is better designed than the above title, but its narrow focus on "Civil War Ghost Stories" makes for a dull read, with a few exceptions.

The Last Continent: New Tales of Zothique edited by John Pelan

(Shadowlands Press) has new stories written in homage to Clark Ashton Smith's creation. I frankly admit that this is just not to my taste, but anyone who loves Smith's work and this particular literary tradition will be quite satisfied. For me, the stories I enjoyed most were those that veered furthest away from that tradition. The beautiful jacket art is by Rob Alexander, and the introduction is by Donald Sidney-Fryer. The book is limited to 550 copies, all signed by the artist, editor, and author of the introduction and with fifty deluxe copies bound in leather.

New Mythos Legends, edited by Bruce Gehweiler (Marietta Publishing), is an excellent anthology of mostly original and quite varied Lovecraftian stories. Five artists provide black and white interior illustrations and the cover art is by Allen Koszowski.

Tales Out of Innsmouth: New Stories of the Children of Dagon, selected and introduced by Robert M. Price (Chaosium), is an entertaining mix of mostly new (three reprints) stories about the town that H. P. Lovecraft created.

Future Crimes, edited by Martin H. Greenberg and John Helfers (DAW), is an all-original science fiction/crime anthology with some very good dark stories.

Writers of the Future, Volume XV, the annual anthology sponsored by Bridge Publications, edited by Algis Budrys, has several good stories tinged with horror by new, upcoming authors.

Divas of Darkness, edited by Greg F. Gifune (Thievin' Kitty Publications), features stories by nine female writers. Nancy Kilpatrick provides the introduction.

Nasty Snips, edited by Christopher C. Teague (MT Publishing, U.K.), is an anthology of short-short horror vignettes.

The Sorcerer's Apprentice: New Tales in the Tradition of Clark Ashton Smith (Sunken Citadel/Tenoka Press) is an original anthology (unseen) of sixteen stories, five poems, and one essay. It has black and white illustrations by a variety of artists and cover art by Mike Minnis.

The Twilight Tales (11th Hour Productions) series of limited edition chapbooks presents original stories and reprints by authors who have participated in the Chicago reading series. During 1999 the group published *Winter Tales, When the Bough Breaks, Play it Again Sam*, and *Animals Don't Knock: Tails from the Pet Shop*. Tina L. Jens edits the series. *Twilight Tales Presents: Book of Dead Things*, also edited by Jens, is the series' first perfect bound book. I'm afraid it fell apart during its first reading, a pity because the cover art and design is by Alan M. Clark. Some of the reprinted material is noteworthy, but most of the ten originals are pretty thin. Twilight Tales also published a collection of stories by Martin Mundt called *The Crawling Abattoir. Mean Time*, edited by Jerry Sykes (Do Not Press/Bloodlines imprint, U.K.), contains mostly original crime stories that take place around the millennium.

Reprint Anthologies

The Antarktos Cycle: Horror and Wonder at the Ends of the Earth, edited by Robert M. Price (Chaosium), the series editor, brings together some excellent fiction by Arthur C. Clarke, Edgar Allan Poe, Jules Verne, and John W. Campbell ("The Thing from Another World"), and others, that while not related to the Lovecraftian mythos—some written prior to Lovecraft—do seem to contain the spirit of Lovecraft; *The Ithaqua Cycle: The Wind-Walker of the Icy Wastes: 14 Tales*, selected and introduced by Robert M. Price (Chaosium), series editor, includes stories by August Derleth, Brian Lumley, and Joseph Payne Brennan; *Great Weird Tales: Fourteen Stories by Lovecraft, Blackwood, Machen, and Others*, edited by S. T. Joshi (Dover), with an introduction by Joshi, contains stories of horror, fantasy, and pseudo-science; *Nightshade: 20th Century Ghost Stories*, edited by Robert Philips (Carroll & Graf), features stories by Truman Capote, Shirley Jackson, Max Beerbohm, Alison Lurie, William Trevor, and others; *Crossing the Border*, edited by Lisa Tuttle (Indigo, U.K.), contains original and reprinted erotic stories about "sexual ambiguity." There isn't a lot of dark fiction in the anthology but there is work by writers known for their genre work, such as Lucy Taylor, Neil Gaiman, Graham Joyce, Angela Carter, Melissa Mia Hall, and the editor herself; Tor's Orb line reprinted *Conjure Wife* and *Our Lady of Darkness*, the two Fritz Leiber classics, in one trade paperback entitled *Dark Ladies; American Gothic: An Anthology 1787–1916* edited by Charles Crow (Blackwell) reprints stories and novellas by Edgar Allan Poe, Edith Wharton, Louisa May Alcott, Emily Dickinson, Henry James, and others, preceding each selection by a brief biographical sketch and essay on how each author's work reflects the genre; *Isaac Asimov's Werewolves* edited by Gardner Dozois and Sheila Williams (Ace); *The Best from Fantasy and Science Fiction*, edited by Edward L. Ferman and Gordon Van Gelder (Tor), reprints stories published 1994–1998—mostly science fiction and fantasy, with a bit of horror; *The Best American Short Stories 1999*, guest edited by Amy Tan with series editor Katrina Kenison (Houghton Mifflin), occasionally includes darker fiction by mainstream authors; *Vampire Slayers: Stories of Those Who Dare Take Back the Night* and *Children of the Night: Stories of Ghosts, Vampires, Werewolves and "Lost Children,"* both edited by Martin H. Greenberg and Elizabeth Ann Scarborough (both from Cumberland House); *The Mammoth Book of Best New Horror:*

Tenth Anniversary Edition, edited by Stephen Jones (Robinson, U.K.), features a few stories and one novella that overlap with our own *Year's Best*. Jones also has an overview and a necrology; *The Best American Mystery Stories 1999*, edited by Ed McBain, series editor Otto Penzler (Houghton Mifflin), reprints nineteen suspense/crime/mystery stories by such varied writers as Joyce Carol Oates, Gary A. Braunbeck, David B. Silva, Ed Gorman, and John Updike; *Technohorror: Inventions in Terror*, edited by James Frenkel (Roxbury Park/Lowell House), reprints stories that intersect both science fiction and horror and contains classics and newer stories by Ray Bradbury, Robert Bloch, Pat Cadigan, Stephen King, Michael Swanwick, and John Shirley, among others; *Bangs & Whimpers: Stories About the End of the World*, edited by James Frenkel (Roxbury Park/Lowell House), collects stories by Neil Gaiman, Philip K. Dick, James Thurber, Connie Willis, James Tiptree, Jr., and others; *The Best of Pirate Writings: Tales of Fantasy, Mystery and Science Fiction*, edited by Edward J. McFadden III (Padwolfe Publishing), reprints thirty stories from the magazine, including stories by Jack Cady, Tom Piccirilli, Jessica Amanda Salmonson; *Jersey Ghouls: Stories and Poetry by the Garden State Horror Writers* selected by John R. Platt, reprints sixteen stories and poems by members of the decade-old writers' group; Ash-Tree Press, run by Barbara and Christopher Roden, continues to bring out collectible hardcover editions of obscure gothic and weird fiction with an abundance of 1999 titles including *The Ash-Tree Press Annual Macabre 1999*, edited by Jack Adrian, bringing back into print six ghost stories originally published between 1908 and 1940 by Neil Gow, Eric Ambrose, and four other writers. The cover illustration is by Rob Suggs; and *The Crow: Shattered Lives & Broken Dreams*, edited by J. O'Barr and Ed Kramer (Del Rey), is a trade paperback edition that differs slightly from last year's hardcover. The Andrew Vachss story has been replaced with an original story by Edward Bryant.

Collections

What You Make It by Michael Marshall Smith (HarperCollins, U.K.) is the first collection by this talented author. Smith burst onto the U.K. horror scene a bit over a decade ago by winning the British Fantasy Award for his first published short story and then winning it again the next year for another. While his novels (*Only Forward, Spares*, and *One of Us*) are science fiction, only a few of his short stories are. Most of them are dark and intense—and many are imbued with a longing for romance. Part of the intensity and immediacy is a result of the first-person point of view Smith often uses. Smith is a terrific storyteller and you can't go wrong paging through the collection to read any of the stories at random. Some of the stories have been in the *Year's Best Fantasy and Horror*.

The Alchemy of Love is a darkly imaginative and hallucinatory trip with Elizabeth Engstrom and Alan M. Clark (Triple Tree Publishing). Clark's art and Engstrom's prose—all original to the book—inspire each other and each piece is a perfect match. Engstrom has been interested in erotic obsession from her earliest fiction, and *The Alchemy of Love* frees her to explore the subject in multiple permutations. The book is appropriately bracketed by two tragic stories about characters with relationship problems. The physical book is beautiful, with a stunning wraparound cover in shades of gray. Unfortunately, it's only available in a hardcover limited edition.

Hearts in Atlantis by Stephen King (Scribner) collects five interconnected narratives set from 1960 to 1999. The first novella, "Low Men in Yellow Coats," is moving and frightening as it depicts strange men who threaten the friendship that has developed between a young boy and a mysterious boarder in his home. At least one of the pieces, "Blind Willie," was previously published.

A Vaudeville of Devils: 7 Moral Tales by Robert Girardi (Delacorte) is a fascinating world tour by a terrific storyteller. Each story or novella involves a moral decision. The most overtly horrific is "The Dinner Party," reprinted herein. As an unnamed Latin American country burns, a group of gods or monsters have a high time, inviting some "lucky" mortals for cocktails. "Arcana Mundi" takes place in a post-apocalyptic future. Insects have attacked a California vineyard but the owner's young daughter prophesies that men will arrive to save the winery. Sure enough, two strange old men calling themselves Mutt and Jeff come and save the day. All they want is one simple thing.

John Shirley's new collection is called *Really, Really, Really, Really, Weird Stories* (Night Shade Books). And that's what they are—the stories that Shirley considers his weirdest. What's in here is a rich mixture of science fiction, fantasy, horror, and just plain strange stories, vignettes, and rants. The attractive trade paperback, with cover art and design by Alan M. Clark, collects stories from 1973 to 1999, with several previously unpublished. One was chosen for an earlier volume of *Year's Best Fantasy and Horror*.

Subterranean Press published George Clayton Johnson's *All of Us Are Dying*, named after his classic tale of shifting identity which was adapted into a *Twilight Zone* episode. Johnson's best work crosses the boundaries from fantasy to dark fantasy and mainstream with ease. This career retrospective contains stories, teleplays, screenplays, articles, and vignettes, some previously unpublished (mostly reminiscences) including the autobiographical mainstream novella "Every Other War." It has an afterword by Dennis Etchison. Limited to 600 signed and numbered copies and 26 signed/lettered sets. The book has really lovely cover art by Burt Shonberg. Subterranean also published *The Lost Bloch by Robert Bloch Volume One*, edited by David L. Schow. This is the first in a projected series of three collections by the father of psychological horror that is to include one or more short "pulp" novels written in the forties and fifties plus several novella-length works. Volume One includes a formerly unpublished interview with Bloch by Schow from 1991. Jacket illustration is by Bernie Wrightson. Available in signed trade and signed and lettered limited editions. Subterranean also published the dreamlike collection, *Lulu and One Other*, by Thomas Tessier, a chapbook of a story and three linked vignettes. Limited to 250 signed and 26 signed and lettered copies. Cover is by Tim Holt.

Waltzes and Whispers by Jay Russell (Pumpkin Books) is the first collection by a writer whose first print appearance in Paul Sammon's *Splatterpunk* anthology under the name J. S. Russell, gave no hint of the range of his horror fiction. But Russell writes wonderfully varied stories about zombies, naive superheroes, former child stars turned private eyes, and a host of other characters. The book comes with an introduction by Michael Marshall Smith and an afterword by Kim Newman. Cover art and interior illustrations are by John Coulthart. Limited to 750 copies in hardcover.

The Wishmaster by Peter Atkins (Pumpkin Books) collects eleven short stories (three originals) and the original screenplay of the horror movie *Wishmaster*, written by Atkins. The book has an introduction by Ramsey Campbell, interior illustrations by Randy Broeckner, and a cover illustration by Les Edwards. Limited to 750 copies in hardcover.

The Longest Single Note and Other Strange Compositions by Peter Crowther (Cemetery Dance Publications) is an excellent showcase for this British author. This limited edition with cover art by Alan M. Clark has nineteen stories, three poems, and an excerpt from a novel-in-progress. One of the stories appeared in a previous volume of *Year's Best Fantasy and Horror*. One poem and three of the stories are original to the volume. *Lonesome Roads*, a collection of three previously published novellas also by Crowther, was published by Razorblade Press in an attractive trade paperback format, with an introduction by Graham Joyce and cover illustration by Chris Nurse.

Night Tales by John Maclay (John Maclay) is the author's third collection of short stories. Two stories in it were first published in 1999, one of these in this collection.

Uncut is by the prolific short story writer Christopher Fowler (Warner, U.K.). Some of the stories have appeared in earlier collections of Fowler's, but others are collected here for the first time and a few are original to the volume. Sharp, witty, and compulsively readable.

The House of the Nightmare by Edward Lucas White (Midnight House) collects ten stories that hold up quite well in the creepiness department, no matter that all but one were published in the collection *Lukundoo* in 1927 and one earlier than that. The jacket art and author illustrations are by Allen Koszowski. Limited to a hardcover edition of 260 copies, 250 of these offered for sale.

My Own Private Spectres by Jean Ray (Midnight House) is the first English language edition of horror stories by Ray in thirty years. The stories were all originally published in French between 1921 and 1974. This excellent collectible edition has been translated and edited by Hubert Van Calenbergh. Jacket art is by Allen Koszowski. Ray's novel *Malpertuis* was published in its first English translation in 1998.

Refugees from an Imaginary Country by Darrell Schweitzer (W. Paul Ganley: Publisher and Owlswick Press) is the author's third short story collection, and includes his dark fantasy work between 1987 and 1997. It has jacket art and interior illustrations by Stephen E. Fabian and is available in a trade paperback and a signed, limited hardcover edition of 300 copies.

Necromancies and Netherworlds: Uncanny Stories by Darrell Schweitzer and Jason Van Hollander (Wildside Press) is a beautifully produced collection of their collaborations written since 1986. Schweitzer, editor of *Weird Tales*, has been writing strange stories as well as writing *about* the weird tale for many years. Van Hollander is a talented artist who provided the beautiful cover art and design and drew the interior illustrations for the book. It's available in hardcover and trade paperback.

Whispers in the Night by Basil Copper (Fedogan & Bremer) feels like a time capsule from an earlier era, despite the fact that most of the eleven stories were written in the past decade. Only one story doesn't work at all, the cautionary science fiction/horror yarn "Out There"—it reminds one of a fifties atomic monster movie. The rest have an old-fashioned feel to them, something traditionalists might very well appreciate. Stephen Jones's introduction notes the influence of Copper's fiction on many British writers and editors. Eight of the stories are original to the collection. Published in a trade edition and a slipcased, limited edition of 100 copies. Jacket art and interior illustrations by Stephen Fabian.

Salt Snake & Other Bloody Cuts by Simon Clark (Silver Salamander Press) is the author's second collection of horror stories and it's a limited run of 860 signed copies, with 850 for sale in three editions: 500 trade paperback, 300 numbered hardcover, plus 50 numbered copies bound in leather. Cover art is by Fredrik King.

The Pit and the Pendulum and other stories by Edgar Allan Poe (Viking) with new illustrations by James Prunier does a superb job of simultaneously attracting and teaching the young readers toward whom it's aimed by using classical (and occasionally nightmarish) illustrations and interesting annotations.

The Nightmare Chronicles by Douglas Clegg (Leisure) is the overdue first collection by a premiere storyteller and author of several novels. Clegg uses a framing device that, while unnecessary, works fine for those readers who need to feel as if they're reading a novel. The thirteen stories are uniformly excellent; three of them were published in earlier volumes of *Year's Best Fantasy and Horror.*

Brotherly Love & Other Tales of Faith and Knowledge by David Case (Pumpkin Books) is an excellent mixture of six stories and novellas of dark fantasy, horror, and dark science fiction by this relatively unknown (at least in the U.S.) British writer. Ramsey Campbell contributed an introduction to this attractive hardcover edition limited to 750 copies. Les Edwards did the jacket art.

Horror Shorts: 1st Collection and *Mystery & Horror Shorts: 1st Collection*, both by Guy N. Smith, were published in the U.K. by the author's own Bulldog Books. They are in magazine format and contain stories spanning two decades.

Neil Gaiman's Midnight Days (DC Vertigo) reprints, for the first time, five tales from Gaiman's early career at DC. Illustrated by Dave McKean, Mike Mignola, Steven Bissette, and others.

The Essential Clive Barker: Selected Fictions (HarperCollins, U.K.) is a selection of fifty-three excerpts from the author's plays and novels, plus four short stories. Each of the thirteen sections has an introduction by the author.

More Binscombe Tales by John Whitbourn (Ash-Tree Press) provides a new batch of reprinted and original occult stories about the town of Binscombe in southeast England. The stories are very homey, and usually leavened with humor no matter how sinister some of them may be.

The Ushers by Edward Lee (Obsidian Press) is the author's first collection. Lee has grown from very rough writing to a more polished style but his work is as raw as ever—it's a question of taste perhaps.

He writes to shock, with gross and gory sexual situations. Cover art and author portrait is by Alan M. Clark. Interior black and white illustrations are by GAK, V. Blast, and Erik Wilson.

Deep into the Darkness Peering by Tom Piccirilli (Terminal Fright Press) gathers together most of the short work by this promising newer writer. The book includes more than forty stories and poems, several new—including a novella that makes a fine addition to the author's ongoing series about a necromancer and his demonic alter ego, "Self." The dust jacket art and interior illustrations are by Chad Savage, there is an overall introduction by Poppy Z. Brite, and publisher Ken Abner provides an introductory essay about the "Self" stories. In addition there is an interview with the author conducted by Richard Laymon. The signed and numbered edition is limited to 1,000 copies and there is a lettered edition as well.

The House Spider and Other Strange Visitors (Delirium Books) by Kurt Newton contains ten stories published between 1993 and 1999, two of them original to the book, with an introduction by Charlee Jacob and art by Roddy Williams. Limited to 50 hardcover signed copies.

Tartarus Press published several excellent collections of new and classic work in the field of the supernatural and weird tale, including: *Forever Azathoth and Other Horrors* by Peter Cannon, a wonderful compilation of new and reprinted stories, most of them parodies and pastiches of H. P. Lovecraft. The excellent cover art and frontispiece is by Jason C. Eckhardt. Limited to 250 numbered and signed copies. *In Violet Veils and Other Tales of the Connoisseur* by Mark Valentine is an entertaining collection of nine stories, all but two originals, about an occult detective. Limited to 200 numbered and signed copies. Cover is by Peter Strausfield. *Uncanny Tales* by F. Marion Crawford, "A Were-Wolf of the Campagna" by Mrs. Hugh Fraser, and "A Mystery of the Campagna" by Von Degan: The latter two stories are by Crawford's two sisters. Richard Dalby provides an introduction to Crawford and his family's works. Limited to a hardcover edition of 250 numbered copies. *The Doll Maker and Other Tales of the Uncanny* by Sarban, last published in 1953, contains two novellas in addition to the title story. Tartarus also published Sarban's short novel *The Sound of His Horn* and the newly discovered novella "King of the Lake" in one volume. The most impressive achievement of Tartarus in 1999 was its publication, in partnership with Durtro Press, of *Robert Aickman: The Collected Strange Stories, Volume I and II* in beautiful hardcover editions. The first volume has an essay by Aickman, an appreciation by publisher David Tibet, and a reminiscence by Ramsey Campbell. Cover art is by Stephen Stapleton.

Antique Futures: The Best of Terry Dowling (MP Books) collects thirteen stories by this versatile writer of science fiction and horror. The cover art is by Nick Stathopoulos and Jack Dann has provided an introduction.

The Lady of Situations by Stephen Dedman (Ticonderoga Publications) is the first collection by this author of two novels and some excellent short stories. It has twelve stories, one original.

Dread in the Beast is Charlee Jacob's first collection (Necro Publications). Of the sixteen stories, six are original to the collection. They're mostly psychological horror pieces that are long on brutality but short on plot. It's a handsome-looking package available in signed limited hardcover and paperback editions, with cover art by Brandy Gill.

The prolific collaborators L. H. Maynard and M. P. N. Sims had two stories published in a chapbook called *Silent Turmoil* (Dream Zone Publications) as the first of a series in the "Haunted Dreams" series of novellas and longer fiction.

The eight stories in S. P. Somtow's *Dragon's Fin Soup* are steeped in Thai traditions and are a mixed bag of the charming, the exotic, and deeply disturbing horror. In contrast, the thirteen stories of David J. Schow's reprinted *Seeing Red*, are flavored with a quintessentially American sensibility and vividly demonstrate the author's love of old monster movies. The other reissue is Dennis Etchison's first collection, *The Dark Country*, with its British Fantasy Award and World Fantasy Award–winning title story. All three are from Alexander Publishing.

In Lovecraft's Shadow (Battered Silicon Dispatch Box/Mycroft & Moran) brings together all of August Derleth's Lovecraftian Mythos stories (excluding his Lovecraft collaborations), three poems (one previously unpublished), and an essay. Illustrated by Stephen Fabian.

The Phantom Coach and Other Ghost Stories of an Antiquary by Augustus Jessop (Richard H. Fawcett Publisher) is edited and introduced by Jessica Amanda Salmonson and illustrated by Wendy Wees. Limited to 400 copies.

Cornish Drolls collects short, predominantly supernatural stories by Joseph Henry Pearce (1854–93) taken from his two collections. Edited by C. D. Pollard with an introduction by Brendan MacMahon (Llanerch Publishers).

Fedogan & Bremer reissued their first title, *Colossus: The Collected Science Fiction of Donald Wandrei*, with two never-before-published stories, a photo gallery, and an updated biography by Richard L. Tierney.

Durtro Press (sister imprint to the Ghost Story Press) published *The Child of the Soul and Other Tales* by Count Eric Stenbock. The book contains four unknown and previously unpublished stories plus the full text of three letters written by Stenbock to the composer Norman O'Neill. Introduction is by David Tibet. Limited to 500 copies.

Sarob Press presented several titles, including *The Blue Room and Other Ghost Stories* by Lettice Galbraith, inaugurating a projected new series reprinting the stories of neglected, but worthy, British "mistresses of the macabre." The second volume is *In the Dark and Other Ghost Stories* by Mary E. Penn. The black and white cover illustration and interior illustrations are by Paul Lowe. Both volumes are edited and introduced by Richard Dalby; *Shadows at Midnight* by L. H. Maynard and M. P. N. Sims in an attractive hardcover edition with jacket and interior illustrations by Douglas Walters. The collection was originally published in 1979 but all ten stories from that edition have been revised, and two new stories have been added; *Margery of Quether and Other Weird Tales* by Sabine Baring-Gould, edited and with an introduction by Richard Dalby with the original magazine illustrations by Harry Furniss and dust jacket illustration by Paul Lowe.

Delta Trade Paperbacks published *More Annotated H. P. Lovecraft*, edited by S. T. Joshi and Peter Cannon.

Nightscape by Michael Pendragon (B.J.M. Press) collects ten stories by the author. There are no publication credits in the chapbook but I believe most, if not all of the stories were previously published.

Odder than Ever by Bruce Coville (Harcourt Brace) is a young adult collection of nine stories, three original.

The Four Corners of the Tapestry by Jared Lobdell (Pulpless.Com) has four original Lovecraftian occult detective stories. An on-demand edition.

Triple Feature (Subterranean Press/Orbit) presents three short original stories by Joe R. Lansdale in an attractive chapbook format limited to 450 signed and numbered copies and 26 signed and lettered. Although not Lansdale's best work, the book should make collectors happy. Illustrations are by Glenn Chadbourne.

Zom Bee Moo Vee and Other Freaky Shows by Mark McLaughlin (Fairwood Press) is an adorable looking paperback chapbook of nine twisted little short stories (one original) about monsters and movies. The attractive cover art and interiors are by Paul Swenson. Definitely worth the money if only for its value as an artifact, but the stories are worth reading as well.

Demons, Freaks, and Other Abnormalities by Michael Laimo (Delirium Books) is an attractive hardcover. Most of the stories are from 1999, with three published for the first time in the collection. Introduction by Tom Piccirilli; artwork by Keith Minnion. Published in a signed, numbered limited edition of 150 copies.

Shadows Before the Maiming by Scott C. Haldstad (Gothic Press) collects thirty-six poems, most with horror elements.

Scrying the River Styx by Wendy Rathbone (Anamnesis Press) collects thirteen poems, six originals.

The Slitherers by John Russell Fearn (Gryphon Books) is a collection of a short science fiction/horror novel and a story that is an early treatment of the same theme. Introduction by Philip Harbottle. Cover by Ron Turner.

The following, all from Ash-Tree Press, are well-made hardcover editions usually limited to 500 to 600 copies, of notable out of print titles: *Norton Vyse Psychic* by Rose Champion de Crespigny edited by Jack Adrian (Ash-Tree Press Occult Detectives Library) is the second volume in the series and presents six stories never before collected in book form. The author switched from writing historical stories and novels to detective fiction after World War I. Later, her fiction began to reflect her abiding interest in psychic research and other aspects of the occult. *The Phantom Coach* by Amelia B. Edwards collects all the supernatural fiction of this Victorian writer. Edited and with an introduction by Richard Dalby. Cover illustration by Paul Lowe. *The Passenger* by E. F. Benson is the second of five volumes edited by Jack Adrian in Ash-Tree's Collected Spook Stories series. The volume covers the period of 1912–21, has an introduction by Adrian and jacket art by Douglas Walters. *Out of the Dark, Volume Two: Diversions* by Robert W. Chambers is edited and has an introduction by Hugh Lamb and presents the best of the author's post-1900 short fiction. Cover illustration by Richard Lamb. *The Night Wind Howls* by Frederick Cowles includes all of the author's supernatural stories taken from his three collections: *The Horror of Abbott's Grange, The Night Wind Howls,* and *Fear Walks the Night,* plus an account of a "true haunting." The book has a foreword by the author's son and an introduction by Hugh Lamb. The cover illustration is by Linda Dyde. *The Wind at Midnight* by Georgia Wood Pangborn is edited and has an introduction by Jessica Amanda Salmonson plus a preface by Patricia A. McKillip. This volume collects all of the author's significant supernatural stories. The jacket art is by Deborah McMillion-Nering. *Six Ghost Stories* by T. G. Jackson, with an introduction by Richard Dalby, is notable for being, with the exception of one story, the first time these stories have been reprinted in book form since 1919. Jackson was one of the foremost architects in England, in his day, and wrote ghost stories for the amusement of his family and friends. *Strayers from Sheol* by H. R. Wakefield incorporates four stories published after the author's death in 1964 with the revised (by Wakefield's notes) texts of the original volume published in 1961. Barbara Roden provides a biographical study of Wakefield, and Paul Lowe did the jacket illustration. *The Terraces of Night* by Margery Lawrence is a companion volume to the earlier *Nights of the Round Table* and has twelve stories. Richard Dalby continues his biography of the author in his introduction. Cover illustration by Paul Lowe. *Ghost Gleams* by W. J. Wintle is the first reprint of a collection originally published in 1921. The new edition has an introduction by Richard Dalby and a cover illustration by Jason C. Eckhardt. *Warning Whispers* by A. M. Burrage, edited by Jack Adrian, is the fourth volume in this series collecting all the prolific author's ghost stories. It contains eight, formerly uncollected tales. Cover illustration is by Doug Walters.

Ancient Exhumations by Stanley C. Sargent (Mythos Books) is a trade paperback collecting seven Lovecraftian tales by a new voice in this subgenre. The cover art is by D. L. Hutchinson with interior illustrations by the author, Peter Worthy, Jeffrey Thomas, Daniel Alan Ross, and Hutchinson. Introduction by Peter Worthy and preface by Robert M. Price.

Down to Sleep by Greg F. Gifune (Goddess of the Bay Publications) is a first collection in trade paperback with an introduction by Trey R. Barker and cover art by Keith Minnion.

Of Pigs and Spiders by Edward Lee, John Pelan, David Niall Wilson, and Brett Savory (Shadowlands Press) collects two collaborative stories in chapbook format. Cover art by H. Ed Cox. Limited to 333 signed copies.

Skull-Job (Hatchet-Job Press) collects Scott Urban's poetry in a chapbook with jacket art and illustrations by Duncan Long. With an introduction by Michael Arnzen.

Five Spots on the Newt & Other Poems of a Curious Nature by Kurt Newton (Yellow Toad Press) is a nicely produced self-published chapbook with excellent cover and interior illustrations by Roddy Williams.

Avatars of the Old Ones are three mythos tales by Jeffrey Thomas, (Mythosian) two of them original to the chapbook. The introduction is by W. H. Pugmire, and Todd H. C. Fischer illustrated it.

Dreams of Lovecraftian Horror by W. H. Pugmire (Mythos Books) collects fourteen original tales by the author. Introduction and artwork is by Stanley C. Sargent.

Miscellany Macabre: Tales of the Unknown by Ken Cowley (BFS) collects ten stories, three originals. The nicely produced chapbook has in an introduction by Ramsey Campbell, and an article on the early days of pulp publishing. The cover photograph is by David J. Howe and interior illustrations are by David Bezzina.

Snakelust by Kenji Nakagami, translated by Andrew Rankin (Kodansha International), collects seven stories, some with ghosts, demons and visions.

Miss or Mrs: the Haunted Hotel, the Guilty River by Wilkie Collins (Oxford University Press, U.K.) collects three long tales (the middle a ghost story) edited and with an introduction and notes by Norman Page and Toru Sasaki.

Mixed-Genre Collections

Beast of the Heartland by Lucius Shepard (Four Walls Eight Windows) is the first U.S. edition of *Barnacle Bill the Spacer*, published in the U.K. in 1997. Although Shepard is better known for his science fiction, throughout his career he has written powerful works combining science fiction with horror, such as his first novel, *Green Eyes*, the novella, *R & R*, and the story "Mengele." And some of his fiction is straight horror such as "How the Wind Spoke at Madaket," "A Little Night Music," and of course, his vampire novel, *The Golden*. *Beast of the Heartland* presents in seven stories and novellas a showcase for Shepard's talent for creating memorable characters and a distinct sense of place, whether it's the Middle East, outer space, or a claustrophobic apartment in Manhattan where a man is going mad.

During her long career, Kit Reed has written science fiction and fantasy stories ranging from the bleak ("Frontiers") to the hilarious ("Like My Dress"). In addition to her science fiction novels, she's written psychological thrillers under the Kit Craig pseudonym. Her newest collection, *Seven for the Apocalypse* (Wesleyan University Press), takes her James Tiptree, Jr. Award–shortlisted novella *Little Sisters of the Apocalypse* (originally published as a chapbook) and puts it with seven other stories. Reed is an expert satirist and her disquieting story about life in a very unusual penal colony is as funny as it is vicious; Charles de Lint's collection of Newford stories *Moonlight and Vines* (Tor) brings together a new batch of tales taking place in the magical town of Newford and includes a few originals. The author does a masterful job of mixing the everyday with the supernatural; *The Oracle Lips* by Storm Constantine (Stark House) has several stories original to the volume and provides a good overview of the author's fantasy and dark fantasy work; *Herland, The Yellow Wallpaper, and Selected Writings* by Charlotte Perkins Gilman (Penguin) combines the utopian feminist science fiction novel, nineteen stories, and eighteen poems; *Haunted Traveller* by Barry Yourgrau (Arcade) is a collection of very short imaginative stories, a few with dark themes; *Patterns* by Pat Cadigan (Tor), after being published in a limited press hardcover in 1989 is finally available in a trade paperback edition. This varied collection of science fiction, fantasy, and horror contains a good representation of Cadigan's short stories up through 1989 and is an excellent introduction to her work; North Atlantic Books continues Paul Williams's project of reprinting all of Theodore Sturgeon's short fiction by publishing *Baby Is Three, Volume VI: The Complete Stories of Theodore Sturgeon*. The volume contains stories written between 1950 and 1952 including the titular story that later evolved into part of the acclaimed novel *More than Human*. Musician David Crosby provides an introduction and the wonderful dust jacket art is by the late great Richard Powers; *Wolves of Darkness: The Collected Stories, Volume 2* by Jack Williamson (Haffner Press) with an introduction by Harlan Ellison. Although known best for his science fiction, Williamson has over his long career written some notable horror, including the novel *Darker Than You Think*, recently reissued by Tor/Orb; *In the Surgical Theatre* by Dana Levin (American Poetry Association) is a marvelous collection of beautiful dark, passionate, and occasionally violent poems; *Strange Travelers* by Gene Wolfe (Tor) collects fifteen recent, sometimes nightmarish stories by this highly respected writer.

Nonfiction Books

The Sandman Companion by Hy Bender (Vertigo/DC Comics) is a classy looking book about the extremely popular comic book series by Neil Gaiman. In addition to synopses and commentary on each story arc and the issues within them, there are extensive interviews with Gaiman about his work and with the many artists who contributed to the series.

No Go the Bogeyman: Scaring, Lulling & Making Mock by Marina Warner (FS&G) considers the persistent popularity and charm of figures of male terror—ogres and bogeymen—their origins and how they relate to contemporary ideas about sexuality and power. She also analyzes how we use myth, fairy tale, and other types of stories to deal with and manage fear. Using art, history, folklore, music, and film, Warner has created a fascinating, page-turning, and ambitious work.

Strange and Secret Peoples: Fairies and Victorian Consciousness by Carole G. Silver (Oxford University Press) is a fascinating book that examines the period of 1798 to 1923, and the vogue of Victorian fairy painting. It opens with various theories regarding the origin of fairies and continues with the concept of "changelings" (fairy children swapped for human ones), goblins, and how the idea of these creatures might have been inspired by the existence of pygmies and other small people foreign to British culture.

Crime Wave by James Ellroy (Vintage Crime) is a collection of reportage and three pieces of fiction, all originally published in *GQ*. Ellroy's nonfiction is as sharp as his fiction as he writes about the murder of his mother, O. J. Simpson, and Hollywood in all its lowlife glory.

Screams & Nightmares: the Films of Wes Craven by Brian Hobb (Overlook) includes more than two hundred black-and-white photographs and a full filmography; *The Cockroach Papers: A Compendium of History and Lore* by Richard Schweid (Four Walls Eight Windows) is a wonderfully informal, anecdotal history of the creatures we love to hate; *The Vampire Lectures* by Laurence A. Rickels (University of Minnesota Press) is based on a college course the author has taught at the University of California, Santa Barbara, and incorporates a variety of pop culture references (even discussing Ed Wood's *Glen or Glenda* in detail, while covering Bela Lugosi's acting career). Lively and chatty if not particularly deep; *American Nightmares: The Haunted House Formula in American Popular Fiction* by Dale Bailey (Bowling Green State University Popular Press) takes a critical look at the subject, using works by Edgar Allan Poe, Nathaniel Hawthorne, Shirley Jackson, and Stephen King; *Imagining the Worst: Stephen King and the Representation of Women*, edited by Kathleen Margaret Lant and Theresa Thompson (Greenwood Press), collects eleven critical essays examining the author's treatment of women as perpetrators and victims of horror. With index and bibliography; *Stephen King Country: The Illustrated Guide to the Sites and Sights that Inspired the Modern Master* by George Beahm (Running Press): the title says it all; *Immortal Monster: The Mythological Evolution of the Fantastic Beast in Modern Fiction and Film* by Joseph D. Andriano (Greenwood Press) examines the evolution of literary and film leviathans and beast-men, from *Grendel* to *King Kong* and *The Island of Dr. Moreau* and on to *Moby-Dick, Jaws, Gravity's Rainbow*, and *Star Trek IV: The Voyage Home; The Fantastic Worlds of H. P. Lovecraft* edited by James Van Hise (James Van Hise) is a series of twenty-seven articles, four original, on Lovecraft, his correspondence, and works. Black-and-white illustrations throughout. Contributors include Robert Weinberg, S. T. Joshi, and August Derleth; *A Cthulhu Mythos: Bibliography and Concordance* by Chris Jarosha-Ernst (Armitage House) is a reference book of bibliographical material and concordance; *Civilization and Monsters: Spirits of Modernity in Meiji*

Japan by Gerald Figal (Duke University Press); *Windows of the Imagination* by Darrell Schweitzer (Borgo Press) collects the author's non-fiction, including book reviews, an article comparing M. R. James and H. P. Lovecraft, and an "interview" with Edgar Allan Poe. ($22.00, prepaid from the author: 6644 Rutland Street, Philadelphia, PA 19149-2128); *Derleth: Hawk . . . and Dove* by Dorothy M. Grobe Litersky (The National Writers Press) is a biography of author and Arkham House founder August Derleth. (Information from the author at Seaside Sanctuary, One Kenmore Lane, Boynton Beach, FL 33435-7309); *Citizens of Somewhere Else: Nathaniel Hawthorne and Henry James* by Dan McCall (Cornell University Press) looks at the possible influence of the two writers on each other; *By Authors Possessed: The Demonic Novel in Russia* by Adam Weiner (Northwestern University Press) is a critical examination of Russian works in which demons appear, focusing on Gogol, Dostoyevsky, Bely, Bulgakov, and Nabokov; *The Witch Must Die: How Fairy Tales Shape Our Lives* by Sheldon Cashdan (Basic Books) is a critical and psychological look at the effects of fairy tales on readers; *Science Fiction, Fantasy and Horror: A Reader's Guide* by Roger Sheppard (Library Association Career Development Group, U.K.), a reference guide to selected recommended works concentrating on the period 1960–95; *Sixty Years of Arkham House* by S. T. Joshi (Arkham House) updates August Derleth's *Thirty Years of Arkham House*. It's a reference work providing information on the more than 230 titles issued by Arkham House in the past six decades; *Fantasy Horror: A Critical and Historical Guide to Literature and Illustration, Film, TV, Radio, and the Internet* by Neil Barron (Scarecrow Press), a critical reference evaluating over 2,300 items of fiction and poetry, with guides to critical scholarship, a chapter on teaching, and lists of recommended works, series, awards, films, and YA works; *The Haunted Mind: The Supernatural in Victorian Literature* edited by Elton E. Smith and Robert Haas (Scarecrow Press) collects nine critical essays; *The Naked and the Undead: Evil and the Appeal of Horror* by Cynthia A. Freeland (Westview) is a critical examination of the appeal of horror movies; *The Blood Is the Life: Vampires in Literature*, edited by Leonard Heldreth and Mary Phare (Bowling Green State University Popular Press), is a critical collection of eighteen essays on vampires in fiction, from early gothic examples to modern works by S. P. Somtow, Nancy A. Collins, and Chelsea Quinn Yarbro; and *Gothic: Four Hundred Years of Excess, Horror, Evil and Ruin* by Richard Davenport-Hines (North Point Press) traces the history of the gothic sensibility, from the seventeenth century to the present day.

Recommended Artists with Work in the Small Press

There are many fine artists who toil for minimal monetary compensation in the small press and I'd like to acknowledge them. The following did excellent work during 1999: GAK, Stephen E. Fabian, Peter Gilmore, H. E. Fassl, Wendy Down, Lubov, Catherine Buburuz, David Martin, Gerald Gaubert, Jamie Obershlake, Andrew Shorrock, Jason Van Hollander, Jack Gaughan, George Barr, Fredrik King, Jill Bauman, Dominic Harman, SMS, James Beveridge, David Checkley, Bob Hobbs, Ron Leming, Augie Wiedemann, Piggy, Roddy Williams, Paul Lowe, Douglas Walters, Dallas Goffin, Alan Hunter, Chris Whitlow, Paul Swenson, Dameon Willich, Keith Boulger, Aryton, Steven Lawler, Anne Kushnick, Shaun Tan, R & D Studios, Gavin O'Keefe, Lisa Fillingham, Paul Joyce, Craig Schultz, Seán Russell Friend, Edgar Franco, Iain Maynard, Frank Mafrici, Trudi Canavan, Donna Johansen, Rob Kiely, Rob Suggs, David Jereboam Gough, Jean-Claude Davreux, Shikhar Dixit, Dan Smith, Yuri Chari, David Fode, Steve Lines, Todd H. C. Fischer, James Matt Frantz, D. L. Sproule, Fiona Griffiths, Thomas Arensberg, Erik Wilson, Peter MacDougall, Ron Lightburn, Andrew Chumbley, and Jean-Pierre Normand.

Magazines and Newsletters

The most important news sources for the field are *DarkEcho*, edited by Paula Guran, and *Hellnotes*, edited by David B. Silva with Paul Olsen; *DarkEcho* has the stamp of Guran's voice, making it more personal and quirky. Both weekly newsletters cover the news of the field equally well. *DarkEcho*, basically a one-woman operation, often has incisive commentary about the field. *Hellnotes* generally has a long interview with a horror notable, short horror reviews by various people, and a view from England by Peter Crowther. *DarkEcho* is free and supports itself with advertising. To subscribe, e-mail darkecho@aol.com with "Subscribe" as your subject. *Hellnotes* is subscription based. E-mail subscriptions are available for $10 per year. Hardcopy subscriptions are available for $40 per year payable to David B. Silva, *Hellnotes*, 27780 Donkey Mine Road, Oak Run, CA 96069. E-mail address: dbsilva @hellnotes.com or pfolson @up.net.

There are several excellent sources of market information available for horror writers: *The Gila Queen's Guide to Markets*, edited by Kathryn Ptacek, is a content-rich newsletter, published about every six weeks and is one of the best guides, covering all kinds of fiction and nonfiction. $45 for a ten issue subscription payable to Kathryn Ptacek, GQ HQ, PO Box 97, Newton, NJ 07860-0097.

The Heliocentric Writer's Network, edited by Lisa Jean Bothell, is published six times a year and is particularly good for its coverage of Internet markets. This useful newsletter also has short articles about writing. Three dollars per issue, $18 a year payable to Bast Media, 17650 1st Avenue S., Box 291, Seattle, WA 98148.

Scavenger's Newsletter, edited by Janet Fox, is a monthly that has remained a reliable source of information for small press genre markets for many years. $18 a year (12), $9 for six months, $34 for two years, payable to Janet Fox, 519 Ellinwood, Osage City, KS 66523-1329.

Necrofile, the critical quarterly on horror edited by Stefan Dziemianowicz, Michael Morrison, and S. T. Joshi has made important contributions to the field with its essays, overviews, and reviews. It's in flux right now and reportedly will have one last print issue, #33, before going to an electronic-only webzine format starting with issue #34.

There are several nonfiction magazines that are worth a look by horror readers: *Video Watchdog*® edited by Tim and Donna Lucas is the best magazine for up-to-date information on various cuts and variants available on video. This digest-sized magazine is always entertaining with its bi-monthly coverage of fantastic video. It is a must for anyone interested in quirky reviews and columns. *VW* went monthly with its fifty-fifth issue.

Scarlet Street, edited by Richard Valley, is a glossy bi-monthly with articles about and reviews of classic mystery, science fiction, and horror films. There are usually at least a couple of excellent interviews or profiles—in 1999 there was an interview with Ian McKellen, who played director James Whale in the acclaimed movie *Gods and Monsters.*

Gauntlet: Exploring the Limits of Free Expression edited by Barry Hoffman covers such provocative issues as the photographing of nude youths by artists Sally Mann, Jock Sturges, and David Hamilton and also the persecution/prosecution of strip clubs in New York City and elsewhere. The magazine often publishes a few fiction originals or reprints. *Gauntlet* is published semi-annually, in November and May, a subscription is $16 a year, payable to *Gauntlet*. Address can be found at the end of this summation.

EsoTerra: The Journal of Extreme Culture edited by Chad Hensley and R. F. Paul. The one issue published in 1999 (they hope to keep to a semiannual schedule) profiles artist Harry O. Morris and has interviews with writers Thomas Ligotti and Iain Sinclair and Durtro Press publisher David Tibet. There were also profiles of musicians. Morris provides the excellent art for the issue. Single issues are $7.50 each and subscriptions are $15 for one year (two issues), payable to Chad Hensley, 410 E. Denny Way #22, Seattle, WA 98122.

Crime Time, edited by Barry Forshaw, is an excellent British magazine in trade paperback format. Issue 2.5 has a very good piece about American crime fiction from the 1960s to the present, which writer Woody Haut dubs Neon Noir, reflecting the "flash that accompanies the portrayal of American culture from street level . . . and suggesting the influence of older pulp crime writers such as Hammett, Thompson, and Woolrich." In addition, there are articles, columns, book and film reviews by Lawrence Block, Maxim Jakubowski, and other crime fiction notables, interviews, and five brief novel excerpts. *CT* provides fine coverage of the field. Twenty pounds sterling for four issues payable to Crime Time Subscriptions, 18 Coleswood Road, Harpenden, Herts AL5 1EQ, U.K.

Most small press magazines come and go with amazing rapidity. It's difficult to recommend buying a subscription to those that haven't proven themselves, but I urge readers at least to buy single issues of those that sound interesting. There isn't room to mention every small press horror magazine being published at any given time, so the following are those that I thought were the best in 1999:

Cemetery Dance, edited by Richard T. Chizmar, just celebrated its tenth anniversary. Professional in appearance and content, this is the one magazine that any serious reader of horror fiction *must* subscribe to. The fiction ranges from dark fantasy and both supernatural and psychological horror to dark crime fiction and so does its nonfiction coverage. Twenty-two dollars for six issues, payable to Cemetery Dance Publications (see address at end).

Weird Tales, edited by George H. Scithers and Darrell Schweitzer, has been around in one form or another for seventy-five years. Now that it's published by DNA Publications, it seems to have gotten back onto its quarterly schedule. The magazine's fiction generally provides a who's who in dark fantasy/horror with originals and reprints by Tanith Lee, Hugh B. Cave, Ramsey Campbell, Thomas Ligotti, and others. Sixteen dollars for four issues, payable to DNA Publications, Inc., PO Box 2988, Radford, VA 24143-2988.

The Third Alternative, edited by Andy Cox, is, along with *Interzone*, the most consistently entertaining magazine of cross-genre fiction in the U.K. In addition to its fiction, *TTA* provides interviews with and articles about genre and cross-genre writers. In 1999, for example, there were interviews with Michael Marshall Smith, Michael Moorcock, Jonathan

Carroll, and Alasdair Gray. It is published quarterly with subscriptions for $22, payable to TTA Press, 5 Martins Lane, Witcham, Ely, Cambs CB6 2LB, U.K.

All Hallows: The Journal of the Ghost Story Society, edited by Barbara and Christopher Roden, is one of the best reasons to join the Ghost Story Society. This attractive, perfect-bound magazine is published thrice yearly and is available only to members. It is an excellent source of news, articles, and ghostly fiction. Another good reason is to support an organization dedicated to providing admirers of the classic ghost story with an outlet and focus for their interest. Membership is only $23 per year.

Kimota, edited by Graeme Hurry, is an excellent mixed-genre magazine published biannually in association with the Preston Speculative Fiction Group. Two pounds fifty sterling for a single issue, £9 payable to Graeme Hurry, 52 Cadley Causeway, Preston, Lancs, PR2 3RX, U.K.

Peeping Tom, edited by David Bell, is a reliable source of good horror fiction and excellent black-and-white illustrations as well. A four-issue subscription is £8 payable to *Peeping Tom*, Yew Tree House, 15 Nottingham Road, Ashby de la Zouch, Leicestershire LE 65 1DJ, U.K.

Enigmatic Tales, edited by Mick Sims and Len Maynard, is a British quarterly that (although it looks like a magazine) calls itself an "anthology"—it's perfect bound with excellent production values. It contains a mix of original and reprinted fiction and a regular section "curated" by Hugh Lamb that contains classic tales. The fiction has been improving steadily, bringing it into the top rung of small press horror magazines. Single issues are £3 or $6 (U.S.) and a four-issue subscription is £10 or $20 (U.S.), payable to M. Sims, 1 Gibbs Field, Bishops Stortford, Herts CM 23 4EY, U.K.

Sackcloth & Ashes, edited by Andrew Busby and Lisa Busby, is another British quarterly that's been publishing good fiction and good art and has a clean and readable design. However, the perfect-bound issues fell apart after one reading. Hopefully, this will be corrected in the future. Four pounds per copy outside the U.K. (in pounds sterling only), payable to Andrew Busby, 8 Woodgreen Close, Hindley, Wigan, Lancs WN2 3JW, U.K.

Not One of Us, edited by John Benson, has been a staple of the small press for several years, publishing semiannually. Benson also publishes a one-off each year. Single issue cost is $5.50 prepaid and a three-issue subscription is $13.50, payable to John Benson, 12 Curtis Road, Natick, MA 01760. The two issues published in 1999 were much improved over the 1998 output—#21 was excellent.

Event Horizon: Science Fiction, Fantasy, and Horror, which I edited, published horror fiction by Kim Newman, Bill Congreve, and Chris Lawson, horror commentary by Douglas E. Winter, and horror book reviews in 1999.

On Spec, edited by Jena Snyder, is a quarterly Canadian magazine specializing in science fiction and fantasy. In 1999 though, there was a bit more horror than usual and those stories were very good. A one-year subscription is $19, payable to *On Spec*, Box 3727, Edmonton, AB T6E 5G6, Canada.

Ghosts & Scholars, edited by Rosemary Pardoe, is an excellent biannual magazine devoted to continuing the M. R. James tradition of ghost stories. Its combination of original and reprinted stories, book reviews, and scholarly articles makes it a must for any reader interested in the traditional ghost story. A four-issue subscription (two years) is $25, (surface/$29 air) cash only to R. A. Pardoe, Flat One, 36 Hamilton Street, Hoole, Chester CH2 3JQ, U.K. Single issues can be purchased for $7 surface/$8 airmail from Richard Fawcett 61 Teecomwas Drive, Uncasville, CT 06382, e-mail: pardos@globalnet.co.uk; FawcettPub @webtv.net.

Dark Regions & Horror Magazine, edited by Joe Morey, Ken Wisman, and Jordan Stoen, is a perfect example of the curse of the fancy font. As often happens to designers with sudden access to a variety of fonts, they seem to want to try them all out immediately, no matter how illegible it makes the text, which is a shame when it hides good fiction. Over the past year the visual readability improved, although there is still the occasional overzealousness.

Wisely, *Horror* has dropped its "news," which tended to be dated by the time the issue came out, and is sticking with author interviews and book and movie reviews. The spring issue settled into a more readable design. Published quarterly. Single-issue price is $4.95 plus $1.25 postage. A four-issue subscription is $15, payable to Dark Regions Press, PO Box 6301, Concord, CA 94524.

Now in its third year, *Lady Churchill's Rosebud Wristlet*, edited by Gavin J. Grant, has already made a splash by having one of its earliest pieces of fiction (by Kelly Link) chosen for the James Tiptree, Jr. Award. It's an eclectic mixture of cross-genre fiction and poetry, travel writing, reviews, and basically whatever interests its editor. For information e-mail the editor at lcrw@hotmail.com.

Tales of the Unanticipated, edited by Eric M. Heideman, came out in the fall of 1999 after a year's planned absence, with an attractive, oversize trade paperback format and excellent cover art by David Roszelle. Although the editorial is rather self-congratulatory, the issue has some very good cross-genre fiction, essays by Maureen McHugh and

Martha Hood, an interview with Neil Gaiman, and at least two real horror stories. Twenty dollars for a four-issue subscription (it's returning to an eight-month schedule with the spring 2000 issue), payable to *Tales of the Unanticipated*, Box 8036, Lake Street Station, Minneapolis, MN 55408.

For consistently interesting dark poetry, you can't go wrong with *Dreams and Nightmares*, edited by David Kopaska-Merkel, who has been doing a masterful job with the magazine since 1986. $12 for six issues ($15 outside the U.S.), payable to David Kopaska-Merkel, 1300 Kicker Road, Tuscaloosa, AL 35404, e-mail: dragontea@earthlink.net.

Some other magazines specializing in poetry are: *Edgar Digested Verse*, a quarterly edited by John Picinich. $2.50 per issue, $10 for four issues, payable to John Picinich, 486 Essex Avenue, Bloomfield, NJ 07003, e-mail: Dragoons5@aol.com; and *Frisson: Disconcerting Verse*, edited by Scott H. Urban. Single issue $2.50, Eight dollars per year, payable to Skull Job Productions, 1012 Pleasant Dale Drive, Wilmington, NC 28412-7617.

Some good horror and dark fantasy can be found in cross-genre professional magazines such as *Asimov's Science Fiction*, edited by Gardner Dozois, and *The Magazine of Fantasy & Science Fiction* edited by Gordon Van Gelder. The latter celebrated its fiftieth anniversary in 1999 (two horror stories from *F&SF* are in this volume). *Realms of Fantasy* edited by Shawna McCarthy, occasionally publishes good dark material (including a story reprinted herein). *Interzone*, edited by David Pringle, often publishes several excellent horror-tinged stories per year. And some mainstream magazines such as *Playboy*, *The Atlantic Monthly*, and *The New Yorker* occasionally publish stories dark enough to be labeled horror. Readers might also want to check out *Crimewave*, the new bi-annual British mystery magazine edited by Mat Coward and Andy Cox—it's got a terrific variety of crime fiction of all sorts, all well-written, some dark. Subscriptions are $22 for two issues (£11), payable to TTA Press, 5 Martin's Lane, Witcham, Ely, Cambs CB6 2LB, U.K. Two Australian magazines deserve reader support, even though they only occasionally publish horror. *Eidolon*, edited by Jeremy G. Byrne, is an important source of excellent fiction, some of it horror. The departure of co-founder Jonathan Strahan was noted with a graceful farewell in an editorial written by Byrne for issue #28, the only issue published during 1999. Hopefully the magazine will return to its quarterly schedule in 2000. The exceptional art direction and some of the art is by Shaun Tan. Subscription rates are in Australian dollars only: A$45 (international airmail) for four issues or A$35 (seamail), payable to Eidolon Publications, PO Box 225, North Perth, WA 6906 Australia;

www.eidolon.net. *Aurealis*: Dirk Strasser and Stephen Higgins are the editors of this semiannual magazine, which features an excellent variety of science fiction and fantasy (and sometimes horror). Issue #24 was especially strong in its horror fiction. Mostly excellent illustrations. A four-issue subscription is A$38 (seamail) or A$46 (airmail) payable to Chimaera Publications, PO Box 2164, Mt. Waverley, Victoria 3149, Australia; www. aurealis.hl.net. Credit card sales acceptable.

Limited Editions, Chapbooks, and Small Press Items

Cemetery Dance Publications had a full schedule in 1999, publishing two novels by Richard Laymon: *Come Out Tonight*, the first edition and only U.S. edition planned for the title, and *Cuts*, the *only* edition scheduled so far. Both titles are available in three hardcover states, all signed, but the 52 copy leather-bound, traycased edition has extra full-color artwork. Jacket art for both titles is by Vince Natale and endpaper artwork is by Gary Geier. *Dahmer's Not Dead* by Edward Lee and Elizabeth Steffen and Ed Gorman's *The Poker Club* (an expansion of "Out There in the Darkness") were published in hardcover trade editions. Ray Garton's science fiction thriller *Biofire* was published in a signed limited edition of 500 copies with jacket art by Scott Vladimir Licina.

CD Publications also continued its attractive hardcover novella series with Nancy A. Collins's *Lynch: A Gothik Western*, about gunslingers, mad scientists, and revenge, with illustrations by Stephen Bissette; Jack Ketchum's *Right to Life*, a raw, brutal, but very moving psychological suspense story about a woman held captive by two sociopaths, dust jacket art by Neal McPheeters; Gary Brandner's *Rot*, a zombie revenge story with dust jacket art by Vince Natale; William F. Nolan's *The Winchester Horror* which makes good use of the famous Winchester House in San Jose, California. Dust jacket art is by Eric Powell and interior illustrations are by Earl Geier. Edward Lee's *Operator "B"* is a surprising departure for the author in that it's a science fiction thriller. Dust jacket, interior illustrations, and endpapers are by Erik Wilson. Each of the novellas is available in a hardcover, 450-copy signed and numbered edition and a traycased edition of 26 signed and lettered copies, except for *Rot*, which is an edition of 1,000 copies.

Obsidian Press published *Dancing with Demons*, a short novel by Lucy Taylor limited to 500 signed hardcover copies with dust jacket art by Alan M. Clark and interior illustrations by Jamie Oberschlake. It includes an introduction by the author.

Gauntlet Press published a hardcover edition of Poppy Z. Brite's *Crow* novel, *The Lazarus Heart* in two signed states, both with an introduction by Brite and an afterword by John Shirley. Jacket art is by J. K. Potter. The 52-copy leather-bound, traycased edition includes photographs by Potter of Brite and a CD of her reading from her most recent collection; *Conspiracies* by F. Paul Wilson is a "Repairman Jack" novel published in a 450-copy numbered edition with an afterword by Ed Gorman and jacket art by Harry O. Morris and in a 52-copy leather-bound, lettered edition in traycase, with additional Morris illustrations and a fifty-minute dramatization from the book; Richard Matheson's *Somewhere in Time* in a 500-copy numbered and 25-copy lettered edition, with an introduction by the author about the genesis of the idea and seven photographs of the film from his personal archives. The lettered edition also comes with a thirty-five-minute CD of Matheson reading two passages from the novel; Caitlín R. Kiernan's award-winning first novel, *Silk*, was published in three states: a 450-copy numbered edition with an afterword by Poppy Z. Brite and jacket art by Clive Barker, a 75-copy deluxe, numbered edition signed by Barker with eight interior full-color illustrations by Barker, and a 26-copy lettered edition signed by all, with an additional piece of art by Barker, a full-color endsheet illustrated by the artist, and a CD with songs from Kiernan's band.

The Overlook Connection Press published a tenth anniversary edition of Kevin J. Anderson's science fiction/horror novel *Resurrection, Inc.* This is the book's first hardcover edition and has cover art by Bob Eggleton. It was released in three states: a trade edition of 1500 copies, a sterling edition of 100 copies, slipcased, and a lettered edition of 52 copies, leather-bound, in a hardwood box. All three editions are signed and have introductions by David B. Silva, Janet Berliner, and Bentley Little. *The Lost Work of Stephen King: A Guide to Unpublished Manuscripts, Story Fragments, Alternative Versions, and Oddities* by Stephen J. Spignesi is a nonfiction book about King's work in two leather-bound hardcover editions limited to 1000 signed and numbered and 52 lettered and boxed. The long-awaited special edition of Michael Marshall Smith's novel *Spares* was published with striking cover art by Alan M. Clark and an introduction by Neil Gaiman. This edition contains the preferred text of the author, a lost first chapter that is printed for the first time, three stories featuring elements of the story, and afterwords by Smith and Clark. The edition was published in three states, all signed: a limited trade edition of 500 copies; the sterling edition of 100 copies with a bound-in bookmark, unique signature page, orginal endpaper art and slipcased; and a lettered edition of 52 copies that is leather-bound, foil embossed in a hardwood case with specially etched glass handcrafted by a wood artisan, and a frontispiece of Clark's cover art.

Terminal Frights Press brought out David Niall Wilson's novel *This Is My Blood* with jacket art by Lisanne Lake in a signed and numbered edition of 1000 copies and a signed, lettered traycase edition of 26 copies. The novel is an expansion of Wilson's story "A Candle in the Sun."

James Cahill Publishing published *Dust of the Heavens*, a book of non-horror material by Jack Ketchum, in two signed, limited editions: 174 numbered and 26 lettered slipcased, copies. The book has an introduction by Edward Lee and illustrations by Aaron Morgan Brown.

Crossroads Press published Joe R. Lansdale's novel *Freezer Burn* in a trade hardcover edition of 400 signed and numbered copies and a deluxe edition of 26 lettered, leather-bound copies, both with gorgeous jacket illustrations by George Pratt.

The Enigmatic Novella series from Enigmatic Press started off with a collaboration by the publishers L. H. Maynard and M. P. N. Sims called "Moths." The second is *The Dark Satanic . . . Two Terror Tales from the North of England* by Paul Finch. The excellent illustrations are by Gerald Gaubert. The third, *Candlelight Ghost Stories*, contains the first two published stories by the promising Anthony Morris. Illustrated by Iain Maynard. Sarah Singleton's excellent "In the Mirror" is the fourth in the series. Illustrated by Gerard Gaubert. Number five presents two stories by Paul Bradshaw as *Alternate Lives*, and is also illustrated by Gaubert. Maynard and Sims have also started the Enigmatic Variations series, which is meant to showcase "slightly harder-edged, and more cross-genre material." First in the series is a good collaboration by Peter Crowther and James Lovegrove called "The Hand that Feeds." The second is *Icarus Descending*, a chapbook of two effective horror stories by Steve Savile. The booklets have black-and-white covers and, beginning with the second, are perfect bound.

Kimota Publishing published Neal L. Asher's three linked stories under the overall title *Mason's Rats*. One is original to the chapbook. The cover illustration is by Jamie Egerton.

Ash-Tree Press published *The Talisman*, a new novel by Jonathan Aycliffe, author of *Naomi's Room, The Lost*, and two other novels of the supernatural. The jacket art is by Jason C. Eckhardt and the edition is limited to 500 copies.

Tartarus Press published, in one volume, new translations of a novel and a collection of poetry and prose poems by Alain-Fournier. *Le Grand Meaulnes,* translated by R. B. Russell, was originally published in 1912, and this is the first English publication of *Miracles*, translated by Adrian Eckersley.

Pumpkin Books brought out *Isle of the Whisperers*, a new novel by Hugh B. Cave. The hardcover, limited to 750 copies, has jacket art and interior illustrations by John Coulthart. *Horror at Halloween*, a "mosaic" novel set in Charles Grant's Oxrun Station, is edited by Jo Fletcher and has cover art by Terry Oakes. It's available in trade paperback.

PS Publishing threw its hat into the ring of small press publishing by inaugurating an excellent novella series with two terrific novellas: James Lovegrove's and Peter Crowther's chilling morality tale, *How the Other Half Lives*. Available in hardcover and paperback limited editions signed by the authors, with a cogent introduction by Colin Greenland and excellent cover art by Japack Photography. Graham Joyce's powerful *Leningrad Nights,* a story of survival during the Nazi siege of Leningrad proves that quirky mainstream work can still be accommodated within the genre of fantastic fiction. Peter Straub wrote the introduction and the book is signed by both writers. Jacket art is by Vasili Ivanovich Surikov. *Andy Warhol's Dracula,* an excellent novella by Kim Newman, was reprinted from the June *Event Horizon*. The chapbook has an introduction by F. Paul Wilson and the cover art is a "variation on 'Self Portrait' " by Andy Warhol (1928–87). *The Vaccinator* by Michael Marshall Smith has an introduction by M. John Harrison and cover art by Simon Turner.

BJM Press published "The Derelict of Death," by Simon Clark and John B. Ford, a new story inspired by William Hope Hodgson. It's a good, creepy story of a strange ship in the tropics that preys on other ships. Ford provides a short biography of Hodgson, and both Ford and Clark also write brief appreciations of the author. The chapbook includes two poems by Hodgson, "Speak Well of the Dead" and "To God." The artwork is by Steve Lines.

Miranda-Jahya Publications has been publishing *The Twilight Garden* chapbooks, a monthly series featuring a selection of stories (some original) and an interview with and biography of one author. Those featured in 1999 include Michael Laimo, Charlee Jacob, Gerard Daniel Houarner, James S. Dorr. The cover art for most of the titles is by Cathy Buburuz.

Black Dog Press published a chapbook of Hugh B. Cave's story "The Desert Host," first published in *Magic Carpet Magazine* in 1933. There is an introduction by the author. The same press collects two stories by Cave (writing as Justin Case) in a chapbook called *White Star of Egypt*. Both stories were originally published in 1942.

MOT Press, an offshoot of the Masters of Terror web site, published its first print title in 1999. It's a very scary novella by Tim Lebbon called "White." Published in an edition of 320 copies, 300 for sale, it's done up in a perfect-bound format with a suitably creepy glossy cover with art by Lisa Busby. The novella is reprinted herein. MOT also put out the limited edition CD-ROM, *Houses at the Borderland*, edited by MOT editor Andy Fairclough. It is available in a 100-copy numbered, limited edition diskette formatted in HTML. It's got fourteen stories, most original, by such writers as Tim Lebbon, Tom Piccirilli, Paul Finch, and Simon Clark. The web site is members.aol.com/andyfair/ house.html.

Subterranean Press published *Veil's Visit: A Taste of Hap and Leonard*—a collection of two Hap and Leonard stories, one by Joe R. Lansdale and Andrew Vachss, a second by Lansdale, this H & L novel excerpts from published novels and an 18,000-word excerpt from an unpublished novel. It also includes an "interview with H & L" conducted by Lansdale, with introductory matter by both authors. The title is available as signed and numbered trade paperback and hardcover editions. "Ella and the Canary Prince" by Michael Cadnum is a subversive retelling of "Cinderella" that appeared as a limited edition chapbook of 250 numbered and 52 lettered copies. Cover and interior illustrations are by Keith Minnion. Charles de Lint's "The Buffalo Man," with cover art by Charles Vess. *The Seed of Lost Souls* by Poppy Z. Brite documents some of what went into the creation of the novel, including a novella from which the novel evolved, an introduction by the author, and an interview with her from around the period of the book's publication, also an unpublished book review by Brite of *Vampires, Wine and Roses* by John Richard Stephens. The cover and interior art is by Dame Darcy. Limited to 500 signed and numbered paperbacks and 52 signed hardcovers. *Waltz of Shadows*, Volume 1 in the Lost Lansdale series of books that the author admits are not among his best but are "interesting." All these titles will be published in hardcover only and will not be reprinted. The jacket illustrations are by Mark A. Nelson and the design, which is quite wonderful, is by Harold Graham. The illustration on the back dust jacket is repeated on the endpapers. The book is available signed, in numbered and lettered editions. *Something Lumber This Way Comes* by Joe R. Lansdale is the second title in the Lost Lansdale series and is a horror story for children about a haunted house, illustrated and with cover by Doug Potter. It was published in signed, limited editions of 500 copies and thirteen lettered copies in traycase. *Seductions* was Ray Garton's first published (but not first written) novel, originally published as a paperback in 1984. This, its first hardcover edition, is signed and limited to 500 copies with a 52-copy lettered edition. It has an introduction by the author, an afterword by Richard Laymon, dust jacket art by Gail Gross, and interior art by Earl Geier. *Peter and PTR: Two Deleted Prefaces and an Introduction* by Peter Straub is a chapbook of material related to the creation of Straub's novel *Mr. X.* It was published in two signed, limited editions of 250 numbered and 52 lettered copies.

Flesh & Blood Press published Michael Laimo's "Within the Darkness, Golden Eyes," a chapbook with an introduction by Edo van Belkom and cover and interior art by Keith Minnion.

Gargadillo Press published a "weird tale" by John Pelan called "An Antique Vintage." Cover art is by GAK, interior illustrations by Allen Koszowski, and the introduction is by Simon Clark. Available in chapbook form in three signed states: a trade paperback, a numbered hardcover, and a lettered hardcover, the latter bound in leather.

Necro Publications published Gerard Daniel Houarner's novel *Road to Hell* in signed, limited hardcover and trade paperback editions. With jacket art by Brandy Gill and an introduction by Brian Hodge.

Babbage Press launched with a revised and updated trade paperback edition of John Shirley's 1985 novel, *Eclipse.* The book is a sturdy, professionally designed format inside and out, with very attractive cover art and design by Lydia Marano. The interiors are designed by Marano and Kristina Etchison.

DNA Publications & Wildside Press published the first *Weird Tales Library #1*, which looks just like an issue of *Weird Tales.* It contains reissues of the novels *Bone Music* by Alan Rodgers and *The White Isle* by Darrell Schweitzer and a short story reprint by John Gregory Betancourt (all in teeny tiny type). At $7.50, for two complete novels, it's a bargain.

Buzzcity Press First Editions published *The Divinity Student* by Michael Cisco in an attractive, reasonably priced trade paperback edition, with a beautifully eerie cover illustration by Harry O. Morris and with Morris's illustrations throughout.

The Desert Island Dracula Library published an attractive hardcover edition of Bram Stoker's first novel, *The Primrose Path*, along with the story, "Buried Treasures." Richard Dalby wrote the introduction and Clive Leatherdale, the series editor, provides an editor's note.

Necropolitan Press published *The Hoegbotton Guide to the Early History of Ambergris by Duncan Shriek* by Jeff VanderMeer. The cover and frontispiece collages are by Jeffrey Thomas.

Sarob Press published *Vampire City* by Paul Feval, translated and edited, with an introduction, afterword, and notes by Brian Stableford. The book, with dust jacket art and interior illustrations by Tim Denton,

is a French gothic parody first published in book form in 1875. Limited
to 250 numbered hardcover copies.

Although not by any definition a small press, Orion, the U.K. publisher brought out the "Criminal Records" series of novellas, edited by
Otto Penzler. The small-sized, very attractive hardcover chapbooks by
such authors as Peter Straub, Ian Rankin, and Ed McBain, are stories
originally published in anthologies edited by Penzler. The Straub, "Pork
Pie Hat," originally published in *Murder for Halloween*, is especially
excellent.

Illustrated Books and Other Odds and Ends

A new illustrated edition of *The Wonderful Wizard of Oz* by L. Frank
Baum, is usually a reason to celebrate and this one, The Kansas Centennial Edition (appropriately enough, from University Press of Kansas)
is illustrated by the respected illustrator Michael McGurdy. Unfortunately, while his woodcuts are beautifully executed, his depiction of
Dorothy is disappointing. She is cast with a perpetually sullen face and
distinct lack of personality. The foreword by Ray Bradbury compares
Baum's classic with Lewis Carroll's *Alice in Wonderland* as being "hot"
vs. "cold." Fans of either may disagree with him.

Two new illustrated versions of Lewis Carroll's classic *Alice's Adventures in Wonderland* are available: Helen Oxenbury's watercolor illustrations (in the Candlewick Press edition) are bright, witty, and
charming, and Lisbeth Zwerger creates fresh and enchanting illustrations
in her version, called simply *Alice in Wonderland* (North-South Books/
A Michael Neugebauer Book).

The Fantastic Art of Beksinski is another gorgeous fine art title from
Morpheus International. It covers thirty years of the Polish artist's work,
which has changed from alien, surreal, lush, horrific painting to com-
posite photography (so far less interesting than his earlier work).

Swift as a Shadow: Extinct and Endangered Animals by the great
photographer Rosamond Purcell highlights preserved animals and birds
from the Collection of Naturalis, National Natuurhistorisch Museum of
Leiden (A Mariner Original) with an afterword by Ross MacPhee. She
documents the loss of such lovely birds as the Carolina Parakeet. whose
habit of staying with its dead or wounded companions allowed hunters
to pick them off one by one, the unlovely California Condor, which
hangs on by the point of its ugly beak, several species of lion and tigers,
and of course the poor dodo.

De Morbis Artificum: A Portfolio of Selected Illustrations by Jason
Van Hollander is a self-published chapbook by this talented artist who

has done cover and interior illustrations for Tor Books as well as work for smaller presses such as Arkham House and Wildside Press. This little book is a good introduction to his work and can be bought for $16 prepaid from the author at 128 Winchester Road, Merion, PA 19066.

The Illusion of Orderly Progress by Barbara Norfleet (Alfred A. Knopf), with a foreword by Edward O. Wilson, is a luscious book for those who enjoy seeing jewel-like beetles and other insects posed in tableaux that explore human and insect nature. Norfleet bought all the insects (dead) from catalogs and explains the experiments that eventually led her to this quirky series of color photographs against natural backdrops.

Opium: A Portrait of the Heavenly Demon by Barbara Hodgson (Chronicle Books) is a charmingly illustrated history of the drug, its cultivation, and its use, in period photographs and illustrations, with depictions in film and print.

New York Noir: Crime Photos from the Daily News Archive by William Hannagan with an introduction by Luc Santé (Rizzoli) is a large coffee-table book of stark black-and-white photos—unfortunately, it missed the boat. It doesn't really add anything to earlier crime-photo books such as *Police Pictures: The Photograph as Evidence, Prisoners* by Arne Svenson, *Death Scenes: A Homicide Detective's Scrapbook* with Katherine Dunn's text, and Luc Santé's own book *Evidence*.

My vote for the most beautiful art book of the year goes hands down to *Spectrum 6: The Best in Contemporary Fantasy Art* edited by Cathy Fenner and Arnie Fenner. It's got a stunning array of art by a variety of artists whose work ranges from light to dark fantasy.

A Straw for Two by Éric Sanvoisin and illustrated by Martin Matje (Delacorte Press) is the sweet follow-up to last year's children's book about vampires who drink the ink from books, *The Ink Drinker*. Will young Odilon overcome his loneliness and meet a girl to share his proclivities?

The Headless Bust: A Melancholy Meditation on the False Millennium by Edward Gorey (Harcourt Brace) is as charming and occasionally grotesque as you'd expect from the great eccentric.

The Book of End Times: Grappling with the Millennium by John Clute (HarperPrism), beneath all its visual overkill is a fascinating critical overview of this blip in time we call the millennium. The book is comprised of science fiction/fantasy critic Clute's own and others' ruminations, commentary, and quotations about a world in crisis as a result of ignorance, stupidity, and greed. But the book design is so glitzy and jangly that it almost overwhelms the intelligent text and illustrations.

The Sandman: The Dream Hunters by Neil Gaiman and Yoshitaka

Amano (DC Comic/Vertigo) is a beautiful hardcover tenth-anniversary celebration of Gaiman's creation. The story, adapted from a Japanese fairy tale, incorporates Gaiman's character Morpheus, King of Dreams. Amano gorgeously illustrates the book in a variety of styles.

The Feejee Mermaid and Other Essays in Natural and Unnatural History by Jan Bondeson (Cornell University Press) presents ten lively essays about various zoological "wonders," such as Toby the learned pig, the Feejee mermaid, and the basilisk, detailing their history and the misinterpretations or cunning manufacture that created and sustained their existence.

Every Creeping Thing: True Tales of Faintly Repulsive Wildlife by Richard Coniff (Henry Holt) is the follow-up to *Spineless Wonders* (1996) and continues with the naturalist's sympathetic and jaunty guide to unloved and underappreciated members of the animal kingdom such as moles, sharks, and snapping turtles. None of the creatures here are really repulsive, but they *are* fascinating when viewed through the eyes of someone who appreciates them.

Waiting for Aphrodite: Journeys into the Time Before Bones by Sue Hubbell (Houghton Mifflin) is by another naturalist fascinated by the less lovable creatures of the earth—in this case, invertebrates. In highly readable prose she interweaves personal experience with her erudition about her subject—earthworms, sponges, and sea urchins—writing about the evolution of various species and why it might be important to pay attention even to creatures with which we have (or want) minimal interaction.

The Big Book of Grimm by the Brothers Grimm (as channeled by Jonathan Vankin) is illustrated in black and white by Charles Vess, Gahan Wilson, and dozens of other lesser-known but talented comics artists. It includes many of the lesser-known tales. The artists' renditions are clever and funny—and occasionally gory.

Blood and Smoke contains three stories, all about smoking, read by Stephen King (Simon & Schuster Audio). Two appear in this audiobook for the first time. The third, "Lunch at the Gotham Café," was reprinted in *The Year's Best Fantasy and Horror: Ninth Annual Collection*.

Small Press Addresses

Ash-Tree Press, P.O. Box 1360, Ashcroft, BC VOK 1AO, Canada. ashtree@ash-tree.bc.ca

Babbage Press, 8740 Penfield Avenue, Northridge, CA 91324. Books@babbagepress.com

The Battered Silicon Dispatch Box, P.O. Box 204, Shelburne, ON LON ISO Canada. gav@gbc.com

BJM Press, 95 Compass Crescent, Old Whittington, Chesterfield, S41 9LX, U.K.

Buzzcity Press, P.O. Box 38190, Tallahassee, FL 32315. annk19@idt.net

CD Publications, P.O. Box 943, Abingdon, MD 21009.

Crossroads Press, P.O. Box 10433, Holyoke, MA 01041. xroads4@juno.com

Dark Tales Publications, P.O. Box 675, Grandview, MO 64030. editor@darktales.zzn.com

Delirium Books, P.O. Box 338, North Webster, IN 46555. deliriumbooks@kconline.com

Desert Island Books, 89 Park Street, Westcliff-on-Sen, Essex 550 7PO, U.K.

Durtro, BM Wound, London WC1N 3XX, U.K.

Enigma Press, 38 Lockley Crescent, Hatfield, Herts, AL10 OTN, U.K.

Enigmatic Press, 117 Birchanger Lane, Birchanger, Bishops Stortford, Hertfordshire, CM23 5QF U.K.

Firebird Distributing LLC, 2030 First Street, Unit 5, Eureka, CA 95501. sales@firebirddistributing.com

Fedogan & Bremer, 3721 Minnehaha Avenue S, Minneapolis, MN 55406. fedbrem@visi.com

Gauntlet Publications, 309 Powell Road, Springfield, PA 19064. gauntlet66@aol.com

Llanerch Publishers, Felinfach, Lampeter, Ceredigion, SA45 8PJ Wales U.K.

MOT Press, 38 Oaklands Drive, Wokingham, Berkshire, RG41 2SB, U.K.

Necro Publications, P.O. Box 540298, Orlando, FL 32854-0298. necropublications@earthlink.net

Night Shade Books, 870 East El Camino Real #133, Mountain View, CA 98040. night@nightshadebooks.com

Obsidian Press, 3839 Whitman Avenue North #303, Seattle, WA 98103. mattj@mmpbooks.com

Overlook Connection Press, P.O. Box 526, Woodstock, GA 30188. overlookcn@aol.com

Owlswick Press, 123 Crooked Lane, King of Prussia, PA 19406-2570.

PS Publishing, 98 High Ash Drive, Leeds LS17 8RE, U.K. pspub@editorial-services.co.uk

Sarob Press, Brynderwen, 41 Forest View, Mountain Ash, Mid Glamorgan, Wales CF45 3DU U.K. SarobPress@hotmail.com

Scarecrow Press, 15200 NBN Way, P.O. Box 191, Blue Ridge Summit, PA 17214-0191.

Tartarus Press titles are distributed in the U.S. by Firebird Distributing LLC, 2030 First Street, Unit 5, Eureka, CA 95501.

Ticonderoga Publications, P.O. Box 407, Nedlands WA 6009 Australia.

Violet Books, P.O. Box 20610, Seattle, WA 98102.

W. Paul Ganley, Publisher, P.O. Box 149 Amherst Branch, Buffalo, NY 14667-0149.

Useful Organizations

The British Fantasy Society is open to everyone. Members receive the informative bi-monthly newsletter, *Prism*, in addition to the fiction magazine *Dark Horizons*, edited by Peter Coleborn and Mike Chinn. The society organizes Fantasycon, the annual British Fantasy Convention, and its membership votes on the British Fantasy Awards. For information write to: The British Fantasy Society, the BFS Secretary, Peter Coleborn, 2 Harwood Street, Stockport, SK4 1JJ, U.K. Web site: www.herebedragons.co.uk/bfs/.

The Horror Writers Association is an organization of writers and publishing professionals dedicated to promoting the interest of writers of horror and dark fantasy. There is a bimonthly newsletter with market reports, useful columns, etc. The HWA also hosts an annual meeting and banquet at which the Bram Stoker Awards for Superior Achievement are given out in several categories. For information write to: P.O. Box 50577, Palo Alto, CA 94303. Web site: www.horror.org/.

Fantasy and Horror in the Media: 1999

Edward Bryant

Once there was a time when you could easily categorize films and get away with it. Whatever else the cusp of millennia has brought us, easy dismissals of it's-broccoli-and-I-know-I-hate-it genres are no longer as simple and die-cut as even, say, ten years ago. Lines blur; distinctions fade. Whether it's a majority opinion or not is arguable, but there's a voice abroad in the land submitting that good is good, no matter what the external trappings.

This is all by way of suggesting that the encroachment of mainstream visual moving art into fantasy and horror from one side, and a broadening of interested approach on the part of genre partisans on the other side, is threatening to meet in the center. It's probably a good thing.

One bit of evidence I'd cite is this year's Academy Awards final ballot. As I write this, I have no idea who will actually win an Oscar, but I'm seeing some good candidates in the running from the side of the dark fantastic.

These are culled from the extremely informative Zentertainment (www. zentertainment.com): Frank Darabont's second Stephen King/ thirties period piece/prison flick *The Green Mile* is up for best picture, male supporting role (for Michael Clarke Duncan), screenplay adaptation, and sound awards. Also with a nod for best picture is M. Night

Shyamalan's *The Sixth Sense*, as well as direction, female supporting role (Toni Collette), male supporting role (Haley Joel Osment), editing, and original screenplay. Tim Burton's *Sleepy Hollow* is in the running for cinematography, art direction, and costume design. Not, strictly speaking, fantasy, but certainly horrific enough, Anthony Minghella's first film since *The English Patient, The Talented Mr. Ripley*, is nominated in the categories of male supporting role (Jude Law), adapted screenplay (from Patricia Highsmith's novel), art direction, costume design, and original score. Nods also went to *The Matrix* for best sound, sound effects editing, and visual effects, to *The Mummy* for best sound, and to *Fight Club* for sound effects editing. I've probably missed a few of the ten zillion Oscar citations, but I hope the catalog I could remember is indicative of the movie industry's reaction to some of the fantastic. I say some because there's an even longer list of notable exceptions.

We live in an often unjust world—or maybe simply one in which not every taste is catered to all the time. Whichever, 1999 had something cool on the screen—large or small—for just about every variety of cinematic taste.

Chills Courtesy of a) the Power of Suggestion, or b) the Slap of a Cold Mackerel Across Your Face

If there really is a true film phenomenon of the year, it has to be *The Blair Witch Project*. Is there anyone out there who didn't go to see this hyper-low-budget supernatural thriller? Well, I suspect some were turned off by the sheer overpowering market thrust placed behind this indie production. *Blair Witch* possessed buzz in spades, and it worked for directors Daniel Myrick and Eduardo Sanchez.

Most of you know the conceit: Several years ago a young documentary film crew investigated a reputed witch in rural Maryland and then vanished. Recently a stash of their videotapes was discovered and assembled into the apparently "true" account of their quest. As we know from movies like *JFK* and *In the Name of the Father*, some audiences have a tough time distinguishing verifiable historical fact from expansive fictive docudrama. The visual image is a potent critter.

Much like the weird audience hysteria factor with *Jaws* (the occasional inland young and impressionable audience member instantly turning phobic about water deeper than a bathtub), *Blair Witch* triggered a spate of criticism for being "way too viscerally disturbing." No, not because of any graphic scenes; rather because of the preponderance of jouncy handheld camera work. The conceit is clever, and it works.

The story itself? Actors Heather Donahue, Michael Williams, and

Joshua Leonard thoroughly convince as raw and often obnoxious young filmmaker characters named Heather, Michael, and Joshua. All the flack aside, the movie worked for several basic reasons. First, the film plugged into potent archetypes: This was a Hansel and Gretel tale. Second, whether deliberately or because they were budgetarily strapped, that expensive contemporary darling, special effects, was shorted. Everything nasty happened off-camera. We saw little concrete manifestation of the growing proximity of evil, save for ominous rock cairns, cool twig sculptures, and one quick glimpse of a small chunk of raw meat with perhaps a tooth attached. The youthful audience, accustomed to endless graphic stabbings and decapitations, seemed intrigued by the revolutionary concept of menace and violence via inference. And third, real thought was put to the story structure. The final few seconds of the film leave us with an image that chills, though not all in the audience immediately get the significance. When the viewer remembers back an hour previous, and recalls some of the recounted details of the Blair Witch legend, then the final image becomes devastating. The haunting effect lingers.

As Linda Prior, a Burkittsville, Maryland, grandmother who sells authentic "Blair Witch" sticks-and-stones constructions online at eBay was quoted as saying, "Kind of weird, isn't it?" Indeed.

Overkill can indeed kill, as may be discovered in the cynically over-wrought reworking of *The Haunting*. But first, check out what can happen with one of the many, many low-budget horror flicks that don't benefit from massive Internet buzz, but which still gets a shot at the brass ring through another medium.

One of 1999's must-see releases is a documentary called *American Movie*. Director Chris Smith took as his subject a small-town Wisconsin filmmaker named Mark Borchardt laboring years to complete a micro-budget horror picture called *Coven*. *American Movie* took the Grand Jury Prize at Sundance last year, and deservedly so. It's a wonderfully unblinking and ultimately affecting story of a young guy simply in love with the movies and aiming, with grit and determination, to break into one of the toughest, most competitive fields of commercial endeavor.

The point is not whether or not his film, *Coven*, is a laudable project. As it happens, *Coven*'s been screened at a number of festivals and art/indie theaters showing *American Movie*. The bottom line seems be that Mark Borchardt is a talented director with a good eye, but he might want to reconsider writing his own scripts. What *American Movie* accomplishes, with heart and humor, is to offer a crisp portrait of screwy individuals struggling to achieve the American Dream on a shoestring.

Ghosts of a Chance—Winners and Losers

A good contrast to *The Blair Witch Project* is the hideous lack of achievement of Jan de Bont's remake of Robert Wise's classic Shirley Jackson adaptation, *The Haunting*. Here was big-budget Hollywood studio excess at its least impressive. The amount of cash lavished on the CGI must have been astronomical. But what the audience quickly realized was that the effects were apparently there to take up the slack and amuse the audience every time the story slipped and stuttered like a loose fan belt—and those times were frequent. Okay, cue the digital gryphon—again.

Liam Neeson, Lili Taylor, Catherine Zeta-Jones, Owen Wilson, Bruce Dern, and Marian Seldes all struggled bravely with a thankless—no, terminal—script.

The barely glimpsed dread of Robert Wise's black-and-white version is totally absent. The haunted house's interior was impressive, gothically lovely on a level soaring gaudily out of human scale, but that's not enough to save an expensive woofer.

I'd like to submit the perfect antidote to 1999's Mr. Yuck version of a haunted/possessed house thriller. I must cheerfully alert you that the remake of 1958's *House on Haunted Hill* is a genuine hoot. I mean in the good sense. You stare at me in horror.

Robert Zemeckis, Gilbert Adler, and Joel Silver are behind the production, so, as you might suspect, some of the *Tales From the Crypt* sensibility is at work here. The original, a cheap William Castle exploitation horror flick with Vincent Price (now remember that—it'll be important), Richard Long, Elisha Cook, Jr., and others, was a pretty fair schlocker about a rich guy paying his guests $10,000 each if they could last the night in a murder-haunted mansion.

The Dick Beebe–scripted remake's got the same gimmick, except that inflation has driven up the ante to a cool million per head for the five schlub guests (counting the grandson of the original builder) who end up trapped in what is evocatively presented as a seaside grotesque deco marvel of a onetime hospital for the criminally loony somewhere in southern California. The mover behind the scenes is Geoffrey Rush(!), playing a not-so-terribly-cuddly high-tech amusement park magnate named Steven Price. And yes, Rush does a good job doing Vincent Price, even to affecting a cheesy moustache. Actor Rush seems to have been having a great deal of fun in this role.

Rush's character may or may not be orchestrating the perfect murder of his perfectly bitchy femme fatale wife. Then again, maybe he's just immersed in weird gamesmanship. In any case, a special effects extravaganza rapidly escalates to manic lethality. Are the guests murdering each other in remarkably gooshy ways? Famke Janssen and Taye Diggs do decently well as halfway palatable characters who try hard to use basic intelligence.

Does the house (where mental patients once faced vivisection and lesser tortures at the hands of an equally deranged medical staff) possess a psychic battery energized by the spirits of the dead? A pathologically homicidal genius loci, the guardian spirit? The remakers of *The Haunting* should have paid some attention.

Not everything makes sense in this melodrama. Actually, most things don't. But the crazed level of direction, cinematography, effects, scoring, and cutting all make up for that. Over the top? You could say that. KNB, Dick Smith, and a variety of other worthies supply diverse effects that frequently evoke a definite tone of Clive Barker-ish imagery. You want a chord by which to peg the picture? Marilyn Manson's "Sweet Dreams (Are Made of This)" accompanies the credit roll. The final scene is a wryly amusing little gem. And don't leave before the post-credits final final scene.

There are cynical retreads of older films and there are lively and affectionate nods of respect. To me, this is the latter. A true B-movie? Definitely. This one'll make you feel like William Castle—or Roger Corman, for that matter—is young again and making no-holds-barred flicks that will shamelessly use any device to make you jump, grab your date, chuckle, and kiss your ticket and popcorn bucks good-bye.

What I'm trying to say is, *House on Haunted Hill* is fun. And there's not a lot of that going around nowadays.

Now back to the Oscars (and alas, Geoffrey Rush got no respect from the Academy for his astonishing revivification of Mr. Vincent Price). Who could have expected the new Bruce Willis vehicle to be one of the finest, most effective chillers of the year? Well, anyone who recalls that Willis really can act when he's in a challenging role a bit more ambitious than *Armageddon* or *Die Hard With a Vengeance*. Remember *Pulp Fiction* and *12 Monkeys*? New director M. Night Shyamalan (what a great name to be appended to a skillful horror flick) accomplished a small triumph with *The Sixth Sense*. This is a ghost tale with the kind of Escheresque plot that guarantees viewer debate after the credits no longer crawl.

Bruce Willis is the shrink attempting to help young Haley Joel Osment, a boy whose dubious talent it is to see the shades of the dead. Toni Collette's his edgy, loving, working, single mom.

As one can usually assume with Christian-based ghost mythology, there's a supernatural purpose angling to be served. Given that premise, the script works fine. But too fine? It's no secret that the story pivots on a dime in the last few scenes. Since some of you in the more impoverished classes, perhaps, are waiting patiently to see *The Sixth Sense* on the small screen, I won't expose the big revelation. Suffice it to say, the surprise is sufficient to generate a quick mental run back through the entirety of the film to see if the director/writer was utterly consistent. As best I can tell, he was.

A non-Oscar contender that still ranks with *The Sixth Sense* as an absolutely terrific ghost story is *A Stir of Echoes*. Written and directed by David Koepp and based on the novel by Richard Matheson, this is a reasonably faithful adaptation and a far more than decent treatment of ghosts in a contemporary urban setting.

Kevin Bacon does well as a Joe Everyman sort of guy who submits to hypnosis at a party and then starts to have those unaccountable experiences that mean he's either going crazy or . . . he can see the spirits of the dead.

As with just about every other fictional character who gets a psychic line out of the mundane world, Bacon first appears to be metamorphosing into an obsessive loon, but then comes to understand he's embarked on a driven quest. A rough justice must be served. But who's the aggrieved party, and who's the beneficiary of what Bacon will eventually do?

Distinctly different treatments of similar bodies of mythology, *The Sixth Sense* and *A Stir of Echoes* are both first-rate examples of supernatural melodrama.

Ditto Tim Burton's autumn entry into the ghost tale sweepstakes, though *Sleepy Hollow* tended to confuse both audiences and critics. Was this wide-ranging elaboration on Washington Irving's classic short story sacrilege or tribute? Was this supposed to be the softer, gentler Burton, the quirky sentimentality of *Nightmare Before Christmas* or *Edward Scissorhands*, but gone hideously awry? Or perhaps a rousing campfire tale of robust, in-your-face Americana?

The answer is probably yes. Across the board. Burton's about as quirky as a commercial director can get, and that's not intended to damn with faint praise. I love his work. But *Sleepy Hollow* does flirt with disaster with an uneasy mixture of diverse tones. Ultimately, however, it works.

Andrew Kevin Walker's script (with an uncredited assist from Tom Stoppard) takes the liberty of changing Ichabod Crane from local teacher to New York City constable, and then has the rebellious lad shipped out to the hinterlands to handle the troubling case of multiple criminal decapitations. Johnny Depp looks great in a goth-dark frock coat. While he's presented as a pioneer of modern forensic science, the script also takes pains to depict him as just as inept and klutzy as Irving's original Ichabod. Presumably a restrained Christina Ricci, playing the daughter of the local wealthy landowner, finds this endearing.

On one hand, cinematographer Emmanuel Lubezki gives *Sleepy Hollow* a terrifically eerie dreamlike quality. At the same time, the appearance of the very real supernatural horseman, played in his human incarnation by an over-the-top Christopher Walken, is presented in jarringly graphic terms. Unstoppable nightmare stalks the dreamscape. The dramatic torque clearly has grated on some viewers' nerves.

Sleepy Hollow works better as dream; forcing it into the mold of a realistic dramatic structure is a chore. Tim Burton's superb quality of a comic worldview grunts and strains a bit here when it squares off with graphic grue. But it's still far more interesting than the neat, solidly mortared dynamic of lesser directors' much less ambitious efforts.

Strong Currents Flow in the Mainstream

Who would have thought that Paul Dale Anderson, whose big splash two years ago was *Boogie Nights*, would have followed up that exuberantly off-center look at the erotic film industry in the seventies with a dark and fantastical outright (well, almost . . .) science fiction film? I speak of *Magnolia*, hailed as a scathing ultra-contemporary view of Southern California. The diverse cast would do justice to a Robert Altman gathering. Perhaps the standout among strong competition was Tom Cruise, clearly enjoying himself as a Tony Robbins-like motivational speaker whose shtick is re-empowering wimpoid men through instilling a frightening sense of misogyny. That's not the speculative element. This is a long (three hours) movie bookended by episodes treating the reality-warping nature of synchronicity and coincidence. The director/screenwriter nails it down shortly before the midpoint when we meet a precocious young boy seated at a library table with a startling array of reading material fanned out before him. Placed in the visual center of the scene is a copy of Charles Fort's *Wild Talents*, one of that century-ago offbeat inquiring mind's collections of weird "true" accounts. About half an hour before the movie ends, at about the time many viewers are consciously wondering when or if this undeniably well-crafted picture will ever wrap up, something startling happens that brings every viewer in the auditorium back to full consciousness. I won't spoil the surprise.

Clearly Paul Dale Anderson knows his material. He's accomplished a clear and deliberate triumph of applied imagination.

It's not every year one finds two appropriate and interesting films that utilize strong elements of misogyny to their benefit. Maybe it's a trend? One hopes not. David Fincher's bleak *Fight Club* doesn't play on misogyny in the same direct way that Tom Cruise's role in *Magnolia* does, but it's effectively there. The surreal and the absurd blend into this postmodern look at men's societal disempowering in the nineties, the effective emasculation that must somehow be countered if red blood is again to flow in masculine veins. At least that's the dilemma for an alienated office dweeb played by Edward Norton. His initial solution to habitual insomnia is to become a twelve-step group addict, attending a different variety of group each night. That scheme is monkeywrenched when he encounters Helena Bonham Carter, playing a similarly habituated group-groupie. Salvation comes from an encounter with powerful, amoral, free-spirited Brad Pitt. Pitt's character lives with a zest and energized spontaneity far beyond Norton's lackluster experience. Pitt and Norton come up with the notion of the Fight Club, a basement environment in which otherwise desolate and isolated men such as themselves can fight in bare-knuckle one-on-one confrontations. Bruises and abrasions bring them back into contact with themselves, their bodies, their male identities. It's a brutal and sad validation. Guy power! And it leads to even more radical, ever more revolutionary approaches to recapturing a male empowerment presumably lost in the relatively recent past to such factors as soulless corporate dronedom and burgeoning feminism. Director Fincher eventually goes for some chilly over-the-top imagery at the end, including a surprise designed to shock as much as the revelation in *The Sixth Sense*. Unlike the latter movie, I'm not convinced that *Fight Club*'s script quite justifies the epiphany. In any case, it's interesting to note that *Fight Club* has become a favored midnight movie in many urban art theaters. I suspect that's because whatever its other virtues or sins, this film touches the kind of nerve in today's young that decades ago was jolted by *Easy Rider* or *Medium Cool*. Go figure.

An indie feature that toys wildly and successfully with what many would label genre tropes is *Being John Malkovich*. Celebrated music videos and commercials director Spike Jonze makes his feature-length debut here; Charlie Kaufman also debuts with his script. Obsessed street puppeteer John Cusack, the self-possessed Orson Bean, an amazingly non-stereotyped Cameron Diaz, a fearsome Catherine Keener, and the rest of the talented cast weave a surreal and magical spell as they bring to life everything from the absurdist half-story corporate level of an office tower to the incredible space-time infundibulum that can place any observer for a brief time into the head of actor John Malkovich. Malkovich plays himself with a certain degree of self-assurance—no surprise there—in what must have been a fascinating experiment in ego contortion. At its heart—and crucial for any story, of course—is the reality that the plot is about character and relationships. The labyrinthine variations contorting relationships in this movie are indeed mind-boggling. How mutable is the very definition of identity.

In a season of long films, *The Green Mile*'s duration was such that one did well to scale up the magnitude of the initial popcorn purchase at least one size. Writer/director Frank Darabont's adaptation of the Stephen King novel runs for a solid three hours or so. Darabont had some good practice for filming this period piece about magical happenings in a southern prison, since he also adapted and directed Stephen King's *The Shawshank Redemption* to good effect several years ago.

More clearly fantastical than its predecessor, *Green Mile* deals with humane prison guard Tom Hanks as he comes to understand and communicate with condemned black prisoner Michael Clarke Duncan. Possibly unjustly convicted of killing two little white girls, Duncan's pending execution may just turn out to be humankind's worst loss in about two millennia. Duncan's character is named John Coffey, and he appears to be a natural healer. He radiates a supernal goodness. And those initials, yes indeed.

The character relationships, the moral views of race relations and capital punishment in the South of the thirties, the whole complex issue of how human beings communicate with each other, and whether they can truly empathize, all get treated at length. Though some audiences got impatient with the length, I saw no problem with spending three hours in these characters' lives. David Morse, Bonnie Hunt, Sam Rockwell, Graham Greene, Harry Dean Stanton, Gary Sinise, James Cromwell, and Barry Pepper all help bring the meditative story to life; that's Stephen King's strong suit, evoking American life as it is—or in this case, as it has been, though the legacies linger on to the present.

Eyes Wide Shut is another long feature (159 minutes). More significantly, it's the late director Stanley Kubrick's swan song. Hurt at the box office by wrongheaded industry buzz (*Eyes Wide Shut* turned out to be a profoundly erotic and sensual intellectual exercise—but without the rumored nude sex scenes between Tom Cruise and Nicole Kidman), it's an extended fantasy well worth the viewing. Kubrick and Frederic Raphael wrote the script using Arthur Schnitzler's surreal novella as a springboard. This is life as twisted daydream, punctuated by moments of sheer nightmare. The demons are no less horrific for being psychological.

Run Lola Run delved into science fiction tropes again, but is especially notable for being probably the most hyperkinetic film of the year, breathlessly keeping up a pace at least a nose ahead of *The Matrix*. The extraordinary Franka Ponte plays a young woman obliged to save her inept boyfriend from a deadly criminal confederate. She has twenty minutes to obtain a certain amount of money and place it in his hands. She tries; she fails. And the whole cycle starts over again. With each time loop, the circumstances and details vary. The suspense builds. Imagine *Groundhog Day* as tight and tense, far more energetic, with cutting-edge music and a neo-punk sensibility. German writer/director Tom Tykwer shows here he's a creative force to watch.

The Red Violin is a fine dark fantasy from Canadian director Francois Gerard in which the possessed instrument of the title is passed down through the centuries. As the violin moves from hand to hand, the film slowly discloses the nature of the instrument's creation and just what the creator ultimately had in mind. The multinational cast of Carlo Cecchi, Irene Grazioli, Samuel L. Jackson, and many others takes it all seriously without stumbling into the ponderous. Jackson plays a contemporary art historian hired to validate the fabled red violin before a stupendous auction but who finds an enigmatic and obsessive relationship growing between him and the artifact.

Imagine, say, *Armageddon* or *Sudden Impact* without many special effects. Imagine a secular apocalypse without the intercession of God or Satan or the Antichrist. Imagine a world resigned to the consensual reality that life on Earth is simply going to end in six hours, at midnight, Toronto time, with no specific reason ever offered. What you're imagining is writer/director Don McKellar's excellent *Last Night*, a "small" movie that shows a diverse group of Toronto citizens figuring out what they're going to do in these last few hundred minutes of the end times. David Cronenberg, Sandra Oh, Genevieve Bujold, and Callum Keith Rennie are among the distinct and distinctive players just trying to make do or get things settled as the end nears. Without a Bruce or Arnie figure on hand to save the day at the very last second, we're left with a growing sense of resignation, whether calm or hysterical, and a rich soup of wry comment, warm sentiment, and a final darkening seriousness.

Spotlighting Anthony Hopkins as an ace primatologist hauled back to the U.S. after committing multiple murder in Rwanda, *Instinct* takes a run at examining speculation about the nature of intelligence, sentience, interspecies communication and empathy, and cultural intolerance. Suggested by a Daniel Quinn novel and directed by Jon Turteltaub, *Instinct*, for better or worse, carves out its own stubborn course. Never entirely successful, the film is aided by a competent supporting cast including Cuba Gooding, Jr., Donald Sutherland, and Maura Tierney. Even when it ultimately staggers, it's still a game try.

For high-quality weirdness (think early David Lynch), I can recommend without qualification *Twin Falls Idaho*. This project is created by identical twins Mark and Michael Polish, who wrote the story and co-star as conjoined twins. Michael Polish directed. This is a sad, dark, and extremely affecting tale of what happens in the present time to society's freaks. The conjoined twins in the story establish a fragile relationship with an apprehensive hooker (Michele Hicks). Once the viewer gets past the barrier of grotesque novelty, the film's tenderness, as it treats pain and loneliness, is extraordinary.

Martin Scorsese's *Bringing Out the Dead* is a stylish look at the difficult, sometimes surreal, lives of New York City's Hell's Kitchen EMT drivers (Nicolas Cage, Tom Sizemore, John Goodman). Paul Schrader's script is properly mean-streetish. Visually it's striking, including some nifty CGI scenes with urban ghosts. In terms of warm fuzzies, it may not make the grade with the more squeamish viewers. If you're of the latter persuasion, try to overcome your trepidation if only to see a desperate Nick Cage extemporize the "healing" of a drug-crazed punk by evoking an evangelical moment and leading the other goths in a prayer circle.

Mike Leigh's *Topsy-Turvy* is one of those aquatic birds that walks like a duck, quacks like a duck, swims like a duck, but is actually something a touch stranger. This period piece about Gilbert & Sullivan's creation of *The Mikado* has been compared to *Shakespeare in Love*, and perhaps it is that to a degree, but it's still very much its own creation in terms of individual notion and nature. As a quasi-fantasy, it does a spectacularly evocative job at recreating a historical period (England in the 1880s) that's now as foreign to us as Imperial Rome; as metaphorical science fiction, I feel it captures the substance of such classic science fiction stories as Murray Leinster's "First Contact." When W. S. Gilbert happens upon a vest-pocket Japanese cultural exchange project in Victorian England, the depiction of initial fascination, the half-grasp of what it really means, but a full apprehension of the significance of the whole experience, makes eloquent statement about both cultural clash and the very nature of the creative experience. Jim Broadbent does terrifically well as Gilbert, but he's matched by the rest of the first-rate cast. The film is capped by the sort of irony beloved by scenarists in any artistic venue: two strong-willed individuals struggle for their heart's desire, only to end up incognizant of the reality that each has realized the other's wish.

Virtual Summer

You want to evoke the classic consensual horror theme of feared loss of control? Three notable science fiction films took different angles of approach, but scored a trio of notable successes with *The Matrix*, *eXistenZ*, and *The Thirteenth Floor*.

The first and most successful of the filmic cyber phenomena was, of course, *The Matrix*. This probably ain't your parents' movie. First impressions of this frenetic, colorful, high-velocity, and loud nonstop melodrama might be that the makers, brothers Andy and Larry Wachowski (*Bound*) misspent their growing-up years far too deeply immersed in comics, rock 'n' roll, action movies, and computer geekdom. Probably so. But that hasn't stopped them from creating a synthesis of high-energy entertainment informed by an ecumenical breakneck dash through what seems like most of the world's philosophies and religion, to create a truly remarkable cinematic diversion. Probably the movie's greatest virtue is that it takes science fiction ideas seriously and doesn't feel any particular need to dumb everything down. *The Matrix* is hardly revolutionary in its science fiction content, but it does take strides forward by comparison with most of its Hollywood competition. The concept is that in the future, a few rebels have discovered that humanity is kept in cyber-thrall (the matrix itself) by a conspiracy of aggressively ambitious artificial intelligences. Led by Laurence Fishburne, startlingly similar in visual effect to a darker version of comics' Mr. X, the rebels keep trying to recruit new allies, even as they become aware that a very special soul, The One, is reputedly coming along to give them a special edge in duking it out in the predicted desperate apocalyptic battle with the machines. But Keanu Reeves? "He doesn't seem very bright," says one of the characters, "but he is cute." The Wachowskis' script gives Reeves the opportunity to shine in a way his somewhat similar role in *Johnny Mnemonic* could never pan out. The cast is full of memorable characters: Carrie-Anne Moss as the smart, tough chick; Hugo Weaving marvelously bringing to life, as it were, Agent Smith, part of the enforcement arm of the machine intelligences. With only one or two real clues shown to identify it, Sydney makes a great anonymous metropolis for the virtual city's location filming. Plenty of expert digital effects, including cranking the human figures into terrific Hong Kong movie martial arts routines, keep the audience awake. As though anyone could sleep through the high-decibel music. Auditorally, visually, this is a full-tilt assault on most of the audience's senses. But are small touches such as the exquisitely choreographed dance of brass shell casings plummeting from a distant helicopter to the pavement below really necessary? Naw, but they certainly are frosting on the cake. Cram the cyberplot together with the always-dependable theme of throwing off the oppressive regime, add all the sensory overload, stir in the new-messiah ingredient, never let up the pace for a second, give us a breathing space with the ultimate mentor figure presented as a Jewish mother, and you've got a Robert Graves mythic farrago that can upstage *Star Wars*.

David Cronenberg's latest extravagant weirdness, *eXistenZ*, may well be his most accessible film, and that's not a bad thing at all. I love his less penetrable work, and I love this one that exhibits a fairly straightforward plot. *eXistenZ* in the context of the film is the latest ultra-hyper-super-virtual gaming project of ace game designer Allegra Geller (Jennifer Jason Leigh). After a disastrous beta group test, Leigh finds herself trapped inside the game with bodyguard and corporate drone, Ted Pikul (Jude Law). Enemy or enemies unknown are after Leigh as her character negotiates level after level of play, avoiding a variety of grotesque traps. No simple shoot 'em up, *eXistenZ* is Cronenberg's favorite form of extrapolation, a mutable environment in which fluid bio-forms merge with virtually anything in our accustomed reality. The game pods take the form of fleshy organs with slick surfaces and nipplelike protrusions. The erotic play functions on a dizzying number of artistic levels, and the edged humor is ever-present. Willem Dafoe takes a terrific turn as a seriously weird service station attendant named "Gas." This is erotic science fiction smoothly merged with apt social commentary, sharp wit, and coherent hyperkinetic energy.

Just another topical ripoff? I suspect few people expected much at all from *The Thirteenth Floor*. Even fewer probably realized the film, in development for virtually forever, is based on *Simulacron-3* by Daniel F. Galouye. Galouye, a recognized science fiction novelist who died in 1976, lived in New Orleans and wrote some still-remembered works, including the modern minor classic, *Dark Universe*. *Simulacron-3* dates back to 1964. *The Thirteenth Floor*'s major virtue is not so much the plot—plotting and corporate chicanery in the hot field of virtual reality—but rather in the visual presentation, particularly that of a virtual destination couched in lovely deco noir decor. *Godzilla* and *Independence Day* principals Dean Devlin and Roland Emmerich did us all a favor in executive producing and muscling *The Thirteenth Floor* into tangible existence.

My Folks Went to the Apocalypse and All They Brought Me Was This Crummy T-shirt

There was a time when I thought science fiction writers, even if they weren't likely to predict future specifics, could still intelligently speculate about general trends in the future, and particularly, that the end of the century would see all sorts of really cool popular art dealing with the cusp of millennia. Wow, did I ever bomb out, particularly in the world of film.

What did 1999 give us? *End of Days* and *The Omega Code*. Directed by Peter Hyams, *End of Days* gives us Arnold Schwarzenegger as a burnt-out New York cop handed the opportunity to save the human race from the devil's return. In the latter role, Gabriel Byrne doesn't do a bad job as Old Scratch's earthly avatar.

And Arnie does his best. So do the special effects. There is plenty of color and action as Satan attempts to find the designated mother (Robin Tunney) only he can impregnate to sire the Antichrist. As so frequently happens, the cause of all real damnation seems to be the script. *End of Days* is written in a sort of shorthand using tired tropes.

The Omega Code is even less successful. Director Bob Macarelli's sneakily camouflaged chunk of orthodox Christian screed sneaked into theaters on little cloven feet, showcasing relatively legitimate actors such as Michael York, Casper Van Dien, and Catherine Oxenberg, all of whom should have known better. The most nuanced acting herein is courtesy of the always splendid Michael Ironside! Despite his effort, though, the Apocalypse was never so dull.

In truth, if you want to see some millennial flicks of genuine ambition and accomplishment, check out videotapes dating back five and nine years ago. For true millennial madness, the ticket is Kathryn Bigelow's 1995 science fiction vision of century's end, *Strange Days*. For an evenhanded, challenging, clear-eyed stare at Bible-rooted apocalyptic drama, the only choice is Michael Tolkin's 1991 directorial debut, *The Rapture*. Mimi Rogers's portrait of a complicated woman frustrated by a dead-end world, an individual embarking with skepticism and trepidation on the next step of spiritual evolution, was the role of a lifetime.

Since the new millennium won't actually start until the end of 2000, I reckon there's still some opportunity for ambitious new apocalyptic material to come along in timely fashion. But I'm not counting on it.

If you still can't get enough theological fantasy, then go ahead and rent *Stigmata*. This time Gabriel Byrne plays the good guy, a skeptical priest investigating miracles for HQ in Rome, only to find himself in conflict with Vatican officials treating an apparent case of divinely triggered stigmata as if it were Linda Blair in *The Exorcism* spewing Satanic soup.

You've got a better chance at thought with your diversion if you obtain Ed Harris as another priestly investigator of the supernatural in Agnieska Holland's serious but still flawed *The Third Miracle*.

Invasion of the B-Keepers

Even though the heyday of double features is long past, the concept of the B-movie still seems to be valid. It's more a value judgment than a pragmatic aspect of budget. Some B-movies are born, others are made. Some are not so ambitious, but fill out the scope of their limits amusingly. Others are ambitious beyond all measure, but fall with sufficient clatter that they trigger our cruel amusement. Guilty pleasures, objects of derision and pity, they all wind up here.

The Faculty is determinedly a classic B-formula picture, and damned proud of it. Both director Robert Rodriguez (*From Dusk 'Til Dawn*) and writer Kevin Williamson (*Scream*) are well aware of their roots here. Much like a deliberately theatrical hair job, the roots are thoroughly showing. As the movie starts, Herrington High is a school that wouldn't shock transfers from *Buffy the Vampire Slayer* one whit. The teachers are increasingly acting like zombies; the kids are divided into broad groups of either stoners or clique clones. Classic geek Elijah Wood one day discovers a peculiar organism on school grounds that just might qualify for some sort of lab dissection. Turns out to be one of the hideous alien parasites that are busily taking over the brains of the faculty. Before you can say "Jack Finney" three times fast, Wood's character and his new and old buds Shawn Hatosy, Josh Hartnett, Laura Harris, and Clea DuVall find themselves suddenly besieged by an insidious alien plot to take over all of humanity. Clea DuVall's goth outsider teen girl character fortunately happens to be a reader of classic science fiction such as *The Puppet Masters* and *Invasion of the Body Snatchers*, so she really does know what's going on. Such oldsters as Salma Hayek, Robert Patrick, Bebe Neuwirth, Famke Janssen, and Piper Laurie do an excellent job playing adults. Clearly not an Oscar aspirant for best picture, *The Faculty* still pegs quite high on the entertainment meter.

For a more artful approach, not to mention an uncompromisingly grisly apprehension of its material, catch Antonia Bird's *Ravenous*. This period Western historical/horror hybrid features Guy Pearce as a

Mexican-American War veteran assigned to an isolated military outpost high in the Sierra Nevada range, where Robert Carlyle staggers in bearing disturbing accounts of cannibalism and starvation. When the army soldiers investigate, they uncover a perverse picture of cannibalism and vampirism. David Arquette, Jeffrey Jones, and Jeremy Davies add to the fermenting character brew. There's plenty of ominous atmosphere and sinister tonal touches here.

I had real hopes for *The Mummy*, directed by Stephen Sommers. It was a vehicle for Brendan Fraser (not necessarily a bad idea), but it also had about a jillion dollars in effects and no particularly enthralling script. The high concept seemed to be Indiana Jones Lite. And since Indy was lite to begin with, we were left with an expensive ($80M) movie so much lighter than air, it kept attempting to home in on Lakehurst, New Jersey.

Comic treatment is a difficult application. There are movies that smile affectionately at the past or other conventions, and then there those that keep poking you in your ribs just to make sure you got the joke. *The Mummy* was of that latter variety. Nudge, nudge, wink, wink. For those unconversant with the cinematic past, it was a good popcorn movie and date flick. For those a little more discriminating about their first-run entertainment, it was a disappointment. Arnold Vosloo's latter-day incarnation of a Terminator-ish Karloff character complemented Fraser's natural comedic bent. But lurid sandstorms and yucky scarab beetles do not a triumph make.

More successful (though not at the box office) was the uneasy mix of rubber history and fantastic adventure, *The 13th Warrior*. Antonio Banderas plays a tenth-century Arab poet who stumbles into a job as an ambassador to the Vikings, and then finds himself enlisted as the extra man in a Scandinavian expedition to take care of a little problem with ancient, evil, flesh-eating critters. Based on Michael Crichton's novel *Eaters of the Dead*, the movie tries to cover a lot of bases, ranging from the Beowulf story to apparent speculation about what eventually happened to the Neanderthals. There's plenty of color here, and a lot of kinetic excitement.

Apart from the remake of *The Haunting*, if there was a major nadir of thwarted expectations in a Hollywood studio production last year, *Star Wars Episode One: The Phantom Menace* was probably it. The long-awaited and much-anticipated first of the three prequels to the now-classic *Star Wars* trilogy simply did not deliver. Perhaps it could not. Action, vivid color, exotic environments, toned-down violence, spectacular effects, hey, all that was there in abundance. Young Jake Lloyd did a pretty good job as the young Annakin Skywalker, later to become

Darth Vader. Liam Neeson did okay as Jedi master Qui-Gon Jinn, as did Ewan McGregor as his apprentice, the young Obi-Wan Kenobi. Perhaps that was part of the problem—everything was "pretty okay." Part of the problem may have been that audience expectations had been driven so high by marketing cranked to eleven on the ten-dial, it would have taken a live telecast of Satan in a Celebrity Death Match with Jesus, both armed with light sabers at the premiere screening, to please the fans. Additionally there was the complication, an intriguing exercise in the theory of dramatic structure, that this picture was the first chapter of an ultimate three, in a story of which the audience has seemingly forever known the outcome. Suspense is a real problem here and now. Then, of course, there's the matter of Jar Jar Binks, a comic relief character from whom most viewers seemingly would rather flee than giggle with. Voiced by Ahmed Best, Jar Jar was perhaps not the best representative of humanoid-kind. If he were a John Bunyan character in *Pilgrim's Progress*, Jar Jar would have been christened "Irritation." Poor Jar Jar must own, to his eternal shame, the world's worst choice in *Star Wars* marketing tie-in toys, the Jar Jar Binks candy tongue. Imagine a plastic head of Jar Jar attached to a syringe-style plunger. Depress the plunger and the hapless alien's jaws gape open. Out slides a long, pink, fleshy, tubular piece of candy which the child is obliged to suck. Jar Jar's one funny scene in the movie which involves a fruit, our man's tongue, and the lightning martial arts grasp of a Jedi is merely cute. *The Phantom Menace* is precisely that—plenty of sound and fury but no edge.

So was Joan of Arc divinely inspired? Simply crazy? Maybe both? *The Messenger* tries to have it all ways and can't seem to draw everything together. The highly suppositional theory is that being witness to a terribly graphic rape was the secular trauma that tipped young Joan in a new direction. Then come the angels of the Lord that evoke nothing so much as a kind of impressionist image of NATO jets on strafing runs. John Malkovich makes a suitably smarmy King Louis. Dustin Hoffman possesses presence but little credibility as a sort of Grand Inquisitor figure. The French political machinations intrigue so far as they go, and the requisite burning at the stake is suitably graphic. Director Luc Besson's got a good camera-eye, and his then-girlfriend Milla Jovovich attempts with great zest to simulate tightly wound hysteria, but the whole recipe never quite jells.

There are some minor classics of the cinema many of us might wish should never be remade, no matter how affectionate the retooled version. I'd place *Mighty Joe Young* in that category. Admittedly this is pure sentiment speaking. Ernest Schoedsack's 1949 original was already something of a spin-off from *King Kong*. Now director Ron Underwood (*Tremors*) updates the action gamely and, for the most part, to good effect. Ray Harryhausen and Willis O'Brien got an Oscar for special effects first time around; in the present version, Harryhausen, along with the 1949 heroine Terry Moore, both make cameo appearances. Vintage movie posters (Ben Johnson, John Ford, Wagon Master) also suggest tributes. Bill Paxton's a solidly masculine hero; Charlize Theron is her customary strong female presence. When Joe's filmed as a non-CGI, John Alexander is the man in Rick Baker's ape suit. Though the human motives have been tweaked, lovable innocent Joe is still the oversized African primate brought to this strange new land of America, struggling to adjust his natural nobility to the weird and troubling landscape of his adoptive home. As remakes go, *Mighty Joe Young* is no *King Kong*. Thank God.

Certainly all of us who remember Robert Conrad and his crew fondly in the vintage TV series went out to see *Wild Wild West* the first weekend. It's always tragic to encounter a comic Western (or comic whatever) that simply isn't funny.

Really now, who would expect a sequel to Brian De Palma's classic of two decades ago, *Carrie*, to have the slightest scintilla of quality and entertainment value? Just for a few nostalgic grins, catch *Carrie 2: The Rage* on video or cable. Newcomer Emily Bergl does an adroit job of capturing the same sort of anguished vulnerability caught in the last generation by Amy Irving. And as a special treat, Irving herself plays a role as one of the last grownups at the local high school who remembers that fatal prom night, oh so long ago.

When it comes to screaming in—and surviving—B-movies, Jamie Lee Curtis did much better this year than last. *Virus*, for all its predictability, was a heck of a lot snappier than *Halloween H$_2$O*. A good part of that doubtless was Gale Anne Hurd's influence as producer. Hurd's history suggests she's got no problems at all with strong female characters in her productions. In *Virus*, adapted from Chuck Pferrar's Dark Horse comic book, Curtis's character comes across as a tough, intelligent woman, as does Joanna Paccula playing the final crew survivor of a Russian science support ship beset by some sort of alien electronic lifeform. The rest of the cast, William Baldwin, Donald Sutherland, and the usual ethnic variety (African American, Cuban—and for a bit of novelty, Maori), go through their paces adequately.

The story's the big problem. Co-written by Pfarrer and Dennis Feldman, directed by John Bruno, the plot gives us a malign alien force infesting the computers and electronic systems of a Russian science vessel in the South Pacific. It's all reasonably good fun, but you know exactly what's going to happen, and you know precisely who's going to survive. There are a few amusing lines, but no surprises.

When he's not creating major television series rating smashes, writer David E. Kelley puts together movies like . . . *Lake Placid*? Well, that's what he did this year. Very consciously the sort of B-movie John Sayles used to crank out for Roger Corman, this is a monster movie about a big old crocodile that has somehow migrated from its natural haunts to a lake in the coastal Northeast. Bridget Fonda, Bill Pullman, Oliver Platt, Brendan Gleeson, Betty White, and Meredith Salenger constitute a wonderful cast. You may have heard complaints that Betty White is miscast as a foul-mouthed old woman. In truth, she's not that foul-mouthed. Critics overreacted. Keep your expectations rationally modest and you won't be disappointed. Although one might argue the aesthetic merits, the high point of the movie's a scene in which a helicopter conveys an indignant cow in a canvas sling over the lake (which is not Lake Placid, by the way) in an effort to bait the monster out of its lair.

If you really can't get your fill of aberrant nature-run-amuck movies, then you may as well spend an unchallenging hour and a half with Louis Morneau's *Bats*. What can I say? In rural America there's a secret government test site set up to do sinister things with bats. When bats apparently start to kill the citizenry, local sheriff Lou Diamond Phillips gets involved. Put it atop a pie, the movie'd be a mildly flavored meringue. And not once does a character say one thing as memorable as David Warner in *Night Wing*: "Bats! That's what I do. I kill bats!" Sic transit, etc.

While there was no *X-Files* feature for the year, series writing veteran Vince Gilligan teamed with director Dean Parisot to create a loose cannon of a small indie picture called *Home Fries*. Plenty of quirky romance with Drew Barrymore and Luke Wilson, rural and small-town irony with Catherine O'Hara and Jake Busey, the literal horror is in the twisted comedy of dysfunctional family relationships. It should be noted that the movie starts with a clearcut case of murder by *X-Files* phenomena.

Robin Williams starring as a robot in Nicholas Kazan's adaptation of Isaac Asimov's story *Bicentennial Man* plus the Asimov/Robert Silverberg novel *The Positronic Man*? A good idea, but not a sure bet as it turned out. Chris Columbus directed, with acting help for Williams from Embeth Davidtz, Sam Neill, Oliver Platt, and Wendy Crewson. Rated PG (I suspect Isaac would have approved). The plot has a two-century span as positronic robot Williams becomes increasingly intrigued by the notion of what makes an individual human, and eventually sheds his metal robot form to try out a fleshly, but mortal, body. Visually sparkling, the movie plays heavily on good old-fashioned sentiment and gentle humor. It doesn't always labor to advantage for the adult nineties jaded sensibility, but this makes for a decent shared experience for an all-ages audience.

You would have seen *Bridge of Dragons* originally on HBO, courtesy of Nu Image. Imagine something of a contemporary variation on *Star Wars*, definitely not so much science fiction as a feel of martial arts cum action adventure cum fairy tale. In an unnamed but definitely eclectically settled modern Graustark, General Ruechang (Cary-Hiroyuki Togawa) has taken power after the death of the king, acting as regent for the too-young princess. A few years go by and the now-adult Princess Halo (Rachel Shane) is ready to take the throne—except that the evil general's planning to share the power by marrying her. Meanwhile, the kingdom's in a nasty political turmoil as out-gunned rebels desperately try to overturn the general's despotic reign. General Ruechang's chief field lieutenant is one Warchild (Dolph Lundgren), doing his best turn on your basic Mel Gibson/*Road Warrior* sort of fighter. It seems the princess has been learning martial arts and venturing out among the commoners in disguise. It's in this role she initially makes Lundren's acquaintance by beating the crap out of him in a tavern mud-pit fighting competition. Naturally a wary mutual attraction kindles and then grows as the princess flees the wedding, Lundgren is dispatched in pursuit, etc. Location shooting in Bulgaria makes for a suitably unfamiliar exotic locale, as the plot chugs along crammed with automatic weapons, faux exploding helicopters, martial arts battling with swords and all manner of other implements, plenty of things that Blow Up Real Good, storm troopers in Nazi helmets, and a variety of bad guys with terrible teeth. It's mostly fun, a guilty pleasure, with a couple of seriously badly edited action scenes.

In *The Astronaut's Wife*, Depp is the astronaut of the title, Charlize Theron's his wife, and she again proves she has acting chops to go along with her looks. The script has a paint-by-numbers story of something terrible happening to shuttle astronauts during a brief, mysterious time they're out of contact with the earth. Rather than see this nineties version, you might want to go back and rent a video of *I Married a Monster from Outer Space*. The suspense is genuine for the first half or so. After that, just go ahead and turn your brain off.

For a lot more sheer goofball fun while your gray matter's on hold, check out *Chill Factor*. Watch Cuba Gooding, Jr. and Skeet Ulrich hijack an ice cream truck and try to evade the terrorists, even as their cargo, yet another disgusting biological superweapon, will be triggered if the temperature rises above 50 degrees.

For a rather more expensive speculative look at the world facing terrible conspiracies, Pierce Brosnan returned as James Bond, in Agent 007's nineteenth film adventure, *The World Is Not Enough*. The Bond franchise is a world unto itself, with its own ground rules, conventions, and family values. This time the unshakeable Mr. Bond has to confront terrorists apparently aiming to blow up an oil pipeline in the former USSR, not to mention figuring out what ace terrorist Robert Carlyle is doing with a nuclear warhead stolen from a Russian disarmament project. Michael Apted's direction and Adrian Biddle's photography give the picture plenty of kinetic action in just about every possible medium for blowing things up. Perhaps more than in any of the previous pictures, James Bond is obliged to function in a grimmer, more realistic world than usual. It should be noted that *The World Is Not Enough* introduces ex-Python John Cleese as R, the possible designated successor to Desmond Llewellyn's Q, the good guys' master supplier of clever gadgets and weapons. As it happens, Mr. Llewellyn died after the film finished shooting, so perhaps the ever-amusing Cleese will return.

Sharks Galore

What would summer be like without an aquatic thriller or two to keep us all deliciously nervous at the shore? *Lake Placid* was supposed to take care of our inland comfort at America's lakes; *Deep Blue Sea* takes us out to *Jaws* country, thanks to director Renny Harlin. At a deep sea corporate research complex, marine scientists have been handed a dandy assignment by their employers. If sharks never get brain deterioration as they age, then why not extract some magic biological agent and do the same thing for humans? One thing leads to another, or there wouldn't be a melodrama. Before you can say "Captain Ahab," the base is isolated by a variety of events, and the humans discover that their experimental shark subjects have become a lot smarter than anyone had expected. The rest is pretty much *Alien* with fins as the crew gets whittled down one at a time. The high point may well be corporate owner Samuel L. Jackson's upbeat farewell speech, delivered providentially enough in front of a pool from which unexpectedly leaps a large and eager-to-snack shark.

I know I haven't sounded properly enthusiastic in my description of the movie, so I'll say that while it's a guilty pleasure, it actually is a slickly made and prettily filmed piece of fluff. Any science fiction suspense thriller could do worse than feature British actress Saffron Burrows as a research scientist.

Nu Image knows where its shagreen is, er, buttered. All the time *Deep Blue Sea* was playing in first run, HBO kept Nu Image's *Shark Attack* in pretty heavy rotation on cable. There's a strong sense of déjà vu in this one. This had a lot cheaper budget and many fewer animatronic shark effects.

Actually *Shark Attack* possesses some virtues. Director Bob Misiorowski filmed it in South Africa, the fictional coastal town of Port Amanzi warping from the real-life Port Alfredo. So the scenery's unfamiliar and quite striking. Casper Van Dien is the studly marine biologist and shark expert who gets to be the New Guy in Town on a mission to figure out why normally disinterested sharks are suddenly attacking locals and tourists every hour or so. The attractive Jennifer McShane fills the love-interest role as the sister of Van Dien's late buddy, a scientist who figures out information he shouldn't and is promptly fed to the sharks by the bad guys. Those self-same baddies are in the palm of an ebulliently menacing Ernie Hudson, an actor of some presence, though his accent shifts as frequently as the trade winds. And naturally there's an obnoxiously wrong-headed scientist (Bentley Mitchum), who's not so much evil as he is boneheadedly monomaniacal. *Deep Blue Sea* was fun but dumb. *Shark Attack*, another harmless guilty pleasure, is less fun and more dumb.

Funny Is As Funny Does

They laughed, many of them—and not laughing with the creators of *South Park: Bigger, Longer & Uncut*—when Trey Parker and Matt Stone announced they were working on a feature-length version of their popular animated Comedy Central series. Presumably those skeptics are not giggling now. *South Park* did gangbusters at the box office and even garnered an Oscar nomination—the slightly risque "Blame Canada" in the best song category. Those few of you, the pioneers on the fringe who have seen the first Trey Parker feature, *Alferd Packer: the Musical* (aka *Cannibal!: The Musical*) know that he's a genuine, if majorly skewed talent. He's thoroughly conversant with what constitutes bravura music and dance numbers for a traditional Hollywood musical.

South Park: Bigger, Longer & Uncut is an astonishingly profligate spew of cultural and political commentary. Just remember that offensive, vulgar, rude, and tasteless aren't equivalent to impermissible or without worth. This is one funny movie with a twenty-gauge scattershot approach to humor.

The *South Park* gang sneaks into an R-rated movie and picks up a few nasty expressions to add to their vocabularies. Irate parents react indignantly, and before you know it, a family values protest has blown out of proportion into a declared war between the U.S. and Canada. Things escalate, and the war reaches down to hell itself. There's the priceless matter of the love affair between Saddam Hussein and Satan, the summary execution of Bill Gates, and a variety of other wacko tangents that need be seen to be appreciated. This is an R-rated movie that thoroughly earns its designation. More important, it's a candid look at our world's warts that, were he alive, Jonathan Swift would probably have ungrudgingly paid full admission price to see. The featured voices of Trey Parker, Matthew Stone, Isaac Hayes, George Clooney, Minnie Driver, Mike Judge, and Eric Idle all add to the alternating pain and merriment. Even the full title of the movie, which the studio didn't comprehend until far too late, adds to the effect.

Perhaps more consistently amusing than a simple laugh-every-second yuk-fest, *GalaxyQuest* gets high marks for an affectionate yet scathing look at the whole *Star Trek* universe, thanks in part to the script by David Howard and Robert Gordon and the direction of Dean Parisot. The gimmick's hardly new in printed science fiction: media stars get mistaken by naive aliens for genuine heroes and get recruited or shanghaied off to save some major sector of an endangered universe. When the movie opens, we encounter the aging stars of the now syndicated, one-time sci-fi hit *GalaxyQuest* at an all-too-horrifyingly-real media convention, all depicted spot-on. Allen's take on William Shatner is absolutely wonderful—though the hair's better. Weaver's a rather stronger and more flamboyant female lead than the *Star Trek* universe featured for decades. Imagine a mutant creation of Ripley interbred with Uhura. Eventually she appears to have a great deal of fun rampaging around an alien landscape in increasingly strategically ripped clothing. Alan Rickman does fine as well as a cranky half-alien science officer.

Mystery Men is one of those comic attempts that's amusing without ever making much headway toward actually being funny. Suspiciously akin in treatment of super-powers to George R. R. Martin's prose fiction series *Wild Cards, Mystery Men* is set in a world of superheroes and super villains, but one in which there are extraordinary individuals whose powers are just plain wonky. Some powers are apparently useless: flatulence on command, for example, or the psychic ability to hurl dinner forks. The cast—Geoffrey Rush, Greg Kinnear, Hank Azaria, Janeane Garofalo, William H. Macy, Paul Reubens, and Ben Stiller—are all good. Would that they had worked from a better script.

Okay, he's back. Mike Myers is no Pierce Brosnan, but rarely does

Mr. Bond have to deal with an antagonist of the caliber of Dr. Evil anymore. In *Austin Powers: The Spy Who Shagged Me*, we meet all our old, uh, friends, plus a few more for frosting on the bundt cake. *Buffy*'s Seth Green is present as Scott Evil, the villain's love child. Myers stays busy here, as before, playing both villain and protagonist. Verne Troyer deserves special notice for playing Dr. Evil's cloned miniature, Mini-Me. Heather Graham, Michael York, Robert Wagner, Mindy Sterling, and Rob Lowe offer solid support. If your comedic taste is broad, very broad, this one is recommended. I probably would have liked the movie better if Doc Evil's pathetic feline, Mr. Bigglesworth, had returned in a more prominent role.

Baby Geniuses probably seemed like a good idea at the time. It isn't. But hey, the Kathleen Turners, Christopher Lloyds, and Dom DeLouises of the world all have to work.

A Little Animation, Please

Other than *South Park: Bigger, Longer & Uncut*, neither of my other two animated favorites this past year was from the usual suspects. Brad Bird, a veteran force behind some of TV's better animated sitcoms, directed *The Iron Giant*. Based on the popular children's book by the late British poet laureate, Ted Hughes, *The Iron Giant* is purely terrific. A boy with a single mom makes friends with a very large mechanical man from space. Loyalty, friendship, and tolerance all make for reasonable thematic bases here. I don't know what the younger viewers think, but for older viewers, some of the real charm lies in the film's nifty setting in the Red-scare era of the fifties. Jennifer Aniston, Eli Marienthal, Christopher McDonald, Vin Diesel, and Harry Connick, Jr. provide solid character voices, particularly Diesel as the weird selection of noises uttered by the title character.

My other favorite was not a completely new release, but was new in the U.S. in its present form, that being *Princess Mononoke*. First released in Japan in 1997, *Princess Mononoke* did better at the box office there than anything until *Titanic*. Director and writer Hayao Miyazaki's epic is a solid two and a half hours. And, as the caution goes, this is an adult animated feature, not a kids' cartoon. The complexity of the story and the amount of appropriate violence make that so. Set in the feudal Japan of the fifteenth century, the writer does not let the story slip off any easy hooks. Relationships among groups and individuals, between mortals and gods, are all realistically complex. The place of humankind in relation to the natural world is examined from a variety of angles. Some of the English voice actors include Minnie Driver, Billy

Crudup, Claire Danes, Gillian Anderson, Billy Bob Thornton, and Jada Pinkett Smith. One of the biggest pluses to the English-language version is the script adaptation by *The Sandman* author Neil Gaiman.

The new Disney version of *Tarzan* is one of the studio's best recent animated epics. Visually it looks spectacular and has perfectly defensible messages. The voices—Tony Goldwyn, Glenn Close, Minnie Driver, Nigel Hawthorne, Brian Blessed, Rosie O'Donnell, and the rest—do their jobs well. Particularly notable as a realistic predator is Sabor the leopard, who doesn't actually have a voice. But clearly he's the meanest mutha in a Disney flick since the unnamed hunter who nailed Bambi's mom.

Toy Story 2 is no slouch either. Disney and Pixar's follow-up to the 1995 blockbuster benefits from the talents of the same creative team, including directors John Lassiter, Ash Brannon, and Lee Unkrich. More than 250 Pixar artists, technicians, and animators brought Buzz Lightyear, Woody, Mr. Potato Head, and a host of new characters to vivid life. Add to that an actual story in the script, and everything comes together impressively.

Addicted to Pixels

People used to rage against the electronic machine when it was just a matter of seeing our offspring as mutant Walter Keene big-eyed-children fixed in front of the sinister TV set for hours and hours on end. As it turns out, those were indeed the good old days.

Nowadays, thanks to satellite dishes and digital cable, at any age you can vegetate in front of a monitor and fill every waking minute with one variety or another of visual horror and fantasy, science fiction and slipstream. I'll make no claims here about its cumulative index of virtue. I'm just speaking of elapsed time.

Suffice it to say, the various series and made-for-the-medium films are legion. As with other media, personal choice is critical. You can't experience it all, and still have a life . . . unless it *is* your life.

The first really big TV event of the dark fantastic for 1999 was ABC's six-hour miniseries presentation of *The Storm of the Century*. This is especially notable for being a faithful translation of a Stephen King script written directly for the small screen. King does well. This exceedingly dark Pied Piper parable about a small New England town isolated by a horrendous blizzard does everything it was supposed to do. The author wielded considerable power here—power, I hasten to point out, that was exercised for good. When the script demanded a grimly downbeat ending, that's exactly what director Craig R. Baxley filmed and what the network ran.

Director of photography David Connell made King's little Maine town an appropriately dark, chilly, and oppressive place, indeed. The cast members are familiar faces, but not intrusive in the manner of major stars. Tim Daly, Debrah Farentino, Casey Siemaszko, Jeffrey De Munn, and the rest all do well at bringing the downeasters to crusty, cranky, three-dimensional life. As the antagonist, Andre Linoge, the blandly chilling little man with the wolf's head cane, Canadian actor Colm Feore performs splendidly. He nails the role. For a more benign image and an indicator of his range, catch Feore as the auctioneer in *The Red Violin*.

Far less ambitious fantasy and science fiction projects ran on cable, particularly on UPN and USA. Generally speaking, these thrillers tended to be concerned with a) plots to spread hideous new bioengineered plagues, b) virtual shenanigans in near-future cyberdramas, or the old dependable, c) incoming extraterrestrials that want to 1) enslave us, 2) eat us, 3) mate with us, 4) steal all our resources, or 5) simply destroy us all on general principles. It's good to know some verities in the universe remain constant.

The SciFi Channel, USA's full-time exponent of the fantastic, displayed more than one of the aforementioned science fiction thrillers. It was also the new adoptive parent of the alternate worlds melodrama *Sliders*, which continues to limp along. Back for a new season, *Farscape* continues to dazzle with wonderful Henson Creature Shop effects and gradually improving plots.

UPN's *Star Trek* franchise is now pared down, at least for the time being, to *Voyager*. Kate Mulgrew's ship still chugs along with increasing self-assurance. The scripts here seem to be on a gradual upswing.

On Fox, Chris Carter's new virtual reality series *Harsh Realm* could find neither an audience nor its sea legs within a sufficient amount of time (the network figured that to be a matter of a few hours, apparently), and was unceremoniously canned after four episodes. Again, it had some real signs of promise, if you were a viewer, but apparently a quite different story if you were a network programmer.

Prior to *Harsh Realm*'s debut, *Millennium* had wound down and crashed at the end of its third season. I, for one, was sorry to see it go. I think Lance Henriksen is a wonderful actor, and his portrayal of beset ex-FBI agent Frank Black was splendid. I suppose the surprise was that the series had lasted for nearly three full years. Unlike *The X-Files*, which evolved fairly smoothly from its beginning to all its variety of later developments, it never seemed as if Chris Carter and his colleagues could ever quite get a handle on what *Millennium* was supposed to be. The first season included a lot of fairly simple serial killer mayhem. The second season dabbled in science fiction and fantasy themes. The third season drowned in conspiracy. At least, when the end came, there was time for the creators to cobble together a somewhat precipitous, but still clear-cut final episode: Frank Black and his daughter literally driving off into the garishly lit sunset.

Solace could be found at the end of the year when the final episode of *The X-Files* for 1999 was titled "Millennium" and guest-starred Lance Henriksen reprising his role as Frank Black. Add a Millennium Group plot utilizing good old-fashioned zombies and an amusing capper as agents Mulder and Scully see in the new year and new millennium together, and you had an entertaining and varietal experience.

As rumors of the principals threatening to defect grew louder, *The X-Files* has continued to preserve the qualities that have kept the audience reasonably interested for the better part of a decade now. Scully and Mulder's alternating personality clashes and connections still work well. FX has continued to run previous season episodes of the series nightly, so fans do not want for something to watch.

Fox continued its deserved reputation as a venue for entertaining adult animation particularly with *The Simpsons* and *King of the Hill*. A terrific addition was Matt Groening's *Futurama*, a great series mining seemingly the entire history of science fiction for imagery, including human brains in bottles. Until this series came along, I think most of the science fiction audience had pretty much forgotten about brains in bottles. No more.

And we must not forget *South Park* over at Comedy Central. Still funny; still extending more prickers than the average adult porcupine.

The Joss Whedon empire on Warner Bros. is growing nicely. Not only has his *Buffy the Vampire Slayer* successfully spun off *Angel*, it's managed to keep intact most of the real humor and scary charm that gave it star power at its inception. Like a variety of other contemporary series, the show has acknowledged the passing of time. The Sunnydale High School kids are now of college age (never mind the real world ages of the actual actors). Some are off to the University of California at Sunnydale, others hang out as townies, and some have left to seek their respective fortunes in Los Angeles. While it remains to be seen if *Buffy* will benefit from an apparently long, long story arc involving a clandestine government project called The Initiative investigating and attempting to deal with paranormal and parahuman phenomena, its greatest asset is still the beguiling cast. A high point recently has been fairly regular appearances by James Marsters as the British punk vampire Spike.

Angel, with a dash of noir sensibility to go along with the sunny atmosphere of L.A., has clearly taken at least a tonal turn away from its parent show. David Boreanaz handles his role well as a repentant vampire attempting to make his way as a not terribly ept private detective. One of the show's brightest spots is Charisma Carpenter as Cordelia, the bitchy Sunnydale coed who's laundered some of her nasty personality as she settles into a prospective show-biz career in L.A. and works as Angel's girl Friday. *Angel*'s less than fully efficient crew is rounded out by Wesley, the self-important but terribly insecure, self-proclaimed British rogue demon hunter. Angel's also found some edgy on-again, off-again romantic interest with a bewildered female L.A.P.D. detective. At any rate, the show hit the ground running and has continued to evolve.

Over on USA, paranoids and cynics continue to delight in the Canadian-filmed *La Femme Nikita*. There's lots of near-future extrapolated surveillance technology and such here, but that's not really the point. As Nikita, the shanghaied female operative of a top secret anti-terrorist agency simply called Section, Peta Wilson gamely hangs in as a character whose mind is getting messed with in virtually every episode. Section's formal enemies only use guns, bombs, and knives. Nikita is constantly having to cope with Section's attempts to control her loyalty absolutely, regulate her self-will, own her brain, and generally exploit her without mercy. It's very much *The Prisoner* for a new generation.

Probably the greatest injustices of last year in terms of good, intriguing, well-executed series not really finding their audiences are Fox's *Action* and the syndicated *Total Recall: 2070*. *Action*, of course, was neither science fiction nor horror, save in the tonal achievement of making Hollywood look even more squamous than usual to the multitude of outsiders who don't actually live in L.A. or its environs. But I loved it for its nasty humor and jagged edges. For about eight episodes, *Action* spun a wondrous tapestry of self-referential and utterly devastating depictions of a major independent producer tottering on the edge of self-immolation. As has been pointed out endlessly with depictions of Hollywood ranging from *The Player* to *Sunset Boulevard*, there really is nothing so outrageous one can say about the American movie industry that it can be classed as too over-the-top for reality. If you can spot late-night re-runs of *Action*, give it a shot. No matter how bleak your own life looks, you'll have the satisfaction of seeing those who have it worse. Much worse.

Total Recall: 2070 started out as part of Showtime's sci-fi Friday night, blocked with shows such as *Poltergeist: The Legacy, Stargate SG-1*, and the weird western, *Dead Man's Gun*. With a nominal nod to Philip K. Dick, the show borrowed liberally for tone and appearance from *Bladerunner*. Essentially the continuing melodrama concerned a homicide cop and his replicant partner working the mean streets of a future metropolis controlled by an enigmatic government trying to hold things together against global combines of oligarchic corporations. Plenty of computers, lots of noir. Ring in the cop's touchy relationship with his wife, and suddenly the viewer realizes that this is not a completely simplistic sci-fi shoot-'em-up. It does a pretty fair job of capturing the technology-cluttered darkness of the projected next century.

Hercules: The Legendary Journeys came to an end last year, but *Xena: Warrior Princess* battles on, still blithely disregarding the slightest pretense of cultural consistency, still exuberantly dispensing one particular variety of female empowerment. At this point, no one seems to know whether the winding-down series will end with Xena dead, married, settled down with sidekick Gabrielle and creating a dynasty, or going somewhere really weird and doing something genuinely strange.

Aaron Spelling's *Charmed* series continues, spotlighting the very contemporary and pulchritudinous witch sisters, Shannen Doherty, Alyssa Milano, and Holly Marie Combs. Humor continues to make occasional welcome appearances.

You just never know what'll survive. *Psi Factor: Chronicles of the Paranormal* has persisted with host Dan Ackroyd. If one stayed up late at night, one might have caught Harlan Ellison guest-starring in an episode as the mysterious "Grifter."

The U.K.'s *Space Island One* made it to U.S. public TV with some nicely produced life-in-orbit episodes. There's a whole new generation of postapocalyptic melodramas with a lot of strong female characters. That's the good news. The bad news is primarily the scripts and, occasionally, the production values.

After a second season in which the writers for *Gene Roddenberry's Earth: Final Conflict* lost their focus, the good news for 1999 was that the stories have once again achieved originality, interest, and direction.

The promising supernatural series *Brimstone* got sucked back to hell after thirteen episodes, but something of a thematic successor appeared in the cryptically titled *GvsE*, which turned out to be a broad comedy about operatives working for something of a God-agency laboring to combat the byzantine plans of Old Scratch. Presently a bit more decipherable as *good vs. evil*, it's over on the SciFi Channel.

Not that the networks didn't get in on the fun. *Now and Again*'s an enjoyable piece of fun about a government high-tech plan to take a middle-class nebbish citizen's mind and plunk it down in the body of an enhanced super-agent.

Then there's the syndicated *7 Days*, which actually has raised some eyebrows. It's not the plots or the characters that are so out-of-the-ordinary. No problem with a government time-machine project that can send an agent back a week to try to remedy terrible things that have recently happened without destroying the present through time paradox. No, the problem came in the sophisticated production methods used to noodle around with virtual product placement in the already-filmed episodes. Tricky, very tricky. And potentially lucrative. The returns are not in yet in terms of whether this practice will prove itself out. Or more to the point, how rapidly it'll spread to other series.

Whistle a Happy Tune . . .

No real space to cover all the dark fantastic in music this time around. Naturally my first suggestion is to check out Terri Windling's wrap essay in this volume. She always gives a wonderfully detailed précis of fantasy influences on the tunes of folk and associated endeavors. My second suggestion would be to catch the music reviews in Patrick and Honna Swenson's eclectic magazine of the fantastic, *Talebones* (details at www.nventure.com/talebones).

While one might suspect that most of the truly weird influences on popular music lurk over there in the shadowy regions of goth, post-punk, metal, and death-rock (and you'd be largely right), I'm always delighted to be presented with the truly grotesque when it's couched in the down-home rhythms and adroitly constructed lyrics of country and western music.

I've always maintained that country and horror are complementary artforms, that they skip cheerfully along the bucolic path through the woods hand-in-claw. Both represent approaches to storytelling often sneered at by the mainstream. Each goes for gut feeling to achieve effect and so, at its core, each is a profoundly visceral medium. Both forms are story oriented. Much of the best of country music encapsulates entire narratives in just a few verses. Finally, country and horror both fully acknowledge and incorporate the notions of violence and death without apology.

I've played a parlor game for a few years now, postulating which country stars have their counterparts in horror fiction and vice versa. The Garth Brooks of horror? Stephen King, of course, only more so.

Brooks was obviously tardy in cobbling up his fictional alter ego Chris Gaines; King had long since abandoned the pretense of Richard Bachman. The E. A. Poe of country? Probably Hank Williams, Sr. The Shania Twain of horror? Lucy Taylor. And so on. Now there is no precise three-way collaboration in horror the equivalent of the Dixie Chicks. But if there were, likely it would be Poppy Z. Brite, Caitlín Kiernan, and Christa Faust.

If those three worthies were cutting albums, I think they'd be reasonably content to be credited with something on the level of the Chicks' 1999 release, *Fly* (Monument NK69678). The album's nifty enough on its own, but the included cut (appropriate word, that) I think would be especially appreciated by fans of the dark is "Goodbye Earl." Now there is a tune with content, narrative drive, violence, evil, death, eventual justice, and plenty of resonance for all too many who hear it.

The point has to do with refusing to countenance evil. The song's protagonist is a woman who makes a very bad choice in marriage. Her husband, Earl, is a classic abuser who beats the crap out of her and puts her in the ICU. She does what she can. Earl violates the court-mandated restraining order without a qualm. The threats mount. There's only one answer; the woman and her friends carry it out to the logical extreme, conventional morality be damned. It's a dark and grim plot counterpointed and augmented through a manic, bouncy, high-energy tune. When she's cranking on all cylinders, Nancy Collins writes horror fiction like this.

Even in country music fandom, there are still those who discount the Dixie Chicks because they're young, adorably cute, and blonde. Violating stereotypes is always a wonderful and energizing thing. These women are sharp, wry, strong, and undeniably saturated with talent. Maybe someday somebody will cut a truly perverse medley of "Goodbye Earl" and Doug Supernaw's hit of several years back, "What'll You Do About Me." Two sides of the same thematic coin; both hyperkinetically danceable, both chilling.

Comics: 1999

Seth Johnson

Let's get one thing straight: despite the dire financial speculations that have been in constant circulation since the bust of the mid-1990s, from a creative standpoint the comics industry is healthier than ever. While some hold up distributor consolidation and lower circulation as evidence that the golden age of comics is past, these same factors have led to greater interest in creator-published comics and a willingness by larger publishers to move into long-fallow territory. The result: diversity—and the return of genre comics.

So this year we're going to take a look at 1999's top comics genre by genre—and yes, some superhero books will indeed be discussed, but I think you'll be surprised by the ground we cover between here and there. Take a moment to glance at the title of this volume, and you'll see why we begin with:

Fantasy Comics

My broad statements of the previous paragraphs shouldn't be taken to mean that genre comics had ever disappeared completely. Many fan-favorites of the last decade were rooted firmly in the fantasy genre. One of those was Neil Gaiman's brilliant and award-winning *The Sandman* (Vertigo/DC), and though the title has sadly wrapped as a monthly series, fans still get their fix of the Dreaming each month in the eponymous *The Dreaming* (Vertigo/DC). Wrapped in the same Dave McKean covers that graced every issue of *The Sandman*, writer Caitlín R. Kiernan's stories explore the fictional territory Gaiman pioneered.

And while Gaiman is concentrating mainly on projects in other media, Vertigo chief editor Karen Berger convinced him to write a new graphic novel for the tenth anniversary of *The Sandman*'s first issue. *The Sandman: The Dream Hunters*, is a fantastical story beautifully illustrated by Japanese artist Yoshitako Amano—video game fans will recognize him as the artistic force behind the wildly popular *Final Fantasy* series.

Though the Avon Books text-only version of Gaiman's fairy tale *Stardust* is a fixture at book superstores, individual issues of the original comic-format release matching the text to Charles Vess's illustrations are harder to find, and laying hands on the limited-edition hardcover collection of all four issues remains a near-impossibility. Happily, DC Comics' Vertigo imprint has remedied the situation by at long last releasing a trade paperback collection, with a new cover by Vess. If you haven't already, snatch up a copy—once read, *Stardust* is sure to be a favorite for years to come.

Mark Crilley's *Akiko* (Sirius), the ongoing tale of an eight-year-old girl's explorations of fantastic alien worlds, remains the comic that all parents should be reading with their children—an opinion shared by Random House Children's Books, who will be releasing four *Akiko* books penned by Crilley. Meanwhile, Crilley's one-time convention-circuit companion under the Trilogy Tour banner, Stan Sakai, moved his comic-action-animal-fantasy *Usagi Yojimbo* under Dark Horse Comics' new Maverick creator imprint in 1999—and with the nine-issue story "Grasscutter" won a well-deserved Eisner Award for best serialized story.

A cornerstone of the Trilogy Tour was (for sadly, the Tour has packed up their amazing fantasy oak convention display and gone their separate ways) Jeff Smith's epic fantasy *Bone* (Cartoon Books). While Smith took some time off in 1999 at the end of "Act II" of the series, Act III is just beginning as of this writing and it appears as though the vacation allowed him to maintain the story's considerable dramatic and comedic momentum.

During his hiatus, Smith arranged to bring Linda Medley's delightful and heretofore self-published *Castle Waiting* under the Cartoon Books banner. We can only hope that this helps Medley find a well-deserved larger audience for her book, a quirky fantasy in the classic fairy-tale mold.

Explorations of godhood was the theme of a pair of enjoyable fantasy comics in 1999. Keith Giffen and Mike McKone's *Vext* (DC) followed the misadventures of the god of mishap and misfortune after his expulsion to earth for "insufficient worship," and while the book was unfortunately canceled before even ten issues could pass, it'll be sure to garner new fans who will find it in the quarter boxes at their local comic shop. Approaching godhood from the opposite direction was *Proposition Player* (Vertigo/DC), written and illustrated by Bill Willingham. Following a lowly house-player at a Vegas casino who inadvertently becomes a soul-dealing deity after buying the souls of his friends for the cost of a round of drinks, it's worth reading for nothing other than the multitude of pantheons Willingham throws together into one great comic mess.

In a similar vein is Garth Ennis and Steve Dillon's *Preacher* (Vertigo/DC), the ongoing quest of preacher Jesse Custer to find an absentee God. The series has drawn a lot of attention for its hard-nosed take on Christian mythology and no-holds-barred sex and violence (which astute readers will remember caused me to place it in the "horror" category last year), but it truly is an epic American adventure (written by a Brit, no less!) with some terrific characters and storytelling. Roaring to a conclusion in 2000, DC has reprinted the entire series in trade paperback for those who have yet to taste its forbidden fruit.

Horror Comics

Ah, the 1950s. Before Fredric Wertham and his accusations that comics were poisoning the minds of America's youth, before the Comics Code Authority put the kibosh on almost the entire EC Comics line. Those were the days . . .

But wait—horror comics have returned! Not just the superhero monsters of titles like *Morbius, the Living Vampire* or the short horror bits hidden away in independent comics or anthology comics like *Dark Horse Presents*, but full-fledged horror comics and anthologies from major talents and publishers:

Mike Mignola's *Hellboy* has been around for a few years now, a title that wears its love of horror on its sleeve. In 1999 Mignola and artist Matt Smith gave us *Hellboy: Box Full of Evil* (Maverick/Dark Horse), pitting earthborn demon turned investigator of the paranormal Hellboy against everything from the duke of hell to gun-toting monkeys. It's good old monsters-and-fisticuffs fun, and Mignola and Dark Horse often use backup features in *Hellboy* miniseries to introduce other terrific horror-comics talents like Gary Gianni's excellent *The Monster-Men*. Also well worth seeking out for horror fans: *ZombieWorld* (Dark Horse), a series created by Mignola and then handed off from creator to creator, telling tales set on an alternate earth overrun by the living dead.

Like Dark Horse, DC's Vertigo line has always been a home to horror-related comics projects. So in 1999, Vertigo launched *Flinch!*, an all-horror anthology comic bringing in talent from across the industry to try their hand at stories ranging from murderous monsters to horror of the more mundane variety. A good book to pick up for a monthly fix of quality horror.

Bright, brash, four-color horror. A contradiction in terms? I submit two examples: First, "Transilvane," a two-issue Superman story in *Legends of the DC Universe* #22–23 that sent Superman and mad scientist Dabney Donnovan to a manmade microscopic world whose genetically created inhabitants were socially programmed via old horror movies. Great B horror movie fun in a very Jack Kirby mold thanks to writers Randy and Jean Marc Lofficer and artist J. O. Ladronn. Second, *Champs* (Fantagraphics), a new graphic novel from Steve Weismann featuring his own eccentric cast of characters, seemingly created by throwing the Peanuts gang and the Universal Studios Monsters in a blender—eight-year-old monster kids from Lil' Bloody and Pullapart Boy to X-Ray Spence and Kid Medusa. Throw in some great tongue-in-cheek set-piece humor, like the local stop on the pro Big Wheel racing circuit, and you'll find it's well worth keeping an eye open for Weismann's irregular appearances on the comics rack.

Science Fiction Comics

Though DC's "Helix" line of science fiction comics collapsed, one great survivor remains, now published under the Vertigo imprint: *Transmetropolitan*, by writer Warren Ellis and artist Darrick Robertson, continues to get better and better as it follows renegade journalist Spider Jerusalem on his quest for truth in a future gone mad. Thankfully, Vertigo continues its policy of maintaining their best titles in trade paperback reprints—this is a series that reads just as well in large chunks as it does in individual issues, and even reveals itself as a comics novel in the making. Edgy, opinionated, even a bit crass at times—but also my nomination for one of the best comics of the year.

At the close of 1999, Vertigo published a select series of titles under a limited "V2K" sub-imprint, two of which fell firmly into science fiction territory. *Pulp Fantastic* was a Dashiell Hammett-esque detective story written by the master of hard-boiled comics, Howard Chaykin, ably illustrated by David Tischman. *Brave Old World*, by William Messner-Loebs with art by Guy Davis and Phil Hester, took the imprint title to heart, asking, "what if the Y2K bug was more powerful than we could have possibly expected—and at the stroke of midnight on December 31, 1999, threw the entire world back to January 1, 1900?" A cool story combining time travel, conspiracy, and healthy dollops of social commentary.

Also from DC: A four-issue science fiction anthology with a title drawn from the heyday of science fiction comics, *Strange Adventures* (Vertigo/DC)—great fun, from the covers all the way through the stories to the creator bios; *Heavy Liquid* (Vertigo/DC), a science fiction tale from Paul Pope of *THB* fame; *Trouble Magnet* (DC), Ryder Windham writing with Kilian Plunkett art, the adventures of a quasi-military unit formed around an artificially intelligent robot; and *Yeah!* (Homage/DC), Peter (*Hate*) Bagge and Gilbert (*Love and Rockets*) Hernandez's tale of the greatest rock band in the universe—a group sadly unknown on their home planet of earth. You know, with this much science fiction material coming out, it might be time for DC to try another Helix experiment. . . .

Not that DC is the only house publishing science fiction comics. The also oft-mentioned Dark Horse Comics is putting out a wide variety of material under its creator-owned Maverick imprint, and one of those titles is writer/artist Richard Delgado's *Hieroglyph*. Beautifully illustrated in a European style, it tells the tale of a lone human scout's exploration of a truly alien world, a tale of solitude and adventure that thankfully ends with a setup for a sequel.

And while it was published in individual issue format long before, I somehow missed *Astronauts in Trouble: Live from the Moon* (AIT/ plaNET Lar) until it was reprinted in trade paperback in late 1999. Now I'm kicking myself for not seeing Larry Young and Matt Smith's great near-future moon launch adventure sooner—and I'm making to sure to catch the new series, *Astronauts in Trouble: Space: 1959* as it comes out in 2000.

Genre Jambalaya

There were some projects in 1999 that jumped across genre lines, or in some cases smashed them altogether:

Early in 1999, Dark Horse Comics arranged to import material from Italy's wildly popular Bonelli Comics line—a company whose comics sell in excess of twenty-five million copies each year. Three Bonelli titles were reprinted by Dark Horse in six issues of their Italian 100-page black-and-white digest format: *Dylan Dog*, "nightmare investigator," who battles monsters and evil (accompanied by a sidekick who looks oddly like Groucho Marx); *Martin Mystery*, "detective of the impossible," journeying around the globe in search of adventure and magical artifacts; and *Nathan Never*, who apparently doesn't get a cool title but who does investigate strange and macabre mysteries in a science-fiction future. All three titles were great pulp adventure fun—and given covers by top American artists such as Mike Mignola, Dave Gibbons, and Art Adams for their Dark Horse reprints. I only hope that they were successful enough for Dark Horse to launch another round of imports, so that we can read more Bonellis. Perhaps the program could even be expanded—if for no other reason than to discover if all Italian comic characters have alliterative names.

Fans have long awaited Bryan Talbot's sequel to his intricate comics novel *The Adventures of Luther Arkwright*; in 1999 he finally presented them with *Heart of Empire: The Legacy of Luther Arkwright* (Dark Horse). An apocalyptic nightmare that ranged across all of time and space to draw in many of the characters from the original *Arkwright, Heart of Empire* was a rousing series worthy of a place next to its predecessor. One request: that the inevitable collection contain some of the wonderful faux Victorian ads created by Talbot for the non-story pages of the original issues.

Burroughs, Philip K. Dick, insanity, messiahs, sorcerers, aliens, and many, many things that are much stranger are all included in Grant Morrison's tale of surreal conspiracy *The Invisibles* (Vertigo/DC). Though the series is literally counting down to an end (the last volume of the series runs from number twelve down to number one), with one of the strangest cult followings of any comic being published, issues are sure to be dissected by fans for years to come.

In the "More Straightforward . . . Or Is It?" category is Warren Ellis and John Cassaday's *Planetary* (Wildstorm/DC), where a three-person team explores mysteries ranging from a cop's ghost still haunting the criminals of Hong Kong to the ruins of a Monster Island strewn with Godzilla and Ghidra-like corpses. A terrific series by one of today's top comics storytellers, of special note is that each issue casts itself in a different genre—from 1930's pulp adventure to Victorian adventure to war epic. Well done, and a great deal of fun, with intriguing underlying mysteries waiting to be revealed to persistent readers.

Superhero Comics

I have a real soft spot for traditional superhero comics. So I'm happy to say that there are some great comics with some amazing storytelling inside that genre.

After years of working on a wide variety of projects—including the spectacular Jack the Ripper tale *From Hell*—comics master Alan Moore warmed up on Image's *Supreme* and then exploded back onto the superhero comics scene with his very own America's Best Comics line of five spectacular titles, all written by Moore and illustrated by some of the best artists in the business: *Tom Strong* (art by Chris Sprouse), a pulp adventure in the four-color Doc Savage mold; *Top 10* (art by Gene Ha), set in a police precinct of a city where every citizen has superpowers; *Promethea* (illustrated by J. H. Williams), the tale of the titular mythic heroine and the young girl who becomes her latest avatar; *The League of Extraordinary Gentlemen* (art by Kevin O'Neill), story of a group of the greatest characters of Victorian literature—Captain Nemo, the Invisible Man, Mina Harker, Dr. Jekyll, and others—drawn together to battle the evil peril of Fu Manchu; and *Tomorrow Stories*, an anthology book of several characters (all written by Moore but illustrated by a variety of artists) and a stunning homage to comics storytellers of the past.

Warren Ellis was the writer for the last few marvelous arcs of Homage Comics' *Stormwatch*, and after a short respite he returned with several of the same characters and *Stormwatch* artists Bryan Hitch and Paul Neary in tow to create *The Authority*, a supergroup to end all supergroups, with high-powered heroes tossed against high-powered menaces, and fights that literally shake the world. Yet it's all done with a surprisingly deft touch, with superbly dramatic plotting and well-crafted characters. The trio held the title for twelve spectacular issues and are now passing it on to the equally talented team of Mark Millar and Frank Quitely, with a promise that the Authority will become just that—and take over the world.

While that story is certain to be well done, it has been done before—most notably in Mark Gruenwald's *Squadron Supreme* (Marvel Comics). A fan-favorite story, it was also a favorite of the author's as well; after his untimely death in 1996, Gruenwald's ashes were mixed into the ink for a new reprint collection of the twelve-issue series.

Another beloved comic reprinted in 1999 following the author's 1998 demise was Archie Goodwin's *Manhunter* (DC), an adventure story written in heavy collaboration with artist Walter Simonson and originally appearing in eight-page backup installments in 1970's *Detective Comics*. A world-spanning story of intrigue, deceit, and thrilling adventure, *Manhunter* is a textbook example of finely crafted storytelling at its best.

An exceptional storyteller made his way over from the realms of television in 1999: J. Michael Straczynski of *Babylon 5* launched his superhero saga *Rising Stars* (Top Cow/Image). Though its publication schedule has been unfortunately sporadic, it is quickly becoming a fan favorite, spinning an intricate story of a killer stalking people who gained superpowers after a meteor crashed in their hometown.

Running with the idea of crossover authors were the editors of DC Comics' Batman line, who destroyed the Dark Knight's hometown of Gotham City with an earthquake and then invited a field of new talent ranging from new comics scribe Devin Grayson and crime writer Greg Rucka to screenwriter Bob Gale in to play. Thus began the epic "No Man's Land" storyline, stretching through eight monthly titles for an entire year—and in the process telling some spectacular stories not just about superheroes, but also about regular people trapped in a terrible disaster. DC is now beginning to reprint the storyline in thick collections, and they would be a fine addition to anyone's comic shelf.

Also taking a look at Batman were writer Karl Kesel and Dave Taylor, who in *World's Finest* (DC Comics) took a close look at the friendship between the grim vigilante and his polar opposite—Superman. Showing the same night each year for the first decade of their relationship, Kesel and Taylor weaved the strings of comic book continuity together to show how the Dark Knight and the Man of Tomorrow could have possibly become first allies, and then friends.

In a similar vein was Mark Waid and Tom Peyer's *The Brave and the Bold* (DC), tracking the friendship of two other DC heroes—the Flash and Green Lantern. While at first glance this sort of retroactive storytelling may seem silly, to those who have come to know and love the characters over the years by following their adventures, these series—by creators who are fans themselves—are a great addition to the characters' mythos and help make them worthy of the fans' admiration.

The Future

I would be remiss if I didn't mention first *SPX99: The Small Press Expo Anthology*, an annual publication collecting together pieces by some of the best up-and-coming talent in the industry, and then the Comic Book Legal Defense Fund (www.cbldf.org), the organization working to make sure that the future remains wide open to any and all sorts of material. If comics fans do nothing each year other than pick up the SPX anthology and donate to the CBLDF, they would be doing a great service to ensure the future of the field.

Of course, if you're interested in picking up any of the titles mentioned in this essay, they should be available along with many others at your local comics store. If you don't frequent a shop, you can find one by calling the Comic Shop Locator Service at 1-888-COMIC-BOOK.

Thanks to FM International and the folks at the late, lamented Pic-a-Book in Madison, Wisconsin, for their help in research and collecting materials for this year's essay.

Obituaries: 1999

James Frenkel

Perhaps it's symptomatic of end-of-century blues, but more likely time, illness, ill fortune, or hard living just caught up with a great number of talented people who enriched our lives with their contributions to the fantastic arts this year. Christian beliefs, among other religious traditions, hold that when a person dies, some part leaves the body and goes . . . somewhere else. When creative people die, they leave a part of their lives with those who remain. In the fruits of their creativity lie the seeds that may bring forth new creative works in generations that follow. Our cultural traditions are built upon the works of genius of preceding generations. So here we list those talented people whose presence have left us, but whose works will stay with us to inspire the rest of us to aspire to reap the fruits of our own creativity.

Marion Zimmer Bradley, 69, was a major figure in fantasy and science fiction. Inarguably, her most major and enduring work was *The Mists of Avalon* (1983), an Arthurian fantasy told from Morgan le Fey's point of view. A major commercial and critical success, a bestseller both in the United States and abroad, it secured her place as a major figure in fantasy and spawned several sequels, *The Forest House* (1993), *Lady of Avalon* (1997), and the forthcoming *Princess of Avalon*. Her "Darkover" novels comprised the other major series she wrote. She was tremendously helpful to young writers, especially in her later years, encouraging them first by allowing them to write in her Darkover universe in collections, then in the magazine she founded in 1988 and edited, *Marion Zimmer Bradley's Fantasy Magazine*. In the years before her death, as she fell victim to a number of strokes, she had some novels edited or written by various writers from her outlines or notes. Her collaborators, who were not formally credited but who she readily acknowledged, included Diana Paxson, Mercedes Lackey, Adrienne Martine-Barnes, and Rosemary Edghill, among others. Marion Zimmer Bradley cast a very long shadow over fantasy, and her works continue to inspire others.

Shel Silverstein, 66, was a multitalented artist and writer. He is probably most famous for his books of children's fantasy and verse, including *Where the Sidewalk Ends* (1974) and *A Light in the Attic* (1981). He also wrote songs—including "A Boy Named Sue," which was a hit for Johnny Cash in 1969—and plays, as well as books of drawings. His work could be dark or whimsical, but never dull.

Stanley Kubrick, 70, was a brilliant and idiosyncratic filmmaker responsible for some of the most enduring film images of the second half of the twentieth century. His satire *Dr. Strangelove, or How I Learned to Stop Worrying and Love the Bomb* (1964) and his brilliantly dark and mercilessly yet clinically horrific drama *A Clockwork Orange* (1971) were both marked by a blurring of the edges of reality. His adaptation of Stephen King's *The Shining* (1980) was a dark, bizarre tale; no doubt his most famous work remains *2001: A Space Odyssey*. Kubrick was a perfectionist; he often co-wrote the screenplays, but will be best remembered as a producer and director.

Joseph Heller, 76, became famous for writing *Catch-22*, a savagely comic novel about World War II, the title of which became part of the English language; he wrote five other novels, including the fantasy *Picture This* (1989).

Clifton Fadiman, 95, was a writer, editor, and radio and television personality. He edited several seminal anthologies in the fifties and sixties, and was involved in books in a variety of ways for the whole of his long professional life. He was a book editor, wrote a book column for *The New Yorker*, and for many years was on the selection committee of the Book-of-the-Month Club. **George C. Scott**, 71, was a powerful, highly acclaimed actor who dominated every production in which he appeared, on stage, and in film and television. He played Sherlock Holmes, or someone who thought he was Holmes, in *They Might Be Giants*. **David Duncan**, 86, was a screenwriter who also wrote some science fiction and fantasy, notably *The Madrone Tree* (1949). Not to be confused with fantasy author Dave Duncan, David Duncan also wrote some scripts for television, including one for *The Outer Limits*. **Larry Sternig**, 90, was a pulp writer and then a literary agent who represented, among others, Andre Norton. **Leonard C. Lewin**, 82, was a writer, journalist, and satirist, who wrote one of the great hoaxes, "Report from

Iron Mountain," supposedly a top-secret government study on the dangers of peace.

John Broome, 85, was a longtime comics writer who penned such well-known comic books as *Green Lantern* and *The Flash*, among others, in a career that lasted over twenty-five years, until his retirement in 1970. He also wrote pulp fiction in the 1930s and 1940s. **Lee Falk**, 87, was the creator of the newspaper comic strips *Mandrake the Magician* and *The Phantom*. He created and started writing *Mandrake* when he was still in college. He created *The Phantom* in 1936; both strips, taken over by others, are still syndicated. After World War II he was also a playwright and theatrical producer. **Vince Sullivan**, 88, was the first comics editor for DC comics and had the perspicacity to buy "Superman" from Jerry Siegel and Joe Shuster and Batman from Bob Kane. **Paul S. Newman**, 75, was a comics writer who wrote for a number of series, some quite unexpected, including *The Twilight Zone*. **Edvin Biukovic**, 30, was a critically acclaimed Croatian artist who worked on various comics, including *Grendel Tales*.

Ray Russell, 74, was an editor, writer, and screenwriter who wrote a handful of dark fantasy novels, many short stories, and screenplays for a number of films. His novels included *The Case Against Satan* (1962) and *Incubus* (1976). He was a fiction editor for *Playboy* in the sixties and seventies, and helped establish that magazine as a major source of science fiction and fantasy, publishing the works of Stephen King, Ray Bradbury, and Arthur C. Clarke, among many others. He also edited, mostly without being credited, dozens of *Playboy* fiction anthologies. He received Lifetime Achievement awards from both the World Fantasy Convention and Horror Writers Association.

Michael McDowell, 49, was a writer of dark fantasy novels and scripts, and short fiction as well. His most commercially successful work was probably the film *Beetlejuice* (1988), which was Tim Burton's first big success. He also wrote the screenplays for Burton's *The Nightmare Before Christmas* (1993), and for *Thinner* (1996). His novels included the *Blackwater* sextet (1983) and a number of others.

Adolfo Bioy Casares, 84, was a major Argentinean author of fantasy and magic realism. Never as famous as Jorge Luis Borges or Julio Cortázar, Casares was one of the most influential and widely acclaimed writers of Latin American magic realism, both as author and editor, for many, many years. **José J. Viega**, 84, also a major magic realist author, was a prolific, award-winning Brazilian author, translator, and newspaper editor. **Dias Gomes**, 76, was a Brazilian playwright, television and screenwriter whose work included some magic realism. **Patrick O'Brian**, 85, was famous for his twenty Jack Aubrey/Stephen Maturin historical novels, novels that were at the same time exciting, historically accurate, and most important, written with great care, sensitivity, and primarily with characterizations that lifted the novels into the ranks of literature. Originally thought to be derivative of C. S. Forester's *Hornblower*, ultimately O'Brian was a spiritual descendant of Jane Austen. He was also something of a small hoax, having claimed for his whole life to be Irish, until in 1998 a biographer unearthed his true history. He was English, though the Irish were pleased to embrace his desire to be one of them. **Gonzolo Torrente Ballester**, 88, wrote twenty-two novels and six plays. This Spanish writer, whose works drew on myths and witchcraft of Galicia, was awarded Spain's Cervantes Prize for Literature in 1985. **Faith Sale**, 63, was an esteemed and successful book editor who worked with a number of fine writers and who edited many award-winning books. Her authors included Kurt Vonnegut, Donald Barthelme, and Amy Tan, among many other literate, literary writers of fiction.

Lord Lew Grade, 91, was a major player in British television. **Quentin Crisp**, 90, was *sui generis*—actor, writer, "performer." He was gay, and flamboyantly so, as chronicled in his 1968 autobiography *The Naked Civil Servant*. He wrote one fantasy novel, the dark *Chog* (1979). **Richard Kiley**, 76, was a versatile actor of stage, screen, and television. His most famous role was his Tony Award–winning creation of the eponymous *Man of La Mancha* (1965), based on Cervantes's seminal picaresque novel. **Sylvia Sidney**, 88, was a powerful, versatile actress who starred in many films for more than fifty years. Her credits included *Beetlejuice* and television's revival last year of *Fantasy Island*. Superb at playing intimidating women in film and on TV, when younger, she was quite a beauty. **Hoyt Axton**, 61, was a popular country singer and songwriter. He also acted, in live-action films and in a number of animated features, including *Charlotte's Web* and *The Jungle Book*, and in shorter animated vehicles. **Victor Mature**, 86, was a matinee idol in his time. He appeared in several fantasy films, including *Androcles and the Lion* (1952) and *Head* (1968). **Oliver Reed**, 61, was a well-known British actor who starred or appeared in several dozen films, including Hammer films such as *Curse of the Werewolf* (1961) and many other films of imagination. He played Athos in Richard Lester's *The Three Musketeers* (1974) and starred in films by David Cronenberg and Ken Russell. **Buck Houghton**, 84, worked in television for decades, most notably as producer of *The Twilight Zone* for more than three years. **Hilary Brooke**, 84, was featured in many films of the 1940s and 1950s, and on television as well. Among her credits were several Sherlock Holmes films and *The Lost Continent*.

Rory Calhoun, 76, was a veteran actor of films and television, among whose credits were such films as *Hell Comes to Frogtown* and various horror films. **Henry Jones**, 86, was a character actor on Broadway, in film, and on television for many years. He played a great variety of roles, including Leroy, the suspicious handyman murdered by the psychotic child in the Broadway production of *The Bad Seed*. **Desmond Llewelyn**, 85, was a British character actor best known as Q, the master of gadgetry for James Bond in many films.

James Turner, 54, was the editor of Arkham House Publishers for many years, and in 1996, when the heirs of founder August Derleth fired him because of disagreement over the direction of the imprint, he founded his own company, Golden Gryphon Press. At both publishers Turner filled a key niche by publishing short story collections by major and up-and-coming fantasy and science fiction writers. This was a change in direction from Arkham's Lovecraft circle origins, but faithful to the imprint's tradition of quality small-press hardcover books.

Howard Browne, 91, was the editor of *Amazing* and *Fantastic* in the 1940s and 1950s, a well-known mystery and scriptwriter, and also wrote some fantasy of his own. He brought *Amazing* back to respectability with a solid and sometimes quite literary roster of writers, after a long series of pseudo-scientific Richard Shaver articles (fostered by his predecessor Raymond A. Palmer) had brought *Amazing* ridicule and to the brink of ruin. His Paul Pine detective series, written mostly in the late 1940s and resumed in the 1980s, is quite highly regarded. He wrote many scripts for TV in the 1950s and 1960s, for such mystery and western shows as *Maverick, Columbo,* and *77 Sunset Strip*, as well as film screenplays. He was awarded a Life Achievement (Shamus) Award by the Private Eye Writers of America.

Arthur Saha, 76, was an editor of science fiction and fantasy, including *The Year's Best Fantasy Stories* for DAW Books after Lin Carter died, until 1988, when the series ended. He was active in fandom for many years in the New York area.

Del Close, 64, was an actor, director, writer, filmmaker, and one of the founders of Chicago's Second City comedy troupe. He produced a few films in the 1970s and 1980s, was an award-winning stage actor, and coauthor, with John Ostrander, of the *Wasteland* comic series (DC). He was a tremendous influence on a generation of comic actors and comedians, and instrumental in the creation of both *Saturday Night Live* and *SCTV*.

Terry Hodel, 61, was producer of the long-running science fiction radio show *Hour 25*, which aired on the Los Angeles Pacifica station, KPFK for some twenty-eight years. *Hour 25* is widely considered the best show focusing on science fiction to have aired over any sustained period of time. Originally working with her husband, the late Mike Hodel, Terry was there for the entire run until her death in March.

Mario Puzo, 78, will be best remembered for his novels about the culture of Italian crime families which began with *The Godfather*, and became a hugely successful series of novels and films. He also wrote other novels, and the screenplay for *Superman, the Movie*. **Paul Bowles**, 88, was a multitalented man. He wrote the existential novel filmed by Bernardo Bertolucci, *The Sheltering Sky*, and also horror fiction; he also wrote music for theatrical productions of Orson Welles and Tennessee Williams; and he was a translator of Moroccan authors, and a photographer. **Robert W. "Buck" Coulson**, 70, was a book reviewer of science fiction and fantasy. Married to writer Juanita Coulson, Buck also wrote a little science fiction himself. He was best known and loved, though, as a fan, both for his zine, *Yandro*, and his generosity and great-heartedness to all. **Gary Jennings**, 70, was best known for his novel *Aztec* (1980), among a number of fine historical novels. He wrote some fantasy stories as well, many of which were published in *The Magazine of Fantasy & Science Fiction*. **Frank MacShane**, 72, was a literary biographer, writer, and translator. His translation work included some fantasy. His best known work was the biography, *The Life of Raymond Chandler* (1976). **David Karp**, 77, was a novelist and film and television writer. He won an Edgar Award and an Emmy during his varied career. Among his novels was *The Day of the Monkey* (1955), considered borderline fantasy. **William Targ**, 92, was a noted editor, publisher, and bookseller. In his long and successful career he published *Best Supernatural Stories of H. P. Lovecraft* (1945), among other strong single-author collections. Possibly his most famous published book was *The Godfather* by Mario Puzo, which he bought for G. P. Putnam.

Evelyn Shrifte, 98, was the longtime president of Vanguard Press, where she published the first books of such talented authors as Joyce Carol Oates, Dr. Seuss, and Saul Bellow, among others, until the company was sold to Random House in 1988. **Michael Avallone**, 74, was a prolific writer of pulp fiction; some of his more than 250 books fell into the category of fantasy or horror. Avallone once boasted that he was the "fastest typewriter in the business," a dubious distinction. His "Ed Noon" detective series was some of his best work. **Charles D. Hornig**, 83, was an editor of several science fiction pulps in the 1930s, and also wrote some fiction himself. **John [Charles Heywood] Hadfield**, 92, was a British author, publisher, and editor. He edited many anthologies, including *A Chamber of Horrors* (1965). **Marie Landis**, 78, was the co-author with Brian Herbert, her cousin, of two science fiction/horror novels, *Merrymakers* (1991) and *Blood on the Sun* (1996). **John L. Goldwater**, 83, was the publisher of Archie Comics, which he started in 1941 with two partners to form MLJ Publications. He helped form the Comics Code Authority, the repressive organization that restricted what comics could show; he was its president for twenty-five years. He was instrumental also in Archie Comics starting a book publishing company, Belmont Books, which published science fiction, fantasy, and horror paperbacks, including works by such talented writers as Frank Belknap Long, Philip K. Dick, and others. **Beverly Lewis**, 51, was a book editor for more than twenty years, editing many fine authors, including Dean Koontz. **Darlene Geis**, 81, was an author and editor whose edited works included *The Fantasia Book* and *Treasury of Stories from Silly Symphonies*, both for Harry N. Abrams. **Tad Dembinski**, 27, was for several years an editorial assistant and then assistant editor for Tor Books, where he worked with a number of fantasy authors. **Gary Louie**, 41, was a bookseller, and a fan who did a lot of behind-the-scenes work on many World science fiction Conventions. **Carl Johan Holzhausen**, 99, was an author, translator, journalist, essayist, and lecturer. Mainly a newspaperman, he also loved fantastic fiction, and he wrote a number of stories and novels, including the children's fantasy, *Drömhunden* (*The Dream Dog*) (1973) and sequels. **Dr. Frederick Albert Thorpe, OBE**, 85, invented and promoted the large print book. **Jack Schiff**, 89, was a managing editor at DC Comics who worked on Superman and Batman. **Charles "Chuch" Harris**, 72, was a very prominent Irish science fiction and fantasy fan who had some short fiction published professionally in addition to his many fannish publications. **Mike Ockrent**, 53, was a British theatrical director whose credits included the musical "Big" and "A Christmas Carol" among a great variety of projects. **Peggy Cass**, 74, was a theatrical and film actress best remembered for her portrayal of Agnes Gooch, the shy, pregnant, unwed secretary in Broadway and film versions of "Auntie Mame."

Anthony Newley, 67, was a very well-known British actor and singer in the 1960s. He also wrote music, in collaboration with several composers, especially Leslie Bricusse, most notably the score for *Willy Wonka & the Chocolate Factory* (1971) and the theme song for *Goldfinger* (1964) (with third collaborator John Barry). He also co-starred in the film *Doctor Doolittle* (1967). **Fredric Morrow**, 59, composed music for theatrical films and television productions, including the horror series *Phantasm*. **Max Hunter**, 78, was a folklorist who collected and recorded thousands of folk songs, jokes, proverbs, and pithy sayings in the Ozarks, saving a part of America's rural cultural tradition from oblivion. **Ranjabati Sircar**, 36, was an Indian dancer and choreographer who fused India's classical and folk dance traditions with experimental Western forms, following in the footsteps of her mother, a famous Indian dancer. **Viola Sheely**, 41, was an actress, singer, and dancer of visionary power, portraying intense, immediate, and primal characters on stage. She was a founding member of the Urban Bush Women dance company. **Muriel Bentley**, 82, was a bright, sprightly ballet dancer who had a long, successful career, dancing prominent roles in many of Jerome Robbins's ballets, including "Fall River Legend," about Lizzie Borden. **Charles Pierce**, 72, was a female impersonator who performed witty, satirical sendups of stage and screen icons, and acted on stage, screen, and television. He never stopped inventing himself as others, and was employed almost constantly for four decades. **David Brooks**, 83, was an actor, director, and producer whose classical opera training helped him win a lead in the Broadway musical fantasy "Brigadoon." **Gene Siskel**, 53, was a film critic for many years, and became known to millions on the film review TV show he shared with Roger Ebert. **Thomas Banyacya**, 89, was a Hopi Indian appointed by his tribe after the explosion of the atomic bomb to tell the rest of the world of Hopi prophecy which warned of grave danger unless we didn't live in harmony with nature; for more than fifty years he performed this difficult task. **Frank DeVol**, 88, was a composer, conductor, and musician who wrote music for numberless television shows and series and acted the part of a bandleader in the TV series *Mary Hartman, Mary Hartman*'s *Fernwood 2Night*.

Kirk Alyn, 88, started in vaudeville, but is best remembered for playing Superman in film serials. He starred in other serials as well, and played Lois Lane's father in the 1978 *Superman* film. **Faith Domergue**, 74, was an actress in a number of science fiction, fantasy, and horror films from the 1950s through the 1970s. **DeForest Kelley**, 79, was a character actor who appeared in more than one-hundred-fifty films and television shows, but is most famous for his role as "Bones" McCoy, the doctor on the original *Star Trek* television series and its sequel films. **Helen Aberson Mayer**, 91, was the author of *Dumbo, The Flying Elephant*, with artist Harold Pearl. Disney made it into an animated film. **Vanessa Brown**, 71, was an actress in films and television who appeared in films such as *The Ghost and Mrs. Muir* and TV series such as *One Step Beyond* and *The Twilight Zone*. **Jean Vander Pyl**, 79, was a radio actor who won anonymous fame as the voice of the animated Wilma on *The Flintstones*. She also voiced seven different characters on *The Jetsons*. **John Bloom**, 54, was 7'4", and starred in various horror and fantasy films, including *Dracula vs. Frankenstein* (1971), and *Harry and the Hendersons* (1987). **Aubrey Schenck**, 90, was a producer of a number of films, high-budget and low, including horror films such as *Shock* with Vincent Price. **Betty E. Box**, 78, was a British film producer whose films included the mermaid fantasy *Miranda* (1948) and others. **Nicholas J. Corea**, 56, was a TV producer and director who produced the fantasy series *The Incredible Hulk*, among a number of action series; he also produced the TV film *Archer: Fugitive from the Empire*. **John Stears**, 64, was a special effects designer whose work garnered him an Oscar. He created some memorable effects for early James Bond films, among many film, theatrical, and television productions. **Joe D'Amato**, 62, was an Italian director of horror films that tended to be quite gory, including the memorable *The Devil's Wedding Night*. **Buzz Kulik**, 76, was a director of television films and series, including episodes of *The Twilight Zone* and the TV film remake of *Around the World in 80 Days* (1989). **Harvey Miller**, 63, was a screenwriter whose credits included *Jeckyll and Hyde . . . Together Again*. **Howard R. Cohen**, 57, was a screenwriter and director who made a number of low-budget films starting in the 1970s, some serious, others satiric. **Edmund Gilbert**, 67, was a veteran voice actor who created many characters for cartoon series including *The Jetsons, Spider-Man, The Tick*, and *Superman*. He also did voices in live-action films, including *The Pagemaster*. **Horst Frank**, 69, was a German character actor whose films included a number of European horror films. **William Sheldon**, 92, was a film director who worked on many productions beginning in the 1920s. He worked on *Freaks* by Tod Browning, and other fantasy productions for at least four decades. **Vittorio Cottavavi**, 84, was an Italian film director whose films included such fantasies as *Hercules Conquers Atlantis* (1961) and a number of others. **Herbert Klynn**, 81, was a pioneer in film and television animation, creating many shorts, including *Mr. Magoo* and *Gerald McBoing-Boing*. **Ross Elliott**, 82, was a veteran actor of films and television, including numerous appearances on such TV series as *Boris Karloff's Thriller, The Twilight Zone*, and *The Wild, Wild West*. **David Allen**, 54, was a stop-motion animator who worked on many fantasy, horror, and science fiction films for more than thirty years. **Sandra Gould**, 73, was a comic actress best known as the nosy neighbor Gladys Kravitz in the TV series *Bewitched*. **Ronny Graham**, 79, an actor, comedian, and writer, co-wrote *Spaceballs* (1987) with Mel Brooks. **Brion James**, 54, appeared as a menacing presence in many fantastic films and television productions, including *Steven Spielberg's Amazing Stories*. **Siegfried Lowitz**, 84, was a German character actor who was featured in *The Invisible Dr. Mabuse*, among many films. **Charles Macauley**, 72, was a screen and TV actor whose roles included Count Dracula in *Blacula* (1972), and *Splash* (1984). **Donal McCann**,

56, was an Irish actor whose credits included *Clive Barker's Rawhide Rex* (1986) and *High Spirits* (1988). **Bobs Watson**, 68, was a child actor who was featured in the 1939 film fantasy *On Borrowed Time* and other films. **Jack Watson**, 84, was a British character actor who acted in many films, including fantasy and horror, and also television. **Jim Weisiger**, 50, was a cinematographer who counted among his credits work on *The X-Files: Fight the Future* (1998). **Sir John Woolf**, 86, was a British film producer who produced television series, including *Roald Dahl's Tales of the Unexpected*. **Douglas Seale**, 85, was a British character actor who appeared in many feature films including *Ghostbusters II* and *Mr. Destiny*, among others. **Rudi Fehr**, 87, was a film editor who had a long career, including fantasy films such as *House of Wax*. **Mary Bergman**, 38, was a versatile, talented voice actress who performed in a number of animated films over the past two decades, including *Beauty and the Beast* and *South Park*, the series and film, for both of which she did a number of different voices. **Mabel King**, 66, was an actress and singer best remembered for her portrayal of Evilene, the Wicked Witch of the West, in the Broadway and film productions of *The Wiz*. She also acted in a number of television shows.

URSULA K. LE GUIN

Darkrose and Diamond

*Ursula K. Le Guin is without doubt one of the greatest living writers
of magical fiction.* Her fantasy works include the acclaimed Earthsea
sequence, Malafrena, *and* Orsinian Tales, *and she has also published
distinguished works of science fiction, contemporary fiction, children's
fiction, poetry, and nonfiction. She has won the American Book Award,
the World Fantasy Award, and the Harold D. Vursell Memorial Award
from the American Academy and Institute of Arts and Letters. She lives
in Portland, Oregon, and describes herself as "a feminist, a
conservationist, and a western American, passionately involved with
West Coast literature, landscape, and life."*

At the end of the first three Earthsea books (A Wizard of Earthsea,
The Tombs of Atuan, *and* The Farthest Shore), *Le Guin considered the
tale completed until she revisited the world of Earthsea with* Tehanu
*(1990), taking up the story of her hero and heroine in their middle age.
Since then, she has published new Earthsea stories in the anthology*
Legends *and in* The Magazine of Fantasy & Science Fiction *(including
the following tale). Let's hope that Le Guin will continue to be drawn
back to Earthsea's wizardly Archipelago for many years to come.*

—T. W.

A Boat-Song from West Havnor

Where my love is going
There will I go.
Where his boat is rowing
I will row.

We will laugh together,
Together we will cry.
If he lives I will live,
If he dies I die.

Where my love is going
There will I go.
Where his boat is rowing
I will row.

In the west of Havnor, among hills forested with oak and chestnut, is the town of Glade. A while ago, the rich man of that town was a merchant called Golden. Golden owned the mill that cut the oak boards for the ships they built in Havnor South Port and Havnor Great Port; he owned the biggest chestnut groves; he owned the carts and hired the carters that carried the timber and the chestnuts over the hills to be sold. He did very well from trees, and when his son was born, the mother said, "We could call him Chestnut, or Oak, maybe?" But the father said, "Diamond," diamond being in his estimation the one thing more precious than gold.

So little Diamond grew up in the finest house in Glade, a fat, bright-eyed baby, a ruddy, cheerful boy. He had a sweet singing voice, a true ear, and a love of music, so that his mother, Tuly, called him Song-sparrow and Skylark, among other loving names, for she never really did like "Diamond." He trilled and carolled about the house; he knew any tune as soon as he heard it, and invented tunes when he heard none. His mother had the wisewoman Tangle teach him *The Creation of Éa* and *The Deed of the Young King*, and at Sunreturn when he was eleven years old he sang the Winter Carol for the Lord of the Western Land, who was visiting his domain in the hills above Glade. The Lord and his Lady praised the boy's singing and gave him a tiny gold box with a diamond set in the lid, which seemed a kind and pretty gift to Diamond and his mother. But Golden was a bit impatient with the singing and the trinkets. "There are more important things for you to do, son," he said. "And greater prizes to be earned."

Diamond thought his father meant the business—the loggers, the sawyers, the sawmill, the chestnut groves, the pickers, the carters, the carts—all that work and talk and planning, complicated, adult matters. He never felt that it had much to do with him, so how was he to have as much to do with it as his father expected? Maybe he'd find out when he grew up.

But in fact Golden wasn't thinking only about the business. He had observed something about his son that had made him not exactly set his eyes higher than the business, but glance above it from time to time, and then shut his eyes.

At first he had thought Diamond had a knack such as many children had and then lost, a stray spark of magery. When he was a little boy, Golden himself had been able to make his own shadow shine and sparkle. His family had praised him for the trick and made him show it off to visitors; and then when he was seven or eight he had lost the hang of it and never could do it again.

When he saw Diamond come down the stairs without touching the stairs, he thought his eyes had deceived him; but a few days later, he saw the child float up the stairs, just a finger gliding along the oaken banister rail. "Can you do that coming down?" Golden asked, and Diamond said, "Oh, yes, like this," and sailed back down smooth as a cloud on the south wind.

"How did you learn to do that?"

"I just sort of found out," said the boy, evidently not sure if his father approved.

Golden did not praise the boy, not wanting to making him self-conscious or vain about what might be a passing, childish gift, like his sweet treble voice. There was too much fuss already made over that.

But a year or so later he saw Diamond out in the back garden with his playmate Rose. The children were squatting on their haunches, heads close together, laughing. Something intense or uncanny about them made him pause at the window on the stairs landing and watch them. A thing between them was leaping up and down, a frog? a toad? a big cricket? He went out into the garden and came up near them, moving so quietly, though he was a big man, that they in their absorption did not hear him. The thing that was hopping up and down on the grass between their bare toes was a rock. When Diamond raised his hand the rock jumped up in the air, and when he shook his hand a little the rock hovered in the air, and when he flipped his fingers downward it fell to earth.

"Now you," Diamond said to Rose, and she started to do what he had done, but the rock only twitched a little. "Oh," she whispered, "there's your dad."

"That's very clever," Golden said.

"Di thought it up," Rose said.

Golden did not like the child. She was both outspoken and defensive, both rash and timid. She was a girl, and a year younger than Diamond, and a witch's daughter. He wished his son would play with boys his own age, his own sort, from the respectable families of Glade.

Tuly insisted on calling the witch "the wisewoman," but a witch was a witch and her daughter was no fit companion for Diamond. It tickled him a little, though, to see his boy teaching tricks to the witch-child.

"What else can you do, Diamond?" he asked.

"Play the flute," Diamond said promptly, and took out of his pocket the little fife his mother had given him for his twelfth birthday. He put it to his lips, his fingers danced, and he played a sweet, familiar tune from the western coast, "Where My Love Is Going."

"Very nice," said the father. "But anybody can play the fife, you know."

Diamond glanced at Rose. The girl turned her head away, looking down.

"I learned it really quickly," Diamond said.

Golden grunted, unimpressed.

"It can do it by itself," Diamond said, and held out the fife away from his lips. His fingers danced on the stops, and the fife played a short jig. It hit several false notes and squealed on the last high note. "I haven't got it right yet," Diamond said, vexed and embarrassed.

"Pretty good, pretty good," his father said. "Keep practicing." And he went on. He was not sure what he ought to have said. He did not want to encourage the boy to spend any more time on music, or with this girl; he spent too much already, and neither of them would help him get anywhere in life. But this gift, this undeniable gift—the rock hovering, the unblown fife—Well, it would be wrong to make too much of it, but probably it should not be discouraged.

In Golden's understanding, money was power, but not the only power. There were two others, one equal, one greater. There was birth. When the Lord of the Western Land came to his domain near Glade, Golden was glad to show him fealty. The Lord was born to govern and to keep the peace, as Golden was born to deal with commerce and wealth, each in his place, and each, noble or common, if he served well and honestly, deserved honor and respect. But there were also lesser lords whom Golden could buy and sell, lend to or let beg, men born noble who deserved neither fealty nor honor. Power of birth and power of money were contingent, and must be earned lest they be lost.

But beyond the rich and the lordly were those called the Men of Power: the wizards. Their power, though little exercised, was absolute. In their hands lay the fate of the long-kingless kingdom of the Archipelago.

If Diamond had been born to that kind of power, if that was his gift, then all Golden's dreams and plans of training him in the business, and having him help in expanding the carting route to a regular trade with South Port, and buying up the chestnut forests above Reche—all such plans dwindled into trifles. Might Diamond go (as his mother's uncle had gone) to the School of Wizards on Roke Island? Might he (as that uncle had done) gain glory for his family and dominion over lord and commoner, becoming a Mage in the Court of the Lords Regent in the Great Port of Havnor? Golden all but floated up the stairs himself, borne on such visions.

But he said nothing to the boy and nothing to the boy's mother. He was a consciously close-mouthed man, distrustful of visions until they could be made acts; and she, though a dutiful, loving wife and mother and housekeeper, already made too much of Diamond's talents and accomplishments. Also, like all women, she was inclined to babble and gossip, and indiscriminate in her friendships. The girl Rose hung about with Diamond because Tuly encouraged Rose's mother the witch to visit, consulting her every time Diamond had a hangnail, and telling her more than she or anyone ought to know about Golden's household. His business was none of the witch's business. On the other hand, Tangle might be able to tell him if his son in fact showed promise, had a talent for magery . . . but he flinched away from the thought of asking her, asking a witch's opinion on anything, least of all a judgment on his son.

He resolved to wait and watch. Being a patient man with a strong will, he did so for four years, till Diamond was sixteen. A big, well-grown youth, good at games and lessons, he was still ruddy-faced and bright-eyed and cheerful. He had taken it hard when his voice changed, the sweet treble going all untuned and hoarse. Golden had hoped that that was the end of his singing, but the boy went on wandering about with itinerant musicians, ballad singers and such, learning all their trash. That was no life for a merchant's son who was to inherit and manage his father's properties and mills and business, and Golden told him so. "Singingtime is over, son," he said. "You must think about being a man."

Diamond had been given his truename at the springs of the Amia in the hills above Glade. The wizard Hemlock, who had known his great-uncle the Mage, came up from South Port to name him. And Hemlock was invited to his nameday party the year after, a big party, beer and food for all, and new clothes, a shirt or skirt for every child, which was an old custom in the West of Havnor, and dancing on the village green in the warm autumn evening. Diamond had many friends, all the boys his age in town and all the girls too. The young people danced, and some of them had a bit too much beer, but nobody misbehaved very badly, and it was a merry and memorable night. The next morning Golden told his son again that he must think about being a man.

"I have thought some about it," said the boy, in his husky voice.

"And?"

"Well, I," said Diamond, and stuck.

"I'd always counted on your going into the family business," Golden said. His tone was neutral, and Diamond said nothing. "Have you had any ideas of what you want to do?"

"Sometimes."

"Did you talk at all to Master Hemlock?"

Diamond hesitated and said, "No." He looked a question at his father.

"I talked to him last night," Golden said. "He said to me that there are certain natural gifts which it's not only difficult but actually wrong, harmful, to suppress."

The light had come back into Diamond's dark eyes.

"The Master said that such gifts or capacities, untrained, are not only wasted, but may be dangerous. The art must be learned, and practiced, he said."

Diamond's face shone.

"But, he said, it must be learned and practiced for its own sake."

Diamond nodded eagerly.

"If it's a real gift, an unusual capacity, that's even more true. A witch with her love potions can't do much harm, but even a village sorcerer, he said, must take care, for if the art is used for base ends, it becomes weak and noxious. . . . Of course, even a sorcerer gets paid. And wizards, as you know, live with lords, and have what they wish."

Diamond was listening intently, frowning a little.

"So, to be blunt about it, if you have this gift, Diamond, it's of no use, directly, to our business. It has to be cultivated on its own terms, and kept under control—learned and mastered. Only then, he said, can your teachers begin to tell you what to do with it, what good it will do you. Or others," he added conscientiously.

There was a long pause.

"I told him," Golden said, "that I had seen you, with a turn of your hand and a single word, change a wooden carving of a bird into a bird that flew up and sang. I've seen you make a light glow in thin air. You didn't know I was watching. I've watched and said nothing for a long time. I didn't want to make too much of mere childish play. But I believe you have a gift, perhaps a great gift. When I told Master Hemlock what I'd seen you do, he agreed with me. He said that you may go study with him in South Port for a year, or perhaps longer."

"Study with Master Hemlock?" said Diamond, his voice up half an octave.

"If you wish."

"I, I, I never thought about it. Can I think about it? For a while—a day?"

"Of course," Golden said, pleased with his son's caution. He had thought Diamond might leap at the offer, which would have been natural, perhaps, but painful to the father, the owl who had—perhaps—hatched out an eagle.

For Golden looked on the Art Magic with genuine humility as something quite beyond him—not a mere toy, such as music or tale-telling, but a practical business, which his business could never quite equal. And he was, though he wouldn't have put it that way, afraid of wizards. A bit contemptuous of sorcerers, with their sleights and illusions and gibble-gabble, but afraid of wizards.

"Does Mother know?" Diamond asked.

"She will when the time comes. But she has no part to play in your decision, Diamond. Women know nothing of these matters and have nothing to do with them. You must make your choice alone, as a man. Do you understand that?" Golden was earnest, seeing his chance to begin to wean the lad from his mother. She as a woman would cling, but he as a man must learn to let go. And Diamond nodded sturdily enough to satisfy his father, though he had a thoughtful look.

"Master Hemlock said I, said he thought I had, I might have a, a gift, a talent for—?"

Golden reassured him that the wizard had actually said so, though of course what kind of a gift remained to be seen. The boy's modesty was a great relief to him. He had half-consciously dreaded that Diamond would triumph over him, asserting his power right away—that mysterious, dangerous, incalculable power against which Golden's wealth and mastery and dignity shrank to impotence.

"Thank you, Father," the boy said. Golden embraced him and left, well pleased with him.

Their meeting place was in the sallows, the willow thickets down by the Amia as it ran below the smithy. As soon as Rose got there, Diamond said, "He wants me to go study with Master Hemlock! What am I going to do?"

"Study with the wizard?"

"He thinks I have this huge great talent. For magic."

"Who does?"

"Father does. He saw some of the stuff we were practicing. But he says Hemlock says I should come study with him because it might be dangerous not to. Oh," and Diamond beat his head with his hands.

"But you do have a talent."

He groaned and scoured his scalp with his knuckles. He was sitting on the dirt in their old play-place, a kind of bower deep in the willows, where they could hear the stream running over the stones nearby and the clang-clang of the smithy further off. The girl sat down facing him.

"Look at all the stuff you can do," she said. "You couldn't do any of it if you didn't have a gift."

"A little gift," Diamond said indistinctly. "Enough for tricks."

"How do you know that?"

Rose was very dark-skinned, with a cloud of crinkled hair, a thin mouth, an intent, serious face. Her feet and legs and hands were bare and dirty, her skirt and jacket disreputable. Her dirty toes and fingers were delicate and elegant, and a necklace of amethysts gleamed under the torn, buttonless jacket. Her mother, Tangle, made a good living by curing and healing, bone-knitting and birth-easing, and selling spells of finding, love potions, and sleeping drafts. She could afford to dress herself and her daughter in new clothes, buy shoes, and keep clean, but it didn't occur to her to do so. Nor was housekeeping one of her interests. She and Rose lived mostly on boiled chicken and fried eggs, as she was often paid in poultry. The yard of their two-room house was a wilderness of cats and hens. She liked cats, toads, and jewels. The amethyst necklace had been payment for the safe delivery of a son to Golden's head forester. Tangle herself wore armfuls of bracelets and bangles that flashed and crashed when she flicked out an impatient spell. At times she wore a kitten on her shoulder. She was not an attentive mother. Rose had demanded, at seven years old, "Why did you have me if you didn't want me?"

"How can you deliver babies properly if you haven't had one?" said her mother.

"So I was practice," Rose snarled.

"Everything is practice," Tangle said. She was never ill-natured. She seldom thought to do anything much for her daughter, but never hurt her, never scolded her, and gave her whatever she asked for, dinner, a toad of her own, the amethyst necklace, lessons in witchcraft. She would have provided new clothes if Rose had asked for them, but she never did. Rose had looked after herself from an early age; and this was one of the reasons Diamond loved her. With her, he knew what freedom was. Without her, he could attain it only when he was hearing and singing and playing music.

"I do have a gift," he said now, rubbing his temples and pulling his hair.

"Stop destroying your head," Rose told him.

"I know Tarry thinks I do."

"Of course you do! What does it matter what Tarry thinks? You already play the harp about nine times better than he ever did."

This was another of the reasons Diamond loved her.

"Are there any wizard musicians?" he asked, looking up.

She pondered. "I don't know."

"I don't either. Morred and Elfarran sang to each other, and he was a Mage. I think there's a Master Chanter on Roke, that teaches the lays and the histories. But I never heard of a wizard being a musician."

"I don't see why one couldn't be." She never saw why something could not be. Another reason he loved her.

"It always seemed to me they're sort of alike," he said, "magic and music. Spells and tunes. For one thing, you have to get them just exactly right."

"Practice," Rose said, rather sourly. "I know." She flicked a pebble at Diamond. It turned into a butterfly in midair. He flicked a butterfly back at her, and the two flitted and flickered a moment before they fell back to earth as pebbles. Diamond and Rose had worked out several such variations on the old stone-hopping trick.

"You ought to go, Di," she said. "Just to find out."

"I know."

"What if you got to be a wizard! Oh! Think of the stuff you could teach me! Shapechanging—We could be anything. Horses! Bears!"

"Moles," Diamond said. "Honestly, I feel like hiding underground. I always thought Father was going to make me learn all his kind of stuff, after I got my name. But all this year he's kept sort of holding off. I guess he had this in mind all along. But what if I go down there and I'm not any better at being a wizard than I am at bookkeeping? Why can't I do what I know I *can* do?"

"Well, why can't you do it all? The magic and the music, anyhow? You can always hire a bookkeeper."

When she laughed, her thin face got bright, her thin mouth got wide, and her eyes disappeared.

"Oh, Darkrose," Diamond said, "I love you."

"Of course you do. You'd better. I'll witch you if you don't."

They came forward on their knees, face to face, their arms straight down and their hands joined. They kissed each other all over their faces.

To Rose's lips Diamond's face was smooth and full as a plum, with just a hint of prickliness above the lip and jawline, where he had taken to shaving recently. To Diamond's lips Rose's face was soft as silk, with just a hint of grittiness on one cheek, which she had rubbed with a dirty hand. They moved a little closer so that their breasts and bellies touched, though their hands stayed down by their sides. They went on kissing.

"Darkrose," he breathed in her ear, his secret name for her.

She said nothing, but breathed very warm in his ear, and he moaned. His hands clenched hers. He drew back a little. She drew back.

They sat back on their ankles.

"Oh Di," she said, "it will be awful when you go."

"I won't go," he said. "Anywhere. Ever."

But of course he went down to Havnor South Port, in one of his father's carts driven by one of his father's carters, along with Master Hemlock. As a rule, people do what wizards advise them to do. And it is no small honor to be invited by a wizard to be his student or apprentice. Hemlock, who had won his staff on Roke, was used to having boys come to him begging to be tested and, if they had the gift for it, taught. He was a little curious about this boy whose cheerful good manners hid some reluctance or self-doubt. It was the father's idea, not the boy's, that he was gifted. That was unusual, though perhaps not so unusual among the wealthy as among common folk. At any rate he came with a very good prenticing fee paid beforehand in gold and ivory. If he had the makings of a wizard Hemlock would train him, and if he had, as Hemlock suspected, a mere childish flair, then he'd be sent home with what remained of his fee. Hemlock was an honest, upright, humorless, scholarly wizard with little interest in feelings or ideas. His gift was for names. "The art begins and ends in naming," he said, which indeed is true, although there may be a good deal between the beginning and the end.

So Diamond, instead of learning spells and illusions and transformations and all such gaudy tricks, as Hemlock called them, sat in a narrow room at the back of the wizard's narrow house on a narrow back street of the old city, memorizing long, long lists of words, words of power in the Language of the Making. Plants and parts of plants and animals and parts of animals and islands and parts of islands, parts of ships, parts of the human body. The words never made sense, never made sentences, only lists. Long, long lists.

His mind wandered. "Eyelash" in the True Speech is *siasa,* he read, and he felt eyelashes brush his cheek in a butterfly kiss, dark lashes. He looked up startled and did not know what had touched him. Later when he tried to repeat the word, he stood dumb.

"Memory, memory," Hemlock said. "Talent's no good without memory!" He was not harsh, but he was unyielding. Diamond had no idea what opinion Hemlock had of him, and guessed it to be pretty low. The wizard sometimes had him come with him to his work, mostly laying spells of safety on ships and houses, purifying wells, and sitting on the councils of the city, seldom speaking but always listening. Another wizard, not Roke-trained but with the healer's gift, looked after the sick and dying of South Port. Hemlock was glad to let him do so. His own pleasure was in studying and, as far as Diamond could see, doing no magic at all. "Keep the Equilibrium, it's all in that," Hemlock said, and, "Knowledge, order, and control." Those words he said so often that they made a tune in Diamond's head and sang themselves over and over: knowledge, or-der and contro————l . . .

When Diamond put the lists of names to tunes he made up, he learned them much faster; but then the tune would come as part of the name, and he would sing out so clearly—for his voice had re-established itself as a strong, dark tenor—that Hemlock winced. Hemlock's was a very silent house.

Mostly the pupil was supposed to be with the Master, or studying the lists of names in the room where the lorebooks and wordbooks were, or asleep. Hemlock was a stickler for early abed and early afoot. But now and then Diamond had an hour or two free. He always went down to the docks and sat on a pierside or a waterstair and thought about Darkrose. As soon as he was out of the house and away from Master Hemlock, he began to think about Darkrose, and went on thinking about her and very little else. It surprised him a little. He thought he ought to be homesick, to think about his mother. He did think about his mother quite often, and often was homesick, lying on his cot in his bare and narrow little room after a scanty supper of cold pea-porridge—for this wizard, at least, did not live in such luxury as Golden had imagined. Diamond never thought about Darkrose, nights. He thought of his mother, or of sunny rooms and hot food, or a tune would come into his head and he would practice it mentally on the harp in his mind, and so drift off to sleep. Darkrose would come to his mind only when he was down at the docks, staring out at the water of the harbor, the piers, the fishing boats, only when he was outdoors and away from Hemlock and his house.

So he cherished his free hours as if they were actual meetings with her. He had always loved her, but had not understood that he loved her beyond anyone and anything. When he was with her, even when he was down on the docks thinking of her, he was alive. He never felt entirely alive in Master Hemlock's house and presence. He felt a little dead. Not dead, but a little dead.

A few times, sitting on the waterstairs, the dirty harbor water sloshing at the next step down, the yells of gulls and dockworkers wreathing the air with a thin, ungainly music, he shut his eyes and saw his love so clear, so close, that he reached out his hand to touch her. If he reached out his hand in his mind only, as when he played the mental harp, then indeed he touched her. He felt her hand in his, and her cheek, warmcool, silken-gritty, lay against his mouth. In his mind he spoke to her, and in his mind she answered, her voice, her husky voice saying his name, "Diamond . . ."

But as he went back up the streets of South Port he lost her. He swore to keep her with him, to think of her, to think of her that night, but she faded away. By the time he opened the door of Master Hemlock's house he was reciting lists of names, or wondering what would be for dinner, for he was hungry most of the time. Not till he could take an hour and run back down to the docks could he think of her.

So he came to feel that those hours were true meetings with her, and he lived for them, without knowing what he lived for until his feet were on the cobbles, and his eyes on the harbor and the far line of the sea. Then he remembered what was worth remembering.

The winter passed by, and the cold early spring, and with the warm late spring came a letter from his mother, brought by a carter. Diamond read it and took it to Master Hemlock, saying, "My mother wonders if I might spend a month at home this summer."

"Probably not," the wizard said, and then, appearing to notice Diamond, put down his pen and said, "Young man, I must ask you if you wish to continue studying with me."

Diamond had no idea what to say. The idea of its being up to him had not occurred to him. "Do you think I ought to?" he asked at last.

"Probably not," the wizard said.

Diamond expected to feel relieved, released, but found he felt rejected, ashamed.

"I'm sorry," he said, with enough dignity that Hemlock glanced up at him.

"You could go to Roke," the wizard said.

"To Roke?"

The boy's drop-jawed stare irritated Hemlock, though he knew it shouldn't. Wizards are used to overweening confidence in the young of their kind. They expected modesty to come later, if at all. "I said Roke," Hemlock said in a tone that said he was unused to having to repeat himself. And then, because this boy, this soft-headed, spoiled, moony boy had endeared himself to Hemlock by his uncomplaining patience, he took pity on him and said, "You should either go to Roke or find a wizard to teach you what you need. Of course you need what I can teach you. You need the names. The art begins and ends in naming. But that's not your gift. You have a poor memory for words. You must train it diligently. However, it's clear that you do have capacities, and that they need cultivation and discipline, which another man can give you better than I can." So does modesty breed modesty, sometimes, even in unlikely places. "If you were to go to Roke, I'd send a letter with you drawing you to the particular attention of the Master Summoner."

"Ah," said Diamond, floored. The Summoner's art is perhaps the most arcane and dangerous of all the arts of magic.

"Perhaps I am wrong," said Hemlock in his dry, flat voice. "Your gift may be for Pattern. Or perhaps it's an ordinary gift for shaping and transformation. I'm not certain."

"But you are—I do actually—"

"Oh yes. You are uncommonly slow, young man, to recognize your own capacities." It was spoken harshly, and Diamond stiffened up a bit.

"I thought my gift was for music," he said.

Hemlock dismissed that with a flick of his hand. "I am talking of the True Art," he said. "Now I will be frank with you. I advise you to write your parents—I shall write them too—informing them of your decision to go to the School on Roke, if that is what you decide; or to the Great Port, if the Mage Restive will take you on, as I think he will, with my recommendation. But I advise against visiting home. The entanglement of family, friends, and so on is precisely what you need to be free of. Now, and henceforth."

"Do wizards have no family?"

Hemlock was glad to see a bit of fire in the boy. "They are one another's family," he said.

"And no friends?"

"They may be friends. Did I say it was an easy life?" A pause. Hemlock looked directly at Diamond. "There was a girl," he said.

Diamond met his gaze for a moment, looked down, and said nothing.

"Your father told me. A witch's daughter, a childhood playmate. He believed that you had taught her spells."

"She taught me."

Hemlock nodded. "That is quite understandable, among children. And quite impossible now. Do you understand that?"

"No," Diamond said.

"Sit down," said Hemlock. After a moment Diamond took the stiff, high-backed chair facing him.

"I can protect you here, and have done so. On Roke, of course, you'll be perfectly safe. The very walls, there . . . But if you go home, you must be willing to protect yourself. It's a difficult thing for a young man, very difficult—a test of a will that has not yet been steeled, a mind that has not yet seen its true goal. I very strongly advise that you not take that risk. Write your parents, and go to the Great Port, or to Roke. Half your year's fee, which I'll return to you, will see to your first expenses."

Diamond sat upright and still. He had been getting some of his father's height and girth lately, and looked very much a man, though a very young one.

"What did you mean, Master Hemlock, in saying that you had protected me here?"

"Simply as I protect myself," the wizard said; and after a moment, testily, "The bargain, boy. The power we give for our power. The lesser state of being we forego. Surely you know that every true man of power is celibate."

There was a pause, and Diamond said, "So you saw to it . . . that I . . ."

"Of course. It was my responsibility as your teacher."

Diamond nodded. He said, "Thank you." Presently he stood up. "Excuse me, Master," he said. "I have to think."

"Where are you going?"

"Down to the waterfront."

"Better stay here."

"I can't think, here."

Hemlock might have known then what he was up against; but having told the boy he would not be his master any longer, he could not in conscience command him. "You have a true gift, Essiri," he said, using the name he had given the boy in the springs of the Amia, a word that in the Old Speech means Willow. "I don't entirely understand it. I think you don't understand it at all. Take care! To misuse a gift, or to refuse to use it, may cause great loss, great harm."

Diamond nodded, suffering, contrite, unrebellious, unmovable.

"Go on," the wizard said, and he went.

Later he knew he should never have let the boy leave the house.

He had underestimated Diamond's willpower, or the strength of the spell the girl had laid on him. Their conversation was in the morning; Hemlock went back to the ancient cantrip he was annotating; it was not till supper time that he thought about his pupil, and not until he had eaten supper alone that he admitted that Diamond had run away.

Hemlock was loath to practice any of the lesser arts of magic. He did not put out a finding spell, as any sorcerer might have done. Nor did he call to Diamond in any way. He was angry; perhaps he was hurt. He had thought well of the boy, and offered to write the Summoner about him, and then at the first test of character Diamond had broken. "Glass," the wizard muttered. At least this weakness proved he was not dangerous. Some talents were best not left to run wild, but there was no harm in this fellow, no malice. No ambition. "No spine," said Hemlock to the silence of the house. "Let him crawl home to his mother."

Still it rankled him that Diamond had let him down flat, without a word of thanks or apology. So much for good manners, he thought.

As she blew out the lamp and got into bed, the witch's daughter heard an owl calling, the little, liquid hu-hu-hu-hu that made people call them laughing owls. She heard it with a mournful heart. That had been their signal, summer nights, when they sneaked out to meet in the willow grove, down on the banks of the Amia, when everybody else was sleeping. She would not think of him at night. Back in the winter she had sent to him night after night. She had learned her mother's spell of sending, and knew that it was a true spell. She had sent him her touch, her voice saying his name, again and again. She had met a wall of air and silence. She touched nothing. He would not hear.

Once or twice, all of a sudden, in the daytime, there had been a moment when she had known him close in mind and could touch him if she reached out. But at night she knew only his blank absence, his refusal of her. She had stopped trying to reach him, months ago, but her heart was still very sore.

"Hu-hu-hu," said the owl, under her window, and then it said, "Darkrose!" Startled from her misery, she leaped out of bed and opened the shutters.

"Come on out," whispered Diamond, a shadow in the starlight.

"Mother's not home. Come in!" She met him at the door.

They held each other tight, hard, silent for a long time. To Diamond it was as if he held his future, his own life, his whole life, in his arms.

At last she moved, and kissed his cheek, and whispered, "I missed you, I missed you, I missed you. How long can you stay?"

"As long as I like."

She kept his hand and led him in. He was always a little reluctant to enter the witch's house, a pungent, disorderly place thick with the mysteries of women and witchcraft, very different from his own clean, comfortable home, even more different from the cold austerity of the wizard's house. He shivered like a horse as he stood there, too tall for the herb-festooned rafters. He was very highly strung, and worn out, having walked forty miles in sixteen hours without food.

"Where's your mother?" he asked in a whisper.

"Sitting with old Ferny. She died this afternoon, Mother will be there all night. But how did you get here?"

"Walked."

"The wizard let you visit home?"

"I ran away."

"Ran away! Why?"

"To keep you."

He looked at her, that vivid, fierce, dark face in its rough cloud of hair. She wore only her shift, and he saw the infinitely delicate, tender rise of her breasts. He drew her to him again, but though she hugged him she drew away again, frowning.

"Keep me?" she repeated. "You didn't seem to worry about losing me all winter. What made you come back now?"

"He wanted me to go to Roke."

"To Roke?" She stared. "To Roke, Di? Then you really do have the gift—you could be a sorcerer?"

To find her on Hemlock's side was a blow.

"Sorcerers are nothing to him. He means I could be a wizard. Do magery. Not just witchcraft."

"Oh I see," Rose said after a moment. "But I don't see why you ran away."

They had let go of each other's hands.

"Don't you understand?" he said, exasperated with her for not understanding, because he had not understood. "A wizard can't have anything to do with women. With witches. With all that."

"Oh, I know. It's beneath them."

"It's not just beneath them—"

"Oh, but it is. I'll bet you had to unlearn every spell I taught you. Didn't you?"

"It isn't the same kind of thing."

"No. It isn't the High Art. It isn't the True Speech. A wizard mustn't soil his lips with common words. 'Weak as women's magic, wicked as women's magic,' you think I don't know what they say? So, why did you come back here?"

"To see you!"

"What for?"

"What do you think?"

"You never sent to me, you never let me send to you, all the time you were gone. I was just supposed to wait until you got tired of playing wizard. Well, I got tired of waiting." Her voice was nearly inaudible, a rough whisper.

"Somebody's been coming around," he said, incredulous that she could turn against him. "Who's been after you?"

"None of your business if there is! You go off, you turn your back on me. Wizards can't have anything to do with what I do, what my mother does. Well, I don't want anything to do with what you do, either, ever. So go!"

Starving hungry, frustrated, misunderstood, Diamond reached out to hold her again, to make her body understand his body, repeating that first, deep embrace that had held all the years of their lives in it. He found himself standing two feet back, his hands stinging and his ears ringing and his eyes dazzled. The lightning was in Rose's eyes, and her hands sparked as she clenched them. "Never do that again," she whispered.

"Never fear," Diamond said, turned on his heel, and strode out. A string of dried sage caught on his head and trailed after him.

He spent the night in their old place in the sallows. Maybe he hoped she would come, but she did not come, and he soon slept in sheer weariness. He woke in the first, cold light. He sat up and thought. He looked at life in that cold light. It was a different matter from what he had believed it. He went down to the stream in which he had been named. He drank, washed his hands and face, made himself look as decent as he could, and went up through the town to the fine house at the high end, his father's house.

After the first outcries and embraces, the servants and his mother sat him right down to breakfast. So it was with warm food in his belly and a certain chill courage in his heart that he faced his father, who had been out before breakfast seeing off a string of timber-carts to the Great Port.

"Well, son!" They touched cheeks. "So Master Hemlock gave you a vacation?"

"No, sir. I left."

Golden stared, then filled his plate and sat down. "Left," he said.

"Yes, sir. I decided that I don't want to be a wizard."

"Hmf," said Golden, chewing. "Left of your own accord? Entirely? With the Master's permission?"

"Of my own accord entirely, without his permission."

Golden chewed very slowly, his eyes on the table. Diamond had seen his father look like this when a forester reported an infestation in the chestnut groves, and when he found a mule-dealer had cheated him.

"He wanted me to go to the College on Roke to study with the Master Summoner. He was going to send me there. I decided not to go."

After a while Golden asked, still looking at the table, "Why?"

"It isn't the life I want."

Another pause. Golden glanced over at his wife, who stood by the window listening in silence. Then he looked at his son. Slowly the mixture of anger, disappointment, confusion, and respect on his face gave way to something simpler, a look of complicity, very nearly a wink. "I see," he said. "And what did you decide you want?"

A pause. "This," Diamond said. His voice was level. He looked neither at his father nor his mother.

"Hah!" said Golden. "Well! I will say I'm glad of it, son." He ate a small porkpie in one mouthful. "Being a wizard, going to Roke, all that, it never seemed real, not exactly. And with you off there, I didn't know what all this was for, to tell you the truth. All my business. If you're here, it adds up, you see. It adds up. Well! But listen here, did you just run off from the wizard? Did he know you were going?"

"No. I'll write him," Diamond said, in his new, level voice.

"He won't be angry? They say wizards have short tempers. Full of pride."

"He's angry," Diamond said, "but he won't do anything."

So it proved. Indeed, to Golden's amazement, Master Hemlock sent back a scrupulous two-fifths of the prenticing fee. With the packet, which was delivered by one of Golden's carters who had taken a load of spars down to South Port, was a note for Diamond. It said, "True art requires a single heart." The direction on the outside was the Hardic rune for willow. The note was signed with Hemlock's rune, which had two meanings: the hemlock tree, and suffering.

Diamond sat in his own sunny room upstairs, on his comfortable bed, hearing his mother singing as she went about the house. He held the wizard's letter and reread the message and the two runes many times. The cold and sluggish mind that had been born in him that morning down in the sallows accepted the lesson. No magic. Never again. He had never given his heart to it. It had been a game to him, a game to play with Darkrose. Even the names of the True Speech that he had learned in the wizard's house, though he knew the beauty and the power that lay in them, he could let go, let slip, forget. That was not his language.

He could speak his language only with her. And he had lost her, let her go. The double heart has no true speech. From now on he could talk only the language of duty: the getting and the spending, the outlay and the income, the profit and the loss.

And beyond that, nothing. There had been illusions, little spells, pebbles that turned to butterflies, wooden birds that flew on living wings for a minute or two. There had never been a choice, really. There was only one way for him to go.

Golden was immensely happy and quite unconscious of it. "Old man's got his jewel back," said the carter to the forester. "Sweet as new butter, he is." Golden, unaware of being sweet, thought only how sweet life was. He had bought the Reche grove, at a very stiff price to be sure, but at least old Lowbough of Easthill hadn't got it, and now he and Diamond could develop it as it ought to be developed. In among the chestnuts there were a lot of pines, which could be felled and sold for masts and spars and small lumber, and replanted with chestnuts seedlings. It would in time be a pure stand like the Big Grove, the heart of his chestnut kingdom. In time, of course. Oak and chestnut don't shoot up overnight like alder and willow. But there was time. There was time, now. The boy was barely seventeen, and he himself just forty-five. In his prime. He had been feeling old, but that was nonsense. He was in his prime. The oldest trees, past bearing, ought to come out with the pines. Some good wood for furniture could be salvaged from them.

"Well, well, well," he said to his wife, frequently, "all rosy again, eh? Got the apple of your eye back home, eh? No more moping, eh?"

And Tuly smiled and stroked his hand.

Once instead of smiling and agreeing, she said, "It's lovely to have him back, but" and Golden stopped hearing. Mothers were born to worry about their children, and women were born never to be content. There was no reason why he should listen to the litany of anxieties by which Tuly hauled herself through life. Of course she thought a merchant's life wasn't good enough for the boy. She'd have thought being King in Havnor wasn't good enough for him.

"When he gets himself a girl," Golden said, in answer to whatever it was she had been saying, "he'll be all squared away. Living with the wizards, you know, the way they are, it set him back a bit. Don't worry about Diamond. He'll know what he wants when he sees it!"

"I hope so," said Tuly.

"At least he's not seeing the witch's girl," said Golden. "That's done with." Later on it occurred to him that neither was his wife seeing the witch anymore. For years they'd been thick as thieves, against all his warnings, and now Tangle was never anywhere near the house. Women's friendships never lasted. He teased her about it. Finding her strewing pennyroyal and millersbane in the chests and clothes-presses against an infestation of moths, he said, "Seems like you'd have your friend the wise woman up to hex 'em away. Or aren't you friends anymore?"

"No," his wife said in her soft, level voice, "we aren't."

"And a good thing too!" Golden said roundly. "What's become of that daughter of hers; then? Went off with a juggler, I heard?"

"A musician," Tuly said. "Last summer."

"A nameday party," said Golden. "Time for a bit of play, a bit of music and dancing, boy. Nineteen years old. Celebrate it!"

"I'll be going to Easthill with Sul's mules."

"No, no, no. Sul can handle it. Stay home and have your party. You've been working hard. We'll hire a band. Who's the best in the country? Tarry and his lot?"

"Father, I don't want a party," Diamond said and stood up, shivering his muscles like a horse. He was bigger than Golden now, and when he moved abruptly it was startling. "I'll go to Easthill," he said, and left the room.

"What's that all about?" Golden said to his wife, a rhetorical question. She looked at him and said nothing, a non-rhetorical answer.

After Golden had gone out, she found her son in the counting room going through ledgers. She looked at the pages. Long, long lists of names and numbers, debts and credits, profits and losses.

"Di," she said, and he looked up. His face was still round and a bit peachy, though the bones were heavier and the eyes were melancholy.

"I didn't mean to hurt Father's feelings," he said.

"If he wants a party, he'll have it," she said. Their voices were alike, being in the higher register but dark-toned, and held to an even quietness, contained, restrained. She perched on a stool beside his at the high desk.

"I can't," he said, and stopped, and went on, "I really don't want to have any dancing."

"He's matchmaking," Tuly said, dry, fond.

"I don't care about that."

"I know you don't."

"The problem is . . ."

"The problem is the music," his mother said at last.

He nodded.

"My son, there is no reason," she said, suddenly passionate, "there is *no* reason why you should give up everything you love!"

He took her hand and kissed it as they sat side by side.

"Things don't mix," he said. "They ought to, but they don't. I found that out. When I left the wizard, I thought I could be everything. You know—do magic, play music, be Father's son, love Rose. . . . It doesn't work that way. Things don't mix."

"They do, they do," Tuly said. "Everything is hooked together, tangled up!"

"Maybe things are, for women. But I . . . I can't be doublehearted."

"Doublehearted? You? You gave up wizardry because you knew that if you didn't, you'd betray it."

He took the word with a visible shock, but did not deny it.

"But why did you give up music?"

"I have to have a single heart. I can't play the harp while I'm bargaining with a mule breeder. I can't sing ballads while I'm figuring what we have to pay the pickers to keep 'em from hiring out to Lowbough!" His voice shook a little now, a vibrato, and his eyes were not sad, but angry.

"So you put a spell on yourself," she said, "just as that wizard put one on you. A spell to keep you safe. To keep you with the mule breeders, and the nut pickers, and these." She struck the ledger full of lists of names and figures, a flicking, dismissive tap. "A spell of silence," she said.

After a long time the young man said, "What else can I do?"

"I don't know, my dear. I do want you to be safe. I do love to see your father happy and proud of you. But I can't bear to see you unhappy, without pride! I don't know. Maybe you're right. Maybe for a man it's only one thing ever. But I miss hearing you sing."

She was in tears. They hugged, and she stroked his thick, shining hair and apologized for being cruel, and he hugged her again and said she was the kindest mother in the world, and so she went off. But as she left she turned back a moment and said, "Let him have the party, Di. Let yourself have it."

"I will," he said, to comfort her.

Golden ordered the beer and food and fireworks, but Diamond saw to hiring the musicians.

"Of course I'll bring my band," Tarry said, "fat chance I'd miss it! You'll have every tootler in the west of the world here for one of your dad's parties."

"You can tell 'em you're the band that's getting paid."

"Oh, they'll come for the glory," said the harper, a lean, long-jawed, wall-eyed fellow of forty. "Maybe you'll have a go with us yourself, then? You had a hand for it, before you took to making money. And the voice not bad, if you'd worked on it."

"I doubt it," Diamond said.

"That girl you liked, witch's Rose, she's runing about with Labby, I hear. No doubt they'll come by."

"I'll see you then," said Diamond, looking big and handsome and indifferent, and walked off.

"Too high and mighty these days to stop and talk," said Tarry, "though I taught him all he knows of harping. But what's that to a rich man?"

Tarry's malice had left his nerves raw, and the thought of the party weighed on him till he lost his appetite. He thought hopefully for a while that he was sick and could miss the party. But the day came, and he was there. Not so evidently, so eminently, so flamboyantly there as his father, but present, smiling, dancing. All his childhood friends were there too, half of them married by now to the other half, it seemed, but there was still plenty of flirting going on, and several pretty girls were always near him. He drank a good deal of Gadge Brewer's excellent beer, and found he could endure the music if he was dancing to it and talking and laughing while he danced. So he danced with all the pretty girls in turn, and then again with whichever one turned up again, which all of them did.

It was Golden's grandest party yet, with a dancing floor built on the town green down the way from Golden's house, and a tent for the old folks to eat and drink and gossip in, and new clothes for the children, and jugglers and puppeteers, some of them hired and some of them coming by to pick up whatever they could in the way of coppers and free beer. Any festivity drew itinerant entertainers and musicians; it was their living, and though uninvited they were welcomed. A tale-singer with a droning voice and a droning bagpipe was singing *The Deed of the Dragonlord* to a group of people under the big oak on the hilltop. When Tarry's band of harp, fife, viol, and drum took time off for a breather and a swig, a new group hopped up onto the dance floor. "Hey, there's Labby's band!" cried the pretty girl nearest Diamond. "Come on, they're the best!"

Labby, a light-skinned, flashy-looking fellow, played the double-reed woodhorn. With him were a violist, a tabor player, and Rose, who played fife. Their first tune was a stampy, fast and brilliant, too fast for some of the dancers. Diamond and his partner stayed in, and people cheered and clapped them when they finished the dance, sweating and panting. "Beer!" Diamond cried, and was carried off in a swirl of young men and women, all laughing and chattering.

He heard behind him the next tune start up, the viol alone, strong and sad as a tenor voice: "Where My Love Is Going."

He drank a mug of beer down in one draft, and the girls with him watched the muscles in his strong throat as he swallowed, and they laughed and chattered, and he shivered all over like a cart horse stung by flies. He said, "Oh! I can't—!" He bolted off into the dusk beyond the lanterns hanging around the brewer's booth. "Where's he going?" said one, and another, "He'll be back," and they laughed and chattered.

The tune ended. "Darkrose," he said, behind her in the dark. She turned her head and looked at him. Their heads were on a level, she sitting cross-legged up on the dance platform, he kneeling on the grass.

"Come to the sallows," he said.

She said nothing. Labby, glancing at her, set his woodhorn to his lips. The drummer struck a triple beat on his tabor, and they were off into a sailor's jig.

When she looked around again Diamond was gone.

Tarry came back with his band in an hour or so, ungrateful for the respite and much the worse for beer. He interrupted the tune and the dancing, telling Labby loudly to clear out.

"Ah, pick your nose, harp-picker," Labby said, and Tarry took offense, and people took sides, and while the dispute was at its brief height, Rose put her fife in her pocket and slipped away.

Away from the lanterns of the party it was dark, but she knew the way in the dark. He was there. The willows had grown, these two years. There was only a little space to sit among the green shoots and the long, falling leaves.

The music started up, distant, blurred by wind and the murmur of the river running.

"What did you want, Diamond?"

"To talk."

They were only voices and shadows to each other.

"So," she said.

"I wanted to ask you to go away with me," he said.

"When?"

"Then. When we quarreled. I said it all wrong. I thought . . ." A long pause. "I thought I could go on running away. With you. And play music. Make a living. Together. I meant to say that."

"You didn't say it."

"I know. I said everything wrong. I did everything wrong. I betrayed everything. The magic. And the music. And you."

"I'm all right," she said.

"Are you?"

"I'm not really good on the fife, but I'm good enough. What you didn't teach me, I can fill in with a spell, if I have to. And the band, they're all right. Labby isn't as bad as he looks. Nobody fools with me. We make a pretty good living. Winters, I go stay with Mother and help her out. So I'm all right. What about you, Di?"

"All wrong."

She started to say something, and did not say it.

"I guess we were children," he said. "Now . . ."

"What's changed?"

"I made the wrong choice."

"Once?" she said. "Or twice?"

"Twice."

"Third time's the charm."

Neither spoke for a while. She could just make out the bulk of him in the leafy shadows. "You're bigger than you were," she said. "Can you still make a light, Di? I want to see you."

He shook his head.

"That was the one thing you could do that I never could. And you never could teach me."

"I didn't know what I was doing," he said. "Sometimes it worked, sometimes it didn't."

"And the wizard in South Port didn't teach you how to make it work?"

"He only taught me names."

"Why can't you do it now?"

"I gave it up, Darkrose. I had to either do it and nothing else, or not do it. You have to have a single heart."

"I don't see why," she said. "My mother can cure a fever and ease a childbirth and find a lost ring, maybe that's nothing compared to what the wizards and the dragonlords can do, but it's not nothing, all the same. And she didn't give up anything for it. Having me didn't stop her. She had me so that she could *learn* how to do it! Just because I learned how to play music from you, did I have to give up saying spells? I can bring a fever down now too. Why should you have to stop doing one thing so you can do the other?"

"My father," he began, and stopped, and gave a kind of laugh. "They don't go together," he said. "The money and the music."

"The father and the witchgirl," said Darkrose.

Again there was silence between them. The leaves of the willows stirred.

"Would you come back to me?" he said. "Would you go with me, live with me, marry me, Darkrose?"

"Not in your father's house, Di."

"Anywhere. Run away."

"But you can't have me without the music."

"Or the music without you."

"I would," she said.

"Does Labby want a harper?"

She hesitated; she laughed. "If he wants a fife player," she said.

"I haven't practiced ever since I left, Darkrose," he said. "But the music was always in my head, and you . . ." She reached out her hands to him. They knelt facing, the willow leaves moving across their hair. They kissed each other, timidly at first.

In the years after Diamond left home, Golden made more money than he had ever done before. All his deals were profitable. It was as if good fortune stuck to him and he could not shake it off. He grew immensely wealthy. He did not forgive his son. It would have made a happy ending, but he would not have it. To leave so, without a word, on his nameday night, to go off with the witchgirl, leaving all the honest work undone, to be a vagrant musician, a harper twanging and singing and grinning for pennies—there was nothing but shame and pain and anger in it for Golden. So he had his tragedy.

Tuly shared it with him for a long time, since she could see her son only by lying to her husband, which she found hard to do. She wept to think of Diamond hungry, sleeping hard. Cold nights of autumn were a misery to her. But as time went on and she heard him spoken of as Diamond the sweet singer of the West of Havnor, Diamond who had harped and sung to the great lords in the Tower of the Sword, her heart grew lighter. And once, when Golden was down at South Port, she and Tangle took a donkey cart and drove over to Easthill, where they heard Diamond sing the *Lay of the Lost Queen*, while Rose sat with them, and Little Tuly sat on Tuly's knee. And if not a happy ending, that was a true joy, which may be enough to ask for, after all.

IAN R. MacLEOD

The Chop Girl

Ian R. MacLeod's alternate history novella The Summer Isles *was one of the finest stories of 1998 (and a Hugo Award finalist)—but it was just too long for us to reprint in last year's edition of* The Year's Best Fantasy and Horror. *Thus it gives me particular pleasure to include an equally fine story by MacLeod in this year's edition.*

MacLeod lives in the British Midlands, where he teaches adult literacy and creative writing classes. His books include the novel The Great Wheel *and* Voyages by Starlight, *a collection of stories. Regarding the following tale, he says, "My parents both served in eastern England during the war, and were helpful to me with some of the details for this story. Chop girls really did exist, by the way, as do many, but not all, of the names of the air bases I've mentioned."*

"The Chop Girl" is reprinted from the December 1999 issue of Asimov's Science Fiction *magazine.*

—T. W., E. D.

Me, I was the chop girl—not that I suppose that anyone knows what that means now. So much blood and water under the bridge, I heard the lassies in the post office debating how many world wars there had been last week when I climbed up the hill to collect my pension, and who exactly it was that had won them.

Volunteered for service, I did, because I thought it would get me away from the stink of the frying pans at home in our Manchester tea room's back kitchen. And then the Air Force of all things, and me thinking, lucky, lucky, lucky, because of the glamour and the lads, the lovely lads, the best lads of all, who spoke with BBC voices as I imagined them, and had played rugger and footie for their posh schools and for their posh southern counties. And a lot of it was true, even if I ended up typing in the annex to the cookhouse, ordering mustard and HP Sauce on account of my, quote, *considerable experience in the catering industry.*

So there I was—just eighteen and WAAF and lucky, lucky, lucky. And I still didn't know what a chop girl was, which had nothing to do with lamb or bacon or the huge blocks of lard I ordered for the chip pans. They were big and empty places, those bomber airfields, and they had the wild and open and windy names of the Fens that surrounded them. Wisbeach and Finneston and Witchford. And there were drinks and there were dances and the money was never short because there was never any point in not spending it. Because you never knew, did you? You never knew. One day your bunk's still warm and the next someone else is complaining about not changing the sheets and the smell of you on it. Those big machines like ugly insects lumbering out in the dying hour to face the salt wind off the marshes and the lights and blue smoke of the paraffin lanterns drifting across the runways. Struggling up into the deepening sky in a mighty roaring, and the rest of us standing earthbound and watching. Word slipping out that tonight it would be Hamburg or Dortmund or Essen—some half-remembered place from a faded schoolroom map glowing out under no moon and through heavy cloud, the heavier the better, as the bombers droned over, and death fell from them in those long steel canisters onto people who were much like us when you got down to it, but for the chances of history. Then back, back, a looser run in twos and threes and searching for the sea-flash of the coast after so many miles of darkness. Black specks at dawn on the big horizon that could have been clouds or crows or just your eyes' plain weariness. Noise and smoke and flame. Engines misfiring. An unsettled quiet would be lying over everything by the time the sun was properly up and the skylarks were singing. The tinny taste of fatigue. Then word on the wires of MG 3138, which had limped in at Brightlingsea. And of CZ 709, which had ploughed up a field down at Theddlethorpe. Word, too, of LK 452, which was last seen as a flaming cross over Brussels, and of Flight Sergeant Shanklin, who, hoisted bloody from his gun turret by the medics, had faded on the way to hospital. Word of the dead. Word of the lost. Word of the living.

Death was hanging all around you, behind the beer and the laughs and the bowls and the endless games of cards and darts and cricket. Knowing as they set out on a big mission that some planes would probably never get back. Knowing for sure that half the crews wouldn't make it through their twenty-mission tour. So, of course, we were all madly superstitious. It just happened—you didn't need anyone to make it up for you. Who bought the first round. Who climbed into the plane last. Not shaving or shaving only half your face. Kissing the ground, kissing the air, singing, not singing, pissing against the undercarriage, spitting. I saw a flight officer have a blue fit because the girl in the canteen gave him only two sausages on his lunchtime plate. That night, on a big raid over Dortmund, his Lancaster vanished in heavy flak, and I remember the sleepless nights because it was me who'd forgotten to requisition from the wholesale butcher. But everything was sharp and bright then. The feel of your feet in your shoes and your tongue in your mouth and your eyes in their sockets. That, and the sick-and-petrol smell of the bombers. So everything mattered. Every incident was marked and solid in the only time that counted, which was the time that lay between now and the next mission. So it was odd socks and counting sausages, spitting and not spitting, old hats and new hats worn backward and forward. It was pissing on the undercarriage, and whistling. And it was the girls you'd kissed.

Me, I was the chop girl, and word of it tangled and whispered around me like the sour morning news of a botched raid. I don't know how it began, because I'd been with enough lads at dances, and then outside afterward fumbling and giggling in the darkness. And sometimes, and because you loved them all and felt sorry for them, you'd let them go nearly all the way before pulling back with the starlight shivering between us. Going nearly all the way was a skill you had to learn then, like who wore what kind of brass buttons and marching in line. And I was lucky. I sang lucky, lucky, lucky to myself in the morning as I brushed my teeth, and I laughingly told the lads so in the evening NAAFI when they always beat me at cards.

It could have started with Flight Sergeant Martin Beezly, who just came into our smoky kitchen annex one hot summer afternoon and sat down on the edge of my desk with his blond hair sticking up and told me he had a fancy to go picnicking and had got hold of two bikes. Me, I just unrolled my carbons and stood up and the other girls watched with the jaws of their typewriters dropped in astonishment as I walked out into the sunlight. Nothing much happened that afternoon, other than what Flight Sergeant Beezly said would happen. We cycled along the little dikes and bumped across the wooden bridges, and I sat on a rug eating custard creams as he told me about his home up in the northeast and the business he was planning to set up after the war delivering lunchtime sandwiches to the factories. But all of that seemed as distant as the open blue sky—as distant, given these clear and unsuitable weather conditions, as the possibility of a raid taking place that evening. We were just two young people enjoying the solid certainty of that moment—which the taste of custard creams still always brings back to me—and Flight Sergeant Beezly did no more than brush my cheek with his fingers before we climbed back onto the bikes, and then glance anxiously east toward the heavy clouds that were suddenly piling. It was fully overcast by the time we got back to the base, driven fast on our bikes by the cool and unsummery wind that was rustling the ditches. Already, orders had been posted and briefings were being staged and the ground crews were working, their arclights flaring in the hangers. Another five minutes, a little less of that wind as we cycled, and there'd have been all hell to pay for me and for Flight Sergeant Beezly, who, as a navigator and vital to the task of getting one of those big machines across the dark sky, would have been shifted to standby and then probably court-martialled.

But as it was, he just made it into the briefing room as the map was being unfolded and sat down, as I imagine him, on the schoolroom desk nearest the door, still a little breathless, and with the same smears of bike oil on his fingers that I later found on my cheek. That night, it was Amsterdam—a quick raid to make the most of this quick and filthy cloud that the weather boffins said wouldn't last. Amsterdam. One of those raids that somehow never sounded right even though it was enemy-occupied territory. That night, GZ 3401, with Flight Sergeant Beezly navigating, was last seen laboring over the North Sea enemy coastal barrages with a full load of bombs, a slow and ugly butterfly pinioned on the needles of half a dozen searchlights.

So maybe that was the first whisper—me walking out of the annex before I should have done with Flight Sergeant Beezly, although God knows it had happened to enough of the other girls. That, and worse. Broken engagements. Cancelled marriages. Visits to the burns unit, and up the stick for going all the way instead of just most of it. Wrecked, unmendable lives that you can still see drifting at every branch post office if you know how and when to look.

But then, a week after, there was Pilot Officer Charlie Dyson, who had a reputation as one of the lads, one for the lassies. All we did was dance and kiss at the Friday hall down in the village, although I suppose that particular night was the first time I was really drawn to him because something had changed about his eyes. That, and the fact that he'd shaved off the Clark Gable moustache that I'd always thought made him look vain and ridiculous. So we ended up kissing as we danced, and then sharing beers and laughs with the rest of his crew in their special corner. And after the band had gone and the village outside the

hall stood stony dark, I let him lean me against the old oak that slipped
its roots into the river and let him nuzzle my throat and touch my breasts
and mutter words against my skin that were lost in the hissing of the
water. I put my hand down between us then, touched him in the place
I thought he wanted. But Pilot Officer Charlie Dyson was soft as smoke
down there, as cool and empty as the night. So I just held him and
rocked him as he began to weep, feeling faintly relieved that there
wouldn't be the usual pressures for me to go the whole way. Looking
up through the oak leaves as the river whispered, I saw that the bright
moon of the week before was thinning, and I knew from the chill air
on my flesh that tomorrow the planes would be thundering out again.
You didn't need to be a spy or a boffin. And not Amsterdam, but a long
run. Hamburg. Dortmund. Essen. In fact, it turned out to be the longest
of them all, Berlin. And somewhere on that journey Pilot Officer Charlie
Dyson and his whole crew and his Lancaster simply fell out of the sky.
Vanished into the darkness.

After that, the idea of my being bad luck seemed to settle around
me, clinging like the smoke of the cookhouse. Although I was young,
although I'd never really gone steady with anyone and had still never
ventured every last inch of the way, and although no one dared to keep
any proper score of these things, I was already well on my way to
becoming the chop girl. I learned afterward that most bases had one;
that—in the same way that Kitty from stores was like a mom to a lot
of the crews, and Sally Morrison was the camp bicycle—it was a kind
of necessity.

And I believed. With each day so blazingly bright and with the
nights so dark and the crews wild-eyed and us few women grieving and
sleepless, with good luck and bad luck teeming in the clouds and in the
turning of the moon, we loved and lived in a world that had shifted
beyond the realms of normality. So of course I believed.

I can't give you lists and statistics. I can't say when I first heard
the word, or caught the first really odd look. But being the chop girl
became a self-fulfilling prophecy. Empty wells of silence opened out
when I entered the canteen. Chairs were weirdly rearranged in the
NAAFI. I was the chop, and the chop was Flight Sergeant Ronnie Fit-
field and Flight Officer Jackie White and Pilot Officer Tim Reid, all of
them in one bad late summer month, men I can barely remember now
except for their names and ranks and the look of loss in their eyes and
the warm bristle touch of their faces. Nights out at a pub; beating the
locals at cribbage; a trip to the cinema at Lincoln, and the tight, cobbled
streets afterward shining with rain. But I couldn't settle on these men
because already I could feel the darkness edging in between us, and I

knew even as I touched their shoulders and watched them turn away that they could feel it, too. At the dances and the endless booze-ups and the card schools, I became more than a wallflower: I was the petaled heart of death, its living embodiment. I was quivering with it like electricity. One touch, one kiss, one dance. Ground-crew messages were hard to deliver when they saw who it was coming across the tarmac. It got to the point when I stopped seeing out the planes, or watching them through the pane of my bunk window. And the other girls in the annex and the spinster WAAF officers and even the red-faced women from the village who came in to empty the bins—all of them knew I was the chop, all of them believed. The men who came up to me now were white-faced, already teetering. They barely needed my touch. Once you'd lost it, the luck, the edge, the nerve, it was gone anyway, and the black bomber's sky crunched you in its fists.

I can't tell you that it was terrible. I knew it wasn't *just*, but then, justice was something we'd long given up even missing. Put within that picture, and of the falling bombs and the falling bombers, I understood that the chop girl was a little thing, and I learned to step back into the cold and empty space that it provided. After all, I hadn't *loved* any of the men—or only in a sweet, generalized and heady way that faded on the walk from the fence against which we'd been leaning. And I reasoned—and this was probably the thing that kept me sane—that it wasn't *me* that was the chop. I reasoned that death lay somewhere else and was already waiting, that I was just a signpost that some crewmen had happened to pass on their way.

Me, I was the chop girl.

And I believed.

Such were the terrors and the pains of the life we were leading.

With the harvest came the thunderflies, evicted from the fields in sooty clouds that speckled the windows and came out like black dandruff when you combed your hair. And the moths and the craneflies were drawn for miles by the sparks and lights flaring from the hangers. Spiders prowled the communal baths, filled with their woodland reek of bleach and wet towels. The sun rippled small and gold like a dropped coin on the horizon, winking as if through fathoms of ocean.

With harvest came Walt Williams. Chuttering up to the Strictly Reserved parking space outside the squadron leader's office in a once-red MG and climbing out with a swing of his legs and a heave of his battered carpetbag. Smiling with cold blue eyes as he looked around him at the expanse of hangars, as if he would never be surprised again. Walt had done training. Walt had done Pathfinders. Walt had done three full tours, and most of another that had only ended when his plane had been shot from under him and he'd been hauled out of the Channel by a passing MTB. We'd all heard of Walt, or thought we had, or had certainly heard of people like him. Walt was one of the old-style pilots who'd been flying before the war for sheer pleasure. Walt was an old man of thirty, with age creases on his sun-browned face to go with those blue eyes. Walt had done it all and had finally exhausted every possibility of death that a bemused RAF could throw at him. Walt was the living embodiment of lucky.

We gathered around, we sought to touch and admire and gain advice about how one achieved this impossible feat—the *we* at the base that generally excluded me did, anyway. The other crew members who'd been selected to fly with him wandered about with the bemused air of pools winners. Walt Williams stories suddenly abounded. Stuff about taking a dead cow up in a Lancaster and dropping it bang into the middle of a particularly disliked squadron leader's prized garden. Stuff about half a dozen top brass wives. Stuff about crash landing upside down on lakes. Stuff about flying for hundreds of miles on two engines or just the one or no engines at all. Stuff about plucking women's washing on his undercarriage and picking apples from passing trees. Amid all this excitement that fizzed around the airfield like the rain on the concrete and the corrugated hangars as the autumn weather heaved in, we seemed to forget that we had told each other many of these stories before, and that they had only gained this new urgency because we could now settle them onto the gaunt face of a particular man who sat smiling and surrounded, yet often seeming alone, at the smoke-filled center of the NAAFI bar.

Being older, being who he was, Walt needed to do little to enhance his reputation other than to climb up into this Lancaster and fly it. That, and parking that rattling sports car the way he did that first day, his loose cuffs and his other minor disregards for all the stupidities of uniform, his chilly gaze, his longer-than-regulation hair, the fact that he was almost ten years older than most of the rest of us and had passed up the chance to be promoted to the positions of the men who were supposedly in charge of him, was more than enough. The fact that, in the flesh, he was surprisingly quiet, and that his long brown hands trembled as he chain-smoked his Dunhill cigarettes, the fact that his smile barely ever wavered yet never reached his eyes, and that it was said, whispered, that the pilot officer in the billet next to his had asked to be moved out on account of the sound of screaming, was as insignificant as Alan Ladd having to stand on a box before he kissed his leading ladies. We all had our own inner version of Walt Williams in those soaringly bright days.

For me, the shadow in bars and dancehall corners, potent in my own opposite way, yet now mostly pitied and ignored, Walt Williams had a special fascination. With little proper company, immersed often enough between work shifts in doleful boredom, I had plenty of time to watch and brood. The base and surrounding countryside made a strange world that winter. I walked the dikes. I saw blood on the frost where the farmers set traps to catch the foxes, and felt my own blood turn and change with the ebb and flow of the bomber's moon. Ice on the runways, ice hanging like fairy socks on the radio spars as the messages came in each morning. The smell of the sea blown in over the land. In my dreams, I saw the figures of crewmen entering the NAAFI, charcoaled and blistered, riddled with bleeding worm holes or grayly bloated from the ocean and seeping brine. Only Walt Williams, laughing for once, his diamond eyes blazing, stood whole and immune.

Walt was already halfway through his tour by the time Christmas came and the consensus amongst those who knew was that he was an unfussy pilot, unshowy. Rather like the best kind of footballer, he drifted in, found the right place, the right time, then drifted out again. I stood and watched him from my own quiet corners in the barroom, nursing my quiet drinks. I even got to feel that I knew Walt Williams better than any of the others, because I actually made it my business to study him, the man and not the legend. He always seemed to be ahead of everything that was happening, but I saw that there was a wariness in the way he watched people, and a mirrored grace in how he responded, as if he'd learned the delicate dance of being human, of making all the right moves, but, offstage and in the darkness of his hut where that pilot who was dead now had said he'd heard screaming, he was something else entirely. And there were things—apart from never having to buy drinks—that Walt Williams never did. Games, bets, cards. He always slipped back then, so smoothly and easily you'd have to be watching from as far away as I was to actually notice. It was as if he was frightened to use his luck up on anything so trivial, whereas most of the other crewmen, fired up and raw through these times of waiting, were always chasing a ball, a winning hand, thunking in the darts and throwing dice and making stupid bets on anything that moved, including us girls.

Watching Walt as I did, I suppose he must have noticed me. And he must have heard about me, too, just as everyone else here at the base had. Sometimes, on the second or third port and lemon, I'd just stare at him from my empty corner and will him, dare him, to stare back at me.

But he never did. Those sapphire eyes, quick as they were, never quite touched on me. He *must*, I thought. He must look *now*. But never, never. Except when I stood up and left, and I felt his presence behind me like the touch of cool fingers on my neck. So strong and sharp was that feeling one night as I stepped down the wooden steps outside the NAAFI that I almost turned and went straight back in to confront him through those admiring crowds. But loneliness had become a habit by now, and I almost clung to my reputation. I wandered off, away from the billets and into the empty darkness of the airfield. There was no moon, but a seemingly endless field of stars. Not a bomber's night, but the kind of night you see on Christmas cards. After a week's rain, and then this sudden frost, I could feel the ground crackling and sliding beneath me. The NAAFI door swung open again, and bodies tumbled out. As they turned from the steps and made to sway arm-in-arm off to bed, I heard the crash of fresh ice and the slosh of water as they broke into a huge puddle. They squelched off, laughing and cursing. Standing there in the darkness, I watched the same scene play itself out over and over again. The splash of cold, filthy water. One man even fell into it. Freezing though I was, I took an odd satisfaction in watching this little scene repeat itself. Now, I thought, if they could see me as well as I can see them, standing in the darkness watching the starlight shining on that filthy puddle, they really would know I'm strange. Chop girl. Witch. Death incarnate. They'd burn me at the stake. . . .

I'd almost forgotten about Walt Williams when he finally came out, although I knew it was him. Instantly. He paused on the steps and looked up at the sky as I'd seen other aircrew do, judging what the next night would bring. As he did so, his shadow seemed to quiver. But he still walked like Walt Williams when he stepped down onto the frozen turf, and his breath plumed like anyone else's, and I knew somehow, knew in a way that I had never had before, that this time he really didn't know that I was there, and that he was off-guard in a way I'd never seen him. The next event was stupid, really. A non-event. Walt Williams just walked off with that loose walk of his, his hands stuffed into his pockets. He was nearly gone from sight into his Nissen hut when I realized the one thing that hadn't happened. Even though he'd taken the same route as everyone else, he hadn't splashed into that wide, deep puddle. I walked over to it, disbelieving, and tried to recall whether I'd even heard the crackle of his footsteps on the ice. And the puddle was even darker, wider, and filthier than I'd imagined. The kind of puddle you only get at places military. I was stooping at the edge of it, and my own ankles and boots were already filthy, when the NAAFI door swung open again, and a whole group of people suddenly came out. Somebody was holding the door, and the light flooded right toward me.

Even though I was sure they must all have seen me and knew who I was, I got up and scurried away.

All in all, it was a strange winter. We were getting used to Allied victories, and there'd even been talk of a summer invasion of France that had never happened. But we knew it would come next summer now that the Yanks had thrown their weight into it, and that the Russians wouldn't give up advancing, that it was really a matter of time until the war ended. But for us, that wasn't reassuring, because we knew that peace was still so far away, and we knew that the risks and the fatalities would grow even greater on the journey to it. Aircrew were scared in any case of thinking further than the next drink, the next girl, the next mission. Peace for them was a strange white god they could worship only at the risk of incurring the wrath of the darker deity who still reigned over them. So there was an extra wildness to the jollification when that year's end drew near, and a dawning realization that, whether we lived or died, whether we came out of it all maimed and ruined or whole and happy, no one else would ever understand.

There was a big pre-Christmas bash in a barn of the great house of the family that had once owned most of the land you could see from the top of our windsock tower. Of course, the house itself had been requisitioned, although the windows were boarded or shattered and the place was empty as we drove past it, and I heard later that it was never reoccupied after the war and ended up being slowly vandalized until it finally burnt down in the fifties. The barn was next to the stables and faced into a wide cobbled yard, and, for once, out here in the country darkness and a million miles from peace or war, no one gave a bugger about the blackout, and there were smoking lanterns hanging by the pens where fine white horses would once have nosed their heads. It was freezing, but you couldn't feel cold, not in that sweet orange light, not once the music had started, and the squadron leader himself, looking ridiculous in a pinny, began ladling out the steaming jam jars of mulled wine. And I was happy to be there, too, happy to be part of this scene with the band striking up on a stage made of bales. When Walt arrived, alone as usual in his rusty MG, he parked in the best spot between the trucks and climbed out with that fragile grace of his. Walt Williams standing there in the flamelight, a modern prince with the tumbling chimneys of that empty old house looming behind him. A perfect, perfect scene.

I did dance, once or twice, with some of the other girls and a few of the older men who worked in the safety of accounts and stores and took pity on me. I even had a five-minute word—just like everyone else, kindly man that he was, and spectrally thin though the war had made him—with our squadron leader. As far away from everything as we were, people thought it was safe here to get in that bit closer to me. But it was hard for me to keep up my sense of jollity, mostly standing and sitting alone over such a long evening, and no chance of going back to base until far after midnight. So I did my usual trick of backing off, which was easier here than it was in the NAAFI. I could just drift out of the barn and across the cobbles, falling through layers of smoke and kicked-up dust until I became part of the night. I studied them all for a while, remembering a picture from *Peter Pan* that had showed the Indians and the Lost Boys dancing around a campfire.

Couples were drifting out now into the quiet behind the vans. I tried to remember what it was like, the way you could conjure up that urgency between flesh and flesh. But all I could think of was some man's male thing popping out like a dog's, and I walked further off into the dark, disgusted. I wandered around the walls of the big and empty house with its smell of damp and nettles, half-feeling my way down steps and along balustrades, moving at this late and early hour amid the pale shadows of huge statuary. It wasn't fully quiet here, this far away from the throb of the barn. Even in midwinter, there were things shuffling and creaking and breaking. Tiny sounds, and the bigger ones that came upon you just when you'd given up waiting. The hoot of an owl. The squeak of a mouse. The sound of a fox screaming. . . .

Perhaps I'd fallen asleep, for I didn't hear him coming, or at least didn't separate out the sound of his footsteps from my thoughts, which had grown as half-unreal as those dim statues, changing and drifting. So I simply waited in the darkness as one of the statues began to move, and knew without understanding that it was Walt Williams. He sat beside me on whatever kind of cold stone bench I was sitting, and he still had the smell of the barn on him, the heat and the drink and the smoke and the firelight. The only thing he didn't carry with him was the perfume of a woman. I honestly hadn't realized until that moment that this was another item I should have added to my long list of the things Walt Williams avoided. But somehow that fact had been so obvious that even I hadn't noticed it. It wouldn't have seemed right, anyway. Walt and just one woman. Not with the whole base depending on him.

I watched the flare of the match, and saw the peaked outline of his face as he stooped to catch it with two cigarettes. Then I felt his touch as he passed one to me. One of those long, posh fags of his, which

tasted fine and sweet, although it was odd to hold compared with the
stubby NAAFI ones because the glow of it came from so far away. No
one else, I thought, would ever do this for me—sit and smoke a fag
like this. Only Walt.

He finally ground his cigarette out in a little shower of sparks beneath his shoe. I did the same, more by touch than anything.

"So you're the girl we're all supposed to avoid?"

Pointless though it was in this darkness, I nodded.

It was the first time I'd heard him laugh. Like his voice, the sound
was fine and light. "The things people believe!"

"It's true, though, isn't it? It *is,* although I don't understand why.
It may be that it's only because . . ." I trailed off. I'd never spoken about
being the chop girl to anyone before. What I'd wanted to say was that
it was our believing that had made it happen.

I heard the rustle of his packet as he took out another cigarette.
"Another?"

I shook my head. "You of all people. You shouldn't be here with
me."

The match flared. I felt smoke on my face, warm and invisible.
"That's where you're wrong. You and me, we'd make the ideal couple.
Don't bother to say otherwise. I've seen you night after night in the
NAAFI. . . ."

"Not every night."

"But enough of them."

"And *I* saw you, that night. I saw you walk over that puddle."

"What night was that?"

So I explained—and in the process I gave up any pretense that I
hadn't been watching him.

"I really don't remember," he said when I'd finished, although he
didn't sound that surprised. This time, before he ground out his cigarette,
he used it to light another. "But why should I? It was just a puddle.
Lord knows, there are plenty around the base."

"But it was *there.* I was *watching.* You just walked over it."

He made a sound that wasn't quite a cough. "Hasn't everyone told
you who I am? I'm Walt Williams. I'm lucky."

"But it's more than that, isn't it?"

Walt said nothing for a long while, and I watched the nervous arc
of his cigarette rising and falling. And when he did begin to speak, it
wasn't about the war, but about his childhood. Walt told me he'd come
from a well-to-do family in the Home Counties, a place that always
made me think of the BBC and pretty lanes with tall flowering hedges.
He was the only child, but a big investment, as was always made clear

to him, of his mother's time, his father's money. At first, to hear Walt talk, he really was the image of those lads I'd imagined I'd meet when I joined the RAF. He'd gone to the right schools. He really had played cricket—if only just the once when the usual wicket keeper was ill—for his county. His parents had him lined up to become an accountant. But Walt would have none of that, and my image of his kind of childhood, which was in all the variegated golds and greens of striped lawns and fine sunsets, changed as he talked, like a film fading. His mother, he said, had a routine that she stuck to rigidly. Every afternoon, when she'd come back from whatever it was that she always did on that particular day, she'd sit in the drawing room with her glass and her sherry decanter beside her. She'd sit there, and she'd wait for the clock to chime five, and then she'd ring for the maid to come and pour her drink for her. Every afternoon, the same.

Walt Williams talked on in the darkness. And at some point, I began to hear the ticking rattle of something which I thought at first was his keys or his coins, the kind of nervous habit that most pilots end up getting. It didn't sound quite right, but by then I was too absorbed in what he was saying. Flying, once Walt had discovered it, had been his escape, although, because of the danger to their precious investment of time and good schools and money, his parents disapproved of it even as a hobby. They cut off his money, and what there was of their affection. Walt worked in garages and then on the airfields, and flew whenever he could. He even toured with a circus. The rattling sound continued as he spoke, and I sensed a repeated sweeping movement of his hand that he was making across the stone on which we were sitting, as if he was gently trying to scrub out some part of these memories.

Then the war came, and even though the RAF's discipline, and the regularity, were the same things that he detested in his parents, Walt was quick to volunteer. But he liked the people, or many of them, and he came to admire the big and often graceless military planes. The kind of flying he'd done, often tricks and arobatics, Walt was used to risk; he opted for bombers rather than fighters because, like anyone who's in a fundamentally dangerous profession, he looked for ways in which he thought, wrongly as it turned out, the risk could be minimized. And up in the skies and down on the ground, he sailed through his war. He dropped his bombs, and he wasn't touched by the world below him. Part of him knew that he was being even more heartless than the machines he was flying, but the rest of him knew that if he was to survive it was necessary to fly through cold, clear and untroubled skies of his own making.

The faint sound of the band in the barn had long faded, and I could see the sweep and movement of Walt's hand more clearly now, and the clouds of our breath and his cigarette smoke hanging like the shapes of the statues around us. I had little difficulty in picturing Walt as he described the kind of pilot he'd once been; the kind who imagined, despite all the evidence, that nothing would ever happen to him. Not that Walt believed in luck back then—he said he only went along with the rituals so as not to unsettle his crew—but at a deeper and unadmitted level, and just like all the rest of us, luck had become fundamental to him.

In the big raids that were then starting, which were the revenge for the raids that the Germans had launched against us, so many bombers poured across their cities that they had to go over in layers. Some boffin must have worked out that the chance of a bomb landing on a plane flying beneath was small enough to be worth taking. But in a mass raid over Frankfurt, flying through dense darkness, there was a sudden jolt and a blaze of light, and Walt's top gunner reported that a falling incendiary had struck their starboard wing. Expecting a fuel line to catch at any moment, or for a night fighter to home in on them now that they were shining like a beacon, they dropped their load and turned along the home flight path. But the night fighters didn't come, and the wind blasting across the airframe stopped the incendiary from fully igniting. Hours went by, and they crossed the coast of France into the Channel just as the night was paling. The whole crew were starting to believe that their luck would hold, and were silently wondering how to milk the most drama out of the incident in the bar that evening when the whole plane was suddenly ripped apart as the wing, its spar damaged by the heat of that half-burning incendiary, tore off into the slipstream. In a fraction of a moment, the bomber became a lump of tumbling, flaming metal.

There was nothing then but the wild push of falling, and the sea, the sky, the sea flashing past them and the wind screaming as the bomber turned end over end and they tried to struggle from their harnesses and climb out through the doorways or the gaping hole that the lost wing had made. Walt said it was like being wedged in a nightmare fairground ride, and that all he could think of was having heard somewhere that the sea was hard as concrete when you hit it. That, and not wanting to die; that, and needing to be lucky. In a moment of weightlessness, globules of blood floated around him, and he saw his co-pilot with a spear of metal sticking right through him. There was no way Walt could help. He clambered up the huge height of the falling plane against a force that suddenly twisted and threw him down toward the opening. But he was wedged into it, stuck amid twisted piping and scarcely able to breathe as the tumbling forces gripped him. It was then that the thought came to him—the same thought that must have crossed the minds of thousands of airmen in moments such as these—that he would give anything, *anything* to get out. Anything to stay lucky. . . .

The darkness had grown thin and gauzy. Looking down now, I could see that Walt was throwing two white dice, scooping them up and throwing them again.

"So I was lucky," he said. "I got the parachute open before I hit the sea and my life-jacket went up and I wasn't killed by the flaming wreckage falling about me. But I still thought it was probably a cruel joke, to get this far and freeze to death in the filthy English Channel. Then I heard the sound of an engine over the waves, and I let off my flare. In twenty minutes, this MTB found me. One of ours, too. Of all the crew, I was the only one they found alive. The rest were just bodies. . . ."

I could see the outlines of the trees now through a dawn mist, and of the statues around us, which looked themselves like casualties wrapped in foggy strips of bandage. And I could see the numbers on the two dice that Walt was throwing.

A chill went through me, far deeper than this dawn cold. They went six, six, six . . .

Walt made that sound again. More of a cough than a chuckle. "So that's how it is. I walk over puddles. I fly through tour after tour. I'm the living embodiment of lucky."

"Can't you throw some other number?"

He shook his head and threw again. Six and six. "It's not a trick. Not the kind of trick you might think it is, anyway." Six and six, again. The sound of those rolling bones. The sound of my teeth chattering. "You can try if you like."

"You forget who I am, Walt. I don't need to try. I believe . . ."

Walt pocketed his dice and stood up and looked about him. With that gaze of his. Smiling but unsmiling. It was getting clearer now. The shoulders of my coat were clammy damp when I touched them. My hands were white and my fingertips were blue with the cold. And this place of statues, I finally realized, wasn't actually the garden of the house at all, but a churchyard. Our bench had been a tombstone. We were surrounded by angels.

"Come on . . ." Walt held out his hand to help me up. I took it.

I expected him to head back to his battered MG, but instead he wandered amid the tombstones, hands in his pockets and half-whistling, inspecting the dates and the names, most of which belonged to the family that had lived in that big house beyond the treetops. Close beside us, there was a stone chapel, and Walt pushed at the door until something crumbled and gave, and beckoned me in.

Everything about the graveyard and this chapel was quiet and empty. That's the way it is in a war. There are either places with no people at all, or other places with far too many. The chapel roof was holed and there were pigeon droppings and feathers over the pews, but it still clung to its dignity. And it didn't seem a sad place to me, even though it was decorated with other memorials, because there's a sadness about war that extinguishes the everyday sadnesses of people living and dying. Even the poor brass woman surrounded by swaddled figures, whom Walt explained represented her lost babies, still had a sense of something strong and right about her face. At least she knew she'd given life a chance.

"What I don't understand," I said, crouching beside Walt as he fed odd bits of wood into an old iron stove in a corner, "is *why*. . . ."

Walt struck a match and tossed it into the cobwebbed grate. The flames started licking and cracking. "It's the same with cards. It's the same with everything."

"Can't you . . ."

"Can't I *what*?" He looked straight at me, and I felt again a deeper chill even as the stove's faint heat touched me. I've never seen irises so blue, or pupils so dark, as his. Like a bomber's night. Like the summer sky. I had to look away.

He stood up and fumbled in his pockets for another cigarette. As he lit it, I noticed that once again his hands were shaking.

"After the war, Walt, you could make a fortune. . . ."

He made that sound again, almost a cough; a sound that made me wish I could hear his proper laugh again. And he began to pace and to speak quickly, his footsteps snapping and echoing as the fire smoked and crackled and the pain of its warmth began to seep into me.

"What should I do? Go to a casino—me, the highest roller of them all? How long do you think *that* would last? . . ."

Walt said then that you were never given anything for nothing. Not in life, not in war, not even in fairy tales. Before that night over Frankfurt, he'd sailed through everything. Up in those bomber's skies, you never heard the screams or the sound of falling masonry.

He slowed then, and crouched down again beside me, his whole body shivering as he gazed into the stove's tiny blaze.

"I see it *all* now," he said, and the smile that never met his eyes was gone even from his lips now. "Every bullet. Every bomb. Even in my dreams, it doesn't leave me. . . ."

"It won't last forever, Walt—"

His hand grabbed mine, hard and sharp, and the look in his eyes made me even more afraid. When he spoke, the words were barely a whisper, and his voice was like the voice of poor dead Pilot Officer Charlie Dyson as he pressed himself to me on that distant summer night under the oak tree.

When Walt said he saw it all, he truly meant he saw *everything*. It came to him in flashes and stabs—nightmare visions, I supposed, like those of the dead airmen that had sometimes troubled me. He saw the blood, heard the screams and felt the terrible chaos of falling masonry. He'd been tormented for weeks, he muttered, by the screams of a woman as she was slowly choked by a ruptured sewer pipe flooding her forgotten basement. And it wasn't just Walt's own bombs, his own deeds, but flashes, terrible flashes that he still scarcely dared believe, of the war as a whole, what was happening now, and what would happen in the future. He muttered names I'd never heard of. Belsen. Dachau. Hiro and Naga-something. And he told me that he'd tried walking into the sea to get rid of the terrors he was carrying, but that the tide wouldn't take him. He told me that he'd thought of driving his MG at a brick wall, only he didn't trust his luck—or trusted it too much—to be sure that any accident or deed would kill him. And yes, many of the stories of the things he'd done were true, but then the RAF would tolerate much from its best, its luckiest, pilots. For, at the end of the day, Walt still *was* a pilot—the sky still drew him, just as it always had. And he wanted the war to end like all the rest of us because he knew—far more than I could have then realized—about the evils we were fighting. So he still climbed into his bomber and ascended into those dark skies. . . .

Slowly, then, Walt let go of me. And he pushed back his hair, and ran his hand over his lined face, and then began stooping about collecting more bits of old wood and stick for the fire. After a long time staring into the stove and with some of the cold finally gone from me, I stood up and walked amid the pews, touching the splintery dust and studying the bits of brass and marble from times long ago when people hadn't thought it odd to put a winged skull beside a puffy-cheeked cherub. . . .

Walt was walking up the church now. As I turned to him, I saw him make that effort that he always made, the dance of being the famous Walt Williams, of being human. From a figure made out of winter light and the fire's dull wood smoke, he gave a shiver and became a good-looking man again, still thinly graceful if no longer quite young, and with that smile and those eyes that were like ice and summer. He turned then, and put out his arms, and did a little Fred Astaire dance on the loose stones, his feet taptapping in echoes up to the angels and the cherubs and the skulls. I had to smile. And I went up to him and we met and hugged almost as couples do in films. But we were clumsy as kids as we kissed each other. It had been a long, long time for us both.

We went to the stove to stop ourselves shivering. Walt took off his jacket, and he spread it there before the glow, and there was never any doubt as we looked at each other. That we would go—stupid phrase—all the way.

So that was it. Me and Walt. And in a chapel—a *church*—of all places. And afterward, restless as he still was, still tormented, he pulled his things back on and smoked and wandered about. There was a kind of wooden balcony, a thing called a choir, at the back of the chapel. As I sat huddled by the stove, Walt climbed the steps that led up to it, and bits of dust and splinter fell as he looked down at me and gave a half-smiling wave. I could see that the whole structure was shot through with rot and woodworm, ridiculously unsafe. Then, of all things, he started to do that little Fred Astaire dance of his again, tip-tapping over the boards.

I was sure, as I stared up at Walt from the dying stove, that he danced over empty spaces where the floor had fallen through entirely.

Walt was due back at base that morning, and so was I: we all were. There had already been talk on the wire that tonight, hangover or no hangover, Christmas or no Christmas, there would be a big raid, one of the biggest. Leaving the chapel and walking back under the haggard trees toward the littered and empty barn, which stank of piss and butt ends, we kept mostly silent. And Walt had to lever open the bonnet of his MG and fiddle with the engine before he could persuade it to turn over. He drove slowly, carefully back along the flat roads between the ditches to the airfield where the Lancasters sat like dragonflies on the horizon. No one saw us as we came in through the gates.

Walt touched my cheek and gave that smile of his and I watched him go until he turned from sight between the Nissen huts and annexes, and then hurried off to get dressed and changed for my work. But for the smudge of oil left by his fingers, I could tell myself that none of it had happened, and get on with banging my typewriter keys, ordering mustard by the tub and jam by the barrel and currants by the sack-load as the ordnance trucks trundled their deadly trains of long steel canisters across the concrete and the ground crew hauled fuel bousers and the aircrew watched the maps being unrolled and the pointers pointed at the name of a town in Europe that would mean death for some of them.

There was never long to wait for winter darkness, and the clouds were dense that day. The airfield seemed like the only place of brightness by the time the runway lanterns were lit and the aircrew, distant figures already, threw their last dart and played their last hand and put on their odd socks and whistled or didn't whistle and touched their charms and kissed their scented letters and pressed their fingers to the concrete and walked out to their waiting Lancasters. Standing away from where everyone else had gathered, I watched the impenetrable rituals and tried without success to figure out which dim silhouette was Walt's as they clustered around their Lancasters. And I listened as the huge Merlin engines, one by one, then wave on wave on wave, began to fire up. You felt sorry, then, for the Germans. Just as the sound became unbearable, a green flare flickered and sparkled over the base. At this signal, the pitch of the engines changed as bombers lumbered up to face the wind and slowly, agonizingly, pregnant with explosives and petrol, struggled up the runways to take flight.

That night, it was dark already. All we could do was listen—and wait—as the sound of the last Lancaster faded into that black bomber's sky without incident.

The way things turned out—thanks to a secret war of homing beams and radar—it was a good, successful raid. But Walt Williams didn't come back from it, even though his Lancaster did, and the story of what had happened was slow to emerge, opposed as it was by most people's disbelief that anything could possibly have happened to him.

I made the cold journey across the airfield late that next afternoon to look at his Lancaster. The wind had picked up by then, was tearing at the clouds, and there was a stand-down after all the day and the night before's activity. No one was about, and the machine had been drained of what remained of its ammunition, oil, and fuel, and parked in a distant corner with all the other scrap and wreckage.

It was always a surprise to be up close to one of these monsters, either whole or damaged; to feel just how big they were—and how fragile. I walked beneath the shadow of its wings as they sighed and creaked in the salt-tinged wind from across the Fens, and climbed as I had never climbed before up the crew's ladder, and squeezed through bulkheads and between wires and pipes toward the gray light of the main cabin amid the sickly oil-and-rubber reek.

The rest of the aircrew had reported a jolt and a huge in-rush of air as they took the homeward flight path, but what I saw up there, on that late and windy afternoon, told its own story. Most of the pilot's bubble and the side of the fuselage beside it had been ripped out—struck by a flying piece of debris from another plane, or a flask shell that refused to explode. Walt had been torn out, too, in the sudden blast, launched into the skies so instantly that no one else had really seen exactly what had happened. They'd all hoped, as the co-pilot had nursed the plane back home through the darkness, that Walt might still have survived, and, Walt being Walt, might even make it back through France instead of ending up as a German prisoner. But the morning had revealed that Walt, either intentionally or through some freak of the way the wind had hit him, had undone all the straps from his seat and had fallen without his parachute. Even now, it was still there, unclaimed, nestled in its well. I was able to bend down and touch it as the wind whistled through that ruined aircraft, and feel the hard inner burden of all those reams of silk that might have borne him.

Then, I believed.

I was transferred to another base in the spring after, when my section was reorganized in one of those strange bureaucratic spasms that you get in the military. They'd had their own chop girl there who'd committed suicide by hanging herself a few months before, and they mostly ignored the rumors that came with me. It was as if that poor girl's sacrifice had removed the burden from me. Her sacrifice—and that of Walt Williams.

Still, I was changed by what happened. There were other men with whom I had dates and longer-term romances, and there were other occasions when I went all instead of just part of the way. But Walt's ghost was always with me. That look of his. Those eyes. That lined, handsome face. I always found it hard to settle on someone else, to really believe that they might truly want to love me. And by the time the war had finally ended, I was older, and, with my mother's arthritis and my father's stroke, I soon ended up having to cope with the demands of the tea room almost single-handed. Time's a funny thing. One moment you're eighteen, lucky, lucky, lucky, and enlisting and leaving Manchester forever. The next you're back there, your bones ache every morning, your face is red and puffy from the smoke and the heat of cooking, and the people over the serving counter are calling you Mrs. instead of Miss, even though they probably know you aren't—and never will be—married. Still, I made a success of the business, even if it ruined my back, seared my hands, veined and purpled my face. Kept it going until ten years ago, I did, and the advent down the street of a McDonald's. Now, my life's my own, at least in the sense that it isn't anybody else's. And I keep active and make my way up the hill every week to collect my pension, although the climb seems to be getting steeper.

The dreams of the war still come, though, and thoughts about Walt

Williams—in fact, they're brighter than this present dull and dusty day. I sometimes think, for instance, that if everyone *saw* what Walt saw, if everyone *knew* what was truly happening in wars and suffered something like these visions, the world would become more a peaceable place and people would start to behave decently toward each other. But we have the telly now, don't we? We can all see starving children and bits of bodies in the street. So perhaps you need to be someone special to begin with, to have special gifts for the tasks you're given, and be in a strange and special time when you're performing them. You have to be as lucky and unlucky as Walt Williams was.

And I can tell myself now, as I dared not quite tell myself then, that Walt's life had become unbearable to him. Even though I treasure him for being the Walt who loved me for those few short hours, I know that he sought me out *because* of what I was.

Chop girl.

Death flower.

Witch.

And I sometimes wonder what it was that hit Walt's Lancaster. Whether it really was some skyborne scrap of metal, or whether luck itself hadn't finally become a cold wall, the iron hand of that dark bombers' deity? And, in my darkest and brightest moments, when I can no longer tell if I'm feeling sad or desperately happy, I think of him walking across that foul puddle in the starlight as he came out of the NAAFI, and as I watched him in an old chapel after we'd made love, dancing across the choir above me on nothing but dust and sunlight. And I wonder if someone as lucky as Walt Williams could ever touch the ground without a parachute to save him, and if he isn't still out there in the skies that he loved. Still falling.

KELLY LINK

The Girl Detective

Short story writer Kelly Link is one of the most exciting new talents in the fantasy field today. This young writer won the James Tiptree, Jr. Award for "Travels with the Snow Queen" and the World Fantasy Award for "The Specialist's Hat," both of which were reprinted in The Year's Best Fantasy and Horror: Twelfth Annual Collection. *Link was raised in North Carolina, currently lives in the Boston area, and will soon be moving to Brooklyn. Her fiction has appeared in* Century, Asimov's, *and on the Internet.*

"The Girl Detective" mixes imagery from myths, fairy tales, teen detective novels, and other literary sources. This impressive (and witty) story first appeared in the March 1999 edition of the Event Horizon *web site, www.eventhorizon.com.*

—T. W.

The girl detective looked at her reflection in the mirror. This was a different girl. This was a girl who would chew gum.   *—CAROLYN KEENE*

The girl detective's mother is missing.

The girl detective's mother has been missing for a long time.

The underworld.

Think of the underworld as the back of your closet, behind all those racks of clothes that you don't wear anymore. Things are always getting pushed back there and forgotten about. The underworld is full of things that you've forgotten about. Some of them, if only you could remember, you might want to take them back. Trips to the underworld are always very nostalgic. It's darker in there. The seasons don't match. Mostly people end up there by accident, or else because in the end there was nowhere else to go. Only heroes and girl detectives go to the underworld on purpose.

There are three kinds of food.

One is the food that your mother makes for you. One is the kind of food that you eat in restaurants. One is the kind of food that you eat in dreams. There's one other kind of food, but you can only get that in the underworld, and it's not really food. It's more like dancing.

The girl detective eats dreams.

The girl detective won't eat her dinner. Her father, the housekeeper—they've tried everything they can think of. Her father takes her out to eat—Chinese restaurants, once even a truck stop two states away for chicken fried steak. The girl detective used to love chicken fried steak. Her father has gained ten pounds, but the girl detective will only have a glass of water, not even a slice of lemon. I saw them once at that new restaurant downtown, and the girl detective was folding her napkin while her father ate. I went over to their table after they'd left. She'd folded her napkin into a swan. I put it into my pocket, along with her dinner roll, and a packet of sugar. I thought these things might be clues.

The housekeeper cooks all the food that the girl detective used to love. Green beans, macaroni and cheese, parsnips, stewed pears—the girl detective used to eat all her vegetables. The girl detective used to love vegetables. She always cleaned her plate. If only her mother were still here, the housekeeper will say, and sigh. The girl detective's father sighs. Aren't you the littlest bit hungry? they ask her. Wouldn't you like a bite to eat? But the girl detective still goes to bed hungry.

There is some debate about whether the girl detective needs to eat food at all. Is it possible that she is eating in secret? Is she anorexic? Bulimic? Is she protesting something? What could we cook that would tempt her?

I am doing my best to answer these very questions. I am detecting the girl detective. I sit in a tree across the street from her window, and this is what I see. The girl detective goes to bed hungry, but she eats our dreams while we are asleep. She has eaten my dreams. She has eaten your dreams, one after the other, as if they were grapes, or oysters. The girl detective is getting fat on other people's dreams.

The case of the tap-dancing bank robbers.

Just a few days ago, I saw this on the news. You remember, that bank downtown. Maybe you were in line for a teller, waiting to make a deposit. Perhaps you saw them come in. They had long, long legs, and they were wearing sequins. Feathers. Not much else. They wore tiny black dominos, with stacks of hair piled up on top, and their mouths were wide and red. Their eyes glittered.

You were being interviewed on the news. "We all thought that someone in the bank must be having a birthday," you said. "They had on these skimpy outfits. There was music playing."

They spun. They pranced. They kicked. They were carrying purses, and they took tiny black guns out of their purses. Sit down on the floor, one of them told you. You sat on the floor. Sitting on the floor, it was possible to look up their short, flounced skirts. You could see their underwear. It was satin, and embroidered with the days of the week. There were twelve bank robbers: Monday, Tuesday, Wednesday, Thursday, Friday, Saturday, Sunday, and then Mayday, Payday, Yesterday, Someday, and Birthday. The one who had spoken to you was Birthday. She seemed to be the leader. She went over to a teller, and pointed the little gun at him. They spoke earnestly. They went away, through a door over to the side. All the other bank robbers went with them, except for Wednesday and Thursday, who were keeping an eye on you. They shuffled a little on the marble floor as they waited. They did a couple of pliés. They kept their guns pointed at the security guard, who had been asleep on a chair by the door. He stayed asleep.

In about a minute, the other bank robbers came back through the door again, with the teller. They looked satisfied. The teller looked confused, and he went and sat on the floor next to you. The bank robbers left. Witnesses say they got in a red van with something written in gold on the side, and drove away. The driver was an older woman. She looked stern.

Police are on the lookout for this woman, for this van. When they arrived, what did they find inside the vault? Nothing was missing. In fact, things appeared to have been left behind. Several tons of mismatched socks, several hundred pairs of prescription glasses, retainers, a ball python six feet long, curled decoratively around the bronze vault dial. Also, a woman claiming to be Amelia Earhart. When police questioned this woman, she claimed to remember very little. She remembers a place, police suspect that she was held hostage there by the bank robbers. It was dark, she said, and people were dancing. The food was pretty good. Police have the woman in protective custody, where she has reportedly received serious proposals from lonely men and major publishing houses.

In the past two months the tap-dancing robbers have struck again. Who are these masked women? Speculation is rife. All dance performances, modern, classical, even student rehearsals are well attended. Banks have become popular places to go on dates or on weekdays, during lunch. Some people bring roses to throw. The girl detective is reportedly working on the case.

Secret origins of the girl detective.

Some people say that she doesn't exist. Someone once suggested that I was the girl detective, but I've never known whether or not they were serious. At least I don't think that I am the girl detective. If I were the girl detective, I would surely know.

Things happen.

When the girl detective leaves her father's house one morning, a man is lurking outside. I've been watching him for a while now from my tree. I'm a little stiff, but happy to be here. He is a fat man with pouched, beautiful eyes. He sighs heavily a few times. He takes the girl detective by the arm. Can I tell you a story, he says.

All right, says the girl detective politely. She takes her arm back, sits down on the front steps. The man sits down beside her and lights a smelly cigar.

The girl detective saves the world.

The girl detective has saved the world on at least three separate occasions. Not that she is bragging.

The girl detective doesn't care for fiction.

The girl detective doesn't actually read much. She doesn't have the time. Her father used to read fairy tales to her when she was little. She didn't like them. For example, the twelve dancing princesses. If their father really wants to stop them, why doesn't he just forbid the royal shoemaker to make them any more dancing shoes? Why do they have to go

underground to dance? Don't they have a ballroom? Do they like dancing, or are they secretly relieved when they get caught? Who taught
them to dance?

The girl detective has thought a lot about the twelve dancing princesses. She and the princesses have a few things in common. For instance, shoe leather. Possibly underwear. Also, no mother. This is
another thing about fiction, fairy tales in particular. The mother is usually missing. The girl detective imagines, all of a sudden, all of these
mothers. They're all in the same place. They're far away, some place
she can't find them. It infuriates her. What are they up to, all of these
mothers?

The fat man's story.

This man has twelve daughters, says the fat man. All of them lookers.
Nice gams. He's a rich man, but he doesn't have a wife. He has to take
care of the girls all by himself. He does the best he can. The oldest one
is still living at home when the youngest one graduates from high
school. This makes their father happy. How can he take care of them if
they move away from home?

But strange things start to happen. The girls all sleep in the same
bedroom, which is fine, no problem, because they all get along great.
But then the girls start to sleep all day. He can't wake them up. It's as
if they've been drugged. He brings in specialists. The specialists all
shake their heads.

At night the girls wake up. They're perky. Affectionate. They apply
makeup. They whisper and giggle. They eat dinner with their father,
and everyone pretends that everything's normal. At bedtime they go to
their room and lock the door, and in the morning when their father
knocks on the door to wake them up, gently at first, tapping, then harder,
begging them to open the door, beside each bed is a worn out pair of
dancing shoes.

Here's the thing. He's never even bought them dancing lessons.
They all took horseback riding, tennis, those classes where you learn to
make dollhouse furniture out of cigarette boxes and doilies.

So he hires a detective. Me, says the fat man—you wouldn't think
it, but I used to be young and handsome and quick on my feet. I used
to be a pretty good dancer myself.

The man puffs on his cigar. Are you getting all this? the girl detective calls to me, where I'm sitting up in the tree. I nod. Why don't you
take a hike, she says.

Why we love the girl detective.

We love the girl detective because she reminds us of the children we wish we had. She is courteous, but also brave. She loathes injustice; she is passionate, but also well groomed. She keeps her room neat, but not too neat. She feeds her goldfish. She will get good grades, keep her curfew when it doesn't interfere with fighting crime. She'll come home from an Ivy League college on weekends to do her laundry.

She reminds us of the girl we hope to marry one day. If we ask her, she will take care of us, cook us nutritious meals, find our car keys when we've misplaced them. The girl detective is good at finding things. She will balance the checkbook, plan vacations, and occasionally meet us at the door when we come home from work, wearing nothing but a blue ribbon in her hair. She will fill our eyes. We will bury our faces in her dark, light, silky, curled, frizzed, teased, short, shining, long, shining hair. Tangerine, clove, russet, coal-colored, oxblood, buttercup, clay-colored, tallow, titian, lampblack, sooty, scented hair. The color of her hair will always inflame us.

She reminds us of our mothers.

Dance with Beautiful Girls.

The father hides me in the closet one night, and I wait until the girls all come to bed. It's a big closet. And it smells nice, like girl sweat and cloves and mothballs. I hold onto the sleeve of someone's dress to balance while I'm looking through the keyhole. Don't think I don't go through all the pockets. But all I find is a marble and a deck of cards with the queen of spades missing, a napkin folded into a swan maybe, a box of matches from a Chinese restaurant.

I look through the keyhole, maybe I'm hoping to see one or two of them take off their clothes, but instead they lock the bedroom door and move one of the beds, knock on the floor, and guess what? There's a secret passageway. Down they go, one after the other. They look so demure, like they're going to Sunday school.

I wait a bit, and then I follow them. The passageway is plaster and bricks first, and then it's dirt with packed walls. The walls open up, and we could be walking along, all of us holding hands if we wanted to. It's pretty dark, but each girl has a flashlight. I follow the twelve pairs of feet, in twelve new pairs of kid leather dancing shoes, each in its own little puddle of light. I stretch my hands up and I stand on my toes, but I can't feel the roof of the tunnel anymore. There's a breeze, raising the hair on my neck.

Up till then, I think I know this city pretty well, but we go down and down, me after the last girl, the youngest, and when at last the passageway levels out, we're in a forest. There's this moss on the trunk of the trees, which glows. It looks like paradise by the light of the moss. The ground is soft like velvet, and the air tastes good. I think I must be dreaming, but I reach up and break off a branch.

The youngest girl hears the branch snap and she turns around, but I've ducked behind a tree. So she goes on and we go on.

Then we come to a river. Down by the bank there are twelve young men, Oriental, gangsters by the look of 'em, black hair slicked back, smooth-faced in the dim light and I can see they're all wearing guns under their nice dinner jackets. I stay back in the trees. I think maybe it's the white slave trade, but the girls go peaceful, and they're smiling and laughing with their escorts, so I stay back in the trees and think for a bit. Each man rows one of the girls across the river in a little canoe. Me, I wait a while and then I get in a canoe and start rowing myself across, quiet as I can. The water is black, and there's a bit of a current, as if it knows where it's going. I don't quite trust this water. I get close to the last boat with the youngest girl in it, and water from my oar splashes up and gets her face wet, I guess, because she says to the man, someone's out there.

Alligator, maybe, he says, and I swear he looks just like the waiter who brought me orange chicken in that new restaurant downtown. I'm so close, I swear they must see me, but they don't seem to. Or maybe they're just being polite.

We all get out on the other side, and there's a nightclub all lit up with paper lanterns on the veranda. Men and women are standing out on the veranda, and there's a band playing inside. It's the kind of music that makes you start tapping your feet. It gets inside me and starts knocking inside my head. By now I think the girls must have seen me, but they don't look at me. They seem to be ignoring me. "Well, here they are," this one woman says. "Hello, girls." She's tall, and so beautiful she looks like a movie star, but she's stern looking too, like she probably plays villains. She's wearing one of those tight silky dresses with dragons on it, but she's not Oriental.

"Now let's get started," she says. Over the door of the nightclub is a sign that says "Dance with Beautiful Girls." They go in. I wait a bit and go in too.

I dance with the oldest and I dance with the youngest, and of course they pretend that they don't know me, but they think I dance pretty fine. We shimmy and we grind, we bump and we do the Charleston. This girl, she opens up her legs for me, but she's got her hands down in an X, and then her knees are back together and her arms fly open like she's going to grab me, and then her hands are crossing over and back on her knees again. I lift her up in the air by her armpits, and her skirt flies up. She's standing on the air like it was solid as the dance floor, and when I put her back down, she moves on the floor like it was air. She just floats. Her feet are tapping the whole time, and sparks are flying up from her shoes and my shoes and everybody's shoes. I dance with a lot of girls, and they're all beautiful, just like the sign says, even the ones who aren't. And when the band starts to sound tired, I sneak out the door and back across the river, back through the forest, back up the secret passageway into the girls' bedroom.

I get back in the closet and wipe my face on someone's dress. The sweat is dripping off me. Pretty soon the girls come home too, limping a little bit, but smiling. They sit down on their beds, and they take off their shoes. Sure enough, their shoes are worn right through. Mine aren't much better.

That's when I step out of the closet and while they're all screaming, lamenting, shrieking, scolding, yelling, cursing, I unlock the bedroom door and let their father in. He's been waiting there all night. He's hangdog. There are circles under his eyes. Did you follow them? he says.

I did, I say.

Did you stick to them? he says. He won't look at them.

I did, I say. I give him the branch. A little bit later, when I get to know the oldest girl, we get married. We go out dancing almost every night, but I never see that club again.

There are two kinds of names.

The girl detective has learned to distrust certain people. People who don't blink enough, for example. People who don't fidget. People who dance too well. People who are too fat or too thin. People who cry and don't need to blow their noses afterwards. People with certain kinds of names are prone to wild and extravagant behavior. Sometimes they turn to a life of crime. If only their parents had been more thoughtful. These people have names like Bernadette, Sylvester, Arabella, Apocolopus, Thaddeus, Gertrude, Gomez, Xavier, Xerxes. Flora. They wear sinister lipsticks, plot world destruction, ride to the hounds, take up archery instead of bowling. They steal inheritances, wear false teeth, hide wills, shoplift, plot murders, take off their clothes and dance on tables in crowded bars just after everyone has gotten off work.

On the other hand, it doesn't do to trust people named George or Maxine, or Sandra, or Bradley. People with names like this are obviously hiding something. Men who limp. Who have crooked, or too many teeth. People who don't floss. People who are stingy, or who leave overgenerous tips. People who don't wash their hands after going to the bathroom. People who want things too badly. The world is a dangerous place, full of people who don't trust each other. This is why I am staying up in this tree. I wouldn't come down even if she asked me to.

The girl detective is looking for her mother.

The girl detective has been looking for her mother for a long time. She doesn't expect her mother to be easy to find. After all, her mother is also a master of disguises. If we fail to know the girl detective when she comes to find us, how will the girl detective know her mother?

She sees her sometimes in other people's dreams. Look at the way this woman is dreaming about goldfish, her mother says. And the girl detective tastes the goldfish, and something is revealed to her. Maybe a broken heart, maybe something about money, or a holiday that the woman is about to take. Maybe the woman is about to win the lottery.

Sometimes the girl detective thinks she is missing her mother's point. Maybe the thing she is supposed to be learning is not about vacations or broken hearts or lotteries or missing wills or any of these things. Maybe her mother is·trying to tell the girl detective how to get to where she is. In the meantime, the girl detective collects the clues from other people's dreams, and we ask her to find our missing pets, to tell us if our spouses are being honest with us, to tell us who are really our friends, and to keep an eye on the world while we are sleeping.

About three o'clock this morning, the girl detective pushed up her window and looked at me. She looked like she hadn't been getting much sleep either. "Are you still up in that tree?"

Why we fear the girl detective.

She reminds us of our mothers. She eats our dreams. She knows what we have been up to, what we are longing for. She knows what we are capable of, and what we are not capable of.

She is looking for something. We are afraid that she is looking for us. We are afraid that she is not looking for us. Who will find us, if the girl detective does not?

The girl detective asks a few questions.

"I think I've heard this story before," the girl detective says to the fat man.

"It's an old story."

The man stares at her sadly, and she stares back. "So why are you telling me?"

"Don't know," he says. "My wife disappeared a few months ago. I mean, she passed on, she died. I can't find her is what I mean. But I thought that maybe if someone could find that club again, she might be there. But I'm old, and her father's house burned down thirty years ago. I can't even find that Chinese restaurant anymore."

"Even if I found the club," the girl detective says, "if she's dead, she probably won't be there. And if she is there, she may not want to come back."

"I guess I know that too, girlie," he says. "But to talk about her, how I met her. Stuff like that helps. Besides, you don't know. She might be there. You never know about these things."

He gives her a photograph of his wife.

"What was your wife's name?" the girl detective says.

"I've been trying to remember that myself," he says.

Some things that have recently turned up in bank vaults.

Lost pets. The crew and passengers of the *Mary Celeste*. More socks. Several boxes of Christmas tree ornaments. A play by Shakespeare, about star-crossed lovers. It doesn't end well. Wedding rings. Some albino alligators. Several tons of seventh grade homework. Ballistic missiles. A glass slipper. Some African explorers. A whole party of Himalayan mountain climbers. Children, whose faces I knew from milk cartons. The rest of that poem by Coleridge. Also fortune cookies.

Further secret origins of the girl detective.

Some people say that she was the child of missionaries, raised by wolves, that she is the Princess Anastasia, last of the Romanovs. Some people say that she is actually a man. Some people say that she came here from another planet, and that some day, when she finds what she is looking for, she'll go home. Some people are hoping that she will take us with her.

If you ask them what she is looking for, they shrug and say, "Ask the girl detective."

Some people say that she is two thousand years old.

Some people say that she is not one girl, but many—that is, she's actually a secret society of Girl Scouts. Or possibly a sub-branch of the FBI.

Who does the girl detective love?

Remember that boy, Fred, or Nat? Something like that. He was in love with the girl detective, even though she was smarter than him, even though he never got to rescue her even once from the bad guys, or when he did, she was really just letting him, to be kind. He was a nice boy with a good sense of humor, but he used to have this recurring dream in which he was a golden retriever. The girl detective knew this, of course, the way she knows all our dreams. How could she settle down with a boy who dreamed that he was a retriever?

Everyone has seen the headlines. "Girl Detective Spurns Head of State." "I Caught My Husband in Bed with the Girl Detective." "Married Twenty Years, Husband and Father of Four, Revealed to Be the Girl Detective."

I myself was the girl detective's lover for three happy months. We met every Thursday night in a friend's summer cottage beside a small lake. She introduced herself as Pomegranate Buhm. I was besotted with her, her long legs so pale they looked like two slices of moonlight when we lay in bed together. I loved her size eleven feet, her black hair that always smelled like grapefruit. When we made love, she stuck her chewing gum on the headboard. Her underwear was embroidered with the days of the week.

We always met on Thursday, as I have said, but according to her underwear, we also met on Saturdays, on Wednesdays, on Mondays, Tuesdays, and once, memorably, on a Friday. That Friday, or rather, that Thursday, she had a tattoo of a grandfather clock beneath her right breast. I licked it, surreptitiously, but it didn't come off. The previous Thursday (Monday, according to the underwear) it had been under her left breast. I think I began to suspect then, although I said nothing, and neither did she.

The next Thursday the tattoo was back, tucked discreetly under the left breast, but it was too late. It ended as I slept, dreaming about the waitress at Frank's Inland Seafood, the one with Monday nights off, with the gap between her teeth and the freckles on her ass. I was dreaming that she and I were on a boat out on the middle of the lake. There was a hole in the bottom of the boat. I was putting something in it—to keep the water out—when I became aware that there was another woman watching us, an older woman, tall with a stern expression. She was standing on the water as if it were a dance floor. "Did you think she wouldn't find out?" she said. The waitress pushed me away, pulling her underwear back up. The boat wobbled. This waitress's underwear had a word embroidered on it: Payday.

I woke up and the girl detective was sitting beside me on the bed, stark naked and dripping wet. The shower was still running. She had a strange expression on her face, as if she'd just eaten a large meal and it was disagreeing with her.

"I can explain everything," I said. She shrugged and stood up. She walked out of the room stark naked, and the next time I saw her, it was two years later and she was disguised as an office lady in a law firm in downtown Tokyo, tapping out Morse code on the desk with one long, petal pink fingernail. It was something about expense accounts, or possibly a dirty limerick. She winked at me and I fell in love all over.

But I never saw the waitress again.

What the girl detective eats for dinner.

The girl detective lies down on her bed and closes her eyes. Possibly the girl detective has taken the fat man's case. Possibly she is just tired. Or curious.

All over the city, all over the world, people are asleep. Sitting up in my tree, I am getting tired just thinking about them. They are dreaming about their children, they are dreaming about their mothers, they are dreaming about their lovers. They dream that they can fly. They dream that the world is round like a dinner plate. Some of them fall off the world in their dreams. Some of them dream about food. The girl detective walks through these dreams. She picks an apple off a tree in someone's dream. Someone else is dreaming about the house they lived in as a child. The girl detective breaks off a bit of their house. It pools in her mouth like honey.

The woman down the street is dreaming about her third husband, the one who ran off with his secretary. That's what she thinks. He went for takeout one night, five years ago, and never came back. It was a long time ago. His secretary said she didn't know a thing about it, but the woman could tell the other woman was lying. Or maybe he ran away and joined the circus.

There is a man who lives in her basement, although the woman doesn't know it. He's got a television down there, and a small refrigerator, and a couch that he sleeps on. He's been living there for the past two years, very quietly. He comes up for air at night. The woman wouldn't recognize this man if she bumped into him on the street. They were married about twenty years, and then he went to pick up the lo mein and the wontons and the shrimp fried rice, and it's taken him a while to get back home. He still had his set of keys. She hasn't been down in the basement in years. It's hard for her to get down the stairs.

The man is dreaming too. He's working up his courage to go upstairs and walk out the front door. In his dream he walks out to the street and then turns around. He'll walk right back up to the front door, ring the bell. Maybe they'll get married again someday. Maybe she never divorced him. He's dreaming about their honeymoon. They'll go out for dinner. Or they'll go down in the basement, down through the trapdoor into the underworld. He'll show her the sights. He'll take her dancing.

The girl detective takes a bite of the underworld.

Chinese restaurants.

I used to eat out a lot. I had a favorite restaurant, which had really good garlic shrimp, and I liked the pancakes too, the scallion pancakes. But you have to be careful. I knew someone, their fortune said, "Your life right now is like a roller coaster. But don't worry, it will soon be over." Now what is that supposed to mean?

Then it happened to me. The first fortune was like a slap in the face. "No one will ever love you the way that you love them." I thought about it. Maybe it was true. I came back to the restaurant a week later, and I ordered the shrimp, and I ate it, and when I opened the fortune cookie, it said, "Your friends are not who you think they are."

I became uneasy. I thought I would stay away for a few weeks. I ate Thai food instead. Italian. But the thing is, I still wasn't safe. No restaurants are safe—except maybe truck stops, or automats. Waiters, waitresses—they pretend to be kind. They bring us what we ask for. They ask us if there is anything else we want. They are solicitous of our health. They remember our names when we come back again. They are as kind to us as if they were our own mothers, and we are familiar with them. Sometimes we pinch their fannies.

I don't like to cook for myself. I live alone, and there doesn't seem to be much point to it. Sometimes I dream about food—for instance, a cake, it was made of whipped cream, mostly. It was the size of a living room. Just as I was about to take a bite, a dancing girl kicked out of it.

Then another dancing girl. A whole troop of dancing girls, in fact, all covered in whipped cream. They were delicious.

I like to eat food made by other people. It feels like a relationship. But you can't trust other people. Especially not waiters. They aren't our friends, you see. They aren't our mothers. They don't give us the food that we long for—not the food that we dream about, although they could. If they wanted to.

We ask them for recommendations about the menu, but they know so much more than that—if only they should choose to tell us. They do not choose to tell us. Their kindnesses are arbitrary, and not to be counted as lasting. We sit here in this world, and the food that they bring us isn't of this world, not entirely. They are not like us. They serve a great mystery.

I returned to the Chinese restaurant like a condemned man. I ate my last meal. A party of women in big hats and small dresses sat at the table next to me. They ordered their food, and then departed for the bathroom. Did they ever come back? I never saw them come back.

The waiter brought me the check, and a fortune cookie. I uncurled my fortune and read my fate. "You will die at the hands of a stranger." As I went away, the waiter smiled at me. His smile was inscrutable.

I sit here in my tree, eating takeout food, hauled up on a bit of string. I put my binoculars down to eat. Who knows what my fortune will say?

What color is the girl detective's hair?

Some people say that the girl detective is a natural blonde. Others say that she's a redhead, how could the girl detective be anything else? Her father just smiles and says, She looks just like her mother. I myself am not even sure that the girl detective remembers the original color of her hair. She is a master of disguises. I feel I should make it clear that no one has ever seen the girl detective in the same room as the aged housekeeper. She and her father have often been seen dining out together, but I repeat, the girl detective is a master of disguises. She is capable of anything.

Further secret origins of the girl detective.

Some people say that a small child in a grocery store bit her. It was one of those children who are constantly asking its parents why the sky is blue and are there really giant alligators—formerly the pets of other small children—living in the sewers of the city and if China is directly below us, could we drill a hole and go right through the center of the earth and if so would we come up upside-down and so on. This child, radioactive with curiosity, bit the girl detective and in that instant the girl detective suddenly saw all of these answers, all at once. She was so overcome she had to lie down in the middle of the aisle with the breakfast cereal on one side and the canned tomatoes on the other, and the store manager came over and asked if she was all right. She wasn't all right, but she smiled and let him help her stand up again, and that night she went home and stitched the days of the week on her underwear, so that if she was ever run over by a car, at least it would be perfectly clear when the accident had occurred. She thought this would make her mother happy.

Why did the girl detective cross the road?

Because she thought she saw her mother.

Why did the girl detective's mother cross the road?

If only the girl detective knew!

The girl detective was very small when her mother left. No one ever speaks of her mother. It causes her father too much pain even to hear her name spoken. To see it written down. Possibly the girl detective was named after her mother, and this is why we must not say her name.

No one has ever explained to the girl detective why her mother left, although it must have been to do something very important. Possibly she died. That would be important enough, almost forgivable.

In the girl detective's room there is a single photograph in a small gold frame of a woman, tall and with a very faint smile, rising up on her toes. Arms flung open, as if to embrace the world outside the photograph. She is wearing a long skirt and a shirt with no sleeves, a pair of worn dancing shoes. She is holding a sheaf of wheat. She looks as if she is dancing. The girl detective supects that this is her mother. She studies the photograph nightly. People dream about lost or stolen things, and this woman, her mother, is always in these dreams.

She remembers a woman walking in front of her. The girl detective was holding this woman's hand. The woman said something to her. It might have been something like, "Always look both ways," or "Always wash your hands after you use a public bathroom," or maybe "I love you," and then the woman stepped into the street. After that, the girl detective isn't sure what happened. There was a van, red and gold, going fast around the corner. On the side was "Eat at Mom's Chinese Restaurant." Or maybe "Eat at Moon's." Maybe it hit the woman. Maybe it stopped, and the woman got in. She said her mother's name then, and no one said anything back.

The girl detective goes out to eat.

I only leave my tree to go to the bathroom. It's sort of like camping. I have a roll of toilet paper and a little shovel. At night I tie myself to the branch with a rope. But I don't really sleep much. It's about seven o'clock in the evening when the girl detective leaves her house. "Where are you going?" I say, just to make conversation.

She says that she's going to that new restaurant downtown, if it's any of my business. She asks if I want to come, but I have plans. I can tell that something's up. She's disguised as a young woman. Her eyes are keen and they flash a lot. "Can you bring me back an order of steamed dumplings?" I call after her, "Some white rice?"

She pretends she doesn't hear me. Of course I follow her. She takes a bus. I climb between trees. It's kind of fun. Occasionally there aren't any trees, and I have to make do with telephone poles, or water towers. Generally I keep off the ground.

There's a nice little potted ficus at Mom's Chinese Restaurant. I sit in it and ponder the menu. I try not to catch the waiter's eye. He's a tall, stern-looking man. The girl detective is obviously trying to make up her mind between the rolling beef and the glowing squid. Listed under appetizers, there's scallion pancakes, egg rolls with shrimp, and wantons (which I have ordered many times, but they always turn out to be wontons instead), also dancing girls. The girl detective orders the dancing girls. Then she asks the waiter, "Where are you from?"

"China," he says.

"I mean, where do you live now," the girl detective says.

"China," he says. "I commute."

The girl detective tries again. "How long has this restaurant been here?"

"Sometimes, for quite a while," he says. "Don't forget to wash your hands before you eat."

The girl detective goes to the bathroom.

At the next table there are twelve women wearing dark glasses. They may have been sitting there for quite a while. They stand up, they file one by one into the women's bathroom. The girl detective sits for a minute. Then she follows them. After a minute I follow her. No one stops me. Why should they? I step carefully from table to table. I slouch behind the flower arrangements.

In the bathroom there aren't any trees, so I climb up on the electric dryer and sit with my knees up by my ears, and my hands around my knees. I try to look inconspicuous. There is only one stall, and absolutely no sign of the twelve women. Maybe they're all in the same stall, but I can see under the door, and I don't see any feet. The girl detective is washing her hands. She washes her hands thoughtfully, for a long time. Then she comes over and dries them. "What next?" I ask her.

Her eyes flash keenly. She pushes open the door of the stall with her foot. It swings. Both of us can plainly see that the stall is empty. Furthermore, there isn't even a toilet in it. Instead there is a staircase, going down. A draft is coming up. I almost think I can hear alligators, scratching and slithering around somewhere further down the stairs.

The girl detective goes to the underworld.

She has a flashlight, of course. She stands at the top of the stairs and looks back at me. The light from the flashlight puddles around her feet. "Are you coming or not?" she says. What can I say? I fall in love with the girl detective all over again. I come down off the dryer. "I guess," I say. We start down the stairs.

The underworld is everything I've been telling you. It's really big. We don't see any alligators, but that doesn't mean that there aren't any. It's dark. It's a little bit cool and I'm glad that I'm wearing my cardigan. There are trees with moss on them. The moss glows. I take to the trees. I swing from branch to branch. I was always good at gym. Beneath me the girl detective strides forward purposefully, her large feet lit up like two boats. I am in love with the top of her head, with the tidy part straight down the middle. I feel tenderly toward this part. I secretly vow to preserve it. Not one hair on her head shall come to harm.

But then we come to a river. It's a wide river, and probably deep. I sit in a tree at the edge of the river, and I can't make up my mind to climb down. Not even for the sake of the part in the hair of the girl detective. She looks up at me and shrugs. "Suit yourself," she says.

"I'll wait right here," I say. There are cute little canoes by the side of the river. Some people say that the girl detective can walk on water, but I see her climb in one of the canoes. This isn't the kind of river that you want to stick your toes in. It's too spick-and-span. You might leave footprints.

I watch her go across the river. I see her get out on the other side. There is a nightclub on the other side, with a veranda, and a big sign

over the veranda. "Dance with Beautiful Girls." There is a woman standing on the veranda. People are dancing. There is music playing. Up in
my tree, my feet are tapping air. Someone says, "Mom?" Someone
embraces someone else. Everyone is dancing. "Where have you been?"
someone says. "Spring cleaning," someone says.

It is hard to see what is going on across the river. Chinese waiters
in elegant tuxedos are dipping dancing princesses. There are a lot of
sequins. They are dancing so fast, things get blurry. Things run together.
I think I see alligators dancing. I see a fat old man dancing with the
girl detective's mother. Maybe even the housekeeper is dancing. It's
hard to tell if their feet are even touching the ground. There are sparks.
Fireworks. The musicians are dancing too, but they don't stop playing.
I'm dancing up in my tree. The leaves shake and the branch groans, but
the branch doesn't break.

We dance for hours. Maybe for days. It's hard to tell when it stays
dark all the time. Then there is a line of dancers coming across the river.
They skip across the backs of the white alligators, who snap at their
heels. They are hand in hand, spinning and turning and falling back,
and leaping forward. It's hard to see them, they're moving so fast. It's
so dark down here. Is that a dancing princess, or a bank robber? Is that
a fat old man, or an alligator, or a housekeeper? I wish I knew. Is that
the girl detective or is it her mother? One looks back at the other, and
smiles. She doesn't say a thing, she just smiles.

I look, and in the mossy glow they all look like the girl detective.
Or maybe the girl detective looks like all of them. They all look so
happy. Passing in the opposite direction is a line of Chinese waiters.
They swing the first line as they pass. They cut across and do-si-do.
They clap hands. They clutch each other across the breast and the back,
and tango. But the girl detectives keep up toward the restaurant, and
bathroom, and the secret staircase. The waiters keep on toward the water, toward the nightclub. Down in that nightclub, there's a bathroom.
In the bathroom, there's another staircase. The waiters are going home
to bed.

I'm exhausted. I can't keep up with the girl detectives. "Wait!" I
yell. "Hold it for just a second. I'm coming with you."

They all turn and look back at me. I'm dizzy with all of that looking.
I fall out of my tree. I hit the ground. Really, that's all I remember.

When I woke up.

Someone had carried me back to my tree and tucked me in. I was snug
as a bug. I was back in the tree across the street from the girl detective's
window. This time the blinds were down. I couldn't see a thing.

The end of the girl detective?

Some people say that she never came back from the underworld.

The return of the girl detective.

I had to go to the airport for some reason. It's a long story. It was an important case. This wasn't that long ago. I hadn't been down out of the tree for very long. I was missing the tree.

I thought I saw the girl detective in the bar in Terminal B. She was sitting in one of the back booths, disguised as a fat old man. There was a napkin in front of her, folded into a giraffe. She was crying, but there was the napkin folded into a giraffe—she had nothing to wipe her nose on. I would have gone over and given her my handkerchief, but someone sat down next to her. It was a kid, about twelve years old. She had red hair. She was wearing overalls. She just sat next to him, and she put down another napkin. She didn't say a word to him. The old man blew his nose on it, and I realized that he wasn't the girl detective at all. He was just an old man. It was the kid in the overalls—what a great disguise! Then the waitress came over to take their order. I wasn't sure about the waitress. Maybe she was the girl detective. But she gave me such a look—I had to get up and leave.

Why I got down out of the tree.

She came over and stood under the tree. She looked a lot like my mother. Get down out of that tree this instant! she said. Don't you know it's time for dinner?

N. SCOTT MOMADAY

The Transformation

Native-American author-artist N. Scott Momaday has published numerous magical books, including The House Made of Dawn, The Man Made of Words, The Ancient Child, *and* In the Presence of the Sun. *Winner of the Pulitzer Prize, the Academy of American Poets Prize, and the Italian "Mondello" literary award, he is a Fellow of the American Academy of Arts and Sciences and a member of the Kiowa Gourd Dance Society. He divides his time between homes in Jemez Springs, New Mexico, and Tucson, Arizona.*

"The Transformation" is a literary rendition of a magical Kiowa folk tale that is central to Momaday's art and fiction, reappearing throughout his oeuvre in many different guises. This lovely piece comes from the author's most recent collection of art, poetry, and short prose, In the Bear's House.

—T. W.

Eight children were there at play, seven sisters and their brother. Suddenly the boy was struck dumb; he trembled and began to run upon his hands and feet. His fingers became claws, and his body was covered with fur. Directly there was a bear where the boy had been. The sisters were terrified; they ran and the bear after them. They came to the stump of a great tree, and the tree spoke to them. It bade them climb upon it, and as they did so it began to rise into the air. The bear came to kill them, but they were beyond its reach. It reared against the trunk and scored the bark all around with its claws. The seven sisters were borne into the sky, and they became the stars of the Big Dipper.

Kiowa Story of Tsoai

The boy.
>> *The boy ran.*
>>> *The boy ran after his sisters. There was a bursting of the boy's heart. He stumbled and gasped and stood still. The cries of his sisters pierced his brain like a madness. He caught his breath—or not his own breath, really, but the breath of something other and irresistible and wild. The ground was almost cold. Dust floated in the long, slanting rays of the sun. Somewhere a raven called. And when the boy looked up his sisters too were standing still, off among the trees, and their faces were pale and contorted with fright. In their eyes was certain disbelief—and certainly love and wonder. And they began to run again, and again he took up the chase.*

No one ever saw the sisters again. Only on the day they left the camp did anyone speak their names. Their names were soon forgotten, though the sisters themselves were remembered, not as individual children, with particular appearances and manners, but collectively. They had become the little sisters to whom it happened. *For the first days and weeks after the children disappeared, the people of the camp gathered themselves up in the dusk and waited for the stars to come out. And when the stars came out and flickered on the black wash of the sky, the people were filled with wonder—and a kind of loneliness. Some of them made exclamations, but most remained silent and respectful, reverent even. In the hold of such events there is little to be said. Then a great storm descended on the hills, and the sky roiled for four days and four nights, and there were no stars to be seen. After that, the people did not convene in the same way, for the same purpose. They went on with their lives as if nothing had happened. Even the parents of the lost children went on with their lives, as if nothing had happened. Of course there was at first the question of whether or not they ought to grieve. It was decided that they ought not, and no one held them up to scorn; no one blamed them in the least. Only old Koi-ehm-toya, one late morning when the snow swirled down and there was a general silence in the camp, emitted a series of sharp tremolo cries and cut off two fingers on her left hand.*

But the boy was seen. One by one, hunters returned from the woods with stories in which a bear figured more or less prominently. Sometimes the bear was said to have run upon its hind legs. Sometimes it was said to have approached the hunter gladly, with eager goodwill, as if it had no sense of danger whatsoever. Sometimes it was said to have been defined in a strange light, as if a blue, smoky shadow lay behind it. One hunter, a man with a withered neck, was so deeply enchanted by the bear's behavior that upon its approach he could do nothing but stand with his arms at his sides. The bear came upon him, breathed the scent of camas upon him, and laid its great flat head to the hunter's genitals. In a strange moment in which there was no fear on either side, there was recognition on both sides, the hunter said. The bear cried in a human voice.

Then, too, a Piegan woman whose name was Thab-san, who had been captured by the Kiowas in the Antelope Plains, told the following story:

One night there appeared a boy child in the Piegan camp. No one had ever seen it before. It was not bad-looking, and it spoke a language that was pleasant to hear, but none could understand it. The wonderful thing was that the child was perfectly unafraid, as if it were at home among its own people. The child got on well enough, but the next morning it was gone, as suddenly as it had appeared. Everyone was troubled. But then it came to be understood that the child never was, and everyone felt better. "After all," said an old man, "how can we believe in the child! It gave us not one word of sense to hold on to. What we saw, if indeed we saw anything at all, must have been a dog from a neighborhood camp, or a bear that wandered down from the high country."

Tsoai, the great stump of the tree, stood against the sky. There was nothing like it in the landscape. The tallest pines were insignificant beside it; many hundreds of them together could not fill its shadow. In time the stump turned to stone, and the wind sang at a high pitch as it ran across the great grooves that were set there long ago by the bear's claws. Eagles came to hover above it, having caught sight of it across the world. No one said so, but each man in his heart acknowledged Tsoai, and the first thing he did upon waking was to cast his eyes upon it, thus to set his belief, to know that it was there and that the world remained whole, as it ought to remain. And always Tsoai was there.

In the clearing, he belonged. Everything there was familiar to him. He began to move toward the woods with the others. They were laughing, and they drew away from him. He followed, and they began to shout, taunting him, entreating him to play the game, and Loki began to run. *Set, Set!* they shouted. "The bear, the bear!" and ran. And he ran after them. "Yes. I am *Set*," Loki called out, flailing his arms and chuffing his breath; he was ferocious. In the trees now, he gained ground. The girls were breathing hard, glancing back and squealing. Suddenly he slowed and began to stagger and reel. Something was wrong, terribly wrong. His limbs had become very heavy, and his head. He was dizzy. His vision blurred. The objects on the ground at his feet were clear and sharply defined in his sight, but in the distance were only vague shapes in a light like fog. At the same time there was a terrible dissonance in his ears, a whole jumble of sound that came like a blow to his head. He was stunned, but in a moment the confusion of sounds subsided, and he heard things he had never heard before, separately, distinctly, with nearly absolute definition. He heard water running over stones, impressing the rooted earth of a bank beyond stands of undergrowth strummed by the low, purling air, splashing upon a drift of pine needles far downstream. He heard leaves colliding overhead, the scamper of a squirrel deep in the density of trees, the wind careening against an outcrop of rocks high on the opposite slope, the feathers of a hawk ruffling in a long stream of the sky. It was as if he could detect each and every vibration of sound in the whole range of his hearing. And the thin air smarted in his nostrils. He could smell a thousand things at once and perceive them individually. He could smell the barks of trees and the rot of roots and the fragrances of grass and wildflowers. He could smell the scat of animals here and there, old and new, across the reach of the hills. He could smell sweet saps and the stench of the deaths of innumerable creatures in the earth. He could smell rain in the distant ranges, fire beyond. He could smell the oils rising to the surface of his skin, and he could smell the breath and sex of his sisters. He caught the sour smell of fear. He looked after his sisters. They too had stopped running. One or two of them had taken steps toward him. He tried to call to them, but he could not; he had no longer a human voice. He saw the change come upon their faces. He could no longer recognize them; they were masks. They turned and ran again. And there came upon him a loneliness like death. He moved on, a shadow receding into shadows.

Shadows.

DELIA SHERMAN

Carabosse

Delia Sherman has published two novels to date, as well as short fiction and poetry in F&SF, Bending the Landscape, The Armless Maiden, The Sandman: Book of Dreams, *and other magazines and anthologies. The following poem takes a sharp look at the Sleeping Beauty story and fairy gifts. It is reprinted from* Silver Birch, Blood Moon, *published by Avon Books.*

—*T. W.*

There were twelve fairies at the feast. Never
Thirteen. The day the queen gave birth, the king
Sent out twelve messengers on horses,
One to each of us, begging us
To bless her, name her, crown her with our favor.
So we came.

There was a banquet—well, there'd have to be,
With jeweled plates and cups, the usual fee
For fairy-godmothering. My sisters returned
The usual gifts: Beauty. Wit. A lovely voice.
Goodness (of course). Good taste (that was Martha,
Wincing at the jeweled cups, the queen's gown).
Grace. Patience. An ear for music. Dexterity
(To help her learn Princessly skills, as sewing,
Dancing, playing the lute). Amiability.
Intelligence.

I had meant to give her a long life.
I raised my wand and caught her eyes. They were
Gray and awake. Her cheeks were flushed with pink,
Her hair transparent down. She batted at
My wand and laughed. The court transfixed me
With expectant eyes—the king and queen,
My sisters, ladies, nobles, serving men,
Waiting for my gift. I considered
Her life, her marriage to a prince raised
Blind to the world behind the jeweled cups,
And said, "Sweet child, I give your life to you
To lead as you will, to go or stay, to use
My sisters' gifts, or let them be. Rule
In your own right, consortless and free.
If you choose."

The king raged; the queen wept; my sisters
Stood aghast. Not marry? The kiss of death,
A harsher curse than marriage to a frog,
Or kissing a hedgehog, or serving a witch, or even
Herding geese, since all these led to mating.
As a good fairy, I did what I could; I gave her
A hundred years' sleep, a hedge of briars, a spell
That would sort her suitors, test them for grace,
For patience, for wit and intelligence and good taste,
For amiability and a lovely voice.
A man who would be her mate,
Not her master.

NEIL GAIMAN

Harlequin Valentine

Neil Gaiman first made his mark as the best-selling author of the Sandman *series and other adult comic books, then proved he was equally adept as a novelist with* Good Omens, *a humorous fantasy written in collaboration with Terry Pratchett. He has gone on to produce dazzling fiction in a more serious vein: the novels* Neverwhere *and* Stardust, *and short stories collected in* Smoke and Mirrors. *The graphic novel version of* Stardust *(illustrated by Charles Vess) won the 1999 Mythopoeic Award, and* Neverwhere *became a BBC television production; both are currently being turned into films. Gaiman has also published rock journalism, children's fiction, and poetry, and wrote the English screenplay for the Japanese animated film* Princess Mononoke.

"Harlequin Valentine" is a dark but lyrical tale in the interstitial realm between fantasy and horror. It was first printed in the program book of the 1999 World Horror Convention.

—*T. W. , E. D.*

It is February the fourteenth, at that hour of the morning when all the children have been taken to school and all the husbands have driven themselves to work or been dropped off, steam-breathing and great-coated, at the rail station at the edge of the town for the Great Commute, when I pin my heart to Missy's front door. The heart is a deep, dark red that is almost a brown, the color of liver. Then I knock on the door, sharply, *rat-a-tat-tat!*, and I grasp my wand, my stick, my oh-so-thrustable and be-ribboned lance, and I vanish like cooling steam into the chilly air . . .

Missy opens the door. She looks tired.

"My Columbine," I breathe, but she hears not a word. She turns her head, so she takes in the view from one side of the street to the other, but nothing moves. A truck rumbles in the distance. She walks back into the kitchen and I dance, silent as a breeze, as a mouse, as a dream, into the kitchen beside her.

Missy takes a plastic sandwich bag from a paper box in the kitchen drawer, and a bottle of cleaning spray from under the sink. She pulls off two sections of kitchen towel from the roll on the kitchen counter. Then she walks back to the front door. She pulls the pin from the painted wood—it was my hat pin, which I had stumbled across . . . where? I turn the matter over in my head: in Gascony, perhaps? or Twickenham? or Prague?

The face on the end of the hat pin is that of a pale Pierrot.

She removes the pin from the heart, and puts the heart into the plastic sandwich bag. She wipes the blood from the door with a squirt of cleaning spray and a rub of the paper towel, and she inserts the pin into her lapel, where the little, white-faced August face stares out at the cold world with his blind silver eyes and his grave silver lips.

Naples. Now it comes back to me. I purchased the hat pin in Naples, from an old woman with one eye. She smoked a clay pipe. This was a long time ago.

Missy puts the cleaning utensils down on the kitchen table, then she thrusts her arms through the sleeves of her old blue coat, which was once her mother's, does up the buttons, one, two, three, then she places the sandwich bag with the heart in it determinedly into her pocket and sets off down the street.

Secret, secret, quiet as a mouse I follow her, sometimes creeping, sometimes dancing, and she never sees me, not for a moment, just pulls her blue coat more tightly around her, and she walks through the little Kentucky town, and down the old road that leads past the cemetery.

The wind tugs at my hat, and I regret, for a moment, the loss of my hat pin. But I am in love, and this is Valentine's Day. Sacrifices must be made.

Missy is remembering in her head the other times she has walked into the cemetery, through the tall iron cemetery gates: when her father died; when they came here as kids at All Hallow's, the whole school mob and caboodle of them, partying and scaring each other; and when a secret lover was killed in a three-car pile up on the interstate, and she waited until the end of the funeral, when the day was all over and done with, and she came in the evening, just before sunset, and laid a white lily on the fresh grave.

Oh, Missy, shall I sing the body and the blood of you, the lips and the eyes? A thousand hearts I would give you, as your valentine. Proudly I wave my staff in the air and dance, singing silently of the gloriousness of me, as we skip together down Cemetery Road.

A low gray building, and Missy pushes open the door. She says "Hi" and "How's it going" to the girl at the desk, who makes no intelligible reply, fresh out of school and filling in a crossword from a periodical filled with nothing but crosswords, page after page of them, and the girl would be making private phone calls on company time if only she had somebody to call, which she doesn't, and, I see, plain as elephants, she never will. Her face is a mass of blotchy acne pustules and acne scars and she thinks it matters, and talks to nobody. I see her life spread out before me: she will die, unmarried and unmolested, of breast cancer in fifteen years' time, and will be planted under a stone with her name on it in the meadow by Cemetery Road, and the first hands to have touched her breasts will have been those of the pathologist as he cuts out the cauliflower-like stinking growth and mutters, "Jesus, look at the size of this thing, why didn't she *tell* anyone?" which rather misses the point.

Gently, I kiss her on her spotty cheek, and whisper to her that she is beautiful. Then I tap her once, twice, *thrice*, on the head with my staff, and wrap her with a ribbon.

She stirs and smiles. Perhaps tonight she will get drunk and dance and offer up her virginity upon Hymen's altar, meet a young man who cares more for her breasts than for her face and will one day, stroking those breasts and suckling and rubbing them, say, "Honey, you seen anybody about that lump?" and by then her spots will be long gone, rubbed and kissed and frottaged into oblivion . . .

But now I have mislaid Missy, and I run and caper down a dun-carpeted corridor until I see that blue coat pushing into a room at the end of the hallway, and I follow her into an unheated room, tiled in bathroom-green.

The stench is unbelievable, heavy and rancid and wretched in the air. The fat man in the stained lab coat wears disposable rubber gloves and has a thick layer of mentholatum on his upper lip and about his nostrils. A dead man is on the table in front of him. The man is a thin, old black man, with calloused fingertips. He has a thin moustache. The fat man has not noticed Missy yet. He has made an incision, and now he peels back the skin with a wet, sucking sound, and how dark the brown of it is on the outside, and how pink and pretty it is on the inside.

Classical music plays from a portable radio, very loudly. Missy turns the radio off, then she says, "Hello, Vernon."

The fat man says "Hello, Missy. You come for your old job back?"

This is the Doctor, I decide, for he is too big, too round, too magnificently well-fed to be Pierrot, and too unself-conscious to be Pantaloon. His face creases with delight to see Missy, and she smiles to see him, and I am jealous; I feel a stab of pain shoot through my heart (currently in a plastic sandwich bag in Missy's coat pocket) sharper than I felt when I stabbed it with my hat pin and stuck it to her door.

And speaking of my heart, she has pulled it from her pocket, and is waving it at the pathologist, Vernon. "Do you know what this is?" she says.

"Heart," he says. "Kidneys don't have the ventricles, and brains are bigger and squishier. Where d'you get it?"

"I was hoping that you could tell me," she says. "Doesn't it come from here? Is it your idea of a Valentine's card, Vernon? A human heart stuck to my front door?"

He shakes his head. "Don't come from here," he says. "You want I should call the police?"

She shakes her head. "With my luck," she says, "they'll decide I'm a serial killer and send me to the chair."

The Doctor opens the sandwich bag and prods at the heart with stubby fingers in latex gloves. "Adult, in pretty good shape, took care of his heart," he said. "Cut out by an expert."

I smile proudly at this and bend down to talk to the dead black man on the table, with his chest all open and his calloused string-bass–picking fingers. "Go 'way, Harlequin," he mutters, quietly, not to offend Missy and his doctor. "Don't you go causing trouble here."

"Hush yourself. I will cause trouble wherever I wish," I tell him. "It is my function." But, for a moment, I feel a void about me; I am wistful, almost pierrotish, which is a poor thing for a harlequin to be.

Oh, Missy, I saw you yesterday in the street, and followed you into Al's Super-Valu Foods and More, elation and joy rising within me. In you, I recognized someone who could transport me, take me from myself. In you I recognized my Valentine, my Columbine.

I did not sleep last night, and instead I turned the town topsy and turvy, befuddling the unfuddled. I caused three sober bankers to make fools of themselves with drag queens from Madame Zora's Revue and Bar. I slid into the bedrooms of the sleeping, unseen and unimagined, slipping the evidence of mysterious and exotic trysts into pockets and under pillows and into crevices, able only to imagine the fun that would ignite the following day as soiled split-crotch fantasy panties would be found poorly hidden under sofa cushions and in the inner pockets of respectable suits. But my heart was not in it, and the only face I could see was Missy's.

Oh, Harlequin in love is a sorry creature.

I wonder what she will do with my gift. Some girls spurn my heart; others touch it, kiss it, caress it, punish it with all manner of endearments before they return it to my keeping. Some never even see it.

Missy takes the heart back, puts it in the sandwich bag again, pushes the snap-shut top of it closed.

"Shall I incinerate it?" she asks.

"Might as well. You know where the incinerator is," says the Doctor, returning to the dead musician on the table. "And I meant what I said about your old job. I need a good lab assistant."

I imagine my heart trickling up to the sky as ashes and smoke, covering the world. I do not know what I think of this, but, her jaw set, she shakes her head and bids goodbye to Vernon the pathologist. She has thrust my heart into her pocket and she is walking out of the building and up Cemetery Road and back into town.

I caper ahead of her. Interaction would be a fine thing, I decide, and fitting word to deed I disguise myself as a bent old woman on her way to the market, covering the red spangles of my costume with a tattered cloak, hiding my masked face with a voluminous hood, and at the top of Cemetery Road I step out and block her way.

Marvelous, marvelous, marvelous me, and I say to her, in the voice of the oldest of women, "Spare a copper coin for a bent old woman, dearie, and I'll tell you a fortune that will make your eyes spin with joy," and Missie stops. She opens her purse and takes out a dollar bill.

"Here," says Missy.

And I have it in my head to tell her all about the mysterious man she will meet, all dressed in red and yellow, with his domino mask, who will thrill her and love her and never, never leave her (for it is not a good thing to tell your Columbine the *entire* truth), but instead I find myself saying, in a cracked old voice, "Have you ever heard of Harlequin?"

Missy looks thoughtful. Then she nods. "Yes," she says. "Character in the *Commedia dell'Arte*. Costume covered in little diamond shapes. Wore a mask. I think he was a clown of some sort, wasn't he?"

I shake my head beneath my hood. "No clown," I tell her. "He was . . ."

And I find that I am about to tell her the truth, so I choke back the words and pretend that I am having the kind of coughing attack to which elderly women are particularly susceptible. I wonder if this could be the power of love. I do not remember it troubling me with other women I thought I had loved, other Columbines I have encountered over centuries now long gone.

I squint through old-woman eyes at Missy: she is in her early twenties and she has lips like a mermaid's, full and well-defined and certain, and gray eyes, and a certain intensity to her gaze.

"Are you all right?" she asks.

I cough and splutter and cough some more, and gasp, "Fine, my dearie-duck, I'm just fine, thank you kindly."

"So," she said, "I thought you were going to tell me my fortune."

"Harlequin has given you his heart," I hear myself saying. "You must discover its beat yourself."

She stares at me, puzzled. I cannot change or vanish while her eyes are upon me, and I feel frozen, angry at my trickster tongue for betraying me.

"Look," I tell her, "A rabbit!" and she turns, follows my pointing finger, and as she takes her eyes off me I disappear, *pop!*, like a rabbit down a hole, and when she looks back there's not a trace of the old fortune-teller lady, which is to say, me.

Missy walks on, and I caper after her, but there is not the spring in my step there was earlier in the morning.

Midday, and Missy has walked to Al's Super-Valu Foods and More, where she buys a small block of cheese, a carton of unconcentrated orange juice, two avocados, and on to the County One Bank where she withdraws two hundred and seventy-nine dollars and twenty-two cents, which is the total amount of money in her savings account, and I creep after her sweet as sugar and quiet as the grave.

"Morning, Missy," says the owner of the Salt Shaker Café, when Missy enters. He has a trim beard, more pepper than salt, and my heart would have skipped a beat if it were not in the sandwich bag in Missy's pocket, for this man obviously lusts after her, and my confidence, which is legendary, droops and wilts. *I am Harlequin, I tell myself, in my diamond-covered garments, and the world is my harlequinade. I am Harlequin, who rose from the dead to play his pranks upon the living. I am Harlequin, in my mask, with my wand.* I whistle to myself, and my confidence rises, hard and full once more.

"Hey, Harve," says Missy. "Give me a plate of hash browns, and a bottle of ketchup."

"That all?" he asks.

"Yes," she says. "That'll be perfect. And a glass of water."

I tell myself that the man Harve is Pantaloon, the foolish merchant that I must bamboozle, baffle, confusticate, and confuse. Perhaps there is a string of sausages in the kitchen. I resolve to bring delightful disarray to the world, and to bed luscious Missy before midnight: my Valentine's present to myself. I imagine myself kissing her lips.

There are a handful of other diners. I amuse myself by swapping their plates while they are not looking, but I have difficulty finding the fun in it. The waitress is thin, and her hair hangs in sad ringlets about her face. She ignores Missy, who she obviously considers entirely Harve's preserve.

Missy sits at the table, and pulls the sandwich bag from her pocket. She places it on the table in front of her.

Harve-the-pantaloon struts over to Missy's table, gives her a glass of water, a plate of hash-browned potatoes, and a bottle of Heinz 57 Varieties Tomato Ketchup. "And a steak knife," she tells him.

I trip him up on the way back to the kitchen. He curses, and I feel better, more like the former me, and I goose the waitress as she passes the table of an old man who is reading *USA Today* while toying with his salad. She gives the old man a filthy look. I chuckle, and then I find I am feeling most peculiar. I sit down upon the floor, suddenly.

"What's that, honey?" the waitress asks Missy.

"Health food, Charlene," says Missy. "Builds up iron." I peep over the tabletop. She is slicing up small slices of liver-colored meat on her plate, liberally doused in tomato sauce, and piling her fork high with hash browns. Then she chews.

I watch my heart disappearing into her rosebud mouth. My valentine's jest somehow seems less funny.

"You anemic?" asks the waitress, on her way past once more, with a pot of steaming coffee.

"Not anymore," says Missy, popping another scrap of raw gristle cut small into her mouth, and chewing it, hard, before swallowing.

And as she finishes eating my heart, Missy looks down and sees me sprawled upon the floor. She nods. "Outside," she says. "Now." Then she gets up, and leaves ten dollars beside her plate.

She is sitting on a bench on the sidewalk waiting for me. It is cold, and the street is almost deserted. I sit down beside her. I would caper around her, but it feels so foolish now I know someone is watching.

"You ate my heart," I tell her. I can hear the petulance in my voice, and it irritates me.

"Yes," she says. "Is that why I can see you?"

I nod.

"Take off that domino mask," she says. "You look stupid."

I reach up and take off the mask. She looks slightly disappointed. "Not much improvement," she says. "Now, give me the hat. And the stick."

I shake my head. Missy reaches out and plucks my hat from my head, takes my stick from my hand. She toys with the hat, her long fingers brushing and bending it. Her nails are painted crimson. Then she stretches and smiles, expansively. The poetry has gone from my soul, and the cold February wind makes me shiver.

"It's cold," I tell her.

"No," she says, "It's perfect, magnificent, marvelous, and magical. It's Valentine's Day, isn't it? Who could be cold upon Valentine's Day? What a fine and fabulous time of the year."

I look down. The diamonds are fading from my suit, which is turning ghost white, pierrot-white.

"What do I do now?" I ask her.

"I don't know," says Missy. "Fade away, perhaps. Or find another role . . . A lovelorn swain, perchance, mooning and pining under the pale moon. All you need is a Columbine."

"You," I tell her. "You are my Columbine."

"Not anymore," she tells me. "That's the joy of a harlequinade, after all, isn't it? We change our costumes. We change our roles."

She flashes me such a smile, now. Then she puts my hat, my own hat, my harlequin hat, up onto her head. She chucks me under the chin.

"And you?" I ask.

She tosses the wand into the air; it tumbles and twists in a high arc, red and yellow ribbons twisting and swirling about it, and then it lands neatly, almost silently, back into her hand. She pushes the tip down to the sidewalk, pushes herself up from the bench in one smooth movement.

"I have things to do," she tells me. "Tickets to take. People to dream." Her blue coat that was once her mother's is no longer blue, but is canary yellow, covered with red diamonds.

Then she leans over, and kisses me, full and hard upon the lips.

Somewhere a car backfired. I turned, startled, and when I looked back I was alone on the street. I sat there for several moments, on my own.

Charlene opened the door to the Salt Shaker Café. "Hey. Pete. Have you finished out there?"

"Finished?"

"Yeah. C'mon. Harve says your ciggie break is over. And you'll freeze. Back into the kitchen."

I stared at her. She tossed her pretty ringlets, and, momentarily, smiled at me. I got to my feet, adjusted my white clothes, the uniform of the kitchen help, and followed her inside.

It's Valentine's Day, I thought. *Tell her how you feel. Tell her what you think.*

But I said nothing. I dared not. I simply followed her inside, a creature of mute longing.

Back in the kitchen a pile of plates was waiting for me. I began to scrape the leftovers into the pig bin. There was a scrap of dark meat on one of the plates, beside some half-finished, ketchup-covered hash browns. It looked almost raw, but I dipped it into the congealing ketchup, and when Harve's back was turned, I picked it off the plate and chewed it down. It tasted metallic and gristly, but I swallowed it anyhow, and could not have told you why.

A blob of red ketchup dripped from the plate onto the sleeve of my white uniform, forming one perfect diamond.

"Hey, Charlene," I called, across the kitchen. "Happy Valentine's Day." And then I started to whistle.

PATRICIA A. McKILLIP

Toad

Patricia A. McKillip has long had my vote as the finest fantasy writer in America today, quietly turning out one exquisite book after another, including Song for the Basilisk, Winter Rose, The Book of Atrix Wolfe, The Riddlemaster Trilogy, *and* The Forgotten Beasts of Eld *(winner of the World Fantasy Award). All of these are highly recommended; magical fiction doesn't come better than this. McKillip was raised in a military family and spent her childhood in England, Germany, and various regions of the United States. She currently lives in a small town in the Catskill Mountains of New York.*

In "Toad," McKillip takes a wry look at an old and familiar fairy tale. The story was written for volume five of Avon Books' adult fairy tale series, Silver Birch, Blood Moon.

—T. W.

The first thing that leaps to the eye is that my beloved had no manners. She behaved like a spoiled brat, once she had what she wanted. If it had not been for her father, where would I have been? Still hanging around the well, instead of dressed in silks and wearing a crown, and being bowed and scraped to, not to mention diving in and out of the dark, moist cave of our marriage sheets, cresting waves of satin like seals, barking and tossing figs to one another, then diving back down, bearing soft, plump fruit in our mouths. "Old waddler," she called me at first, with a degree of accuracy missing from subsequent complaints. She never could tell a frog from a toad.

Why, you might wonder, would any self-respecting toad, having been slammed against a wall by a furious brat of a princess, want, upon regaining his own shape, to marry her? Not only was she devious, promising me things and then ignoring her promises when threatened by the cold proximity of toad, she was bad-tempered to boot. The story that has come down doesn't make a lot of sense here: why are lies and temper rewarded with the handsome prince? She didn't want to let me into the castle, she didn't want to feed me, she didn't want to touch me, above all she didn't want me in her bed. When I pleaded with her to show mercy, to become again that sweet, weeping, charming child beside the well who promised me everything I asked for, she picked me up as if I were the golden ball that I had rescued for her, and bounced me off the stones. If she had missed the wall and I had gone flying out a window, what might have happened? Would I have waddled away, muttering and limping, under the moonlight, to slide back into the well until fate tossed another golden ball my way?

Maybe.

She'll never know.

Her father comes out well in the stories. A man of honor, harassed by his exasperating daughter, who tries to wheedle and whine her way out of her promises. A king, who would consent to eat with a toad at his table, for no other reason than to make his daughter keep her word. "Papa, please, no," she begged, her gray eyes awash with tears, the way I had first seen her, her curly hair, golden as her ball, tumbling out of its pins to her shoulders. "Papa, please don't make me let it in. Don't make me share my food with it. Don't make me touch it. I'll die if I have to touch a frog."

"It's a toad," he said at one point, watching me drink wine out of her goblet. She had his gray eyes; he saw a bit more clearly than she, but not enough: only enough to use me as a lesson in his daughter's life.

"Frog, toad, what's the difference? Papa, please don't make me!"

"Toads," he said accurately, "are generally uglier than frogs. Most have nubby, bumpy skin—"

"I'll get warts, Papa!"

"That's a fairy tale. Look at its squat body, its short legs, made for insignificant hops, or even for walking, like a dog. Observe its drab coloring." He added, warming to his subject while I finished his daughter's dessert, "They have quite interesting breeding habits. Some lay eggs on land instead of water. Others give birth to tiny toads, already fully formed. Among midwife toads, the male carries the eggs with him until they hatch, moistening them in—"

"That's disgusting!"

"I would like to be taken to bed now," I said, wiping my mouth with her embroidered linen.

"Papa!"

"You promised," I reminded her reproachfully. "I can't get up the stairs; you'll have to carry me. As your father pointed out, my limbs are short."

"Papa, please!"

"You promised," he said coldly: an honorable man. A lesson was to be learned simply at the expense of a stain of well water on her sheets, a certain clamminess in the atmosphere. What harm could possibly come to her?

I have always thought that her instincts were quite sound. For one thing: consider her age. Young, beautiful, barely marriageable, she might have kissed—though, contrary to common belief, not me—but she had most certainly never taken anyone to bed with her besides her nurse and her dolls. Who would want an ugly, dank, and warty toad in her bed instead of what she must have had vague yearnings for? And after all that talk of breeding habits! Something bloated and insistent, moving formlessly under her sheets while she tried to sleep, something cold, damp, humorless—who could blame her for losing her temper?

Then why did she make those promises?

Because something in her heart, in her marrow, recognized me.

Let's begin with the child sitting beside the well, beneath the linden tree. She thinks she is alone, though her world, she knows, proceeds in familiar and satisfactory fashion within the elegant castle beyond the trees. The linden is in bloom; its creamy flowers drift down into her hair, drop and float upon the dark water. Breeze strokes her hair, her cheeks. She tosses her favorite plaything, her golden ball, absently toward the sky, enjoying the suppleness and grace of her body, the thin silk blowing against her skin. She wears her favorite dress, green as the heart-shaped linden leaves; it makes her feel like a leaf, blown lightly in the wind. She throws her ball, takes a breath of air made complex and intoxicating by scents from the tree, the gardens, the moist earth at the lip of the well. She catches her ball, throws it again, thinks of nothing. She misses the ball.

It falls with a splash into the middle of the well, and, weighted with its tracery of gold, sinks out of sight. She has no idea how deep the water is, what snakes and silver eels might live in it, what long grasses might reach up to twine around her if she dares leap into it. She does what has always worked in her short life: she weeps.

I appear.

Her grief is genuine and quite moving: she might have dropped a child into the well instead of a ball. She scarcely sees me. I make little impression on her sorrow except as a means to end it. In her experience, help answers when she calls; her desperation transforms the world so that even toads can talk.

All her attention is on the water when she hears my voice. She speaks impatiently, wiping her eyes with her silks, to see better into the rippling shadows. "Oh, it's a frog. Old waddler, I dropped my ball in the water—I must have it back! I'll die without it! I'll give you anything if you get it for me—these pearls, my crown—anything! So will my papa."

She scarcely listens to herself, or to me. I am nothing but a frog, I while away the time eating flies, swimming in the slime, sitting in the reeds and croaking. Her pearls might resemble the translucent eggs of frogs, but I would have no real interest in them. Yes, of course I can be her playmate, her companion; she has had fantasy friends before. Yes, I can eat out of her plate; they all do. Yes, I can drink from her cup. Yes, I can sleep in her bed—yes, yes, anything! Just stop croaking and fetch my ball for me.

I drop it at her feet. I am no longer visible; I have become a fantasy, a dream. A talking frog? Don't be silly. Frogs don't talk. Even when I cry out to her as she runs away, laughing and tossing her ball, that's what she knows: frogs don't talk. Wait for me! I cry. You promised! But she no longer hears me. All her fantasy friends vanish when she no longer needs them.

So it must have been with a first, faint sense of terror that she heard my watery squelching across the marble floor as she sat eating with her father. They were not alone, but who among her father's elegantly bored courtiers would have questioned the existence of a talking frog? The court went on with their meal, secretly delighting in the argument at the royal table. I ate silently and listened to their discreet murmurings. Most took the princess's view, and wished me removed with the salmon bones, the fruit peelings, and tossed unceremoniously out the kitchen door. Others thought her father right: I would be a harmless lesson for a spoiled daughter. Most saw a frog. A toad with its poisonous skin touching the princess's goblet, leaving traces of its spittle on her plate? Unthinkable! Therefore: I was a frog. Others were not so sure. The king recognized me, of course, but, setting aside the fact that I could talk, seemed to believe that for all other purposes, I would behave in predictable toad-fashion toward humans, desiring mainly to be ignored and not to be squashed.

But the princess knew: to journey up the stairs with me dangling between her reluctant fingers would be to turn her back to that fair afternoon, the sweet linden blossoms, the golden-haired child tossing her ball, spinning and glinting, toward the sun, then watching it fall down light cascading over leaves into shadow, until it fell, unerringly, back into her hands. When the ball plummeted into the depths of the well, she wept for her lost self. Faced with the future in the form of a toad, she bargained badly: she exchanged her childhood for me.

Who am I?

Some of the courtiers knew me. Their wealth and finery did not shelter them from air or mud, or from the tales that are breathed into the heart, that cling to boot soles and breed life. They whisper among themselves. Listen.

"Toads mean pain, death. Think of the ugly toadfish that ejects its spines into the hands of the unwary fisher. Think of the poisonous toadstool."

"If you kill a toad with your hands, the skin of your face and hands will become hardened, lumpy, pimpled. Toads suck the breath of the sleeper, bring death."

"But consider the midwife toad, both male and female involved with life."

"If you spit and hit a toad, you will die."

"A toad placed on a cut will heal it."

"If you anger a toad it will inflate itself with a terrible poison and burst, taking you with it as it dies."

"Toads portend life. Consider the Egyptians, who believe that the toad represents the womb, and its cries are the cries of unborn children."

"She is life."

"It is death."

"She belongs to the moon, she croaks to the crescent moon. Consider the Northerners, who believe she rescues life itself, when it ripens into the shape of a red apple, and falls down into the well."

"She is life."

"It is death."

"She is both."

To the princess, carrying me with loathing up the stairs, a wisp of linen separating the shapeless, lumpy sack of my body from her fingers. I am the source of an enormous and irrational irritation. I rescued her golden ball; why could she not be gracious? I would be gone by morning. But she knew, she knew, deep in her; she heard the croaking of tiny, invisible frogs; she recognized the midwife toad.

If she had been gracious, I would indeed have been gone by morning. But her instincts held fast: I was danger, I was the unknown. I was what she wanted and did not want. She could not rid herself of me fast enough, or violently enough. But because she knew me, and part of her cried Not yet! Not yet!, she flung me as far from her as she could without losing sight of me.

Changing shape is easy; I do it all the time.

The moment she saw me on the floor, with my strong young limbs and dazed expression, rubbing my head and wondering groggily if I were still frog-naked, she tossed her heart into my well and dove after it herself. She covered me with a blanket, though not without a startled and curious glance at essentials. She accepted her future with remarkable composure. She stroked my curly hair, whose color, along with the color of my eyes, I had taken from her favorite doll, and listened to my sad tale.

A prince, I told her. A witch I had accidentally offended; they offend so easily, it seems. She had turned me into a toad and said . . .

"You rescued me," I said gratefully, overlooking her rudeness, as did she. "Those who love me will be overjoyed to see me again. How beautiful you are," I added. "Is it just because yours is the first kind face I have seen in so long?"

"Yes," she said breathlessly. "No." Somehow our hands became entwined before she remembered propriety. "I must take you to meet my father."

"Perhaps I should dress first."

"Perhaps you should."

And so I increase and multiply, trying to keep up with all the voices in the rivers and ponds, bogs and swamps, that cry out to be born. Some tales are simpler than others. This, like pond water, seems at first glance as clear as day. Then, when you scoop water in your hand and look at it, you begin to see all the little mysteries swarming in it, which, if you had drunk the water without looking first, you never would have seen. But now that you have seen, you stand there under the hot sun, thirsty, but not sure what you will be drinking, and wishing, perhaps, that you had not looked so closely, that you had just swallowed me down and gone your way, refreshed.

Some tales are simpler than others. But go ahead and drink: the ending is always the same.

BECKIAN FRITZ GOLDBERG

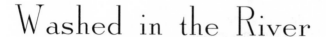

Washed in the River

Beckian Fritz Goldberg is an associate professor of English at Arizona State University. She received her B.A. and M.A. in English at Arizona State Uni- versity and took an M.F.A. in Creative Writing at Vermont College. Her poetry has appeared in numerous journals and in such anthologies as The Best American Poetry 1995 and Fever Dreams: Contemporary Arizona Poetry. She's received several prizes for her work, including a 1998 Pushcart Prize and the Gettysburg Review Annual Poetry Award. Goldberg has published three full-length collections: Body Betrayer and In the Badlands of Desire, with the Cleveland State University Press, and her latest, Never be the Horse, with the University of Akron Press.

"Washed in the River" is a heartbreaking poem based on old folk tales. It comes from The Iowa Review, Volume 29, Number 3.

—T. W.

Of course the woman with the mouse-child was famous,
as grace is famous
a rarity

at the end of suffering. She kept him in
a nest in the dry bathtub
and washed in the river.

And although only children were meant
to believe this, I still believe this.
The fate of the body
is to confound

itself with everything. That's why
in another tale, the fair sister
opened her mouth and spoke
rubies

and the plain sister, vipers and toads.
Meanwhile the mother

of the gray thing
bathed him in a teacup.
Plucked him out and let him
run along the shore

to the window. Where both of them
were struck with longing—
he behind the great glass,
she behind the gray boy.

The second you see yourself in the suffering
the story's over.

ROBERT GIRARDI

The Dinner Party

Robert Girardi is the author of three novels: Madeleine's Ghost, The Pirate's Daughter, *and* Vaporetto 13. *His work has appeared in* The New Republic, The Washington Post, *and* Tri-Quarterly. *He lives in Washington, D.C., with his wife and daughter.*
   "The Dinner Party" was published in his collection of novellas, A Vaudeville of Devils: Seven Moral Tales.

—*E. D.*

Kurt pulled the Lagonda onto the drive of the ugly pink mansion that had once belonged to Claudio Pouffon, the industrialist. He stopped the big car precisely beneath the porte cochere and waited for me to finish dressing. Two brass carriage lamps burned on either side of the archway; phosphorescent lizards scurried up the stucco into the wavering shadows. A footman stood on the veranda at the top of the front steps. Behind him the great doors were thrown open, and from the ballroom came a sad and jittery music and the muted swell of conversation.

A crowd of neighbors watched silently from the black-and-white mosaic sidewalk of the Esplanade, across the Avenida Perquitos. It must have seemed terrible to them, an outrage. Still, no one raised a voice or threw a rock or came over to demand an explanation. The neighbors seemed to understand the dinner party was beyond shame and suffering, beyond morality itself.

I saw Kurt's dark, piggy eyes in the rearview. He picked up the speaking tube.

"Your tie, sir," he said.

"Shut up, Kurt," I said, but I straightened it in the privacy glass. Then I twisted the cuff links and fixed the red sash with the few modest orders they had provided for me and slipped my feet into the polished slippers. If you've got to go to a dinner party, I told myself, you might as well be dressed. Or perhaps there were other reasons I did not care to examine.

Kurt came around the car to open the door. I stepped from the Lagonda's leathery interior into calm night air that did not hold the slightest breath of the green inferno that consumed the city below. The wall of flame began just the other side of the rose garden, neatly pruned bushes running up to it, not a single petal singed to the line.

"A moment, sir," Kurt said as I turned toward the steps. He touched me on the shoulder and pulled a glittering cigarette case from the pocket of his double-breasted jacket. "It would never do to enter a dinner party late without a cigarette. A question of style."

"Then I'm late as usual?" I said.

"Perfectly late, sir."

"You always had an eye for the smallest particulars, Kurt," I said, taking the cigarette.

He lit it and touched his cap.

"Till next time," I said.

"Enjoy your meal, sir," Kurt said.

"Never," I said.

He was one of their creatures. He smiled his lackey's smile, utterly without humor. Then he got into the Lagonda and pulled away.

The footman stood hollow-eyed and shivering at the door. His uniform did not fit him well; the scuffed dress shoes on his feet were at least a size too large. At the last minute his agency had called him to work this party on the hill. How was he to know what would happen? He had a wife, an apartment in the Rua Coutora. She was helpless without him. Had I heard anything? Was there anything I could do? He must have recognized that though I was not exactly one of them, I was no longer quite human. They have a gleaming quality that is startling, like platinum static, and unmistakable.

"The Cini District, the docks," I said shaking my head.

He rolled his eyes. There was a painful twitch.

"You mean?"

"Gone this afternoon," I said. "Cinders. Also the Palace of the President, the Botanical Gardens, the Alcaron Library. I'm sorry."

He was weeping now. The flames had come up so quickly. It was almost impossible that his wife had gotten any farther through the mad tangle of refugees than the Praca Olvidos, a raging gully of green fire by ten o'clock. The tears shone on his cheeks in the light from the tall windows.

"Don't let them see that," I whispered. "If there's one thing they can't stand, it's weakness. Courage, my friend."

"What does it matter now?" the footman said. He slumped down at the base of one of the columns that supported the entranceway and covered his face with his hands.

I could see into his life suddenly, the narrow, comfortable limits: a small, neat apartment, blue curtains in the window, a young wife from the country. They made love twice a week, Sunday and Wednesday. And on his rare night off she put on her best dress, and they went to the Olympia and laughed at the pantomime with the rest. Or to the Yoruba Ballroom to watch the young toughs and their hard women at the latest dances, maybe stepping in timidly for a tango or two. There was a bottle of Aracon on the table—an extravagance, but one must be extravagant now and then—and the moon in the street on the way home. I envied him his lost routine, his vanished certainties.

"Stand up," I said. "Let me help you." I lifted him by the elbows. There was a clean handkerchief in the pocket of my tux. I gave it to him, and he blew his nose.

The music squealed and tittered from inside, a stiff orchestral arrangement of a popular dance number. I turned toward the door to this sour accompaniment, and at that moment Maité appeared in the threshold. The same aquiline profile and startling blue eyes. I was not surprised to see her. This time she wore a black evening gown that exposed her breasts. Her shoulders were smooth and muscular, her breasts splendid, nipples teased into a state of perpetual excitement. The straps of the gown and her tiara were encrusted with diamonds as big as my thumbnail. Her black hair, streaked attractively with blue to match her eyes, curled cleverly around her ears. She was a little drunk. She held her martini at the same precise angle, always about to spill a drop, though she never did.

"Finally," she said, her voice a throaty, beautiful purr. "We didn't think you were going to make it, darling. There's always that possibility." She offered her white cheek for a kiss, which I ignored.

"Listen," I said, taking a step to the side. "This poor fellow here. His wife—"

She pulled back angrily. "Don't be ridiculous. Do you avoid stepping on ants? Do you feel sorry for bacteria?"

The footman stared at her, confused; then his face stiffened with rage. "Medusa! Bitch!" he spit at her through his teeth.

Maité drew herself up like a snake about to strike, but the footman held his ground. He was not a coward. His tears had been for others, not for himself.

Maité leaned down till her face was an inch away from his. He didn't flinch at first; then he began to wail softly.

"You will be cursed," she said quietly. "Not only now but through the generations."

"Who are you?" The footman began to back away.

"Don't you know?" She straightened, triumphant. "We are the gods!"

I almost laughed. "That's ridiculous," I said. "Sheer melodrama. Don't believe her for a second."

The footman was already halfway down the drive, his ill-fitting shoes flopping against the gravel. He veered off into the roses, hand out to the wall of flame as if pushing open a door. Then came a small flash when he fell into the poisonous green and was consumed.

In the ballroom an orchestra played on a small stage draped with maroon velvet set in between two forlorn rubber plants. The horn players could barely keep the instruments to their lips, which were white with fear. The sound of distant explosions interrupted their harmless melody. It was the oil tanks along the canal at Isola Iguenol blowing one by one, or perhaps a last regiment of the Civil Guard dynamiting the suburbs in a desperate attempt to stop the spread of the flames. A bright green flash lit the room with each shudder, the faces of the guests saved in green for a moment from the soft illumination of chandeliers clattering nervously above.

They had invited a crowd of about fifty for cocktails. The dinner later was always a private affair. Just myself and them. I recognized some of these unfortunate drinkers, but couldn't say from where. Famous people, no doubt: generals, cabinet ministers, actresses, millionaires. Maybe even the president of the republic himself, though—I realized with a shock—I no longer remembered what the man looked like.

A few of the guests put up a good show, sipping gin fizzes with false smiles, telling jokes, trying to take the measure of their new masters. Making conversation as their world burned around them. These were the ones who could knife their own mothers should the need arise, then go smiling to breakfast. Most of the others looked shaken and scared. Many sobbed openly, huddled together at the windows. It wouldn't go well for them.

I remembered my family with a painful jolt. Yes, I had a wife, children. They were out in the country, at Las Cruzas, visiting Mother.

How long would it take the flames to reach them there? I remembered a bright noon ten years gone, buying a yellow parrot, a gift for my wife's birthday. The parrot's eyes had been yellow like its feathers, its voice sweet and musical. For a moment I could see the yellow parrot with the yellow eyes quite clearly. I had taken this happy bird in his cage from a dim shop in the Alfama District into the sun and shadows of the arcade. But all that was fading, replacing itself with what had been before.

Now Maité had me by the arm. Her touch, the sight of her breasts filled me with a heat I could not name. Were they sexual beings or too inhuman for such human passions? Were they still flesh? Yes, they were flesh but altered. I had once known everything, been among them.

Joris stood talking to a frightened blonde in a blue dress. The blonde's skin showed the clear pallor of a recent beauty treatment; she had been to the spa at Criscol or La Maya from the look of her. Drowsing in the shade of a colorful silk umbrella on the beach during the long, lazy mornings, playing baccarat in the casino long past midnight. Joris was impeccably dressed. Pinned to the sheeny lapel of his tuxedo, a silver rose to match his lustrous silver hair. He was without age; there were no lines on his face. It was perfectly smooth. He ran his hand down the blonde's arm and over her nicely rounded rump. She shuddered but did not stop him. How could she?

"Joris is up to his usual filthy tricks, as you can see," Maité said. "He'll take the little vermin to bed in a bit, I'm sure. I can't imagine what he gets out of the experience. It's too disgusting. Anyway, have a drink, darling. You look utterly parched." She held out an exotic cocktail afloat with cherries and paper umbrellas that hadn't been in her hand a second before.

Suddenly I was struck with a terrible thirst that I recognized as one of their tricks. "No, thanks," I managed, trying not to look at the moisture sweating down the sides of the glass.

She raised an eyebrow. "You're sure?" The cocktail trembled a moment between her fingers.

I said nothing, and she let it drop to the polished tiles. It was a signal. As the glass shattered, the others turned toward us out of the crowd. I saw Petra, Ani, Jane, Colum. Their white, too-perfect faces were like the faces of marble giants. Their too-perfect marble lips were touched with cold smiles of incalculable disdain.

"We throw a dinner party because we haven't seen you for ages, darling, and you refuse to drink a little drink with us, with your good friends?" Maité sounded hurt.

"Not a drop," I said. "Not now, not ever."

She brought her face close. The smell of her breath was an intoxi-
cant, a drug. "Listen, after we have a few drinks and after dinner, we
can go upstairs, just the two of us, and make love. Like old times. It's
been so long for me. Too long. After dinner you'll resume your true
shape; we'll give it back to you. It must be terrible to be trapped in
such a body. It must be terrible making love to earthly women. The
smells and the whimpering and the wetness."

"Making love is an exchange of vulnerability," I said. "What's the
use of two invincible beings making love? It would be like trying to
breathe in a vacuum."

"You're cruel." Maité sniffed. "Awful. We had so much together
once. I know you remember."

She was talking just to talk, just for the drama. I had only the
vaguest intimations of that ancient life. Nothing more than a dark flash
upon waking, a shudder in the moment before sleep. A series of dark,
confused images recognized now as the dreams that had haunted me
since childhood: black mountain peaks lit by an ebony moon; reflections
of naked bodies in a pane of silvered glass; the heavy glitter of jewelry
against bare flesh; a face among all the faces that did not want to be
remembered. It wasn't much, a damning nostalgia. But I knew now it
was more than they had.

A few seconds later a brilliant explosion shook the old house to the
frame. Probably the refineries at Port Doux. The orchestra stopped playing; a gasp went up from the guests. In the silence that followed, Maité
said in a loud voice, "So, you no longer care for me?"

"I guess not," I said.

A single theatrical tear slid down her cheek and fell into her martini.
The liquid froze instantly, and the glass cracked in her hand. She threw
it to the floor in another shatter of glass and ice across the polished tiles
and stormed off.

I wandered the mansion to get away from the pathetic scene in the
ballroom. I went into the empty salons and drawing rooms, up the winding stairs into the onion-domed turret. The furnishings on the second
floor were elegant, if a bit dusty. Faded photographs showed people
dressed in the formal style of the last generation. Through the door to
the master bedroom I heard the sound of the blonde and Joris going at
it. I tried to get water from the faucet in an old bathroom in the servants'
quarters on the third floor to cool my burning mouth. That wouldn't
count, I thought. As long as I didn't accept anything from them, not a
drop to drink, not a bite of food. This was civic water, from the public
works; I had actually paid taxes for the privilege of drinking the foul

stuff. But when I turned the handle, there was just a bare rusty trickle and then nothing.

In the big kitchen Ward and Colum were on their knees, shooting dice with the cook. Jane sat up on the butcher-block table, a bottle of excellent champagne in one hand, laughing that high, pointless laugh of hers. The cook seemed the only one in the house not afraid of them.

"You're lucky, old man, damn lucky," Ward was saying to him. "You don't know it, but you're the luckiest man in the world right now."

They always pick one each time for their special favors, their whimsical magnanimity. This cook would be a prince in his next life, a ruler of men. He didn't look as if he would care much for that sort of thing. Pots boiled over on the stove behind him. He checked over his shoulder every now and then, from habit, and shrugged.

"Right. It don't matter no more," he said in a thick accent. "I seen that quick enough." He was a Montagnard, dark and rugged, with a head as big as a mule's. These people had never cared about much to begin with, toughened by wars, persecutions, blood feuds, and the rigors of life in the mountains. Now he was calmly winning at dice against Ward. He would be a prince, and he didn't care one way or the other. I had to admire his complacency.

When I stepped from the hallway into the light, Jane looked up.

"Here he is," she said. "Mr. Gloom. A drink?" She held up the bottle.

I shook my head.

"No, of course not," Colum said. "The jerk's going to make us go through the whole routine one more time."

The three of them made up the younger set, the fun crowd, lighter in attitude than Joris and the rest. They fancied themselves characters in a dizzy farce, all champagne and imported cigarettes and practical jokes. Though of course it was only a question of style. There was no difference in substance, none at all. I knew there was no chance with them, but I always tried.

"There are a billion stars," I said. "You could leave me alone on any speck of dust to the windward of just one of them. A normal lifetime. Then the end."

Jane laughed and tipped up the bottle. She was the girl dancing on the table at the party, the tease with the gleam in her eye. Her heart was black.

"Oh, boy," she said. "You're a scream."

Colum straightened and brushed the wrinkles out of his tuxedo. The cook had just shot a seven against his eight.

Ward was swearing under his breath.

"You're getting a little too lucky, cookie," Ward said.

"I'll lose if you want, sir," the cook said.

Jane laughed again at this. A sharp, unpleasant sound that rose to perfect pitch and set the copper pots ringing above the stove.

"Listen, we'd like to help you out," Colum said to me as he rummaged in his pockets for a cigarette. "But what can we do? Joris is an absolute tyrant, you know that."

"Just a swallow, old sport," Ward said, looking up. "That's all it would take on your part. A morsel, a smidgen."

"A crumb," Jane said.

"Naturally you'd have to sit down at the table with us for a minute or two," Colum said. "For the sake of ceremony."

"No." I said. "I won't eat with you. That's out of the question."

"Then . . ." Ward pursed his lips.

"What do you think, cookie?" Colum said, nudging the man with the toe of his polished pump.

The big Montagnard shrugged. "I don't know," he said. "He does not want to eat. He is not hungry."

In truth I was very hungry. I hadn't eaten in three days, just as they had intended. Sausages and hams hung on hooks from a beam in the ceiling; dried peppers and heads of garlic were strung together in ropes over the stove; marmalades and jars of honey marinade gleamed like gold in a rack along the windowsill. In a wire bowl on the table, christophines and starfruit ripened audibly. The cook went back to his game, a pile of colorful ten-thousand escudo notes stacked up before him, probably more money than he had seen in his entire life. But he seemed to know now that money no longer had any value. He was playing for something far more important.

"You're an idiot and a drip," Jane hissed at me from her perch on the butcher block. "You know at last we'll make you do it. You'll stop begging, you'll stop refusing, and you'll just eat. You'll stuff your face with it. We'll find a way to make you."

"You won't," I said. "You never will."

A row of silenced clocks stood along the mantel in the darkened library. On the walls, in cases, hung regimental flags from the last war. The young blonde who had gone with Joris earlier was here now and had pulled a chair over to the open window. She sat unmoving in green shadow, watching the city burn.

I came up behind and put a hand on her shoulder. "Are you all right?" I said.

She didn't turn around. "That's a ridiculous question."

Her blue dress was torn. She couldn't go back to the party looking like that. I pulled up another chair and sat beside her in the green semidarkness.

We stayed like that for about fifteen minutes without speaking, really the first bit of quiet I'd had in days. And it was only now that I could feel myself becoming hollow, each second riven of the things that had made me human. Suddenly I wanted badly to remember, to call back every moment of the life that was leaving.

"I have to tell someone before it's too late, before it's all gone," I began in a trembling voice.

The blonde said nothing.

"And you, I've seen you before. I know you," I said.

"No, you don't know me," she said in a tired voice. "I was famous, I was in films. From the cover of magazines, probably. My face."

"It's just that I'm forgetting," I said.

"Forgetting what?"

"Everything. This life."

"What's wrong with that?"

"You don't understand. It's like the floor falling out from under your feet. It's horrible."

"Once the fires reach the pampas," she said, "the whole countryside will go up. Who knows where it will stop?"

"It will not stop," I said.

Lying open on the big library table, the atlas showed a map more real than the landscape it portrayed, already gone, gutted, unrecognizable.

The green light was almost pleasant for a moment. The music and ballroom conversation seemed natural from this distance. It could be any Saturday, any slightly dull society party, except for the unquenchable flames consuming the city below.

"I'm responsible," I said. "I'm responsible for all of it." I bowed my head and told her everything I knew. I wouldn't eat with them; I wouldn't take a drink. I had refused time and time again. They pursued me across the aeons, through so many lives, and still I wouldn't eat with them. A mouthful of food was worth ten million souls, a drop of wine another million. For a whole meal they would spare this world—or what was left of it now. But I would never eat with them. Never.

"Who are you?" she said. She did not seem surprised at anything I told her.

"I don't know," I said.

"You're a man?"

"Yes," I said. "In this life."

"No. You're a monster."

"So you believe me?"

"Yes." She leaned back against the brocade fabric of the chair, her face lit green by the blaze. Her irises were green now. There was a swollen circle of bite marks on her shoulder, darkening into bruises.

"You know what," she said. "I don't care. It can all go to hell."

"It is."

"You look so normal," she said. "Dumpy, really. No one could tell from looking at you."

There was a mirror strung at an angle over the fireplace. I stood and walked over to it. I had already forgotten this face, this body. A small man, about fifty. Balding, a slight paunch, uncomfortable in dinner clothes. Used instead to open collars and dusty linen suits, to cheap cigars on a patio in a less fashionable suburb and commonplace meditations over a glass of beer. The eyes were a little short-sighted from squinting at copy, the skin tinged with an unhealthy yellow from too many hours out of the sun, too many late nights at the typewriter in the city room, too much coffee. Still, I saw something likable about him: Something that had made people listen.

A few other scenes glimmered in the mirror as well, deep in the heart of the glass. I could see a long road of red dirt, banana trees. The tumbledown walls of kitchen gardens on either side. Old-fashioned country houses built in the days when country houses weren't so far from the city. We had a house there, my wife and I. It was small, and the backyard of scrabble grass faded into the scrub of hills, but it was ours. Had she been happy?

I remembered the patio crowded with plants in terra cotta pots. Cactus, Wandering Jew. She had collected them in the hills, her hands protected by a pair of my old army gloves, a wide-brimmed straw hat shading her brown face. Her father had been a captain in the commercial service. We still had a chest in the attic full of his moldering uniforms, gold braid gone brittle with age, brass buttons tarnished. I remembered making love late one night after the cinema, very quietly so as not to wake the children asleep upstairs. Her eyes filled with tears as she put a sentimental tune on the gramophone and unhooked her dress, as we lay down together on the old divan. Those tears were nothing, she'd explained afterward in my arms, just the melancholy of life. How many more evenings would there be like this?

I stared up at my face in the mirror now, a stranger's face visited with uncertainty and weakness, green in the dreadful green light. Not daring a hope, I waited for another forgotten evening to recall other evenings farther back, links in a chain receding into the murk of vanished lives. Perhaps the whole picture would emerge at last, perhaps . . .

In the distance the black mountains touched with snow beneath the black moon, and everywhere through the gloom along the agate path, red ants struggle with small bits of bloody flesh. There is the unsteady breathing of a wounded man hidden in the underbrush and the snorting of the horses. On the steps of the palace, crushed and broken-faced, my cousin . . . then in a prison cell. . . .

No. It was impossible.

From the chair the girl called to me. I sat down again beside her and took her hand.

"My lower half has gone numb," she said. "I can't feel a thing."

"That will happen," I said. "To you it would be like poison."

"But it doesn't feel bad," she said. "It feels quite pleasant."

"Yes," I said.

"And the places where he touched me, they're going numb too."

"I remember you now," I said. "Once I saw you riding up the Avenida Alberto Liku in a big car. You came through my district with your windows closed, and you didn't even wave, but still people lined the street to get a look at you passed."

"That little jaunt was my publicist's idea," she said. "The district just south of the Alfama is full of radicals. Bomb throwers. Of course I kept the window up."

"My newspaper offices were there," I said. "In the Via dos Prazeres."

"*La Prensa.*"

"I can't remember."

"Try, please." The green light in her eyes was going dim. "Keep talking, please."

"I wrote editorials," I said, speaking quickly. "We were closed by the Secretariat and closed again. But we always managed to reopen. There was a fan in my office that made a strange clattering noise. We wanted people to have cleaner water to drink. We wanted people to be able to walk the streets without being stopped by the police for their papers and arrested on a whim. I had a secretary, an earnest girl from the provinces, Rio Platos. She had nice legs. Once, just before the general strike, working late, we—"

"Will you kiss me?" the blonde said. Her voice sounded faint. She let go of my hand. When I reached her lips with mine, they were cold. She was already dead.

I waited the last hour in the garden. This was the part of the dinner party I hated most. Joris liked to go around popping heads. He'd just look at them, the poor beggars, and narrow his eyes a bit, and that would be it. An ugly spectacle.

"The process is painless for the animals," he said once. Then I hit him, and we never made it to dinner that time. How could they be so cruel and so stupid after all this time? Stars had come and gone, and still they behaved like spoiled children out on a spree. Consciousness is about knowledge or nothing; they think it's about sensation. How idiotic.

Most of the city was gone now. Soon dawn would reveal the final vista: a broken plain of smoldering rubble as far as the eye could see. They always left a few servants alive until the end, and one came into the garden to fetch me. A boy, fifteen or sixteen, with a tear-stained face.

"They told me to tell you dinner was ready, sir," he said. "They said they'll kill me if you don't come."

"I know," I said.

"Hurry, please." I followed him through the garden and up the grand staircase. The dining room was on the second floor, a long, elegant room with arched windows overlooking the holocaust. They were all waiting at the table, and as I came through the door, they greeted me with a light smattering of applause.

"There you are, old boy," Joris said. "Was busy earlier, didn't have a chance to really say hello."

"I saw that, Joris," I said. "She died in the library."

"Who?" he said, genuinely perplexed.

"We were about to start without you," Maité said, holding out her hand. My place had been set next to hers at the far end of the table facing Joris. Jane sat between Colum and Ward on one side, across from Ani and Petra, grim-faced on the other. To them it was a solemn occasion.

The table looked wonderful, as usual. All ice swans and fresh-cut flowers and sterling flatware and a bewildering array of food arranged on heaping platters down the center. Everything smelled delicious. I saw game and mutton, pork, fish, fowl, roast beef, lobsters, oysters in their shells, mounds of fresh shrimp, noodle dishes, goulashes, vegetable casseroles, salads, salmon molds, desserts, flavored ices, fruit, cheese, wine. Enough food for a hundred guests. The sight of all that food made me weak. Pierced with hunger, I felt my will begin to bend.

"Sit down, darling, sit down," Maité insisted.

I hesitated, but sat beside her, and there was another smattering of applause. The empty black plate set before me reflected candlelight and the shame on my face. I didn't usually sit down. They knew that.

"Well done," Ward said.

"Yes, maybe we can finally conclude this business in a civilized manner," Jane said. "Maybe we can get on with it!"

"Shut up, you little cunt!" Maité said, her hand over mine. "Can't you see it's hard for him?"

I felt feverish, my mouth watering. The smell of all that food was more than I could bear. *Don't give in!* I whispered to myself, and looked around the room for anyone who might help. Waiters in white jackets stood, teeth chattering, at their busing stations. A cold green fire burned in the fire place. Joris's eyes were lead. I was alone.

"Just one little swallow, baby, that's all it will take," Maité said in my ear. "One little swallow, and you will be with us again. Such a small thing, a swallow." She was very close. Her white limbs gleamed at the edge of my vision.

Ward leaned across the table. "Remember all the fun we used to have, old sport," he said. "We'll have all that fun and more again. Just a nibble, just a sip. In fact I'm going to propose a toast." He stood and lifted his glass; then everyone stood. "To good times again," he said. "And to you, old sport." He nodded at me, his smile gruesome and red-lipped. He could almost get away with the makeup; he almost looked natural. But the smile was horrible. They shared it, looking down at me, glasses raised.

I stood slowly. A wineglass was put into my hand. The room seemed to be swimming in food. The wineglass got closer to my lips. But before I drank, I forced a breath and peered into the blood-colored liquid and saw something there at the bottom that made me remember. I set the glass down beside the black plate.

"No," I said. "Not a bite. Not a single swallow. It will always be the same."

I was remembering everything now, all of it, every moment of a thousand lives in a mad rush of passion and regret, foolishness, squalor, perversity, courage, cowardice, grace, love. Then the first life in which I had walked with them on the streets of a vast city, moon like a black pearl suspended above mountain peaks in the distance upon which there was always snow. I was remembering faces in the crowd, the first crowd, and then the first ghastly meal. Never again. Worlds could perish, galaxies implode, but I would not eat with them again.

When I looked back at the table, the food was gone, as I knew it would be, the cutlery and place settings gone. Only one plate remained, my plate. And at the center of that plate a single black pill.

"There it is," Maité said. "Swallow it. Go ahead."

"Swallow . . . swallow," they all murmured.

I turned my face from them and left the room.

Before I reached the staircase, the wall of heat that was their undying rage hit the mansion. Everything around me seemed to float for a suspended moment. Then the south facade crashed away to a great hollow booming, and green flames sprang up all around. The fire would spread; the planet would be reduced to cinders. Another dark hunk of rock circling a nameless sun, another billion burned souls on my conscience. The great roof beam of the house cracked with a roar. Flames consumed the foundation. The floors buckled and opened at my feet. This was always happening. As I fell, I caught a last glimpse of the burning city. Green flames followed the columns of refugees all the way to the sea.

In this life, barely a generation ago, my father had owned a house there, a big ramshackle place in the middle of a pine grove by the sea beneath the cliffs at Isola Verde. In the spring, armies of blind caterpillars used to come marching down off the trees in long lines of undulating fur. Touching head to tail, they always followed the leader straight for my mother's flower garden. Once, they stripped the petals off every one of her prize-winning bearded irises in a single afternoon. From there they got into the house and into everything else: shoes left beneath the bed, clean sheets folded in the linen closet, bowls of soup on the table in the kitchen, water freshly drawn for the bath.

The caterpillars were beautiful soft things, which given time would become iridescent green moths, but in this stage they were poisonous to the touch. Their fur carried a powdery substance that caused a terrible rash. So every spring Father waged a merciless war against them: He would wait until the caterpillars had almost reached the garden, pour kerosene along each line, strike a match, and they would go up in flames in a straight shot right back into their nests in the trees. It was a tricky business. You had to run when the wind shifted; even the smoke from their burning bodies could give you a rash, make your eyes swollen and red.

When the flames burned out, Father would sweep the charred, tarry bodies of the caterpillars into neat piles, bag them up, and bury them in the woods. But the acid stink of kerosene and burned flesh would linger in the yard for days.

STEVE RASNIC TEM

Heat

Steve Rasnic Tem's stories have been published in numerous anthologies, including MetaHorror, Forbidden Acts, Dark Terrors 3, The Best New Horror, *and earlier volumes of* The Year's Best Fantasy and Horror, *as well as in various magazines. His first English language collection,* City Fishing, *was recently published by Silver Salamander Press. A chapbook in collaboration with his wife, Melanie Tem,* The Man on the Ceiling, *was also just published by American Fantasy.*

"Heat" is one of a series of stories he's been working on over the years concerning the four elements of the ancients—earth, wind, fire, and water. He still has one left to do—a wind story.

"Heat" originally appeared in White of the Moon: New Tales of Madness and Dread, *edited by Stephen Jones.*

—E. D.

Ignition point, the minumum temperature for burning. She knew the temperature at which paper would burn because of that book by Bradbury. She did not know the right temperature for the combustion of flesh. Whenever she asked her doctor he just shook his head, patted her shoulder. For her part, she did not tell him about the things she saw when she looked out his window. Or the way his office smelled of char.

"Just tell me about whatever pops into your head," he said, smiling. She found herself wondering how much internal body heat was used to make a smile.

But "a calorie is the amount of heat required to raise the temperature of one gram of water one degree Centigrade" is what she replied.

He looked at her appraisingly. She wondered how much heat he used to suppress his initial reaction and to reconsider his words. "And that is a fact which is important to you?" he asked, obviously knowing the answer.

"Cotton batting ignites at four hundred forty-six degrees Fahrenheit," she replied. "Wool blankets at four hundred one, fiberboard at four twenty-one."

"Try this on for size," he said, softly. "Sometimes knowing the facts and figures makes what we fear seem more comprehensible. They present the possibility that this might, after all, be dealt with."

She gazed out his window without speaking. In the middle distance smoke had appeared. Dozens of fires moved through the streets. With their blazing heads and torsos and two or more legs, she could not tell if they were people on fire writhing in agony or a new form of fiery life performing an ecstatic dance.

Eventually she tore her eyes away long enough to look at the doctor. "Did you know, Doctor," she asked, "that the world was without fire until Prometheus brought it down to us? He'd stolen it from Heaven."

It was one of those hot, shimmering days so common in Arizona this time of year. Or so Sandra had been told. She'd been here for two of those years, leaving Colorado in almost frantic haste the third summer after the plane went down and burned up her ex-husband along with their only child.

David. He would have been thirteen in another month. Hair a runaway blaze of copper. He would have hated Arizona, but then she would never have lived here if he'd been alive. He'd liked it cool, sought it out in swimming pools and shade trees and ski runs, fall evenings curled up on the porch swing with his mom just like a little kid, his babyish face in the moonlight a pale antidote to his dazzle of hair.

The heated air shuddered over the car lot beyond her balcony, or maybe it was her eyesight going from grief held adamantly at bay. If she started crying now she wouldn't stop for a week, and she'd had a few weeks like that back in Colorado before the move.

Don't get me started! she'd say to David when he used to question her, question everything with an energetic resentment only a child that full of life could maintain. Just don't get me started, not today. I have to get dressed, get to work. I can't start crying today.

One of the legs of her pantyhose developed a run under her shaking hands. Dammit. She hurried around the apartment, bumping into things and cursing. She'd had to settle for a smaller place than they'd owned in Colorado, but the thought of finding something to do with all that room was terrifying in any case. *Smaller, hell—we had a house! Big shade trees in the backyard and flowers everywhere, orange and red like scattered match heads.* . . . She found another pair of hose with only a couple of snags, willed herself to slip them on carefully, easing them over her raw-feeling legs like a second skin. Her friends at the bank teased her over this insistence of hers that she wear pantyhose every day, whatever the heat. And makeup—she couldn't go outside without makeup. She couldn't bear to look people in the face if she wasn't wearing makeup. They might see too much.

Outside in the black asphalt lot a child screamed. Sandra stamped shoeless out onto the balcony. Down below a father held the crying child, mother frantically brushing at the little one's bare feet as if she could clean the pain away. Their shiny white car had Indiana plates. Sandra closed her eyes and swore. Every summer some tourist permitted his child to walk barefoot on the asphalt. And if the child was a toddler, reaction times being slow at that age, the burns could be . . .

Sandra felt heat on her eyelids, saw the fire licking at the edges of the shutters she'd made to keep the world out, saw dancing flames through closed eyes.

She managed to get herself back inside before the attack subsided, fireworms leading her, racing ahead over the tops of bookcases and trailing across the back of the charcoal-upholstered couch. This wasn't an unfamiliar sensation—she'd had the experience several times since the hot weather began. Something was wrong with her eyes, of course, but she just couldn't bring herself to see her doctor about it, to describe the phenomenon and be questioned about her diet, her habits, her losses. She kept thinking she should be shaking this off, calling an ambulance for those poor people outside. But she could hear the sounds of excited conversation now, other people in the complex coming out to help. It probably wasn't very serious anyway, just a little burn, and she would have embarrassed everyone with her hysterical overreaction. It wouldn't have taken much, perhaps just a glance from the hurt child, and she'd have fallen down on that hot asphalt, burning herself, burning herself all over and not even caring.

She looked around—she was on the couch although she couldn't remember sitting down. With a feeling surprisingly akin to disappointment she noted that the flames were gone from her apartment. But still a hint of smoke in the air. Not that that was confirmation of anything; this time of year, people said, it always smelled like smoke.

She gradually became aware of an ache in her lower extremities. Then saw that she was kicking her right foot over and over in anxious rhythm, against the coffee table leg, against some book wedged beneath the couch, the stocking toe torn as if chewed. She made herself stop, reached down and freed the leather-bound volume.

Her fingers trembled over the cover. She thought she'd gotten rid of it, then remembered she couldn't figure out how: throw it away and someone might find it, trace it back to her, ask her embarrassing questions about herself, her life without David. Her face suffused with heat visualizing the look on the questioners' faces. At one point she'd actually thought she'd burn it, had even brought the matches up out of the jumble at the back of the drawer where she'd banished them, but could not will them to strike.

She opened the scrapbook for the terrible reassurance that the clippings were still there: glued to the pages in no particular order or alignment: a chronicle of human disaster, a catalogue of all the myriad ways a human body might lose warmth, color, thought, and urgency. A narrative chronicling the departure of heat from human life. All the ways a life might discorporate. A collage of suicides, murder, fatal activity, accident (in which she found it increasingly difficult to believe), disease, earth, wind, water, and especially fire.

And included among these clippings, but with no special handling or delineation, were the stories about the one particular fire, the singular plane crash which had changed her life forever. Her own audacity in this one aspect of this book of disasters still did not fail to take her breath away.

She'd never shown the book to her doctor; she'd never shown it to anyone. She would have been ashamed. For the whole purpose of this tome was to keep other people, their lives, their messy tragedies, at bay. She'd discovered simply too much pain out there. And if anyone else were to read this scrapbook they would know what she had discovered about herself: she didn't really care what happened to them, not really. She couldn't afford to.

"It's a charter," her ex-husband had said. "I'm not going to tell you how much, but it's worth it. We'll fly up for two days of skiing, the prettiest snow country David's ever seen, then back in time for school on Monday. He'll love it."

And he did, of course. David had told her so himself when he called, thirty minutes before boarding the return flight.

She fingered the strips of newsprint carefully, as if handling brittle historic documents. They were unexpectedly yellowed—it hadn't been that long ago, after all. But the clippings looked so old, and the chronicle—of how the ice had weighed heavy on one wing, resulting in a loss of control after take-off, the plane rolling, the search for survivors, and finally the list of names, David's name—read like a piece of history, too far away to touch her.

But the evidence of how much she had been touched, changed, transformed was here in abundance, in the very existence of such a scrapbook, and the jumble of hundreds of notations and extended commentary, scribblings in a tiny, intense handwriting inserted among the clippings, using up every bit of available space, added to daily before she'd managed to free herself and move away from Colorado. Forty killed. A hundred twenty killed. Chemical oxidation is a common source of heat. Pilot error. Class B fires are fires in flammable petroleum products. Wreckage scattered over ten square miles. The emperor Augustus instituted a night patrol of slaves to watch out for fire. Varnished fabrics are prone to spontaneous ignition. The Wilson family, who missed the flight, expressed their sympathy. The five stages of combustion, freeburning, smoldering, and total loss, total involvement.

But she'd brought the book with her, hadn't she? Once she'd made it, it almost seemed too dangerous to be gotten rid of. And now, after slipping into shoes to cover the tears in her stocking, pulling on a suit jacket—"in *this heat*, Sandra?"—she unaccountably tucked the scrapbook under her arm for the long, hot drive to work.

The couple sitting across from Sandra's desk smiled fiercely. *What is it with all the smiling people in my life?* she thought, and imagined a fire under their feet, the heat radiating up through their bodies forcing the lips to stretch into an impossibly wide line before evolving further into a grimace. What else could such a smile mean? The man occasionally glanced at the coffeemaker on the credenza behind Sandra, no doubt wondering why she hadn't offered them any. He probably felt entitled— that's what the coffee was for, for loan department employees to offer to the customers and he had certainly seen other customers get their share so where was his? Sandra could hear the machine bubbling away behind her, liquid dripping and sizzling down the hot sides. She never went near that death machine; no way was she going to start today. You never saw an open flame, but that was the worst, the absolute worst. The heat was still there, disguised, waiting for you to make a mistake.

The man smiled anyway. As did his wife. A fact which made Sandra profoundly uncomfortable as they'd come in so that she might tell them *in person* that there was no way Southwest was going to give them a loan, a loan which might allow them to keep their home. The reason she had to deliver this bad news in person was because Southwest was the Bank with the Personal Touch.

The idea of touching these people made her shudder. They were probably good people, they probably worked hard and were great neighbors to have around, decent company. But a truck was about to run them down, smear them across the hot asphalt, and Sandra desperately did not want to be there when it happened.

The more they smiled the more Sandra fidgeted. Maybe they always smiled like this, whatever the news. "I'm sorry," she repeated. Even more smiles, as if they couldn't help themselves. Only the small child sitting between them seemed unhappy, seemed to understand exactly what Sandra was trying to tell them, and Sandra found herself peering over at that child more and more, as if appealing for help.

But the child, a little girl with luxurious wavy brown hair, looked elsewhere. Under the desk, by Sandra's feet, where Sandra had quickly hid the scrapbook when the couple came in ten minutes early for their appointment. Sandra glanced nervously between her legs: the book had fallen open, several rather graphic photos of car crashes displayed themselves. Her handwriting looked large and crazy on these pages; she worried that the little girl might be able to read the words. She should never have left it out—she should have stuck it into a drawer. Now this child might be damaged by what she had done. The central picture on the exposed page was of a burned-out vehicle: a large one, she thought it might be a van. In blocky lettering by the picture, her emphatic writing: OXYGEN. Underneath that was an observation she thought she remembered.

> Human beings breathe in oxygen. Burning is a rapid oxidation. If there were no nitrogen in the air to retard oxygen, all fires would burn uncontrolled. Perhaps they would burn forever.

Across from her, as if in answer, the woman breathed heavily. The little girl looked up at Sandra with an annoyed expression. The man continued to smile, but Sandra could detect the beginnings of an unraveling at the corners of his mouth. "Well, perhaps you could try again sometime, when your credit history improves," Sandra began, looking for a way to initiate the goodbyes and head the family toward the door. Someone had a radio on their desk, listening to the news. Something about a fire downtown. Sandra glanced down at her scrapbook of disasters, her purse. It was almost lunchtime; she could reach the site of the fire in less than ten minutes. If only these two would stop smiling. If they'd just stop smiling she might be able to get them to leave. Perhaps their English wasn't very good, although nothing on the application had suggested immigration. She looked from the man to the woman—maybe if she could bring herself to go to the coffee machine, and brought the man back a cup, then he would leave. She could give him a styrofoam cupful, something he could take with him. Hell, she could give him one of those complimentary thermoses they had for people opening new savings accounts, the ones with the bank logo embossed in red on the side.

She looked at the little girl again, asleep in her mother's arms now. Face so still, pale. Children that age could sleep so deeply it seemed more akin to hibernation than to normal slumber. Barely breathing, almost no perceptible signs of life. Terrifying. The cheeks and forehead appeared so cool, all heat color gone from the face. More than once she had wrestled David out of just such a sleep to make sure he was still alive. The bubbling from the coffeemaker was louder behind her now, an anxious sizzle from the cherry wood credenza top. The couple's eyes appeared to widen in alarm, but the smiles held.

She looked down at the little girl, who held Sandra's scrapbook in her lap, turning the pages, playing with the brittle yellow flaps of newsprint. She looked up at Sandra and laughed. The mother tilted her head toward the scrapbook and began to read.

"Oh, you really don't want to see that!" Sandra exclaimed, reaching over the desk and snatching one edge of the book. The pages fluttered, clippings dangling precariously as she pulled, the little girl resisting, then finally letting go so suddenly Sandra stumbled backwards. She clasped the book to her chest, a sick panic growing in her stomach when she saw that some of the clippings had fallen out, littering the carpet around her desk like soiled underwear. She looked around to see who among her co-workers might be watching, suddenly convinced she wouldn't be able to work here anymore. She turned back to the family and tried stammering an apology.

A yellow finger of flame tapped the man's right shoulder, grew into a hand reaching for his high, stiff collar, pouted its lips to kiss, then whisper into his ear. Unless she was mistaken, his smile grew even more, engorged with warmth, his eyes shiny with reflected heat.

Flame spread its legs and leapt from husband to wife, a nimbus behind their heads, so that they were two saints smiling beneficently at her. Their clothing began to glow as if wrapping hot coals.

"So . . . please try us again," she said, her purse and scrapbook ready in her hands. She set her purse on the desk and reached out to shake whatever hand might be offered, then pulled back when hands enveloped in blue flame floated up from the other side. She grabbed her purse again and clutched it with the scrapbook in front of her, turning her head away from the fiery pupa the little girl had become in her mother's arms, and racing out the door.

———————

Downtown, Sandra drove through layered soot and falling debris, so much smoke, so much ash floating through the air. There were fire trucks everywhere, and roadblocks. A police officer stopped her a block from the fire. "You can't go this way, ma'am."

"But I have to get closer. I have to see."

The policeman waved his arms in irritation. Car horns pierced the overheated air behind her. Beyond the officer, where she wanted to be, great white hoses like prehistoric snakes meandered down the street, over curbs and sidewalks, slipped into ragged, darkened cavities seeking to drink the fire. "Lady, back this vehicle up *now* if you don't want to spend the night in jail!"

She turned her car around jerkily, backing it against one of the great hoses, which sent the cop cursing, chasing after her. She stepped on the gas, nearly sideswiping several parked cars as she made a quick right into the next alley. She pulled behind some battered trash cans, got out with her scrapbook and ran toward the other end where she saw firefighters running past, their giant-beetlelike forms fleeing the conflagration.

She burst out of the mouth of the alley into heavy black smoke and sparking air. She felt small and helpless, an insect chased from a burning log. Up and down the street empty windows full of fire, black rectangular spaces alive with flames. Across the street, paramedics attended to several firefighters with their masks off, faces black-caked and androgynous. A few feet away, a dead fireman wrapped in a gray blanket, another bending over him, face scarred by fire and tears. She stepped back, anxious to keep her distance. She worried about being seen, of a policeman confiscating her scrapbook, reading it, and arresting her for its contents. She thought of the newspaper stories that would be appearing tomorrow, the picture of this dead fireman on the front page. She thought about where that clipping might go into her scrapbook.

Small groups of firefighters charged several doorways, long axes in hand. Sandra knew then why she envied them, why her admiration of them was never compromised. Their job was clear: they put out fires. An army of good against a nebulous evil.

An explosion over the rooftops, and Sandra gazed up to see fire wrapping the buildings like a giant woman's hair, like tornadoes devouring the firefighters who struggled there. Falling hot cinders beat her to the pavement. She crawled over to a Dumpster whose lid had been spread open like a wing. There she cowered, opening the scrapbook to one article and then to another, gazing at the pictures, trying to visualize the burned bodies the newspapers refused to show. They would not tell the truth. No one wanted to tell her the truth.

She read how fire was like any living thing: it ate, it breathed. Sometimes the fire would leave a room and go into the walls in search of air. Sometimes it was like an animal, hiding wherever it found the right place, then attacking when it was cornered.

When fire came into you it ate up everything: all memory, all hope, all that had made you a presence when you were in the world.

And yet when fire left you it left you empty and cold, the spark and the gleam gone, so that those who'd loved you would find nothing there.

"I had a wonderful time," David said, his voice distorted by distance and static. In the dark she could feel the embers of every word her sweet child had ever said to her burning through her clothes.

Sandra awakened into a land of disintegration. Black shadows of furniture leered out of vanished walls, their shapes stark and distinctive.

Firemen stalked through this gray other world, killing the bright creatures wherever they showed themselves.

Beneath her trembling hands the scrapbook crumbled to ash.

Sssss, a doll's melted face whispered.

"Here, let me help you," the fireman said softly at her side. "Here, try not to move."

She looked up into his mask. "I love you," she whispered through burning lips.

The masked head nodded silently, flames dancing in the bright plastic where there might have been eyes, heat warping the lips into well-intentioned smile.

LINNET TAYLOR

The Wedding at Esperanza

Linnet Taylor was born in London and studied English Literature at Cambridge University. Her careers thus far have included theater directing, horse training, house painting, and financial television. Her radio play Carmini Catulli *won the Woolrich Young Playwrights Award in England. She has written plays, fiction, and journalism for a variety of publications ranging from* Vogue *to* The Christian Science Monitor. *She currently lives in Vermont.*

The following story is part of a collection of fiction dating from the author's two years in Mexico, where she wrote journalism on indigenous issues, human rights, and escalating guerilla conflicts. "The Wedding at Esperanza" is reprinted from the Winter 1999 edition of Pleiades.

—*T. W.*

There was a huge tree in the center of the village square. Isabella's first memory was of the time her brother had placed her high in its branches to watch a meeting, where she had stayed until her grandmother had seen her peering from the foliage like a bird and let out such a cry that everyone stopped arguing and helped retrieve the toddler from her swaying crow's nest. Guillermo was beaten by their father for that, but Isabella remembered it as one of the best times of her childhood. When she sat under it working on her embroidery or talking to José, her lover, or peeling corn for dinner she would stop occasionally to close her eyes and lean back against the great trunk, imagining the life flowing inside it and remembering how it felt to be part of a branch, almost as high as a cloud, omniscient and invisible, smelling the sweet-sour tang of the leaves and feeling the breeze in the heat of the afternoon touch the tendrils of green that encircled her.

The tree was named El Viejo, the old one, and was the heart of the village. Couples came there to kiss late at night when their parents were home in bed, children climbed it and the birds surveyed their kingdom from its leaves. It was as old and as unshakable as life in Esperanza itself.

Guillermo had left to be a soldier while she was still a child. He had gone to the capital where a meal cost a day's wage and along with the other troops had cut the grass in the president's palace grounds to earn his keep. Years later he was posted back to a base near home, to guard them all from the guerillas. Occasionally he would come by, his features fixed in professional gravity, standing in a rumbling open-topped truck packed with identically dressed young men, all with anti-quated guns in their hands, looking nervously into the trees for signs of danger.

The danger came mostly from Isabella's oldest brother, Roberto. He had left home a few days after Guillermo, saying he was going to town to pick up a donkey from a friend, and had never come back. It was well known that he had joined the guerillas, but Isabella had occasion-ally received news from the boys who had been his companions: first that he had become a lieutenant, then a subcommandante, and now a commandante. Sometimes, out in the sierra, she imagined she heard him calling across the hills to his men; sometimes she thought she caught a smudge of darker green amongst the trees, following her, watching as she had once watched from among leaves. She liked the idea that Rob-erto was there. It made her feel safe.

That evening she sat with José under El Viejo's spreading branches, watching darkness stalking the last vestiges of the day. They were silent: it was too hot to speak. The air pressed on them like a heavy garment, crushing thought and speech. Periodically José would take her hand and stroke it, then when the action began to make the sweat trickle down his arm he would let it go and sit still once again, his head, like hers, resting against the rough bark behind them, all their minds concentrated on summoning the cool air of night.

Eventually the breath of dark sighed through the square and they could turn their heads to look at each other. Isabella spoke.

"We're going to have a child," she said.

Her grandmother Assunta was against it from the start.

"He's not ready yet," she warned. "He'll be off with other women, he'll not support you, you'll be having to go out and work in the fields when your belly's so big all you need to do is stay inside and have him look after you. And besides, he's too young. You're a woman of fifteen, but he's not a man yet, for all he's two years older than you."

Isabella only smiled and said, "You will make me a dress. I want it to be white."

Assunta grumbled and worried and made the dress.

In the weeks before the wedding, the war in the sierra worsened. The patrols came through every day, the sweating army sergeant asked questions and shouted and once even poked his gun into the face of Isabella's father, the mayor. "Tell me where they are, Antonio Marquez Santo, you liar. I know your dog of a son is out there. Tell me where they are or you'll see how the army finds runaway children." But Isabella's father kept quiet, looking at the embarrassed Guillermo in the line of wilting troops. He did not know which of his sons disappointed him more.

The guerrillas were coming down from the sierra with increasing regularity to attack the patrols for their weapons and bullets. Every other day there were reports of ambushes, the sierra suddenly divulging a flood of men the color of leaves who moved with the ease of jaguars, ransacking the trucks and leaving bloodied, wriggling boys where there had been trained military units. Walking to the cornfield to take her father his lunch, Isabella saw blood mixed with dust in the road, tatters of military fatigues, sometimes a shoe left behind as if it had pinched its wearer. But still she did not see Roberto.

Then, twelve days before the wedding, the world exploded into madness. It was a blazing day in the sierra, hot and fierce, the sky glaring at the earth which shook off the heat in rippling waves of air. The men were at work tending the young corn, and Isabella was sitting under a tree at the edge of the field sheltering from the morning heat. All was silent, as if sound, like the breeze, could not cut a path through the sweltering jungle of air. The men's bare backs glistened and darkened, and Isabella fanned herself with a leaf, absent-mindedly probing her belly with inquiring fingers. It did not feel different yet, though her breasts felt heavier and she would feel queasy in the early mornings until her grandmother rose and made the tea to calm her stomach.

The sound began almost imperceptibly, like a distant swarm of bees. Nothing was visible over the treetops, the men were so absorbed that no one heard the far-off murmur which neared and swelled until they were all standing up, looking into the sky, wondering what it was that sounded so like a giant fleet of insects in a season when none were due. Isabella peered up through the leaves curiously, unwilling to move from the shade.

Then the sky erupted. The machines soared raging into view, shaking and searing the still air like a flight of demented bumblebees hauling their misshapen bulk over the trees. Isabella had a glimpse of the men hanging from the open sides with their huge guns pointing down at the fields. For an insane moment she thought she saw Guillermo, his face aflame with strange murderous fervor. The men below were looking up with incomprehension, transfixed as if by a grotesque god descending from the heavens. Then the gunships opened fire and the earth exploded in plumes of dry soil and she could see no more.

She remembered the terror of that day as something vague, experienced through a curtain of leaves as if once more she were hidden away, watching the adults go about their business. She remembered how the dust cleared so gradually in the sucking whirlpools of wind that the figures remained unclear for a long time, hidden by shifting clouds where it was impossible to see who was standing and who had fallen. The helicopters finally turned away, gathering their force and tilting their heavy abdomens with the updraft of their wings to fall forward into the clean air and the unbroken green of the hills.

The field was still covered with swirling dust as if creation were happening over again, gradually settling to reveal a mess of moving bodies which Isabella could increasingly make out were wounded and dead and unhurt all mingling. She ran to Antonio, who was crouching on the ground by the unmoving body of his friend Andres, cradling his head in his lap and rocking slowly to and fro as she remembered her grandmother rocking with her mother's quiet body many years ago, after her little brother Miguel was born.

"What can I do?" she asked.

"Run and get help," her father answered, his voice shaking with tears, and Isabella ran for all she was worth down the steep path to the village, her heart in her throat as if she were very young and had done something for which she knew terrible punishment awaited her.

Reports reached the village that night that the army was saying that a guerrilla band had been destroyed in the sierra, that the General was on television all over the country proclaiming that a great blow had been struck against terrorism and that the bodies of six guerillas were in the mortuary. They said the television showed the bodies, Andres and the rest, naked, covered only with rags of clothing, lying on slabs in the cellar at the base. No one could believe that they could say such things except Antonio Marquez Santo. He went back to the field and mourned his friends silently as he worked, his hands molding the damaged corn, Esperanza's life, back into the earth, stroking its leaves in silent communion and praying under his breath for his grandchildren to live in better times. Isabella went with him, kneeling on the ground as he did because it seemed the right thing to do. Late into the night they tended the young corn, replanting it gently as a mother lays down a baby to sleep.

Her grandmother warned against going on with the plans to marry José. "It is a bad time," she said, rocking in her chair, her strong fingers making clothes for the great-grandchild growing inside Isabella. "How can we expect God to be listening when he is busy with the dead?"

But Isabella set her face and went to the church. She took flowers with her, a bride's bouquet, young corn interwoven with wildflowers from the borders of the field still spattered with blood. She laid it at the feet of the Virgin, kneeling and looking up into her sad, white face. "Give me a husband," she prayed. "Let me marry José. Don't let God take him as He took the others, and I swear I will put myself and the village in your protection."

She prayed for a long time, motionless before the white altar. Her grandmother, coming to look for her, saw her in the gloom of the church in her white dress with her hair falling loose over her shoulders like the Virgin's robes above her, looking like a lost child who has found her mother. Approaching she heard her grandchild's quiet prayers, saw her lips moving in faithful supplication, and could not speak. She knelt down next to her and, placing her arms on the cushioned rail next to Isabella's, prayed for a happy marriage.

When they came out of the church together, she stopped everyone they passed and told them to prepare for the marriage in three days' time. Such was her certainty that no one questioned her change of heart. Isabella, beside her, glowed with happiness.

On Sunday morning the heat lifted and the village came out of mass to find a breeze blowing that was almost cool, lifting El Viejo's leaves like the veil of a bride. The tree had come out in its spring raiment of white flowers, which nodded and bobbed with the sighs of cool air as if accepting a compliment. "It is a good omen, the Virgin is watching over us," people said as they went to work setting up tables and chairs in the square for the wedding party that evening.

Isabella stood in the center of her home's only room, her arms raised above her head as her grandmother put the finishing touches to her dress. Having made her decision, the old woman had decided that it would be the best wedding the village had ever seen, and had dedicated herself to perfecting the white dress with lace taken from her own, lifted from its box with ceremony and yellowing with age. She had sent out Miguel to pick the sweetest wildflowers, little blue and white sprays, corn for life and renewal, and trailing white-flowered bindweeds to bind her granddaughter to her new husband. When her family walked Isabella to the church, she looked to them the image of her mother twenty-five years before, and Antonio's eyes swelled with tears as he saw his daughter's unexpected splendor.

The party was in full swing by the time darkness fell, the band playing raucously and everyone so full they could hardly drink from the bowls of pulque that stood on every table. Isabella took the first dance with José, her face glowing with happiness, his pride so evident it brought tears to the eyes of even the most hardened old couple sitting around the square. The dance ended and Antonio got up to speak. José swept up Isabella in a flurry of underskirts and sat her on the lowest branch of El Viejo, standing below her with pride as his father-in-law made a speech about his hopes for the couple, the gifts they had been given by the village and the welcome he gave his new son. Isabella sat, perfectly happy in the arms of the tree, thinking of her child and her lover, feeling the light breeze rustle the leaves and mingle their scent with the sweeter fragrance of the flowers.

Only half-listening to her father, her attention was caught by a movement outside the ring of listeners. She peered into the night to see what it was, moving outside the low walls enclosing the square. Slowly she made out dark figures creeping amongst the uneven adobe houses, more and more of them, slouching out of the narrow openings between and settling in the darkest places, becoming shadows. She looked over to the opposite side of the square and saw other figures, less bulky and more sinuous, moving there too under cover, threading their way from darkness to darkness like jaguars. Eventually the last of the figures on each side slipped into the refuge of shadow within shadow and all was still. She could feel the gaze of either side burning across the square through the illuminated crowd which separated them, and she knew with terrible certainty that her brothers had come to attend her wedding-dance.

She leaped down from the branch in a shower of petals and leaves. "Dance," she commanded, "everybody dance." The band struck up as she caught José by the hand and led him to the center of the square, surrounded by couples finding their partners and moving to join them. The melody they played for her was not a wedding tune, but an ardent, wild music of incantation that caught their bodies like moths in candlelight and made everyone dance as they had danced when they were young, the rhythm taking them, leading them whirling and stamping and twisting in the light of the great church candles and strings of colored bulbs like spiraling birds. Isabella spun her desperate supplication in the midst of the crowd, urging them on to greater passion with her swirling skirts flying around her and her clapping hands intoxicating her body with prayer.

The dark figures watched silently, fused with the night, unable to see the shapes on the other side of the square for the whirling crowd, but waiting with murderous patience for the dance to end.

But when the musicians looked to be tiring, Isabella called out to them to play on, winding her way through the crowd with José, spurring her guests to dance faster and with more abandon, until the band played on without asking, song after song, caught in the collective spiral of the dance, mesmerizing the eyes watching from the darkness, hypnotizing the night itself, drawing on the moon and the stars in their arcs above in distant imitation, spinning a web of prayer and magic around the whirling village.

They awoke to perfect silence. In the dust the soldiers and guerillas one by one sat up, rubbing their eyes and stretching as if waking from a sleep of intoxication. They had slept where they fell, forgetting their intent along with themselves. The wedding party was gone; so were the adobe shacks of the villagers, the livestock that had run free in the streets, the dirty children and the tired men. The smells, the voices, all the evidence of habitation, all was gone, vanished without a trace. The wall that had surrounded the square had disappeared to leave only the old tree which no longer had a name, holding its white blossoms up to the sky as if to deny that anything but itself had ever existed there in the clearing in the sierra.

They stood up sleepy and unsure, shaking off the dust and brushing themselves down. They looked about them with incomprehension like men who had drunk from the river of oblivion. Without a glance at those who the night before had been enemies, they trooped silently out of the village onto the dusty road, setting off in opposite directions into the morning that was scented with nothing but white spring blossoms.

URSULA K. Le GUIN

Redescending

Ursula Le Guin is the award-winning author of more than thirty books of fiction, nonfiction, and poetry. The following poem, reprinted from her most recent volume of poetry, Sixty Odd: New Poems, *takes another look at the classical myth of Orpheus, the great musician who descended into the Underworld to bring his beloved Euridice back from the dead. In the original tale, Orpheus wins permission to take her back to the world above, provided that during the long journey upward he never once looks back. He breaks this taboo and Euridice is lost to him—until this poem.*

—*T. W.*

He who turned upon her sings
striking his lyre, the lover
sweeter than ever.
      Beasts go about their business,
trees are indifferent,
rocks hard as any heart.
Only the women in the bushes,
wild girls, hair unbraided,
listen, peering from cover.
As he sobs in the melodic
climax of his art,
they grunt and snigger
with anger, they come at him
loose-chapped as lionesses.
      He is rent from the center,

gutted, dismembered.
 The head floats,
mouth open on a high note.
 Bearing the lyre the river
runs to the entrance and falls.

Down in the silence
Euridice gathers him.
By Lethe she pieces him,
on those dark margins,
the sands of remembrance.
 Holding the hollow
lyre unstrung, and dumb,
he faces her once more.
"This time follow me,"
she says, and he follows.
She does not look back.

A long way in silence
by the dry sea with one shore,
a long way without turning
to the place of returning.
 There she can turn to him
at last, and he into her; there
the curved hand strikes the doubled chord
and other is no longer; there
are interpenetrations of bodies
of words, fecund, there
under the roots of the hair of the mothers
in the realm of the maidens
where the unborn surrounds
the womb, and the fathers
dream in the curled
hands of the child who comes to be
in the world, braiding
and twining vibrations
rejoining and voices
rejoined.

KIM NEWMAN

You Don't Have to Be Mad...

Novelist, critic, and broadcaster, Kim Newman has worked extensively in theater, radio, and television. His most recent novels include Anno Dracula, Judgment of Tears: Anno Dracula 1959, *and* Life's Lottery. *Under the name Jack Yeovil, he has written gaming novels. His short stories are collected in* The Original Dr. Shade and Other Stories, Famous Monsters, Seven Stars, *and* Where the Bodies Are Buried. *He has won the Bram Stoker Award, the British Science Fiction Award for Best Short Fiction, the Children of the Night Award, the Fiction Award of the Lord Ruthven Assembly, and the International Horror Critics' Guild Award for Best Novel.*

Of this story, first published in White of the Moon: New Tales of Madness and Dread, *Newman says, "I'm returning here to characters introduced in 'The End of the Pier Show' from* Dark of the Night, *and the world of late 1960s to early 1970s British popular culture. This time, I was thinking specifically of shows like* The Avengers, Adam Adamant Lives!, The Champions, *and* The Prisoner, *which often dealt with bizarre and cruel 'therapies' and sinister superscientific retreats in British country house settings. In these stories, I'm hoping to make the purple-haze period between* Sergeant Pepper *and the oil crisis as fantastical and ambiguous a playground as the fog-shrouded London of Sherlock Holmes or the 1940s of Philip Marlowe."*

—E. D.

Prologue
A Graduate of the Laughing Academy

He arrived bright and early in the morning. At eight o'clock, the entire workforce was assembled in the open air. The managing director introduced him as an outside consultant with bad news to deliver and handed him the loud-hailer. Barely restraining giggles, Mr. Joyful announced the shipyard would close down at the end of the year and they were all sacked.

Escorted off-site by armed guards, ignoring the snarls and taunts of to-be-unemployed-by-1971 workmen, he was back in his bubble car, stomach knotted with hilarious agony, by eight-fifteen. He managed to drive a few miles before he was forced to pull over and give vent to the laughter that had built up inside him like painful gas. Tears coursed down his cheeks. The interior of his space-age transport vibrated with the explosions of his merriment.

At nine o'clock, chortling, he told a young mother that her son's cancer was inoperable. At ten, snickering, he personally informed the founder of a biscuit factory that he'd been unseated in a boardroom coup and would be lucky to escape prosecution over a series of mystery customer ailments. At eleven, in full view of a party of schoolboys, he wielded a length of two-by-four to execute an aged polar bear that a small zoo could no longer afford to feed. At twelve, almost unable to hold the saw steady for his shaking mirth, he cut down a seven-hundred-year-old oak tree on the village green of Little Middling by the Weir, to make way for a road-widening scheme. The chants of the protesters were especially rib-tickling.

From one until two, he had a fine lunch in a Jolly Glutton motorway restaurant. Two straight sausages and a helping of near-liquid mash. An individual apple pie with processed cream. It was a privilege to taste this, the food of the future. Each portion perfect, and identical with each other portion. That struck him as funny too.

At two-thirty, controlling himself, he murdered three old folks in a private home, with the hankie-over-the-mouth-and-nose hold. Their savings had run out and this was kinder than turning them loose to fend for themselves. His five o'clock appointment was something similar, a journalist working on a news item about hovercraft safety for the telly program *Tomorrow's News*.

"I've got some bad news for you," he told the surprised young woman.

"Who are you?" she demanded.

"I'm Mr. Joyful. Aren't you interested in my news?"

"Why are you grinning like that? Is this a joke?"

He was about to go off again. Amused tears pricked the backs of his eyes. Laughter began to scream inside his brain, clamoring for escape.

"Your contract is cancelled," he managed to get out.

It was too, *too* funny.

He produced the silenced pistol. One quick *phut* in the face and he could knock off for the day.

He was laughing like a drain.

What this woman didn't know—but would find out unless stopped—was that the Chairman of the Board of Directors of her employer, Greater London Television, was also responsible for Amalgamated British Hoverlines, and had personally authorized the cost-cutting scheme that resulted in the deaths of twenty-eight day-trippers.

His gun barrel shook as it pointed.

The look on the woman's face was too much. He barked laughter, like the policeman in the comedy record. His sides literally split, great tears running down from his armpits to his hips.

His shot creased the woman's shoulder.

That was funny too. People held him down, wrestling the gun out of his grip. Someone even kicked him in the tummy. It was too much to bear.

He kept on laughing, blind with tears, lances of agony stabbing into his torso. Then he stopped.

Act I: Vanessa Is Committed

She was comfortably lotused among orange and purple scatter-cushions in the conference room of the Chelsea mansion, rainbow-socked feet tucked neatly into the kinks of her knees. Vanessa wore a scarlet leotard with a white angora cardigan. Her long red hair was in a rope-braid, knotted end gripped in a giant turquoise clothes peg. Fred Regent sat nearby, on a wire-net bucket chair, in his usual jeans and jean jacket, square head almost shaven.

Jazz harpsichord tinkled out of the sound system concealed behind eighteenth-century wood panelling. Matched Lichtenstein explosions hung over the marble mantelpiece. A bundle of joss sticks smoked in a Meissen vase on a kidney-shaped coffee table.

Richard Jeperson, silver kaftan rippling with reflected light, nested cross-legged in a white plastic chair that hung from the ceiling on an anchor chain. It was shaped like a giant egg sliced vertically, with yolk-yellow padding inside.

He showed them a photograph of a happy-looking fat man. Then another one, of the same man, lying on the floor in a pool of mess.

"Jolyon Fuller," he announced.

Vanessa compared the shots. Fuller looked even happier in the one where he was dead.

"He made his living in an interesting way," Richard said. "He delivered bad news."

"I thought that was Reginald Bosanquet's job," put in Fred.

"Fuller doesn't look gloomy," Vanessa ventured.

"Apparently, he wasn't," Richard said. "He laughed himself to death. Literally. Matters you or I would consider tragic were high comedy to him. His wires were crossed somewhere up here."

He tapped his head.

Taking back the pictures, hawk brows momentarily clenched, he gave them consideration. Shoulder-length black ringlets and the mandarin's moustache gave his face a soft, almost girlish cast, but the piercing eyes and sharp cheekbones were predatory. After all they'd been through together, Vanessa still hadn't got to the bottom of Richard Jeperson.

It had been weeks since the last interesting problem to come along, the business of the Satanist Scoutmaster and his scheme to fell the Post Office Tower. Richard had summoned his assistants to announce that they were to investigate a string of strangenesses. This was often the way of their affairs. At the Diogenes Club in Pall Mall, a group of clever and wise minds—under the direction of Edwin Winthrop, Grand Old Man of the Ruling Cabal—constantly sifted through court records, police reports, newspapers, and statements from members of the public, earmarking the unusual and red-flagging the impossible. If the inexplicabilities mounted up, the matter was referred to one of the Club's Valued Members. Currently, Richard was reckoned the Most Valued Member.

"Here's another pretty fizzog. Harry Egge."

Richard showed them a glossy of a boxer, gloves up, bruises on his face.

"He was supposed to be the next 'Enery Cooper," said Fred, who followed sport. "He could take the Punishment for fifty rounds. Couldn't feel pain or didn't care about it. No matter how much battering he took, he kept on punching."

"I read about him," Vanessa said. "Didn't he die?"

"Indeed he did," Richard explained. "In his home, in a fire caused by faulty wiring."

"He was trapped," she said. "How horrible."

"Actually, he wasn't trapped. He could have walked away, easily. But he fought the fire, literally. He punched it and battered it, but it caught him and burned him to the bone. Very odd. When you put your hand in flame, you take it out sharpish. It's what pain is for, to make you do things before you think about them. Nature's fire alarm. Harry Egge kept fighting the fire, as if he could win by a knockout."

"Was he kinky for pain?"

"A masochist, Vanessa? Not really. He just wasn't afraid of being hurt."

"And that makes him barmy?"

"Quite so, Fred. Utterly barmy."

Vanessa wondered what Jolyon Fuller and Harry Egge had in common, besides being mad and dead.

"There are more odd folk to consider," Richard continued, producing more photographs and reports. "Nicholas Mix-Elgin: head of security at a multinational computer firm. He became so suspicious that he searched his children's pets for listening devices. Internally. Serafine Xavier: convent school teacher turned high-priced call girl, the only patient ever hospitalized on the National Health with 'clinical nymphomania.' We only know about her because several male patients on her ward died during visits from her. Lieutenant Commander Hilary Roehampton: a naval officer who insisted on volunteering for a series of missions so dangerous only a lunatic would consider them."

"Like what?" asked Fred.

"Sea-testing leaky submarines."

"Cor blimey!"

Vanessa had to agree.

"These people held more or less responsible positions. It's only by chance that their files were passed on to us. The *grande horizontale* was, I believe, retained by the FO for the intimate entertainment of visiting dignitaries."

"They all sound like loonies to me," Fred said.

"Ah, yes," Richard agreed, extending a finger, "but their lunacies *worked* for them, at least in the short term. You are familiar with that allegedly humorous mass-produced plaque you see up in offices and other sordid places? 'You Don't Have to Be Mad to Work Here'—asterisk—'But it Helps.' Sometimes being mad really does help. After all, a head of security should be a bit of a paranoiac, a boxer needs to have a touch of the masochist."

"Don't most firms and all government agencies make prospective employees take a battery of psychiatric tests these days? To weed out the maniacs?"

"Indeed they do, my dear. I have copies here."

He indicated a thick sheaf of papers. She reached out.

"Don't bother. All our interesting friends were evaluated within the last three years as one hundred percent sane."

"The tests must be rigged," Fred said. "You don't just go bonkers overnight. This lot must have been in and out of nut-hatches all their lives."

"As a matter of fact, they were all rated with Certificates of Mental Health."

Fred didn't believe it.

"And who gave out the certificates?" she asked.

Richard arched an eyebrow. She'd asked the right question. That was the connection.

"Strangely enough, all these persons were certified as sane by the same practitioner, one Dr. Iain Menzies Ballance. He is Director of the Pleasant Green Center, near Whipplewell in Sussex."

"Pleasant Green. Is that a private asylum?"

"Not officially," he told her. "It offers training courses for executives and other high-earners. Like a health farm for the mind. Sweat off those unsightly phobias, that sort of thing."

She looked at a glossy prospectus that was in with all the case files. A Regency mansion set among rolling downs. Dr. Ballance smiling with his caring staff, all beautiful young women. Testimonials from leaders of industry and government figures. A table of fees, starting at £500 a week.

"Let me get this straight," said Fred. "Sane people go in . . ."

"And mad people come out," Richard announced.

She felt a little chill. There was something cracked in Dr. Ballance's half-smile. And his staff couldn't quite not look like the dolly bird wing of the SS.

"The question which now presents itself, of course, is which of us would most benefit from a week or two under the care of the good Dr. Ballance."

Richard looked from Fred to her. Fred just looked at her.

"You're the sanest person I know, Ness," Fred said.

"That's not saying much," she countered.

Richard was about to give a speech about knowing how dangerous the assignment would be and not wanting her to take it unless she was absolutely sure. She cut him off. After all, she owed him too much— her sanity, at least, probably her life—to protest.

"Just tell me who I am," she said.

Richard smiled like a shark and produced a folder.

In the garage of the Chelsea house, her white Lotus Elan looked like a Dinky toy parked next to Richard's Rolls Royce ShadowShark, but it could almost match the great beast for speed and had the edge for maneuverability. She should get down to Sussex inside an hour.

Fred was already in Whipplewell. If asked, he was a bird-watcher out after a look-see at some unprecedented avocets. Richard had given him an *I-Spy Book of Birds* to memorize. He would watch over her.

Richard had turned out to see her off. He wore an orange frock coat with matching boots and top hat, over a psychedelic waistcoat and a lime-green shirt with collar points wider than his shoulders. He fixed her with his deep dark eyes.

"My love, remember who you are."

When they had met, she'd been a different person, not in command of herself. Something it was easiest to call a demon had her in a thrall it was easiest to call possession. He'd been able to reach her because he understood.

"We have less memory than most. That's why what we have, what we are, is so precious."

Richard was an amnesiac, a foundling of the war. He had proved to her that it was possible to live without a past that could be proved with memory. Once, since the first time, she had come under the influence of another entity—she shuddered at the memory of a pier on the South Coast—but had been able to throw off a cloak dropped over her mind.

"You'll be pretending to be a new person, this Vanessa Vail. That's a snakeskin you can shed at any time. While the act must be perfect, you must not give yourself up to it completely. They can do a great deal to 'Vanessa Vail' without touching Vanessa the Real. You must have a core that is you alone."

She thought she understood.

"Vanessa," he repeated, kissing her. "Vanessa."

She vaulted into the driving seat of the Lotus.

"What's your name?" he asked.

She told him, and drove off.

"You are an army officer?" Dr. Ballance asked, looking up from the folder. He had a hard Scots accent of the sort popularly associated with John Laurie, penny-pinching, wife-beating, and sheep abuse.

Vanessa nodded. She was supposed to be a paratrooper. Looking at her long legs and big eyes, people thought she must be a fashion model, but she had the height to be a convincing warrior woman. And she could look after herself in hand-to-hand combat. It wasn't a great snake-skin but it was wearable.

"Things have changed since my day, Lieutenant Vail."

She hated her new name. The double V sounded so cartoony. But you couldn't be in the army without a surname.

"Were you in the services, Dr. Ballance?"

He nodded and one side of his mouth smiled. The left half of his face was frozen.

She imagined him in uniform, tunic tight on his barrel chest, cap perched on his butter-colored cloud of hair, tiger stripes on his blandly bespectacled face. She wondered which side he had been on in whichever war he had fought.

"You will be Lieutenant Veevee," he said. "For 'vivacious.' We rename all our guests. The world outside does not trouble us here in Pleasant Green. We are interested only in the world inside."

She crossed her legs and rearranged her khaki miniskirt for decency's sake. Dr. Ballance's one mobile eye followed the line of her leg down to her polished brogue. She was wearing a regimental tie tucked into a fatigue blouse, and a blazer with the proper pocket badge. Richard had suggested medal ribbons, but she thought that would be over-egging the pud.

"I'll have Miss Dove show you to your quarters," said Dr. Ballance. "You will join us for the evening meal, and I shall work up a program of tests and exercises for you. Nothing too strenuous at first."

"I've passed commando training," she said.

It was true. Yesterday, getting into character, she had humped herself through mud with an incredulous platoon of real paratroopers. At first, they gallantly tried to help her. Then, when it looked like she'd score the highest marks on the course, they did their best to drag her back and keep her down. She gave a few combat-ready squaddies some nasty surprises and came in third. The sergeant offered to have her back to keep his lads in line.

"Your body is in fine shape, Lieutenant Veevee," said Dr. Ballance, eye running back up her leg, pausing at chest-level, then twitching up to her face. "Now we shall see what we can do about tailoring your mind to fit it."

Dr. Ballance pressed a buzzer switch. A young woman appeared in the office. She wore a thigh-length flared doctor's coat over white PVC knee-boots, a too-small T-shirt, and hot pants. Her blonde hair was kept back by an alice band.

"Miss Dove, show Lieutenant Veevee where we're putting her."

The attendant smiled, making dimples.

Vanessa stood and was led out of the office.

Pleasant Green Manor House had been gutted, and the interior remodeled in steel and glass. Vanessa took note of various gym facilities and therapy centers. All were in use, with "guests" exercising or playing mind games under the supervision of attendants dressed exactly like Miss Dove. They looked like Pan's People rehearsing a hospital-themed dance number. Some processes were obvious, but others involved peculiar machines and dentist's chairs with straps and restraints.

She was shown her room, which contained a four-poster bed and other genuine antique furniture. A large window looked out over the grounds. Among rolling lawns were an arrangement of pre-fab buildings and some concrete block bunkers. Beyond the window was a discreet steel grille, "for protection."

"We don't get many gels at Pleasant Green, Lieutenant Veevee," said Miss Dove. "It's mostly fellows. High-powered executives and the like."

"Women are more and more represented in all the professions."

"We've one other gel here. Mrs. Empty. Dr. Ballance thinks she's promising. You'll have competition. I hope you'll be chums."

"So do I."

"I think you're going to fit in perfectly, Lieutenant."

Miss Dove hugged her.

Vanessa tensed, as if attacked. She barely restrained herself from popping the woman one on the chin. Miss Dove air-kissed her on both cheeks and let her go. Vanessa realized she had been very subtly frisked during the spontaneous embrace. She had chosen not to bring any obvious weapons or burglar tools.

"See you at din-din," Miss Dove said, and skipped out.

Vanessa allowed herself a long breath. She assumed the wall-size mirror was a front for a camera. She had noticed a lot of extra wiring and guessed Dr. Ballance would have a closed-circuit TV setup. She put her face close to the mirror, searching for an imaginary blackhead, and thought she heard the whirring of a lens adjustment.

There was no telephone on the bedside table.

Her bags were open, her clothes put in the wardrobe. She hoped they had taken the trouble to examine her marvelously genuine army credentials. It had taken a lot of work to get them up to scratch, and she wanted the effort appreciated.

She looked out of the window. At the far end of the lawns was a wooded area and beyond that the Sussex downs. Fred ought to be out there somewhere with a flat cap, a thermos of tea, and a pair of binoculars. He was putting up in the Coach and Horses at Whipplewell, where there were no bars on the windows and you could undress in front of the mirror without giving some crackpot a free show.

Where was Richard all this time? He must be pulling strings somehow. He was supposed to be following up on the graduates of Pleasant Green.

She felt sleepy. It was late afternoon, the gold of the sun dappling the lawn. She shouldn't be exhausted. There was a faint hissing. She darted around, scanning for ventilation grilles, holding her breath. She couldn't keep it up, and if she made an attempt the watchers would know she was a fake. She decided to go with it. Climbing onto the soft bed, she felt eiderdowns rise to embrace her. She let the tasteless, odorless gas into her lungs, and tried to arrange herself on the bed with some decorum.

She nodded off.

Something snapped in front of her face and stung her nostrils. Her head cleared. Everything was suddenly sharp, hyper-real.

She was sitting at a long dinner table, in mixed company, wearing a yellow-and-lime striped cocktail dress. Her hair was done up in a towering beehive. A thick layer of makeup—which she rarely used—was lacquered over her face. Even her nails were done, in stripes to match her dress. Overhead fluorescents cruelly illuminated the table and guests, but the walls were in darkness and incalculable distance away from the long island of light. The echoey room was noisy with conversation, the clatter of cutlery, and the Move's "Fire Brigade." She had a mouthful of food and had to chew to save herself from choking.

"You are enjoying your eyeball, Lieutenant?"

The questioner was a slight Oriental girl in a man's tuxedo. Her hair was marceled into a Hokusai wave. A name tag identified her as "Miss Lark."

Eyeball?

Chewing on jellying meat, she glanced down at her plate. A cooked pig's face looked back up at her, one eye glazed in its socket, the other a juicy red gouge. She didn't know whether to choke, swallow, or spit.

The pig's stiff snout creaked into a porcine smile.

Vanessa expectorated most of the pulpy eye back at its owner.

Conversation and consumption stopped. Miss Lark tutted. Dr. Ballance, a tartan sash over his red jacket, stared a wordless rebuke.

The pig snarled now, baring sharp teeth at her.

A fog ocean washed around Vanessa's brain. This time, she struggled. Flares of light that weren't there made her blink. Her own eyeballs might have been Vaselined over. The room rippled and faces stretched. The guests were all one-eyed pigs.

Some eye slipped down her throat. She went away.

This time, the smell of cooking brought her to. She was in an underground kitchen or workshop. Sizzling and screeching was in the air. Infernal red lighting gave an impression of a low ceiling, smoky red bricks arched like an old-fashioned bread-oven.

In her hands were a pair of devices which fit like gloves. Black leather straps kept her hands around contoured grips like the handles of a skipping rope, and her thumbs were pressed down on studs inset into the apparatus. Wires led from the grips into a junction box at her feet.

She was wearing black high-heeled boots, goggles that covered half her face and a rubber fetish bikini. Oil and sweat trickled on her tight stomach, and down her smoke-rouged arms and calves. Her hair was pulled back and fanned stickily on her shoulders.

Her thumbs were jamming down the studs.

Jethro Tull was performing "Living in the Past."

And someone was screaming. There was an electric discharge in the air. In the gloom of the near distance, a white shape writhed. The goggles were clouded, making it impossible to get more than a vague sense of what she was looking at.

She relaxed her thumbs, instantly. The writhing and screaming halted. Cold guilt chilled her mind. She fought the fuzziness.

Someone panted and sobbed.

"I think you've shown us just what you think of the cook, Lieutenant Veevee," said Dr. Ballance.

He stood nearby, in a kilt and a black leather Gestapo cap. A pink feather boa entwined his broad, naked chest like a real snake.

"Have you expressed yourself fully?" he asked.

She could still taste the eyeball. Still see the damned pig-face making a grin.

Red anger sparked. She jammed her thumbs down.

A full-blooded scream ripped through the room, hammering against the bricks and her ears. A blue arc of electricity lit up one wall. The white shape convulsed and she kept her thumbs down, pouring her rage into the faceless victim.

No. That was what they wanted.

She flipped her thumbs erect, letting go of the studs.

The arc stopped, the shape slumped.

Half Dr. Ballance's face expressed disappointment.

"Forgiveness and mercy, eh, Lieutenant? We shall have to do something about that."

Attendants took down the shape—was it a man? a woman? an animal?—she had been shocking.

Vanessa felt a certain triumph. They hadn't turned her into a torturer.

"Now cook has the switch," said Dr. Ballance.

She looked into the darkness, following the wires.

Shock hit her in the hands and ran up her arms, a rising ratchet of voltage. It was like being lashed with pain.

Her mind was whipped out.

She was doing push-ups. Her arms and stomach told her she had been doing push-ups for some time. A voice counted in the mid-hundreds.

Staff Sergeant Barry Sadler's "The Ballad of the Green Berets" was playing.

She concentrated on shoving ground away from her, lifting her whole body, breathing properly, getting past pain. Her back and legs were rigid.

Glancing to one side, she saw a polished pair of boots.

Numbers were shouted at her. She upped the rate, smiling tightly. This, she could take. She was trained in dance (ballroom, modern, and ballet) and Oriental boxing (judo, karate, and *jeet kune do*), her body tuned well beyond the standards of the commandos. She reached her thousand. Inside five seconds, she gave ten more for luck.

"On your feet, soldier," she was ordered.

She sprung upright, to attention. She was wearing fatigues and combat boots.

A black woman inspected her. She had a shaved head, three parallel weals on each cheek, and "Sergeant-Mistress Finch" stenciled on her top pocket.

Her tight fist jammed into Vanessa's stomach.

She clenched her tummy muscles a split second before hard knuckles landed. Agony still exploded in her gut, but she didn't go down like a broken doll.

Sergeant-Mistress Finch wrung out her fist.

"Good girl," she said. "Give Lieutenant Veevee a lollipop."

Miss Dove, who was dressed as a soldier, produced a lollipop the size of a stop sign, with a hypnotic red and white swirl pattern. She handed it to Vanessa.

"By the numbers," Sergeant-Mistress Finch ordered, "lick!"

Vanessa had a taste-flash of the pig's eyeball, but overcame remembered disgust. She stuck her tongue to the surface of the lollipop and licked. A sugar rush hit her brain.

"Punishments and rewards," commented a Scots voice.

She woke with the taste of sugar in her mouth and a gun in her hand. She was wearing a kilt, a tight cut-away jacket over a massively ruffled shirt, and a feathered cap. Black tartan tags stuck out of her thick gray socks and from her gilt epaulettes.

Sergeant-Mistress Finch knelt in front of her, hands cuffed behind her, forehead resting against the barrel of Vanessa's pistol.

"S-M Finch is a traitor to the unit," said Dr. Ballance. Vanessa swiveled to look at him. He wore the full dress uniform of the Black Watch.

They were out in the woods somewhere, after dark. A bonfire burned nearby. Soldiers (all girls) stood around. There was a woodsy tang in the air and a night chill settling in. A lone bagpiper mournfully played "Knock Knock, Who's There?", a recent chart hit for Mary Hopkin.

"Do your duty, Lieutenant Veevee."

Vanessa's finger tightened on the trigger.

This was some test. But would she pass if she shot or refused to shoot? Surely, Dr. Ballance wouldn't let her really kill one of the attendants. If he ran Pleasant Green like that, he would run out of staff.

The gun must not be loaded.

She shifted the pistol four inches to the left, aiming past the Sergeant-Mistress's head, and pulled the trigger. There was an explosion out of all proportion with the size of the gun. A crescent of red ripped out of Finch's left ear. The Sergeant-Mistress clapped a hand over her spurting wound and fell sideways.

Vanessa's head rang with the impossibly loud sound.

She looked out through white bars. She was in a big crib, a pen floored with cushioning and surrounded by a fence of wooden bars taller than she was. She wore an outsized pinafore and inch-thick woolen knee-socks. Her head felt huge, as if jabbed all over with dental anesthetic. When she tried to stand, the floor wobbled and she had to grab the bars for support. She was not steady on her feet at all. She had not yet learned to walk.

Veevee crawled. A rattle lay in the folds of the floor, almost too big for her grasp. She focused on her hand. It was slim, long-fingered. She could make a fist. She was a grown-up, not a baby.

A tannoy was softly broadcasting "Jake the Peg (With the Extra Leg)" by Rolf Harris.

She picked up the rattle.

The bars sank into the floor and she crawled over the row of holes where they had been. She was in a playroom. Huge alphabet blocks were strewn around in Stonehenge arrangements, spelling words she couldn't yet pronounce. Two wooden soldiers, taller than she was, stood guard, circles of red on their cheeks, stiff Zebedee moustaches on their round faces, shakoes on their heads, bayonet-tipped rifles in their spherical hands.

Plumped in a rocking chair was Dr. Ballance, in a velvet jacket with matching knickerbockers, a tartan cravat frothing under his chin, a yard-wide tam o'shanter perched on his head.

"Veevee want to play-play?" he asked.

She wasn't sure anymore. This game had been going on too long. She had forgotten how it started.

There were other children in the playroom. Miss Dove and Miss Lark, in identical sailor suits. And others: Miss Wren, Miss Robin, and Miss Sparrow. Sergeant-Mistress Finch was home sick today, with an earache.

The friends sang "Ring-a-ring-a-rosy" and danced around Veevee. The dance made her dizzy again. She tried to stand, but her pinafore was sewn together at the crotch and too short to allow her body to unbend.

"You're it," Miss Dove said, slapping her.

Veevee wanted to cry. But big girls didn't blub. And she was a very big girl.

She was a grown-up. She looked at her hand to remind herself. It was an inflated, blubbery fist, knuckles sunk in baby fat.

The others were all bigger than her.

Veevee sat down and cried and cried.

Act II: Richard Is Rumbled

Alastair Garnett, the Whitehall man, had wanted to meet in a multi-story car park, but Richard explained that nothing could be more conspicuous than his ShadowShark. Besides, two men exchanging briefcases in a car park at dead of night was always something to be suspicious about. Instead, he had set a date for two in the morning in the Pigeon-Toed Orange Peel, a discotheque in the King's Road.

He sat at the bar, sipping a tequila sunrise from a heavy glass shaped like a crystal ball. An extremely active girl in a polka-dot halter and matching shorts roller-skated behind the long bar, deftly balancing drinks.

Richard was wearing a floor-length green suede Edwardian motorist's coat over a tiger-striped orange-and-black silk shirt, zebra-striped white-and-black flared jeans and handmade zigzag-striped yellow-and-black leather moccasins. In place of a tie, he wore an amulet with the CND peace symbol inset into the eyes of a griffin rampant. In his lapel was a single white carnation, so Garnett could identify him.

He lowered his sunglasses—thin-diamond-shaped emerald-tint lenses with a gold wire frame—and looked around the cavernous room. Many girls and some boys had Egyptian eye motifs painted on bare midriffs, thighs, upper arms, throats, or foreheads. The paint was luminous and, as the lights flashed on and off in five-second bursts, moments of darkness were inhabited by a hundred dancing eyes.

A band of long-haired young men played on a raised circular stage. They were called the Heat, and were in the middle of "Non-Copyright Stock Jazz Track 2," a thirty-five minute improvised fugue around themes from their debut album *Neutral Background Music*.

A pleasantly chubby girl in a cutaway catsuit, rhinestone-studded patch over one eye, sat next to Richard and suggested they might have been lovers in earlier incarnations. He admitted the possibility, but sadly confessed they'd have to postpone any reunion until later lives. She shrugged cheerfully and took his hand, producing an eyebrow pencil to write her telephone number on his palm. As she wrote, she noticed the other number tattooed on his wrist and looked at him again. A tear started from her own exposed eye and she kissed him.

"Peace, love," she said, launching herself back onto the dance floor and connecting with a Viking youth in a woven waistcoat and motorcycle boots.

Across the room, he saw a thin man who wore a dark gray overcoat, a black bowler hat, and a wing-collar tight over a light gray tie, and carried a tightly furled Union Jack umbrella. Richard tapped his carnation and the man from Whitehall spotted him.

"What a racket," Garnett said, sitting at the bar. "Call that music? You can't understand the words. Not like the proper songs they used to have."

" 'Doodly-Acky-Sacky, Want Some Seafood, Mama'?"

"I beg your pardon?"

"A hit for the Andrews Sisters in the 1940s," Richard explained.

"Harrumph," said Garnett.

A boy dressed in tie-dyed Biblical robes, with an enormous bush of beard and hair, paused at the bar while buying a drink and looked over Garnett. The Whitehall man held tight to his umbrella.

"That's a crazy look, man," the boy said, flashing a reversed V sign.

A crimson undertone rose in Garnett's face. He ordered a gin and tonic and tried to get down to business. Though the Heat were playing loud enough to whip the dancers into a frenzy, there was a quiet-ish zone at the bar which allowed them to have a real conversation.

"I understand you're one of the spooks of the Diogenes Club," the Whitehall man said. "Winthrop's creature."

Richard shrugged, allowing the truth of it. The Diogenes Club was loosely attached to the Government of the Day and tied into the tangle of British Intelligence agencies, but Edwin Winthrop of the Ruling Cabal had kept a certain distance from the Gnomes of Cheltenham since the war, and was given to running Diogenes more or less as a private fiefdom.

It was said of one of Winthrop's predecessors that he not only worked for the British Government but that under some circumstances he *was* the British Government. Winthrop did not match that, but was keen on keeping Diogenes out of the bailiwick of Whitehall, if only because its stock in trade was everything that couldn't be circumscribed by rules and regulations, whether the procedures of the Civil Service or the laws of physics. Richard was not a civil servant, not beholden to the United Kingdom for salary and pension, but did think of himself as loyal to certain ideals, even to the Crown.

"I'm afraid this is typical of Diogenes's behavior lately," Garnett said. "There's been the most almighty snarl-up in the Pleasant Green affair."

Garnett, Richard gathered, was one of the faction who thought the independence of the Diogenes Club a dangerous luxury. They were waiting patiently for Winthrop's passing so that everything could be tied down with red tape and sealing wax.

"Pleasant Green is being looked into," Richard said.

"That's just it. You're jolly well to stop looking. Any expenses you've incurred will be met upon production of proper accounts. But all documentation, including notes or memoranda you or your associates have made, must be surrendered within forty-eight hours. It's a matter of national security."

Richard had been expecting this curtain to lower.

"It's ours, isn't it?" he said, smiling. "Pleasant Green?"

"You are not cleared for that information. Rest assured that the unhappy events which came to your notice will not reoccur. The matter is at an end."

Richard kept his smile fixed and ironic, but he had a gnawing worry. It was all very well to be cut out of the case, but Vanessa was inside. If he wanted to extract her, there would be dangers. He had been careful not to let Garnett gather exactly what sort of investigation he had mounted, but it had been necessary to call in favors from the armed forces to kit the girl up with a snakeskin. Garnett might know Vanessa was undercover at Pleasant Green, and could well have blown her cover with Dr. Iain M. Ballance.

Garnett finished his g and t and settled the bar bill. He asked the surprised rollergirl for a receipt. She scribbled a figure on a cigarette paper and handed it over with an apologetic shrug.

"Good night to you," the Whitehall man said, leaving.

Richard gave Garnett five minutes to get clear of the Pigeon-Toed Orange Peel and slipped out himself.

The ShadowShark was parked round the corner. Vanessa usually drove for him, and Fred was occasionally allowed the wheel as a treat, but they were both down in darkest Sussex. He slid into the driver's seat and lowered the partition.

"You were right, Edwin," he told the man in the backseat.

Winthrop nodded. Though he wore a clipped white moustache and had not bulked out in age, there was a certain Churchillian gravity to the old man. He had fought for king and country in three world wars, only two of which the history books bothered with.

"Ghastly business," Winthrop snorted, with disgust.

"I've been asked to cease and desist all investigation of Pleasant Green and Dr. Ballance."

"Well, my boy, that you must do. We all have our masters."

Richard did not need to mention Vanessa. Winthrop had made the call to an old army comrade to help outfit "Lieutenant Vail" with a believable life.

"The investigation was a formality, anyway," Winthrop said. "After all, we knew at once what Ballance was up to. He drives people off their heads. Now, we know who he mostly does it for. He has private sector clients but his major business is to provide tailor-made psychopaths who are placed at the disposal of certain official and semi-official forces in our society. It's funny, really. The people behind Ballance are much like us, like the Diogenes Club. Governments come and go, but they're always there. There are times when any objective observer would think them on the side of the angels and us batting for the other lot. You know what our trouble is, Richard? England's trouble? We won all our wars. At great cost, but we won. We needed a new enemy. Our American cousins might be content to clash sabers with the Soviets, but Ivan was never going to be our dragon. We made our own enemy, birthed it at home, and raised it up. Maybe it was always here and we are the sports and freaks."

Richard understood.

"I know what Garnett wants me to do," he said. "What does Diogenes want?"

"Obviously, you are to stop investigating Dr. Ballance's business. And start dismantling it."

Act III: Vanessa Is Valiant

In the morning room, comfortable armchairs were arranged in a full circle. Group sessions were important at Pleasant Green.

In the next seat was a middle-aged man. Dr. Ballance asked him to stand first.

"My name is Mr. Ease," he said.

"Hello, Mr. Ease," they all replied.

". . . and I cheat and steal."

"Good show," murmured an approving voice, echoed by the rest of Group. She clapped and smiled with the rest of them. Dr. Ballance looked on with paternal approval.

He was a businessman. It had apparently been difficult to wash away the last of his scruples. Now, after a week of Pleasant Green, Mr. Ease was unencumbered by ethics or fear of the law. He had been worried about prison, but that phobia was overcome completely.

"My name is Captain Naughty," said a hard-faced man, a uniformed airline pilot. "And I want to punish people who do bad things. Firmly. Most of all, I want to punish people who do nothing at all."

"Very good, Captain," said Dr. Ballance.

Next up was the patrician woman who always wore blue dresses, the star of Group.

"My name is Mrs. Empty," she announced. "And I feel nothing for anyone."

She got no applause or hug. She earned respect, not love. Mr. Ease and Captain Naughty were clearly smitten with Mrs. Empty, not in any romantic sense but in that they couldn't stay away from the sucking void of her arctic charisma. Even Dr. Ballance's staff were in awe of her.

"My name is Rumor," drawled a craggy Australian. "And I want everything everyone thinks to come through me."

"Good on you, sir," Captain Naughty said, looking sideways to seek approval, not from Dr. Ballance—like everyone else in Group—but from Mrs. Empty.

"My name is Peace," said a young, quiet Yorkshireman. "I like killing women."

Peace, as always, got only perfunctory approval. The others didn't like him. He made them think about themselves.

She was last. She stood, glancing around at the ring of encouraging faces.

The Group was supportive. But this would be difficult.

"My name is Lieutenant Veevee," she said.

"Hello, Veevee," everyone shouted, with ragged cheer.

She took a deep breath, and said it.

". . . and I will kill people."

There. She felt stronger, now.

Mr. Ease reached up, took her hand and gave a friendly squeeze. Miss Lark gave her a hug. She sat down.

"Thank you all," said Dr. Ballance. "You are very special to Pleasant Green, as individuals and as Group. You're our first perfect people. When you leave here, which you're very nearly ready to do, you'll accomplish great things. You will take Pleasant Green with you. It won't happen soon, maybe not for years. But I have faith in you all. You are creatures of the future. You will be the Masters of the 1980s."

Already, complex relationships had formed within Group. Mr. Ease and Captain Naughty competed to be friends with Mrs. Empty, but she liked Rumor best of all. Peace was drawn to Veevee, but afraid of her.

"Would anyone like to tell us anything?" Dr. Ballance asked.

Captain Naughty and Mr. Ease stuck hands up. Mrs. Empty flashed her eyes, expecting to be preferred without having to put herself forward.

"It's always you two," Dr. Ballance said. "Let's hear from one of the quiet ones."

He looked at her, then passed on.

"Peace," the doctor said. "Have you thoughts to share?"

The youth was tongue-tied. He was unusual here. He had learned to accept who he was and what he wanted, but was nervous about speaking up in the presence of his "betters." Whenever Mrs. Empty made speeches about eliminating laziness or what was best for people, Peace opened and closed his sweaty hands nervously but looked at the woman with something like love.

"I was wondering, like," he said. "What's the best way to a tart's heart. I mean, physically. Between which ribs to stab, like?"

Captain Naughty clucked in disgust.

Peace looked at her. She lifted her left arm to raise her breast, then tapped just under it with her right forefinger.

"About here," she said.

Peace flushed red. "Thank you, Veevee."

The others were appalled.

"Do we have to listen to this rot?" Captain Naughty asked. "It's just filth."

Peace was a National Health referral, while the others were private.

"You've just run against your last barrier, Captain," Dr. Ballance announced. "You—all of you—have begun to realize your potential, have cut away the parts of your personae that were holding you back. But before you can leave with your Pleasant Green diploma, you must acknowledge your kinship with Peace. Whatever you say outside this place, you must have in your mind a space like Pleasant Green, where you have no hypocrisy. It will ground you, give you strength. We must all have our secret spaces. Peace will get his hands dirtier than yours, but what he does will be for Group just as what you do will be for Group."

Mrs. Empty nodded, fiercely. She understood.

"That will be all for today," Dr. Ballance said, dismissing Group. "Veevee, if you would stay behind a moment. I'd like a word."

The others got up and left. She sat still.

She didn't know how long she had been at Pleasant Green, but it could have been months or days. She had been taken back to the nursery and grown up all over again, this time with a direction and purpose. Dr. Ballance was father and mother to her psyche, and Pleasant Green was home and school.

Dr. Ballance sat next to her.

"You're ready to go, Veevee," he said, hand on her knee.

"Thank you, Doctor."

"But there's something you must do, first."

"What is that, Doctor?"

"What you want to do, Veevee. What you like to do."

She trembled a little. "Kill people?"

"Yes, my dear. There's a 'bird-watcher' on the downs. Fred Regent."

"Fred."

"You know Fred, of course. A man is coming down from London. He will join Fred in Whipplewell, at the Coach and Horses."

"Richard."

"That's right, Lieutenant Veevee. Richard Jeperson."

Dr. Ballance took a wrapped bundle out of his white coat and gave it to her. She unrolled the white flannel, and found a polished silver scalpel.

"You will go to the Coach and Horses," he told her. "You will find Fred and Richard. You will bring them back here. And you will kill them for us."

"Yes, Doctor."

"Then, when you have passed that final exam, you will seek out a man called Edwin Winthrop."

"I've met him."

"Good. You have been brought up for this purpose specifically, to kill Edwin Winthrop. After that, you can rest. I'm sure other jobs will come up, but Winthrop is to be your primary target. It is more important that he die than that you live. Do you understand?"

She did. Killing Winthrop meant more to her than her own life.

"Good girl. Now, go and have dinner. Extra custard for you today."

She wrapped the scalpel up again and put it in her pocket.

"You've been in there five days, Ness," Fred told her.

"It seems longer," she said. "Much longer."

Richard nodded sagely. "Very advanced techniques, I'll be bound."

They were cramped together in her Elan. She drove carefully, across the downs. After dark, the road could be treacherous.

"I was close to you in the wood on the first night," Fred said. "For the soldier games. What was that all about?"

She shrugged.

Richard was quiet. He must understand. That would make it easier.

She parked in a layby.

"There's a path through here," she said. "To Pleasant Green."

"Lead on," Richard said.

They walked through the dark wood. In a clearing, she paused and looked up at the bright half-moon.

"There's something," Fred said. "Listen."

It was the bagpiper, wailing "Cinderella Rockefeller." Dr. Ballance stepped into the clearing. Lights came on. The rest of the Pleasant Green staff were there, too: Miss Lark, Miss Wren, and the others. To one side, Mrs. Empty stood, wrapped up in a thick blue coat.

"It seems we're expected," Richard drawled.

"Indeed," said Dr. Ballance.

Fred looked at her, anger in his eyes. He made fists.

"It's not her fault," Richard told him. "She's not quite herself."

"Bastard," Fred spat at Dr. Ballance.

Mrs. Empty cringed in distaste at the language.

Dr. Ballance said "Veevee, if you would . . ."

She took her scalpel out and put it to Richard's neck, just behind the ear. She knew just how much pressure to apply, how deep to cut, how long the incision should be. He would bleed to death inside a minute. She even judged the angle so her ankle-length brown suede coat and calfskin high-heeled thigh boots would not be splattered.

"She's a treasure, you know," Dr. Ballance said to Richard. "Thank you for sending her to us. She has enlivened the whole Group. Really. We're going to have need of her, of people like her. She's so sharp, so perfect, so pointed."

Richard was relaxed in her embrace. She felt his heart beating, normally.

"And quite mad, surely?" Richard said.

"Mad? What does that mean, Mr. Jeperson. Out of step with the rest of the world? What if the rest of the world is mad? And what if your sanity is what is holding you back, preventing you from attaining your potential? Who among us can say that they are really sane? Really normal?"

"I can," said Mrs. Empty, quietly and firmly.

"We have always needed mad people," Dr. Ballance continued. "At Rorke's Drift, Dunkirk, the Battle of Britain, the Festival of Britain, we must have been mad to carry on as we did, and thank mercy for that madness. Times are a-changing, and we will need new types of madness. I can provide that, Mr. Jeperson. These women are perfect, you know. They have no conscience at all, no feeling for others. Do you know how hard it is to expunge that from the female psyche? We teach our daughters all their lives to become mothers, to love and sacrifice. These two are my masterpieces. Lieutenant Veevee, your gift to us, will be the greatest assassin of the era. And Mrs. Empty is even more special. She will take my madness and spread it over the whole world."

"I suppose it would be redundant to call you mad?" Richard ventured.

Dr. Ballance giggled.

Vanessa had Richard slightly off-balance, but was holding him up. The line of her scalpel was impressed against his jugular, steady.

"Ness won't do it," Fred said.

"You think not?" Dr. Ballance smiled. "Anybody would. You would, to me, right now. It's just a matter of redirecting the circuits, to apply the willingness to a worthwhile end. She feels no anger or remorse or hate or joy in what she does. She just does it. Like a tin-opener."

"Vanessa," Richard said.

Click.

That was her name. Not Veevee.

Just his voice and her name. It was a switch thrown inside her.

Long ago, they had agreed. When she first came to Richard, under the control of something else, she had been at that zero to which the Pleasant Green treatment was supposed to reduce her. She had escaped, with his help, then built herself up, with his love and encouragement. She was the stronger for it. Her name, which she had chosen, was the core of her strength. It was the code word which brought her out of a trance.

Everything Pleasant Green had done to her was meaningless now. She was Vanessa.

Not Veevee.

She didn't change, didn't move.

But she was herself again.

"That's all it takes," Richard said, straightening up. "A name. You don't really make people, Doctor. You just fake them. Like wind-up toys, they may work for a while. Then they run down. Like Mr. Joyful . . . Mr. Achy . . . Mr. Enemy . . . Miss Essex . . . Lieutenant-Commander Hero?"

He enunciated the names clearly. Each one was a jab at Dr. Ballance. The living half of his face froze, matching the dead side.

"This Group is better than them."

"No more crack-ups, eh? They're just mad enough, but not too broken to function?"

Mrs. Empty's cold eyes were fixed on them.

"To survive in the world we are making," Dr. Ballance said, "everybody will have to be mad."

He reached into his coat and brought out a gun. In a blink, Vanessa tossed her scalpel. It spun over and over, catching moonlight, and embedded its point in Dr. Ballance's forehead. A red tear dripped and he crashed backwards.

When he had gone for the gun, he had admitted defeat. He had doubted her. At the last, he had been proved wrong.

It all came crashing in. The programming, the torture, the disorientation—there had been drugs as well as everything else—fell apart.

With a scream, Miss Dove flew at her. She pirouetted and landed a foot in the attendant's face. The girl was knocked backwards and sprawled on the ground. She bounced back up, and came for her.

It was no match. Miss Dove was a master of disco-style roughhouse. All her movements came from her hips and her shoulders. Vanessa fell back on the all-purpose *jeet kune do*—the style developed by Bruce Lee which was starting to be called kung fu—and launched kicks and punches at the girl, battering her on her feet until she dropped.

The others backed away. Mrs. Empty walked off, into the dark.

Fred checked Dr. Ballance, and shook his head.

"Well done," Richard said. "I never doubted you."

She was completely wrung out. Again, she was on the point of exploding into tears.

Richard held her and kissed her.

"I trusted you here, rather than go myself or send Fred, because I know your heart," he said, kindly. "Neither of us could have survived Pleasant Green. We're too dark to begin with. We could be made into killers. You couldn't. You can't. You're an angel of mercy, my love, not of death."

Over his shoulder, she saw Ballance stretched out with a stick of steel in his head. She loved Richard for what he felt about her, but he was wrong. The Pleasant Green treatment might have failed to make her a malleable assassin, but Dr. Ballance had turned her into a killer all the same. After his doubt, had he known a split-second of triumph?

"It was about Winthrop," she said. "After you and Fred, he wanted me to kill Winthrop. It was part of some plan."

He nodded grimly, understanding.

Coda: Mrs. M. T.

On the croquet lawn of the Pleasant Green manor house, Richard found an Oriental woman feeding a bonfire with an armful of file folders. Fred took hold of her and wrestled her to the ground, but she had done her job with swift efficiency. Filing cabinets had been dragged out of the pre-fab buildings and emptied. Documents turned to ash and photographs curled in flame.

Vanessa, cloaked with his coat, was still pale. It would take a while for her to recover fully, but he had been right about her. She had steel.

The Oriental—Miss Lark—produced a stiletto and made a few passes at Fred's stomach; forcing him back. Then, she tried to slip the blade into her own heart. Vanessa, snapping out of her daze, grabbed the woman's wrist and made her drop the knife.

"No more," she said.

Miss Lark looked at them with loathing. Dr. Ballance would never have approved of an emotion like that.

The rest of the stuff had vanished into the night, melting away to wherever it was minions languished between paying jobs. Bewildered folks in dressing gowns, among them the electric-eyed woman who had been in the wood, had drifted out to see what the fuss was all about and found themselves abandoned. The other members of the Group.

Car headlights raked the lawns, throwing shadows against the big house. Doors opened and people got out. They were all anonymous men.

"Jeperson," shouted Garnett.

The Whitehall Man strode across the lawns, waving his umbrella like a truncheon.

Richard opened his hands and felt no guilt.

"I think you'll find Dr. Ballance exceeded his authority, Mr. Garnett. If you look around, you'll find serious questions raised."

"Where is the Doctor?" demanded Garnett.

"In the wood. He seems to be dead."

The civil servant was furious.

"He has a gun in his hand. I think he intended to kill someone or other. Very possibly me."

Garnett obviously thought it a pity Ballance hadn't finished the job. It was a shame this would end here, Richard thought. Important folk had been sponsoring Dr. Ballance, and had passed down orders to act against the Diogenes Club. Winthrop would be grimly amused to learn he was the eventual target of the plan.

"It wasn't working, though," Richard said.

"What?" Garnett said.

"The Ballance Process or whatever he called it. He was trying to manufacture functioning psychotics, wasn't he? Well, none of them ever functioned. Didn't you notice? Look at them, poor lost souls."

He indicated the people in dressing gowns. Ambulances had arrived, and the Pleasant Green guests were being helped into them.

"What use do you think they'll be now?"

By the ambulances was parked a car whose silhouette Richard knew all too well. There were only five Rolls Royce ShadowSharks in existence; and he owned three of them, all in silver. This was painted in night black, with opaque windows to match. A junior functionary like Garnett wouldn't run to this Antichrist of the road.

He would know the machine again. And the man inside it, who had ordered his death and Edwin's.

Garnett turned away and scurried across the lawn, to report to the man in the ShadowShark. The woman from the wood firmly resisted orderlies who were trying to help her into an ambulance. She asked no questions and made no protests, but wouldn't be manhandled, wouldn't be turned.

"Who is that?" he asked Vanessa.

"Mrs. Empty," she said. "The star pupil."

He shuddered. Mrs. Empty was quite, quite mad, he intuited. Yet she was strong, mind unclouded by compassion or uncertainty, character untempered by humor or generosity. In a precognitive flash that made him momentarily weak with terror, he saw a cold blue flame burning in the future.

She was assisted finally into an ambulance, but made the action seem like that of a queen ascending a throne, surrounded by courtiers.

The ambulances left. The ShadowShark stayed behind a moment. Richard imagined cold eyes looking out at him through the one-way black glass. Then, the motor turned over and the Rolls withdrew.

He looked at Fred and Vanessa. "Let's forget this place," he said.

"That might not be easy," Vanessa said.

"Then we shall have to try very hard."

THOMAS WHARTON

The Paper-Thin Garden

Canadian author Thomas Wharton was born in Grande Prairie, Alberta. He received an M.A. in English from the University of Alberta in 1993, and completed his Ph.D. in English at the University of Calgary in 1998. He currently lives in Edmonton with his wife and two children, and teaches English at Grant MacEwan College. Wharton's first novel, Icefields, *won the Grand Prize at the Banff Mountain Festival (1995); the Writers Guild of Alberta Best First Book Award (1996); and the Commonwealth Prize for Best First Book (Canada/Caribbean) in 1996.* Icefields *has also been published in the U.S., Great Britain, Germany, and France. He has recently completed his second novel,* Salamander, *which will be published by McClelland and Stewart early in 2001.*

The story that follows, "The Paper-Thin Garden" is a brief tale of crystalline prose poised halfway between fairy tale and surrealism. It comes from the Canadian journal Descant *105, Summer 1999 edition.*

—T. W.

The Emperor, in addition to being a lover of dioramas, models, and automata, also collects books. I have heard tales of some of the wondrous volumes in his library, such as that of the book which is said to be made entirely of glass. As you read, the ghostly words of adjacent pages shine through from below, like memory. If you breathe upon its surface, the book opens like a crystalline lotus and changes the order of its pages. Yet no one is allowed to read this book. No one has ever read it. Such a miraculous artifact is too precious to be handled as one would handle a book of accounts, an astrological treatise, a novel.

However, this is just a story I have heard. Of course I myself have never seen the book made of glass. I have never even set foot in the imperial library. I am only a gardener, one of the many whose daily task it is to care for the emperor's perfect garden. In the early years of his benevolent majesty's reign, twice five miles of fertile ground were set aside for this garden, girdled with walls and towers. Then the earth in this enclosure was covered in tiles of green porcelain to create a lawn that would never wither or go to seed. Trees of copper and brass were erected and painted in lifelike colors, and every morning incense-bearers perfume these metallic boughs with their swinging censers so that if any members of the court chance to walk that way they will inhale sweet odors of jasmine, peach blossom, and honey. The flowers that line the paths are all fashioned of jade, crystal, and amethyst. You might imagine there would be no need of gardeners amid this landscape of artifice, but our daily ministrations are of great importance. Everything must be kept polished, free from stain or blemish. Any dry leaves, twigs, or nests of mice that happen to stray over or under the walls must be rooted out: nothing is allowed to remain that suggests decay and death, for this garden is to be paradise.

Through its gates on summer mornings stroll ministers and courtiers, celestial beings arrayed in silk and cloth of gold. The emperor himself is pleased to wander through the garden from time to time, to enjoy the warblings of ceramic birds, to trail an imperial finger in the sinuous rills where bronze goldfish glitter and flash. At such times we gardeners must retire from view, but woe to us should the emperor discover a blight, a trace of imperfection in his path. One dead sparrow in the grass cost our former Superintendent of Gardens his head. Altogether four superintendents have met with the emperor's wrath since I first came to work here. Not that a perfect attention to duty is ultimately rewarded: gardeners are not permitted to grow old and thus mock the timelessness of the garden, and so after the age of forty they are unceremoniously dismissed. If the present rate of replacement continues, soon I will become superintendent, but I no longer dread that eventuality: For unbeknownst to anyone, I have found, in the immaculate garden, a book.

I was picking up straw blown over the wall by the autumn winds when I saw the crimson tongue of its place-marking ribbon poking up between two tiles. The sight was partially hidden by a mimosa bush of artfully wrought copper. Under pretense of inspecting the stalks of the plant for stray wisps of straw, I knelt and levered up a tile with my trowel, exposing one angular corner of the interloper. With painstaking effort I was able to dig the book free of the alarmingly hairy, fibrous roots that anchored it to the dark earth. I only had time for a quick glance at my find before concealing it in my tunic. The book's cover was made of wood, its damp, heavy pages giving off a pungent odor of earth, rain, leaf rot. As I hurried back to my cell, I debated what I should do with the book. Cart it, with all the other chaff, to the bonfire outside the garden wall? Or give it to the superintendent to pass on upward through the courtiers and ministers to the emperor, to add to his unread library of marvels? After a morning of indecision, I did neither and instead kept my discovery hidden.

In private moments I take up the volume and the rough, thorny binding hums in my hand like a beehive. As I turn the pages coniferous sap sticks to my fingers. In the rustle of its paper I hear the nocturnal stirring of owls. Letters become iridescent beetles that uncase their wings with a click and whir into the air. This book is a wild tangle of words, a shadowy ravine through which unseen beasts prowl, rustling the pages as they pass.

As I read, each page slowly turns yellow and sere and falls softly from the book to the tiled lawn, where I hurriedly gather it up and bury it in the place where I first saw the book. I have been reading all through the summer, and now approaches the time of year when not even imperial decree may halt the inevitable. This is the season when the emperor takes flight to his palace far to the south, to escape the sight of gray skies and trees, even artificial trees, laden with snow. This is the season when we must battle vigilantly against ice and sleet, against rust and rot.

I have no doubt that in the spring, the book will be the first sign of green to emerge from winter's white sleep, the pale, dog-eared corners of its pages shivering in the cool wind. During the rains I will come out with my umbrella to inspect the tender shoots, watch the snails crawl across their delicately veined surfaces, knowing that soon I will be reading it again, a book both familiar and entirely new.

I used to wonder how this book reached me and who authored it, but I soon grew weary of pondering these unimportant matters. I know only that the book's leaves have come from another garden, a far-off, legendary garden as thin as paper, a garden weaving across thousands of miles like a labyrinthine wall that keeps no one out and nothing in. A garden I dream of every night in my narrow cell, and which I know to be real, if unapproachable. It is not down on any map, you cannot see it, but when you pass unsuspecting through its shimmering verdant curtain you will know, and remember. There will be a moment where all your senses will tremble with a cool, humid joy. At night, when I tuck the book away under my straw mattress and blow out the candle,

I can see, through my cell window, the towers of the emperor's palace above the artificial forest. And on certain wet and gusty nights I see a light appear in a high window, a light that then burns until morning. And then I know that in his vast canopied bed, under sheets of the purest peach-blossom silk, the emperor too has dreamt of this garden, and has woken in terror.

MARY SHARRATT

The Anatomy of a Mermaid

Mary Sharratt lives in Munich, Germany, where she publishes New Voices, *a journal dedicated to the work of emerging writers from around the world. Her own fiction has appeared in* Hurricane Alice, The Long Story, The Evergreen Chronicles, Pica, *and* Writing for Our Lives. *Her first novel,* Summit Avenue, *set in early twentieth-century Minnesota, was published by Coffee House Press in May 2000.*

About the following story, Mary says, " 'The Anatomy of a Mermaid' arose from my fascination with industrial northern England, where my ancestors originate, and with the lives of working class women." This lyrical piece of historical fantasy is reprinted from the Winter 1999 edition of Lynx Eye, *a small but lively literary journal published in Los Angeles.*

—T. W.

In the ugly and landlocked town of Oldham I met her, my mermaid with her sea-colored eyes and hair like an angry sunset. She saw my dressmaker's placard in the apothecary window and came to my attic room in the Bridewell Lane Female Boarding House. After deciding that I was better and cheaper than the dressmakers she'd had before, she took to coming every fortnight, always on Monday and always at noon, when the church bells were ringing and the smell of boiled pudding and frying bread was rising through the floorboards. Her lungs would be bursting from dashing up the four flights of stairs. She always seemed to run and skitter, never to walk slow and sedate like a grown woman should. I never mustered up the nerve to ask her how old she was or how long she had been earning her bread as a woman of pleasure at the Mermaid Inn. All I knew was that she was young—younger than my twenty-four years—still more girl than woman.

She called herself Miranda Fontaine, a name she could have only invented. "My stage name, it is," she told me gravely. "Every actress must have a stage name. And never forget, Sara Doolan, I am an actress and not a whore. It's just the part I play, and I play it so well I've all those poor bastards completely fooled." I knew her real name had to be something plain and homely like Noreen, Bridie, or even Philomena. Like me, she was Irish, but unlike me, she had lost her accent after coming to England. It only came back to her when she was cursing, such as the time she rammed her shin against my coal bucket: "Shite, oh shite, oh Mother of God!"

The dresses I made her were certainly fit for an actress. She had me sew gowns of white brocade with gold and silver thread, and robes of Indian cotton as diaphanous as silk. Miranda was no common street-walker. She wore no paint, no gaudy low-cut satins, no dyed ostrich feathers in her hair. It was not working men or soldiers who came to her. The Mermaid Inn was a place where gentlemen went, and she had to prove that she was worth the money they paid for her. I poured all my dressmaker's cunning into cutting the gowns to flatter her figure, which wasn't as easy as one might think, for she did not have the ideal proportions for her line of work. Her chest was flat and her hips were wide, her thighs and bottom heavy. But I padded the bodice with quilted silk and lawn, adorned the neckline with mock pearls and ivory lace as filmy as the foam of a wave. Of all my customers, she was the most grateful and the most gratifying to serve. Each time she stepped into a new dress and modeled it in front of my beveled mirror, she became another woman. I think it was because she was born in the month of May, under Gemini, the sign of the Twins, which meant she had more than one nature, more than one face. As she stood in front of my mirror in her white brocade, I had an inkling of how her men saw her—not as a clumsy young girl who bolted up stairs two at a time and scraped her shin on coal buckets, but a woman of mystery, silent in her beautiful gown. The only word I could think to describe it was *queenly*. She appeared like a queen from another time and place, a *bean sidhe*, a fairy woman from the hollow hills. Not a queen of love, mind you. There was no tenderness in her eyes nor even coyness, but fire and steel and defiance. She was like Maeve in her chariot, a queen of war with a brazen spear. But as soon as she took the gown off and changed back into her everyday dress with the gray and white stripes, the enchantment was gone.

Then she was a coltish girl again, flying around my room, bumping her head against the low, slanting ceiling. I often wondered how such a small room could contain her. The floor shuddered under her feet. She was motion itself, never shutting her mouth, either. She would always be singing, usually a song too bawdy for the Bridewell Lane Female Boarding House. A blessing my landlady was nearly deaf. She fluttered around inspecting my things as if she were family or a dear friend. She leafed through my Bible and my missal, which I still kept, though I hadn't been to mass since coming to Oldham. Then she picked up my book of poetry and my book on the interpretation of dreams. But what seemed to delight her most were the seashells and dried starfish on the mantelpiece. I had gathered them with my sister when we were little girls, back when I still breathed sea air and drank fresh milk. If you held the shells close, you could not only hear the ocean, you could also smell it.

With her grasping arms and flying skirts, she nearly always broke something, though none of my treasures—not my starfish, or my glass thimble, not the Singer machine or the beveled mirror. The things she broke were old and ugly, evidence of my low station, like the mismatched crockery I had bought at the penny stalls in the marketplace already chipped. Whatever she broke she replaced with something shamelessly extravagant and dear, which explained how a poor seamstress like me came to acquire a tea set of bone china with hand-painted cherry blossoms like the month of May. It was useless trying to refuse her gifts; to refuse her gifts would be to lose her, and she was my best customer, the only one who paid on time, who said please and thank you, who praised instead of complained, and never sent a dress back to be done over again.

I always asked myself why she chose to linger on in my room, fingering my things and reading my books, sometimes for more than half an hour after the fittings were over. My other customers couldn't wait to get out the door and be away from my shabby little room, but the shabbiness did not seem to bother her. I think she liked the place as much as she did because it was a house of women. No man and no boy over the age of twelve could pass through the door. The Bridewell Lane Female Boarding House was as far removed from the demimonde as one could get without entering a convent.

Once I asked her in a light and jesting way how she came to work in the Mermaid Inn. For all my poverty I could never imagine doing what she did. I would sooner work in a factory or slave away as a charwoman hauling around buckets of slops.

In the same bantering tone, she replied, "Because I am one, of course. A mermaid. Look!"

Before I could stop her, she was sitting in the middle of my floor, tugging off her shoe and stocking to show me her right foot. I'd seen plenty of feet before but none like hers. First of all it was scrupulously clean and didn't smell at all. It was soft pink like the inside of a shell and more shapely and graceful than I ever thought a foot could be. For some reason the sight of her foot affected me more than the sight of her posing in the beautiful dresses I made her. Then she spread her toes.

"Mother of God," I whispered. I couldn't help it. Her toes were connected with a loose web of skin. I had heard there were people with webbed feet, but I had never thought I would see one sitting on my floor.

Pleased with her performance, Miranda put her sock and shoe back on and pulled down her skirts.

Though I was dying to know what her life was really like—her working life, I mean—she never told me, never said a word about the men who came to see her and how she could do what she did night after night. But I knew her money didn't come for nothing, and her life was not as luxurious as it seemed. A few times a year the police came to inspect the Mermaid Inn. Then Miranda and her sisters-in-sin, as she called them, were carted off to the Oldham Jail and inspected at Her Majesty's Pleasure to see if they carried the plague of syphilis. The next day, if they were found healthy, they were released. Miranda never talked about that either, but I could imagine her walking out the jail door, her chin stuck high in the air, her gait jaunty but unsteady after the forced examination.

One day in June, though, I got to see for myself. She had just been let out of the jail, but instead of going directly back to the Mermaid, she came to my door and started shouting to be heard over the racket of my sewing machine: "Sara Doolan, it's me! Let me in."

I must admit that I opened the door reluctantly and in a bad temper, for I had a christening gown and riding skirt to finish by tomorrow morning. I was late on my rent again and couldn't afford to lose an hour's work. I was about to send her on her way when I saw that her arms were full of parcels of food, the grease leaking through the paper wrapping.

"It's nigh on noon," she said, stepping past me into my room without an invitation and laying her greasy parcels all over the table where I cut out my dress patterns. "I'll bet anything you haven't eaten yet today. How can you work without eating? What you need, Sara Doolan, is someone to look after you."

Unable to think of the words that would send her back out the door, I watched her unwrapping parcel after parcel. She must have stopped at every hot cooking shop and bakery and greengrocer's between the Oldham Jail and the Bridewell Lane Female Boarding House. She had brought steaming fish cakes, chicken pie, hot brown bread, damson plums, lemon custard, sticky buns, ginger biscuits, a hunk of Stilton as big as my fist, and a bottle of dark ale—well concealed in newspapers, for no alcohol of any kind was permitted in the house. "It's just the right color," said Miranda, pouring the ale into the fabulously delicate cups with their cherry blossoms. "It looks like tea, once you lick the foam away."

She went to the cupboard, found the plates she had bought me and filled one, pressing it in my hands, pressing me to eat, though she herself only drank the ale and picked at her fish cake, sucking the hot oil from her fingers. Her eyes were hooded and her chin was drooping. I had never seen her like this. What amazed me most was not her despondency or eccentric behavior after her night in the jail, but the fact that they kept letting her go again, month after month, year after year. How long would her luck run, I wondered, and how long could she ply her trade without getting ill? The clap, I'd heard, wasn't so bad, though I had worried enough about it when I was married to Gabriel, my sailor, the one I eloped to Liverpool with. "Sara, Sara, Queen of May," he called me before we sickened of each other. He sickened of my eternal weeping and homesickness. I sickened of his temper and gambling and faithlessness. After eleven months of wedlock, I had finally had enough. That's when I shrieked, "The Devil take you, Gabriel Doolan." An answered prayer is a frightening thing, but an answered curse is even worse. The next day he left for sea, and nine days later a storm sank his ship and everyone on it. If Miranda was a mermaid, I was a witch; but this is her story, not mine, so let me get on with it.

Amongst the whores was a saying that the clap was a blessing. With any luck it would make you barren. But syphilis! Ever since meeting Miranda, I had taken to reading the stories on the back page of the Saturday papers: the cautionary tales of harlots who had gone blind or mad or both, with weeping cankers covering their ruined flesh like barnacles on the bottom of a ship. By the time you finally died of it, you were ready to quit this world even if it did mean the eternal fires of hell.

Miranda and I ate without speaking. I did not know what to say to her. I needed her to go away, so I could do my work. What had she been thinking of, buying all this food for me? It was enough to feed a sedentary seamstress like myself for an entire week. And it was so unnerving to see her sitting there, limp and mute. It was up to me to drag the conversation along. I wanted to shout at her the way Gabriel used to shout at me. "Woman, have you no eyes in your head? Can't you see I've work to do?" Yet I could hardly turn her out the door when she was like this. She looked like she might start crying at any moment. If I shouted or said anything unkind, I knew she would burst into tears and not be able to stop. Finally I got my *Treasury of English Poetry* down from the shelf and began to read to her as I had once read to my sisters to send them off to sleep.

> *On that fair isle where Venus holds her court,*
> *And every Grace, and all the Loves resort—*

"I'd rather you read from your book of dreams," she said.

So I put the poetry away and brought down *The Gypsy Book of Portents and the Meaning of Dreams*. This was not one of those occult tomes full of strange diagrams and mystical rambling, but a straightforward treatise written in plain language—written for sailors, for they are a superstitious lot. It was Gabriel's book, the only thing besides his gambling debts that he left me when he died. His name was still scrawled on the inside cover, the handwriting of a nineteen-year-old boy who believed in dreams and portents and curses. I opened to a page at random and began to read, "A dream of water foretells a journey." *A dream of a closed box foretells a death,* it said, but that I did not read. I skipped down to the bottom of the page. "A dream of fish portends a great feast."

"Last night in jail," she said, "I dreamt I was a procuress. Do you know, Sara Doolan, what a procuress is?"

I nodded, returning to my chair, taking a cautious sip of ale, then nearly spitting it out. I had work to do. I had to keep a clear head. "The one you work for," I said. "She would be a procuress, would she not?"

"Yes," she said. "A quick one you are. At any rate I dreamt I was a procuress. There was a new girl in my establishment. Just a child. It was a travesty she was even there. Fourteen she was, though she looked even younger. She was from the East Indies. I don't know how she came to Oldham. Maybe a sailor brought her here and sold her to me. A lot of men fancy those girls with their golden skin, and she was a beauty. She was also frightened out of her wits, but I made her get to work. I said, 'You want to eat, don't you? You can either earn your bread here, or try your luck at the factories, where you'll go deaf from the machinery, maybe lose an arm or leg. In any case, you'll contract consumption before the year is out; and in a whole year at the factory you won't earn as much as you will in a month at the Mermaid.'

"She did as she was told. The gentleman who came to her room was a solicitor, fifty years old, with a great white belly covered in hair. He made her crouch naked on the floor in front of him as if he were an idol she had to worship. He made her kneel. He didn't want to touch her right away, just look at her while he decided what he was going to do with her. Then he left the room to get a cigar and a glass of brandy, and that's when the girl came to life. She grabbed her clothes, put them on as fast as she could, and made a dash for the door, except I was standing in her way. It was my duty to stop her, give her a good slap, and send her back to work, but the way she looked at me! She was crying and she was just a child. I couldn't do anything. I was like the woman in the Bible who was turned into a pillar of salt. I could not move. She gave me a grateful look and slipped past me into the alley, running away, whether to try her luck in the factories or mills, I don't know. But I let her run away.

"And then the gentleman came back. He was drinking my brandy, smoking my cigars, railing at me, absolutely furious. I was half afraid he would hit me. He said, 'How could you let that chit get away?' I nearly wanted to run away from him myself, but then I remembered that this was my establishment. I folded my arms in front of myself and said, 'You fool, she's just a child. Are you not ashamed?' "

As Miranda told her tale, her voice was thick with hate. When she had finished her tale, I realized the hate was pointed at herself.

She was quiet for a long time afterward. So was I. I had no answers for her. I closed my book of dreams and put it back on the shelf. Finally I said, "But *you* aren't a procuress. You never brought harm on any young girls."

"I was the girl," she said. "I'm not from the Indies, but I was four-teen when I started working for the old bitch." Before I could say anything, she continued, speaking too fast for me to interrupt. "I won't go back there yet, not today. I fancy a night of peace for once, if you know what I mean. Will you let me stay here with you? Please, Sara. Just one night. I'll sleep on your floor. I'll bring you hot bread and chocolate buns in the morning. Sara, please." Her eyes were as imploring as a child's.

I told her about the christening gown and riding skirt I had to finish by tomorrow morning.

"You can sew all you want. I won't get in your way. I promise."

"I can't work with you in the room. You know I can't."

She stood up, her fingers plucking at her skirt. Her eyes were fixed on my shoes. "How much?" she asked.

"How much *what*?" I was trying not to lose my patience. She really was worse than a child.

"How much will they pay you for the skirt and christening gown?"

"Miranda . . ."

"If I give you the money, you won't have to do the work. It will be a holiday for you."

"Don't you dare try to bribe me, girl. Maybe *you* can be bought for shillings and pence but not me!"

Her face split in two. Her blue-green eyes turned red. I thought they would burst. *There you go now, Sara, you did it again. The same thing you did to Gabriel.* She would run out my door and get struck down by a milk wagon. She would be dead on the pavement, another curse hanging on my soul. Before I knew what I was doing, I had placed myself between her and the door. I was touching her arm and yelling at her as roughly as before, but I was saying, "Yes, you can stay, but I have to work, maybe all night, and you mustn't disturb me."

The relief on her face was the relief of a child who has been expecting a beating but gets a sudden and unexpected reprieve. Her rush of gratitude was too much for me to bear after the way I had spoken to her. And her eyes were the color of the sea I had not seen for five years, the sea that separated me from my mother who had died grieving my elopement and my sisters who would not forgive me for it. I turned away from her, sat at my sewing machine, and didn't look up until the midsummer sun had set, around ten o'clock, and it was too dark to continue. This time I did not have to waste any lamp oil for night labor, though; both the christening gown and the riding skirt were finished. I hobbled from my chair, my back stiff, my legs numb, and saw that Miranda had thrown away the oily wrapping paper, wiped down my table, and arranged the leftover food on the cherry blossom plates. She had gone downstairs to the landlady's kitchen to warm the fish cakes and chicken pie. Now she was pouring me a teacup of sweet, dark ale.

"Cakes and ale," she said, shyly this time, as if fearful I would still change my mind and turn her out. "It can't do you any harm, Sara. Your work is done. You *do* need someone to look after you, you know. When's the last time you had a cooked meal?"

I didn't know what to say, because I couldn't remember. In truth I lived most days on bread and jam.

"It's very good tea brack," she said. "Remember in Ireland at Halloween? The tea brack with the wedding ring hidden inside it?" But I didn't want to talk about Ireland or wedding rings, not to her or anyone else.

When we had eaten our fill, I helped her put the leftovers away in the cupboard and went down with her to the scullery to wash up the plates and cups.

"I'll sleep on the floor," she said when we returned to my room.
"You'll do no such thing."

I did not have a proper bedroom, just a curtained alcove hiding my
bed from the ladies who came to be measured for the clothes I sewed
them. Now I pulled the curtain back and turned down the sheets. I never
had trouble sleeping. By the time night came around, I was weary to
my bones, as the saying goes. Night was a few hours of oblivion before
the sun rose and with it another day's work. I lay down on the side of
the bed by the wall, leaving the outside half for her. I was too tired to
think too much about sharing my bed with a woman who sold her body
to strangers. I only wanted sleep. She lay beside me and blew out the
candle. But then I *couldn't* fall dead asleep as I always did, because she
smelled of summer, of the summer I never saw anymore, now that I
lived in the middle of Oldham at the top of this boarding house in this
gray street. All I could see from my window were factories and mills,
no meadows or forest or ocean. She smelled of summer from the perfume she wore, not the cheap cologne the women in my boarding house
rubbed into their bosom or their hair to disguise the scent of their sweat
when they didn't have time or enough hot water to wash themselves.
This was real perfume, the perfume they sold in beautiful bottles with
French names, the kind ladies wore. It smelled of flowers that could not
grow in this climate, but only on faraway islands where it was always
summer.

In the darkness, my back to her, I finally asked her what I had been
longing to ask her in all the months I had known her. "How can you
bear it, night after night? I would die if a stranger touched me."

She inhaled sharply. For a long time she was silent. For a long time
I thought she wouldn't answer. "It's not me they touch, Sara Doolan.
Have you not heard of the children who are stolen away by the fairies?
They stole me away long ago. You see, I have the ability to steal *myself*
away. I leave my body behind. I leave behind a block of wood that
looks like me. But I have powers, Sara Doolan, I swear I do. There are
women who can bless and curse."

I buried my face in the pillow. She could not see it, but I was crying
for all I had done and could never undo.

"I can fly to the moon. I can swim to the bottom of the sea. Do you
not believe me?"

"I believe you, Miranda. I saw your mermaid feet with my own
eyes. I believe you."

"If you let me stay with you one night a week, I'll teach you, too.
I'll teach you how to fly. I can send my soul out of my body. It flies

like an owl far away over the sea. Do you not miss the smell of the
sea?"

"Aye. But sleep now. Don't get yourself overexcited."

I could feel the mattress shifting. She was rolling over, her front to
my back. "I'll take you with me. Just lie still and sleep as you always
do. I'll take you along. You'll go there in your dreams. I'll take you
over the sea tonight." Her arm wrapped around my waist. She buried
her face in my hair. I could feel her breath, hot and moist, against the
back of my neck. "Pretend we're sisters," she whispered.

"Maíre," I said.

She made a noise in her throat. "What are you saying, Sara Doolan?"

"My sister's name, the sister I was close to, her name was Maíre.
And if you want to be my sister, that's what I'll call you."

She made that noise again, somewhere between a gasp and a whimper. That was when I knew that Maíre was her name, too, her real name.

"Go to sleep, Maíre." And I whispered the poem about that fair isle
where Venus holds her court until her breathing was deep as the sea
and her arm around my waist was limp and warm as a sleeping cat. I
listened to the night sounds of the boarding house. Crying babies and
creaking floorboards. From down the alley came the sound of breaking
glass, and from somewhere very far away was the sound of the wind
blowing through midsummer trees, wind skimming the grass of open
fields full of broom and cow parsley, wind skimming ocean waves. We
were flying over the endless saltwater, Maíre and me. We were on the
strand down the hill from my mother's cottage. We were hitching up
our skirts to gather seaweed. We were scraping mussels off the salty
black rocks in the bay. The sun was setting over the western ocean, and
we saw a sleek head emerging from the foam of a wave. It was a seal
bobbing in the surf, her tail as graceful as a mermaid's and her eyes as
melting.

The moment just before you fall asleep is the moment of enchantment. For one eternal moment I was there, between the worlds where
everything is possible, where all mistakes can be undone. I called Gabriel back up from the bottom of the sea, gave him back his ring, and
set him free with a blessing instead of a curse. And I was a maiden
again. I had never left my mother and sisters, never betrayed their love
and their faith in me. Maíre and I still gathered shells and made fish
cakes every Friday. The shells and starfish were on my mantelpiece and
the sea itself was in the mermaid eyes of the girl who slept beside me.
She *was* a mermaid, not just another lost child who had become a
woman too soon. We were sisters. And for one moment, we were home.

ELEANOR ARNASON

The Grammarian's Five Daughters

Eleanor Arnason has published numerous works of science fiction and fantasy since her debut in Michael Moorcock's New Worlds Quarterly *in 1973. Her fantasy novels include* The Swordsmith, Daughter of the Bear King, *and* A Woman of the Iron People *(winner of the very first James Tiptree, Jr. Award in 1991).*

The following story about the magic of language is one of the most charming modern fairy tales I have ever encountered. "The Grammarian's Five Daughters" comes from the June issue of Realms of Fantasy.

—*T. W.*

Once there was a grammarian who lived in a great city that no longer exists, so we don't have to name it. Although she was learned and industrious and had a house full of books, she did not prosper. To make the situation worse, she had five daughters. Her husband, a diligent scholar with no head for business, died soon after the fifth daughter was born, and the grammarian had to raise them alone. It was a struggle, but she managed to give each an adequate education, though a dowry—essential in the grammarian's culture—was impossible. There was no way for her daughters to marry. They would become old maids, eking (their mother thought) a miserable living as scribes in the city market. The grammarian fretted and worried, until the oldest daughter was fifteen years old.

Then the girl came to her mother and said, "You can't possibly support me, along with my sisters. Give me what you can, and I'll go out and seek my fortune. No matter what happens, you'll have one less mouth to feed."

The mother thought for a while, then produced a bag. "In here are nouns, which I consider the solid core and treasure of language. I give them to you because you're the oldest. Take them and do what you can with them."

The oldest daughter thanked her mother and kissed her sisters and trudged away, the bag of nouns on her back.

Time passed. She traveled as best she could, until she came to a country full of mist. Everything was shadowy and uncertain. The oldest daughter blundered along, never knowing exactly where she was, till she came to a place full of shadows that reminded her of houses.

A thin, distant voice cried out, "Oyez. The king of this land will give his son or daughter to whoever can dispel the mist."

The oldest daughter thought a while, then opened her bag. Out came the nouns, sharp and definite. *Sky* leaped up and filled the grayness overhead. *Sun* leaped up and lit the sky. *Grass* spread over the dim gray ground. *Oak* and *elm* and *poplar* rose from grass. *House* followed, along with *town* and *castle* and *king*.

Now, in the sunlight, the daughter was able to see people. Singing her praise, they escorted her to the castle, where the grateful king gave his eldest son to her. Of course they married and lived happily, producing many sharp and definite children.

In time they ruled the country, which acquired a new name: Thingnesse. It became famous for bright skies, vivid landscapes, and solid, clear-thinking citizens who loved best what they could touch and hold.

Now the story turns to the second daughter. Like her sister, she went to the grammarian and said, "There is no way you can support the four of us. Give me what you can, and I will go off to seek my fortune. No matter what happens, you will have one less mouth to feed."

The mother thought for a while, then produced a bag. "This contains verbs, which I consider the strength of language. I give them to you because you are my second child and the most fearless and bold. Take them and do what you can with them."

The daughter thanked her mother and kissed her sisters and trudged away, the bag of verbs on her back.

Like her older sister, the second daughter made her way as best she could, coming at last to a country of baking heat. The sun blazed in the middle of a dull blue, dusty sky. Everything she saw seemed overcome with lassitude. Honeybees, usually the busiest of creatures, rested on their hives, too stupefied to fly in search of pollen. Plowmen dozed at their plows. The oxen in front of the plows dozed as well. In the little trading towns, the traders sat in their shops, far too weary to cry their wares.

The second daughter trudged on. The bag on her back grew ever heavier and the sun beat on her head, until she could barely move or think. Finally, in a town square, she came upon a man in the embroidered tunic of a royal herald. He sat on the rim of the village fountain, one hand trailing in water.

When she came up, he stirred a bit, but was too tired to lift his head. "Oy—" he said at last, his voice whispery and slow. "The queen of this country will give—give a child in marriage to whoever can dispel this stupor."

The second daughter thought for a while, then opened her bag. *Walk* jumped out, then *scamper* and *canter, run* and *jump* and *fly*. Like bees, the verbs buzzed through the country. The true bees roused themselves in response. So did the country's birds, farmers, oxen, housewives, and merchants. In every town, dogs began to bark. Only the cats stayed curled up, having their own schedule for sleeping and waking.

Blow blew from the bag, then *gust*. The country's banners flapped. Like a cold wind from the north or an electric storm, the verbs hummed and crackled. The daughter, amazed, held the bag open until the last slow verb had crawled out and away.

Townsfolk danced around her. The country's queen arrived on a milk-white racing camel. "Choose any of my children. You have earned a royal mate."

The royal family lined up in front of her, handsome lads and lovely maidens, all twitching and jittering, due to the influence of the verbs.

All but one, the second daughter realized: a tall maid who held herself still, though with evident effort. While the other royal children had eyes like deer or camels, this one's eyes—though dark—were keen. The grammarian's daughter turned toward her.

The maiden said, "I am the crown princess. Marry me and you will be a queen's consort. If you want children, one of my brothers will bed you. If we're lucky, we'll have a daughter to rule after I am gone. But no matter what happens, I will love you forever, for you have saved my country from inaction."

Of course, the grammarian's daughter chose this princess.

Weary of weariness and made restless by all the verbs, the people of the country became nomads, riding horses and following herds of great-horned cattle over a dusty plain. The grammarian's second daughter bore her children in carts, saw them grow up on horseback, and lived happily to an energetic old age, always side by side with her spouse, the nomad queen. The country they ruled, which had no clear borders and no set capital, became known as Change.

Now the story turns back to the grammarian. By this time her third daughter had reached the age of fifteen.

"The house has been almost roomy since my sisters left," she told her mother. "And we've had almost enough to eat. But that's no reason for me to stay, when they have gone to seek their fortunes. Give me what you can, and I will take to the highway. No matter what happens, you'll have one less mouth to feed."

"You are the loveliest and most elegant of my daughters," said the grammarian. "Therefore I will give you this bag of adjectives. Take them and do what you can with them. May luck and beauty go with you always."

The daughter thanked her mother, kissed her sisters, and trudged away, the bag of adjectives on her back. It was a difficult load to carry. At one end were words like *rosy* and *delicate*, which weighed almost nothing and fluttered. At the other end, like stones, lay *dark* and *grim* and *fearsome*. There seemed no way to balance such a collection. The daughter did the best she could, trudging womanfully along until she came to a bleak desert land. Day came suddenly here, a white sun popping into a cloudless sky. The intense light bleached colors from the earth. There was little water. The local people lived in caves and canyons to be safe from the sun.

"Our lives are bare stone," they told the grammarian's third daughter, "and the sudden alternation of blazing day and pitchblack night. We are too poor to have a king or queen, but we will give our most respected person, our shaman, as spouse to anyone who can improve our situation."

The third daughter thought for a while, then unslung her unwieldy bag, placed it on the bone-dry ground, and opened it. Out flew *rosy* and *delicate* like butterflies. *Dim* followed, looking like a moth.

"Our country will no longer be stark," cried the people with joy. "We'll have dawn and dusk, which have always been rumors."

One by one the other adjectives followed: *rich, subtle, beautiful, luxuriant.* This last resembled a crab covered with shaggy vegetation. As it crept over the hard ground, plants fell off it—or maybe sprang up around it—so it left a trail of greenness.

Finally, the bag was empty except for nasty words. As *slimy* reached out a tentacle, the third daughter pulled the drawstring tight. *Slimy* shrieked in pain. Below it in the bag, the worst adjectives rumbled, "Unjust! Unfair!"

The shaman, a tall, handsome person, was nearby, trying on various adjectives. He/she/it was especially interested in *masculine, feminine,* and *androgynous.* "I can't make up my mind," the shaman said. "This is the dark side of our new condition. Before, we had clear choices. Now, the new complexity puts all in doubt."

The sound of complaining adjectives attracted the shaman. He, she, or it came over and looked at the bag, which still had a tentacle protruding and wiggling.

"This is wrong. We asked for an end to starkness, which is not the same as asking for prettiness. In there—at the bag's bottom—are words we might need someday: *sublime, awesome, terrific,* and so on. Open it up and let them out."

"Are you certain?" asked the third daughter.

"Yes," said the shaman.

She opened the bag. Out crawled *slimy* and other words equally disgusting. The shaman nodded with approval as more and more unpleasant adjectives appeared. Last of all, after *grim* and *gruesome* and *terrific,* came *sublime.* The word shone like a diamond or a thundercloud in sunlight.

"You see," said the shaman. "Isn't that worth the rest?"

"You are a holy being," said the daughter, "and may know things I don't."

Sublime crawled off toward the mountains. The third daughter rolled up her bag. "All gone," she said. "Entirely empty."

The people looked around. Their land was still a desert, but now clouds moved across the sky, making the sunlight on bluff and mesa change. In response to this, the desert colors turned subtle and various. In the mountains rain fell, misty gray, feeding clear streams that ran in the bottoms of canyons. The vegetation there, spread by the land-crab *luxuriant* and fed by the streams, was a dozen—two dozen—shades of green.

"Our land is beautiful!" the people cried. "And you shall marry our shaman!"

But the shaman was still trying on adjectives, unable to decide if she, he, or it wanted to be feminine or masculine or androgynous.

"I can't marry someone who can't make up her mind," the third daughter said. "Subtlety is one thing. Uncertainty is another."

"In that case," the people said, "you will become our first queen, and the shaman will become your first minister."

This happened. In time the third daughter married a young hunter, and they had several children, all different in subtle ways.

The land prospered, though it was never fertile, except in the canyon bottoms. But the people were able to get by. They valued the colors of dawn and dusk, moving light on mesas, the glint of water running over stones, the flash of bugs and birds in flight, the slow drift of sheep on a hillside—like clouds under clouds. The name of their country was Subtletie. It lay north of Thingnesse and west of Change.

Back home, in the unnamed city, the grammarian's fourth daughter came of age.

"We each have a room now," she said to her mother," and there's plenty to eat. But my sister and I still don't have dowries. I don't want to be an old maid in the marketplace. Therefore, I plan to go as my older sisters did. Give me what you can, and I'll do my best with it. And if I make my fortune, I'll send for you."

The mother thought for a while and rummaged in her study, which was almost empty. She had sold her books years before to pay for her daughters' educations, and most of her precious words were gone. At last, she managed to fill a bag with adverbs, though they were frisky little creatures and tried to escape.

But a good grammarian can outwit any word. When the bag was close to bursting, she gave it to her fourth daughter.

"This is what I have left. I hope it will serve."

The daughter thanked her mother and kissed her one remaining sister and took off along the highway, the bag of adverbs bouncing on her back.

Her journey was a long one. She made it womanfully, being the most energetic of the five daughters and the one with the most buoyant spirit. As she walked—quickly, slowly, steadily, unevenly—the bag on her back kept jouncing around and squeaking.

"What's in there?" asked other travelers. "Mice?"

"Adverbs," said the fourth daughter.

"Not much of a market for them," said the other travelers. "You'd be better off with mice."

This was plainly untrue, but the fourth daughter was not one to argue. On she went, until her shoes wore to pieces and fell from her weary feet. She sat on a stone by the highway and rubbed her bare soles, while the bag squeaked next to her.

A handsome lad in many-colored clothes stopped in front of her. "What's in the bag?" he asked.

"Adverbs," said the daughter shortly.

"Then you must, like me, be going to the new language fair."

The daughter looked up with surprise, noticing—as she did so— the lad's rosy cheeks and curling, auburn hair. "What?" she asked intently.

"I'm from the country of Subtletie and have a box of adjectives on my horse, every possible color, arranged in drawers: *aquamarine, russet, dun, crimson, puce.* I have them all. Your shoes have worn out. Climb up on my animal, and I'll give you a ride to the fair."

The fourth daughter agreed, and the handsome lad—whose name, it turned out, was Russet—led the horse to the fair. There, in booths with bright awnings, wordsmiths and merchants displayed their wares: solid nouns, vigorous verbs, subtle adjectives. But there were no adverbs.

"You have brought just the right product," said Russet enviously. "What do you say we share a booth? I'll get cages for your adverbs, who are clearly frisky little fellows, and you can help me arrange my colors in the most advantageous way."

The fourth daughter agreed; they set up a booth. In front were cages of adverbs, all squeaking and jumping, except for the sluggish ones. The lad's adjectives hung on the awning, flapping in a mild wind. As customers came by, drawn by the adverbs, Russet said, "How can we have *sky* without *blue*? How can we have *gold* without *shining*? And how much use is a verb if it can't be modified? Is *walk* enough, without *slowly* or *quickly*?

"Come and buy! Come and buy! We have *mincingly* and *angrily, knowingly, lovingly,* as well as a fine assortment of adjectives. Ride home happily with half a dozen colors and a cage full of adverbs."

The adverbs sold like hotcakes, and the adjectives sold well also. By the fair's end, both Russet and the fourth daughter were rich, and there were still plenty of adverbs left.

"They must have been breeding, though I didn't notice," said Russet. "What are you going to do with them?"

"Let them go," said the daughter.

"Why?" asked Russet sharply.

"I have enough money to provide for myself, my mother, and my younger sister. *Greedy* is an adjective and not one of my wares." She opened the cages. The adverbs ran free—slowly, quickly, hoppingly, happily. In the brushy land around the fairground, they proliferated. The region became known as Varietie. People moved there to enjoy the brisk, invigorating, varied weather, as well as the fair, which happened every year thereafter.

As for the fourth daughter, she built a fine house on a hill above the fairground. From there she could see for miles. Out back, among the bushes, she put feeding stations for the adverbs, and she sent for her mother and one remaining sister. The three of them lived together contentedly. The fourth daughter did not marry Russet, though she remained always grateful for his help. Instead, she became an old maid. It was a good life, she said, as long as one had money and respect.

In time, the fifth daughter came of age. (She was the youngest by far.) Her sister offered her a dowry, but she said, "I will do no less than the rest of you. Let my mother give me whatever she has left, and I will go to seek my fortune."

The mother went into her study, full of new books now, and looked around. "I have a new collection of nouns," she told the youngest daughter.

"No, for my oldest sister took those and did well with them, from all reports. I don't want to repeat someone else's adventures."

Verbs were too active, she told her mother, and adjectives too varied and subtle. "I'm a plain person who likes order and organization."

"How about adverbs?" asked the mother.

"Is there nothing else?"

"Prepositions," said the mother, and showed them to her daughter. They were dull little words, like something a smith might make from pieces of iron rod. Some were bent into angles. Others were curved into hooks. Still others were circles or helixes. Something about them touched the youngest daughter's heart.

"I'll take them," she said and put them in a bag. Then she thanked her mother, kissed her sister, and set off.

Although they were small, the prepositions were heavy and had sharp corners. The youngest daughter did not enjoy carrying them, but she was a methodical person who did what she set out to do. Tromp, tromp she went along the highway, which wound finally into a broken country, full of fissures and jagged peaks. The local geology was equally chaotic. Igneous rocks intruded into sedimentary layers. New rock lay under old rock. The youngest daughter, who loved order, had never seen such a mess. While neat, she was also rational, and she realized she could not organize an entire mountain range. "Let it be what it is," she said. "My concern is my own life and other people."

The road grew rougher and less maintained. Trails split off from it and sometimes rejoined it or ended nowhere, as the daughter discovered by trial. "This country needs engineers," she muttered peevishly. (A few adverbs had hidden among the prepositions and would pop out now and then. *Peevishly* was one.)

At length the road became nothing more than a path, zigzagging down a crumbling mountain slope. Below her in a valley was a town of shacks, though town might be the wrong word. The shacks were scattered helter-skelter over the valley bottom and up the valley sides. Nothing was seemly or organized. Pursing her lips—a trick she had learned from her mother, who did it when faced by a sentence that would not parse—the fifth daughter went down the path.

When she reached the valley floor, she saw people running to and fro.

"Madness," said the daughter. The prepositions, in their bag, made a sound of agreement like metal chimes.

In front of her, two women began to argue—over what she could not tell.

"Explain," cried the fifth daughter, while the prepositions went "bong" and "bing."

"Here in the Canton of Chaos nothing is capable of agreement," one woman said. "Is it age before beauty, or beauty before age? What came first, the chicken or the egg? Does might make right, and if so, what is left?"

"This is certainly madness," said the daughter.

"How can we disagree?" said the second woman. "We live topsy-turvy and pell-mell, with no hope of anything better." Saying this, she hit the first woman on the head with a live chicken.

"Egg!" cried the first woman.

"Left!" cried the second.

The chicken squawked, and the grammarian's last daughter opened her bag.

Out came the prepositions: *of, to, from, with, at, by, in, under, over*, and so on. When she'd put them into the bag, they had seemed like hooks or angles. Now, departing in orderly rows, they reminded her of ants. Granted, they were large ants, each one the size of a woman's hand, their bodies metallic gray, their eyes like cut and polished hematite. A pair of tongs or pincers protruded from their mouths; their thin legs, moving delicately over the ground, seemed made of iron rods or wire.

Somehow—it must have been magic—the things they passed over and around became organized. Shacks turned into tidy cottages. Winding paths became streets. The fields were square now. The trees ran in lines along the streets and roads. Terraces appeared on the mountainsides.

The mountains themselves remained as crazy as ever, strata sideways and upside down. "There is always a limit to order," said the daughter. At her feet, a handful of remaining prepositions chimed their agreement like bells.

In decorous groups, the locals came up her. "You have saved us from utter confusion. We are a republic, so we can't offer you a throne. But please become our first citizen, and if you want to marry, please accept any of us. Whatever you do, don't go away, unless you leave these ingenious little creatures that have connected us with one another."

"I will stay," said the fifth daughter, "and open a grammar school. As for marriage, let that happen as it will."

The citizens agreed by acclamation to her plan. She settled in a tidy cottage and opened a tidy school, where the canton's children learned grammar.

In time, she married four other schoolteachers. (Due to the presence of the prepositions, which remained in their valley and throughout the mountains, the local people developed a genius for creating complex social groups. Their diagrams of kinship excited the awe of neighbors, and their marriages grew more intricate with each generation.)

The land became known as Relation. In addition to genealogists and marriage brokers, it produced diplomats and merchants. These last two groups, through trade and negotiation, gradually unified the five countries of Thingnesse, Change, Subtletie, Varietie, and Relation. The empire they formed was named Cooperation. No place was more solid, more strong, more complex, more energetic, or better organized.

The flag of the new nation was an ant under a blazing yellow sun. Sometimes the creature held a tool: a pruning hook, scythe, hammer, trowel, or pen. At other times its hands (or feet) were empty. Always below it was the nation's motto: WITH.

For Ruth Berman

GENE WOLFE

The Tree Is My Hat

Gene Wolfe is best known for his Book of the New Sun *series and his tetralogy* The Book of the Long Sun. *He is currently in the middle of his trilogy* The Book of the Short Sun, *the second volume of which,* In Green's Jungles, *has just been published. He has also written some amazing novellas and short stories, including the interconnected trio of novellas called* The Fifth Head of Cerberus *and the stories collected in* The Island of Doctor Death and Other Stories. *His most recent collection is* Strange Travellers. *His work has won two Nebula Awards and three World Fantasy Awards, including the Lifetime Achievement Award.*

"The Tree Is My Hat," originally published in the anthology 999, *edited by Al Sarrantonio, shows off the author's work at its most exotic and perhaps its strangest.*

—*E. D.*

3 0 Jan. I saw a strange stranger on the beach this morning. I had been swimming in the little bay between here and the village; that may have had something to do with it, although I did not feel tired. Dived down and thought I saw a shark coming around the big staghorn coral. Got out fast. The whole swim cannot have been more than ten minutes. Ran out of the water and started walking.

There it is. I have begun this journal at last. (Thought I never would.) So let us return to all the things I ought to have put in and did not. I bought this the day after I came back from Africa.

No, the day I got out of the hospital—I remember now. I was wandering around, wondering when I would have another attack, and went into a little shop on Forty-second Street. There was a nice-looking woman in there, one of those good-looking black women, and I thought it might be nice to talk to her, so I had to buy something. I said, "I just got back from Africa."

She: "Really. How was it?" Me: "Hot."

Anyway, I came out with this notebook and told myself I had not wasted my money because I would keep a journal, writing down my attacks, what I had been doing and eating, as instructed; but all I could think of was how she looked when she turned to go to the back of the shop. Her legs and how she held her head. Her hips.

After that I planned to write down everything I remember from Africa, and what we said if Mary returned my calls. Then it was going to be about this assignment.

31 Jan. Setting up my new Mac. Who would think this place would have phones? But there are wires to Kololahi, and a dish. I can chat with people all over the world, for which the agency pays. (Talk about soft!) Nothing like this in Africa. Just the radio, and good luck with that.

I was full of enthusiasm. "A remote Pacific island chain." Wait . . .

P. D.: "Baden, we're going to send you to the Takanga Group."

No doubt I looked blank.

"It's a remote Pacific island chain." She cleared her throat and seemed to have swallowed a bone. "It's not going to be like Africa, Bad. You'll be on your own out there."

Me: "I thought you were going to fire me."

P. D.: "No, no! We wouldn't do that."

"Permanent sick leave."

"No, no, no! But, Bad." She leaned across her desk and for a minute I was afraid she was going to squeeze my hand. "This will be rough. I'm not going to try to fool you."

Hah!

Cut to the chase. This is nothing. This is a bungalow with rotten boards in the floors that has been here since before the British pulled out, a mile from the village and less than half that from the beach, close enough that the Pacific-smell is in all the rooms. The people are fat and happy, and my guess is not more than half are dumb. (Try and match that around Chicago.) Once or twice a year one gets yaws or some such, and Rev. Robbins gives him arsenic. *Which cures it.* Pooey!

There are fish in the ocean, plenty of them. Wild fruit in the jungle, and they know which you can eat. They plant yams and breadfruit, and if they need money or just want something, they dive for pearls and trade them when Jack's boat comes. Or do a big holiday boat trip to Kololahi.

There are coconuts too, which I forgot. They know how to open them. Or perhaps I am just not strong enough yet. (I look in the mirror, and ugh.) I used to weigh two hundred pounds.

"You skinny," the king says. "Ha, ha, ha!" He is really a good guy, I think. He has a primitive sense of humor, but there are worse things. He can take a jungle chopper (we said *upanga* but they say *heletay*) and open a coconut like a pack of gum. I have coconuts and a heletay but I might as well try to open them with a spoon.

1 Feb. Nothing to report except a couple of wonderful swims. I did not swim at all for the first couple of weeks. There are sharks. I know they are really out there because I have seen them once or twice. According to what I was told, there are saltwater crocs, too, up to fourteen feet long. I have never seen any of those and am skeptical, although I know they have them in Queensland. Every so often you hear about somebody who was killed by a shark, but that does not stop the people from swimming all the time, and I do not see why it should stop me. Good luck so far.

2 Feb. Saturday. I was supposed to write about the dwarf I saw on the beach that time, but I never got the nerve. Sometimes I used to see things in the hospital. Afraid it may be coming back. I decided to take a walk on the beach. All right, did I get sunstroke?

Pooey.

He was just a little man, shorter even than Mary's father. He was too small for any adult in the village. He was certainly not a child, and was too pale to have been one of the islanders at all.

He cannot have been here long; he was whiter than I am.

Rev. Robbins will know—ask tomorrow.

3 Feb. Hot and getting hotter. Jan. is the hottest month here, according to Rob Robbins. Well, I got here the first week in Jan. and it has never been this hot.

Got up early while it was still cool. Went down the beach to the village. (Stopped to have a look at the rocks where the dwarf disappeared.) Waited around for the service to begin but could not talk to Rob, he was rehearsing the choir—"Nearer My God to Thee."

Half the village came, and the service went on for almost two hours. When it was over I was able to get Rob alone. I said if he would drive us into Kololahi I would buy our Sunday dinner. (He has a jeep.) He was nice, but no—too far and the bad roads. I told him I had personal troubles I wanted his advice on, and he said, "Why don't we go to your place, Baden, and have a talk? I'd invite you for lemonade, but they'd be after me every minute."

So we walked back. It was hotter than hell, and this time I tried not to look. I got cold Cokes out of my rusty little fridge, and we sat on the porch (Rob calls it the veranda) and fanned ourselves. He knew I felt bad about not being able to do anything for these people, and urged patience. My chance would come.

I said, "I've given up on that, Reverend."

(That was when he told me to call him Rob. His first name is Mervyn.) "Never give up, Baden. Never." He looked so serious I almost laughed.

"All right, I'll keep my eyes open, and maybe someday the Agency will send me someplace where I'm needed."

"Back to Uganda?"

I explained that the A.O.A.A. almost never sends anyone to the same area twice. "That wasn't really what I wanted to talk to you about. It's my personal life. Well, really two things, but that's one of them. I'd like to get back together with my ex-wife. You're going to advise me to forget it, because I'm here and she's in Chicago; but I can send E-mail, and I'd like to put the bitterness behind us."

"Were there children? Sorry, Baden. I didn't intend it to hurt."

I explained how Mary had wanted them and I had not, and he gave me some advice. I have not E-mailed yet, but I will tonight after I write it out here.

"You're afraid that you were hallucinating. Did you feel feverish?" He got out his thermometer and took my temperature, which was nearly normal. "Let's look at it logically, Baden. This island is a hundred miles long and about thirty miles at the widest point. There are eight villages I know of. The population of Kololahi is over twelve hundred."

I said I understood all that.

"Twice a week, the plane from Cairns brings new tourists."

"Who almost never go five miles from Kololahi."

"Almost never, Baden. Not never. You say it wasn't one of the villagers. All right, I accept that. Was it me?"

"Of course not."

"Then it was someone from outside the village, someone from another village, from Kololahi, or a tourist. Why shake your head?"

I told him.

"I doubt there's a leprosarium nearer than the Marshalls. Anyway, I don't know of one closer. Unless you saw something else, some other sign of the disease, I doubt that this little man you saw had leprosy. It's a lot more likely that you saw a tourist with pasty white skin greased with sun blocker. As for his disappearing, the explanation seems pretty obvious. He dived off the rocks into the bay."

"There wasn't anybody there. I looked."

"There wasn't anybody there you saw, you mean. He would have been up to his neck in water, and the sun was glaring on the water, wasn't it?"

"I suppose so."

"It must have been. The weather's been clear." Rob drained his Coke and pushed it away. "As for his not leaving footprints, stop playing Sherlock Holmes. That's harsh, I realize, but I say it for your own good. Footprints in soft sand are shapeless indentations at best."

"I could see mine."

"You knew where to look. Did you try to backtrack yourself? I thought not. May I ask a few questions? When you saw him, did you think he was real?"

"Yes, absolutely. Would you like another one? Or something to eat?"

"No, thanks. When was the last time you had an attack?"

"A bad one? About six weeks."

"How about a not-bad one?"

"Last night, but it didn't amount to much. Two hours of chills, and it went away."

"That must have been a relief. No, I see it wasn't. Baden, the next time you have an attack, severe or not, I want you to come and see me. Understand?"

I promised.

"This is Bad. I still love you. That's all I have to say, but I want to say it. I was wrong, and I know it. I hope you've forgiven me." And sign off.

4 Feb. Saw him again last night, and he has pointed teeth. I was shaking under the netting, and he looked through the window and smiled. Told Rob, and said I read somewhere that cannibals used to file their teeth. I know these people were cannibals three or four generations back, and I asked if they had done it. He thinks not but will ask the king.

"I have been very ill, Mary, but I feel better now. It is evening here, and I am going to bed. I love you. Good night. I love you." Sign off.

5 Feb. Two men with spears came to take me to the king. I asked if I was under arrest, and they laughed. No ha, ha, ha from His Majesty this time, though. He was in the big house, but he came out and we went some distance among hardwoods the size of office buildings smothered in flowering vines, stopping in a circle of stones: the king, the men with spears, and an old man with a drum. The men with spears built a fire, and the drum made soft sounds like waves while the king made a speech or recited a poem, mocked all the while by invisible birds with eerie voices.

When the king was finished, he hung this piece of carved bone around my neck. While we were walking back to the village, he put his arm around me, which surprised me more than anything. He is bigger than a tackle in the NFL, and must weigh four hundred pounds. It felt like I was carrying a calf.

Horrible, *horrible* dreams! Swimming in boiled blood. Too scared to sleep anymore. Logged on and tried to find something on dreams and what they mean. Stumbled onto a witch in L.A.—her home page, then the lady herself. (I'll get you and your little dog too!) Actually, she seemed nice.

Got out the carved bone thing the king gave me. Old, and probably ought to be in a museum, but I suppose I had better wear it as long as I stay here, at least when I go out. Suppose I were to offend him? He might sit on me! Seems to be a fish with pictures scratched into both sides. More fish, man in a hat, etc. Cord through the eye. Wish I had a magnifying glass.

6 Feb. Still haven't gone back to bed, but my watch says Wednesday. Wrote a long E-mail, typing it in as it came to me. Told her where I am and what I'm doing, and begged her to respond. After that I went outside and swam naked in the moonlit sea. Tomorrow I want to look for the place where the king hung this fish charm on me. Back to bed.

Morning, and beautiful. Why has it taken me so long to see what a beautiful place this is? (Maybe my heart just got back from Africa.) Palms swaying forever in the trade winds, and people like heroic bronze statues. How small, how stunted and pale we have to look to them!

Took a real swim to get the screaming out of my ears. Will I laugh in a year when I see that I said my midnight swim made me understand these people better? Maybe I will. But it did. They have been swimming in the moon like that for hundreds of years.

E-mail! God bless E-mail and whoever invented it! Just checked mine and found I had a message. Tried to guess who it might be. I wanted Mary, and was about certain it would be from the witch, from Annys. Read the name and it was "Julius R. Christmas." Pops! Mary's Pops! Got up and ran around the room, so excited I could not read it. Now I have printed it out, and I am going to copy it here.

"She went to Uganda looking for you, Bad. Coming back tomorrow, Kennedy, AA 47 from Heathrow. I'll tell her where you are. Watch out for those hula-hula girls."

SHE WENT TO UGANDA LOOKING FOR ME

7 Feb. More dreams—little man with pointed teeth smiling through the window. I doubt that I should write it all down, but I knew (in the dream) that he hurt people, and he kept telling me he would not hurt me. Maybe the first time was a dream too. More screams.

Anyway, I talked to Rob again yesterday afternoon, although I had not planned on it. By the time I got back here I was too sick to do anything except lie on the bed. The worst since I left the hospital, I think.

Went looking for the place the king took me to. Did not want to start from the village, kids might have followed me, so I tried to circle and come at it from the other side. Found two old buildings, small and no roofs, and a bone that looked human. More about that later. Did not see any marks, but did not look for them either. It was black on one end like it had been in a fire, though.

Kept going about three hours and wore myself out. Tripped on a chunk of stone and stopped to wipe off the sweat, and Blam! I was there! Found the ashes and where the king and I stood. Looked around wishing I had my camera, and there was Rob, sitting up on four stones that were still together and looking down at me. I said, "Hey, why didn't you say something?"

And he said, "I wanted to see what you would do." So he had been spying on me; I did not say it, but that was what it was.

I told him about going there with the king, and how he gave me a charm. I said I was sorry I had not worn it, but anytime he wanted a Coke I would show it to him.

"It doesn't matter. He knows you're sick, and I imagine he gave you something to heal you. It might even work, because God hears all sorts of prayers. That's not what they teach in the seminary, or even what it says in the Bible. But I've been out in the missions long enough to know. When somebody with good intentions talks to the God who created him, he's heard. Pretty often the answer is yes. Why did you come back here?"

"I wanted to see it again, that's all. At first I thought it was just a circle of rocks, then when I thought about it, it seemed like it must have been more."

Rob kept quiet; so I explained that I had been thinking of Stonehenge. Stonehenge was a circle of big rocks, but the idea had been to look at the positions of certain stars and where the sun rose. But this could not be the same kind of thing, because of the trees. Stonehenge is out in the open on Salisbury Plain. I asked if it was some kind of temple.

"It was a palace once, Baden." Rob cleared his throat. "If I tell you something about it in confidence, can you keep it to yourself?"

I promised.

"These are good people now. I want to make that clear. They seem a little childlike to us, as all primitives do. If we were primitives ourselves—and we were, Bad, not so long ago—they wouldn't. Can you imagine how they'd seem to us if they didn't seem a little childlike?"

I said, "I was thinking about that this morning before I left the bungalow."

Rob nodded. "Now I understand why you wanted to come back here. The Polynesians are scattered all over the South Pacific. Did you know that? Captain Cook, a British naval officer, was the first to explore the Pacific with any thoroughness, and he was absolutely astounded to find that after he'd sailed for weeks his interpreter could still talk to the natives. We know, for example, that Polynesians came down from Hawaii in sufficient numbers to conquer New Zealand. The historians hadn't admitted it the last time I looked, but it's a fact, recorded by the Maori themselves in their own history. The distance is about four thousand miles."

"Impressive."

"But you wonder what I'm getting at. I don't blame you. They're supposed to have come from Malaya originally. I won't go into all the reasons for thinking that they didn't, beyond saying that if it were the case they should be in New Guinea and Australia, and they're not."

I asked where they had come from, and for a minute or two he just rubbed his chin; then he said, "I'm not going to tell you that either. You wouldn't believe me, so why waste breath on it? Think of a distant land, a mountainous country with buildings and monuments to rival ancient Egypt's, and gods worse than any demon Cotton Mather could have imagined. The time . . ." He shrugged. "After Moses but before Christ."

"Babylon?"

He shook his head. "They developed a ruling class, and in time those rulers, their priest and warriors, became something like another race, bigger and stronger than the peasants they treated like slaves. They drenched the altars of their gods with blood, the blood of enemies when they could capture enough, and the blood of peasants when they couldn't. Their peasants rebelled and drove them from the mountains to the sea, and into the sea."

I think he was waiting for me to say something; but I kept quiet, thinking over what he had said and wondering if it were true.

"They sailed away in terror of the thing they had awakened in the hearts of the nation that had been their own. I doubt very much if there were more than a few thousand, and there may well have been fewer than a thousand. They learned seamanship, and learned it well. They had to. In the ancient world they were the only people to rival the Phoenicians, and they surpassed even the Phoenicians."

I asked whether he believed all that, and he said, "It doesn't matter whether I believe it, because it's true."

He pointed to one of the stones. "I called them primitives, and they are. But they weren't always as primitive as they are now. This was a palace, and there are ruins like this all over Polynesia, great buildings of coral rock falling to pieces. A palace and thus a sacred place, because the king was holy, the gods' representative. That was why he brought you here."

Rob was going to leave, but I told him about the buildings I found earlier and he wanted to see them. "There is a temple, too, Baden, although I've never been able to find it. When it was built, it must have been evil beyond our imagining. . . ." He grinned then, surprising hell out of me. "You must get teased about your name."

"Ever since elementary school. It doesn't bother me." But the truth is it does, sometimes.

More later.

Well, I have met the little man I saw on the beach, and to tell the truth (what's the sense of one of these if you are not going to tell the truth?) I like him. I am going to write about all that in a minute.

Rob and I looked for the buildings I had seen when I was looking for the palace but could not find them. Described them, but Rob did not think they were the temple he has been looking for since he came. "They know where it is. Certainly the older people do. Once in a while I catch little oblique references to it. Not jokes. They joke about the place you found, but not about that."

I asked what the place I had found had been.

"A Japanese camp. The Japanese were here during World War Two."

I had not known that.

"There were no battles. They built those buildings you found, presumably, and they dug caves in the hills from which to fight. I've found some of those myself. But the Americans and Australians simply bypassed this island, as they did many other islands. The Japanese soldiers remained here, stranded. There must have been about a company, originally."

"What happened to them?"

"Some surrendered. Some came out of the jungle to surrender and were killed. A few held out, twenty or twenty-five, from what I've heard. They left their caves and went back to the camp they had built when they thought Japan would win and control the entire Pacific. That was what you found, I believe, and that's why I'd like to see it."

I said I could not understand how we could have missed it, and he said, "Look at this jungle, Baden. One of those buildings could be within ten feet of us."

After that we went on for another mile or two and came out on the beach. I did not know where we were, but Rob did. "This is where we separate. The village is that way, and your bungalow the other way, beyond the bay."

I had been thinking about the Japs, and asked if they were all dead, and he said they were. "They were older every year and fewer every year, and a time came when the rifles and machine guns that had kept the villages in terror no longer worked. And after that, a time when the people realized they didn't. They went to the Japanese camp one night with their spears and war clubs. They killed the remaining Japanese and ate them, and sometimes they make sly little jokes about it when they want to get my goat."

I was feeling pretty rocky and knew I was in for a bad time, so I came back here. I was sick the rest of the afternoon and all night, chills, fever, headache, the works. I remember watching the little vase on the bureau get up and walk to the other side, and sit back down, and seeing an American in a baseball cap float in. He took off his cap and combed his hair in front of the mirror, and floated back out. It was a Cardinals cap.

Now about Hanga, the little man I see on the beach.

After I wrote all that about the palace, I wanted to ask Rob a couple of questions and tell him Mary was coming. All right, no one has actually said she was, and so far I have heard nothing from her directly, only the one E-mail from Pops. But she went to Africa, so why not here? I thanked Pops and told him where I am again. He knows how much I want to see her. If she comes, I am going to ask Rob to re-marry us, if she will.

Started down the beach, and I saw him; but after half a minute or so he seemed to melt into the haze. I told myself I was still seeing things, and I was still sick; and I reminded myself that I promised to go by Rob's mission next time I felt bad. But when I got to the end of the bay, there he was, perfectly real, sitting in the shade of one of the young palms. I wanted to talk to him, so I said, "Okay if I sit down, too? This sun's frying my brains."

He smiled (the pointed teeth are real) and said, "The tree is my hat."

I thought he just meant the shade, but after I sat he showed me, biting off a palm frond and peeling a strip from it, then showing me how to peel them and weave them into a rough sort of straw hat, with a high crown and a wide brim.

We talked a little, although he does not speak English as well as some of the others. He does not live in the village, and the people who do, do not like him although he likes them. They are afraid of him, he says, and give him things because they are. They prefer he stay away. "No village, no boat."

I said it must be lonely, but he only stared out to sea. I doubt that he knows the word.

He wanted to know about the charm the king gave me. I described it and asked if it brings good luck. He shook his head. "No *malhoi.*" Picking up a single palm fiber, "This *malhoi.*" Not knowing what *malhoi* meant, I was in no position to argue.

That is pretty much all, except that I told him to visit when he wants company; and he told me I must eat fish to restore my health. (I have no idea who told him I am ill sometimes, but I never tried to keep it a secret.) Also that I would never have to fear an attack (I think that must have been what he meant) while he was with me.

His skin is rough and hard, much lighter in color than the skin of my forearm, but I have no idea whether that is a symptom or a birth defect. When I got up to leave, he stood too, and came no higher than my chest. Poor little man.

One more thing. I had not intended to put it down, but after what Rob said maybe I should. When I had walked some distance toward the village, I turned back to wave to Hanga, and he was gone. I walked back, thinking that the shade of the palm had fooled me; he was not there. I went to the bay, thinking he was in the water as Rob suggested.

It is a beautiful little cove, but Hanga was not there, either. I am beginning to feel sympathy for the old mariners. These islands vanished when they approached.

At any rate, Rob says that *malhoi* means "strong." Since a palm fiber is not as strong as a cotton thread, there must be something wrong somewhere. (More likely, something I do not understand.) Maybe the word has more than one meaning.

Hanga means "shark," Rob says, but he does not know my friend Hanga. Nearly all the men are named for fish.

More E-mail, this time the witch. "There is danger hanging over you. I feel it and know some higher power guided you to me. Be careful. Stay away from places of worship, my tarot shows trouble for you there. Tell me about the fetish you mentioned."

I doubt that I should, and that I will E-mail her again.

9 Feb. I guess I wore myself out on writing Thursday. I see I wrote nothing yesterday. To tell the truth, there was nothing to write about except my swim in Hanga's bay. And I cannot write about that in a way that makes sense. Beautiful beyond description. That is all I can say. To tell the truth, I am afraid to go back. Afraid I will be disappointed. No spot on earth, even under the sea, can be as lovely as I remember it. Colored coral, and the little sea-animals that look like flowers, and schools of blue and red and orange fish like live jewels.

Today when I went to see Rob (all right, Annys warned me; but I think she is full of it) I said he probably likes to think God made this beautiful world so we could admire it; but if He had, He would have given us gills.

"Do I also think that He made the stars for us, Baden? All those flaming suns hundreds and thousands of light years away? Did God create whole galaxies so that once or twice in our lives we might chance to look up and glimpse them?"

When he said that I had to wonder about people like me, who work for the federal government. Would we be driven out someday, like the people Rob talked about? A lot of us do not care any more about ordinary people than they did. I know P. D. does not.

A woman who had cut her hand came in about then. Rob talked to her in her own language while he treated her, and she talked a good deal more, chattering away. When she left I asked whether he had really understood everything she said. He said, "I did and I didn't. I knew all the words she used, if that's what you mean. How long have you been here now, Baden?"

I told him and he said, "About five weeks? That's perfect. I've been here about five years. I don't speak as well as they do. Sometimes I have to stop to think of the right word, and sometimes I can't think of it at all. But I understand when I hear them. It's not an elaborate language. Are you troubled by ghosts?"

I suppose I gawked.

"That was one of the things she said. The king has sent for a woman from another village to rid you of them, a sort of witch-doctress, I imagine. Her name is Langitokoua."

I said the only ghost bothering me was my dead marriage's, and I hoped to resuscitate it with his help.

He tried to look through me and may have succeeded; he has that kind of eyes. "You still don't know when Mary's coming?"

I shook my head.

"She'll want to rest a few days after her trip to Africa. I hope you're allowing for that."

"And she'll have to fly from Chicago to Los Angeles, from Los Angeles to Melbourne, and from there to Cairns, after which she'll have to wait for the next plane to Kololahi. Believe me, Rob, I've taken all that into consideration."

"Good. Has it occurred to you that your little friend Hanga might be a ghost? I mean, has it occurred to you since you spoke to him?"

Right then, I had that "what am I doing here" feeling I used to get in the bush. There I sat in that bright, flimsy little room with the medicine smell, and a jar of cotton balls at my elbow, and the noise of the surf coming in the window, about a thousand miles from anyplace that matters; and I could not remember the decisions I had made and the plans that had worked or not worked to get me there:

"Let me tell you a story, Baden. You don't have to believe it. The first year I was here, I had to go to town to see about some building supplies we were buying. As things fell out, there was a day there when I had nothing to do, and I decided to drive up to North Point. People had told me it was the most scenic part of the island, and I convinced myself I ought to see it. Have you ever been there?"

I had not even heard of it.

"The road only goes as far as the closest village. After that there's a footpath that takes two hours or so. It really is beautiful, rocks standing above the waves, and dramatic cliffs overlooking the ocean. I stayed there long enough to get the lovely, lonely feel of the place and make some sketches. Then I hiked back to the village where I'd left the jeep and started to drive back to Kololahi. It was almost dark.

"I hadn't gone far when I saw a man from our village walking along the road. Back then I didn't know everybody, but I knew him. I stopped, and we chatted for a minute. He said he was on his way to see his parents, and I thought they must live in the place I had just left. I told him to get into the jeep, and drove back, and let him out. He thanked me over and over, and when I got out to look at one of the tires I was worried about, he hugged me and kissed my eyes. I've never forgotten that."

I said something stupid about how warmhearted the people here are.

"You're right, of course. But, Baden, when I got back, I learned that North Point is a haunted place. It's where the souls of the dead go to make their farewell to the land of the living. The man I'd picked up had been killed by a shark the day I left, four days before I gave him a ride."

I did not know what to say, and at last I blurted out, "They lied to you. They had to be lying."

"No doubt—or I'm lying to you. At any rate, I'd like you to bring your friend Hanga here to see me if you can."

I promised I would try to bring Rob to see Hanga, since Hanga will not go into the village.

Swimming in the little bay again. I never thought of myself as a strong swimmer, never even had much chance to swim, but have been swimming like a dolphin, diving underwater and swimming with my eyes open for what has got to be two or two and a half minutes if not longer. Incredible! My God, wait till I show Mary!

You can buy scuba gear in Kololahi. I'll rent Rob's jeep or pay one of the men to take me in his canoe.

11 Feb. I let this slide again, and need to catch up. Yesterday was very odd. So was Saturday.

After I went to bed (still full of Rob's ghost story and the new world underwater) and *crash!* Jumped up scared as hell, and my bureau had fallen on its face. Dry rot in the legs, apparently. A couple of drawers broke, and stuff scattered all over.

I propped it back up and started cleaning up the mess, and found a book I never saw before, *The Light Garden of the Angel King*, about traveling through Afghanistan. In front is somebody's name and a date, and "American Overseas Assistance Agency." None of it registered right then.

But there it was, spelled out for me. And here is where he was, Larry Scribble. He was an Agency man, had bought the book three years ago (when he was posted to Afghanistan, most likely) and brought it with him when he was sent here. I only use the top three drawers, and it had been in one of the others and got overlooked when somebody (who?) cleared out his things.

Why was he gone when I got here? He should have been here to brief me, and stayed for a week or so. No one has so much as mentioned his name, and there must be a reason for that.

Intended to go to services at the mission and bring the book, but was sick again. Hundred and nine. Took medicine and went to bed, too weak to move, and had this very strange dream. Somehow I knew somebody was in the house. (I suppose steps, although I cannot remember any.) Sat up, and there was Hanga smiling by my bed. "I knock. You not come."

I said, "I'm sorry. I've been sick." I felt fine. Got up and offered to get him a Coke or something to eat, but he wanted to see the charm. I said sure, and got it off the bureau.

He looked at it, grunting and tracing the little drawings on its sides with his forefinger. "No tie? You take loose?" He pointed to the knot.

I said there was no reason to, that it would go over my head without untying the cord.

"Want friend?" He pointed to himself, and it was pathetic. "Hanga friend? Bad friend?"

"Yes," I said. "Absolutely."

"Untie."

I said I would cut the cord if he wanted me to.

"Untie, please. Blood friend." (He took my arm then, repeating, "Blood friend!")

I said all right and began to pick at the knot, which was complex; and at that moment, I swear, I heard someone else in the bungalow, some third person who pounded on the walls. I believe I would have gone to see who it was then, but Hanga was still holding my arm. He has big hands on those short arms, with a lot of strength in them.

In a minute or two I got the cord loose and asked if he wanted it, and he said eagerly that he did. I gave it to him, and there was one of those changes you get in dreams. He straightened up, and was at least as tall as I am. Holding my arm, he cut it quickly and neatly with his teeth and licked the blood, and seemed to grow again. It was as if some sort of defilement had been wiped away. He looked intelligent and almost handsome.

Then he cut the skin of his own arm just like mine. He offered it to me, and I licked his blood like he had licked mine. For some reason I expected it to taste horrible, but it did not; it was as if I had gotten seawater in my mouth while I was swimming.

"We are blood friends now, Bad," Hanga told me. "I shall not harm you, and you must not harm me."

That was the end of the dream. The next thing I remember is lying in bed and smelling something sweet, while something tickled my ear. I thought the mosquito netting had come loose, and looked to see, and there was a woman with a flower in her hair lying beside me. I rolled over; and she, seeing that I was awake, embraced and kissed me.

She is Langitokoua, the woman Rob told me the king had sent for, but I call her Langi. She says she does not know how old she is, and is fibbing. Her size (she is about six feet tall, and must weigh a good two-fifty) makes her look older than she is, I feel sure. Twenty-five, maybe. Or seventeen. I asked her about ghosts, and she said very matter-of-factly that there is one in the house but he means no harm.

Pooey.

After that, naturally I asked her why the king wanted her to stay with me; and she solemnly explained that it is not good for a man to live by himself, that a man should have someone to cook and sweep, and take care of him when he is ill. That was my chance, and I went for it. I explained that I am expecting a woman from America soon, that American women are jealous, and that I would have to tell the American woman Langi was there to nurse me. Langi agreed without any fuss.

What else?

Hanga's visit was a dream, and I know it; but it seems I was sleep-walking. (Perhaps I wandered around the bungalow delirious.) The charm was where I left it on the dresser, but the cord was gone. I found it under my bed and tried to put it back through the fish's eye, but it will not go.

E-mail from Annys: "The hounds of hell are loosed. For heaven's sake be careful. Benign influences rising, so have hope." Crazy if you ask me.

E-mail from Pops: "How are you? We haven't heard from you. Have you found a place for Mary and the kids? She is on her way."

What kids? Why, the old puritan!

Sent a long E-mail back saying I had been very ill but was better, and there were several places where Mary could stay, including this bungalow, and I would leave the final choice to her. In fairness to Pops, he has no idea where or how I live, and may have imagined a rented room in Kololahi with a monkish cot. I should send another E-mail asking about her flight from Cairns; I doubt he knows, but it may be worth a try.

Almost midnight, and Langi is asleep. We sat on the beach to watch the sunset, drank rum-and-Coke and rum-and-coconut-milk when the Coke ran out, looked at the stars, talked, and made love. Talked some more, drank some more, and made love again.

There. I had to put that down. Now I have to figure out where I can hide this so Mary never sees it. I will not destroy it and I will not lie. (Nothing is worse than lying to yourself. *Nothing.* I ought to know.)

Something else in the was-it-a-dream category, but I do not think it was. I was lying on my back in the sand, looking up at the stars with Langi beside me asleep; and I saw a UFO. It was somewhere between me and the stars, sleek, dark, and torpedo-shaped, but with a big fin on the back, like a rocket ship in an old comic. Circled over us two or three times, and was gone. Haunting, though.

It made me think. Those stars are like the islands here, only a million billion times bigger. Nobody really knows how many islands there are, and there are probably a few to this day that nobody has ever been on. At night they look up at the stars and the stars look down on them, and they tell each other, "They're coming!"

Langi's name means "sky sister" so I am not the only one who ever thought like that.

Found the temple!!! Even now I cannot believe it. Rob has been looking for it for five years, and I found it in six weeks. God, but I would love to tell him!

Which I cannot do. I gave Langi my word, so it is out of the question.

We went swimming in the little bay. I dove down, showing her corals and things that she has probably been seeing since she was old enough to walk, and she showed the temple to me. The roof is gone if it ever had one, and the walls are covered with coral and the sea creatures that look like flowers; you can hardly see it unless somebody shows you. But once you do it is all there, the long straight walls, the main entrance, the little rooms at the sides, everything. It is as if you were looking at the ruins of a cathedral, but they were decked in flowers and bunting for a fiesta. (I know that is not clear, but it is what it was like, the nearest I can come.) They built it on land, and the water rose; but it is still there. It looks hidden, not abandoned. Too old to see, and too big.

I will never forget this: How one minute it was just rocks and coral, and the next it was walls and altar, with a fifty-foot branched coral like a big tree growing right out of it. Then an enormous gray-white shark with eyes like a man's came out of the shadow of the coral tree to look at us, worse than a lion or a leopard. My god, was I ever scared!

When we were both back up on the rocks, Langi explained that the shark had not meant to harm us, that we would both be dead if it had. (I cannot argue with that.) Then we picked flowers, and she made wreaths out of them and threw them in the water and sang a song. Afterward she said it was all right for me to know, because we are us; but I must never tell other *mulis*. I promised faithfully that I would not.

She has gone to the village to buy groceries. I asked her whether they worshipped Rob's God in the temple underwater. (I had to say it like that for her to understand.) She laughed and said no, they worshiped the shark god so the sharks would not eat them. I have been thinking about that.

It seems to me that they must have brought other gods from the mountains where they lived, a couple of thousand years ago, and they settled here and built that temple to their old gods. Later, probably hundreds of years later, the sea came up and swallowed it. Those old gods went away, but they left the sharks to guard their house. Someday the water will go down again. The ice will grow thick and strong on Antarctica once more, the Pacific will recede, and those murderous old mountain gods will return. That is how it seems to me, and if it is true I am glad I will not be around to see it.

I do not believe in Rob's God, so logically I should not believe in them either. But I do. It is a new millennium, but we are still playing by the old rules. They are going to come to teach us the new ones, or that is what I am afraid of.

Valentine's Day. Mary passed away. That is how Mom would have said it, and I have to say it like that, too. Print it. I cannot make these fingers print the other yet.

Can anybody read this?

Langi and I had presented her with a wreath of orchids, and she was wearing them. It was so fast, so crazy.

So much blood, and Mary and kids screaming.

I had better backtrack or give this up altogether.

There was a boar hunt. I did not go, remembering how sick I had been after tramping through the jungle with Rob, but Langi and I went to the pig roast afterward. Boar hunting is the men's favorite pastime; she says it is the only thing that the men like better than dancing. They do not have dogs and do not use bows and arrows. It is all a matter of tracking, and the boars are killed with spears when they find them, which must be really dangerous. I got to talk to the king about this hunt, and he told me how they get the boar they want to a place where it cannot run away anymore. It turns then and defies them, and may charge; but if it does not, four or five men all throw their spears at once. It was the king's spear, he said, that pierced the heart of this boar.

Anyway it was a grand feast with pineapples and native beer, and my rum, and lots of pork. It was nearly morning by the time we got back here, where Mary was asleep with Mark and Adam.

Which was a very good thing, since it gave us a chance to swim and otherwise freshen up. By the time they woke up, Langi had prepared a fruit tray for breakfast and woven the orchids, and I had picked them for her and made coffee. Little boys, in my experience, are generally cranky in the morning (could it be because we do not allow them coffee?) but Adam and Mark were sufficiently overwhelmed by the presence of a brown lady giant and a live skeleton that conversation was possible. They are fraternal twins, and I think they really are mine; certainly they look very much like I did at their age. The wind had begun to rise, but we thought nothing of it.

"Were you surprised to see me?" Mary was older than I remembered, and had the beginnings of a double chin.

"Delighted. But Pops told me you'd gone to Uganda, and you were on your way here."

"To the end of the earth." (She smiled, and my heart leaped.) "I never realized the end would be as pretty as this."

I told her that in another generation the beach would be lined with condos.

"Then let's be glad that we're in this one." She turned to the boys. "You have to take in everything as long as we're here. You'll never get another chance like this."

I said, "Which will be a long time, I hope."

"You mean that you and . . . ?"

"Langitokoua." I shook my head. (Here it was, and all my lies had melted away.) "Was I ever honest with you, Mary?"

"Certainly. Often."

"I wasn't, and you know it. So do I. I've got no right to expect you to believe me now. But I'm going to tell you, and myself, God's own truth. It's in remission now. Langi and I were able to go to a banquet last night, and eat, and talk to people, and enjoy ourselves. But when it's bad, it's horrible. I'm too sick to do anything but shake and sweat and moan, and I see things that aren't there. I—"

Mary interrupted me, trying to be kind. "You don't look as sick as I expected."

"I know how I look. My mirror tells me every morning while I shave. I look like death in a microwave oven, and that's not very far from the truth. It's liable to kill me this year. If it doesn't, I'll probably get attacks on and off for the rest of my life, which is apt to be short."

There was a silence that Langi filled by asking whether the boys wanted some coconut milk. They said they did, and she got my heletay and showed them how to open a green coconut with one chop. Mary and I stopped talking to watch her, and that's when I heard the surf. It was the first time that the sound of waves hitting the beach had ever reached as far inland as my bungalow.

Mary said, "I rented a Range Rover at the airport." It was the tone she used when she had to bring up something she really did not want to bring up.

"I know. I saw it."

"It's fifty dollars a day, Bad, plus mileage. I won't be able to keep it long."

I said, "I understand."

"We tried to phone. I had hoped you would be well enough to come for us, or send someone."

I said I would have had to borrow Rob's jeep if I had gotten her call.

"I wouldn't have known where you were, but we met a native, a very handsome man who says he knows you. He came along to show us the way." (At that point, the boys' expressions told me something was seriously wrong.) "He wouldn't take any money for it. Was I wrong to offer to pay him? He didn't seem angry."

"No," I said, and would have given anything to get the boys alone. But would it have been different if I had? When I read this, when I really get to where I can face it, the thing I will miss on was how fast it was—how fast the whole thing went. It cannot have been an hour between the time Mary woke up and the time Langi ran to the village to get Rob.

Mark lying there whiter than the sand. So thin and white, and looking just like me.

"He thought you were down on the beach, and wanted us to look for you there, but we were too tired," Mary said.

That is all for now, and in fact it is too much. I can barely read this left-handed printing, and my stump aches from holding down the book. I am going to go to bed, where I will cry, I know, and Langi will cuddle me like a kid.

Again tomorrow.

17 Feb. Hospital sent its plane for Mark, but no room for us. Doctor a lot more interested in my disease than my stump. "Dr. Robbins" did a fine job there, he said. We will catch the Cairns plane Monday.

I should catch up. But first: I am going to steal Rob's jeep tomorrow. He will not lend it, does not think I can drive. It will be slow, but I know I can.

19 Feb. Parked on the tarmac, something wrong with one engine. Have I got up nerve enough to write about it now? We will see.

Mary was telling us about her guide, how good-looking, and all he told her about the islands, lots I had not known myself. As if she were surprised she had not seen him sooner, she pointed and said, "Here he is now."

There was nobody there. Or rather, there was nobody Langi and I or the boys could see. I talked to Adam (to my son Adam, I have to get used to that) when it was over, while Rob was working on Mark and Mary. I had a bunch of surgical gauze and had to hold it as tight as I could. There was no strength left in my hand.

Adam said Mary had stopped and the door opened, and she made him get in back with Mark. *The door opened by itself.* That is the part he remembers most clearly, and the part of his story I will always remember, too. After that Mary seemed to be talking all the time to somebody he and his brother could not see or hear.

She screamed, and there, for just an instant, was the shark. He was as big as a boat, and the wind was like a current in the ocean, blowing us down to the water. I really do not see how I can ever explain this.

No takeoff yet, so I have to try. It is easy to say what was not happening. What is hard is saying what was, because there are no words. The shark was not swimming in air. I know that is what it will sound like, but it (he) was not. We were not under the water, either. We could breathe and walk and run just as he could swim, although not nearly so fast, and even fight the current a little.

The worst thing of all was he came and went and came and went, so that it seemed almost that we were running or fighting him by flashes of lightning, and sometimes he was Hanga, taller than the king and smiling at me while he herded us.

No. The most worst thing was really that he was herding everybody but me. He drove them toward the beach the way a dog drives sheep, Mary, Langi, Adam, and Mark, and he would have let me escape. (I wonder sometimes why I did not. This was a new me, a me I doubt I will ever see again.)

His jaws were real, and sometimes I could hear them snap when I could not see him. I shouted, calling him by name, and I believe I shouted that he was breaking our agreement, that to hurt my wives and my sons was to hurt me. To give the devil his due, I do not think he understood. The old gods are very wise, as the king told me today; still, there are limits to their understanding.

I ran for the knife, the heletay Langi opened coconuts with. I thought of the boar, and by God I charged them. I must have been terrified. I do not remember, only slashing at something and someone huge that was and was not there, and in an instant was back again. The sting of the wind-blown sand, and then up to my arms in foaming water, and cutting and stabbing, and the hammerhead with my knife and my hand in its mouth.

We got them all out, Langi and I did. But Mark has lost his leg, and jaws three feet across had closed on Mary. That was Hanga himself, I feel sure.

Here is what I think. I think he could only make one of us see him at a time, and that was why he flashed in and out. He is real. (God knows he is real!) Not really physical the way a stone is, but physical in other ways that I do not understand. Physical like and unlike light and radiation. He showed himself to each of us, each time for less than a second.

Mary wanted children, so she stopped the pill and did not tell me. That was what she told me when I drove Rob's jeep out to North Point. I was afraid. Not so much afraid of Hanga (though there was that, too) but afraid she would not be there. Then somebody said "Banzai!" It was exactly as if he were sitting next to me in the jeep, except that there was nobody there. I said "Banzai" back, and I never heard him again; but after that I knew I would find her, and I waited for her at the edge of the cliff.

She came back to me when the sun touched the Pacific, and the darker the night and the brighter the stars, the more real she was. Most of the time it was as if she were really in my arms. When the stars got dim and the first light showed in the east, she whispered, "I have to go," and walked over the edge, walking north with the sun to her right and getting dimmer and dimmer.

I got dressed again and drove back and it was finished. That was the last thing Mary ever said to me, spoken a couple of days after she died.

She was not going to get back together with me at all; then she heard how sick I was in Uganda, and she thought the disease might have changed me. (It has. What does it matter about people at the "end of the earth" if you cannot be good to your own people, most of all to your own family?)

Taking off.
We are airborne at last. Oh, Mary! Mary starlight!

Langi and I will take Adam to his grandfather's, then come back and stay with Mark (Brisbane or Melbourne) until he is well enough to come home.

The stewardess is serving lunch, and for the first time since it happened, I think I may be able to eat more than a mouthful. One stewardess, twenty or thirty people, which is all this plane will hold. News of the shark attack is driving tourists off the island.

As you see, I can print better with my left hand. I should be able to write eventually. The back of my right hand itches, even though it is gone. I wish I could scratch it.

Here comes the food.

An engine has quit. Pilot says no danger.

He is out there, swimming beside the plane. I watched him for a minute or more until he disappeared into a thunderhead. "The tree is my hat." Oh, God.

Oh my God!
My blood brother.
What can I do?

MICHAEL MARSHALL SMITH

Welcome

Michael Marshall Smith is no stranger to The Year's Best Fantasy and Horror *series, having appeared here many times already—but this talented author's tales usually fall in the horror half of the book. "Welcome" is a beautifully penned story on the border between fantasy and horror, distinguished by the rich characterization that is the trademark of his fiction.*

Smith was born in England in 1965, and grew up in the United States, South Africa, and Australia. He has won three British Fantasy Awards, and the August Derleth Award for his first novel, Only Forward. *Other novels include* Spares *and* One of Us *(both optioned for film); his short fiction has appeared in* Omni *magazine, the* Mammoth *anthologies,* Dark Terrors, Lethal Kisses, Best New Horror, *and numerous other volumes. "Welcome" comes from* White of the Moon: New Tales of Madness and Dread, *an anthology edited by Stephen Jones and published by Pumpkin Books in the U.K. Smith lives with his wife and two cats in North London, where he is at work on a new novel and screenplays for feature films.*

—T. W.

Paul swore imaginatively and at some length, glaring at the screen in front of him. His current sentence already boasted three *and*'s and two *actually*'s, and was moreover set firmly on a course into the realms of pure nonsense. Its end dangled in space, peering nervously about for something to mean, but he despaired of even just getting it to the point where he could legitimately put a full stop after it.

He reached for the cigarettes on the windowsill, glancing dully at the clock in the corner of the screen. 11:14 P.M. When he'd started work that evening, "Send in the Clones" had stood at eight hundred words. Three hours of effort had merely made it slightly shorter. The individual sentences stood up—he could usually come up with a trenchant observation or a fairly *bon mot*—but they were like a group of strangers trapped together on a bus, with no relationship to each other apart than the fact they appeared on the same page. Chances were that by the time Paul had massaged any coherence into the piece some bastard scientist would have invented a new technique and the whole thing would be out of date anyway. Again.

Enough, already. Paul command-clicked a "save" and listened to the 1's and 0's on the hard disk feverishly playing musical chairs. Eventually the machine pinged at him and he quit out, yawning and slumping forward, noticing just how much his back hurt. And how tired he was. As ever: feeling shattered as a way of life. Haul yourself out of bed too tired to even focus. Drag your body around for the day, then go home. Work some more, then go to bed too late. Repeat until dead.

Suddenly the solution to the sentence he'd been working on popped into his head, a way of making it both say something intelligible and remain conventional English. The boys in the back room had evidently been beavering away at the problem, not noticing he'd given up for the night. He considered reloading the word processor, found that he couldn't be bothered, and decided to jot it down in the document's information window instead.

Selecting "Clones" with a click on the document's icon, Paul hit the required key combination and typed the revised sentence into the little window that popped up. It didn't look quite as stirring on the screen, but it was going to have to do. He moved the cursor up toward the box that would close the window, his eyes straying over the information underneath.

Last Modified: Wednesday, December 15, 1999, 11:17 P.M. Type: AllWrite Document. Document Size: 7K. File Created . . .

Suddenly he stopped and leaned closer to the screen. Mouth open, he stared at the final line in the information window.

File Created: Mon, September 9, 1957, 5:02 P.M.

He shut the information window, then opened it again. It was still there. Obviously it was just a glitch of some kind, some binary dancer left standing when the music stopped, but in a funny sort of way he liked it. There was something appealingly odd about seeing "1957" up there, a year when the computer displaying it would have been a piece of science fiction.

Taking a gulp of cold tea, Paul started to apply some scientific method. The clock in the corner of the screen was showing the correct time, which proved that the motherboard battery was still functioning. He reloaded the word processor and checked the story, which appeared fine. Then he created a test document, typing in a few words, saving it and quitting. Opening the new document's information window showed a file creation date of December 15, 1999. Pleased, Paul opened the "Clones" window again.

File Created: Mon, September 9, 1957, 5:02 P.M.

It was still just a glitch, a five and a seven snatched out of the ether instead of two nines, but it was a weird and one-off glitch, and Paul felt vaguely cheered by it. He switched the computer off and rubbed his eyes. Time to give Jenny a ring.

In preparation he walked into the kitchen to make a fresh cup of tea, circling the phone as if it were an animal that had been recently and only partially tamed. Telephones are fine for conducting business, essential even. The whole edifice of commerce would come crashing down if people could see the chasm of boredom in the faces of those they dealt with. Over the phone it was possible to pretend things were important, when actually they were just jobs. Personal conversations were different, and Paul had come to dread them, even though the distance between him and Jenny meant that the phone mediated about eighty percent of their relationship. Maybe if things were okay you could just breezily chat to each other, update on the unimportant things because the real things were okay. But things were not okay. They were not okay to the tune of two miserable years and a score line of Jenny: three affairs, Paul: nil. The last six months had been a little better, and they had at least been together, but bridge-building had in reality been limited to dropping a slim and fragile plank between the two sides, occasional weekends spent precariously in the middle. Unhappiness at not feeling needed or wanted had become a part of Paul's life, his every thought, like an interfaceless application running in the background of every moment. His mental soundtrack had become a litany of miserable bitterness, and he hated himself for being that way.

Settling back into the flat's one comfortable chair, Paul propped the handset under his chin—the skill a legacy of long hours at work spent listening to people whining at him over the phone—and dialed the Cambridge number. A ringing tone eventually emerged and Paul lit a cigarette in preparation. Five, six rings. Christ, how long did it take to get from her room to the hall—ten seconds? Nine, ten.

After twenty or so rings Paul quietly replaced the handset, chewing the inside of his lip. He tried again, looking at his watch. 11:30. Another twenty rings. No reply. Breathing deeply he put the phone down again.

What this time? Aerobics class go into overtime? *Another* drink with the people from work? Why was she never bloody *in* when he called?

"I went to the cinema with Val. I *told* you I was going to."

"Till half eleven?"

"We stopped off for a drink, alright? It's Christmas. God, aren't I even allowed to . . ."

Been there, done that, seen it all before.

Of course that was all it was. Or one of a hundred variants. In a way it was better than getting the engaged signal. That always made him think she was curled up happily in her flat, chatting to the Last One. She couldn't win either way. But then neither could he.

Closing his eyes, Paul slowly calmed down. It wasn't fair to be suspicious, to envy her friends and social life. But the Paul who had been able to take things in his stride, to forgive and forget and trust, was a Paul who'd never been lied to and never seen infidelity, never sat at home knowing his girlfriend was at that moment sleeping with someone else, someone older, taller, and more exciting than himself. He missed that Paul, mourned the nicer man he thought he'd probably once been, but recognized the inevitability of his passing. He just hadn't been up to the job. Reality demanded psyches with crumple zones. He'd walked into the world with his head held high, and had the shit kicked out of him so many times that now he was hiding somewhere deep inside, waiting for a miracle without much hope.

It was time for sleep. Looking like a hard-drugs user might be part of what stopped him ever getting the small consolation of someone appearing to fancy him. That and being only average-looking, and not having a tan, and only being five feet nine inches tall. Not that short, above average height, in fact, but ever since hearing Jenny's description of the Last One he'd gone around marveling at how close the ground was to his head, feeling like a bloody dwarf.

But he didn't feel tired enough to trust himself to bed. It was there, and in this sort of mood, that he saw most clearly Jenny's kisses on someone else's neck and stomach, imagined scenarios that should have burned themselves out long ago, but which just got clearer every time. He tried the television, which offered two yobs in track clothes talking about a group of musical yobs in track clothes, and three conventionally suited old twonks gassing on about women in the church. Paul, who believed that the only priests who could be taken halfway seriously were Irish males in their fifties, turned it off again.

For want of anything better to do, he sat back down at his desk and turned the computer back on again, calling up the "Clones" information window again. It was still there.

File Created: Mon, September 9, 1957, 5:02 P.M.

The strange thing was that it didn't look like a mistake. The "57" looked unremarkable, and solid. Paul reached for his diary and checked September 9th, 1999. It had been a Thursday. So the day was wrong too.

Or was it? On a sudden whim he fired up his Organizer application, and asked it to go to the relevant month in 1957, aware that he was feeling nervously excited.

And there it was. September the 9th, 1957, had been a Monday.

That was something else. Throwing up a couple of random numbers that happened to make a date was one thing, but getting the right *day* was, well it was something different again. Too intrigued to notice that for once neither Jenny nor work had a place in his mind, Paul sat back and smiled. He couldn't explain what he was seeing, and he was glad. He knew that basically it was still just a glitch, and that he ought to be worrying about system file corruption or I/O errors, but he didn't care. For some reason it was interesting, and exciting. It seemed to point to unusual territories, something intangible beyond the everyday. A glimpse of a land beyond the icy wastes of normality was worth having, even if it was just a code-generated mirage.

What it called for, of course, was a story. A little piece. Relaxing, blowing smoke up toward the ceiling, Paul worked around the idea, trying to see where it could lead. Man finds that a document he's created shows a creation date many years before his computer was invented, but which is still a genuine date. Computer time versus real time. Unreliability of binary truths. The millennium bug. Something.

Nothing came, and he wasn't too concerned. He was beginning to feel sleepy, which meant that he could safely go to bed. It didn't matter if he couldn't get a story out of the glitch. It was still good that it had happened.

And, of course, he had to go to work tomorrow.

He woke abruptly, hammered from sleep by his alarm. After turning it off by hitting it with his fist until it stopped, he hauled himself upright and lurched to the bathroom, still well over half-asleep and feeling terrible. Sitting blankly in the bath, working up the energy to wash, he found that he was almost in tears.

As he shaved, he remembered the dream. He and Jenny had been at an event of some kind, a big party full of people in formal wear, and things between him and Jenny had been okay in a way they hadn't been for a while. As if there was a future to look forward to. Then she had been called away to the telephone. When she came back, she said that the Last One was coming to visit her, and that he'd be there for two weeks this time. Paul had been distracted by a sound of some kind, and before he'd had time to argue she'd disappeared into the crowd. He'd searched for her, and asked people if they'd seen where she went. All he got was smiles, and then the windows had burst inward as an endless pack of wolves poured into the room.

More awake now, he knew he wouldn't cry, but also that he'd spend the day even more bitterly than normal. The thought of breakfast made him feel as nauseous as usual, and he smoked a few cigarettes instead, staring out the window with a cup of tea. He realized that Jenny and he still hadn't made any plans for what to do on December the 31st. With less than two weeks to go, he was beginning to suspect it wasn't going to happen. What then? Arbitrary or not, surely it should herald a new beginning. Surely not just more of the same.

It rained as he walked to the station.

During the forty-minute tube journey he climbed slowly toward the hard and brittle self he used these days, reading fitfully. The mornings were always the worst. Often he would find his mind working away at old hurts, and would have to force himself to read, to try to block them out. Sometimes he even found himself inventing things that might have happened, or could happen. Bringing bad things into being for the sake of it. Some part of him was locked away in a circle of hurt, and couldn't think about anything else. It couldn't hate her, so it hated him, instead, punished him with make-believe and foreshadowing all possibilities— so that nothing would ever come as a surprise again. It was completely out of Paul's control, and all he could do was try to coat it with white noise. Reading wasn't working, so he looked around the carriage instead, trying to find something to look at, something to tether his attention to the outside world for a change.

In front of him stood a gaggle of girls in their late teens, gossiping in mock outraged terms about something some acquaintance of theirs had done. Paul silently bet that the girl's name was Laura. There seemed to be hundreds of Lauras out there, bad-mouthing their bosses, stealing other people's boyfriends, and never traveling on the tube. Just along from the girls was a man who looked like someone had found an enormous pear, painted it like a suit, and stuck a copy of the *Financial Times* in its mitts. Apart from that, the carriage looked as if it had been filled by extras from the "Random Commuters" department of central casting: pink eyes, clothes hastily de-crumpled, faces still half-asleep.

But two stops later, she got on.

Paul had no idea of her name, and no intention of trying to find out. She was in her late thirties, early forties, with dark brown hair, slim, tall. Unexceptional really, except that she looked nice, and friendly, and trustworthy, and seeing her gave him his customary pang of quiet desire and misery. A fat man in a brown suit oozed onto the train after her and blocked his sight line, and Paul turned back to his book, almost with relief. Better not to look.

After a while the words began to swim in front of his eyes, and to head his mind off from its accustomed paths, Paul worried at the problem of the story idea from the night before, feeling sure that something must be possible from a premise like that. Perhaps it could generate the kind of quirky piece that all the magazines seemed to be after, a piece led by personality rather than information. Maybe he might be able to sell something for once, start turning the dream of journalism into something approaching a reality. Nothing came, though. The idea seemed unwilling to be diluted, and just sat there by itself.

In front of him Paul noticed a quiet couple holding hands, and knew immediately that they had just spent the night together for the first time, probably after an office party. Her hair, still wet from its morning wash, her normal routine disrupted; his face, smarting from using a razor found lying around in the bathroom, feeling oddly put together, wearing yesterday's shirt and smelling of someone else's deodorant. Neither of them quite sure what to say, how to be, struggling to deal with the suddenly widened perception of someone they saw every day at work. Confused memories of the night before, of the shock of so much skin.

The next stop was theirs and they stood up together, wavered, and then didn't hold hands as they got off the train.

Paul got off at Oxford Circus and trudged up Great Portland Street to the office. Everyone else was already at their desks. As always. One or two grunted at him as he went to the kitchen. He poured himself a cup of coffee and took it into his office, shutting the door behind him. Normally he left it open, to catch what stray gusts of camaraderie might come. This morning he needed ten minutes' peace, and wasn't in the mood for saying "Oh, really?" Then the phone rang and the first hassle of the day started. He opened the door.

He took his lunch at 2:00 P.M., as always. The short afternoon seemed to make the day go quicker, and he was generally so busy doing mindless things to unrealistic schedules that there wasn't a breathing space for time to drag in. Lunchtimes were often when he felt worse, in fact. He had time to resent the fact that the days went so quickly without him getting anything out of them, that he had no power in his job, only responsibility. And time to feel yet more fury at himself for apparently having nothing else to think about, his neverending self-absorption, for the constant black mass in his head. He was terribly, terribly bored with himself. Perhaps it wasn't surprising if Jenny was too.

He walked out past the others, feeling their eyebrows rise. Taking your lunch break was deemed a sign of weakness, a lack of dedication. It made him feel as if he'd said something rude about the Queen Mother. The thing Paul found hardest to bear was having to pretend that he cared about the office, that it was his life. The others didn't seem to have to pretend. Egerton in particular appeared to *live* at the bloody place: virtually every day he'd proclaim with smug self-deprecation that he'd been there since 8:30 A.M. or even earlier. The required response seemed to be one of mingled awe and businesslike respect. It made Paul want to grab him by the lapels and shake him vigorously, shouting "*Why*, you dull bastard?" loudly in his face.

A queue of people strung out of the snack bar, all waiting to take their sandwiches away so they could eat them at their desks with a telephone under each ear. Paul walked a further fifty yards to the Burger King. A blank-faced waitress sold him a hamburger and told him to enjoy his meal.

"I'll try," Paul said. She didn't smile, didn't look like she ever had, in fact.

Determined to relax, Paul lit a cigarette after his burger and tried to read. A middle-aged man nursing a coffee a few tables away asked for the time. Paul told him. "Oh," the man said, and went back to staring at the table, nothing else to do, nothing to be on time for. Waiting the day away.

On the way out, Paul shoved his rubbish into a bin that said "Thank You" on it. A passing Oriental table-clearer with cataclysmic acne thanked him too.

Adam was waiting for him when he got back to the office, sitting on his desk and using his phone, making no effort to cut the call short.

"Here," he said, eventually, thrusting a sheaf of papers at him. "These have to be at the printers by four."

Paul stared at the bundle. The association he worked for produced a stupendously dull magazine, which was nothing to do with him. He'd somehow ended up with the responsibility of proofreading the non-stories on non-issues, however—at some stage he must have made some ill-advised comment about being interested in journalism—and he was never given it until the last possible minute. In front of him was forty pages of galleys, the whole magazine.

"Adam, got rather a lot to do, actually . . ." he said, forcing himself to play his polite part in what was a monthly ritual.

"Got to go off today, alright?" Adam replied, looking past him, and then abruptly turned and walked away, dropping the proofs on Paul's desk.

An hour later, and less than a third of the way through, Paul paused to get a cup of coffee. As he passed Whitehead's office, the director stepped out.

"Proofing done, is it?" he said, looking at the coffee in Paul's hand.

"Almost," Paul replied, trying to sound like a colleague, not a minion. "I'm about . . ."

"Got to go off today, you know," Whitehead said, and stepped back into his office, closing the door.

He finally finished at 6:10, having got none of his own work done. Adam took the proofs without a word. Through his door Paul saw he and Whitehead conferring over them. Adam looked at his watch and shook his head. Paul half-rose from his chair to go over and explain to Whitehead just why the proofs were late, then sat heavily down again. He could picture exactly what sort of reply he'd get. Brutally polite, like a genteel and slow-motion punch in the mouth. Instead he tidied his desk until they had gone and then left the office, feeling the customary thread of weak relief at the end of something unpleasant and boring, amidst quiet despair in anticipation of the next.

The tube station was full of people, milling into a funnel struggling toward the one escalator out of three that was working. Paul let fluid hatred wash over him: surely it wasn't *that* difficult to keep escalators working? It was happening all over the Underground. Was the magic that kept them going really that arcane and impenetrable? Had someone forgotten the spell? For years they'd all worked fine, then suddenly it was apparently impossible to keep them running for more than ten minutes at a time. The week before, he'd noticed that one side of the steps leading out of the station had been roped off too. Not working either, presumably.

The platform was crowded, the destination board blank, sightless eyes and sagging shoulders jostling in an ether of irritation. It emerged that someone had thrown themselves under a train. Paul felt that he could see their point. How long would you have to stand, surrounded by desperate commuters, people angrily pacing in smaller and smaller circles until they were almost standing still, before you simply couldn't take it anymore? Before you realized that there could be a new and unusual journey that you could start with a single step? He could almost see the bored fury seeping out of the rumpled and glowing bodies of the commuters around him, swirling like a hot mist around their feet. Perhaps when it reached head height they would all jump together, piling into the trench in front.

When a train finally arrived it was packed, and going somewhere he didn't want to go via somewhere he'd never even heard of. The doors opened into a battle-zone of elbows and sweating flesh. Pressed from all sides, too close to faces, surrounded by dry red skin and sallow foreheads. Brutal stupidity and vapid waste hanging from straps, cheap suits and fat white calves. For a moment Paul experienced an alarming feeling of vertigo, unable to believe that there was anyone in the bodies around him, convinced that he was trapped in a humid abattoir and that what surrounded him were just bodies, hung meat. Then a flick of greasy hair across his face and the unwelcome pressure of a man's hip brought him back, and it was a little better. But also worse.

Too hemmed in to read his book, he succumbed to the thoughts that came, feeling nastier and more twisted with each one.

When the tube reached Leytonstone, Paul had to fight his way off to avoid going down the wrong line. It was raining quite hard and he hunched into a corner of the open platform, lighting a cigarette with trembling hands. Of course it was illegal to smoke, but he was going to do it anyway. He forced a ten-minute train of thought concerning Jenny to stop by repeating a line over and over in his head until it was gone. Only then did he realize what the line actually was.

File Created: Mon, September 9, 1957, 5:02 P.M.

Gradually he calmed down, diffusing the hatred with a childlike fantasy about the woman on the morning train. Nothing sexual, nothing sordid, just thoughts of sitting with her, talking to her, and seeing her looking at him as if she loved him. It made him feel about four years old, which wasn't so bad. Except that he was standing alone on a platform in the rain, and when he got home his mother wouldn't be there, just a flat full of empty space and objects he couldn't remember buying.

Eventually another train meandered into the station, probably by accident, and Paul ducked through the nearest doors. The air was hot and rancid. The carriage seemed deserted with its only five or six bedraggled survivors, as if all the other casualties had already been dragged out by the feet to the morgue. As he sat down Paul looked at his watch. Nearly 8:00 P.M. Another half hour to get home. Shower, eat, try to wind down. Goodbye evening. And tomorrow's another day.

As the train pulled out, the girl sitting opposite went through a complex rigmarole of half-standing contortions as she tried to pull her skirt down. Not that it was riding up, as such: if you wear a skirt that ends about nine inches above the knee, Paul thought, then surely you must expect your legs to be a little bit visible. Presumably that was the point. So why the prim self-righteousness, the baleful stare?

Not wanting to read, but feeling compelled to make a show of not looking at the girl in the way she clearly thought he was going to, Paul stared at his book instead.

She got off two stops later, leaving the carriage empty. Savoring the almost surreal feeling of space, he lounged back in the seat and relaxed, breathing deeply, looking around at the debris. Coke cans, tissues, burger wrappers, and strewn pieces of newspaper. It looked like an urban back street painted by someone who wanted to live in the countryside.

Two minutes later the train was stationary again. Not at a station, of course, just stationary. Staring drowsily in front of him, Paul noticed an intact newspaper on one of the opposite seats and leaned forward to pick it up. In his current frame of mind he would be very unlikely to make any headway with either "Clones" or the new idea for a story. He might as well find out what was on television.

Before his hand was even close to it, he noticed something odd about the paper. At first he'd just taken it for a crumpled *Evening Standard*, but as he got nearer to it the stock seemed to get whiter, cleaner. He leaned back again, frowning. Slowly he moved his head, thankful that no one was in the carriage to witness what would have seemed like a very strange series of maneuvers, and slightly worried that staring at computer screens might finally have damaged his eyes. At first the paper was a nasty gray, but as you got closer it became whiter, so white that the edges almost seemed blue. Then he realized that the paper was actually just white, but that there seemed to be an area of color around it, a field of rich blue-purple. The paper wasn't crumpled and mauled as he'd first thought, but crisp, with edges that looked razor-sharp.

Tentatively he reached toward it again. The colors in the air about it grew stronger. He moved his head from side to side, but the field stayed where it was, proving that it wasn't his eyes at fault. The effect was hard to come to terms with, a pocket of super-intense hues which at the same time didn't interfere with the color of the seat underneath it.

When his fingers touched the paper the riot of color blinked out, leaving the carriage even more drab than before. Carefully, he picked it up. It felt very light. The paper was indeed very clean and new-looking, and the typeface seemed unfamiliar. Intrigued, Paul turned to the front page. At the top was just one word, the name of the paper. It was "Welcome."

As the train started to move again, the driver presumably having finished whatever crossword he'd been working on, Paul looked more closely at the front page. He realized that the header typeface was in fact merely a standard Times or Plantin or whatever: it was the contents of the columns of type underneath it that made it look different. It was simply a list of names. Hundreds of them.

The next page was the same, and the next. Page after page, column after column, right down to the foot of the back page. Names. No headings, no photos, no adverts. Just names.

Paul scanned the edges of pages, looking for clues as to what the paper might be, but there was no publisher listed, or address. It was just a newspaper full of names, on crisp white paper. He looked down the columns, trying to pick out a pattern, but there was none. The names weren't in alphabetical order, were both men's and women's. And that title. Still frowning, Paul turned back to the front page.

"Welcome."

Apart from being the nicest thing anyone had said to him all day, what did it mean? Welcome to what? Who were all these people, and what on earth was the point of printing all their names? Then his eyes caught something they'd only flicked over before. In the top right-hand corner, the newspaper had a date. It was Monday, September the 9th, 1957.

A grunt of surprise escaped as Paul's mouth dropped open, and his chest felt suddenly very cold. The sound of doors opening made him look up. It took him a moment to realize that the tube had reached his station. By that time they were closing again.

Still clutching the paper in his hands, Paul leaped through the doors onto the empty platform. The train pulled off, and Paul stood and watched it go, dazed. He looked down, saw the paper in his hand, and tucked it inside his coat pocket to protect it from the rain. Then he put his head down and started walking quickly.

When he got to his front door he was tired and out of breath. Normally he took his time up the final hill, but tonight he had stalked up it rapidly and his heart was thudding painfully. He showered quickly and changed his clothes. Then he sat next to the phone. He didn't think Jenny would actually be very interested, but she would have to do. Paul was as open to the idea of coincidence as the next man, but also aware of its limitations. This, he felt, was way beyond them. This erased the possibility of a computer glitch. What it opened up instead was far from clear. For the first time in what seemed like forever, he felt excited.

Hooking the phone under his chin and lighting a cigarette, he stabbed out the number. As it rung he reached out behind him and felt in the coat pocket for the paper, scrabbling it out just as the phone was picked up at the other end.

"Hi, it's me," he said.

There was a slight pause, and then Jenny said "Oh, hello."

Paul felt his heart give its customary lurch at the tonelessness of her greeting, at the complete absence of any hint of interest or satisfaction at hearing his voice, and also felt a thread of anger. He brushed it aside and launched into a description of what had happened, spreading the paper out in front of him. He'd got as far as the title of the paper, speaking into a void, as far as he could tell for all of Jenny's exclamations of interest, when he looked down.

On his lap was a copy of the *Evening Standard.* It was very grubby and had a picture of Tony Blair on the front and a footballer on the back and was dated December 16th, 1999.

Feeling both foolish and betrayed, Paul rapidly leafed through the paper, blood rising to his face. Adverts for upcoming sales. Share prices. Bollocks about the housing market. It was just the *Evening Standard.*

As was her custom, Jenny covered the silence by not saying anything.

Ten minutes later Paul put the phone down. Jenny had started saying she had work to do, and that anyway she was expecting a call from her mother. It had got bad long before that, though not because of what was said. They saved that up for the little time they had together. Another duel of silences. Paul jollied along for as long as he could, as always, talking about his day, trying to get her to talk about hers, saying her name occasionally to check that she was still there. After a time he lost heart, and asked her what was wrong. She said that nothing was wrong. Why wasn't she saying anything then? She denied that she was. Silence. Well she obviously *wasn't* saying anything, was she? How was she supposed to say anything when he was having a go at her for not saying anything. He wasn't having a go: something was obviously wrong, what was it? Nothing was wrong. Silence.

Glad that he hadn't done it in front of her again, Paul sat in the silent flat and cried. No mention had been made of how they were going to spend the Millennium.

After he was done he got up and switched the television on. There wasn't anything he wanted to watch. He had the *Evening Standard* now, didn't he, so he knew what was on. He just needed some background noise. Something to link him to real time, the real world. Something also to dampen the constant noise of thought, the endless whirl of sentences with nowhere to go and nothing to absolve them. When he was honest with himself he could admit that he'd long ago given up all hope of getting anything he wrote published. All it was about now was trying to find some sticky lines to attach the thoughts to, to fasten them down and stop them tearing around his head like a flock of damaged birds, pecking viciously at him until the pain threatened to push him into a state of mind where he didn't feel safe with knives in the kitchen. One of the things the last two years had taught him was that you didn't have to have nothing to lose to sometimes want to lose it anyway.

He got some food together and ate it. Every now and then he looked at the newspaper, but it was still just an ordinary paper. His supper finished, he busied himself with washing up and making yet more tea. Tea and cigarettes, the pillars of his days. Until a couple of years ago, he had never cried. Now he seemed to be on the verge of tears all the time. He tried to ration himself, and never wanted to cry in front of Jenny again. He had used to feel strong, had used to feel her equal. Crying in front of her made him feel demeaned and weak, pathetic. It wasn't terribly manly, even for the postmodern neo-sensitives that women allegedly wanted these days. But sometimes he couldn't help it. What can you do if the only person you have to talk to is the person who makes you feel as bad as you do?

Sitting in his chair again, he stared belligerently at the paper on the floor. Obviously he'd just dozed off on the train and the date on his mind had woven a dream for him. When he'd jumped off at Loughton he'd felt disorientated and strange, and clearly that had been the result of being awakened by the opening doors and having to leap off the train still half-asleep. It didn't really matter. He just felt very disappointed that it hadn't happened, that the glitch was still a glitch. For when he'd dreamed he'd seen that date on the paper he had been frightened at the thought that it was no longer just a mistake on the computer: but he had also been very happy.

By half past ten the evening's viewing had got too boring to even just sit vacantly in front of. Paul thought about listening to a CD, but couldn't be bothered. He couldn't seem to really hear music anymore. Going to bed would be a definite mistake.

So by default he ended up in front of his computer, listening to the system load itself up. Maybe if he tacked yesterday night's sentence onto the end of "Clones," he would be able to see where to take it from there. Maybe he could actually get it finished. Maybe world peace would break out.

The machine pinged at him to signify readiness, and Paul called up the "Clones" information window to copy down the sentence. After reading it twice he realized something he hadn't noticed the night before. It was crap.

He deleted it, all desire to work on the story gone, and sat with his head in his hands. The television burbled in the background, in excited transition from one late-night slot-filler to the next.

The file creation date was still there, still just a glitch. Discredited though it was, it still made him smile wanly. His glazing eyes wandered down the screen as he absently moved the cursor in circles over it, watching it move over numbers and letters as if it was actually above them. As he tried to motivate himself into doing something constructive, the words he was circling over slowly came into focus. He read them, and the circle came to an abrupt halt. The "Clones" information window said: *Document Size: 341K*

Three hundred and forty-one kilobytes? That couldn't be right: "Clones" was only two pages long, for God's sake. And the night before it had said 7K. He was sure it had. It must have done. Two pages was about 6 or 7K. 341K must be a few hundred pages, and "Clones" sure as hell wasn't that long. His collected works weren't that long.

That meant problems. That meant Problem City, in fact. Something bad must be happening to the desktop file or extents tree, which meant not only that the file creation date *was* most likely just a glitch, but that if he wasn't careful everything on his hard disk would be crapped out of existence. Paul hurriedly loaded the word processor. If it was just "Clones" that was affected, maybe it was okay. If not, then it was all hands to the floppy disks, with women and journalism off first.

The document took a while to load, much longer than just two pages should. Then the machine pinged again, and a blank page filled the screen, surrounded by the word processor's scroll bars and menus. That was as expected: he always left a blank page at the top of a document to fill the title and his address in when he'd finished, as a sort of completion ritual. He clicked on the scroll bar, bringing up the next portion of the page.

He saw that the first page was not blank as he'd left it, that the document now had a title. That title was "Welcome."

Paul clicked the scroll bar once more, and again. The second page came up. It was divided into three neat columns, something his word processor was not capable of doing. In each of those columns was a list of names.

It took Paul nearly ten minutes to click down through the document, one screen at a time. A few of the names he half-recognized, and he knew why. The list was similar to the one he'd seen on the train, but longer. One hundred and seventy pages of names. As he got toward the end of the document the scrolling seemed to get slower, more sluggish. At the bottom of the last page was a new line. It said "To all of you, Welcome."

Paul had just time to read this, and then the screen jittered and went blank.

He stared at it for some time, not smoking, not thinking. Just hearing names, seeing them in their orderly rows like some kind of roll call. Eventually he got up and turned the stalled computer off at the back. He could rebuild his desktop file, and had a fairly recent backup of all his documents. None of it seemed very important. He noticed his cheeks were wet, and realized that he had been crying. But he didn't feel sad. He didn't really know what he felt. Something was there, but just out of reach.

He made a cup of tea, sat in his chair, and waited.

The time seemed to pass very quickly, easily, his mind an almost total and blessed blank. After a time he fell asleep, and did not dream.

As he smoked his breakfast the next morning the letter box clanged. Some post, for a change. The contents of a large manila envelope he knew before he opened it. Sure enough, it was another rejection for another piece, with a form letter politely telling him to fuck off and die.

There was also a small light-blue envelope, with handwriting he recognized. A letter from Jenny, which could only mean bad news. He couldn't remember the last time she'd bothered to write. He opened it slowly, hands trembling.

The Last One, he read—although she of course used his real name, not realizing the vertiginous double-thump it always caused in Paul's heart—was coming to visit. Paul had known that it would happen sooner or later, but seeing his name again still made him feel dizzy. The Last One was an American. Every now and then he got a job as a courier and thus a free return flight to Britain. It was on one of these jaunts that Jenny had met him, and now he was coming over again, but with a difference. He had only been able to get a flight to Paris. And so Jenny was going to go over there for the weekend to see him.

There was a lot more, of course. A wealth of stuff about how it was reasonable of her to want to see someone that she'd had a relationship with; how it was important that she sorted out her feelings for him and that seeing him was the only way she could do that; how they would have different hotel rooms. But all of it was irrelevant. The fact was that he was coming, and she was going, and how Paul felt about it meant absolutely nothing to anyone.

Paul fought hard, his face reddening and neck spasming. However she dressed it up, it wasn't fair. And how like her not to mention it on the phone the night before, but instead wait for the letter to arrive, to give him time to lose his anger before they spoke of it. Time to become just a terribly hurt little boy, who could no more shout at her than he could leave her. She didn't realize that he couldn't hate her, that all he could do, whatever she did, was love her.

Putting his coat on, he left the house to go to work.

The train was late and he had to stand, clenching his fists tight to keep himself under control, the muscles in his face working. He'd been to Paris. He knew where they'd go, the sights they'd see. And he knew that they would sleep together. They always did.

The woman got on as usual, but this morning all that her demure beauty did was push him closer to the edge. At the next stop a man got on and stood and talked to her. Paul could hear her laughing.

To one side another couple stood face to face with their arms around each other. She looked at his lips when he talked, her head tilted up, smiling. In the stillness of a tunnel, with the train stationary, Paul could hear the rustle of her hand on his coat. He loved women's hands. They were so real.

He was late to work. Someone had been using his desk, and left a couple of pastry wrappers and a polystyrene cup amidst circular coffee marks on the surface. Paul shut the door and sat down. Over the course of ten minutes he calmed down a little, telling himself that perhaps this time things would sort themselves out. Even her leaving him would be something, a relief almost.

Eventually he opened his door and started the work he should have finished the day before. When his word processor was loaded he ran his eyes down the list of documents, half-hoping that there would be one there called "Welcome." But there wasn't, and he felt confused and foolish for looking.

Fetching a cup of coffee mid-morning he ran into Adam, who stopped him.

"Lot of mistakes in those galleys, you know," Adam said. "I had to go over them again myself."

Paul turned slowly and looked at him. "Who gives a shit?" he asked.

Walking back through the main office he regretted it, even though the look on Adam's face had been worth seeing. Antagonizing the assistant director was a bad idea. He wished the secretary, Susan, wasn't on holiday. She was the sole straightforward person in the office, and a chat with her might have brought him down a bit, earthed him. The sleep he'd had the night before didn't seem to have done him much good. His head felt cloudy and distanced from what was going on. At 2:00 P.M. he decided to skip lunch, but went out for a walk anyway to try to clear his head.

He wandered without paying attention where he was going, and looked up suddenly to find himself in a deserted back street that he'd never seen before. Which was odd, because he knew the area quite well. The street could have been anywhere, in any town. On a map it would have been just a straight little line, of no relevance to anything around it. At the far end was a newspaper kiosk. He walked up to it but there was nobody there, despite the fact that it was evidently open for business. On the counter was a single newspaper.

It was "Welcome."

Looking up and down the street, Paul picked it up. It seemed to be a different edition to the one he'd seen before, and an even stranger one: the columns of names petered out halfway down the second page. The rest were just blank. What on earth was the point of a mostly blank newspaper? He looked at the second page again, then with a yelp dropped the paper and walked quickly away.

The columns on the second page had just gotten longer.

By the time he got back to the office he regretted not keeping the paper, though he knew it would probably just have been an *Evening Standard* by then. He sat at his desk and tried to work, but a date kept running through his mind over and over, blanking out most other thoughts. Monday, September the 9th, 1957. The only thoughts it left room for were ones he didn't want. A hand on Jenny's thigh, her arm around the waist of a man he'd never seen, whose face he couldn't picture. A smile he never saw these days, and crumpled sheets.

He kept looking up, expecting Whitehead to be standing behind him. But there was only the wall, with a calendar left by the previous occupant. It showed scenes of European capitals by night.

Lists of names marched through his head, and he typed to the pattern of their syllables. But they didn't fit the lines, and when he read what he'd typed nothing made sense except the rhythm. It sounded like the rhythm of a train.

He deleted it all and stumbled out to get a coffee, past Whitehead's office—where he and Adam and Egerton stood in a huddle. They didn't look at him as he passed. He was invisible. He was fading. He was being left behind.

By 5:00 P.M. all he'd managed to do was put five pages of gibberish on the screen, green type on black with blue underlining that swirled into purple before his eyes. He saved it and turned the machine off. People looked up as he walked out of the office. This was early even for him. Emerging blinking into the light, he set off toward the tube. The winter afternoon was giving way to a storm and the dark clouds grew blue-black behind the buildings. Somewhere a child was crying, a hitching wail that spiraled up into the sky.

On the platform deep in the earth he leaned against the wall and rubbed his forehead with the back of his hand. Despite the perspiration on his forehead he felt very cool, and everything he saw seemed very clear. A middle-aged black man walked past slowly, with a boxed computer under his arm, a Christmas present for his son, who was holding his other hand. Both were quiet and smiling at the end of a perfect day.

A train rocketed into the station and Paul ducked to look in the windows as they flashed past: a smear of yellow flickers smudged with torsos and arms. As the train slowed he moved toward it, ready to fight for a place. But no one else seemed interested. They were all looking elsewhere.

Doors opened in front of him and he stepped into the warmth alone. The train pulled out of the light and into the waiting dark, and as he rocked to the rhythm of the names it came as no surprise to realize that the bodies hung around him were just that. Empty shells. The lights were no longer on, there was nobody home, and with that realization there came no fear at all.

Then he turned and saw the woman sitting there, looking straight at him. There was an empty seat beside her, just as there never was in the mornings. He knew that she'd been born on the 9th of September, and that she'd be there forever for him, and he knew that when he talked she'd listen, and she'd be looking at his lips.

The doors opened again, onto a deserted platform he'd never seen before, with a destination board that was blank. He let them close without a thought: it was a last chance he didn't want. The next thousand years could get along without him. There would be delays in the service later, but he knew at least some of the other commuters would understand.

He threaded his way toward the woman, watching the dawning of her smile.

"Welcome," she said.

DOUGLAS E. WINTER

The Pathos of Genre

Douglas E. Winter, an attorney in Washington, D.C., is a member of the National Book Critics Circle and the editor of Prime Evil *and* Revelations. *His nonfiction books include* Stephen King: The Art of Darkness, Faces of Fear, *and* Clive Barker: The Dark Fantastic. *Born in St. Louis, Missouri, and raised in southern Illinois, he is an honors graduate of Harvard Law School. His first novel,* Run, *was published this year by Alfred A. Knopf.*

Winter has been a respected critic and commentator on the horror field for more than fifteen years. "The Pathos of Genre" was originally a speech given by Winter at the 1998 Bram Stoker Awards banquet of the Horror Writers Association. It was later adapted as an essay for the June issue of Event Horizon.

—E. D.

Not long ago, a likable, intelligent editor for one of the major New York publishers asked me to read the manuscript of a first novel she was publishing. She hoped that I would offer some suitable words of wisdom for the book's cover—a "blurb." I agreed to read the novel, whose title and premise were enticing, but I withheld any promise to deliver a quotable quote. When I turned to the manuscript a few weeks later, I was mesmerized, caught up in an intense and certifiably weird masterpiece.

I wrote to the editor and offered a lengthy and enthusiastic paragraph, reporting that this was no ordinary book, but probably the most original and unnerving first novel that I had read in years. In concluding,

I noted that here, at last, was what readers had been waiting for: a new horror for the nineties.

I soon received a gracious call from the editor, thanking me for taking the time to help her with marketing that most problematic of commodities, a first novel; but then came a curious request. She wanted to use my impassioned remarks on the back cover of the book, but she wondered: Would I mind if she edited them slightly? Would I agree to eliminate . . . one word? The word, of course, was horror.

When Jack Williamson and William Peter Blatty—the men honored at the 1998 Horror Writers Association banquet for their lifetimes of achievement—sat down to create their masterworks, the word "horror" did not describe a kind of book. But since the early 1980s, we have been besieged by this word. Horror. For better—and, more often, for worse—"horror" has come not only to define, but also to dictate, a kind of fiction. The writer whose bestselling novels brought new credence to the literature of fear was labeled the "King of Horror." Publishers eagerly branded their products as "horror" through cover copy and publicity; some went so far as to use the word as an imprint. Magazines proclaimed their devotion to it. Entire shelves and sections in bookstores and libraries wore the name.

A World Horror Convention was born. Writers gathered, like lost sheep, into a Horror Writers Association.

The word, the word: the horror, the horror.

In this sudden quest for identity, for a way of labeling whatever impulse had given readers and filmgoers the particular appetite for chaos that marked the fading 1970s, the coming 1990s, the moment was what mattered: for writers, notoriety and income; for booksellers and publishers, sales. Few considered the long-term consequences, and those who raised their voices were ignored, shouted down. We witnessed, in the name of "horror," a curious entropic journey in which readers, writers, editors, publishers, and booksellers ventured into a seemingly limitless frontier, but soon circled the wagons, claiming a known and seemingly solid ground, around which signifying fences—brand name writers, book cover art, even book titles, icons, styles—were erected to define, describe . . . and confine. Horror. The Horror.

A fiction whose fundamental impulse was the unsafe—the breaching of the taboo, the creation of physical and metaphysical unease— was being made safe for mass consumption. Soon a "horror" existed that was as recognizable as science fiction, the western, or the romance—and thus as capable of reproduction, marginalization, and, indeed, denigration.

And why? Because a fiction whose hallmark was the unexpected had become, as a genre, a fiction of the expected.

Genre is the bastard child of expectation . . . anticipation.

We love anticipation. Waiting and hoping, wondering with the eyes and heart of a child . . . the promise of spring, the summer crop of film releases, the fall list of books dark and dangerous, and then the stuff of Christmas. The best is yet to come, we are told; it is yet to come. But all too often what comes is disappointment, particularly in popular entertainment, where the prospect of a new work by a favorite writer or filmmaker now rarely can be matched by the work itself. In the postmodern era of information overload, where we have entertainment news, and even entertainment about entertainment, each coming attraction is previewed and reviewed to the extent that we often know so much about a book or film or video that, when we finally have the chance to experience it, there is little room for surprise or wonder. We are told what we will enjoy or dislike, deny or denounce, what we should buy, what we should rent, what we should boycott, what we should ignore.

Deprived of the need to exercise our own imaginations, we sit in mindless confirmation of the judgment of others . . . or we become serial readers and viewers, eagerly consuming each new work by our admired, without discretion, just as we eat without thinking at any and every McDonald's, knowing that the burgers and fries, although by no means particularly tasteful or wholesome, will be pretty much the same wherever we eat them. Hence we find ourselves surrounded by artists and entertainers who are nothing more than manufacturers, whose redeeming virtue is not so much quality as quality control—the ability to deliver not necessarily great, not even necessarily good, but simply consistent product year after year after year.

Little wonder that Stephen King, victimized by the ever-encroaching fences of his success, would write a compelling triptych—*Misery*, *The Dark Half* and "Secret Window, Secret Garden" (in *Four Past Midnight*)—about bestselling writers haunted by their literary pasts; and then, as a coda, destroy his trademark setting, the town of Castle Rock, in *Needful Things*.

Little wonder that Peter Straub, in the wake of his bestselling *Floating Dragon*, would bravely turn away from the structure and content that was expected of him, and reinvent his art in the likes of *Koko*—and, to my mind, the first great horror novel of this decade, *The Throat*.

The eternal debate about what constitutes "horror"—and what it should be called—proceeds from the misguided belief that a definition has significance to anyone but the middleman. A category is important to publishers and their distribution network, particularly the publishers whose reputations and finances depend upon placing a kind of product on the shelf; but consider the plight of these selfsame publishers who, after pushing a product called "horror"—often with little regard for its quality, slowly but surely eroding the audience of interested readers—find that this product does not sell.

But we cannot blame the publishers. At least, not most of them. The bubble known as "horror" burst at the same time that merger-mania gripped the publishing industry and that mass-market book distribution suffered a nervous breakdown. And let's be fair: many publishers have stood by the literature of horror, out of love for the fiction or its writers; but more important, because they know what I know—horror sells. It sells.

Indeed, at times—like in the 1980s—it sells too well. It sells so well that almost anyone thinks they can write it.

And it is the writers of horror fiction who must accept the blame, because it is ours. Believe me, it is ours. We have failed to provide publishers with fiction of a quality—and more specifically, an originality—that could sustain reader interest, and thus sales.

We have failed in our essential mission of educating publishers, and thus readers, about our art. About horror.

We have allowed ourselves to become typecast as writers of a kind of fiction, by agreeing to the notion that horror is a marketing category—and a genre.

When, in the late 1980s, the name "horror" began to lose its already suspect veneer, the inevitable next step was to find a mask, some more palatable description. When the name proves a hindrance, then, as my editor friend suggested, the simple solution, some believed, was to change it. In the home audio and kitchen appliance industries, this tactic is known as "bait and switch."

Some writers, principally those made nervous by the word "horror" and its adolescent and visceral connotations, opted for the gentler sound of "dark fantasy." Others flirted briefly with something known as the "new horror," and a repeated catchword was "cutting edge," which underscored, rather dramatically, the reality that the blade of horror had indeed dulled.

Perhaps the most honest of the alternative names is "dark suspense" or "dark fiction"—horror indeed, but without the pejorative use of its name. A literature of "dark suspense" is nothing new, given the likes of Jim Thompson and David Goodis, but the lines have blurred; where once Thompson may have been classified as a crime writer, now he has stepped beyond that category and into the mainstream—and because, I should note, a fundamental impulse of his fiction was the horrific.

The penumbra of "dark suspense" seems also to embrace "terror," which once described psychological horror as made famous by Robert Bloch. One of its spiritual successors was V. C. Andrews, a critically maligned but immensely popular novelist whose dysfunctional family sagas were resonant with autobiography. Virginia Andrews invited me to her home in 1985 for what sadly proved to be her last interview. She told me about the novels she wanted to write, and some that she had written—a children's book, a fantasy, a science fiction novel. When she died the following year, her estate commissioned a series of novels ghost-written "in her tradition" while ignoring the unfinished manuscripts she left behind, which diverged from her publisher's expectations. There is no better paradigm for the pathos of genre: even in death, Virginia Andrews cannot escape its clutches.

As the name game was being played out, the once-expansive, now defined, landscape of horror was being divided up—Balkanized, if you will—as writers and their publishers sought to find cliques, movements, subgenres, some palpable (and, of course, marketable) means of distinguishing "us" from "them."

Notable among the subsets was the suddenly commercial category of vampire fiction. It is an unsettling truth, but in recent years an audience has emerged—one of considerable size—that is capable of experiencing the literature of horror (if not literature itself) only through a type of character: the vampire.

There's a framed letter in my office, written exactly one hundred years ago on the stationery of the Lyceum Theatre. My brother, a historian and writer, found the letter in St. Louis, among a trove of documents concerning the American Civil War, where surely it had been misplaced.

The letter was written by Bram Stoker, and his scurrying pen queries his literary agent, Colles, about—what else?—money, and his publisher's terms for his new novel, the novel being prepared in the wake of *Dracula*.

Beyond its confirmation that the writing life hasn't much changed, the letter is an artifact of painful irony. Who remembers the novel that Stoker was writing in 1899? It was *The Mystery of the Sea* (1902), which Conan Doyle found "admirable" but which, along with so much else that Stoker wrote, is long out of print. And who does not doubt that, if Stoker were alive today, his publisher, and possibly his agent, would be encouraging, if not demanding, that Stoker write something else: a sequel to *Dracula*.

The vampire was not Stoker's creation, but *Dracula* has proved such convincing propaganda for "the Un-Dead" (to indulge Stoker's original title) that it has found immorality in repetition and imitation while its author, and most of what he wrote, has been drained to a marginal memory. Even the 1995 motion picture *Bram Stoker's Dracula* was marketed by a novelization—another sad sign of the pathos of genre.

Consider, too, the writing career that is staked on writing vampire novels. In a market gone batty, with endless titles sucking blood—and thus life—from the market, a disgruntled vampire writer told me recently that she was writing a "completely different kind of book." Oh, really? Yes . . . a werewolf novel.

That's not writing horror fiction.

That's repeating horror fiction.

But you say: Anne Rice did it, Doug.

And yes, she did, but . . . that's Anne Rice. And you are you. Think for a moment about the cadre of the bestselling horror writers of our time—Rice, King, Straub, Clive Barker, Thomas Harris . . . what do they have in common? The fact that they each write different kinds of books.

When a handful of younger writers, encouraged by Barker's bloody surge to fame, took the name "splatterpunks," they found both notoriety and derision as a trend—a "movement." While the original writers of "splatterpunk" worked from principle or jesterdom, their heirs, ever eager to distinguish themselves, worked only from a kind of delusional hope that the "shocking" would get them noticed. A subgenre of violent horror resulted, but its appeal was limited, of course, to a smaller audience—a subset—of readers.

So . . . what followed splatter? After explicit violence, why not explicit sex? Erotic horror. The erotic thriller. Sex, sex, and more sex. And then, of course, violent sex. As Clive Barker's villainous Mamoulian observes in *The Damnation Game*: "It wasn't difficult to smudge sexuality into violence, turns sighs into screams, thrusts into convulsions. The grammar was the same; only the punctuation differed." Hence the semi-professional "sexpunks" whose obsession with genitalia is rivaled only by that of twelve-year-old boys.

The latter crew, in particular, represents the lunatic child of inbreeding: genre begetting subgenre begetting sub-subgenre until, sooner or later, its writers are not communicating to anyone but an initiated few. I could offer you further analysis, but in the end, I think that Johnny

Rotten said it best: "This is what you want, this is what you get. This is what you want, this is what you get."

A more recent incarnation of horror is the "new gothic"—which, like splatterpunk, seeks by name and aesthetic stance to distinguish its peculiar wheat from genre chaff. Where the splatpack's selling point was an insistent dialogue about (and in too many cases, pandering to) sex and violence, the new gothic is a more clever and constructive proposition, invoking, of all things, horror's literary tradition in order to set itself apart from generic perdition. Although the darling of academics, mainstream critics, and dilettantes who prefer their fear dolloped out in fluted crystal (rather than, say, in splatterpunk's barf bags), the new gothic is a curious self-exile to a land of literary make-believe. Because its manifesto—that horror will always survive and prosper as literature— is a foregone conclusion, the implicit conceit is revealed: by whose authority do these writers represent the literature of our time?

This is not to say that writers of the "new gothic" lack talent; it is abundant, for example, in the work of Patrick McGrath and, of course, Joyce Carol Oates. Oates, by the way, readily embraces the term "horror," although she favors "the grotesque" in describing her own fiction; but that term doesn't lend itself well to jacket copy or writers' associations.

The "new gothic" is a variant of the "old school" perspective of academia, whose proponents, like literary Luddites, eschew the modern (and especially the popular) and hold that horror's glory days lurk in the "weird fiction" of its past. Acolytes of weird fiction rely on the company of M. R. James and the Bensons for legitimacy, but tend to obsess about that dour and dear gentleman from Providence, H. P. Lovecraft.

For some time, the "weird fiction" clique embraced Ramsey Campbell as its contemporary savior, based upon his Lovecraftian roots and layered, at times baroque, narrative style. One wonders what these folks make of Campbell's recent novels. . . . A more likely rallying point for connoisseurs of the "weird" is Thomas Ligotti, whose *Noctuary* includes this wonderful opening sentence: "No one needs to be told about what is weird."

And that, my friends, brings us full circle. Because it's true: no one needs to be told about what is weird. . . . Names, movements, subgenres—letting ourselves or our publishers decide what is horror—is a siege mentality, a refusal to look outside the nonexistent boundaries, those ridiculous fences, that have haunted the horror fiction of the past decade. A publisher can, in the short term, use different names just like it uses different marketing strategies to sell its product. But let's be honest with ourselves. You can call something deceased, expired, gone to meet its maker. You can say that, like Elvis, it's left the building. But in the end, folks, it's dead.

And horror is dead.

The "death of horror" is a self-fulfilling prophecy. Once given life, a fiction category of "horror" was doomed to die—consigned to the purgatory of specialty stores and specialty shelves where its fate is that of the romance or the western: to function as a certain kind of fiction for a certain kind of audience. The phone call from my editor friend was not unexpected: at last the implied had become explicit. Horror has reached, it would seem, the exalted stature of a *Babylon 5* novel, trapped in a virtually inescapable ghetto of its own making.

So: horror is dead. You've heard that rumored, argued, and just plain said with increased persistence over the past few years—and over this weekend. And that's true: horror, as defined as a publishing category in the 1980s, is dead. It's gone. Forever. And you'd better get used to it.

But the winner is . . . horror.

Because the fiction of horror, like its favorite creatures of the night, does not perish so easily. The doomsayers forget its persistence, its uncanny ability to mutate and survive, which ought to serve as the most powerful clue that this fiction is not easily consigned to a category—it exists, thrives, lingers, and occasionally triumphs because, unlike any other supposed kind of fiction, horror invokes an emotion.

I've said that before, and unfortunately, I'm probably going to have to say it again. And again. But horror, my friends, is not a genre. It is a progressive form of fiction, one that evolves to meet the fears and anxieties of its times.

Do you need proof? Just when so-called horror fiction seemed to find its nadir late in the eighties, along came a novel by a gentleman named Thomas Harris. Although published as a crime novel, to be sure, no one can gainsay that *The Silence of the Lambs* was a horror novel. Or that its progeny have sold, and sold well, over the past decade.

What we are witnessing, then, is not the "death of horror," but the death of a short-lived marketing construct that, although it wore the name of "horror," represented but a sideshow in the history of the literature. Horror will never escape us—indeed, our literary history is proof positive that fear is the only constant of storytelling. Great horror fiction is being published today; sometimes it wears other names, other faces, marking the fragmentation and meltdown of a sudden and ill-conceived thing that many publishers and writers foolishly believed could be called a genre. Probably the most welcome result is the departure of the bottom-feeders and lemmings, who will move along to writing the flavor of the new decade and allow the conscientious writers of the horrific to flourish.

In closing, I want to echo some of the thoughts from my afterword to *Revelations*, a book in which I sought to showcase the many facets of this immortal fiction.

In the final years of the nineteenth century, the Western literature of horror and the supernatural experienced a profound change. In the space of little more than a decade, an astonishing number of seminal works of horror were published, including Robert Louis Stevenson's *The Strange Case of Dr. Jekyll and Mr. Hyde* (1886); Oscar Wilde's *The Picture of Dorian Gray* (1891); Arthur Machen's *The Great God Pan* (1894); H. G. Wells's *The Island of Dr. Moreau* (1896) and *War of the Worlds* (1897–98); Bram Stoker's *Dracula* (1897); Henry James's *The Turn of the Screw* (1898); Arthur Conan Doyle's *The Hound of the Baskervilles* (1901); W. W. Jacobs's "The Monkey's Paw" (1902); and Joseph Conrad's *Heart of Darkness* (1902).

The year 1900 marked the transition of this literature from the gothic to the iconic. With the new century, and the advent of visual media (motion pictures and, later, comic books and television), the personification of horror in a visual construct—the creature—became paramount. The aesthetics of seeing have dominated our popular culture ever since, spawning the "monster movies" of the fifties and the blood-splattered special effects films of the eighties and nineties, in which optical illusion took primacy over plot—and, in the worst cases, the only human role was that of victim.

A deft morality play for television, Rod Serling's "The Monsters Are Due on Maple Street" warned of the dangers of seeking the monstrous in skin other than our own. Just as Jane Austen's *Northanger Abbey* (1818) signaled the certain sunset of the gothic by critiquing its preoccupation with the external, Serling's simple scenario, in which everyday people hasten with McCarthyite fervor to condemn each other as monsters, underscored the fragile reign of the creature. Horror, these writers from different centuries remind us, is not the safe pretense of twisted houses or twisted bodies—or even twisted minds. It is that which cannot be made safe—evolving, ever-changing—because it is about our relentless need to confront the unknown, the unknowable, and the emotion we experience while in its thrall.

Now that we have seen the monsters—now that they have arrived on Maple Street—we have learned that certain truth: they are us. Although we will no doubt endure, and occasionally enjoy, their reign for years to come, the success of Christopher Pike and R. L. Stine in mediating the imagery of monsters to young readers suggests that, as the Bible reminds us, there comes a time to put away childish things.

As creators and consumers of horror, we find ourselves at a turning point not unlike that faced by the dreamers and devotees who confronted the end of the nineteenth century. Perhaps the correlation is fortuitous, the product of social and technological forces that have no concern for calendars. But I insist that there is one certainty. It is time to move on: to another horror, one that, like each new day, has unlimited possibilities.

Think of our mission like that of the demolition experts who bring down old and rotten buildings. Do you know what they call their craft? They call it making sky.

If you believe in horror, then join me, in the name of horror . . . let's go make some sky.

PETER CROWTHER

Shatsi

Peter Crowther has sold some seventy-five stories to magazines and anthologies on both sides of the Atlantic. A number of them are collected in Lonesome Roads *and* The Longest Single Note, *both published in 1999. He has edited twelve anthologies (including, this year,* Taps and Sighs *and, in 1999, with Martin H. Greenberg,* Moonshots) *and written a collaborative novel,* Escardy Gap, *with James Lovegrove, with whom he also wrote the chapbook "The Hand That Feeds." In addition, he writes regular columns for* Interzone, Hellnotes, *and* The Third Alternative, *and has published eight titles in a projected series of novella-length books under the PS imprint. Crowther lives in Harrogate, England, with his wife, Nicky.*

Crowther seems to have a love affair with the United States. Many of his best stories are set here, including "Shatsi," which was originally published in The Longest Single Note and Other Strange Compositions.*

—E. D.*

When the wind is just right you can smell the dreams.

They're almost palpable, a thick mixture of smog, sweat, and hope, drifting along Wilshire, Sunset, and Hollywood Boulevards, pooling in the hollowed-stone footsteps and handprints of Marilyn Monroe and Hank Fonda, Jimmie Stewart and Jeannie Crain, and all the others that litter the sidewalk and courtyard of Grauman's Chinese Theater.

For Benjamin Wassermann, it would always be Grauman's. Fuck Teddy Mann.

Bennie Wassermann, whose resumé now has him as Sherman Tyler, sets the black valise down on the cracked paving stones beside the public phone kiosk and shuffles in his pocket for some change. He drops a quarter into the slot and dials. A woman's voice answers.

"Thank you for calling," the voice says. Then, "Herman Morris's office, how may I help you?"

Bennie had heard the line before, albeit with a different name maybe, but it always seems like the words or the phrases are in the wrong sequence.

"Hi there," he says, sounding real friendly. "Is Mr. Morris in right now?"

"Oh, I'm sorry, Mr. Morris is in a meeting this afternoon."

Bennie has to give it to her, her patter is well rehearsed. The woman sounds genuinely distraught that the guy can't take the call: the only problem is that Bennie knows he *can*.

"Can he be interrupted?" Bennie asks, oozing concern and sincerity, spreading on a little bit of Peter Falk in *Columbo*, the re-runs for which Bennie always watches on Channel 13. "It's important."

"I'm sorry," comes the response.

He waits.

"What is it regarding?" the voice asks, covering her ass. "Maybe somebody else—"

"It's a . . . it's a personal matter," Bennie says, sticking to his script, smiling as he delivers the hesitation. He pours sunshine into the mouthpiece, sunshine and professionalism. A Fuller Brush salesman with a hint of Jimmy Stewart, awkwardly playing with his hat brim, shifting it around in his hands. "But I think he'll want to take this call."

There's a two-second delay before the voice says, "I see. May I tell him who's calling?"

"He won't know me . . . *doesn't* know me."

"Well, as I said, Mr. Morris is busy right now. Is this something you could write him about?"

Bennie shakes his head and then remembers that the woman can't see him. "No, no this is something that really needs to be dealt with over the telephone."

"I see." But her tone says that she doesn't see. She doesn't see at all. "Well, may I tell him what it concerns?"

"It's personal," Bennie says. "I already told you that." A harder edge gleams in the words like a discarded razor-blade catching the light, Martin Balsam in *Psycho*.

"Yes, well, as I told you, Mr. Morris is—"

"Tell him it's about his cat."

"Pardon me?"

Bennie shifts the handset to his other hand and frowns. In the mirror on the wall in front of him, Bennie thinks maybe he just caught a glimpse of DeNiro in that shitty remake of *Cape Fear*, even down to the Hawaiian shirt. He says, "Look lady, you heard me. Just tell him."

Another pause. "Hold the line please."

Bennie fishes a handful of coins from his pocket and drops them onto the open directory beside the phone.

A man's voice says, "What *is* this?"

Bennie is still Max Cady. "Mr. Morris?" he says.

"This is Morris. What is this? Something about my cat? Is she okay?"

Bennie says, "Mr. Morris the theatrical agent?"

"Who is this? Is this some kind of stunt?"

Bennie shakes his head and thinks Damon Runyon. "No, this is some kind of telephone call," he says.

There's a long silence on the line before Morris says, "So what about my cat?"

Bennie can't keep the grin out of his voice. "She's fine, Mr. Morris, just fine. She's missing you."

"Where's Rita?"

"Rita?"

"Yeah, Rita. She's looking after Shatsi. Is there something wrong with her?"

"Is that Rita or Shatsi?"

"Listen you dumb fuck, don't mess around with me. I'm asking you if my cat's okay."

"I already told you, Mr. Morris, the cat's fine." He moves the handset back to the other hand again, frowning at the moisture glistening on the plastic. "Your cat's name is *Shatsi*? What *is* that? Is that German? French? It sounds French. . . ."

"Who are you?"

Bennie says, "Me? I'm a Samaritan, Mr. Morris. Call me . . . call me the patron saint of animals."

"You're a fucking animal you—What you doing to my cat?"

"Hey," Bennie giggles. "Hey, I'm not doing anything to your cat, Mr. Morris. I love cats. Really." He waits to see if Morris is going to say anything. When there's no response, he says, "Next to caviar, I love cats the best. Cat stew maybe, or cat carbonnade . . . or maybe ca—"

"What the fuck are—"

"Don't shout at me, Mr. Morris." He flexes his shoulders. That wasn't right, he thinks. A little too much Tony Perkins, too vulnerable, too weak. He closes his eyes and, pushing a smile into his tone, he pictures Christopher Walken in *True Romance*, talking to Dennis Hopper. Reasonable but firm. "I don't like it when people shout at me," he says. "Like I say, I only like cats next to caviar or fillet steak. Thing is," he continues, the smile broadening into a real shit-eating grin, "I can't afford caviar. Can't even afford fillet steak."

"What have you done with Rita?"

"Ah, Rita." He pauses. "She the little Spanish bitch?"

"What have you done with her?"

"Rita's fine. Everybody's doing just fine, Mr. Morris. We're all fine here."

"Put her on. Put Rita on the line."

Bennie clucks, put on his regret voice, his *Oh gee whiz, I don't think we can do that* voice. "She's not here, Mr. Morris. Rita isn't here."

"Where is she?"

Bennie shrugs. "Back where I left her?"

"Oh, Jesus Chri—"

"Hey, now hold on. Don't go getting—"

"What have you done with Rita, you sick fuck?"

"Now you're shouting at me again, Mr. Morris and I told you I don't like that. I'll call you again soon and we'll talk." He slams the handset down onto the cradle and glares at it, feels the muscles at the side of his jaw twitching. He turns and kicks the concertina door to the phone booth until it shakes, kicks it once more and watches the top pane of glass slide slowly out of place and down onto the floor. He lifts the handset again and listens, hears the dial tone and slams it down again, then kicks the pane to the back of the booth next to the valise, watches it shatter against the wall, his jaw still twitching.

Sick fuck? Was this any way for a theatrical agent to speak? He'd heard that Morris was connected and that proved it. He picks up the valise and makes like he's going to throw it out into the street and suddenly feels a shift of movement inside. He leans against the glass and shakes his head, laughing a little, the twitching fading away now. He's getting too much into the part. Time to settle down.

"Looks like it's me and you for now," he says, his mouth against the shiny black leather. "Shatsi." He shifts the word around in his head until it feels right, like well-chewed gum. He puts the valise under his arm and steps out of the booth.

Somewhere over west, a siren wails like a banshee. Bennie figures it probably isn't for him.

Back in his apartment, Bennie tips some more bourbon into the funnel and watches it pool in the bum's mouth, thin rivulets pouring over the unshaven chin. The bum shakes his head from side to side, and Bennie grabs hold of the guy's nuts, tight, like he's going to tear them right off through the stained crotch of his jogging pants. The bum makes to call out and that relaxes his throat. The level of bourbon falls rapidly and the bum swallows, reluctantly at first and then gratefully. He coughs and splutters while Bennie looks at the bottle. Looking down at the bum, Bennie dials the number on his mobile phone.

"Hello?"

"Mr. Morris?"

"Yeah, it's me. What do you want?"

Bennie smiles across at the cat and whispers, "Don't record me." Then he kills the call, waits a minute, and dials again.

"Hello?"

"Hey, long time no speakee, Mr. Morris." He chuckles and then stops—it was sounding like Frank Gorshin's Riddler. "How you doin'?"

"Will you tell me what you want?"

"Hey, you're shouting again. No shouting, okay?"

There's no response, just the electronic hum of silent frustration, the all-pervading darkness of murderous anger seeping down the line.

Bennie says, "I said, okay?" He slaps the table with his free hand. Special effects.

"Okay, okay. Take it easy."

"That's better Mr. Morris. You recording me again?"

"No, I'm not recording you."

"You're lyin' to me, Mr. Morris. Are you lyin' to me?"

"No, no I'm not lying."

"Because if you are then it might be that little Shatsi here says nighty night to her master, you know what I'm sayin' here? Shatsi go beddy-bye permanent, you unnerstand?" He holds his breath, hoping he's not overdoing it.

"I understand. I hear you loud and clear."

"Good. Hey . . . loud and clear: I like that. It's like out of the movies, you know what I mean?" Bennie lets the silence hover and then says, "But you know all about the movies, am I right here Mr. Morris?"

"What do you want?" Morris's voice is calm and quiet. "Is it money?"

Bennie laughs and affects a nasal whine. "Izzit money?" He laughs again. "You bet your life it's fucking money, Mr. Morris. Second thoughts, you bet your cat's life. Little Shatsi here. You catch my drift?"

"Yes, like I said, loud and clear."

"Yeah, right: loud and clear." Bennie throws in a giggle and is only a little surprised at how realistic it sounds. "I still like that," he says.

"Good. So everybody's fine?"

"Everybody's fine."

"Then," Morris says, hesitantly, "we have to make sure everybody stays that way, yes?"

"Right."

A pause. "So how do we do that?"

Bennie draws in his breath, making like he's thinking about it. "Well, it's gonna be expensive, you know what I mean?"

Morris says, "How much?"

Bennie says, "Pardon me?"

"How fucking much do you want?"

"Ah, well—"

Morris sighs and Bennie thinks he can hear other voices whispering somewhere near. He pictures them all crouched by the telephone or maybe a couple of handsets, everyone advising and suggesting. And Morris getting suddenly pissed at the whole thing.

Sure enough, Morris says, "Now listen to me, you shitwipe, and listen good."

Bennie smiles and punches the air. He says, "Hey, you're—" and sure enough Morris interrupts.

"*Hey,* you're nothing, fuck-up. *Listen* to me. Rita is in the hospital and—"

"Rita?"

"My maid."

"Right. The Spanish bitch."

Morris lets it ride and says, "She saw you."

Bennie stays silent, breathes a little heavy . . . like he's trying to think back, trying to remember.

"She said you were like a superhero."

Bennie can't stop the snigger. "Like a *what?*"

"A superhero. Like in the comic books, she said. Big black cape."

Bennie looks across at the bed, across at the bundled-up black cape lying over the headboard. "That's some ID," he says.

"It is with the sneaker."

Bennie smiles. Bingo! "S-sn-sneaker?" he says, dragging the word out like he's suddenly gotten nervous.

"You left your sneaker on my front lawn."

"So what are you, huh? Prince Fuckin' Charmin'? You gonna go round town tryin' on an old Nike to everyone you see? Shee-it!"

"You drinking?"

The question catches Bennie on the hop. "Huh?"

"I said, are you drinking? Think about it, asswipe. It's an easy question. Look at your fucking hand and tell me if there's a glass in it."

"So what if I'm—"

Morris lowers his voice, like he's breaking a confidence, and says, "So this. You bring my cat back and we call it quits. Maybe I even let you have a bottle for your trouble. Like a reward for finding Shatsi? Plus I give you back your shoe and maybe a few dollars to fold up in your back pocket. What do you say to that?"

Bennie gulps in three or four mouthfuls of air, swallows hard and then lets out with a belch, right into the mouthpiece.

"What say we forget the reward and I eat your cat, Mr. fuckin' hot-shot theatrical agent?" He thinks a second for a suitable exit line, smiles and adds, "My momma always tol' me never to drink on an empty stomach." He presses the "end" key and smiles across at the sleeping bum.

Outside the window behind the bed, the sky is black and moody.

"Okay," Bennie says, "time to go walkees." This time, he's using his normal voice.

It is almost midnight.

Bennie drags the unconscious bum out into the yard and lays him beside the car. Then he dresses him in the cape and bundles him into the backseat. He throws the valise in after him.

The drive takes a little under forty minutes. When he gets to the top of Beaconsfield Drive, Bennie turns off the ignition and lights and rolls down to the clump of trees and parkland adjacent to Morris's house. He sits there for almost fifteen minutes to make sure he hasn't been seen, then he gets out of the car.

A minute later, he pulls the bum out of the backseat and drags him around the front of the car, lays him half on the road and half on the sidewalk.

Bennie gets back into the car and starts it up, drives forward over the bum. Slowly. He hears the bones crunch even over the sound of the engine.

"A Dodge is one heavy fuckin' car, man," Bennie says to the night, his voice a cross between the Fonz and Jim out of *Taxi,* in the days before Christopher Lloyd was a wacked-out scientist in the *Back to the Future* films or a Klingon spaceship captain in that *Star Trek* movie— the one where they rescued Spock from the planet that was blowing itself apart with the Genesis project doo-hicky.

Bennie gets out of the car and runs around to the crumpled body, kneels down beside it and feels for a pulse. The bum is as dead as dead can be.

Bennie takes the knife from his pocket, cleans it on his jacket, and slides it into the bum's outstretched hand, curling the dead-as-dead-can-be fingers around the handle. Then he runs back to the car and grabs the valise out of the back seat, pulls out the drugged cat, and throws the valise back in. He slams the door. With the cat under his arm, he runs back to the body and goes into the performance.

"Oh my *God!* Oh my good *lord!*" Bennie shouts to the night. He stands up and yells, "Hey! Anybody! There's been an accident out here." He runs back to the car and leans on the horn, cringing at the sound as it rings through the early morning stillness.

He moves back to the body, stares down at it.

Somewhere behind him a light comes on.

He hears footsteps and muffled conversation.

Then the bum groans.

Bennie says, "Jesus Fucking Christ!" and kicks the bum in the side of the head.

Someone shouts, "Who's out there?"

He considers dropping the cat, getting in the car and driving the hell away from the whole mess. But he's come too far to stop now.

"There's been an accident out here!" he shouts, loud, so nobody can hear the dull thud of his shoe hitting the bum's head again. *What is he, this guy—a fucking Kryptonian?* "Over here!"

Bennie turns around and sees a dim movement over by the front door behind the gates. Still a ways off. He braces himself and jumps into the air, landing with both feet on the bum's head. It splits like a melon.

"What you say?" a voice asks.

Wiping his shoes on the grass as he walks toward the voice, trailing them behind him like he has two club feet—or maybe like Boris Karloff in the Frankenstein movies—Bennie says, "I knock this guy down and . . . and he pulls a knife on me. Guy's carrying a cat, for crissakes, and he pulls a knife on me."

"Who're you?" Gene Herman Morris says, his voice filled with sleep.

"Me? I'm—"

"What are you doing here?" Another voice, over to the left.

Bennie turns around and looks into the beam of a flashlight, shielding his eyes with his free hand. The beam moves off and illuminates the figure on the road.

Bennie waits, dreading some telltale movement, half expecting the bum to stand up and—

Truth, Justice, and the American Way!

—just dust himself down. But the body doesn't move, not even when the guy holding the flashlight bends over him and lifts his one bare foot.

Bennie sighs with relief. That was just what he didn't need: a near-dead vagrant brought back to life by somebody tickling his feet.

The voice speaks again. "I said, what are you doing here?"

Bennie shrugs. "I was . . . you know, I was out driving." He points across at the house and waves his arm around the whole deserted street. "Hey, I often drive around the movie people's houses. You know?" He shrugs again. "I'm an actor myself but—" Another shrug. "I'm between roles right now." He laughs disarmingly. "Looking for the big break."

"Looking for the big break at one o'clock in the morning?" the voice asks. It comes from the figure alongside Morris.

Bennie turns around to make sure the bum's still on the ground. "He dead?" he asks.

The man stands up, shines the flashlight at Bennie's car. "Yeah, he's dead. Good car," the man says as he walks to the Dodge.

Bennie laughs. "*Old* car, more like. Still it gets me around."

The man is running his hand along the front of the hood, like he's caressing it. "No, I mean there's not even an impact mark."

"No?" Bennie shifts from one foot to the other. "Huh. Well, I hit him a good one." He shrugs. "Maybe I wasn't going fast enough to do any real damage."

"Did plenty of damage to him," the man says, swinging the flashlight's beam back to the crumpled body.

Bennie decides that the statement doesn't need a response from him so he lets it go.

The two men in the shadows are muttering.

Morris steps forward. Bennie recognizes him from photographs in the movie magazines.

"So you're an actor?" he says.

Bennie gives another shrug, laughs a little and looks down at his feet. "Well, trying anyway."

"Maybe I can help you out," Morris says, holding his hands out.

Bennie does a surprised stutter, a kind of who and why, both abbreviated to wh—.

"That's *my* cat," Morris says. "Guy stole my fucking cat." He nods to the bum. "Can you believe that?"

Bennie hands Shatsi to Morris and shakes his head. "It's a weird world," he says, slapping his leg.

"Well, I figure I owe you," Morris says, tickling the cat under the chin, frowning at the lack of response he's getting.

"He looks traumatized," Bennie says, pleased with himself at changing the cat's gender without even thinking.

"It's a she," Morris says.

"Oh," says Bennie. "Sorry."

The man in the shadows steps forward. "So he pulled a knife on you *after* you'd hit him? Or before?"

More shrugs from Bennie. "I er . . . I hit him—well, first off, he just suddenly appears, you know? Across the street?"

The man with the flashlight is opening the Dodge's door. Bennie can hear the click.

"And?"

"Oh," says Bennie. "Let me think." He laughs and clasps his hands together. "It all happened so fast," he says. "Yeah, that's it," Bennie says, "I hit him and he goes down—" He claps his hands. "Boom. Like that, you know? And I get out of the car and go around to him and he pulls a knife!"

Now Morris says, "The guy pulls a knife on you when he's lying in the road?" He chuckles. "I guess you really pissed him off."

Bennie falls in with the chuckling. "I guess I did."

"Then what?" says the man.

"Well, I . . . I kicked him in the head," Bennie says, suddenly realizing that that all makes some kind of sense—it also explains the guy's head looking like a fruit crumble. "Yeah, I kicked him in the head—" He demonstrates. "Twice, like this, and I take the cat from him." He flashes his open palms and smiles. "And then you guys appear."

A voice behind him—from the Dodge—says, "This is your car, right?"

"Sure it's my car," Bennie says, turning around. "You think I'm a thief? Hey, he's the thief," he says, pointing. "That guy over there."

The man is standing with the door open, leaning on the roof, looking across at Bennie. He lifts something into view. The valise. "This yours?"

Bennie feels whole sections of his guts tearing off and sliding down to the tops of his legs. He starts to laugh a little and gives a little shrug, looks around at Morris—who's even now taking a step toward them, frowning—and glances at the other man, who's watching him, a slight smile tugging at the corners of his mouth.

"Well?" the man says again.

Bennie nods. "Well, it's my sister's," he says.

The man nods. "Well, I guess that must make your sister pretty small."

"I didn't mean—" Bennie starts to say.

"There a problem, Joe?" Morris asks.

Joe slams the Dodge's door and walks around holding the valise like it's a trophy. "I think so, Mr. Morris," he says. "No sign of impact on the hood or the fender, car stinks of booze, bag stinks of pussy— and not the kind you'd want spend a night with—and—" He points across at the still prone figure on the street "Guy there shleps across town with one bare foot and there's not a mark on it. That's what set me off wondering in the first place."

"Wondering? Hey, you know," Bennie says, indignantly, "I did you a favor, but this is all getting a little strange for me and I'd just as soon—"

Morris nods to the second man and the man takes hold of Bennie's arm. He has a firm grip.

"Like I said," Morris says, "looks like I owe you."

Joe has now reached him and taken his other arm, swinging the valise by his side. The first man has pulled something out of his pants pocket. Bennie can't see it fully but he doesn't think it's a contract. It looks too solid.

What's the phrase? *Cast iron.*

"Let's go inside . . . discuss your part," Morris says. "Frank, bring him inside. Get rid of the car, Joe. And clear the street."

As the other man—Frank—starts to walk him toward the gates and the waiting house beyond, Bennie tries to think of something to say.

"Say goodnight, Gracie," Joe whispers as he lets go of his arm.

NEIL GAIMAN

Keepsakes and Treasures:
A Love Story

Neil Gaiman is a transplanted Briton who now lives in the American Midwest. Among his many works are the award-winning Sandman *series of graphic novels, the novel and BBC TV series* Neverwhere, *and his collaboration with artist Dave McKean on the brilliant book* Mr. Punch. *Gaiman is also a talented poet and short-story writer whose work has been published in various anthologies on both sides of the Atlantic, including* The Year's Best Fantasy and Horror. *His short work has been collected in* Angels and Visitations *and* Smoke and Mirrors. *He has won the World Fantasy Award, the Mythopoeic Award, and the Julia Verlanger Award for Best Novel published in France. He recently finished a new novel, tentatively titled* American Gods.*

According to the author, "Keepsakes and Treasures: A Love Story" seems to polarize reviewers—for some it was a favorite, while for others it was in poor taste. "For the record," he says, "I'm very fond of it. And yes, it's in poor taste, but then, so many love stories are."

It was originally published in 999, *edited by Al Sarrantonio.*

—E. D.

I am his Highness' dog at Kew
Pray tell me, sir, whose dog are you?
ALEXANDER POPE
"ON THE COLLAR OF A DOG WHICH
I GAVE TO HIS ROYAL HIGHNESS"

You can call me a bastard if you like. It's true, whichever way you want to cut it. My mum had me two years after being locked up "for her own protection"; this was back in 1952, when a couple of wild nights out with the local lads could be diagnosed as clinical nymphomania, and you could be put away "to protect yourself and society" on the say-so of any two doctors. One of whom was her father, my grandfather, the other was his partner in the North London medical practice they shared.

So I know who my grandfather was. But my father was just somebody who shagged my mother somewhere in the building or grounds of Saint Andrews Asylum. That's a nice word, isn't it? Asylum. With all its implications of a place of safety: somewhere that shelters you from the bitter and dangerous old world outside. Nothing like the reality of that hole. I went to see it, before they knocked it down in the late seventies. It still reeked of piss and pine-scented disinfectant floor wash. Long, dark, badly lit corridors with clusters of tiny, cell-like rooms off them. If you were looking for hell and you found St. Andrews you'd not have been disappointed.

It says on her medical records that she'd spread her legs for anyone, but I doubt it. She was locked up, back then. Anyone who wanted to stick his cock into her would have needed a key to her cell.

When I was eighteen I spent my last summer holiday before I went up to University hunting down the four men who were most likely to have been my father: two psychiatric nurses, the secure ward doctor, and the governor of the asylum.

My mum was only seventeen when she went inside. I've got a little black-and-white wallet photograph of her from just before she was put away. She's leaning against the side of a Morgan sports car parked in a country lane. She's smiling, sort of flirtily, at the photographer. She was a looker, my mum.

I didn't know which one of the four was my dad, so I killed all of them. They had each fucked her, after all: I got them to admit to it, before I did them in. The best was the governor, a red-faced, fleshy old lech with an honest-to-goodness handlebar moustache, like I haven't seen for twenty years now. I garotted him with his Guards tie. Spit-bubbles came from his mouth, and he went blue as an unboiled lobster.

There were other men around St. Andrews who might have been my father, but after those four the joy went out of it. I told myself that I'd killed the four likeliest candidates, and if I knocked off everyone who might have knocked up my mother it would have turned into a massacre. So I stopped.

I was handed over to the local orphanage to bring up. According to her medical records, they sterilized my mum immediately after I was born. Didn't want any more nasty little incidents like me coming along to spoil anybody's fun.

I was ten when she killed herself. This was 1964. I was ten years old, and I was still playing conkers and knocking off sweet shops while she was sitting on the linoleum floor of her cell sawing at her wrists with a bit of broken glass she'd got from heaven-knows-where. Cut her fingers up, too, but she did it all right. They found her in the morning, sticky, red, and cold.

Mr. Alice's people ran into me when I was twelve. The deputy head of the orphanage had been using us kids as his personal harem of scabby-kneed love slaves. Go along with him and you got a sore bum and a Bounty Bar. Fight back and you got locked-down for a couple of days, a really sore bum and concussion. "Old Bogey" we used to call him, because he picked his nose whenever he thought we weren't looking.

He was found in his blue Morris Minor in his garage, with the doors shut and a length of bright green hosepipe going from the exhaust into the front window. The coroner said it was a suicide and seventy-five young boys breathed a little easier.

But Old Bogey had done a few favors for Mr. Alice over the years, when there was a chief constable or a foreign politician with a penchant for little boys to be taken care of, and he sent a couple of investigators out, to make sure everything was on the up-and-up. When they figured out the only possible culprit was a twelve-year-old boy, they almost pissed themselves laughing.

Mr. Alice was intrigued, so he sent for me. This was back when he was a lot more hands-on than today. I suppose he hoped I'd be pretty, but he was in for a sad disappointment. I looked then like I do now: too thin, with a profile like a hatchet blade, and ears like someone left the car doors open. What I remember of him mostly then is how big he was. Corpulent. I suppose he was still a fairly young man back then, although I didn't see it that way: he was an adult, and so he was the enemy.

A couple of goons came and took me after school, on my way back to the home. I was shitting myself, at first, but the goons didn't smell like the law—I'd had four years of dodging the Old Bill by then, and I could spot a plainclothes copper a hundred yards away. They took me to a little gray office, sparsely furnished, just off the Edgware Road.

It was winter, and it was almost dark outside, but the lights were dim, except for a little desk lamp casting a pool of yellow light on the desk. An enormous man sat at the desk, scribbling something in ball-point pen on the bottom of a telex sheet. Then, when he was done, he looked up at me. He looked me over from head to toe.

"Cigarette?"

I nodded. He extended a Peter Stuyvesant soft pack, and I took a cigarette. He lit it for me with a gold and black cigarette lighter. "You killed Ronnie Palmerstone," he told me. There was no question in his voice.

I said nothing.

"Well? Aren't you going to say anything?"

"Got nothing to say," I told him.

"I only sussed it when I heard he was in the passenger seat. He wouldn't have been in the passenger seat, if he was going to kill himself. He would have been in the driver's seat. My guess is, you slipped him a mickey, then you got him into the Mini—can't have been easy, he wasn't a little bloke—here, mickey and Mini, that's rich—then you drove him home, drove into the garage, by which point he was sleeping soundly, and you rigged up the suicide. Weren't you scared someone would see you driving? A twelve-year-old boy?"

"It gets dark early," I said. "And I took the back way."

He chuckled. Asked me a few more questions, about school, and the home, and what I was interested in, things like that. Then the goons came back and took me back to the orphanage.

Next week I was adopted by a couple named Jackson. He was an international business law specialist. She was a self-defense expert. I don't think either of them had ever met before Mr. Alice got them together to bring me up.

I wonder what he saw in me at that meeting. It must have been some kind of potential, I suppose. The potential for loyalty. And I'm loyal. Make no mistake about that. I'm Mr. Alice's man, body and soul.

Of course, his name isn't really Mr. Alice, but I could use his real name here just as easily. Doesn't matter. You'd not have heard of him. Mr. Alice is one of the ten richest men in the world. I'll tell you something: you haven't heard of the other nine, either. Their names aren't going to turn up on any lists of the hundred richest men in the world. None of your Bill Gateses, or your Sultans of Brunei. I'm talking *real* money here. There are people out there who are being paid more than you will ever see in your life to make sure you never hear a breath about Mr. Alice on the telly, or in the papers.

Mr. Alice likes to own things. And, as I've told you, one of the things he owns is me. He's the father I didn't have. It was him that got me the medical files on my mum, and the information on the various candidates for my dad.

When I graduated (first class degrees in business studies and international law), as my graduation present to myself, I went and found my-grandfather-the-doctor. I'd held off on seeing him until then. It had been a sort of incentive.

He was a year away from retirement, a hatchet-faced old man with a tweed jacket. This was in 1978, and a few doctors still made house calls. I followed him to a tower block in Maida Vale. Waited while he dispensed his medical wisdom, and stopped him as he came out, black bag swinging by his side.

"Hullo, grandpa," I said. Not much point in trying to pretend to be someone else, really. Not with with my looks. He was me, forty years on. Same fucking ugly face, but with his hair thinning and sandy gray, not thick and mousy brown like mine. He asked what I wanted.

"Locking mum away like that," I told him. "It wasn't very nice, was it?"

He told me to get away from him, or something like that.

"I've just got my degree." I told him. "You should be proud of me."

He said that he knew who I was, and that I had better be off at once, or he would have the police down on me, and have me locked away.

I put the knife through his left eye and back into his brain, and while he made little choking noises I took his old calf-skin wallet—as a keepsake, really, and to make it look more like a robbery. That was where I found the photo of my mum, in black-and-white, smiling and flirting with the camera, twenty-five years before. I wonder who owned the Morgan.

I had someone who didn't know me pawn the wallet. I bought it from the pawn shop when it wasn't redeemed. Nice clean trail. There's many a smart man who's been brought down by a keepsake. Sometimes I wonder if I killed my father that day, as well as my grandfather. I don't expect he'd have told me, even if I'd asked. And it doesn't really matter, does it?

After that I went to work full time for Mr. Alice. I ran the Sri Lanka end of things for a couple of years, then spent a year in Bogota on import-export, working as a glorified travel agent. I came back home to London as soon as I could. For the last fifteen years I've been working mainly as a troubleshooter, and as a smoother-over of problem areas. Troubleshooter. That's rich.

Like I said, it takes real money to make sure nobody's ever heard of you. None of that Rupert Murdoch cap-in-hand to the merchant bankers rubbish. You'll never see Mr. Alice in a glossy magazine, showing a photographer around his glossy new house.

Outside of business, Mr. Alice's main interest is sex, which is why I was standing outside Earl's Court station with forty million U.S. dollars' worth of blue-white diamonds in the inside pockets of my macintosh. Specifically, and to be exact, Mr. Alice's interest in sex is confined to relations with attractive young men. No don't get me wrong, here: I don't want you thinking Mr. Alice's some kind of woofter. He's not a nancy or anything. He's a proper man, Mr. Alice. He's just a proper man who likes to fuck other men, that's all. Takes all sorts to make a world, I say, and leaves a lot more of what I like for me. Like at restaurants, where everyone gets to order something different from the menu. *Chacun a son goût* if you'll pardon my French. So everybody's happy.

This was a couple of years ago, in July. I remember that I was standing in the Earls Court Road, in Earls Court, looking up at the Earl's Court Tube Station sign and wondering why the apostrophe was there in the station when it wasn't in the place, and then staring at the junkies and the winos who hang around on the pavement, and all the time keeping an eye out for Mr. Alice's Jag.

I wasn't worried about having the diamonds in my inside pocket. I don't look like the sort of bloke who's got anything you'd want to mug him for, and I can take care of myself. So I stared at the junkies and winos, killing time till the Jag arrived (stuck behind the road works in Kensington High Street, at a guess) and wondering why junkies and winos congregate on the pavement outside Earl's Court station.

I suppose I can sort of understand the junkies: they're waiting for a fix. But what the fuck are the winos doing there? Nobody has to slip you a pint of Guinness or a bottle of rubbing alcohol in plain brown bag. It's not comfortable, sitting on the paving stones or leaning against the wall. If I were a wino, on a lovely day like this, I decided, I'd go down to the park.

Near me a little Pakistani lad in his late teens or early twenties was papering the inside of a glass phone box with hooker cards—CURVY TRANSSEXUAL and REAL BLONDE NURSE, BUSTY SCHOOLGIRL and STERN TEACHER NEEDS BOY TO DISCIPLINE. He glared at me when he noticed I was watching him. Then he finished up and went on to the next booth.

Mr. Alice's Jag drew up at the curb and I walked over to it and got in the back. It's a good car, a couple of years old. Classy but not something you'd look twice at.

The chauffeur and Mr. Alice sat in the front. Sitting in the backseat with me was a pudgy man with a crewcut and a loud check suit. He made me think of the frustrated fiancé in a fifties film; the one who gets dumped for Rock Hudson in the final reel. I nodded at him. He extended his hand, and then, when I didn't seem to notice, he put it away.

Mr. Alice did not introduce us, which was fine by me, as I knew exactly who the man was. I'd found him, and reeled him in, in fact, although he'd never know that. He was a professor of ancient languages at a North Carolina university. He thought he was on loan to British Intelligence from the U.S. State Department. He thought this, because this was what he had been told by someone at the U.S. State Department. The professor had told his wife that he was presenting a paper to a conference on Hittite Studies in London. And there was such a conference. I'd organized it myself.

"Why do you take the bloody tube?" asked Mr. Alice. "It can't be to save money."

"I would have thought the fact I've been standing on that corner waiting for you for the last twenty minutes demonstrates exactly why I didn't drive," I told him. He likes it that I don't just roll over and wag my tail. I'm a dog with spirit. "The average daytime speed of a vehicle through the streets of Central London has not changed in four hundred years. It's still under ten miles an hour. If the tubes are running, I'll take the tube, thanks."

"You don't drive in London?" asked the professor in the loud suit. Heaven protect us from the dress sense of American academics. Let's call him Macleod.

"I'll drive at night, when the roads are empty," I told him. "After midnight. I like driving at night."

Mr. Alice wound down the window and lit a small cigar. I could not help noticing that his hands were trembling. With anticipation, I guessed.

And we drove through Earls Court, past a hundred tall, red-brick houses that claimed to be hotels, a hundred tattier buildings that housed guest houses and bed and breakfasts, down good streets and bad. Sometimes Earls Court reminds me of one of those old women you meet from time to time who's painfully proper and prissy and prim until she's got a few drinks into her, when she starts dancing on the tables and telling everybody within earshot about her days as pretty young thing, sucking cock for money in Australia or Kenya or somewhere.

Actually, that makes it sounds like I like the place and, frankly, I don't. It's too transient. Things come and go and people come and go too damn fast. I'm not a romantic man, but give me South of the River, or the East End, any day. The East End is a proper place: it's where things begin, good and bad. It's the cunt and the arsehole of London, they're always close together. Whereas Earls Court is—I don't know what. The body analogy breaks down completely when you get out to there. I think that's because London is mad. Multiple personality problems. All these little towns and villages that grew and crashed into each other to make one big city, but never forget their old borders.

So the chauffeur pulls up in a road like any other, in front of a high, terraced house that might have been a hotel at one time. A couple of the windows were boarded over. "That's the house," said the chauffeur.

"Right," said Mr. Alice.

The chauffeur walked around the car and opened the door for Mr. Alice. Professor Macleod and I got out on our own. I looked up and down the pavement. Nothing to worry about.

I knocked on the door, and we waited. I nodded and smiled at the spyhole in the door. Mr. Alice's cheeks were flushed, and he held his hands folded in front of his crotch, to avoid embarrassing himself. Horny old bugger.

Well, I've been there too. We all have. Only Mr. Alice, he can afford to indulge himself.

The way I look at it, some people need love, and some people don't. I think Mr. Alice is really a bit of a *don't*, all things considered. I'm a *don't* as well. You learn to recognize the type.

And Mr. Alice is, first and foremost, a connoisseur.

There was a bang from the door, as a bolt was drawn back, and the door was opened by an old woman of what they used to describe as "repulsive aspect." She was dressed in a baggy, black one-piece robe. Her face was wrinkled and pouched. I'll tell you what she looked like. Did you ever see a picture of one of those cinnamon buns they said looked like Mother Teresa? She looked like that, like a cinnamon roll, with two brown raisin eyes peering out of her cinnamon roll face.

She said something to me in a language I did not recognize, and Professor Macleod replied, haltingly. She stared at the three of us, suspiciously, then she made a face, and beckoned us in. She slammed the door behind us. I closed first one eye, then the other, encouraging them to adjust to the gloom inside the house.

The building smelled like a damp spice rack. I didn't like anything about the whole business; there's something about foreigners, when they're that foreign, that makes my skin crawl. As the old bat who'd let us in, who I had begun to think of as the Mother Superior, led us up flight after flight of stairs, I could see more of the black-robed women, peering at us out of doorways and down the corridor. The stair carpet was frayed and the soles of my shoes made sticking noises as they pulled up from it; the plaster hung in crumbling chunks from the walls. It was a warren, and it drove me nuts. Mr. Alice shouldn't have to come to places like that, places he couldn't be protected properly.

More and more shadowy crones peered at us in silence as we climbed our way through the house. The old witch with the cinnamon bun face talked to Professor Macleod as we went, a few words here, a few words there; and he in return panted and puffed at her, from the effort of climbing the stairs, and answered her as best he could.

"She wants to know if you brought the diamonds," he gasped.

"Tell her we'll talk about that once we've seen the merchandise," said Mr. Alice. He wasn't panting, and if there was the faintest tremble in his voice, it was from anticipation.

Mr. Alice has fucked, to my personal knowledge, half a bratpack of the leading male movie stars of the last two decades, and more male models than you could shake your kit at; he's had the prettiest boys on five continents; none of them knew precisely who they were being fucked by, and all of them were very well paid for their trouble.

At the top of the house, up a final flight of uncarpeted wooden stairs, was the door to the attic, and flanking each side of the door, like twin tree trunks, was a huge woman in a black gown. Each of them looked like she could have held her own against a sumo wrestler. Each of them held, I kid you not, a scimitar: they were guarding the treasure of the Shahinai. And they stank like old horses. Even in the gloom, I could see that their robes were patched and stained.

The Mother Superior strode up to them, a squirrel facing up to a couple of pit bulls, and I looked at their impassive faces and wondered where they originally came from. They could have been Samoan or Mongolian, could have been pulled from a freak farm in Turkey or India or Iran.

On a word from the old woman they stood aside from the door, and I pushed it open. It wasn't locked. I looked inside, in case of trouble, walked in, looked around, and gave the all-clear. So I was the first male in this generation to gaze upon the Treasure of the Shahinai.

He was kneeling beside a camp bed, his head bowed.

Legendary is a good word to use for the Shahinai. It means I'd never heard of them and didn't know anyone who had, and once I started looking for them even the people who had heard of them didn't believe in them.

"After all, my good friend," my pet Russian academic said, handing over his report. "You're talking about a race of people the sole evidence for the existence of which is half a dozen lines in Herodotus, a poem in the *Thousand and One Nights*, and a speech in the *Manuscrit Trouvé à Saragosse*. Not what we call reliable sources."

But rumors had reached Mr. Alice and he got interested. And what Mr. Alice wants, I make damned sure that Mr. Alice gets. Right now, looking at the Treasure of the Shahinai, Mr. Alice looked so happy I thought his face would break in two.

The boy stood up. There was a chamber pot half-sticking out from beneath the bed, with a cupful of vivid yellow piss in the bottom of it. His robe was white cotton, thin and very clean. He wore blue silk slippers.

It was so hot in that room. Two gas fires were burning, one on each side of the attic, with a low hissing sound. The boy didn't seem to feel the heat. Professor Macleod began to sweat profusely.

According to legend, the boy in the white robe—he was seventeen at a guess, no more than eighteen—was the most beautiful man in the world. I could easily believe it.

Mr. Alice walked over to the boy, and he inspected him like a farmer checking out a calf at a market, peering into his mouth, tasting the boy, and looking at the lad's eyes and his ears; taking his hands and examining his fingers and fingernails; and then, matter-of-factly, lifting up his white robe and inspecting his uncircumcised cock before turning him round and checking out the state of his arse.

And through it all the boy's eyes and teeth shone white and joyous in his face.

Finally Mr. Alice pulled the boy toward him and kissed him, slowly and gently, on the lips. He pulled back, ran his tongue around his mouth, nodded. Turned to Macleod. "Tell her we'll take him," said Mr. Alice.

Professor Macleod said something to the Mother Superior, and her face broke into wrinkles of cinnamon happiness. Then she put out her hands.

"She wants to be paid now," said Macleod.

I put my hands, slowly, into the inside pockets of my mac and pulled out first one, then two black velvet pouches. I handed them both to her. Each bag contained fifty flawless D or E grade diamonds, perfectly cut, each in excess of five carats. Most of them picked up cheaply from Russia in the mid-nineties. One hundred diamonds: forty million dollars. The old woman tipped a few into her palm and prodded at them with her finger. Then she put the diamonds back into the bag, and she nodded.

The bags vanished into her robes, and she went to the top of the stairs and as loud as she could, she shouted something in her strange language.

From all through the house below us there came a wailing, like from a horde of banshees. The wailing continued as we walked downstairs through that gloomy labyrinth, with the young man in the white robe in the lead. It honestly made the hairs on the back of my neck prickle, that wailing, and the stink of wet rot and spices made me gag. I fucking hate foreigners.

The women wrapped him up in a couple of blankets, before they would let him out of the house, worried that he'd catch some kind of a chill despite the blazing July sunshine. We bundled him into the car.

I got a ride with them as far as the tube, and I went on from there.

I spent the next day, which was Wednesday, dealing with a mess in Moscow. Too many fucking cowboys. I was praying I could sort things out without having to personally go out there: the food gives me constipation.

As I get older, I like to travel less and less, and I was never keen on it in the first place. But I can still be hands-on whenever I need to be. I remember when Mr. Alice said that he was afraid that Maxwell was going to have to be removed from the playing field. I told him I was doing it myself, and I didn't want to hear another word about it. Maxwell had always been a loose cannon. Little fish with a big mouth and a rotten attitude.

Most satisfying splash I've ever heard.

By Wednesday night I was tense as a couple of wigwams, so I called a bloke I know, and they brought Jenny over to my flat in the Barbican. That put me in a good mood. She's a good girl, Jenny. Nothing sluttish about her at all. Minds her P's and Q's.

I was very gentle with her, that night, and afterward I slipped her a twenty-pound note.

"But you don't need to," she said. "It's all taken care of."

"Buy yourself something mad," I told her. "It's mad money." And I ruffled her hair, and she smiled like a schoolgirl.

Thursday I got a call from Mr. Alice's secretary to say that everything was satisfactory, and I should pay off Professor Macleod.

We were putting him up in the Savoy. Now, most people would have taken the tube to Charing Cross, or to Embankment, and walked up the Strand to the Savoy. Not me. I took the tube to Waterloo Station and walked north over Waterloo Bridge. It's a couple of minutes longer, but you can't beat the view.

When I was a kid, one of the kids in the dorm told me that if you hold your breath all the way to the middle of a bridge over the Thames and you made a wish there, the wish would always come true. I've never had anything to wish for, so I do it as a breathing exercise.

I stopped at the call box at the bottom of Waterloo Bridge. (BUSTY SCHOOLGIRLS NEED DISCIPLINE. TIE ME UP TIE ME DOWN. NEW BLONDE IN TOWN.) I phoned Macleod's room at the Savoy. Told him to come and meet me on the bridge.

His suit was, if anything, a louder check than the one he'd worn on Tuesday. He gave me a buff envelope filled with word processed pages:

a sort of homemade Shahinai-English phrase-book. *"Are you hungry?"* *"You must bathe now." "Open your mouth."* Anything Mr. Alice might need to communicate.

I put the envelope in the pocket of my mac.

"Fancy a spot of sightseeing?" I asked, and Professor Macleod said it was always good to see a city with a native.

"This work is a philological oddity and a linguistic delight," said Macleod, as we walked along the Embankment. "The Shahinai speak a language that has points in common with both the Aramaic and the Finno-Ugric family of languages. It's the language that Christ might have spoken if he'd written the epistle to the primitive Estonians. Very few loan-words, for that matter. I have a theory that they must have been forced to make quite a few abrupt departures in their time. Do you have my payment on you?"

I nodded. Took out my old calfskin wallet from my jacket pocket, and pulled out a slip of brightly colored card. "Here you go."

We were coming up to Blackfriars Bridge. "It's real?"

"Sure. New York State Lottery. You bought it on a whim, in the airport, on your way to England. The numbers'll be picked on Saturday night. Should be a pretty good week, too. It's over twenty million dollars already."

He put the lottery ticket in his own wallet, black and shiny and bulging with plastic, and he put the wallet into the inside pocket of his suit. His hands kept straying to it, brushing it, absently making sure it was still there. He'd have been the perfect mark for any dip who wanted to know where he kept his valuables.

"This calls for a drink," he said. I agreed that it did, but, as I pointed out to him, a day like today, with the sun shining and a fresh breeze coming in from the sea, was too good to waste in a pub. So we went into an off-license. I bought him a bottle of Stoli, a carton of orange juice, and a plastic cup, and I got myself a couple of cans of Guinness.

"It's the men, you see," said the Professor. We were sitting on a wooden bench looking at the South Bank across the Thames. "Apparently there aren't many of them. One or two in a generation. The Treasure of the Shahinai. The women are the guardians of the men. They nurture them and keep them safe.

"Alexander the Great is said to have bought a lover from the Shahinai. So did Tiberius, and at least two Popes. Catherine the Great was rumored to have had one, but I think it's just a rumor."

I told him I thought it was like something in a storybook. "I mean, think about it. A race of people whose only asset is the beauty of their men. So every century they sell one of their men for enough money to keep the tribe going for another hundred years." I took a swig of the Guinness. "Do you think that was all of the tribe, the women in that house?"

"I rather doubt it."

He poured another slug of vodka into the plastic cup, splashed some orange juice into it, raised his glass to me. "Mr. Alice," he said. "He must be very rich."

"He does all right."

"I'm straight," said Macleod, drunker than he thought he was, his forehead prickling with sweat, "but I'd fuck that boy like a shot. He was the most beautiful thing I've ever seen."

"He was all right, I suppose."

"You wouldn't fuck him?"

"Not my cup of tea," I told him.

A black cab went down the road behind us, its orange "For Hire" light was turned off, although there was nobody sitting in the back.

"So what is your cup of tea, then?" asked Professor Macleod.

"Little girls," I told him.

He swallowed. "How little?"

"Nine. Ten. Eleven or twelve, maybe. Once they've got real tits and pubs I can't get it up anymore. Just doesn't do it for me."

He looked at me as if I'd told him I liked to fuck dead dogs, and he didn't say anything for a bit. He drank his Stoli. "You know," he said, "back where I come from, that sort of thing would be illegal."

"Well, they aren't too keen on it over here."

"I think maybe I ought to be getting back to the hotel," he said.

A black cab came around the corner, its light on this time. I waved it down, and helped Professor Macleod into the back. It was one of our Particular Cabs. The kind you get into and you don't get out of.

"The Savoy, please," I told the cabbie.

"Righto, governor," he said, and took Professor Macleod away.

Mr. Alice took good care of the Shahinai boy. Whenever I went over for meetings or briefings the boy would be sitting at Mr. Alice's feet, and Mr. Alice would be twining and stroking and fiddling with his black-black hair. They doted on each other, you could tell. It was soppy and, I have to admit, even for a cold-hearted bastard like myself, it was touching.

Sometimes, at night, I'd have dreams about the Shahinai women—these ghastly, batlike, hag-things, fluttering and roosting through this huge rotting old house, which was, at the same time, both Human History and St. Andrews Asylum. Some of them were carrying men between them, as they flapped and flew. The men shone like the sun, and their faces were too beautiful to look upon.

I hated those dreams. One of them, and the next day was a write-off, and you can take that to the fucking bank.

The most beautiful man in the world, the Treasure of the Shahinai, lasted for eight months. Then he caught the flu.

His temperature went up to 106 degrees, and his lungs filled with water and he was drowning on dry land. Mr. Alice brought in some of the best doctors in the world, but the lad just flickered and went out like an old lightbulb, and that was that.

I suppose they just aren't very strong. Bred for something else, after all, not strength.

Mr. Alice took it really hard. He was inconsolable—wept like a baby all the way through the funeral, tears running down his face, like a mother who had just lost her only son. It was pissing with rain, so if you weren't standing next to him, you'd not have known. I ruined a perfectly good pair of shoes in that graveyard, and it put me in a rotten mood.

I sat around in the Barbican flat, practiced knife-throwing, cooked a spaghetti bolognaise, watched some football on the telly.

That night I had Alison. It wasn't pleasant.

The next day I took a few good men and we went down to the house in Earls Court, to see if any of the Shahinia were still about. There had to be more Shahinai young men somewhere. It stood to reason.

But the plaster on the rotting walls had been covered up with stolen rock posters, and the place smelled of dope, not spice.

The warren of rooms was filled with Australians and New Zealanders. Squatters, at a guess. We surprised a dozen of them in the kitchen, sucking narcotic smoke from the mouth of a broken R. White's Lemonade bottle.

We searched the house from cellar to attic, looking for some trace of the Shahinai women, something that they had left behind, some kind of clue, anything that would make Mr. Alice happy.

We found nothing at all.

And all I took away from the house in Earls Court was the memory of the breast of a girl, stoned and oblivious, sleeping naked in an upper room. There were no curtains on the window.

I stood in the doorway, and I looked at her for too long, and it painted itself on my mind: a full, black-nippled breast, which curved disturbingly in the sodium-yellow light of the street.

MICHAEL MARSHALL SMITH

What You Make It

Michael Marshall Smith's story "Welcome" appears elsewhere in this volume. "What You Make It," the title story of Smith's first story collection, demonstrates the sly wit common to much of his fiction.

—*E. D*

Finding a child was easy. It always was. You waited outside one of the convenience stores that lined the approach, or trawled a strip mall at the nearby intersections for half an hour. There were always kids hanging around at night, panhandling change for a burger or twenty minutes on a coin-op video game in one of the arcades. Or sometimes just hanging there, with nothing in particular in prospect. You have to have seen something of the world to know what's worth looking for. These kids, the just-hanging kids, had seen nothing—and were mainly willing to be shown pretty much whatever you had in mind.

The only question was which one to pick. Too old, either age, and it looked weird at the gate. Too young, and people tend to wonder where the kid's mother is at. And of course sometimes it depended, and you had to find one that looked just right for the night. Early teens was usually best, acquiescent, not too scuffed up.

It only took Ricky ten minutes to find one. She was sitting by herself on a bench outside the Subway franchise, looking at her feet or nothing in particular, alone in a yellow glow. Ricky cruised by the sandwich store twice in the twilight, noted that though there were two groups of kids nearby, one just a little along the sidewalk and another loitering

outside Publix, the girl didn't seem to have a link to either. He parked
the car up, let the motor tick down to silence, and watched her a little
while. The nearest group of kids walked right by her, in and out of her
pool of light, without a word being exchanged. She didn't even look
up. She wasn't expecting friends.

Ricky grabbed his cigarettes off the dash, locked the car, and walked
over to her.

She glanced at him as he approached, but not with much curiosity.
Something told him that this wasn't indifference, but a genuine ignorance of the kind of situations the world could provide. This meant she
was even more likely to be what he needed, and it was just good luck
for her that it was Ricky's eye she'd caught, instead of some kind of
fucking pervert.

"Waiting for someone?" he asked, stopping when he was a couple
of yards away. She looked up, then away. Didn't even shake her head.
He took the last few steps, sat down casually on the next bench along.
"Right. I know. Just a good place to sit."

There was no response. Ricky took out a cigarette and lit it, un-
hurried. She looked maybe twelve years old, pretty face. Blue eyes, fair
hair in a ponytail. White T-shirt, blue jeans. Both recently clean. He
noticed her eyes follow his match as it skittered across the way and
went out. Despite appearances, he had her attention.

"You hungry?"

She blinked, and her head turned a little way toward him. Something
changed. It always did. It's a very elemental question. Even if you've
just eaten enough to kill a man, you think about it. Am I hungry? Have
I had enough? Will I be okay? And if you're really hungry, the question
comes at you like you've just been goosed, like someone's just guessed
your worst secret, how close you are to being cancelled out. Ricky knew
how it worked. He'd been hungry. You answered the hungry question
quietly, so the vultures wouldn't hear.

"Kinda," she said, eventually.

He nodded, looking out across the parking lot for a while. Partly to
check how many couples were hefting grocery bags to their breeder
wagons; mainly just to let the conversation settle.

"I could buy you something," he said then, casually. "What's the
matter? Your mom didn't feed you tonight?"

"Don't have a mom," she said.

"What about your old man? Where's he at?"

The girl shrugged. Didn't matter whether she didn't know or just
didn't want to know. Ricky knew she was his.

Ten minutes later, as he watched her wolf down her sandwich and fries, Ricky asked the big question.

"How'd you like to visit Wonder World tonight?"

It was well after eight by the time they got to the entrance. The queue was pretty short. Ricky knew it would be: they had a parade every night at eight-thirty, down First Street, and anyone with park-visiting in mind made sure they were already inside by then. Even the girl, whose name was Nicola, knew about the parade. Ricky told her that this week it was at nine-fifteen because it was a special parade. She looked at him dubiously, but seemed hopeful.

As he turned into one of the lanes and pulled up to the gate Ricky felt a familiar flicker of anxiety. This was the part where it could all go wrong. It hadn't yet, because the kids had always wanted what they thought they were getting, but it could. It could go wrong tonight. It could go wrong any time. He wound the window down.

The gateman's head immediately bobbed down to grin at him. "Hi there! I'm Marty the Gateman! How you doing?"

Marty the Gateman was in his late fifties, and dressed in an exaggerated version of the uniform of a cop from the 1940s. His face was pink with good cheer or makeup. Or alcohol most likely, Ricky thought. The other gatemen in all the other lanes looked the same, and said exactly the same things.

Ricky grinned right back. "I'm good. You?"

"Me? I'm great!" the man said, and then laughed uproariously. When he did this, he leaned back from the waist, placed a splayed hand on either side of his ribcage, and rubbed them up and down with each chortle, like a cartoon. Nicola giggled, twisted in her seat.

Ricky let one hand drop to where the gun rested down between the seat and the door, waited for the man to stop. Fucking loser. He imagined the guy going home after his shift, taking off his stupid fucking costume, whacking off in front of the television or a stack of porno. He had to do something like that. Rick knew *he* would have done, that's for sure. Couldn't be any other way.

Eventually the man stopped laughing, wiped his eyes. "Shee! So! Two happy travelers for Wonder World! You just here for rides and fun and all the magic you can find?"

"No," Nicola said, leaning over Ricky so she could smile up at him through the window. "We're visiting Grandma too!"

Ricky relaxed. The girl was going to behave. Better still, she'd got into the part. They did, sometimes. Kids love make-believe.

Marty winked. "Lucky Grandma! She know you're coming?"

"It's a surprise," Nicola said, confidingly. "She lives in Homeland 3."

"Okey dokey!" the gateman yelped joyously, pulling a deck of tickets out of one of the oversize pockets on his uniform. "So, Mr. Dad—
how long you going to be spending with us?"

"An hour, maybe two." Ricky smiled. "Depends on how strong
Grandma's feeling."

"Why don't we say three? Can always get you a rebate when you
come out."

"Sure, Marty. That'd be great."

"All-righty!" Tongue sticking out of the corner of his mouth, Marty
the Gateman tapped some buttons on the control unit on the side of his
booth. As he tapped, the buttons got a little larger, and started moving
around, so he had to keep his hand darting back and forth to keep up.
Two twinkling animatronic eyes appeared at the top of the control unit,
and one of them winked at Nicola. Within a few seconds the buttons,
which were brightly colored in primary hues, were a few inches long
and bending every which way. Still the man poked at them, huffing and
puffing.

"Hey!" he said, and Nicola laughed, when a couple of the buttons
got even longer and started poking him back. When this gag was done,
the gateman held a ticket out toward the machine, a slit opened in the
unit in the shape of a cheerful mouth, and the ticket was popped inside,
chewed for a moment, and then spat out, authorized. The eye winked
at Nicola again, and then suddenly the control unit returned to normal
and Marty was waggling the ticket right under Ricky's nose.

Any other time or place, Marty would have lost his hand. But Ricky
gave him the money, and the gate opened. The gateman waved at Nicola
through the back window.

As the car started to pull forward, all of the faces in the gate structure—each a classic character from a Wonder World cartoon, every one
hand-tweaked by liars into joyous perfection—swiveled their eyes toward the car and started to sing.

China Duck was there, Loopy Hound and Careful Cat, Bud and
Slap the Happy Rats and Goren the fucking Gecko and countless others,
every face already hot-wired into your mind no matter how hard you'd
always ignored them.

"The magic is what you make it," they sang, a sonic tower of sac-
charine harmonies, "make it, make it . . . the magic is what you . . ."

Ricky wound the windows up.

Lit a cigarette and stepped on the gas.

———

The kid was quiet as they headed toward Homeland 3. She had plenty to look at, and she drank it in as though even in darkness it was the greatest thing she had ever seen. Maybe it was. Unlike her, Ricky had seen it all before.

Monorail tracks arced gracefully in all directions, linking park to park. Mostly quiet for the evening, but occasionally a streamlined shape would swoosh past the road or over their heads. Taking happy families out, or back, for the evening: out to ridiculous themed restaurants, or back to dumb-looking resort hotels where overexcited kids would make so much noise you'd want to throttle them, and parents would reconcile themselves to another night without screwing and send out for room service booze instead. Probably even that was delivered by a fucking chipmunk.

Actually, Ricky had never stayed in one of the hotels. Never even been in one: the security was too good. But he felt he knew exactly how it would be. A great big stupid con, like everything else in Wonder World. Set up fifty years ago, and now so vast and sprawling it put most cities in the shade. Rides and enclosures and parks and theaters and "experiences" and crap, all based around a bunch of cartoons and some asshole's idea of the perfect world. There was a fake big game reservation. A bunch of fake lakes, where fish and dolphins and shit swam about, like anyone cared. A fake downtown strip the size of a whole town, where people who were too scared to walk to the corner store in their own stupid bergs could wander around and buy up all the shit they wanted. Some sort of stupid futuristic park, where it was supposed to be like what it would be in a hundred years: like we were all going to be shopping from home and wearing pastel nylon and using videophones—standing in tight little nuclear family groups and talking to Gramps on Mars.

Ricky knew what it was really going to be like in a hundred years, and it wasn't going to be cutesy characters walking around, posing for photographs and making the little kids laugh. It wasn't going to be restaurants where the family could go and get good food and great service for ten bucks a head; it wasn't going to be endless fucking stores full of T-shirts and candy in painted tins, and being able to leave your door unlocked at night and no litter anywhere. It was going to be guns, and stealing things. It was going to be dog eat dog, and he wasn't talking the kind of dog which had some fuckass pimply kid inside, earning chump change for blow. It was going to be taking what you wanted, and fucking up anyone who got in your way. It was getting that way already, and only fools pretended otherwise. That's what kids needed to learn, not crap about talking bunnies. Wonder World pained Ricky personally, which is one of the reasons why he did what he did for a living. He hated the bright colors, the cheer, the stupid, kiddie nonsense, the lies about how the world really was, the conspiracy to believe that there was magic somewhere in the world. He hated it all.

It was a crock of utter shit.

The kid stayed good as he drove, even though weird and miraculous buildings kept appearing in the darkness, each promising fun and games. She didn't ask to stop at every one, like most of them did. She kept quiet until the car swung around in the front of the massive portal into the heart of Wonder World, the original Beautiful Realm park. The gate was like a massive googie castle, every ludicrous '50s drive-in and coffee shop-erama mashed joyously together into an eight-story extravagance that would have taken the Jetsons' breath away. Whirling spotlights sent beams of light chopping merrily through the night, and characters capered around the entrance, beckoning people in. The girl had wound her window back down by then, and could hear in the distance the sound of drums and music, the singing and dancing inside.

"The parade," she said.

He shrugged. "Fuckers did it early. Or maybe it's just beginning."

She was calm, reasonable. "You said we'd see the parade."

"We will. It goes on for, like, an hour. We'll just do this thing, and then we'll go catch the end. It's better that way. Most of the people have gone home, you get closer to all the characters."

"Really?" She was looking at him closely, her mouth wanting to smile, but nervous of being let down. Just then one of the lights cut through into the car, showing her in every detail. Pretty little face, red lips that had never been kissed. Big eyes, wanting him to tell her good news, wanting to see nice things.

And tiny new breasts outlined in a T-shirt one size too small. She was perfect, all the more so because she wouldn't even understand what he was thinking.

Ricky decided this one was going to play the game a little longer than most of the others, that she going to learn the facts of life. The facts that had to do with taking whatever he wanted to put inside her. A training session. Save some guy time and effort later on, except Ricky knew there wasn't going to be a later. Usually he lay the kid over the backseat on the way out, put a blanket over them like they were just sleeping, winked at some guy at the gate and laughed with him about how the child had too much excitement for one day. Tonight he'd find a way of getting this one out alive. He'd work it out.

"Really," he said. "Trust me."

She smiled.

Ten minutes later he was scanning street names as he cruised slowly down Homeland 3's main drag. Every now and then they'd pass a toon character, who'd stop and wave at Nicola. Ranging from three-foot dancing toadstools to six-foot ducks, they were freaking Ricky out. You didn't normally see characters roaming this late: they were only there to magic the place up through the day, during the most popular visiting hours. Ricky was having trouble sorting through the names of the streets, which were also the names of fucking characters. Loopy Drive IV, Careful Crescent VI—how the fuck were you supposed to keep track? Nicola wasn't helping, having decided to tell him her life story. She was thinking of shortening her name, and spelling it Nicci, because she thought it was classy and presumably didn't know how Gucci was actually pronounced. She liked cats, like Careful Cat, but dogs were sometimes cute too. She didn't know where Daddy was because she'd never known. She said she didn't have a mommy because real mommies didn't do what hers did, and so two days ago she'd run away from home and she wasn't going back this time.

Jesus, only two days, Ricky was thinking. Are you lucky you ran into me so quick. Going to save you six months of turning into your mommy, then a short lifetime waiting for the hammer to fall. You're a lucky girl, little Nicola. Lucky, lucky, lucky.

Part of him was also shaking, because of what he knew he was going to do later. He didn't normally do it. He just disposed of them. Take a drive down the 'glades, dump the body, no one's going to know or give a shit. He didn't like doing anything else, made him feel like a pervert though he wasn't—he was a professional. Every now and then was okay though, even if it was clouding his mind right now, making it hard to make the street names out. Some guys bought themselves new guns, went on a coke bender, hired a couple of whores. Everyone needs a treat. Incentive scheme. Keeps your wheels turning.

Ricky gripped the wheel tightly, tuned out the noise of the kid's nattering, got himself straight. Eventually he turned the car in what looked like the right direction. Found his way down the grid of streets, each lined with houses, some streets like the 1940s, some the 1950s or 1960s. Or like those times would have been if they hadn't been shit, anyhow. Like those decades were if you looked back at them now and forgot everything that was wrong with them. The streets were quiet, because mostly the people in the houses were too old to be out walking this late.

Homeland 3, along with the four other near-identical districts which spread in a fan around the Beautiful Realm, was one of the newest parts of Wonder World. Five years ago, the suits who ran the parts realized they had yet another goldmine on their hands: managed communities of old farts. Cutesy little neighborhoods in the sun, where the oldsters could come waste their final years, safe from the world outside and bad afternoons where they could be walking home from the store they'd used all their lives and suddenly find three guys with knives standing on the corner. Not only safe, but coddled, living somewhere where their grandkids could be guaranteed to want to come see them. You want to go visit Granny in Roanoke? I don't think so. Wonder World?—that's a pretty easy sell. They built the houses, any size, any style, so everyone from trailer trash to leather-faced zillionaires had somewhere to hang their trusses: houses that looked like whatever you wanted from a space podule to a mud hut on the planet Zog. All this and stores and banks and shit, all built to look like what they sold. That's what made it so difficult to find your way around. Was like being in a toy store on acid.

It got so popular that even the smallest houses started getting expensive, and a year ago Ricky had an idea. You've got house after house of old people. With money. People who can't defend themselves too well. With things worth stealing. You get yourself into one of the Homelands—with a cute kid, who's going to question you?—and you help yourself to some stuff, using the kid's voice to get the door open. You're in and out before anyone knows there's a few old people gone to meet their maker sooner than intended: kid's the only living witness, and not for very long. All you got to do is make sure you never get recognized at the gate, and with millions of people going in and out every week, it's never going to happen.

And the kicker—Wonder World covered the burglaries up. Of course they did. Very bad for business, because they showed the magic retreat was a crock of shit. Plus, and here Ricky witnessed something which made perfect sense to him, something which placed the whole world in context as he understood it—the families often didn't make too much fuss. Why? Same reason that, after a couple months, Ricky had a new idea and moved on to a different line of business, made himself a professional.

Lot of times the families weren't exactly too sad to see the old folks go, because they wanted the old people's money. Which is why Ricky didn't bother to steal anymore. Now Ricky took contracts instead, made it look natural. Much safer, more secret, more lucrative—for the time being. Sooner or later the suits would catch on and increase security somehow, and Ricky would move out, and start blackmailing the families instead. Even the kind of people who'd pay to have Gramps whacked had to be living in a Wonder World of their own, if they didn't realize it would come back to haunt them some day.

Ricky finally found Gecko Super Terrace III, drove a little way along it. Pulled over to the curb, looked up at a house, and checked the address. Grunted with satisfaction. He was in the right place.

Margaret Harris, eighty-four years old, was worth maybe three hundred and fifty thousand dollars, all told, including the Homeland house. Not such a hell of a lot, but her son and daughter-in-law could get the bigger boat a couple years earlier, and without working all those unsociable hours and missing cocktail hour. Upgrade the satellite, get a widescreen TV for the den. Maybe they'd throw their children a bone too. A games station. A bike. A last visit to Wonder World.

As John Harris, the son, had put it while slurping a large scotch to blur his conscience: they were just realizing an unwanted asset.

Margaret Harris had herself a kind of tiny Tudor mansion, dark beams and whitewash, exaggerated leans in the walls and gingerbread thatch. There was a light on in a downstairs room, behind a curtain. The grass in the front yard was all the same perfect fucking length. Maybe it was animatronic grass. Maybe it sang a happy wake-up call in the morning, a million blades in unison.

Nicola looked at the house too. "Is this where she lives?"

"That's right. You remember what I want you to do?"

She looked away, didn't answer for a moment.

"I had a grandma," she said. "I saw her twice. She gave me a ring, but Mommy took it. She died when I was six. Mommy got so drunk she wet herself."

Ricky nearly hit her then, but stopped himself just in time. It was like that with the ones like her. Part of wanting to fuck them was finding them just too fucking irritating to bear. He forced himself to speak calmly. "This isn't your grandma, okay? Do you remember, Nicola? What I want to you to do?"

"Of course," the girl said. She opened the door and got out.

Swearing quietly, Ricky got out his side, slipped the gun into his pocket, then followed her up the path to the Harris house.

Nicola rang the doorbell a second time, and Ricky heard someone moving inside the house. He stepped back into shadow. Nicola stood in front of the door, waiting.

"Who is it?" The voice was old, cracked but not quavery. The kind of voice that says, I'm pretty old but not ready to drop just yet.

"Hi, Grandma!" Nicola piped, leaning forward to peer through the diamond of swirled glass in the door. She waved her hand. "I've come to see you!"

"Theresa?" The oldster's voice was uncertain, but Ricky caught the sound of locks being tentatively drawn. This was the second key moment. This was the moment where the kid had to be good enough so that the old woman didn't press the Worry Button put beside the door of every Homeland house. The button that would alert Wonder World's version of security that something was sharp and spiky in the dream tonight.

The final slide bolt, and the door opened a crack. "Theresa?"

Margaret Harris was small, maybe five feet tall. She was grandma-shaped and had white hair done up in a curly style. Her face was plump and lined and she was wearing one of the those dresses that old people wear, flowers on a dark background. You opened a dictionary and looked up "grandma" and she was pretty much what you'd see.

"You're not Theresa," she said.

"Oh, no." Nicola laughed. "I'm Theresa's friend. Theresa said if we were passing by we should call in and say hello."

Ricky stepped into the light, an apologetic smile on his face. "Hi there, Mrs Harris. Hope this is okay—Theresa's telling Nicola here about you all the time. John said you probably wouldn't mind. Meant to call ahead, but you know how it is."

"You're a friend of John's?"

"Work right across the hall from him at First Virtual."

Mrs Harris hesitated a final moment, then smiled back, her face crinkling in a pattern which started from the eyes. "Well, I guess it's okay then. Come on in."

The hallway looked like a painted background from an old Wonder World cartoon: higgledy stairs, everything neat, colors washed and clean. When the door was shut behind them, Ricky knew the job was done.

"You can't be too careful these days," the old woman said, predictably, leading Nicola through to the kitchen to make some coffee. Right, thought Ricky, following at a distance, and you haven't been careful enough.

He hung outside for a moment, scoping the place, listening with half an ear to the sound of Nicola chatting with the old bag in the kitchen. Jeez, the kid could lie: what's happening at school, party she went to with Theresa last week, Theresa borrowing her shoes. Listening to her, you'd think she really *did* know the woman's granddaughter. Make-believe again, some life she wished she had.

Ricky debated disabling the Worry Button, finally decided it wasn't necessary. Difficult to do, anyhow—and just smashing it would leave a clue. This one was too easy to make it worth taking the risk.

The kitchen was small, cozy, tricked up to look like the kind of place where there would always be something in the oven, instead of ready-made shit in the microwave. Pots, pastry cutters, a rolling pin. Probably Wonder World sent someone into everyone's house every day, made sure the props looked just right. Grandma Harris turned as Ricky entered and handed a cup of coffee up to him. She smiled, twinkle-eyed, relaxed—the kid had put her at ease.

Ricky made a mental note that the cup and saucer would need wiping when he was done. Nicola had a glass of Dr. Pepper—that would need washing too. He sipped the coffee—might as well—and deflected a couple of questions about working with the great John Harris. Pathetic, really, the way the old woman was eager for any news of her son, wanted telling how people liked him. Suddenly, he just wanted to lash out and shove his cup right down the old fart's throat. It would be a whole lot quicker, and put her out of misery she didn't even know she was in. But he knew how it had to look, and death by ingestion of china tea set wouldn't play.

Meanwhile, Nicola and Grandma sat at the table, yakking nineteen to the dozen. Nicola had a lot of Grandma-talking to do, even if she had to make do with someone else's. Ricky let his eyes glaze over, mulling what he was going to do to the kid later. He enjoyed doing that, getting the comparison, just like he liked looking at girls in the street and imagining them on the job, their hands or mouth busy, face wet with sweat. They'd never know, but they'd been his. Ricky rode that line, that fine line, between the life they lived and the life that could come and find them in the night.

"Isn't that right, Daddy?"

"Huh?" Ricky looked at the girl dully, having missed the question. "What's that?"

"Nicola was just saying how you and John were planning a joint vacation for the families later in the year," Mrs Harris said. "That's wonderful news. Do you think you might be able to make it up here again? We'd have such fun."

"Sure," Ricky said, abruptly deciding this had gone on long enough and was getting out of hand. "No question. Hey, Mrs. Harris—meant to ask you something."

"Of course." Grandma was beside herself at the prospect of another visit later in the year. She'd have agreed to anything. "What is it?"

"John told me about some pictures, old photos, you've got at the top of the stairs? Kind of an interest of mine. He said you might not mind me taking a peek at them."

"I'd be delighted." The old woman beamed. "Come, let's go up." Nicola jumped to her feet, but Ricky flashed a glare at her.

Grandma raised an eyebrow. "Wouldn't you like to come too, dear?"

Nicola avoided Ricky's eye. "Could I have another Dr. Pepper first?"

"Help yourself, then follow us up. Now come on—Ricky, isn't it?—let's go take a look."

Ricky sent another "Stay here" look at the kid, followed Grandma out. Made interested grunts every now and then as the old woman talked and led him across the hall to the stairs. A couple of objects caught Ricky's eye on the way, and he planned on picking them up later, before he left. Little bonus.

Up the stairs behind her. Feeling very little. No fear, no excitement. Just watching for the best moment. Mrs. Harris walked up the stairs slowly, hitching one leg up after the other. Her voice might be strong but her body was saying goodbye. She wouldn't be losing much.

They got to the first landing, and Ricky saw that there were indeed a whole bunch of really fucking dull-looking black-and-whites in frames there on the wall. John Harris had the whole thing planned out, gave Ricky this way of getting her up to the scaffold. Ricky debated telling the old woman about that, letting her see what lay beyond her wonder world, that the son she'd raised had sat in his study one night drinking cheap scotch and working it all out. But by then Margaret Harris was standing right by him, and he knew the time was right and he wanted to get it over with. The real bonus was waiting for him in the kitchen. He didn't need any cheap thrills first.

This picture was her mother, that one her grandpapa. Gone-away people, stiff in fading monotone.

Ricky leaned toward her, apparently to get a closer look at a bunch of people grouped in front of a raggedy farm building—but actually to get the right angle.

For a moment then he was distracted, by a scent. It seemed to come from the old woman's clothes, and was a combination of things: of milk and cinnamon, rich coffee and apples cooking on the stove. Leaves barely on the trees in fall, and the smell of sun on grass in summer. These things weren't a part of his life, but for a moment he had them in his mind—like they were part of some story he'd read long ago, as a child, and just dismissed.

Then he pushed her down the stairs.

Palm flat against her shoulder, feeling the bones inside the old, thin flesh. He straightened his arm firmly, which was enough—and wouldn't leave a bruise that some forensic smartass might be able to talk up into evidence.

The old woman teetered, without making a sound, and then her center of gravity was all wrong and she just tumbled over sideways, over the edge and down the stairs.

Thump, crash, thud, splat. Like a loose bag of sticks.

Ricky walked briskly down the stairs after her, reached the bottom bare seconds after she did. Held back from kicking her head, which would have been risky and was clearly unnecessary. Huge dent in the skull already, eyes turned upward and out of sight. Arm twisted a strange way, one leg bent back on itself. The usual anticlimax.

Job done.

He stepped quickly over the body and to the kitchen, stopping Nicola already on her way out. She ran into him, crashed against his body. He grabbed her shoulders, warm through the thin T-shirt.

"What happened? I heard a crash."

Usually he killed the kid at this point, before they got hysterical and made too much noise or ran out of the house. Ricky pushed Nicola gently back into the kitchen, felt his temperature rising. Needed her alive to do things with, but he couldn't do them here. "Nothing. Just an accident. Mrs. Harris fell down the stairs."

"Grandma?"

"She's not your grandma, sweetie. You know that."

"We've got to get help. . . ."

Ricky smiled down at her. "We will. That's exactly what we'll do. We'll get in the car, go find one of the security wagons. They'll help her out. She'll get fixed up and we'll catch the end of the parade."

The girl was near tears. "I want to stay here with her."

He pretended to think about it, then shook his head. "Can't do that. Security gets here while I'm away, finds you with an old lady at the bottom of the stairs, what are they going to think? They're going to think you pushed her."

"They won't. She was my grandma. Why would I hurt her?"

Ricky glared at her, good humor fast disappearing. "She wasn't your fucking grandma. Just some old woman."

Nicola pushed hard against him, momentarily rocking him on his heels. "She was *too*. She knew about me. She knew things. She said not to worry about my mom anymore. She said she loved me."

Ricky lashed out with his hand, shoved the kid hard. She flew back, ricocheted off the table and knocked the coffeepot flying. It struck the wall, spraying brown gunk everywhere, just as Nicola crashed to the floor. Ricky cursed himself. Not clever. Just going to make it more difficult to get her out of the house, plus it was going to look like signs of a struggle. He took a deep breath, stepped toward her. Maybe he was going to have to just kill her after all.

"Nicola? Are you okay, dear?"

Ricky froze, foot just hitting the floor. Turned slowly around.

Grandma stood in the doorway. One eye fluttered slowly, the one below the huge dent which pulled most of the side of her face out of kilter. The arm was still bent way out of place. Her body was completely fucked up, but somehow she'd managed to drag herself to the door, to her feet.

Nicola struggled into a sitting position against the wall behind Ricky. "Grandma—are you all right?"

Of course she's not fucking all right, Ricky thought. No way.

Grandma leaned against the door frame, as if tired. "I'm fine, dear. Just had a little fall, isn't that right, Rick?" Her working eye fixed on him.

Ricky felt the hairs on the back of his neck rise like a thousand tiny erections. Then her other eye stopped flickering. Closed for a moment, reopened—and then he had two strong eyes looking at him. Tough old bitch.

Ricky reached for the table, grabbed the rolling pin lying there. This job was getting very fucked up, but he was going to finish it now.

"Close your eyes, dear," Grandma said. She wasn't talking to him, but the kid. "Would you do that, for Grandma? Just close your eyes for a while."

"Close them tight?" Nicola asked, voice small.

"Yes, close them extra tight," Grandma nodded, trying to smile. "And I'll tell you when you can open them again."

Ricky saw the girl shut her eyes and cover her ears. He shook his head, turned back to the old woman, rolling pin held with loose ease. He took a measured stride toward her, not hurrying. Ricky had been in bad situations all his life, had been beaten up and half-killed on a hundred occasions, starting with the times that happened in his own bedroom, a room that had no posters on the walls or books on shelves or little figures of cartoon animals. Ricky's old man hadn't believed in make-believe either, was proud of being cynical—"That's what I am, boy, I'm nobody's fool"—and working the angles and telling God's honest truth however fucking dull it was. His lessons had been painful, but Ricky knew he'd been right.

Ricky wasn't afraid of an old woman, no matter how tough she might be, and he just grinned at her, looking forward to seeing what the pin was going to do to her face. She looked back at him, head tilted up, gray hair awry and skin papery, and then her head popped back out.

One minute her skull was caved in, the next it was back where it should be, like someone pumped exactly the right amount of air back into a punctured balloon. It made a sound like cellophane.

Ricky gawped, arm aloft.

Grandma swallowed, blinked, then did something with her fucked-up arm. Swung it around from behind her—and as it came it seemed to become more solid, find the right planes to rotate on again. She bent it experimentally, found it worked, and used it to pat her dry hair more or less back into place.

"You're a very bad boy, Ricky," she said, softly, too quietly for Nicola to hear. "And bad boys never see Santa Claus. Hear what I'm saying, motherfuck?"

Before Ricky could even process this sentence, Margaret Harris had hurled herself at him. He tried to turn, bring the pin down, but only managed to twist halfway around at the waist. She smacked into him sideways, and the two of them spun off the corner of the table to crash into the wall. Ricky felt his nose bend and melt, and realized there was going to be blood to clean up as well as everything else.

He tried to push the old woman away, but she looped a fist straight into his face. It cracked hard against his cheekbone, far too hard. The rolling pin went spinning across the floor.

Ricky kicked and scrambled, lashing out feet, hands, and elbows in a flurry of compact violence. Each time he thought he was finally going to be able to dislodge her, she seemed to gain a notch in strength. They rolled back and forth under the table, smashing a chair to firewood, and out the other side. Ricky heard Nicola squeal, and a small part of his mind was able to hope their neighbors hadn't heard. Then he found himself with two gnarled hands tight around his throat, and almost wished they had, and were sending help. For him.

He finally managed to pull his knee up under the old bitch, and gradually forced his hands in between hers. When they were in position he steadied himself for a second, got his breath—and then threw everything he had, chopping his hands in opposite directions, and kicking out hard.

The old woman flew a yard and hit the stove like an egg.

Ricky was on his feet almost immediately, hands on his knees and coughing like a bastard. When he swallowed, something clicked alarmingly in his throat. Nicola was still squeaking, eyes shut, but he heard it as from a great distance. He could taste his blood, and see it spattered on the wall and floor—in amongst the coffee and a few lumps of gray hair that he managed to yank out of the robot.

A fucking animatronic. Had to be. He'd been set up. John Harris had changed his mind, or more likely been a plant from minute one and there'd never been a real Grandma Harris. Fuckers. Wonder World weren't working with the cops. They were settling things their own way.

And so would Ricky. The job was over, and it didn't matter how much mess he left. He was getting out, and then going to find Mr. Harris. The fee had just gone up to include everything the bastard owned, including his wife. And his daughter.

Grandma Harris was slumped on the floor, back against the cooker. Her throat was arced up like a twisted branch, a perfect target, but jerked back into position as Ricky pulled out his gun. No matter. The face would do just as well.

He held the gun in a straight-arm grip, sighted down the barrel.

"Don't even fucking think about it," the rolling pin said.

Ricky turned very slowly to look. "Excuse me?"

It had grown legs, and was standing with little hands on where its hips would be. Two stern eyes glared out of the wooden cylinder of its body, and it looked like a strange wide crab.

Ricky stared at it. Knew suddenly that it wasn't a machine, but an actual rolling pin with eyes and arms. He fired at it. The pin flipped out of the way, then switched direction and flick-flacked toward him, like a crazy little wooden gymnast. Ricky backed hurriedly, fired another shot. It missed, and the rolling pin flicked itself into the air like a mus-cular missile. Ricky wrenched his head out of the way just in time, and the pin embedded itself in the wall.

"Careful," said the wall, slowly opening its eyes.

Over at the stove, Grandma Harris was pulling herself upright. Ricky blinked at her. She smiled, a sweet old lady smile that wasn't for him. Ricky decided he didn't have to mop up this mess. He'd go straight to talk with John Harris. He fired a couple of rounds into the wall, just between its huge eyes. It made a grumpy sound, but didn't seem much inconvenienced. A huge mouth opened sleepily, as if yawning, as it was only just getting up to speed. The pin meanwhile pushed itself out with a dry popping sound, and turned its beady eyes on Ricky.

"Shit on this," Ricky muttered, as it scuttled toward him. He swung a kick at the rolling pin, sent it howling across the room. Fired straight at Margaret Harris, but didn't wait to see if it hit.

He turned on his heel in the kitchen door, bounded across the hall-way and yanked at the door. It wouldn't open, and when Ricky tried to pull his hand away, he saw the handle had turned into a brown wooden hand and was gripping his like he was a prime business opportunity and they were testing each other's strength. Ricky braced his foot against the wall and tugged, for the first time hearing the sound of the beams whispering above. He glanced up and saw some of them were wriggling in place, limbering up, getting ready for action. He didn't want to see their action.

The door handle wasn't letting go, and so he placed the muzzle of the gun against it and let it have one.

It took the tip of one of Ricky's fingers with it, but the fucker let go. Ricky reared back, kicked the door with all his strength. It splintered and he barrelled through it, tripped and fell full length on the lawn. Face to face with the grass for a moment, he saw that he'd been right, and there was a little face on every blade. He heard a noise like a million little voices tuning up and knew that its song wasn't likely to be one he wanted to hear.

He scrabbled to his feet and careened down the path toward the car, bloody hand scrabbling for the keys. Before he could get even halfway there two trash cans came running around from next door. They made it to the car before him, and started levering one side off up the ground. Meanwhile the rolling pin shot out of the house from behind him, narrowly missed his head, and went through the windscreen of the car like a torpedo. Barely had the spray of glass hit the ground before the pin emerged the other side, turned in midair and looped back to punch through a door panel. It kept going, faster and faster, looping and punching, until the car began to look like a battered atom being mugged by a psycho electron.

Ricky began to realize just how badly his hand hurt, and that the car wasn't going to be a viable transportation option. He diverted his course in mid-stride, just heading for the road, for a straight line to run. He cleared the sidewalk, barely keeping his balance, and leaned into the turn. Ricky could run. He'd had the practice, down many dark streets and darker nights, and always running away instead of to. The way was clear.

Then a vehicle appeared at the corner in front of him, and he understood what the grass had been singing. Not a song, but a siren.

Wonder World's designers hadn't stinted themselves on the cop wagon. It was black and half as big as a house, all superfins and intimidating wheel arches spiked with chrome. The windows in the sides were blacker still, and the doors in the back might just as well have had ABANDON HOPE ALL YE WHO ENTER HERE scrawled right across them.

Ricky skidded to a halt, whirled around. An identical vehicle had

moved into position just the other side of the remains of his car. Behind
it a bunch of mushrooms and toadstools were moving into position.

The doors of the first wagon opened, and a figure got out each side.
Both seven feet tall, with very long tails and claws that glinted. Bud
and Slap, though rats, had been friendly rats in all the countless cartoons
they'd appeared in over the last thirty years. They were almost as popular as Loopy and Careful and China Duck, and even Ricky recognized
them. Cute, well-meaning villains, they always ended up joining the
right side in the end.

But this Bud and Slap weren't like that. These toons were just for
Ricky. As he held his ground, knowing there was nowhere to run, they
walked toward him with heavy tread. They were stuffed into parodies
of uniforms, torn at the seams and stained with bad things. Bud had a
lazy, damaged eye, and was holding a big wooden truncheon in an
unreassuring way. Slap had a sore on his upper lip, and kept running a
long blue tongue over it, to collect the juice. Both had huge guns stuffed
down the front of their uniforms. At least that's what Ricky hoped they
were. From five yards away he could smell the rats' odor, the gust of
sweat and stickiness and decay, and for a moment catch an echo of all
the screams and death rattles they'd heard.

"Hey there, Ricky," said Slap, winking. His voice was low and oily,
full of unpleasant good humor. "Got some business with you. Lots of
different kinds of business, actually. You can get in the wagon, or we
can start it right here. What d'you say?"

Behind him Bud giggled, and started to undo his pants.

Nicola stood at the window with Grandma, and watched the parade in
the road. It wasn't the real parade, like the one in the Beautiful Realm
where they had fireworks and Careful Cat and Loopy, but they were
going to see that tomorrow. This was a little parade, with just Bud and
Slap, and Percival Pin and Terrance and Terry the Trash Cans: sometimes they put on little parades of their own, Grandma said, just because
they enjoyed it.

They laughed as they watched the characters play. Nicola had
thought the man she'd come with had been a bad man, but he couldn't
have been as bad as all that. Bud and Slap the Happy Rats were each
holding one of his hands, and they were dancing with him, leading him
to the wagon. They looked like they liked him a lot. The man's mouth
opened and shut very wide as he danced, and Nicola thought he was
probably laughing. She would be, in his position. They all looked like
they were having such fun.

Finally, the wagon doors were shut with the man inside, and Bud and Slap bowed up at Grandma's window before getting back into their police car. The trash cans went somersaulting back to next door's yard, and the rolling pin came hand-springing up the path, leaving a trail of little firework stars in its wake. Nicola clapped her hands and Grandma laughed, and put her arm around the little girl.

Now it was time for supper and pie, and tomorrow would be a new and different day. They turned away from the window, and went to start cooking, in a kitchen where the tables and chairs had already tidied everything up as if nothing bad had ever happened, or ever could.

Meanwhile, well outside Wonder World, over on a splintered porch outside a small house the other side of the beltway, Marty the Gateman sat in his chair enjoying his bedtime cigarette. His back ached a little, from standing up all day, but it didn't bother him too badly. It was a small price to pay for seeing all the faces as they went into the parks, and when they came out again. The kids went in bright-eyed and hopeful, the parents tired and watchful. You could see them thinking how much it was all going to cost, and wondering whether it would be worth it. Then when you saw them come out, hours or days later, you could see that they knew that it had been. For a little while the grown-ups realized their cynicism was an emotional shortcut which meant they missed everything worth seeing along the way, and the children had proof of what they already believed: the world was cool. The gateman's job was important, Marty knew. You said the first hello to the visitors, and you said goodbye. You welcomed them in and helped them acclimatize; and then you sent them on their way, letting them see in your eyes the truth of what they believed—they were leaving a little lighter inside.

Marty's house was small and looked like all the others nearby, and he lived in it alone. As he sat in the warmth of the evening, looking up at the stars, he didn't mind that very much. His wife now lived with someone who was better at earning money, and who came home after a day's work in a far worse mood. Marty missed her, but he'd survive. The house could have been fancier, but he'd painted it last summer and he liked his yard.

He had the last couple of puffs of his cigarette, and then stubbed it out carefully in the ashtray he kept by the chair. He yawned, sipped the last of his iced tea, and decided that was that. It was early yet, but a good time for sleep. It always is, when you're looking forward to the next day.

As he lay in his bed later, gently settling into the warm train which would take him into tomorrow, he dimly wondered what he'd do with the rest of his life. Work for as long as he could, he supposed, and then stop. Sit out on the porch, most likely, live out his days bathed in the memory of faces lit for a moment by magic. Smile at passersby. Drink iced tea in the twilight.

That sounded okay by him.

DELIA SHERMAN

The Parwat Ruby

Delia Sherman was born in Japan, raised in New York City, and holds a Ph.D. in Renaissance Studies from Vassar College. Her first novel, Through a Brazen Mirror, *was published as part of the Ace Fantasy Special; her second novel,* The Porcelain Dove, *won the Mythopoeic Award. Her recent novella* The Fall of the Kings *(co-written with Ellen Kushner) was nominated for the World Fantasy Award, and her young adult novel* Freedom's Maze *is forthcoming from HarperCollins. Sherman is also a consulting editor for Tor Books and co-editor of the anthologies* The Horns of Elfland *and* The Essential Bordertown. *She divides her time between New York, Massachusetts, and travels abroad.*

"The Parwat Ruby" grew out of the author's recent interest in the works of Anthony Trollope. (Sherman's thoughts on the relationship of Anthony Trollope to modern fantasy fiction can be found on the Young Trollopes Web page, www.endicott-studio.com/yt.html. This delightfully Victorian fantasia can be enjoyed without a special knowledge of Trollope's oeuvre, but the tale is absolutely delicious if one has spent time with his Palliser books.

—T. W.

Whether the disaster of the Parwat Ruby would have taken place if Sir Alvord Basingstoke had not married Margaret Kennedy is a matter of conjecture. Given his character, Sir Alvord would undoubtedly have married a woman like Margaret if Margaret herself had never been born. For Sir Alvord was a gentle man, silent in company, devoted to solitude—in short, the natural mate of a woman who talked a great deal and loved society. In her youth, Margaret Kennedy had been much courted, being lively and clever and very well dressed, as well as mistress of three thousand pounds a year. Over time, she grew domineering and unpleasant as well, but as Sir Alvord spent the best part of the next thirty years exploring uncharted wildernesses, it is likely that he did not notice. When ebbing vital forces put a period to his travels, Lady Glencora Pallister prophesied a speedy separation. But months passed, and still the reunited couple showed every sign of mutual affection, demonstrating that even the most dedicated hunters of human weakness must sometimes draw a blank.

Some two years after returning from his last journey, Sir Alvord called upon his sister, Mrs. Mildmay. A certain coolness having long ago arisen between Mrs. Mildmay and Lady Basingstoke, Mrs. Mildmay had seen little of her brother in that time. Consequently, she was much astonished, one evening as the Season began, to hear her maid announce the name of Sir Alvord Basingstoke. It was time to be thinking of changing for supper; nevertheless, she had him shown into her sitting room, and received him with a sisterly embrace.

"So here you are, Alvord," she said. "Handsome as ever, I see." It had been a schoolroom joke that they looked very alike, although the heavy jaw and pronounced nose that made him a handsome man kept her from being considered anything but plain.

He pressed her hands and put her from him. "I have something very particular to say to you, Caroline. You're my only sister—indeed, my only living blood relation—and I am an old man."

Somewhat distressed by this greeting, Mrs. Mildmay bade her brother sit and indicated her readiness to hear what he had to tell her, but he only sighed heavily and rubbed his forehead with his right hand, which was decorated with a ring set with a large cabochon ruby. The ring was familiar to her, as much a part of Sir Alvord as his pale blue eyes and his indifferently tailored coats. He had brought the stone back from a journey to Ceylon in his youth and it had never left his hand since. Massy as it was, it had always looked perfectly at home on his broad hand, but now it hung and turned loosely on his finger.

The white star that lived in its depths slid and winked, capturing Mrs. Mildmay's eye and attention so fully that when Sir Alvord spoke, she was forced to beg him to repeat his words.

"It's this ring of mine, Caroline," said Sir Alvord patiently. "It's more than a trinket."

"Indeed it is, brother. I've never seen such a fine stone."

"A fine stone indeed. Your true, clear star is very rare and very precious in a ruby of this size. But that is not what I meant. There is a history attached to this ring and a responsibility."

He seemed to experience some difficulty in continuing, a difficulty not remarkable in a man who all his life had been accustomed to let first his mother and then his wife speak for him. Mrs. Mildmay sat quietly until he should find words.

"This is unexpectedly difficult," he said at length.

Mrs. Mildmay looked down at her hands. "I have often wished us better friends," she said.

"I have wished the same. But my wife had a claim upon my loyalty."

Mrs. Mildmay flushed and would have retorted that she hoped that his sister had at least an equal claim, but he held up his hand to forestall her, his ruby flashing like a diamond as the star caught the afternoon sun.

He continued, "I have not come to quarrel with you. Margaret has been a good wife to me. However, I don't mean for her to have this ring. I had hoped to leave it to a son of mine"—here he sighed once again—"but that was not to be. I have it in my mind to put in my will that you're to have it when I die, and that it must pass to Wilson after you." Wilson was Mrs. Mildmay's oldest son, a likely young man of four-and-twenty.

Mrs. Mildmay, much moved, reached out and patted her brother's hand. "There's no need to be talking of wills and dying, brother. I've no doubt you'll see out your century with ease."

"And I have no doubt that I will not see out the year. No, Caroline, don't argue with me. The ring must stay in the family." He rose slowly and tottered as he stood, so that Mrs. Mildmay sprang to her feet to steady him. Once more he kissed her cheek. "God bless you, Caroline. I don't suppose I'll see you again."

After this conversation, Mrs. Mildmay was not much amazed when, not three days later, she received word that Sir Alvord had suffered an apoplectic fit. At first, his life was despaired of, and even when it seemed sure he would live, he could no longer move his arms or legs, but must be fed and turned and bathed like an infant. In this great exigency, Lady Basingstoke displayed all the careful tenderness that could be hoped from a loving wife and, although she was herself not a young woman, undertook the entire burden of his nursing. To be sure, there were nurses hired to tend him, but Lady Basingstoke considered them all worthless baggages and would not leave any of them alone with him for more than a few moments. So it was that when Mrs.

Mildmay called to inquire after her brother's health, Lady Basingstoke did not come down to her, but received her in Sir Alvord's dressing room with the communicating door ajar.

She was seated in a shabby wing-chair, her head inclined upon her hand in an attitude eloquent of the most complete dejection, but she lifted her head at Mrs. Mildmay's entrance and waved her feebly to a chair. "Please forgive me not rising to greet you, dear Caroline," she said. "I am utterly prostrate, as you see. He had a very bad night, and this morning was discovered to be unable to speak. Sir Omicron Pie has warned me to prepare myself for the worst."

Mrs. Mildmay may have considered her brother's wife a harpy and a fool, but it would be a harder heart than hers to have denied Lady Basingstoke a sister's comfort at such a time. "My dear Margaret," she said. "I am so very sorry. You must let me know if there is anything I may do to help you. Sit with Alvord, perhaps, so that you can take some rest?"

"No, no. You are too kind, Caroline, but no. Dear Alvord will suffer no one about him but me." Her voice faltered and she raised her hand to her eyes, as though to hide springing tears. The gesture reminded Mrs. Mildmay irresistibly of her brother's when he had come to call, the more so that it displayed Lady Basingstoke's hand, well-kept and very large for a woman, just now made to look delicate by a great gold ring set with a single large, red stone: the Parwat Ruby.

"I beg your pardon, Margaret," said Mrs. Mildmay, "but is that not Alvord's ring?"

The question caused Lady Basingstoke to have recourse to her hand-kerchief, and it was not until she had composed herself that she said, "He gave it to me last night. It was as though he knew he'd soon be beyond speech, for he took it from his finger and put it upon mine, saying that it was the dearest wish of his heart to see it always upon my hand. It is, of course, far too big; but I have tied it on with a bit of cotton, which I trust will hold it until I can bear to be parted with it long enough to have it made to fit."

"How very touching," said Mrs. Mildmay. There was nothing so very exceptionable in her tone, but Lady Basingstoke absolutely frowned at her and requested her to explain what she meant.

"Only that dear Alvord was not commonly so fluent in his speech."

"I think, dear Mrs. Mildmay, that you are hardly qualified to have an opinion," said Lady Basingstoke, "considering that you have hardly spoken to him twice in twenty years. I assure you it took place just as I have told you."

"No doubt," answered Mrs. Mildmay, and took her leave not many minutes afterward. It is not, perhaps, necessary to say that Mrs. Mildmay had every doubt as to the accuracy of Lady Basingstoke's recollection, but she could hardly say so. An evening call is not a will, after all, and her brother had every right to change his mind as to the distribution of his own property.

Now Lady Basingstoke was even more indispensable to Sir Alvord than when he had been merely bed-bound, for she was the only one who could make shift to understand his gruntings and gesturings and bring him a little ease. In fact, she dispensed with the nurses altogether and snatched her rest when she might upon a trundle bed in Sir Alvord's dressing room, for he would become unbearably agitated in her absence. Sir Omicron Pie continued to call each morning, but he could do nothing above prescribing a calming draught. Given the tenor of her last visit, Mrs. Mildmay was not surprised when the butler turned her from the door when next she came to call. But she was much astonished the following morning, when she read the notice of Sir Alvord Basingstoke's death in *The Times*.

"It's a bad business," she exclaimed to her husband, who was enjoying the text of Mr. Gresham's latest speech. "It's a bad business when a sister must read of her brother's passing in the public press."

"Not at all, my dear. Devoted wife, prostrate widow. Likely it slipped her mind. Here's Gresham rabbitting on about the poor again, as if *he* could do anything with his party feeling as it does about taxes. It's a crime, that's what it is. A crime and a sin."

"I daresay, Quintus, but do pay attention. When I called yesterday afternoon, the curtains were not drawn, there was no crepe on the knocker, and the butler said only that his mistress was not at home to visitors."

"Man wasn't dead yet," said Mr. Mildmay reasonably.

"Nonsense," said his wife. "I defy even the most energetic widow to get a notice of death in *The Times* in anything under a day, and if he were alive when I called, she could have had only a few hours. I call it a bad business."

"Odd, anyway," said Mr. Mildmay. "Wonder if he left you anything?"

"As if I cared about that! He did mention his ruby ring to me when last I saw him, but I doubt that anything will come of it."

Mr. Mildmay put down his paper. "His ruby, eh? Worth a good few hundred pounds, I'd think. The ruby would be worth having indeed."

"The ring may be worth what it will, Quintus. My point is that

Alvord expressed the wish that it remain in the family, and yet I saw it upon Lady Basingstoke's hand."

"Woman's his wife, Caroline. A wife is part of a man's family, I hope."

"Not when she's a widow, Quintus, for she may then marry again and take her husband's property into another man's family."

"Then we must hope that your brother put the thing down in his will." Mr. Mildmay took up his paper again to show that the subject was closed, firing as he did so a warning shot around its crackling edges: "Won't look well to make a fuss, Caroline."

Mrs. Mildmay so far agreed with her husband that she was able to pay her condolence call and support the grieving widow at Sir Alvord's funeral without adverting to the subject of Sir Alvord's last visit. Yet as she stood next to Lady Basingstoke at the graveside, she could not suppress a shudder at the sight of the Parwat Ruby glowing balefully against the deep black of the widow's wash-leather gloves. She could not think it well done of Margaret to have worn it, hoping only that her grief had blinded her to the impropriety of flaunting a ruby at a funeral. Yet, as the first shovelfuls of dirt fell upon the casket, Mrs. Mildmay could have sworn that the widow was smiling.

"But she was heavily veiled," exclaimed her bosom friend Lady Fitzaskerly when Mrs. Mildmay had unburdened herself of her righteous anger.

"Nonetheless," said Mrs. Mildmay. "You know what she looks like."

"A horse in a flaxen wig," replied Lady Fitzaskerly, who disliked Lady Basingstoke as heartily as the most exacting friend could wish.

"Precisely. And the heaviest veil to be purchased at Liberty's would be insufficient to hide the most subtle of her expressions. The woman was grinning like an ape. And there was no mention of the ring in the will—not a single word, though many of his collections are dispersed and the entire contents of his library are to be given to his club."

"Perhaps he fell ill before the lawyer might be called."

"Perhaps. And perhaps he didn't. I thought Mr. Chess wished to speak to me when the document had been read, but Lady Basingstoke entirely engaged his attention. And now here is a note from Mr. Chess in the first mail this morning, begging me to receive him at four this very afternoon. What do you think of that?"

Lady Fitzaskerly did not know what to think, but she found the whole matter so very interesting that she could not forbear mentioning it to Lady Glencora Pallister when next she had occasion to call upon her. Lady Glen was sitting, as she often was, with Madam Max Goesler of Park Lane.

"Why, it's just like the Eustace diamonds!" Lady Glencora exclaimed when Lady Fitzaskerly had done. "You remember the fuss, when that silly girl Lizzie Eustace stole her own diamonds to keep them from the hands of her husband's family?"

"It's not so very much like it, not to my mind," said Madam Max. "No one has stolen anything, so far as I can tell. A gentleman in his dotage has changed his mind about the disposition of his personal property and created an unpleasantness."

"Well, I think Mrs. Mildmay is hardly used in the matter."

"Consider, my dear. Lady Basingstoke is his widow. She cared for him in his last illness and shared his interests."

"His interests!" Lady Glencora was scornful. "We best not inquire too closely into his interests, if all I hear be true."

"Surely, Lady Glen, you can't believe he was a wizard," exclaimed Lady Fitzaskerly. "Why, he wasn't even interested in politics."

"Well, he *was* a member of the Magus," said Lady Glen. "And he left all his books to his club. What else am I to believe?"

"If he was a wizard," said Lady Fitzaskerly, "he was a decidedly odd one."

"Perhaps he wasn't, then," Lady Glen said. "Wizards like nothing better than talking, and they seldom travel. Well, how could they? Sir Alvord barely said a word in company, and he was forever in some foreign land or another."

"Be that as it may," said Madam Max. "If he was a wizard, it is foolhardy at best for Lady Basingstoke to keep his ring if he wished it to go otherwise."

"No doubt," said Lady Fitzaskerly dryly. "But I knew Margaret Kennedy at school. She was the sort of girl who *always* ate too many cream buns, even though she was invariably sick after."

So Mrs. Mildmay had her partisans among the most highly placed persons in the land—a fact that might have brought her some comfort as she sat listening to her brother's lawyer set forth his dilemma in her drawing room. Mr. Chess was a man of substance, silver-haired and solid as an Irish hound, with something of a hound's roughness of coat and honesty of spirit, which had brought him to confess to Mrs. Mildmay that he had misplaced the most recent codicil to her brother's will.

"It was the day he was taken ill, you know, or perhaps a day or two before that. He came by my chambers without the least notice, and would have it drawn up then and there and witnessed by two clerks. It described the ring most particularly—'The stone called the Parwat

Ruby, and the Ring in which it is set, the bezel two Wings of gold tapering into the Shank'—and gave it to you for your lifetime and to your son Wilson on your death, with the testator's recommendation that neither ring nor stone be allowed to pass out of the hands of his descendants. He insisted on the exact wording."

"And you said that the codicil was not in the document box when you removed the will to read it?"

"The document box was quite empty, Mrs. Mildmay, save for the will itself, some few papers pertaining to his investments, and a quantity of fine dust. Nevertheless, knowing his wishes in the matter, I did not think it wise to drop the matter without consulting with Lady Basingstoke."

"And Lady Basingstoke laughed in your face," said Mrs. Mildmay.

"I only wish she had done something so relatively predictable." Mr. Chess extracted his handkerchief from his pocket and wiped his forehead with it. "She heard me out quietly, then gave me to understand that the ring would have to be cut from her hand before she'd give it up. Furthermore, she impugned my memory, my competence as a lawyer, even my motives in coming to see her, and all in such a tone of voice as I hope never in my life to hear again."

"It was doubtless very rude of her," said Mrs. Mildmay soothingly.

"Rude!" Mr. Chess gave his neck a surreptitious dab. "She was most intemperate. If she were not very recently widowed, I would question her sanity."

"And the ring?"

"Unless the codicil should come to light, the ring is hers, along with all her husband's chattels and possessions not otherwise disposed of. We might file a case in Chancery on the basis of my recollection of the afternoon call, supported by affidavits from my two clerks who witnessed the document, but it would almost certainly cost more than the ring is worth, and success is by no means sure."

Mrs. Mildmay thought for a moment, than gave a decided nod. "I'll let it go, then. It's only a ring, after all. May she have joy of it, poor woman."

And there the matter would have rested had it not been for Lady Basingstoke herself, who, some two weeks after her husband's death, wrote to Caroline Mildmay requiring her attendance in Grovesnor Square. *You know I would come to you if I might,* she wrote, *but I am grown so ill that I cannot stir a foot abroad.*

"You shouldn't go," said Mr. Mildmay when his wife showed him Lady Basingstoke's letter. "You owe her nothing and she'll only be unpleasant."

"I owe her kindness as my brother's widow, and if she is unpleasant, I need not prolong my visit."

Mr. Mildmay smiled knowingly upon his wife. "I know how it is, Caroline. You're eaten up with curiosity over what she could have to say to you. Wild horses would not keep you from her, were she five times worse than she is."

"I don't expect to find her so ill as all that," said Mrs. Mildmay provokingly. But she did not deny her husband's allegation, nor, in good conscience, could she. Indeed, she did not think Lady Basingstoke likely to be ill at all. But when she was shown into the parlor where Lady Basingstoke was laid down upon a sofa with a blanket over her feet, Mrs. Mildmay observed that she looked withered and drawn, with the bones of her cheeks staring out through her skin and great dark smudges beneath her eyes, which seemed to have retreated under her brows. The Parwat Ruby glowed like a live coal on her hand.

She was attended by a dark-skinned person in a white turban, who was introduced to Mrs. Mildmay as Mr. Ahmed, an Arab gentleman learned in the study of medicine and the arcane arts.

"Mr. Ahmed has been invaluable to me," said Lady Basingstoke, and held out her hand, which he kissed with great grace; though it seemed to Mrs. Mildmay, looking on with some disgust, that the salute was bestowed rather upon the Parwat Ruby than on the gaunt hand that bore it. "It is at his suggestion, in fact, that I called you here, Caroline. You know, of course, that dear Alvord was a great wizard?"

Mrs. Mildmay drew off her gloves to cover her confusion. "A wizard, Margaret?"

"I think I spoke clearly. Are you going to pretend that you don't believe in wizards when the country is ruled by them? Why, half the members of the House of Lords, two-thirds of the Cabinet, and the Prime Minister himself are members of the Magus!"

"I hardly know what I do believe, Margaret."

"There was never a wizard living as powerful as Alvord, and it was all the ruby, Caroline, the ruby."

"The ruby?" Mrs. Mildmay faltered, convinced that Lady Basingstoke's complaint was more serious than a mere perturbation of the spirit. Alvord a wizard! What would the woman say next?

Lady Basingstoke plucked angrily at the fringe of her shawl. "Why do you mock me, Caroline? You must know what I mean. Alvord must have spoken to you. Why else would he have called on you so soon before he fell ill?"

"I assure you, Margaret, that Alvord told me nothing. Only . . ."

Lady Basingstoke leaned forward, a horrid avidity suffusing her countenance. "Only what, dear Caroline? It is of the utmost importance that you tell me every word."

"I'm afraid it must cause you some distress."

The Arab gentleman added his voice to Lady Basingstoke's, and reluctantly Mrs. Mildmay recounted her conversation with Sir Alvord substantially as it has been recorded here, noting Lady Basingstoke's almost comical expression of malicious triumph when Caroline mentioned her brother's intention to change his will. When she had made an end, Lady Basingstoke turned to the Arab gentleman and burst out, "Is there anything there, Ahmed? Is she telling the truth?"

"As to that, gracious lady, I cannot say without subjecting the lady to certain tests."

He smiled beguilingly at Mrs. Mildmay as he spoke, as if proposing a rare treat. Mrs. Mildmay was not to be beguiled. "Tests!" she exclaimed. "Are you both mad?"

Both Lady Basingstoke and the Arab gentleman ignored her. "Your husband certainly meant his sister to have the ring, lady, and I do not think he told her why."

"Well, I think he did. I think he told her all about it, and she's come here to frighten me out of it. Well, I won't frighten, do you hear? I won't frighten and I won't give up the Parwat Ruby. It's going to make me great, isn't it, Ahmed? Greater than Mr. Gresham, greater than the Queen herself, and once I learn its secret, the first thing I shall do is destroy *you*, Caroline Mildmay!"

With every word of this extraordinary speech, Lady Basingstoke's voice rose, until at last she was all but screaming at her hapless sister-in-law, at the same time rising from her sofa and menacing her with such energy that Mrs. Mildmay thought it best to take her leave.

After such an interview, Mrs. Mildmay did not, of course, call in Grosvenor Place again. Nor did she ever tell a soul, saving only her husband, what had passed between her and her sister-in-law. She did, however, hear what the world had to say concerning Lady Basingstoke's subsequent behavior. For that lady, far from hiding herself in the seclusion expected of a widow, began to go abroad in the world.

"I saw her in Hyde Park, my dear, *astride* her horse, if you please. I would not have credited it had I not seen it with my own eyes. And looking quite brown and dried-up, for all the world like a farm wife, and so hideously plain you'd think that horrid Darwin justified in declaring us all the grandchildren of apes."

"Lady Glencora!" Madam Max admonished her, with a glance at Mrs. Mildmay.

Lady Glencora was at once contrite. "Oh, Mrs. Mildmay, I *beg* your pardon to speak so of a close connection, but surely the woman is not mistress of herself, to be riding astride in the company of a gentleman in a turban."

"Mr. Ahmed," murmured Mrs. Mildmay.

"He might be the Grand Cham of Arabia if he chose; it still wouldn't be proper. And it is common knowledge that her servants have left her without notice, and Lizzie Berry says her new boot boy tells such blood-curdling stories of Lady Basingstoke's household that the servants all suffer from nightmares."

Feeling Lady Glencora's curious eyes upon her, Mrs. Mildmay schooled her features to gentle dismay. "How difficult for Lady Berry," was all she said, but her heart burned within her, and she thought of Lady Basingstoke's astonishing remark, that England was governed by wizards. Lady Glencora's husband, Plantagenet Palliser, was said to be performing miracles as Chancellor of the Exchecquer. Were they miracles indeed? Did Lady Glencora think she knew, or was she deriving amusement from her ignorance? Prey to melancholy reflections, Mrs. Mildmay brought her visit to an end as soon as she might do so without betraying the agitation the conversation had caused her, and went home again wishing that Alvord had seen fit to take her more fully into his confidence.

A month passed. The Season's round of balls and card parties was enlivened by stories of Lady Basingstoke's eccentricities, which grew wilder with each telling. Lady Basingstoke had thrown scones at the waiter at Liberty's Tea Room; Lady Basingstoke had snatched a fruit woman's basket of apples and run away with it; Lady Basingstoke had bitten a policeman on the arm. Mrs. Mildmay was privately mortified by her sister-in-law's behavior, and took full advantage of her own state of mourning to regret all invitations that might bring her into Lady Basingstoke's erratic orbit. But she could not avoid the morning calls of ladies eager to commiserate and analyze, nor the occasional glimpse of her brother's widow, gaunt, unkempt, and draped in black, dragging on Mr. Ahmed's arm as if it were all that kept her upright.

Then, as suddenly as she'd emerged, Lady Basingstoke disappeared once again into Grovesnor Place. Society looked elsewhere for its amusement, and as the Season wore on, Mrs. Mildmay ventured to hope that she had heard the end of the matter. In mid-July, her hope was frustrated by Mr. Chess, who called upon her once again, this time accompanied by one of his clerks.

"I don't know how sufficiently to beg your pardon," Mr. Chess told her, his honest hound's eyes dark with distress.

"It wasn't Mr. Chess's fault, madam," his clerk said. "It was all mine. If you intend to go to law with someone, it'll have to be me, and I won't contest the charge, indeed I won't."

"Let us have no talk of going to law," said Mrs. Mildmay. "Please, tell me what has happened."

And so the unhappy story came out. Apparently, the afternoon of the day upon which Sir Alvord had changed his will, he had returned to Mr. Chess's chambers and left in the possession of the clerk (whose name was Mr. Rattler) a thick packet, with instructions that it be conveyed to Mrs. Mildmay as soon as possible.

"But it *wasn't* possible, not if it were ever so, not with the Queen vs. Phineas Finn coming up to trial, and me run clear off my feet until ten of the clock. So I took it home so as to be sure and deliver it next morning on my way to chambers, and my old mother was taken ill in the night, and that's the last I thought of the packet until I was sorting through things yesterday—for she died of her illness, I grieve to say, and the house is to be sold—and found it, dropped behind the boot rack."

The poor man looked so close to tears that Mrs. Mildmay was moved to give him her full forgiveness. "I have the packet in my hand now, after all, and we must hope that there's not too much harm done. Why don't you wait in the library while I read it, Mr. Chess, in case there is something in it I don't understand?"

"Certainly, Mrs. Mildmay," said Mr. Chess, and withdrew, herding the wretched clerk before him.

Now, if the reader be tempted, like Mrs. Mildmay, to pity Mr. Rattler, the reader may put his mind at ease. Mr. Rattler, less honest than provident, was not to be pitied; for upon discovering Sir Alvord's packet behind the boot rack, he had lifted its seal with the aid of a heated knife, read it through, whistled thoughtfully, and immediately set himself to copy it all over. It was a long document, and the task took him the better part of the night, but his labor was well paid, for he sold the copy to one of the more sensational papers for a sum sufficient to buy passage to America, where we may only hope he found honest employment. Mr. Rattler's industry, in the meantime, has relieved the present writer of reproducing the whole text of Sir Alvord's letter to his sister, as the document was published in full soon after the Grovesnor Place affair became public, and may be read by anyone who cares to ask for the July _____ edition of *The People's Banner*.

In brief, the letter recounted how, not long after his marriage to Margaret Kennedy, Sir Alvord Basingstoke had taken himself off to Ceylon, where he had wandered, lost in impenetrable forests, for nearly two years. His adventures in this period were numerous, but in the letter, he restricted himself to the month he spent with a tribe of savages who worshipped an idol in the shape of a great ape carved of wood and inlaid with gold and precious stones.

"*Its teeth were pearls, perfectly matched, the largest I have ever seen, and it was crowned with beaten gold set, in the Eastern manner, with rough-cut sapphires, emeralds, and rubies. But its chiefest glory were its eyes, that were perfectly matched cabochon rubies of great size, each imprisoning a perfect, clear, bright star that gave the creature an air of malevolent intelligence. I chaffered with the king of those people, who was a wise and far-sighted woman, and brought her to understand that it would be much to her advantage to accept from me half the arms and ammunition I had brought with me, along with certain cantrips I had learned of a warrior-wizard in Katmandu. In exchange for all this, which would almost certainly ensure her victory over some two or three neighboring tribes, I would receive the left eye of the ape-god.*

"*The gift came hedged around with warnings and restrictions, the greater part of which I have been able to circumvent or neutralize. I could do little, however, with the fundamental nature of the stone, which is likely to manifest itself in the form of a dreadful curse. I am exempt from this curse, as are all persons related to me by blood. But anyone else who wears it upon his finger, be it the Queen of England or Mr. Gresham or His Grace the Archbishop of Canterbury, will most assuredly and inevitably regret it. If you do not feel equal to the role of caretaker, dear Caroline, or harbor any doubts as to the fitness of young Wilson to undertake this responsibility, I enjoin you to send to (mentioning the name and direction of a gentleman whose position in Society commands our complete discretion) and tell him how the land lies. He'll know what to do. You'll need to call upon him in any case, to initiate you and your boy into the uses and rituals of the stone.*"

In the course of reading this extraordinary document, Mrs. Mildmay was forced to ring for brandy, and when she had finished, sat for a few minutes with the sheets of her brother's narrative spread on her knees. Poor Alvord, she thought. And poor Margaret. She rang again for Mr. Chess and his clerk, and her hat and cloak, and her carriage to take them all to Grovesnor Place.

"For I'll certainly want you for witnesses or help, or both," she told them. "And there's not a moment to be lost, not that it probably isn't too late already."

When the carriage pulled up to Lady Basingstoke's house, all seemed as it should be, save that the steps clearly had not been swept nor the door brass polished in some time.

"There, you see?" said Mrs. Mildmay. "Something is dreadfully amiss. It is unlike Margaret not to have hired new servants."

"Perhaps she couldn't hire any," Mr. Chess suggested.

"Servants are always to be had in London," said Mrs. Mildmay, "times being hard as they are."

A distant crash within put an end to idle conversation and inspired Mr. Chess to try the door, which was locked. A thin, inhuman screech from an upper floor sent him backing hastily down the steps, drawing Mrs. Mildmay, protesting, by the arm. "This is a matter for the police, dear lady, or perhaps a mad doctor. Rattler, find a constable."

While Rattler was searching out a member of the constabulary, Mr. Chess suggested that some tale be agreed on to explain the necessity of breaking into the town residence of a respectable baronet's widow, but in the event, no explanation was demanded, for such a screeching and crashing greeted the constable's advent as to lend considerable weight to Mrs. Mildmay's plea that the door be forced at once.

With a blow of the constable's truncheon, the lock was broken. He set his broad shoulder to the door, and, with the help of Mr. Chess and Mr. Rattler, thrust it open upon a scene of chaos. The rugs had been tumbled about and smeared with filth. Furniture had been overturned, paintings ripped from the walls, draperies torn, and a display of native weapons cast down from the wall. The noise had ceased upon their entrance, and a deathly, listening silence brooded over the ruined hall.

Mrs. Mildmay was the first of the quartet to regain her presence of mind. She stepped forward to the foot of the stairs and called, "Margaret, are you there? It is Caroline Mildmay, with Mr. Chess and a constable. Answer us if you can."

At the sound of her voice, the noise began again, a wild gibbering and screeching like a soul in torment, and suddenly a figure appeared upon the gallery above the hall. Mrs. Mildmay at first supposed it to be Lady Basingstoke, rendered thin and stooped by illness, for it was wrapped in a voluminous, pale dressing gown. But then the figure tore off the gown, threw it down upon the pale faces turned up to it, and swung itself from the gallery high over their heads to the great central chandelier, where it crouched, chattering angrily.

"It's an ape," said Mr. Chess unnecessarily.

"And a bleedin' 'uge un," said the constable, "beggin' the lady's parding."

But Mrs. Mildmay hardly noticed, for she was examining the creature—which was indeed one of the great apes that make their homes in the remoter reaches of the East—with more dismay than fear. "Why, it's Margaret," she exclaimed. "I'd know that chin anywhere. Oh, Mr. Chess!"

"Pray calm yourself, Mrs. Mildmay. Mr. Rattler shall alert this rude fellow's superiors of our predicament so that he may have help in subduing the creature, after which we may search the house for news of Lady Basingstoke."

"But we *have* news of Lady Basingstoke, I tell you! Look at her!" Mrs. Mildmay indicated the ape in the chandelier, whereupon the creature burst into a frenzy of hooting and bounced furiously up and down.

"*Pray*, Mrs. Mildmay, don't agitate it, or you'll have it down on our heads. Perhaps you'd best step outside until it is disposed of. This is no place for a lady, madam. Let the official gentlemen do their jobs and we'll sort it all out later."

But Mrs. Mildmay would not have it so, not unless Mr. Chess were to carry her bodily from the house. They were still arguing the point when the ape gave an almost human scream of rage and leapt from the chandelier.

Its intention was clearly to land upon Mrs. Mildmay's head, which would certainly have snapped her neck, given the height of the chandelier and the weight of the ape. Fortunately, the constable, who had in the interval snatched a wicked-looking spear from the pile of weapons, cast it at the ape, catching it squarely in the chest. The ape screamed again and fell to the marble floor with a terrible thud.

In a moment, Mrs. Mildmay was kneeling beside it, careless of the spreading pool of blood, examining its leathery paws while Mr. Chess wrung his hands and begged her for heaven's sake to come away and leave the filthy thing to the authorities.

"Do be silent, Mr. Chess," said Mrs. Mildmay abstractedly. "I can't find the ring. We must find it—don't you see?—before it does further harm. I made sure it would be upon her finger, but it is not."

As she commenced gently to feel over the inert body, the ape groaned and opened its eyes. Mrs. Mildmay's hand flew to her mouth, and at this last extremity, she was at some trouble to stifle a scream. For the ape's right eye was gray and filled with pain and fear. And the ape's left eye—the ape's left eye was red as fire, smooth and clouded save for a clear star winking and sliding in its depths: the Parwat Ruby.

"Poor Margaret," said Mrs. Mildmay, and plucked the stone from the creature's head. As soon as the ruby was in her hand, the ape was an ape no more, but the corpse of an elderly woman with a spear in her breast.

As to the aftermath of this terrible story, there is little to say. Soon after the appearance of the ape, Mr. Rattler crept out the door to the offices of the sensational paper and thence to the shipping office. Mr. Chess and the constable together searched the house in Grovesnor Place. Of Mr. Ahmed, no trace was found, saving a quantity of bloody water in a copper hip-bath and some well-chewed bones in my lady's bedchamber. In the ruins of Sir Alvord's study, Mr. Chess discovered some papers that suggested that Lady Basingstoke had extracted the codicil from the document box in Mr. Chess' chambers by means into which he thought it best not to delve too deeply. He thought it likely, also, that Lady Basingstoke had been instrumental in her husband's death, an opinion shared by Mrs. Mildmay and her husband, when she told him the story. Yet all were agreed that Lady Basingstoke, having suffered the most extreme punishment for her crimes, should not go to her grave with the stigma of murder upon her name. There was a brief period when no London jeweler could sell any kind of ruby, even at discounted prices, and no fashionable gathering was complete without a thorough discussion of the curse, its composition, and effect. But then came August and grouse-shooting, with house parties in the country and cubbing to look forward to, and the nine-day's wonder came to an end.

As for the ruby itself, Mrs. Mildmay wore it on her finger. It was perhaps a coincidence that Mr. Mildmay's always lively interest in politics soon became more active, and that he successfully stood for the seat of the borough of Lessingham Parva for the Liberals. After he became Minister of Home Affairs, he introduced and forced through the House the famous Poor Law of 18__, which guaranteed employment to all able-bodied men and women, and a stipend for the old and helpless. In all his efforts, he was ably seconded by his wife, who became in her later years a great political hostess and promoter of young and idealistic Liberal MPs. After her husband's death, at an age when most women are thinking of retiring to the country, Mrs. Caroline Mildmay mounted an expedition to the impenetrable forests of Ceylon, from which journey neither she nor the Parwat Ruby ever returned.

GEOFFREY BROCK

Odysseus Old

Geoffrey Brock's poems have appeared in New England Review, Southern Review, Gettysburg Review, *and other journals. He received the 1998 Raiziss/de Palchi Translation Fellowship from the Academy of American Poets for his work on Cesare Pavese's poetry. He lives in Kansas.*

The beautiful poem that follows (reprinted from the Autumn 1999 issue of The Hudson Review) *is based on the magical adventures of Odysseus, but takes place long after the events in Homer's great epic are over.*

—T. W.

In darker hours, I try recalling why
I left her. Gazing into wine, perhaps,
or at a girl, I'll call back that lost island

of permanent sun, that woman immune to the passage
of all that passes. Memory's a ragged sail,
and years have faded to a wash of gasping

fascination: long months mapping the pale
shores of her skin, the smooth peninsulas,
the inlets; then the roads into her frailer

interior. Calypso frail? She was.
When told she had to let me go, such tears!
But loss couldn't mean for her what it does

for us, I'd thought. How vain! And how sincere
my vanity! I was bored, and blessed or cursed
to know Penelope still waited here.

Such faithfulness: ambrosia-sweet at first,
maddening later on. Wasn't she human?
Didn't lack of water make her thirsty?

And am I so weak, who float through this dry room
nightly, dreaming water? If offered again—
but just what was I offered? And by whom?

No matter. This one offers all a mortal can
and more, and still this glooming. For how should I,
who once was envied by every Ithacan,

who have known with naked ears the song of sirens,
and who now am neither sung to by beauty nor envied,
be glad? I chose this, chose to slowly die.

And chose the woman sleeping by that window,
her gray hair silvering in the moon's weak light.
Her eyes flicker beneath their lids. Her fingers

twitch and clutch, and with some inward sight
she weaves and unweaves me, her days, this night.

KENT MEYERS

The Smell of the Deer

Kent Meyers is the author of one novel, The River Warren, *a book of essays,* The Witness of Combines, *and short fiction published in* The Georgia Review, The Southern Review, Crazy Horse, *and* Best of the West. *Meyers has won the Minnesota Book Award and the Friends of American Writers Award, and fellowships from National Endowment for the Arts and the South Dakota Arts Council. He lives in Spearfish, South Dakota, with his wife and children.*

The following tale is drawn from Meyers's recent story collection, Light in the Crossing. *It is a subtly fantastic tale, reworking the myth of Artemis and Actaeon.*

—T. W.

Before her death, Sara Sinclair became the most bitter woman in this town, so like a nail in the way she regarded the world that she berated the boys who shoveled her walk in the winter for the small patches of snow they missed, accused them of preying on old women, and refused to pay them what she'd agreed to, poking a few musty bills into their palms before shooing them away. The cowed boys retreated up the sidewalk with their scoop shovels never to return, so that in the worst blizzards, snow piled up around Sara's house at the edge of town until her gray shingles appeared as a dirty extension of the drifts. Once or twice some men who'd hunted with her husband, Jerrod, tunneled their way to her door but upon knocking were met by a woman so fierce and thankless, so dried of all human grace, that she might have been the bones and eyes of an owl.

Some of us remembered Sara as a sweet girl who wore dandelion-chain necklaces and flowers in her hair. We commented on how age changes people. Or marriage does. Jerrod Sinclair came from a strange family, and in the years before he died, he haunted the town park, half drunk by midafternoon, with a voice like the quaver of a stick against a window. He approached young mothers watching their children, lovers holding hands, evening walkers escaping family, and he pinned them down, if he could, with stories of what he'd done in the river valley when he was younger and the valley was wilder.

We never understood why Sara married him, and we never expected the marriage to last. When it did until death, we nevertheless observed that Sara's bitterness and isolation were the end result of marriage to a man who cared for hunting, and later for alcohol, more than he cared for his wife. Satisfied with this easy truth, we left Sara in her snow-muffled house, where she would have been completely alone had it not been for Diane Bourdeaux.

Diane appeared in town one day with her two dogs, the strangest-looking mongrels any of us had ever seen, hungry, lean, orange-gray, looking like some mad mix of greyhound and pit bull—dogs that, though invariably placid, looked like they would enjoy only one thing more than running prey down, and that would be tearing it apart once they caught it. Diane herself was ageless, elegant and earthy both. Her name wasn't German or Scandinavian, and no one knew where she came from. Some said she'd moved to Cloten to work in the gambling hall the Indians had opened in Graniteville, but this was speculation. With her black hair and light brown eyes, her cinnamon skin that even in the winter shone burnished and coppery, and her laugh like sudden bells, she moved among the gullpale folks of Cloten like a mythical bird lost in migration.

It was apparently pure accident that brought her to be Sara Sinclair's caretaker. They met in Aisle 3, Breads and Cereals, of the Red Owl on Diane's first day in town—or at least her first day in the Red Owl. Kenny Christianson, the Red Owl's owner, noticed her pass by the meat counter and decided right then he needed to check inventory. He says she was standing in the middle of Aisle 3 when Sara—then only a few weeks into her widowhood—pushed her cart toward her. Diane, her back to Sara, didn't notice Sara attempt to squeeze through the narrowed aisle next to the cereal boxes and then reach out to move Diane's cart aside.

When Sara touched it, however, the cart lurched around on a wild wheel, transforming itself from a peaceful carrier of groceries into a vicious wire dog. Fluorescent light gleaming off its frame, it attacked the cereal boxes, boring into the shelf with such force that it surprised even Kenny, who knew more about the nature of grocery carts than anyone in Cloten. The cart rammed the shelf with its blunt nose, swept through a good four feet of boxes, then danced to the other side of the aisle, bobbing like a boxer on its uneven wheels, and butted with the force of a battering ram the shelves stacked with Wonder Bread.

The aisle collapsed as if a natural force had hit it. There was a single moment of silence after the last cornflakes box crashed to the tile. Then Diane, unstartled, turned. Her heel scraped the tile. Light glanced off her cheekbone, and Kenny saw her face, stern as a rock, swing around, saw Sara's shoulders collapse under the pitiless eyes, micalike in the grocery-store light, that found her.

But then Diane laughed. None of us had ever heard anything like it in Cloten, though in the few years that Diane stayed with us, we all became familiar with the sound. It was a laugh so infectious, like the music of meadowlarks, under pressure to be happy, that Kenny, owner of the smashed bread, laughed too, and so did the checkers at the front of the store, without knowing what had happened.

The only one in the store not laughing was Sara. We would later say that this was the first sign of her descent into who she became. She gazed at Diane's face for a moment, then turned away, her own face a face of ash. She pushed her cart through the chaos of cereal and past Kenny as if it were a four-legged cane for a cripple, and her eyes, Kenny says, had the hammered look that all of us eventually noticed.

Yet from this inauspicious beginning, Diane became the single person in Cloten who could deal with Sara. Perhaps when she learned of Sara's widowhood she felt guilty for laughing. She visited Sara once— to apologize, we assumed—then visited her again, then again, bringing baskets of fruit and cheese. Neighbors heard Sara shouting, rebuffing Diane's attempts at reconciliation, demanding that Diane "leave me alone!" Anyone else in town—much to our discredit—would have acceded to the demand, but Diane persisted in her friendliness, until finally she was Sara's sole companion. And, as Sara grew more isolated, Diane became her only contact with the outside world, even doing her grocery shopping for her.

We realized just how mysteriously attached Diane had become to Sara when she brought the single pup born of the mating of her dogs into the Red Owl and announced that she was giving it to Sara. "Maybe it'll cheer her up," she said, "having a puppy to take care of." It melted some hearts, though others thought there was something imperious in the way she announced it.

Sara—who had loved all animals when she was a teenager, feeding stray cats and dogs with scraps off her own plate—declaimed more loudly against the pup than against anything else the neighbors could report of her muffled shouts from inside the house including, "Take the bastard away!" and "I don't want the sonofabitch!" Diane left the pup nevertheless.

All of this would mean nothing if it weren't for the unusual way Sara died—so unusual that it made us reassess Jerrod's drunken ramblings. The Sinclairs were one of the oldest families in Cloten. The story goes that when old James Cloten first came to the place that would bear his name, the Sinclairs were already there, as distrustful and secretive as the native animals, and friends only with the Indians.

Jerrod's great-grandfather virtually lived in the river valley, hiking across country to his farm only to sleep with his wife and look in on the resultant children, three sons who took over the farm—such as it was—when he died, and who, like their father, lived more in the valley than in the rundown house guarding its weedy acres. While around the Sinclairs the land began to sprout crops, rich beyond even the immigrants' expectations, the Sinclairs' farm remained a patch of native prairie and scrubby corn. The Germans fought the weeds with a bulldog single-mindedness, and the Scandinavians hunched their huge shoulders to their implements with a strength that rivaled their horses'—but on the Sinclairs' farm the old land held sway, their efforts to subdue it only a nod to convention so that they could return to the mosquito-infested woods.

Into this family Jerrod's father and then Jerrod himself were born. But even the Sinclairs couldn't hold off progress forever. Without their noticing, their land increased in value, borrowing from the neighbors' efforts. Jerrod's father came home from the river one day to find his wife—a thin woman, gray as a dusty leaf—holding an envelope that turned out to be a tax notice asking for more money than the farm had netted that year. Jerrod's father cursed the system and cast himself in the role of savior of the land, ranting that his farm contained the last virgin prairie in the entire county.

However, taxes don't concern themselves with the preservation of species. He had no choice but to sell in order to pay the bill. Big Jim Anderson—one of a long line of Big Jims, each owning more land than his father—bought the Sinclair farm, bulldozed the ratty house and the tired trees where fox and pheasant escaped winter storms, and loosed his equipment upon it, transforming the virgin prairie into fields to do the work that, in Big Jim's eyes, land was meant to do.

Jerrod's father, rather than escaping to the river as we expected, escaped to the bottle, and became a bar regular. His wife divorced him and moved to Clear River, where she married a man who provided her with the luxuries she'd never had. She became obese beyond description, happily settling her great jellylike mass into the wheelchair with which her devoted husband transported her to church. She sighed, content to be pushed up the quiet streets and to remember the bare shack she'd once occupied alone, waiting by the single window for her husband to appear, walking through the wildflowers. Remembering this, she would reach back and place her palm on the sweating hand of her new husband and deliberately jiggle her flesh whenever the wheelchair bumped over a crack, in order to feel the extent of her existence, the flesh she occupied like a queen a kingdom, expanding inexorably, nibbling away at her new husband's resources, taking them into herself.

Then one day she died—perfectly alive, content, and self-satisfied when she left the house, and perfectly dead when she arrived at church, with so little change in her appearance that the four men who helped carry the wheelchair up the church steps stooped over her and grunted in their usual way, speaking lightly about the weather with her husband in order to hide their guilt at how they truly felt about this, their selfless and Christian duty to a God who accepted all weaknesses.

They got her up the sixteen cement steps and to the front pew before one of them detected something he later described as "congealed" about her and tactlessly asked one of his companions, "How do we know she's alive?"—a comment her husband overheard and then remembered she hadn't reached back to touch his hand on the walk to church. He threw himself onto her stupendous bosom, soaking her dress with his tears.

Jerrod, having lost his mother to contentment and his father to bitterness, did what everyone expected a Sinclair to do: he took even more deeply to the woods. Abandoning the shotguns and rifles of his forebears, he killed noiselessly, with a bow, and he treated fence lines—for the valley was just then beginning to be domesticated—as part of the natural world, no more firm in their denial of access than a swamp, which he waded, or the river, which he swam. Landowners could no more prove his presence on their land than they could prove the bobcats and cougar that they also suspected, and soon sign of Jerrod Sinclair became as much a part of local wildlife lore as sign of those elusive cats.

For the few supplies he needed beyond venison and fish, he did carpentry, which he'd been doing even as a teenager, since his father's dissipating when he'd first began living in Ivy Bercovitch's basement. Ivy, a German widow, was Cloten's first landlady. Determined not to be dependent on anyone she turned her cramped basement into an apartment, convinced beyond any reasonable hope that the creation of a rental would create a renter—which, in the small, miraculous way of such things, it did.

Ivy pinned her remaining worries and hopes on Jerrod. When he was gone to the woods, as he usually was, she worried that he might be attacked by wild animals, and when he was in her basement, she worried about his social life and hoped he would marry and have children who would come up the basement steps, surrogates for the grandchildren Ivy'd never had. When Jerrod finally did marrry, however, he disappointed Ivy by moving out of the basement and into a house he built at the edge of town, where Sara kept the shades drawn all day and night.

Later in his life, after he, like his father, had taken to alcohol he would sneak up on people in the park, approaching them as silently as he must have once approached other prey, and if they didn't start and run, he would begin telling them stories—or rather, we realized later, perhaps a single story heard in bits and pieces by various people. He would speak in a voice so distant and low that the stories he told seemed distant too, as untouchable as the world spoken by high, gabbling geese.

Because no one heard the entire story—everyone eager to escape Jerrod's mosquito-insistent voice—it seeped into the town, slow as ice forming at the beginning of winter, built privately and incrementally. It was retold only in quiet places, and never in groups: two men on a boat waiting for a channel cat to find the three-inch sucker dangling in the current below; two lovers watching the moon rise over the river bluffs, whispering the story one of them has heard, a prelude to greater intimacy.

Through such quiet transmission, everyone in Cloten learned the story, but because the moment of hearing it was marked by trust and vulnerability, everyone thought that only two others knew—the person from whom one had heard it, always assumed to have heard it from Jerrod himself, and the one to whom one told it. It was only after Sara's bizarre death that someone flushed the story into the open by asking whether there might be a connection between the two things, death and story.

We all looked at one another then and asked, "You too? You too?" In the cafes, the bars, on church steps after services, we talked of little else, unable to quite believe that everyone knew Jerrod's story. It was as if the whole town woke from a long dream of secrecy, from which we are still waking.

It begins with rain. He'd seen six grown men struggle to lift his mother's casket, and he'd noted, with an eye that would make him the most sought-after carpenter in Cloten, the reinforcing bands that kept her from bursting through the bottom. He left the funeral reception early, put on his hunting clothes, and went to a willow over the river, to stand in a fork within the rain and falling leaves. The river was covered with leaves—brittle, cupped hands, curled inward, holding nothing. He stood for hours, his heart colder than the rain, like a turtle's heart sinking into mud at the bottom of the river.

He grew so still, he said, that he felt as his mother must have felt in that casket, an infinitude of heaviness sinking down. Rain smacked against his camouflaged rainsuit. And then, drifting through the rain came the scents of faraway deer, a buck and three does, like ribbons woven through the trees.

The scent was so strong and distinct that he could picture the animals circling each other as they grazed. He lifted his face to the sky and let the rain fall into it, then climbed down from the tree and set off through the rigid, dead weeds, under the thick hardwood canopy. Night was settling under the trees, filling the cavities alongside trunks. It was too dark for anyone with a conscience to shoot, but he went on anyway, the scent taking him away from the river. He simply wanted to see deer, to watch them graze as night fell: their spindle legs, their nostrils flaring.

For a while he lost the scent, the ribbons sheared by a shifting wind. He waited for the breeze to return, and he remembered the carpentry tools he'd abandoned in Gene Svenson's house, walking out between pounding one nail and the next when Gene had come to him with news of his mother's death. But when the scent returned, he went on.

Then he peered into a triangular clearing at trampled grass where deer had moved and fed. Rain streaked the empty light against a background of gray trees. He walked into the clearing and saw with his practiced eye that deer had recently departed. Grass was dragged into long lines by their hooves. He knelt and touched a hoofprint, the abrupt crescent of it in the earth, then looked around at the hollowness that remains when animals have been frightened off, and thought of bobcat or lion, felt his own back, exposed and bent. But he didn't rise.

The rain turned to snow. Squatting, Jerrod let his eyes drift upward against the descending flakes. His spine felt bowed and taut, as if one touch of a claw would rupture it and his body would fly like a broken spring across the clearing. His eyes sought yellow eyes, a furred and whiskered face. He focused on a fork in a tree where something seemed unnecessary, a concentration of foliage or an outgrowth of bark. He stared until he realized he was looking into a pair of eyes that stared back at him.

Jerrod should have been startled. He noticed the brownness of the eyes first, and then the curled lashes and the brows shaped and arched. The rest of the face faded into the trees. He should have been startled, but he'd been expecting yellow eyes with slits that regarded him as prey, and these brown eyes, though unexpected, were merely appraising.

Without rising, he said, "You scared them away."

The eyes blinked.

"You scared them away," he repeated.

Lips formed. "You saw me," they said.

"Why'd you scare them away?"

"How did you see me?"

"I looked," he said tersely.

He saw a smile and then the tip of a tongue behind white teeth. Only then was he startled.

"I didn't want you to shoot," she said, finally answering.

Though it was freezing in the clearing, the backs of his hands felt warm.

"I wasn't going to shoot."

She disappeared for a moment; then she was on the ground, moving over the damp grass. She stopped in front of him.

"Men usually shoot."

Jerrod had never met a woman bow-hunting before. He glanced at the bow she carried lightly in her left hand, an ancient thing. He'd never seen camouflage like hers, a pattern that made her face seem without surface, made it, even close up, part of the background. He listened for the sound of someone else in the woods, a man who accompanied her, but the falling snow made the only sound.

She knew what he was thinking. "No," she said. "I'm quite alone."

It seemed a brazen statement. Too confident. A challenge. He was twenty years old. Too young to think of himself as a dangerous man. Too young, almost, to think of himself as a man. Yet he suddenly felt dangerous. Or—he wasn't sure—in danger. To keep the thoughts at bay, he asked, "What are you doing here?"

A shadow of irritation passed over her face. "What are you?"

"Of course. Yes." What would anybody be doing but hunting? "Have you seen many deer?"

She gazed at him, her eyes brown as oak leaves before they fall. He turned from her gaze to the falling snowlines, the dripping trees, the closing dark—but in spite of his looking away, it seemed to him that the death of his mother, and his father's desertion, and the orphaning off of his land had all been for this: that he would climb the willow and smell the deer and come to meet her and want her, this woman, here in the danger of snow.

"How did you know there were deer here?" she asked.

"I smelled them. A buck and three does."

He had the courage to meet her eyes again. She smiled. Her teeth were white as the snow that now formed a layer over the grass and seemed to be the sole source of remaining light. She laid her bow on the ground and rose and took his head in her hands. For a moment he thought to jerk away like a wild animal, but her lips touched his, and he smelled the sweet grass she had chewed to scent and disguise her breath.

So it is said.

They lay next to each other, on their clothes. Jerrod stared upward into a darkness so deep he couldn't see the snow falling onto his face and body. Next to him the woman lay still, her skin unnaturally warm against his. He wondered if he were in a delirium of winter, dreaming of her heat.

Her joints slid past each other as she rose. He groped for his clothes and was surprised to smell the four deer again in the woods outside the clearing, standing under the dark trees damphaired, a smell like old, wet paper. Then her sweet smell rose out of the scent of the deer. He opened his arms. She stepped into them. Shivering, he pulled her in.

"I've got to go now," she said.

"I'll come with you." He had no past to return to.

"No."

"Why not?"

He thought that his reasons were hers, that she too had no past, that their lovemaking had given them the same future.

"Sweet boy," she said. In all versions of the story, through whichever channel it flowed, these words are the same.

Sweet boy.

He couldn't imagine any man containing her, any more than he was able to contain her as she slipped from his arms and he felt cold air fill the space next to his skin. Yet he couldn't imagine why she would leave him if not to preserve a past, and he was struck by jealousy for the man who wasn't here. He stepped toward her but couldn't find her.

"Is there someone else?" he called, groping for her. "Will I see you again?"

"It all depends." Her voice came from a distance, but he didn't know which question she answered, if she answered one at all.

His total disappearance into the woods was hardly noticed. Gene Sven-son complained about his unfinished wall, while his wife Ruthie berated him for hiring a Sinclair. And Ivy Bercovitch heard in her house the same silence she'd heard after her husband died, and she told her plants that her tenant had fallen hard, either for a woman or for the bottle—those quiet types fell hard either way. Unable to decide which it was, Ivy prayed prayers of thanks in the morning for the children who might soon grace her upstairs rooms, and in the evenings, having fretted all day, she prayed that Jerrod might be delivered from the amber curse.

The weather warmed again, the early snow melted, and the woods glowed with orange light. Beginning always in the willow along the river, Jerrod made his way through the burdock and preacher's lice and wild hemp to the clearing. He carried his bow but never shot. If he saw deer on the trails that wound like faint threads through the undergrowth, he watched them go by.

She was always waiting for him, concealed next to a trunk, or higher up where the branches thinned and multiplied. It was always her eyes that he saw first. She taught him all the ways of love, her knowledge greater than his imagination, until the clearing grass was pressed flat, like a deer's bedding area. She told him that she had watched countless men go by who had never seen her, men who stared right at her and didn't see, men who smoked tobacco within two feet and gazed through their own cloud at her face and didn't see. Jerrod didn't care if she was lying or telling the truth; he had seen her, and she was his.

One day he opened his eyes as they were making love and found the buck and does grazing around them, unperturbed. The sight stilled and awed him, their bodies joined and the animals accepting them, content to graze. "Look," he exclaimed.

And the whole town of Cloten, in different places and situations—some yearning, some horrified; some disbelieving, some awed; some drunk, some sober; some staring into darkness, some staring into light; but all of them in pairs: man and woman, adult and adolescent, friend and friend—all of them look, and willfully or in spite of their will, see what Jerrod wishes his lover to see: the four deer accepting their lovemaking.

He reached out to touch her face, from which she had never removed her camouflage. He had given up ever seeing her face for the same reason he'd given up knowing her name—because he thought she protected another life outside the woods, something domestic and calm. But now she kissed his palm as he ran it over her cheek. Then she stood and went to her quiver, opened a pouch and took out a small cloth. She brought this and her canteen back to him and knelt in front of him and poured water on the cloth and held it out.

He touched her face with it. A drop of water rolled down her cheek.

He washed the camouflage off. It was, he said, the tenderest thing he'd ever done, the two of them kneeling together, her nostrils dilated as she breathed with shut eyes. The camouflage streaked at first, the colors mixing to form muddy gray lines that ran down her neck, streaked her shoulders and breasts. Jerrod rinsed the cloth in the water from the canteen, wiped the streaks off. He cleaned her brow, washed her cheekbones.

Without opening her eyes, she said, "You've seen my face now."

"Yes," he said. "You're beautiful."

"I am," she said—as if beauty, for her, were fact.

The long Indian summer ended. She stood in his arms one evening, both of them wrapped in the same blanket.

"There'll be snow in the morning," she said. "Staying snow."

"How do you know?"

"This is the last evening."

"The last evening for what?"

"We can't come here in the winter."

"We'll meet in town somewhere."

"That's not possible. We have to wait until spring."

He pled with her. Her eyes turned hard. She walked away from his pleading into the woods, promising impatiently to return in the spring, when the snow had melted. He stood in the clearing, forbidden to follow her while dry trees clattered about him. He felt her absence turn in his chest like tumbling and shattered glass.

He showed up at Gene Svenson's the next day and in a grim precision of loss, picked up the hammer where he'd left it lying, and the eight-penny nail he'd dropped back into his pouch, and with one blow drove the nail below the surface of a two-by-four. Working nonstop like this for thirty-six hours, he finished the entire remodeling Gene and Ruthie had asked for. After the first twelve hours, Ruthie complained, and Gene went to Jerrod and suggested that maybe he'd think of quitting—beings as how they'd waited this long for the room, there wasn't so much urgency to all of a sudden finish it. Jerrod turned and looked at Gene. Periodically throughout the night Gene tried to tell Ruthie about that look, both of them listening to the incessant hammer and whining saw.

"It was like a lake looks just after the ice's melted—but like it had ideas to drown you, Ruthie. You wouldn't argue with that, would you?"

"I would if it was in my house."

But Gene, having actually seen the look he couldn't describe, ignored Ruthie's implication of cowardice.

"It ain't, Ruthie," he said. "Not your house again till he's finished and gone."

When he had finished and gone, Jerrod returned to the basement apartment. Ivy, staring through the window, said a prayer of thanks. For a few months, as winter deepened and snow swept across the frozen fields, filling the valley with snowdrifts five and six feet deep, Jerrod entombed himself in Ivy's basement. No one saw him except for the checkers at the Red Owl. Maude Grabow, an old woman now, says he looked like death warmed over, coming in sporadically for a few groceries, smelling of mildew and damp places.

Sara Jacobson was working in the Red Owl then, a sixteen-year-old girl too gentle, almost, for life. She wept when her father sold cattle, and she could hardly bring herself to touch the packets of meat wrapped in white paper that customers laid on her belt at the store. People with too many kittens or puppies, and too little fortitude, dropped them off near the Jacobson place. Sara found them and adopted them all, to her father's exasperation.

Why such a girl would be attracted to a Sinclair, hunters without qualm for generations, is a mystery. But Jerrod had the look of a lost puppy in the weeks before Sara spoke to him, and Maude Grabow believes Sara couldn't resist this look. She had to talk to him when he came through her line, had to reach out furtively and touch his hand when she took the few crumpled bills he held out, and meet his eyes and smile shyly.

And Jerrod?

There is only this in the various remnants of his story: one night, in the middle of a blizzard, he heard a tentative knock on the door at the top of the steps, and he went up, thinking that someone was looking for Ivy at the wrong door. He found Sara Jacobson there, capless, her hair spraying about her face in the wind, her cheeks flushed red, a denim barn coat pulled to her chest with crossed arms.

"I was on my way home," she said. "I saw you in the store again today, and I thought I'd see . . ."

Then the confidence dropped out of her voice, the casual lie shattered by the eyes that gazed at her, and the hand that floated up and took hers to lead her down the dark steps.

For three months they lived together in Ivy's basement. Sara's parents, though distraught, had long ago given up trying to influence their strange daughter, made willful by her own gentleness. And Ivy Bercovitch, though she fretted, couldn't bring herself to kick them out, her hopes that a child might be conceived overcoming her Lutheran morals.

Then, on a spring morning, Jerrod woke from a dream of the last snow in the woods melting, turning transparent in the sun. Sara lay in bed beside him, and he touched her shoulder, knowing that in spite of her love, he would betray her—though he had been surprised by the possessiveness in her otterlike body, the hunger there, as if she would save him by her fierce abandon.

When he woke her and told her he was going to the woods, she asked, "To hunt?"

He sensed a fight bubbling under the surface. He could see the set of her jaw, a stoniness about her mouth, her stubbornness hardening. She might demand he choose between hunting or her. He didn't have time for justification. Or for choice. Or truth. He shrugged her away.

"Just to go," he said.

The woods smelled of sap rising and animal droppings thawed. His heart loosened like the sweep of the river flooding open fields. He breathed deeply, forcing the basement air that he and Sara had shared out of his lungs. Dulled from the first winter he'd ever spent entirely in town, he didn't smell the deer until he was almost in the clearing. He entered it and found her among the deer—his lover, watching him, there as she'd promised.

He returned to the basement at one in the morning. Sara, alone and awake, heard his foot on the step. The door to the apartment opened silently. Jerrod had taken the door off its hinges and run a graphite pencil over the hinge posts, coloring them gray, and when he replaced the door, it was noiseless. But air moved on Sara's face, and she knew Jerrod stood in the doorway. He stepped into the room; she could see him in the few rays of light coming through the small window from a distant street lamp. Without rising or moving, she said, "Talk to me, Jerrod."

He walked, unnervingly silent, to the bed and sat down. He took her hand. Until he touched her, he might have been a wild animal stalking toward her in the dark.

"What is it?" she asked. "Talk to me."

"It's the river," he said. "The valley."

She waited for him to go on. He looked away, at the shadows cast by the thin light onto the back wall. Even though he was betraying her, he wanted her to know something of his passion. He thought of when it had all started, the rain in the willow, the river full of brittle hands.

"I've been going to the valley all my life," he said. "Before my mother died. Before we lost the farm. There's a willow by the river. If I sit in it, so still that squirrels think I'm part of the tree and run up and down me—if I stay that still, Sara, I'll smell deer."

Sara gasped. She jerked her hand to her mouth and half-rose from the bed, choking, her face working.

His heart sank, that she'd intuited the truth.

Then he realized she was gazing past him.

He turned. A shadow moved across the back wall as he did, in the sweep of a passing automobile's headlights, and something clattered on the street, and a wind from nowhere gusted hard against the house.

Sara pointed to the narrow, low window of the basement. But it was blank, a dark glass to the night.

"What? There's nothing there."

Her mouth worked. Her throat convulsed. When she met his eyes, his hair stood on end.

"There was," she whispered. "A deer. When you were talking. Looking at us."

In the morning he returned to the woods. Sara begged him to stay. He told her she might have seen a dog, and so what if it was a deer, they wander through town sometimes.

"No," she said. "It wasn't like that. It was watching *us*."

She told him she wouldn't be there when he returned. If he was going to live in the woods, she wouldn't wait for him. Even as he walked up the steps she was putting her things—a few of her father's shirts, some jeans—into a small bag, to return to her parents' farm.

In the clearing the woman waited, while the four deer that had grown accustomed to Jerrod grazed around her. Jerrod watched them carefully but saw nothing unfamiliar about them. They were wild animals living wild, alert only to the woods.

He reached for his lover.

She stepped away from him.

"You betrayed me." He'd never heard so cold a voice.

Yet he never knew, as would be repeated in all the story's manifestations through all the years, whether it was a statement or a question. It was as if, in telling the story again and again, he was trying to capture the precise intonation and so know what had been said.

"Betrayed you?"

"I asked you to wait a winter. That's all I asked."

He didn't deny Sara to her. He lost his one chance to deny Sara, and as he would say later—the only moral he ever offered—there is only one chance, ever, for denial, momentary as a whirlwind, and if missed, gone forever.

"I didn't know," he said desperately. "I didn't know what to think."

He stopped, sensing how little the words would clutch and hold what he intended them to say, how they would turn against themselves and speak what would seem a lie—that he'd betrayed her because he loved her, and in her absence didn't know what else to do. A truth—but if spoken it would seem cheap and empty.

"If I ever see your face again"—she hissed like fire consuming drought-killed grass—"I'll kill you. How dare you betray me? I showed you my face, and you think you can *betray* me?"

And she turned and was gone, swallowed by the woods.

For weeks he drifted through the valley, as he'd drifted after he lost the farm, and again after seeing his father glassy-eyed, who'd once been keen with a rifle. He felt as if his life were being taken from him piece by piece, even as he found and gathered it. We forgot that he existed, made of him a wild thing, the last denizen of the valley, more mythical than the cougar and bobcats that had become mere sign and spoor told of.

Only Ivy waited for him. And Sara—doing her daily routine at the checkout counter of the Red Owl, passing desultory items through her listless hands. Perhaps her waiting drew him back, and Ivy's ungrounded and ridiculous love. Or perhaps the intractable silence of the valley forced him back. In any case he appeared in the Red Owl one day and wandered through the store, plucking from the shelves a single can of coffee. He carried it to Sara's checkout lane and laid it on the belt. She didn't look up. She stated the price in a monotone.

"Sara," he said.

Her hand rested on the keys of the cash register. She stared at her fingers there.

"You want the woods, stay there," she said.

She looked small, drowning in a shirt too large for her. He reached out and placed a diamond ring on the coffee can. It was his mother's ring, from her marriage to his father. She had given it to him a few months before she died, the ring tiny in her overgrown hand.

"If we still had that farm," she'd said, "I'd never give you this. You'd be just like your father—haul a girl out there and forget her. But it's a curse gone from your life. Praise the Lord, son. You find a good girl, you give her that ring. Settle down in town. Make her happier than your father ever made me. Make that ring worth something."

Sara looked at the ring on the can of coffee.

"Why should I, Jerrod?"

He looked around as if he'd just discovered where he was and found it incomprehensible—the magazines on the rack, the paperback books, the candy, the large window, the great red owl with pointed ears and hollow, friendly eyes overseeing all the aisles from its vantage on the front wall.

"I don't know, Sara," he said. "If you need a reason, you probably shouldn't."

He tried to do as his mother had instructed. He built Sara the house at the edge of town, the way she wanted it built and better than she knew, with seams so tight and alignments so true that nothing ever loosened in it, no nail ever budged. It still stands, empty now but refusing to decay.

Jerrod applied himself to carpentry, deserted the woods. He grew rich in the way of small-town riches, nothing ostentatious but more than enough. But neither work nor possessions nor Sara nor the dogs and cats she still attracted and fed could drive the unknown woman from his mind or dreams. He tried to push her out with the nails he pounded, or excise her with the saws that snarled through the fibers of wood, but at night she resided in him, oak-leaf eyes that watched him sleep.

Three years after he married Sara, he woke one fall night from a dream where he had clearly seen the pattern of the camouflage the woman had worn to hide herself. He woke remembering each line and shading, each weave of color. He smelled rain outside and put on his robe and went into it, stood under the maple in the yard and let the water-weighted leaves fall onto his hair, and he felt with a certainty that rooted him till the sun rose over the fields outside of town, where the corn was standing brown to be harvested, that without a death, the heart can never be certain of its losses.

He walked into the house and took his bow off the wall, where it had gathered a thick layer of dust. When Sara woke, he was at the kitchen table, sharpening broadheads.

"What are you doing?" she asked.

"I'm going hunting. It's time I did it again."

She poured orange juice, stood with her back to him for a moment, then turned.

"How can you do it?"

"Do what?" The razor edges barely missed his fingers.

"How can you shoot arrows into animals? I hate the thought of it."

He stopped sharpening. He remembered how his mother used to

fight with his father over this. He'd hated those fights. He'd sided with his father, and he hated his mother's unreasonableness, her certainty of moral rightness. She'd never wanted to understand; even as a child, he knew that.

But Sara wasn't his mother. And she loved him. He could see it in her beautiful face, made slack by the sorrow of incomprehension.

Still, he made no attempt to console or help or even to fight her.

"Quit eating then," he said. "Plants, animals. One way or the other, something dies. You don't like it, starve."

He'd never hurt her like that. He saw a dull, glazed coating of shock in her eyes, a look like galvanized metal.

He went into the bathroom and shaved his face smooth. He remembered the woman's face, the camouflage applied so perfectly that he saw only the eyes, the rest of the face like light turned off a leaf, or shadow in a leaf crease. He began to copy onto his own face the image of hers, applying old camouflage paint that he hadn't used for years in fits and starts of correction, until he heard Sara leave the house for work, speaking quietly to the dogs and cats, petting each one. He stopped for a moment to listen, then when the door shut, went on with the camouflage, until staring out of the mirror was the face of the woman as he'd first seen her, his own face, hardly a face at all.

Out of sight of the clearing, he dropped to his hands and knees, then to his stomach, sliding his bow forward. He moved through the preacher's lice and wild hemp like a snake, parting the stems with his body. It took him most of the morning before he saw the clearing through the weed stems.

Within it, the four deer grazed, raising their heads to the wind. He inched back into the trees until he came to a large oak, and behind it, he stood.

He backed into the shadow of the trees until he was looking down a narrow passageway between trunks. He waited, more still than the trunks he stood among. One of the does grazed into the lane, grazed out, in the careless time of animals, while the sun moved in the sky and the faraway river flowed, and leaves dropped out of trees. He heard the muffled clacking of his heart valves inside his chest.

A twig appeared in the lane. Still he didn't move. The twig came farther, forked. Only then did he slowly raise the bow, letting it drift upward as if on a slow breeze, and he drew back the string to the corner of his mouth as the buck's rack, lowered for grazing, moved forward along the ground. The deer's head and shoulders appeared, then its rib cage. Jerrod centered the thin line of sharpened steel there.

The buck took one more step. It raised its head. Jerrod Sinclair would later say it looked down the lane at him with an expression human and sensible, and quizzical, looked at him in the shadows with drawn bow, motionless. And he would repeat again and again that the buck knew him. Not only saw, but knew. And knew what he was doing. And yet merely waited.

He released the arrow.

It glittered and spun light, arcing down its flattened parabola through the line of trees. It disappeared into its own thinness. The buck took a step forward, a second. Jerrod's heart leaped with exultation and disappointment, whirled in his chest like an out-of-round wheel, that he had missed, that his decision had been stolen from him.

Then the buck plunged.

And only at the last moment, as its knees buckled and its head snapped forward to strike the ground, its long neck like a curling whip, and one of its antlers cracked with the force of the fall—only then did it take its accusing and compassionate eyes off the spot where Jerrod stood.

Even the leaves stopped moving, he said.

He waited for her scream.

None came.

Remorse deepened in his heart like thick mud filling it.

He walked into the clearing, but before he entered it, he turned down his face.

The buck shed its heat in great waves. Jerrod stood within that heat, breathing it, his tongue dried stiff and thick in his mouth. He knelt and touched the animal's coarse hair. He looked into its eyes, so dead they didn't even reflect him kneeling there.

He sank further into the grass until it rose around his face. He slowly turned his head and he heard a folding of cloth as he did. His heart beat hard under the shining point of the arrow he felt centered on it.

Then he turned his face full on the spot where the sound came from. He found her even as she screamed at last, in rage and disbelief. "If I ever see your face," she'd said. And he knew, even as he found the brown eyes that burned out of a shifting, blurry space that those eyes saw only the same thing—his eyes floating, not part of a face seen, but peering like part of the earth from the ground itself.

She'd been tricked. She shrieked, a sound worse than a great tree splintering. He saw, with a yearning too large for his heart, her white teeth, her tongue. But his blood went cold at her inhuman shriek. He tried to call to her, but the heat of the dead buck had dried his tongue to a stick.

That was the story he told—or the story we put together out of whatever it really was he told, which may have been nothing more than the rags and scraps of a drunk rummaging through his memory. When he gave up his hunting and then his carpentry and followed his father into the bottle, we thought it was nothing more than the way of the Sinclairs, which may still be a truer view than any explanation offered by the things he said. If it hadn't been for Sara's odd death, none of us would have attached anything but personal meaning to what we knew.

One day he simply disappeared, didn't return home in the evening. Some men who had known him when he was younger came to Sara's aid. They crowded into her living room to plan a search. Sara no longer kept animals, perhaps because keeping Jerrod was mercy enough, but the house still smelled faintly of their years-old presence.

"Where do you think he might have gone?" one asked.

Sara gazed at him. He felt like a bad student.

"The river," she said tiredly. "Where else?"

They searched the valley and eventually found his car. Starting from there, they combed all the wild places they knew. Unsuccessful at the end of the day, they returned to Cloten and insisted to Sara's gray face that they'd looked everywhere.

"No," she said. "You haven't."

The next morning they returned. A new snow had fallen overnight. All morning they puffed through the woods calling. Finally one of them, walking from one patch of woods to another across a field of cornstalks long cleared of trees and fenced now, saw snowblurred tracks and followed them. He found Jerrod's frozen body, naked, clothes scattered about, lying within an area trampled by deer. An empty bourbon bottle lay nearby.

Local wisdom held that freezing people, their delirious minds deprived of oxygen, often tear off their clothes as blood rushes to their skin, making them feel hot, and alcohol only makes it worse. The editor of the local paper, in fact, followed the story of Jerrod's death with an article about the warning signs of hypothermia and freezing—a bit tactless many of us thought, but certainly to the point.

The only real dissenter in this opinion was Ivy Bercovitch, by now an ancient resident of the Cloten Manor, who spent her days staring out the big picture window of the manor at the field across the highway. She wrote a letter to the editor, a nearly incoherent thesis of paranoia, that was nevertheless printed. Ivy's point—if she had one—was that strange forces operated in the woods, disguising themselves to seem innocuous, and that she'd always known that her old tenant would be taken by them.

Then Sara died. And our horror at the way she died has left us with no certainties. It wasn't just the way she died; it was that none of us did a thing to prevent it. We let a stranger take over a job we should have done ourselves, even if Sara was cantankerous and difficult. We were too happy to let Diane Bourdeaux make our lives easier.

For a year and a half she was Sara's caretaker. She became part of the routine of the town—her weekly visits to the Red Owl, her dogs that followed her around and played with the children, her laughter at the smallest things, her glowing skin, bright eyes. We forgot she was a stranger.

One week, in an already cold winter, the biggest blizzard many of us could remember struck, a white-out that lasted three days and confined us all to our houses except for the farmers who had to feed their livestock. Snow fell so hard and heavy it came down in long, solid ribbons that unfurled on the ground—sheets of snow, planes of snow.

And the wind. We'd never heard such wind. It came from all directions at once, shrieking with a sound that battered at our sanity as we huddled in our houses. It knocked down power lines, leaving the entire town without electricity for the three days of the blizzard and the two following it.

Sara's house disappeared, which was one of the reasons we forgot about her, along with the fact that she'd been gone from our lives for so long. Her house had turned into one large drift that blended with Earl Jensen's field—a big drift, true, but there were big drifts everywhere. We just didn't stop to remember that there was a house under that drift. It was a place that for a few days ceased to exist, a blank spot in the geography of our memories.

It wasn't until three days after the blizzard that Kenny Christianson looked up from the meat counter, puzzled—and then realized that he expected to see Diane Bourdeaux coming toward him on her weekly shopping trip for Sara, buying cereal, bread, fruit, dog food for the now-grown pup.

Kenny walked into the aisles, his head buzzing like the fluorescent lights above him, astonished at the emptiness of the store. Only then did he think of Sara.

We tunneled in, blindly, not even sure where her door lay.

We found it, entered.

Only the pup greeted us, fawning, licking our faces, whining with joy over our attention and the chance to finally escape the closed-in house.

"Sara?" we called, but she didn't answer.

We found her on the bed.

What was left of her.

Men whose faces the pup had licked washed for days, and their wives refused for a long time to kiss them.

The coroner claimed she'd frozen to death first. Who could blame the pup? There was no food in the house. There was nothing at all.

Once we recovered from our shock, someone thought to shoot the dog. Then we discovered it was gone. We'd left the door open a crack, wedged by snow, and the pup had escaped while we gazed in horror at the exposed bones and chewed flesh of what had been, when younger, the beautiful face of Sara Sinclair. There were reports of a dog as large as a deer streaking across farmland toward the river, its body curling and straightening like a steel leaf-spring over the frozen clods of plowed earth.

That—again—might have been the end of it. Except that someone got to thinking about what he'd heard of Jerrod's story, and he brought the story into the open. Then we all looked at one another as if waking from a dream. And since then, none of us has figured out where any of this ends, or where it started, or whether the whole thing is a single story, or two, or more than we can count.

SARAH VAN ARSDALE

Chorion and the Pleiades

Sarah Van Arsdale has published one well-received novel, Toward Amnesia, *and is currently at work on a second. She teaches English at the University of Vermont and Vermont College.*

In "Chorion and the Pleiades," Van Arsdale makes ingenious use of classical myths about the stars known as the Pleiades, or Seven Sisters. The poem is reprinted from the Winter 1999 special fairy-tale issue of Columbia: A Journal of Literature and Art *from Columbia University in New York City.*

—*T. W.*

It wasn't so much the night sky raising
its bulk above the dark town, or the light
fractured house to house, lamp to lamp, split
to huntress' smoky meadow firelight
and forest light of cat eye, firefly—
surely not the actual night sky, bowl
bending black and seamless over everything,

Because we don't know where the sinister
germinates, but it seems to ooze from soil,
smears from wet rocks' slippery undersides,
dank and musty and full of all that's bad.
Or maybe it just opens up the earth
in meadow's midst, and like Persephone
we all fall in.

Living on the hamlet's rim, this village
with its stone-planked walks and candled houses,
streets clogged with cattle and scattered hay,
with the smell of gristle, firesmoke, dog,
in this gravity the seven sisters
born into evil
stanched their own wounds, pressed palm to fevered head,
bit down on kerchief or flax-seed sheet
as night seeped in the casements, old dog asleep
at doorway's stoop, mother punched down in her bed.
Together, they bore what can't be borne
each one in her turn, seven feigning sleep
backs arced against what night had come to mean,
small girl hands covering their child eyes.

Seven sisters like girls everywhere, you, me
never told the moon's shape in its orbit,
never taught the shape of their own desire,
never shown the path Artemis parted in the meadow,
her dark wolves just ahead, nosing the grass.

One night beneath the sky's vast tilt and lean,
the mother, in her last expiration,
severs the sisters' slim tendril of hope,
dies in her straw bed, vomit everywhere,
and the seven sisters huddle in their room.
They hear the voice outside the door, know
its meaning, smell it now, hear the dog
lift its jowls from stone stoop, hear the latch
click up and this time they're prepared: poker
and stick, blackened urine pot and dried brick,
but for all their preparation, the man
bulks up the doorway with his laughter.

This is the story we know too well, my darling,
it's the discolored truth that's become
our companion, the stories of girls
roped out across the patches of countryside;
Pleiades drifting, unnoticed, above them,
sky bowl bending its back in agony.

Tell me we don't need divine intervention.

But in our hamlet, there appeared that night
Chorion, goddess of little girls,
huge and imposing, like a blue-robed angel,
feet sandled, dark wolf-mane hair tangling down,
sharp sword of victory weighting her belt
the coat of a tiger she'd killed with her teeth
slapped over one muscled shoulder.
She stands in the room, and the man stops laughing.
He knows in this moment he's lost everything,
and Chorion opens a sack made of bear fur;
she lifts the girls in one by one, giving them each
a piece of Turkish Delight, and they are so young
and she is so big and so capable,
they all fit in her sack, and at last they are safe.

She hoists the girls up onto her back
and tells them a story, says she knows a big cow
with horns that tip out into the night
who's been wanting some riders, a passel of girls
girls who like stories, who want to go for a ride
through the night sky, escaping from evil, escaping from
shame,
and she flies them up to the stars, all the way up to Bovis
and there you can see them, still to this day,
girls living a girl-life, like a brand on the shoulder
of Bovis the Cow, protected by Chorion,
the seven young sisters—you can only see six
the oldest girl, cursed with memory,
looks away from the earth.

ELIZABETH ENGSTROM

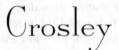

Crosley

Elizabeth Engstrom is the author of six books and dozens of short stories, articles, and essays. Her most recent book, The Alchemy of Love, *is a collaborative work with artist Alan M. Clark. Engstrom runs the Maui Writers Retreat and is director of their Program of Continuing Education. She lives in the Oregon woods with her husband and dog.*

Engstrom notes that she wrote the bulk of this story while in the midst of a tropical downpour on Oahu. She lived in the tropics for seventeen years and goes back twice a year, and each time is "surprised anew by the salubrious air. There's a sensuality in the tropics that is conducive to bare skin, cold drinks, hot sun, salt-sweaty lovemaking, and broken hearts."

"Crosley" was originally published in The Alchemy of Love.

—*E. D.*

I have always been fascinated by evil. I've flirted with it, been tempted by it, but only once have I fallen in love with it.

I live on an island in the South Seas. How I came to be here is a story of young love, foolishness, and weakness—both his and mine—and therefore a tale for a different time.

I pour drinks in a poor man's bar. In the tropics, no walls are necessary, just a good roof, bar stools, a couple of tables, an old sofa that had seen too many sunrises, and a room at the back where Godfrey used to live. The liquor shelves have a lockable grate to keep out the monkeys and the thieves. Daily rain washes the island and the open air dance floor which, at the time of Godfrey's ownership, hadn't seen a dancer in years—not since the tour boat stopped docking here.

Godfrey was a harmless old drunk who began each day with an impressive head of optimism and a mug of thick black coffee, and ended it with a rant of some sort and sometimes a roundhouse punch at a hallucination.

Many times I hauled Godfrey to bed, locked up the booze, and slept on the couch next to his bed, afraid he had finally taxed his liver to the maximum. Surely he couldn't survive this level of toxicity much longer. But he had done so since long before I met him, and God seems to look out after old drunks for some reason.

I worked for Godfrey. I poured drinks, mopped the floor, received shipments of liquor, collected overdue accounts from the locals, endured their hard luck stories, listened to their weary tales, parried amorous advances, and generally did whatever was called for, including tending Godfrey. I did all this outwardly patient, while inside I seethed, waiting for the next adventurer to sail into the harbor and bring either news of something familiar, something of my old life perhaps, or an offer of something magnificent, a gateway to a new life.

They came, the adventurers, not frequently, but steadily. We had a protected anchorage and a stocked bar, the locals were skilled handymen, and UPS knew our address.

But when they came, they mostly came in couples, and they shared what adventure they had in their souls, but it was either not enough or of the wrong kind, or pointed in the wrong direction. And when they hoisted their main and caught a freshening breeze out of the bay, their names and faces faded immediately into obscurity and I would go back to fixing something that the jungle was trying to reclaim.

The morning that Crosley arrived, Godfrey and I sat at the bar drinking coffee and watching deluge rain soak the already sodden earth. It fell as a solid sheet from the gutterless roof all around, splashing mud from the rain-gouged trenches to mix with the water that splashed up from the dance floor, bits of grout and other evidence of its deterioration floating closer to our bare feet.

I felt the tropical depression in my soul and sipped coffee silently, feeling desperately claustrophobic, penned in by the humidity and the liquid walls, the vinyl of the stool sticking uncomfortably to the backs of my thighs.

Godfrey, on his second cup, was full of enthusiastic remodeling talk, but his enthusiasm was not infectious—I'd heard it all too many times before.

And then, characteristic of many tropical storms, the rain ceased abruptly, and Godfrey was caught mid-sentence. My thighs peeled off the stool without thought as we both stood at the sight of the long, sleek black yacht at anchor in the center of the bay. It had appeared as if by magic.

An astonishing array of seaworthy and not-so-seaworthy craft came and went from this bay. Generally they came one at a time, but occasionally cruisers would arrive in tandem, and now and then, enough showed up at once to raft up together. Their drunken parties could even wake Godfrey.

But never had such a craft arrived with such little fanfare nor during such a storm. The entrance to the bay through the coral reefs was treacherous during the best of times. Who would chance it during such a blinding downpour?

Someone stupid. Someone stupidly lucky. Someone with supermortal navigating skills. Or perhaps someone who had been here before.

And the boat itself—sixty feet if it was an inch. Sails were neatly furled under black covers, and what lines we could see from this distance had been coiled at their ends. No gear was visible on deck. The boat looked not as if it had been sailed at all, but as if it had been freshly groomed and polished, ready for a show.

All hatches were tightly closed.

"Know that boat, Godfrey?" I asked, entranced.

"Nope, and not the type of thing I'd be likely to forget," he said, and he was right, of course, even with his cheesecloth memory.

It floated, mysterious, anonymous, and somehow untouchable—not even the local islanders rowed out to investigate—for two days with no visible signs of life.

I went about my normal daily duties, but with a difference. There was a spark of excitement in my soul. There would soon come an alteration to my mundane routine, brief though it was sure to be. My eyes drifted out to that floating yacht, dark like a hole in the brilliant blue of the bay, and my imagination, long dormant, came alive.

On the second night, when the regulars drifted in for their beer or tequila, to retell old jokes, reopen old wounds, and reignite old jealousies, the topic was exclusively the Black Yacht. Godfrey had come to believe it was the Reaper's yacht come for him, and the idea that the Reaper had a yacht fueled the hilarity for most of the evening.

But when Godfrey's head hit the bar and he began to snore, a man stepped out of the dark, thick tropical night and sat on the stool next to him.

Conversation faded as we all observed the outsider. That he belonged to the black boat was obvious. He looked like the yacht. Tall, swarthy, with black hair just beginning to silver, dressed in black shirt and black cotton pants, he smiled a charming, white-toothed smile at me and ordered a grappa.

As it happened, a bottle of grappa collected cobwebs under the cabinet and I opened it and poured him a shot.

"Grappa for all," he said quietly, and he became an instant hero to these drunken fools as I set up a row of shot glasses and began to fill them.

Mingo was the first to thank him, patting his shoulder and trying to include him in the ring of camaraderie, but the stranger merely flicked his eyes in acknowledgement at the procession of gratitude and kept his attention focused on me.

I wished I had fixed myself up a little more, but the light was dim and he seemed to like whatever it was he saw in me, so I warmed to his attentions.

And why not? It had been two years since I had the attentions of a man, and my femininity suffered for it.

He savored his grappa, though the others drank theirs as fast as he bought and I poured, and soon they all stumbled home. Someone had seen to Godfrey, and we were alone. I could tell it was going to be a long night—I hoped it was—so I ran myself a shot of espresso and slugged it down. "Last call," I said.

"A waltz," he said.

"Pardon?"

"I call for a waltz," he said, and held out his hand.

Damned if I couldn't hear "Stardust" coming from somewhere. I took his hand, came around the bar, and he twirled me into his arms.

"I am Crosley," he said, and I had no response for him, my senses were completely overwhelmed. He smelled like a spice I couldn't identify—something exotic. His hands held me firmly, competently, self-assuredly, and he directed our dance in a slow, comfortable rhythm, completely in time with the music in my head.

His broad chest, the hard muscles of his arms, his breath warm in my hair made me want to lose myself in him. *Take me*, my mind ordered my mouth to say. *Take me away from here. Give me a new life, an easy life, a pampered life, a loved life.* But I said nothing. I merely swayed with him.

When the music ended, Crosley held me steadily, then disengaged himself, his hands on my hips pushing me gently away. He kissed my fingertips with warm lips. "So lovely," he said, then he turned and disappeared into the night.

I stood alone in the center of the dance floor and for one awful disorienting moment, wandered if I had imagined it all. Did I just dance by myself to music in my head? Were Godfrey's drunken hallucinations contagious? Or was my own loneliness and dissatisfaction with life pushing me over the edge?

Then I heard a small splash in the bay, as if from an oar, and I heard his voice in my heart as clearly as I heard the music, and I didn't care about the consequences of loving this man, this drifter, this unconventional sailor. I only knew that I must have him, some way, some how, no matter how briefly.

Godfrey woke me the next morning, and I was surprised to find myself sleeping on the old sofa next to the bar. He handed me my coffee and he paced back and forth on the dance floor. "Bet that guy's got money," he said. "Bet he'd be smart enough to invest in an operation that could give him a good return on his investment."

"What guy?" I asked, but I already knew.

"That black boat guy."

"Crosley," I said, and sipped my coffee.

"You met him?"

I ran my fingers through my tangled hair, damp with tropical moisture. "He came in last night and we fed the home team all the grappa."

"Money, you think?"

I shrugged. I wasn't about to get in the middle of one of Godfrey's schemes. "Stay awake tonight and you can ask him yourself."

"Think he'll come?"

I did. I did indeed. "Where else?"

"Do we have any steaks? Let's cook him a steak. Think he eats meat? Is there any grappa left?" Godfrey made another pot of coffee and stuck with it all day long. Perhaps Crosley would make a difference in everybody's life.

I found it difficult to concentrate, and ended up wasting most of the day on daydreams of dark hair, dark eyes, and an exciting life of sailing the seas with Crosley. When the sun went down, I walked the quarter mile to my home, showered, shaved, powdered, perfumed, and made up my face. There were a few whistles and knowing elbow jabs among the regulars when I got back. They knew who had captured my eye and my imagination and they couldn't help but approve. After all, he had bought drinks for the house.

They all teased Godfrey about going on the wagon, too, and he took their ribbing good-naturedly. They'd seen Godfrey sober before, always when he rode high on a fantasy. His sobriety ended when his dream—

which was never based on reality—ended. This one was no exception, and we all knew it. I suspected Godfrey knew it as well.

Talk was of the usual nonsense, the locals sensing Godfrey and me both pegging a dream on Crosley and not wishing to interfere. But it was clear that a sense of excitement ran through their conversation. Many brought their spouses, hoping the free booze would run again.

The party was wild and rambunctious when he stepped out of the night and into the circle of warmth.

An involuntary cheer went out, and people moved aside so he could take his former barstool—an honor among this group of barflies.

Godfrey slid right over and placed a napkin on the bar. I urged everyone to quit gawking and get back to drinking. I poured a few more, opened a couple of sweaty beers, my heart pounding and my breath coming hard at the sight of him. And when I glanced at him, he was looking at me.

I had to hold on to the bar to keep myself from floating right over to him. I smiled, a smile I hope looked full of promise, then busied myself with Godfrey's business while Godfrey talked with Crosley. He talked earnestly and passionately, with many gestures, and I tried not to look, although I stole a glance now and then. Crosley's drink sat before him, untouched.

After a while, Godfrey came over to me, poured himself a double shot of whiskey and slugged it down. "Fully invested," he muttered, and took over my end of the bar.

I was glad. I'd never throw my lot in with Godfrey on purpose, but the bar paid me enough to live simply in this simple place.

I wandered toward Crosley, although I'm sure it was more like a making a beeline to him.

He picked up his drink, held it up to me in a toast, then drank it.

A moment later, he was gone.

I was disappointed beyond reason, and blamed Godfrey. I was tempted to walk down to the water and borrow one of the islanders' boats to go to him to explain—explain what? Godfrey?

I wouldn't. I wouldn't be chasing after a man like Crosley.

Instead, I went home.

Disappointed and distressed with my choices in life, I crawled into my lonely bed and cried.

In the night, when the banana moon turned the jungle black and silver and the nightlife was at its noisiest, I heard a step on my porch. A human step.

I kept a small bat by my bed and a machete between mattresses for self-defense. Although it had never happened, one of those drunken locals could get an idea. . . . And then there were always the transients, the cruising sailors with no resume, no history, no real accountability.

I grabbed the bat, and the book of matches. In my heart-pounding haste to light a bedside candle—my little shack had no electricity—I kept crumbling the humidity-damp matches.

Then a lighter flicked open and a flame illuminated my bedside table. Crosley lit the candle and sat down next to me.

My hair was a mess, my eyes were swollen, I had a terrible taste in my mouth.

"I must leave in five days," he said, and I moved over and held open the covers for him.

His skin was cool and smooth and felt good next to my sleep-warmed body.

His hand moved slowly from my knee, across my hip, waist, around my breast to my neck and lay quietly on my cheek, leaving a trail of fire in its wake. With studied slow, self-assured movements, he manipulated my passions and drove me to a frenzied wildness like I'd never known before. By the time our bodies merged, our mouths locked together as if transferring our souls, the orgasm that had threatened to overwhelm me burst forth in all its Technicolor glory.

We continued the dance as if we'd done it a thousand times before, until he slid from me with a sweat-slick sigh and entwined my fingers in his.

"From the first moment I saw you . . ." he whispered, then his breathing slowed and a soft snore took its place.

Likely a line used a thousand times on a thousand women, I thought, but that did not diminish its effectiveness.

For five days, I never set foot inside Godfrey's bar, as Crosley and I lived, loved, and spoiled each other. We explored my island, swam naked, gorged on native fruits, and licked the juices from one another's bodies. His boat was as dark, mysterious, and as free of affectations on the inside as it was on the outside, and though I longed to learn more of Crosley—his history, his family, his aspirations—there was nothing to be gleaned from his possessions. Nor from him. He remained an enigma, revealing everything of his exterior, revealing little of his substance.

We slept together in my bed, on the beach, in his stateroom, in the jungle, on the hills under the stars. We made love and laughed, swam in the lagoon with the dolphins and whiled away rainy afternoons, making up silly poems. We wove garlands of flowers for our hair, and buried ourselves in the warm sand. We showered together and made soapy love in the flimsy, tin shower stall. We melded.

And every morning, when I watched the sky grow light with the fire of dawn, the fire of panic grew within my gut as it was another day closer to his departure. Desperate to not cling to him, I clung to his words, his gestures, his amusements, his kisses. I let his actions speak, and they eloquently spoke of love and desire and delight.

Surely he would never leave me.

We didn't speak of the future, but it was not far from my tongue. Five days with Crosley was not going to be enough—perhaps a lifetime of him would not be enough—and my heart broke on an hourly basis for five days as I knew he would, eventually, leave.

And then he said it.

We lay together in the lee of a rock outcropping on the beach. We had picnicked and finished a bottle of wine, then thrown the leftover food to the crabs and engaged in what seemed to be the next event of our continual lovemaking on the chenille bedspread I laid out. We had discovered gourmet sex, funny sex, quickie sex, instant sex, and slurpy, delicious sex, but this was emotional sex. We both cried when it was over, and he kissed the tears from my cheeks and told me he loved me.

We lay quietly together after that, watching the sun sink, his arm protectively around me, until the chill came over us, and with one thought, we got up and slowly made our way back to my cabin.

We showered, crawled into bed, and held each other, neither of us speaking of the fact that this was our last night, if it was. There is always hope, I told myself. Always hope.

With hope in my heart and our arms and legs entwined, we slept.

In the morning, when I woke, I was alone. At first, sleepy-brained, I thought he was in the bathroom, or he had gone to fetch breakfast. But when I sat up and saw the fresh gardenia leaning next to the bedside candle, I knew.

"No," I wailed. I jumped out of bed and threw on my clothes, desperate to make him stay, to remind him that he loved me, to convince him that I could sail with him, to beg him not to abandon what we had created.

By the time I was out the door and running for the bay, I was desperate only to say goodbye. I had to hold him one more time, to kiss him once more, to tell him how he had restored me, to wish him well on his journey.

But the bay was empty.

Far off on the horizon, I saw a black sliver with its mainsail illuminated in the dawn.

I felt gutshot. Numb. Dead.

I wandered to Godfrey's bar, made myself some espresso and mixed in some Jack Daniels. After two drinks, I eliminated the coffee. After two more, I began to cry.

My name is Winston. I came to the island on the run from the law when I was only twenty-four. Today I am twenty-nine and hopelessly in love with Francine, the bartender. I am short and dark like a chimpanzee, and a deep scar runs through my right eyebrow and down my cheek, pulling my nose out of alignment. It would be so romantic to tell of some knifefight over a noble cause, but the truth is, I stumbled off the path and fell into a ravine one night while drunk, and lay unconscious at the bottom with my face impaled on the sharp edge of a banana stump until morning. Infection raged, and this scar is the result. On my best days I tell myself that my look is unique, particularly among these beautiful Polynesian locals, and on my worst days I view myself as a deformed Quasimoto, barely fit to breathe this fragrant air.

I am short, I am ugly, I am unskilled, but I am also devoted. I work at the landfill, and every day after work I bathe and then go to Francine's bar. She is always there, smiling and pouring drinks for the regulars, the home team she calls us, cracking jokes and buying rounds for the house.

Francine was here when I arrived. She is somewhat older than I am, but age on her makes her only more beautiful. Age is not the only difference between us; while my upbringing was dictated by the toughs in the streets, she led a white-bread life of privilege. When I left North America, it was to escape the law, and no one has ever missed me. When she escaped North America, it was to escape from her parents, and toward eternal bliss, and mail arrives for her every week in the pouch without fail.

Everyone on the island has a crush on Francine, but they indulge themselves in fruitless, fanciful fantasy, for Francine beds no one.

No one, that is, but the boy who brought her here ten years or so ago, and the European devil who sent her into the depths of despair. This man came shortly after I discovered Francine's bar, although at that time it was owned by a drunk named Godfrey. I had already lost my heart to her. I had lost that upon first sight.

And my crush on her is not fanciful, because I love her, and have vowed to protect her regardless of the frivolous antics that bring her nothing but heartbreak. Some day she will see me for who I am, and until that happens, I can be patient.

And it is because of this love I have for her, and my self-sworn duty to protect her, that I, and only I, know what happened that night. I know, and Francine knows. And we are the only two.

The story begins with Godfrey's yellow death.

Francine, still heavy with grief over the European, came to work one morning to find the coffeepot cold and Godfrey even colder. He had been turning yellow the last few months, and when she came upon him in his bed, he was the color of urine. His face wore not the mask of peaceful repose, but a grimace of pain, and he was doubled over and frozen in that position.

Francine called Mingo, who gathered several of the home team together. We built a pyre on the outcropping that formed an arm of the bay, and it was there we set fire to Godfrey and sent his spirit to its reward. Mingo danced and spoke in his native tongue, while Francine sat numbly watching the flames, smelling the ambiguous odors of roasting meat and roasting Godfrey. And when we had all had enough, I helped her up and walked her back to the bar.

She took her place behind the counter, and I put a bill on the bar and bought a round for the house, in Godfrey's name.

She bought the next round, and it wasn't long before everybody began patting her on the back and congratulating her on inheriting the bar.

She didn't understand at first, but after a moment, she realized it was true. Godfrey had no family, no heirs, there was no paperwork, the bar just passed from him to her and that was that.

This is what brought her out of her grief for the devil.

I began coming by on weekends and doing repair work around the place. I regrouted the dance floor, and strung up tiny fairy lights as she began to plan her grand opening. Apparently, the bar brought in plenty of money, it was just that Godfrey drank up all the profits. Francine had a different business sense.

Every week UPS brought some other prize she'd ordered through a catalog, and she was selling raffle tickets, and getting the community organized. There is a poor mission not too far from here, and once a year doctors come and minister to the sick children. Francine was raising money for them, they need so much, and it was a nice thing for the community to rally behind. Soon the island women were coming around as well. When Godfrey owned the bar, the island women hated the place. Their men would come in, get drunk, and go home and beat them and their kids. No wonder they hated it.

But now, Francine wouldn't let the men get that drunk in her place, and it was clean, and the women were welcome, and she sat and chatted with them while their children played on the fresh dance floor with their toys. And the women arranged flowers, so the bar always had a festive, tropical atmosphere.

The day of the grand opening dawned sunny and clear. Francine was up and about early, pouring coffee for all her workers, the same people who would later attend the party in their nicer clothes, but in the morning they were wearing work clothes and breaking their backs to launch her new enterprise right.

Women delivered elaborate flower arrangements, men set up tables to display the gifts, boys mixed juices for the refrigerator and stowed fresh kegs for chilling. Another crew put up a small stage in the corner of the dance floor for the band that would arrive later, and even the priest from the mission came by and had a cup of coffee, and ended up sweeping the floor. A couple of cruising sailors who happened to wander into the bay joined in, and Francine put them to work preparing food.

I had appointed myself foreman for the whole remodeling project, and wandered around with a coffee cup, making suggestions and helping everywhere I could. Francine joined me periodically, wiping a sweaty lock of hair from her forehead, and consulting with me on a point or two. Whenever she did that, I felt as though we were doing it together. A joint project. A couple. It made me feel important.

Then, when everything looked ready and all the locals went home, it was just Francine and me taking a final look around before going to our respective places to get cleaned up.

"Francine," I said, and she turned those lovely eyes on me. She was dirty and sweaty and never lovelier. She looked at me with familiarity born of long association and respect. "May I have the first dance tonight?"

Her face softened at the question, and she smiled. I know there was affection in her heart, but I also recognized that she didn't want to foster any false hopes of romance between us. "Sure," she said, and put her hand on my shoulder. "We've done a good job here, haven't we, Winston?"

"You have," I said. She gave my shoulder a squeeze and I went home to get ready for my dance with the love of my life.

And it was every bit as wonderful as I imagined.

The crowd was young, the band barely warmed up, but I knew that Francine would be frantically working after a few minutes, and if I was going to get my dance, it would indeed have to be the first.

The sun had gone beyond the horizon, but the clouds still blazed. The fairy lights seemed like a net of jewels over our heads. Those who had come early stood around the edges of the dance floor, watching the band hit its stride, and when they played "Stardust," I held out my hand, and Francine accepted.

The crowd yelled and applauded, and she moved into my arms gracefully.

She is taller than I am, so I didn't have the pleasure of her face against my chest, but our cheeks did touch and I rested my hands on her hips and she put her arms on my shoulders. I felt everybody watching us for the first part of the dance, and it felt wonderful. Soon, other couples swarmed the new floor, and I was proud that so far, Francine's evening was perfect, and the new dance floor was having a fine inauguration.

Then a hand on my shoulder. I smiled. Someone wanting to cut in. Yeah, sure. No way. I held her tighter and turned to refute the friend, but it was no friend.

It was the European, and Francine froze in my arms, an expression of stunned pleasure on her face. An expression that struck terror into my heart.

I had no intention of giving her up, yet he moved right in and took her from me. My face heated and I had to walk away, out into the jungle to calm my rage. He had come back to hurt her one more time, and I couldn't bear it.

After an hour or so, I went back to the bar, and Francine was dancing around her guests like a young girl at her coming-out party. She looked lithe and youthful, more beautiful even than she had when the party started, and my jealousy burned ever brighter at the thought that it was this wretched womanizer who made her feel thus, when my love only turned her gaze to one of pitiful tolerance.

She danced and she flitted, and she smiled and she laughed, and never far from her was the devil, smiling and acting the host, the role that I had intended to play.

The party wore on, and I watched from the sidelines, but before it was over, Francine got one of the boys to bartend, and she and the European slipped off the far end of the dance floor and escaped into the night. I followed them to the bay, and watched as he rowed her to his black yacht, almost invisible in the dark night.

I went home and tried not to think about her in his arms. Tried to think, instead, of the day she would be in my arms, but my dreams were flat and without substance. Francine would never be mine, not as long as she could still be tempted by such as he.

What did I want with such a woman, I kept asking myself. But she was not to blame for her weakness. She was a good girl, a clean girl, she just had a soft spot for the rogue. And he capitalized on it. I hated him with all the hate that was in me and all the hate that should be in her. I cast about, trying to imagine what I could do to rescue her, but I could think of nothing. She was an adult. She was her own woman.

When the devil smashed her heart again, I would be there to hold her and kiss away her tears.

It was this thought that consoled me in the night, and toward morning, when I knew they slept exhausted in each others' arms, I, too, eventually slept.

I didn't mean to watch them. I didn't mean to follow them. It was never my intention to spy on them. But they were so easy with one another. Francine laughed so easily, so gaily that I was attracted beyond my willpower. I watched the European effortlessly make a lei of flowers for her head with deft fingers, the type of romantic thing that I imagine all women love, but I would never have thought of it. That he did intrigued me as much as it pleased Francine. He was physically affectionate, always touching her. His white teeth flashed in the tropical sun often, and she put her face down in modest shyness just as often. What did he say to her to elicit that type of response?

I felt completely inadequate as a man.

And I could not take my eyes off them, I could not keep from studying them. All hope for a romance, a relationship, a marriage with Francine vanished as I watched the magic he wove about her head and into her heart. I wanted to run and shake her and say, "Don't you see? Can't you see what he is, what he is doing?" But I couldn't do that, because I was as entranced as she was. The European, Crosley his name, was busy teaching us both. He taught her what it meant to be a warm and wonderful, delightful woman, and he taught me what it meant to be an ugly, scarfaced runt.

Still I could not stop watching them.

I followed within the cover of the jungle as they walked up the beach that first morning, to the party-ravaged bar. She fixed them each an espresso, and then arranged for Kenny, one of the home team, to take over the bar for the next five days. She said she was going to take some time off.

Five days.

That concept immobilized me with dread. I would have to watch them together for five days. On the other hand, Crosley was sure to leave after the five days were up, and so my agony, while intense, would be short-lived. And then I would hold her while she healed. Perhaps she would come to me then, tired of the razzle-dazzle that ends in heartache, preferring instead the solid and steadfast.

Hope is a strange and wonderful thing.

Five days turned out to be an eternity—an eternity of waiting in the weeds. Waiting and watching as they made love, as they talked and laughed and spent endless idle hours together. I barely ate, barely slept, didn't work, didn't bathe. I was afraid to leave them, afraid I'd miss the moment where he revealed his nature to her, the moment when she saw the truth of him, the moment where what they had fell apart and I could swoop down and rescue my damsel from the evil one.

I waited and I watched, tirelessly, with undying devotion, and all I saw was more love and more affection and more touching and more kissing and more madness grew inside my head until I spent all my time hating myself for watching. "She would never look at the likes of you," I said to myself in disgust. "Look at you!"

And still I followed and watched.

Now and then I thought of the home team's opinions of Francine and her affair. They were crude about it all, and while I was tempted to go to the bar and defend her honor, I could not leave her. For five days I watched from the doorstep of the eroding shrine of love I had built for her in my soul.

And on the fifth night, when they were back at her shack, I went home. I bathed and shaved and tried to ignore the wildness in my eyes. Then I went to the bar, ate a decent meal, and tried to ignore the prodding questions from the regulars. I tried even harder to ignore the things they said about Francine. They were not mean things, these were her friends, but they were hurtful to my ears.

And so, dressed for the occasion, I went back to her place to await the final hour, when the evil Crosley would drive a spike through my beloved's heart and I would be the first one she would cling to upon its completion.

Five years later, he returned. Could not stop thinking of me, he said. Could not forget the silken feel of my skin, the amber scent of my hair. Could not escape the way the dimples in the small of my back fill with perspiration when we make love. Lies I lived to hear, lies that rolled off his tongue so smoothly and delicately and sounded so sweet when I listened only to his words and not to his duplicitous soul.

Godfrey failed to wake one morning, so I inherited the bar by default. I cleaned it up and changed the menu, instituted some policies and began making it the social center of our side of the island as it should have been all along, instead of a smelly drunk's hangout. I had the dance floor fixed, and staged a gigantic grand opening party, including a dance band and a raffle. It was a great party, and it had barely kicked off when Crosley swept me into his arms for a dance.

I had been too busy to notice the arrival of his yacht, and my surprise was authentic and overwhelming.

I'd been expecting him. I'd expected his return since the moment he left me. I'd expected to see his smile at the end of my bar every night for five years, but when I actually saw him, smelled him, felt him, and then tasted him, it was a sight, a smell, a sensation totally beyond that of my meager imagination. He was dark and pungent and his hands strong and familiar and bold. When he tasted me, I felt as though I had never been tasted before. My spirit soared. He could not have chosen a better time than my grand opening ceremony.

I continued acting the hostess for the night, but as the party wound down, I set others to see to the wrapping up, paid the musicians, grabbed the dusty bottle of grappa I had stashed in the back of the cabinet for just exactly this anticipated event, and let myself be led to his boat, to his bed.

Again, I was stunned into silent submission by my own inadequate fantasies of what Crosley had been like. What Crosley had been to me.

After stormy, insistent, almost desperate lovemaking, we lay quietly in his bunk listening to the snapping and popping of little creatures as they fed on the boat's bottom growth. The anchor rope squeaked as the yacht pulled on it, and somewhere high above, a halyard clanged.

My fingers toyed in the thick, curly black hair that grew in a line downward from his navel. The cabin smelled like seafaring, like diesel, like weathered teak, like lovemaking.

"I must leave in five days," he said softly.

I had expected that, but the sound of it sliced my heart. I took a steeling breath and vowed to make the most of these five days he allowed me.

Early the next morning, I delegated responsibilities around the bar, and told the home team that I was taking a few days off. Then Crosley and I set about recreating who we had been five years previously. We did many of the same things of sensual pleasure. He had five years' worth of new seafaring stories to delight me, and his storytelling skills had sharpened.

I was like a young girl. I knew I could have Crosley for five days and survive. I had decided long ago that if ever given another chance, I wouldn't ruin the poetry of the moment by superimposing the inevitability of the future. Whenever the sinking feeling would come into my belly at the thought of either his string of women, all in five-day increments, or at the thought of his leaving me yet again, I squashed that thought and put it right out of my mind. I had business at hand. I had to make these five days last a lifetime. I needed to experience the depth and breadth of all that he brought to me. I was experiencing myself for the first time, and it was through the catalyst of Crosley's attentions.

I wondered continually if his other women whined about his leaving them and what he thought or did about that. Perhaps he came back to me simply because I never mentioned it. But while I was young and free this time, not whining internally or externally, Crosley was not. Perhaps it was exactly my lack of concern for the future that made him nervous. Perhaps he was falling in love with me. Perhaps the years were beginning to wear on him. Perhaps his cast aside litter of broken hearts was beginning to wear on him. Regardless, Crosley had become paranoid.

It began the very first night, as we lay in each others' arms in his stateroom. "I feel as though someone is watching us," he said, and twice during the night he took his binoculars topside and scanned the edge of the bay.

He has dealt with too many cuckolded husbands and jealous boyfriends, I thought to myself.

And the next day, as we swam in the ocean and made love in the sand, then, too, he felt as though we were being observed. But nobody was interested in two middle-aged people having sex on the beach. If they saw us, they went on their way. It was the island way.

But Crosley was not convinced of that.

And after a while, I began to feel it, too. Eyes. Desperate eyes fronting an unsettled mind. "Crosley," I said, "please stop this. You're making me afraid in my own home."

"I'm sorry, darling," he responded, "but there is something not right. There is a harmful energy here. Deeply bubbling. Your lover?"

"Of course not."

"You're sure."

After repeating that same conversation in what must have been a hundred different ways, I stopped responding. I had no desire to be infected with his fear.

And a tiny voice of hope spoke through the tangled mess of my emotions that asked if Crosley was considering me for a lifetime mate and wanted to make certain that I was unencumbered.

But I knew that wasn't the case.

On the fourth night, I sat straight up in bed out of a sound sleep and said, "Winston." And then I knew. Winston was afraid for me. Shy, reclusive, scarred Winston. Lonely Winston. Winston had a little crush on me, and I knew it, I knew it when he started coming to the bar after

Godfrey's death, looking for work and then accepting no pay for what he did. I did nothing to encourage his ardor; perhaps he encouraged it himself, and needed no help from me.

Winston. Winston was keeping an eye on Crosley to make certain Crosley behaved in an honorable manner. Winston should not have wasted his time. Crosley had no honor.

That Winston was looking after me was a comfortable feeling, and I felt just a tiny twinge of shame to know that Crosley and I had made love so openly, so blatantly, so passionately in full view of poor little Winston's feelings. Yet I was not responsible for Winston's clandestine activities, nor his uninvited attentions.

On the fifth day, Crosley and I spent the day tangled among each other in the hammock, reading. Plates of fresh fruit and bottles of wine kept us company, and we dozed and touched and dozed and read. My mind began to flirt with the bar, wondering what had transpired since I was last there a week ago. I wondered if Carola had had her baby; I wondered if Pico got his promotion. I wondered if the bar was being kept clean, swept and mopped daily. I wondered if anyone was stealing the receipts, or guzzling free booze. I didn't worry; I had chased worry from my life when I moved to this slow-moving tropical place. I was more curious. I missed it. I was eager to get back to it in the morning.

And that said a lot about my relationship with Crosley. Maybe he was right to keep his affairs to five days. Five days was perhaps enough.

As evening drew near, he began to get restless, looking behind him all the time. That, too, was becoming tiresome. "Is there a lock on your door?" he asked.

"No," I said, although I had a way of locking it when I felt unsafe. This was the fifth day. Crosley would be leaving me before dawn—without a word, without a goodbye—and I felt like tormenting him a little bit. "Put it out of your head, Crosley," I said, "and come make love to me."

He did, and it was the transcendental experience of souls merging that every woman longs to have. We spent half the night murmuring to each other, stroking softly, urgently, gently and then stopping to talk and laugh, only to begin again, slowly building. That peak, when finally attained, left me disoriented and fragmented. Words from different languages, partial thoughts from what certainly must be different minds shot through my head like stray bullets. I saw colors I'd never seen before, and could not follow a concept. I'd never had an experience like that before, and while at first afraid, I thought perhaps sleep would heal it. Crosley was already snoring.

Afraid I would sleep through his departure, I got up and moved a chair in front of the door. And when I next heard the scrape of that chair, Crosley was dressed and making his escape.

"Crosley," I said softly.

"Yes, darling?"

"One last kiss?" He looked at me; I saw the reflection in his eyes from the distinct starlight that shone through the large windows in my shack. "Please?"

He slipped off his shoes and got back into my bed, clothes and all. I held him to me, the emotion rising up from my belly to clog in my throat. I unbuttoned his shirt and kissed his chest, then rested my head against his breast.

"Francine . . ." he began.

"Shhh," I said, and spent a long, concentrated moment memorizing him, for this would be the last time his heart would beat against my cheek.

My plan was to confront him as he slipped away like a coward during the early morning hours. It doesn't take a lot of intelligence to count to five, and I sat not far from her front door in those the pre-dawn hours, waiting for that door to open. I didn't know what I would do with him, I just knew that if he wanted to cruise the world breaking hearts and wreaking emotional havoc, he could do as he pleased, but not on my island, and not with Francine.

But when the door opened it wasn't Crosley standing there, it was Francine, dressed in that gauzy white fabric she was prone to wear. "Winston," she said, and my astonishment could not have been more complete. More paralyzing was the shame that she had known. She had known that I watched, and yet she acted in that wanton way—it was too much to think about. I had to have time to ponder all the ramifications of that one word spoken clearly in the dark. Her summons. "Winston," she said.

I stood up and walked calmly to the door, as if entirely by prearrangement.

"I need your help," she said, and it was then I saw the blood on her hand. She saw it, too, and rinsed her hand in a bucket by the front door that had captured rainwater, then threw the water on the banana trees.

Crosley was in her bed, dressed. His shirt was unbuttoned, and the stub of a bamboo shoot protruded from his chest. Blood leaked out around the wound and stained his shirt.

"There is a consequence for every action," Francine said to me, her eyes calm but sad. "Crosley's has come and gone. I will wait for mine."

Together we carried him to his tender, and Francine drove it to his yacht, while I followed in my whaler. With difficulty, we loaded him aboard his boat, weighed anchor, and motored out of the bay to the calm, deep-green water. Not a word passed between us.

I secured Crosley in his stateroom, then opened the seacocks on both toilets, and together she and I sat in my boat and watched the black yacht settle ever lower in the water, until with great burbles and gasps, it sank beneath the surface.

I motored us back to the bay just as the rain began. We ran through the deluge for the bar, and arrived soaking wet. Francine made us each a double espresso and threw in a shot of Jack Daniels.

We clicked coffee cups and made our private toasts silently.

The morning that Crosley left, Winston and I sat at the bar drinking coffee and watching deluge rain soak the already sodden earth. It fell as a solid sheet from the gutterless roof all around, splashing mud from the rain-gouged trenches to mix with the water that splashed up from the dance floor, bits of confetti and other leftover party debris floating closer to our bare feet.

I felt the tropical depression in my soul and sipped coffee silently, feeling desperately claustrophobic, penned in by the humidity, the liquid walls, and my self-limiting choices in life, the vinyl of the stool sticking uncomfortably to the backs of my thighs.

PAUL J. McAULEY

Naming the Dead

Paul J. McAuley, who lives in London, has published nine novels, including Child of the River, Ancients of Days, *and* Shrine of Stars, *which form the* Confluence *trilogy. His latest,* The Secret History of Life, *will be published in the U.K. later this year. Although McAuley is best known for his science fiction, he also writes the occasional fantasy or horror story.*

McAuley notes that "in 1999, a year or two after the events in 'Naming the Dead,' the Reading Room of the British Library has been closed and emptied, more Roman graves have been found close to Spitalfields Market, and the Marquess Estate along Essex Road is being demolished."

"Naming the Dead" was originally published in Interzone *149.*

—*E. D.*

I want you to prove he killed my Emma," the woman told me.

"You realize, madam—"

"I only want to know."

"—that the police will not use anything I find as evidence."

"I have to know."

"Perhaps you should talk with someone else first."

"My husband divorced me. My mother and father are dead. My Emma is dead. I am alone, Mr. Carlyle."

She was wrong, of course. None of us are alone. Neither the living nor the dead. Even in my sanctuary there were the feeble ghosts of the silkmaker and his wife. And there was the thing clinging to my would-be client's shoulder.

Her hands tightened on the straps of her handbag. She said, "I know what you are. I know what you can do. I want you to help me find my Emma."

I said, in my very best soothing voice, "Perhaps you would like some more tea, Mrs. Stokes? And perhaps one of the delicious chocolate bourbon biscuits."

"I am quite calm, Mr. Carlyle. I have no need of the sovereign remedy, and I think that you have eaten all the biscuits."

I had to admit that Mrs. Strokes was a formidable woman. Although she was made uneasy by the steady hiss of the gas mantles, the green wallpaper, the heavy walnut furniture, and the crowded ranks of books, she tried not to show it as she sat bolt upright in the wing armchair, clutching her quilted blue handbag to her lap as if it contained her life. It was four o'clock on a dreary wet November day, darkness already lying deep in the narrow streets outside, made more sepulchral by a distant glimpse of the bright neon of the curry houses and Bangladeshi video shops of Brick Lane. The coal fire gave out a withering heat, but Mrs. Strokes had kept on her gabardine raincoat. She lived alone but she took trouble over her appearance out of habit, her lined face softened with pancake and blusher, her thin lips reddened with "Autumn Maple" lipstick, the white helmet of her hair stiffened by a new perm. When she leaned forward, she gave off an acrid little cloud compounded of the scent of face powder and Arpege. The thing at her shoulder glared at me with a mixture of spite and fear. It was her own ghost, but it had the heart-shaped face of her dead daughter, whose photograph lay on the walnut table between us. She had spent much money and more energy finding me. I knew I was her last hope. I am the last hope of all who manage to find me.

Mrs. Stokes—although she was divorced, she would never give up the "Mrs."—picked up the photograph. "He killed her, Mr. Carlyle," she said. "I know that he did. He cut off her face. That was how she was found, naked, without a face. Like his other victims. But he wouldn't confess."

She said this quite dispassionately. Her eyes were hard and bright. She was long past crying. Years past. Emma had run away to London and been killed twelve years ago. Her body had been dumped in wasteland behind King's Cross. A year later, Robert Summers had been caught in a burnt-out lockup close by, wearing the face of his victim and doing something so unspeakable to her body that two of the three policemen who made the arrest took early retirement after the trial. He was found sane, was sent down for the one murder. There was no evidence—blood, DNA, fingerprints, fiber—to tie him to the other six murders, nothing but the method of killing, the strangulation and partial flaying of the victims. His brief made a good case that he was a copycat killer. He had no previous criminal record, had held the same job, as an inventory clerk in one of the big Oxford Street department stores, for fifteen years. He got the usual tariff, reduced for good behavior. He spent his last year in an open prison, had been on the streets for three weeks.

Emma Stokes's mother had started to look for someone like me as soon as she knew that Summers would be released. She had sold the house her husband had been forced to give her after the divorce. She had rented a room in Dalston, among the sound systems and Turkish restaurants. Money meant nothing to her. She wanted nothing except to know. To know that he had done it. To purge any of Emma's ghosts, if they still remained.

I could cure her at once, of course, but I would not. I needed the money. Still, I felt sorry for her. I tried to explain again that anything I found could not be used in a court. There were still a few old-fashioned policemen who were sympathetic, but the system had changed.

"In any event," I said, "it is unlikely that any of Emma's ghosts will remember anything useful, something I can give the police so they can find some piece of tangible evidence. Ghosts rarely do remember what happened when they were cast off."

"That doesn't matter, Mr. Carlyle. I have no faith in the police."

I knew a flat in one of the point blocks off Kingsland Road, not far from where she was renting a room, where you could hire a gun for fifty pounds an hour, no questions asked. But I doubted that she wanted revenge. And it was none of my business anyway. My business was with the dead.

I told her my terms. She had done her research. She had the money, and the other things. She handed over the money without a qualm, but it took a visible effort for her to give up the rest.

"You will find her," she said.

"I will get in contact with you when it is over."

She started to tell me the number of the pay telephone in the rooming house, but I said, "I do not use the telephone, Mrs. Stokes. But be assured that I will be in contact with you when it is over. Not before. It might take some time."

"I have been waiting twelve years, Mr. Carlyle."

On the way out, she asked the question most of my clients have not dared to ask. "Why do you live like this?"

She said it with a trace of her old prim, suburban judgmentalism. I said, "You will not need to come here again."

"I don't mind it. But it makes what you do seem like . . . an act. I hope it is not, Mr. Carlyle. I have put my Emma in your hands."

I went to King's Cross first, but there was nothing of Emma Strokes there, nor anything of the other victims. There were plenty of other ghosts, of course, mostly scraps of spent lust mingled with sparks of rage from the clients of the whores who still work the station, despite the security cameras and the extra police patrols. I dispatched them all, and afterward became aware of an old woman watching me among the weeds on the far side of a tangle of rusting tracks. Her long black dress and shawl looked to be Victorian, and I made a note to investigate once the case was over. Long-lived ghosts are rare, even in London. I thought that I knew them all, and I have a particular affinity for Victorian ghosts.

Later, when I asked the librarian about her, he smiled faintly and said, "There are many of us you do not know about, Carlyle. The living cannot know all the names of the dead."

"But you know who she was?"

"As a matter of fact I do not. But I could make enquiries . . ."

"Not now."

"Because you wish me to observe this murderer of young girls. How poorly you must think of me, Carlyle, for you always force me to associate with these unsavory characters."

"You don't have to do it." I had the things Mrs. Stokes had given me in the pockets of my trenchcoat. The librarian knew that they were there; his eyes, faint stars in his pale face, kept straying toward them.

"It is a living," he said. "Where is he?"

I told him, and he said, "Ah, the tea gardens, and the New River. I spent many a happy afternoon there in the bosky meadows."

There were no tea gardens there now. They had been built over long ago, and built over again with the interlocked decks of the Marquess Estate. Robert Summers had been given a one-bedroom flat there. I had watched him for most of the afternoon as he sat hunched on one of the benches in the triangular Green in Islington, at the junction of Upper Street and Essex Road, had waited outside the nearby branch Sainsbury's while he spent an hour buying half a carrier bag's worth of groceries. A scrawny harmless man, unshaven, his iron-gray hair sticking up in a cowlick over a bland, unlined face. He wore a new black suit and a dirty white shirt. People knew to give him a wide berth as he shuffled along.

But no ghosts clung to him. Perhaps he had lost them in prison to someone more powerful. Most ghosts are unfaithful, short-lived things.

The librarian was one of the more persistent ghosts, the death shell of a man who had died in the mid-nineteenth century. He was, like many ghosts, vague about the person who had cast him off. He had not been a librarian, but something to do with the book trade, perhaps a bookseller or a bookbinder or a printer. He had taken up semi-permanent residence in the reading room of the British Library, which was where I had come to consult with him, pretending to read a trade union history while conducting a whispered conversation. No one took any notice. A lot of the scholars and journalists who worked on the curved ranks of cubicles talked to themselves. It was raining, and the rain pattered on the high ceiling overhead.

I said, "What will you do, when this place is closed?"

"There are plenty of other accommodations. Or perhaps I will choose to pass over at last. The twentieth century is becoming tiresome, and I do not look forward to the millennium. Now, the stuff, if you please, and I will be gone as quickly as Puck or Ariel."

I took out the things Mrs. Stokes had given me, and laid them on the reading desk. A square of blue nylon cut from one of Emma's old sheets. An old lipstick, dried out. A pair of plain white Marks & Spencer knickers. A photograph, formally posed.

The librarian lowered his face to them, as greedy as an addict. He sighed, and said, "Yes, it is so strong, so good . . ." and then faded, the stars of his eyes going last of all. As I gathered up the material the electric bell rang. It was closing time.

Like the librarian, I find the late twentieth century tiresome. Because of my dress and the furnishing of my house, most people assume that I affect a late Victorian style to express this distaste, but that is not the case. It is simply a style I have never outgrown. And it was the time in which my family first gained influence over the dead.

We had a long and honorable history as sin-eaters and scriers, but it was grandfather who began the trade in what is now known, inaccurately, as the paranormal. It was he who codified a systematic approach to the matter of the dead. I am the last of my line. My mother and father died when our house was destroyed by an ill-advised experiment, and when I had recovered I moved from Edinburgh to London, and bought a house in Spitalfields.

It was a Georgian house in poor repair, and I have done nothing since to modernize it, or, like some of my neighbors, to restore it to its original state. (I have several times resisted visits from well-meaning members of the self-styled historical society, who give conducted tours of their restored houses dressed in Georgian costume; but my black suit, paisley waistcoat, homburg, walking stick, and fob watch are not a costume.) There is no electricity, and no telephone, but those things are not necessary. As light attracts moths, so electricity attracts too many partial ghosts, and I do not need the distraction. I have gas mantles, and coal fires in the winter. And anyone who wants to find me will eventually do so, or they will discover in the process of trying to find me that they do not, after all, need my help.

But the most important thing is that it is a quiet house, a quiet place, and well protected. How difficult that is to find in any large city! All who died here died natural deaths; they led contented and happy lives. When I found it, there were no ghosts thrown off by hate or fear, by ecstasy or enlightenment. Ghosts of the original owners, a Huguenot silkmaker and his wife, sometimes drift through the rooms, and the ghost of the cobbler who lived and worked in the basement for more than fifty years can sometimes be heard, but they are all weak and harmless fragments, no more of a nuisance than the mice which rustle behind the walnut paneling. A few imps of delirium left by the hippies who squatted there in the early 1970s were easy to disperse, and other ghosts are kept at bay by soul catchers at doors and windows, and regular asperging with rosemary, moly, and rue.

Such places are increasingly rare as ghosts multiply. Fewer people seem inclined to a quiet death, and the jostle of the city's population fills its streets with malevolent ghosts cast off in moments of intense anger or fear. Traffic intersections are crowded with the remnants of motorists' frustrations; I am unable to visit hospitals, or to travel on the Underground, or pass near casinos (although they do not know it, gamblers are quite right to use fresh decks of cards with each session, for the ghosts which cling to used cards strongly affect the laws of chance). Many churches are still peaceful, as are certain graveyards. After all, very few die in either place, and those mourning the dead do not shed ghosts for mourning is an emotional state akin to exhaustion, not a state of heightened awareness.

The long-dead, such as the librarian, find the press of ghosts as tiresome as I. And of course for them certain ghosts are dangerous. There are lions and tigers and bears loose in the world. More of them, it seems, every year, as if the millennium on whose brink we tremble will after all be the threshold of the pit. London is crowded with ghosts, imps, and other revenants, but the truly long-lived manifestations are dwindling. They are being eaten by those of their kind which require the energy of others to sustain them.

But that was not the immediate threat, which manifested itself as two men who materialized on either side of me as I was making my way through the crowded Spitalfields market the Sunday after Mrs. Stokes had visited me. I had bought walnut bread at one stall, organic potatoes and cabbage at another, and a water-stained edition of Hick's *Death and Eternal Life*, which promised to be amusing. It was difficult to disengage as the two men took me by the elbows and steered me into a corner by one of the gates.

"We've been looking for you," the smaller one said. He was sweating despite the cold, a slight, sandy-haired man with a narrow moustache, wearing an immaculate London Fog raincoat. There were imps clinging to his thinning hair, spiky black things that chittered like bats. He said, "You are a hard man to find."

"I am glad to hear it," I said. "My house is protected."

"But *you* aren't protected," the smaller man said, and told his companion, "Show him what I mean."

The larger man opened his leather jacket to show me the jointed metal truncheon tucked into the inside pocket.

"This is in the nature of a warning," the smaller man said.

"You have an infestation," I said. "Who is it that marked you?"

"Don't play games. I was warned about you and I don't believe in all that shit, all right?" The imps were whispering in his ears, and he said his piece defiantly, but his eyes glittered. He knew that he was trapped, although he did not understand how.

"Then you are in great danger, my friend."

"You be quiet! Roddy here has a lot of toys, and he likes using them. We could go back to your house and he'll give you a free trial."

"I do not think I could allow you to find my house. I expect that you have been looking for it all morning, and you have not found it. Nor will you. Give me the message, and leave."

The sandy-haired man handed me an envelope. "This will explain everything. You are threatening the interests of a powerful man, Mr. Carlyle."

"And who would he be?"

The imps chittered. The man said, "No names, no pack drill."

"Ah. One of those."

"You just stop. All right? Remember Edinburgh."

"What do you know about—"

But the little man was already walking away, head down, the big man at his back, toward the black 500 series BMW parked on the double yellow lines just outside the gate. I watched as they got into the back of the car; someone was waiting inside, but I saw only a shadow before the door closed and the car drove off.

There was a speck of an imp in the seal of the envelope, and I crushed it by reflex. It was designed to do but one thing, squeal that the envelope had been opened, and I gave it no chance to do that. It could have told me nothing more than its existence already told me, that the man who had sent the message knew something about the matter of the dead.

Inside, the message was crude and shocking. I did not look at it again, but called upon an old friend.

We met early the next morning near Smithfield Market, in one of the public houses which are licensed to open at 6:30 A.M. Superintendent Rawles looked at the photograph that had been inside the envelope and said that it was part of the crime-scene documentation.

"I'll look into how it was leaked," he said. He was a tall, slender, upright man, with close-cropped white hair and a military bearing, and one of the most honest men I have ever met. He was working on his second pint of bitter while I ate the excellent full English breakfast— the pinnacle of the cuisine of this wretched country I have adopted— which the public house served.

"It is not where the photograph came from which is important."

I described Mrs. Stokes's commission, the two men who had delivered the envelope, and my suspicion that this was the work of a would-be necromancer who believed that he had some use for the murderer, Robert Summers.

"There's an incident room already set up," Inspector Rawles said. "Perhaps you can come in and look at the books, see if you can spot these bad boys. But that's all I can let you do. It's out of my hands, Carlyle."

"You know that they will not be among your mug-shots."

"No, I suppose not. She was your client. What was she doing there?"

"She had rented the room. I believe that she had sold her house."

"Keep away from Summers. We're watching him. Your client is dead; you don't have that job anymore."

The librarian was watching Summers. I said, "I do not need to go near him. Do you think he killed her?"

"You look pale," Rawles said. "Paler than usual, although I see that your appetite is as healthy as ever. You think this necromancer chap might actually be dangerous?"

"Only if he is more ignorant than usual. It is not the thought of him which makes me uncomfortable, despite this excellent repast, but the proximity of the market."

Rawles smiled. "The ghosts of cows?"

I used the last of the blood pudding—they served two kinds there, white and black—to wipe up the last of the egg yolk. "Animals leave no ghosts. It is not the meat market, but the public executions that were held here. Mary Tudor had two hundred martyrs burned; before that heretics and witches were roasted, burned, or boiled alive. Traces remain, even after all these years. Effluvia from the crowd rather than the ghosts the poor tormented victims cast off at the death. Still, it is not as bad as the public transport system."

"You're too sensitive for this city, lad." Rawles looked at the Polaroid again. "It has your artist's mark. But whoever did it didn't know much about skinning. Summers used a proper flensing knife, and he has had practice using it. Unfortunately he used a different knife each time, which is why the forensic boffins couldn't pin the full slate to him. But this wasn't done with a flensing knife. We think this was done with the same combat knife that the murderer used to cut her throat. We found the weapon, no prints of course, and it could have been bought in any one of a hundred shops. We're canvassing them, but I doubt if we'll get anywhere. This is a professional hit."

"It was meant as a message, to me. Summers is more than he seems."

"You stay away. We can handle it."

"He has no ghosts. He murdered at least fifteen girls and he has no ghosts at all."

"Is that strange? He was in prison a long time."

Rawles was a practical man; he had grasped many of the nuances of the matter of the dead instinctively.

"Not strange, but it is unusual, given the interest in him."

Rawles drained his pint. "Perhaps this chap who put the heavies on you took Summers's ghosts."

"Then why is Summers still of interest? You drink too much, Robert."

"And you have a healthy appetite. I have to see my chief in a couple of hours. A bloodless Ph.D. in sociology who did about six hours on the beat before getting a desk job. He's fifteen years younger than me. He talks like a company executive, quotas and efficiency and targets. I'll retire next year. They'll probably put a computer in to replace me. This isn't like the old days, Carlyle."

"As I am all too unfortunately aware."

As we parted, he added, "I hope that's just a walking stick these days. If some eager young bobby thinks to take a look, he'll do you for carrying a concealed weapon."

It was not the last warning I was to receive that day.

My house is, as I have said, protected. There are not many streets at the heart of old Spitalfields, a brief grid with the market on one side and the exotic glamour of Brick Lane on the other, but for anyone searching for my house with malice in their hearts they can become impossibly tangled.

But my next warning did not knock upon my door. Instead, it came roaring and gurgling out of the slate sink in the kitchen, which took up the basement where the cobbler had once worked. The noise shook the whole house, but I was already coming down the stairs with a candle; I had felt the wind of its approach.

The water spout had formed a thick column of water that shook and shivered as it spun around and around. It glowed with a faint, greenish light. It stank horribly.

A face formed on its shivering surface, the kind of face you might imagine seeing on the trunk of a tree where a branch has been torn away, or the kind of face which rises toward you out of the scintillae you make when you press your fingertips against your closed eyelids. An approximation of a face. It had no eyes but I knew it could see me as it whirled around. It made a horrid gargling sound when it spoke.

It spoke in Latin, and I knew at once what it was. The oldest of all the ghosts of London. At once, I made obeisance.

He had never been a person, and that made him more terrible and powerful than any ordinary ghost. He was something like the effluvia which had made me uncomfortable near Smithfield Market, the accumulated blood-lust of the tens of thousands of men and women who had come to watch the executions for sport. Like that, but far more powerful and focused, for he had been formed and reinforced by the sacrificial ceremonies of those who had worshipped at the Temple of Mithras, founded by Ulpius Silvanus, a veteran of the II Legio Augusta during the Roman occupation of Britain. Archaeologists found a relief sculpture of a god killing a bull, a sculpture of a river god, and other remains in the middle of the Walbrook, the long-buried tributary around which the Romans had built their original settlement, but only I knew precisely where the temple had stood, and the nature of the rituals. There had been sacrifice of bulls, but also human sacrifice: the victims had been sealed in the belly of a brazen bull, and fires lit beneath it.

The thing which manifested itself through the drain of my kitchen sink was the remnant of the river god which worship and sacrifice had created. You might say that it was the echo of a collective mania so strong it had lasted for two thousand years. It spoke only in Latin, but because of my long apprenticeship to my father I was not only fluent in Latin but knew (unlike all living scholars of that dead language) how to pronounce it correctly. I even knew that Mithras had a Spanish accent; Ulpius Silvanus, like many of the legionaries who had occupied Britain, had come from the Mediterranean shore of Spain.

"You will not disturb the murderer," Mithras said. "You will leave all alone, and all will be well."

"Why is that? What is your interest?"

"I speak for all the dead."

"Then I am honored that you should visit me." I took a steak from the meat safe and threw it into the whirling unstable column of water. It vanished at once, shredding into pulp and blood. It was to have been my supper, but I felt that propitiation of the old god was more important. I had only ever seen Mithras once before, on an ill-advised expedition beneath London with the young engineer and Dr. Pretorius, and that had been long ago, in my salad days.

Mithras said, "The sacrifice is acceptable. You may ask a question."

Once, dozens of bulls had been slaughtered in a single day in his honor. Men drunk on the thick red wine called Bull's Blood had run through the streets ahead of the animals before they had been sacrificed. The men who had fallen to the bulls had been as much sacrifices to Mithras as those roasted inside the brazen bull. Mithras had been very powerful. He had protected the Roman settlement from ancient indigenous ghosts of the wild lands outside the stockade walls. He survived only because he had once been so powerful. He was an echo, a revenant, but not without influence. I wondered how long it had been since someone had given him tribute.

"One question," he said again. "Ask!"

"Is Robert Summers owned by a living man?"

"There is no such person as Robert Summers."

"Then what is he?"

"You have asked your question. It is answered. Ask no more. Seek no more. You have some protection here, but I could remove it all if I wished."

"Where is the librarian? Bring him here and I will speak with him."

The speed of the revolving column of water increased. Greasy droplets dashed against my face. The whirling water made a high wailing sound, and out of it Mithras said, "He no longer exists."

"Did Summers kill him? Or the man who has taken control of him?"

"Ask no more. Remember you live here upon my sufferance."

"Hmm. With respect, that is not quite true. This place lies to the east of the walls of your city."

"Some of my dead lie nearby. It is enough."

I remembered then that a Roman cemetery had been discovered four hundred years ago, in the fields to the east of the priory of St. Mary Spital. I opened my mouth to ask one more question, but the face dissolved or spread out across the glowing surface of the unstable column of water. The force which held the water together vanished.

I stepped back and dropped the candle as the flood spun out in an splattering arc across the kitchen. I was alone in darkness.

I could not let the mystery lie. Although my client was dead and the contract dissolved, it was clear that taking Mrs. Stokes's money had put me in danger. Oh, not yet, but if I let it go then the amateur who was meddling with the ghosts of Robert Summers would do something stupid. Better to stop it now, whatever Mithras said, than wait until it got worse.

And besides, I had always liked the librarian.

As I mopped the flood of stinking drain water from the old linoleum, I thought of a ghost who might be able to help me. I finished the work and carefully sprinkled dried rue and wild garlic on the last of the water before pouring it down the drain. It would not keep out the river god, of course, but it would stop imps and other sprites from following his path.

I made no other precautions. It would not to do attract attention.

I ate lunch at one of the fine Bangladeshi restaurants in Brick Lane, and then set off north. I could not ride in public transport because I needed to keep my mind clear (and taxis were worse repositories of shed moments of anger than buses). It was cold, a sharp dry cold, the sky clear except for a few high strands of cirrus, darkening in the east.

It took an hour to walk to the rooming house where Mrs. Stokes had been murdered. I was happy to be alone with my thoughts. At one point I passed a mosque under construction, and wondered what ghosts it would add to the city, but for the most part I thought hard about what must be done.

Mrs. Stokes had rented a room in one of the houses in the Victorian terraces behind Ridley Road Market. They had been poor things when they had been thrown up to help accommodate the increasing population of factory laborers, and they had not lasted well. There were three lidless dustbins and a broken pram among the dead weeds in the mean little garden, and a bored young constable stood in front of the door, which had been sealed with blue and white crime-scene tape. The circus which accompanied any murder—and I do not mean the police, the forensic team, the ambulance, and the crowd of morbid onlookers—had passed on.

But something lingered.

I had bought a slab of cheesecake in the twenty-four-hour Jewish bakery, and I walked to the end of the road and ate it while I waited. The streetlights came on and the sky beyond them darkened. It was cold, and I wished that I had bought some coffee with the cheesecake.

But at last I caught a faint scent of face powder and Arpege, and without turning around I knew that she had come to me.

The ghost of Mrs. Stokes was remarkably composed, but from my brief meeting with her when she had been alive I had expected nothing less. I had been counting on it, in fact. She knew that she was dead, although like all ghosts she did not remember dying. I remembered the photograph I had been given and thought it a mercy.

When the traffic had thinned out—she found the rushing cars a terrible distraction, as if each promised to bear her away to paradise—I walked along Balls Pond Road. She was at my back, talking about her Emma. I think that she had become fused or mixed with the thing which had been at her back when she had come to see me, or perhaps this was the same ghost, strengthened by the death of the woman who had thrown it off.

It would not matter soon. All that did matter was that it would do as I asked.

"I will see her again. My Emma, just as she was."

"Yes, you will see her again."

I could have removed the ghost at Mrs. Stokes's back when she had first come to see me. She would have lost her obsession, and gone away. It was something I could have done with most of my clients, but I had needed the money. Now, I thought that it was fortunate that I had no scruples. For otherwise I would not have known what kind of creature Robert Summers was, and of the man who had an interest in him, until too late.

But I knew that it would still be difficult to stop them.

I tried to tell the ghost, but she babbled happily that it did not matter. "I know what I must do and I know I can do it. I can do it for my Emma. I know I can." And, "I will take her to the arms of Jesus, Mr. Carlyle. I will find the way." And, "How strange everything looks! Some things so bright, the rest so dark. I had a television once which showed pictures like this. The thing controlling its picture had broken.

It was all light or all dark. I had to take it back to the shop and there was quite an argument over replacing it, although I was fully within my rights. Is this how it looks to you, Mr. Carlyle?"

"Sometimes."

"No wonder you live the way you do. I know now why you have no electricity. I think I can see electricity now. Every car is a scrawled outline of electric wires, like the filaments in a light bulb."

No, she did not really understand. She seemed much younger. I think that she was assuming the form in which she remembered her daughter, but I did not dare look around to see.

The big, black BMW was parked on double yellow lines on Essex Road, by the stairs which led to the first floor deck of the block of flats. Its motor was idling—a white plume of exhaust waved in the air from its tailpipe—but I could not see who was inside because the windows were tinted.

Mrs. Stokes knew that her Emma was not inside the car. I nearly lost her as she went gadding away toward Summers's flat, light and limber as a young girl. It was all I could do to restrain her as I went puffing up the stairs, but the swirling graffiti helped divert her attention.

At the top were the two men who had accosted me in Spitalfields Market. I had expected nothing less.

"You're not wanted here," the sandy-haired one said sharply. "You clear off, granddad."

His boldness was a mask. I could smell his fear. His imps were a ruff of sharply angled black bodies tangled around his head, squeaking with fury.

"My business is with your master," I said. "I believe that he is in Robert Summers's flat. Stand aside, sir."

I was afraid, of course, but determined to see this through. It occurred to me that Mrs. Stokes's obsession had transferred to me.

The sandy-haired man raised a hand. He wore black leather gloves.

I unlatched my cane and whipped it up. The cover flew off, revealing the short, double-edged blade.

The sandy-haired man barked a brief laugh and took a step backward. "Who d'you think you are? Zorro? Put it away or you'll get hurt."

"Will you stand aside?"

"Get him," the sandy-haired man said. His hand was inside his London Fog raincoat and I knew that he had a revolver. But he did not want to use it because it would immediately attract attention.

The big man stepped forward, his hands working, and I pointed the blade at his face so that he went cross-eyed as he tried to focus on it, then whipped it down and drew a line on the dirty rippled concrete of the walkway. The man's eyes followed and stayed there, and something in him relaxed. It was a small trick, but effective. He would stare at the line I had scratched into the concrete until I released him. He would not be able to move his eyes from it at all, even if all the women he most desired paraded naked in front of him. Already he was trying to break free—I could see sweat gathering on his forehead, and tears swelling in his unblinking eyes—but I knew that he could not.

The sandy-haired man drew his revolver with a convulsive movement when I pointed my sword at him. "You stay there," he said. "Just keep still or you'll regret it."

I was tired of his threats. I dismissed his retinue of chattering imps and he batted wildly at the air around his head and looked at me as if for the first time. His mouth opened, but there was nothing to put words into it.

"Wait by the car," I suggested.

He nodded violently. "Yes. That's what I should do. He wants to see you. And I'll go and wait . . . ."

"In the car."

After he had gone, I went past the big man—who strained and failed to lift his eyes—to the door of Robert Summers's flat. It had been painted pale blue a long time ago. Someone had sprayed a crude graffito of male genitalia on it in black touch-up paint. Someone else—or perhaps it had been the graffiti artist—had tried to kick in its lower panel, which was chipped and splintered around three smashed dents. It was ajar, and light spilled around it. As I raised my hand to push it open, a voice from inside said, "You are welcome to enter, ghost eater, but know that you do so of your own free will."

There was a short corridor with a kitchen on one side and a bathroom on the other. Both were unspeakably filthy. The light came from the room at the end, which was lit by the pitiless glare of an unshaded hundred-watt bulb. There were no carpets, only stained and cracked chipboard. The wallpaper, pink and silver stripes, had been sprayed with scribbled tags and obscenities. It smelled of urine and unwashed bodies, and moldy dampness. It smelt of despair. It was the most evil place I had ever been in. If not for the ghost of Mrs. Stokes clinging to my back I would have turned around and fled to the safety of my house, never to come out again.

Robert Summers stood in the middle of the room, his hands laced before his crotch. He did not acknowledge my entrance. He was as still as the man I had charmed. The harsh light shone off the bald patch on the crown of his head. He wore his expensive black suit. There was something wrong with his face. It was more wrinkled than I remembered, and seemed to have slipped, so that its bottom part rested on the collar of his stained white shirt.

Then I realized what it was. A mask. A mask made from the skinned face of Mrs. Stokes.

Behind me, a man said, "You should not have come here, Mr. Carlyle."

I turned. A man of medium height, his face masked by a trimmed beard and mirrored sunglasses, sat on a plastic chair of the kind sold as cheap patio furniture. He wore an impeccably tailored chalk-stripe suit, a Turnball & Asser shirt, oxblood loafers. His shirt cuffs were fastened by onyx studs. There was a £10,000 oyster Rolex on his right wrist, and several heavy gold bracelets on his left. A circle had been drawn around him on the warped chipboard; even before I saw the black lamb dead in a corner I knew that the circle had been drawn with blood.

"Oh, I am well protected," the man said.

He had a cultivated voice, salted with an Eastern European accent. Lithuanian, perhaps, or Slovak. Although he was immaculately dressed and manicured, there was something indescribably filthy about him, as if an invisibly thin film of excrement covered him.

I held out my hand. "I am pleased to meet you, sir."

For a moment, I thought that he was about to stand up, but then he flattened his palms on the flimsy arms of the plastic chair and relaxed and smiled. "You know that I will not leave the circle."

"I do not know you."

The man's smile broadened. He placed the tips of his forefingers to the end of his neat beard. "Ah, it is not so easy to learn my name."

"Yet I believe you know mine."

"Then I have the advantage. I see that you have a companion."

"Your creature did not eat all of her."

"Eat? Ah. I see. No, he does not do what you do. You have made a grave mistake, Mr. Carlyle. You really should not have come here. *Why* did you come here?"

"Mrs. Stokes is my client."

"The poor thing which clings to you is not your client. It is merely all that is left of her."

I thought it better to say nothing. I could have walked out of the room. Mrs. Stokes would stay, of course. In a way, she would become united with her daughter again, and so I would have fulfilled the conditions of my contract. Even now she was yearning toward Summers, as someone in the desert will stretch toward a handful of cool water. But if I let her go and left the room I knew that I could not stay in

London. Perhaps there would be no place in the world which would be safe.

The man said, "I shall tell you why you are here. You came because you believe that you are the self-appointed spiritual guardian of the city. You believe that things must be always as they are, not as they should be. You hate change as much as the ghosts you fondly believe are your charges. You came here because you are a fool who believes his own boasts. You are nothing but a tricked-out ghost eater who makes a living duping the bereaved. I am here because it is long past time for change. There are new things loose in the world, wonderful things."

I said unwillingly, "Lions and tigers and bears."

"Yes. Fierce wild creatures created by the unique pressures at the end of this century. It is not your century, Mr. Carlyle. You do not belong here."

I said, "Summers is your creature."

"I found him." The man could not resist boasting. It was his fatal flaw. It was the fatal flaw of all his kind. He said, "He was never really alive. A shell of a man, a bundle of habits. His work was trivial and meaningless. He had no personal life. On weekends he would sit on the edge of the sagging bed in his greasy bedsit staring at the patch of sky visible beyond the chimneypots and hoping for escape. That was his strongest desire, and at last it turned inward. He vanished into himself. He became as empty as his bedsit, and a new tenant arrived."

"It is lonely, is it not? That is why it kills."

"It has no human weakness, Mr. Carlyle. It kills because that is what it is. That is its power."

He said this in such a gloating way that I felt physically ill. But I knew that he was wrong. If it killed only for the sake of killing, it did not need to wear the faces of its victims. And I knew then that the man did not fully understand his creature.

He said, "What will you do, Mr. Carlyle? Run away? But where will you run to? Try and hide? But your hiding place will not last forever. Join me? But I do not need your help. Try and run me through with that pig-sticker of yours. Go on. I know that you want to."

"I want to, but I will not. You are protected. But I will give you what you want."

And I released the ghost of Mrs. Stokes.

She had been straining so hard to be released that it was a relief to let her go. She went with a joyful noise, as straight as an arrow.

I do not think that the man saw her—I do not think that he could see ghosts. He was sensitive to their presence, but that is not unusual. He was not interested in the matter of the dead, but only in power. The problem is not that the people do not believe, but that they believe in the wrong things, in numerology, spiritualism, tarot, crystals, and so on. As Lewis's devil remarked in *The Screwtape Letters,* the first step to damnation is to replace God with some other belief. The man's weakness was that he believed in his own power, but it is easy enough to find enough of the matter of the dead to dabble. The old necromancers were vain enough to write down their knowledge, and their encryption systems are no match for modern computers.

But knowledge and vain self-belief are not enough.

If the man did not see the poor woman's ghost, the Summers creature did. Its head snapped up and it yawned, showing stained false teeth, and gulped her down.

For a moment, nothing happened. The man clapped his clean pink palms together in soft applause.

Then Summers tipped back his head and howled, and I knew that Mrs. Stokes had found her daughter.

It was all she wanted; all that she had left behind was a single desire, hot and strong and vibrant. As sharp as a knife through cloth, she had cut through the ghosts the Summers creature had bound about itself, the ragged garment it had woven as a disguise or an attempt to become human. Now it burst apart.

It was as if a magnesium flare had been exploded in a cave full of bats.

For a moment the room was full of ghosts and other revenants. Behind me, the man screamed and screamed, but I hardly heard him. The lightbulb blew in a flurry of brief sparks. Ghosts flew around me in the darkness. I like to think that I glimpsed Mrs. Stokes and her daughter, but I cannot be sure. There were so many. And at the core of their whirling flight was the thing which had bound them, shaggy and black. It was not something new but something very old. I believe that it may have been prehistoric, some remainder of a shamanistic dream or ritual. How badly it wanted to be human! That is why it had killed, assembling a persona from fragments of the dead. I dispatched it and the ghosts fled in every direction.

There is not much left to tell. The man had buried his face in his hands. Blood leaked between his fingers. I could smell the stench of his voided bladder and bowels. I left him sitting within his protective circle and walked home alone.

In the next few days I learned from the newspapers of an increase in murders, suicides, and other acts of violence. A man threw himself among the lions in Regent's Park Zoo; a woman set herself alight and jumped from Hungerford Bridge; another woman was found chewing on the stringy corpse of one of the ravens of the Tower of London.

It would pass, but I knew that things were changed. There were new and terrible things awake in the world, and not all of them belonged in the realm of the dead. For a very long time I had lived as if things had not changed, as if this great and terrible century was nothing more than a dream from which I would at last awake, free of the burden of my past, my own ghosts.

I knew now that no one could free me but myself. It was time to take up my own life, and walk freely in the city, among the living and the dead.

JUAN GOYTISOLO

The Stork-men

I'm a fan of magic realism, an avid reader of García Márquez, Isabel
Allende, and their illustrious followers. I love novels and stories that
are rich in fantastical characters and fabulous happenings: wise
grandmothers, blood falling as rain, flying children, galleons mysteriously stranded amidst the greenery of the virgin jungle. These "romans
de pays chaud," as they were labeled by one defender of outmoded,
anemic literary values, represent fresh energy and vitality, and bring an
element of poetry into the prosaic narrowness of our lives. So, when I
heard the tale of the *Thousand Minus One Nights* of my esteemed colleague from the Circle, with its reference to the stork's nest next to the
little house Eusebio rented in the Alcazaba district, by the *mechouar,* I
recalled certain paragraphs by my fellow Spaniard, Alí Bey, on the

subject of these migratory waders whose company he enjoyed in Marrakech thanks to the sultan's credulity.

According to an old Moroccan tradition, Berber peasants believe that storks are human beings who adopt that form temporarily in order to travel and experience other lands, and then, when they return to their own country, they recover their original shape. So, on my arrival in Marrakech in pursuit of the elusive Eusebio, I decided to abandon risky and fruitless enquiries, and with the help of the historian Hamid Triki I made my way to the ancient stork refuge next to the Mosque of Ibn Yusef.

After a great deal of searching and asking for directions, I came upon Dar Belarx and managed to find the guide. Encouraged by my generous tip, he produced a bunch of keys and led me through a side door, along a gloomy corridor, and into a large, magnificent patio, though dirty and neglected. Heaps of rubble covered the central area, adorned with a fountain; but the fine arcades, the moldings in the side rooms, and the tile friezes had resisted the ravages of time. There were piles of feathers and pigeon droppings, and even the recent corpse of one of those birds, attracted, like her companions, by the silence and benevolence of the spot. The refuge had been closed up a century earlier, on the death of a grandson of its founder.

I mentioned to my escort the legend of the stork-men. To my great surprise, he corrected my terminology. It was no legend, but the absolute truth. He himself knew someone who emigrated in that fashion to Europe and returned home a few months later, having recovered his former shape. The man lived in that very alley, and my guide needed no prompting to introduce me to him.

The quick-change artist—how else to describe him?—was a placid, serene old man, of a very similar appearance to the one my colleagues have attributed to Eusebio, with intensely blue eyes and a carefully tended white beard, sitting at the door of his house, his right hand resting on the handle of his stick. To avoid any boring preamble I will let him tell his own story; I don't know if it's true, or his own invention, or taken from folklore.

"Some forty years ago, my wife—may she be with God!—managed to get a contract to work in a thread mill in France and so she emigrated in order to improve our modest fortunes, leaving me behind to take care of the children. At first, we received regular news of her, together with a postal order representing her savings for the month; but gradually the money began to arrive on its own, with no accompanying letter. This strange, long silence, pregnant with fears and doubts, plunged me into a profound melancholy. My own letters went unanswered; as did my requests for her to telephone. I wrote enquiring after her to a neighbor who had also gone to work in a thread mill in the same area. Her laconic telegram—'all well, your wife working'—far from dispelling my unease, only increased it. If all was so well, why the silence? Had she forgotten her position as wife and mother of four children? At night I would toss and turn in my bed, unable to sleep. Meanwhile, the chances of getting a passport had decreased: the economic crisis and unemployment in the Christian countries meant all doors were closed to foreigners, and the French consulate did not issue tourist visas to poor artisans like me: a humble cobbler. They asked me for a bank reference and goodness knows what else. In short: I had to give up the idea. But I still yearned to make the trip and one day, as I was gazing at the storks nesting on the top of the walls of the royal palace, I thought to myself, if only I could be like them and fly to where my wife is working in her thread mill in faraway Épinal. As though led by a presentiment, I went to see my eldest brother: I told him I had decided to go to Europe and I gave him temporary charge of the care and education of my children. That uneasy period of my life came to a sudden end.

"The next day, I was on my way with a flight of storks, in a state of bliss and delight difficult to express in words. The world was both tiny and immense: landscapes and towns like toys, seas glinting like mirrors, white mountains. . . . Height, weightlessness, speed of movement, made me feel superior to humans, slow as tortoises, tiny as insects. I was flying with a sense of utter happiness toward the prosperous and enlightened continent from which Christians had ventured forth in order, apparently, to educate us, and incidentally offer us work, distracted by the rapture of soaring from the precise purpose of my journey. Those were weeks of freedom and contentment, untrammeled by borders and official stamps. Carrying no papers of any kind, we crossed the boundaries of separate territories, we broke their petty laws, eluded customs barriers and police checks, laughed at the mean discrimination represented by visas. Once we had passed a huge chain of mountains, covered with snow like the Atlas range, the view changed: the fields were greener, woods more frequent and thicker, the towns with ochre tiles gave way to others with roofs of gray slate. We were following the course of a river on whose banks stood cities and factories. A few days later, after many a long days' flight, halting by night on towers and belfries, I felt my drive weaken, I could not keep up with my companions, I was falling hopelessly behind, I could scarcely move my wings. Unable even to hover, I nearly plummeted to the ground, but landed as best I could in a garden.

"My appearance startled the owner of the house, a Frenchman of

about forty who was pruning some trees and trimming the lawn with
shears. 'Look, Aicha, a stork,' he cried. The name of my beloved wife
set my heart fluttering wildly. Who was this fellow, and how dare he
address her so intimately? When she appeared at the door, I was ready
to faint. I kept staring at her and my eyes flooded with tears. 'That's
incredible,' she said in French. 'There are lots of them in my country.
I'm sure that's where it's come from.' She came over to me, without
recognizing me, and stroked my feathers. 'How tame it is! It has probably fallen ill and can't fly on. I'm going to take care of it and feed it
raw fish. Where I come from they say it brings good luck; it's a guest
out of the blue and it deserves our respect and hospitality.'

"Aicha's sweet, welcoming words, instead of easing my pain, increased it. Her use of 'our' and her obvious intimacy with the man
confirmed my suspicions: she was living with him as man and wife,
sharing his bed and table. Still bewildered, and full of bitterness, I wondered whether they had children. I was afraid I might hear a baby crying,
and I scrutinized the washing line, fortunately without spotting any nap-
pies or baby clothes. But the sense of superiority and pride I had previously felt, up in the sky, gave way to feelings of impotence and rage.
I was two steps away from my wife and her lover, incapable of responding to her adultery, with my awkward wader's movements and my dis-
cordant squawks. The affection and maternal instinct Aicha showed, her
eagerness to care for me, choose my food, build me a kind of nest on
the roof of a shed, degraded, rather than exalted, my temporary status
as a bird. The sight of me reminded her of home, she covered me with
kisses and caresses, but at night when they both came back from work—
she from her thread mill, he from a branch of a major bank—they would
go inside and close the door, leaving me standing one-legged on my
nest.

"After the first weeks of sadness, I grew bolder: I resolved to go
on the offensive. I left my wretched nest and, without further ado,
stalked into the house. At first, the intruder tried to shoo me away, but
she stopped him.

" 'This stork is a blessed creature that reminds me of everything I
left behind. If it wants to live in the house it shall live in the house.
God sent it to us, his will be done.'

"The fellow oozed bad temper. 'That's all very poetic, but who's
going to clean up its droppings?'

" 'I will! Haven't I told you a thousand times it's a sacred animal?'

"He muttered something about India and its sacred cows, she
shrugged her shoulders and got her own way. From now on, if I wanted,
I would share their home day and night.

"The new situation brought about by my wife's energy and determination favored my plans for revenge. Taking advantage of their absence during working hours, I rifled through the drawers and poked around in every corner of the house; I discovered that Aicha treasured her children's photos, paid her entire wages into a savings account, and regularly sent a proportion of this money to my address. The shopping—including the fish and maggots intended for me—and the gas and electricity bills, were all paid by the intruder. This evidence of provision for our future, together with her kindness toward me, made me bolder: I increased the frequency with which I soiled objects and garments belonging to the intruder; I parked myself on their bed.

"As I had hoped, the rows and domestic quarrels got worse.

" 'Surely you're not going to let it dirty the sheets!'

" 'If she does, I'll wash them.' (She often referred to me in the feminine.) 'The poor soul, she's had a long journey, then she fell ill, and she feels comfortable here, she's part of the family.'

"I pretended to give in to the fellow's irritation, and surrendered the field in a dignified manner. I waited till they had turned off the light and he had begun to move around and touch her, then I hopped onto the bedspread and soiled it. He immediately snapped on the bedside light.

" 'Right, that's it! This time it's gone too far! Enough is enough!'

" 'If you so much as touch a feather on that bird, you'll be sorry! If you must know, I'm tired of you mauling me. I just want to get to sleep!'

" 'If you want to sleep, sleep, but not with that creature. I've told you a thousand times, I can't stand it.'

" 'In that case, go and sleep on the sofa. I'm staying here.'

" 'Honestly, anyone would think you were married to it. Ever since it arrived, you've been behaving oddly. These mad ideas and superstitions may be all very well where you come from, but they don't suit a modern, civilized nation.'

" 'My country is better than yours, do you hear? This stork belongs to me, and if you don't like it, I'll leave and that'll be that.'

"From then on, there were quarrels every day. I wanted to sleep on the bed with my wife, and the intruder was beginning to give in and migrate to the sofa. I could feel that Aicha preferred me and was thinking about me. Sometimes she would sit at the kitchen table and write letters home, to the house next to the stork refuge founded centuries ago. She and the *nsrani* fought like cat and dog. When she was out, I would fly to the roof of the shed and take up my position on the nest. I feared the intruder might slit my throat with a knife, or club me to death. My success was reassuring and I began to recover my pleasure in flying. One day, after swallowing my ration of fish, I bade a silent goodbye to Aicha, waited till my flock came into view, joined them, and began the flight back to Marrakech.

"As soon as I arrived there, I regained my human form. I turned up at my house as though I had only just left it and embraced my children. My brother had taken good care of them, they were attending school, and they danced for joy to see me. Beside the clock in my bedroom there was a pile of letters from Aicha. They spoke of the stork's visit, of her deep longing for her homeland and her family. She was still working in the thread mill in order to save enough to buy a little business on her return. When she did return, two years later, she was radiant with joy and came loaded down with presents. I forgave her, of course I forgave her: I forgot her betrayal and lived happily with her until God called her to His side and we buried her in Bab Dukala.

"I never told her about my visit, nor did I tell anyone else, except one neighbor and also a gentleman of European origin living in the neighborhood, whose Moroccan friend was killed in a traffic accident and who ever since then had withdrawn from the world; he wrote poetry and in the evenings would go and sit quietly in the Mosque of Ibn Yusef. His name was Eusebio.

"I remember that he listened to me attentively and then he wrote down word for word the same story that I have just related to you."

STEVEN MILLHAUSER

The Disappearance of Elaine Coleman

It is a pleasure to welcome Steven Millhauser back to the pages of
The Year's Best Fantasy and Horror *with this disquieting, typically
Millhauserean tale, first published in the November 22 issue of* The
New Yorker.

*Millhauser is one of our top fantasists today. His magical (and
highly recommended) books include* The Knife Thrower, Little
Kingdoms, The Barnum Museum, In the Penny Arcade, Martin Dressler,
From the Realm of Morpheus, *and* Enchanted Night. *He has won the
Pulitzer Prize, the World Fantasy Award, and been honored by the
American Academy of Arts and Letters. Millhauser lives in upstate New
York, where he teaches at Skidmore College.*

—T. W.

The news of the disappearance disturbed and excited us. For weeks
afterward, the blurred and grainy photograph of a young woman
no one seemed to know, though some of us vaguely remembered
her, appeared on yellow posters displayed on the glass doors of
the post office, on telephone poles, on windows of the CVS and the
renovated supermarket. The small photo showed a serious face turned
partly away, above a fur collar; the picture seemed to be an enlargement
of a casual snapshot, perhaps originally showing a full-length view—
the sort of picture, we imagined, taken carelessly by a bored relative
with a borrowed camera to commemorate an occasion. For a time

women were warned not to go out alone at night, while the investigation pursued its futile course. Gradually the posters became rain-wrinkled and streaked with grime, the blurred photos seemed to be fading away, and then one day they were gone, leaving behind a faint uneasiness that itself dissolved slowly in the smoke-scented autumn air.

According to the newspaper reports, the last person to see Elaine Coleman alive was a neighbor, Mrs. Mary Blessington, who greeted her on the final evening as Elaine stepped out of her car and began to walk along the path of red slates leading to the side entrance of the house on Willow Street where she rented two rooms on the second floor. Mary Blessington was raking leaves. She leaned on her rake, waved to Elaine Coleman, and remarked on the weather. She noticed nothing unusual about the quiet young woman walking at dusk toward the side door, carrying in one arm a small paper bag (probably containing the quart of milk found unopened in her refrigerator) and holding her keys in the other hand. When questioned further about Elaine Coleman's appearance as she walked toward the house, Mary Blessington admitted that it was almost dark and that she couldn't make her out "all that well." The landlady, Mrs. Waters, who lived on the first floor and rented upstairs rooms to two boarders, described Elaine Coleman as a quiet person, steady, very polite. She went to bed early, never had visitors, and paid her rent unfailingly on the first of the month. She liked to stay by herself, the landlady added. On the last evening, Mrs. Waters heard Elaine's footsteps climbing the stairs as usual to her apartment on the second floor in back. The landlady did not actually see her on that occasion. The next morning, she noticed the car still parked in front, even though it was a Wednesday and Miss Coleman never missed a day of work. In the afternoon, when the mail came, Mrs. Waters decided to carry a letter upstairs to her boarder, who she assumed was sick. The door was locked. She knocked gently, then louder and louder, before opening the door with her own key. She hesitated a long time before calling the police.

For days we spoke of nothing else. We read the newspapers ardently, the local *Messenger* and the papers from neighboring towns; we studied the posters, we memorized the facts, we interpreted the evidence, we imagined the worst.

The photograph, bad and blurry though it was, left its own sharp impression: a woman caught in the act of looking away, a woman evading scrutiny. Her eyes were half closed, the turned-up collar of her jacket concealed the line of her jaw, and a crinkled strand of hair came straggling down over her cheek. She looked, though it was difficult to tell, as if she had hunched her shoulders against the cold. But what struck some of us about the photograph was what it seemed to conceal. It was as if beneath that grainy cheek, that blurred and narrow nose with the skin pulled tight across the bridge, lay some other, younger, more familiar image. Some of us recalled dimly an Elaine, an Elaine Coleman, in our high school, a young Elaine of fourteen or fifteen years ago, who had been in our classes, though none of us could remember her clearly or say where she sat or what she did. I myself seemed to recall an Elaine Coleman in English class, sophomore or junior year, a quiet girl, someone I hadn't paid much attention to. In my old yearbook I found her: Elaine Coleman. I did not recognize her face. At the same time, it didn't seem the face of a stranger. It appeared to be the missing woman on the poster, though in another key, so that you didn't make the connection immediately. The photograph was slightly overexposed, making her seem a little washed out, a little flat—there was a bright indistinctness about her. She was neither pretty nor unpretty. Her face was half turned away, her expression serious; her hair, done up in the style of the time, showed the shine of a careful combing. She had joined no clubs, played no sports, belonged to nothing.

The only other photograph of her was a group picture of our homeroom class. She stood in the third row from the front, her body turned awkwardly to one side, her eyes lowered, her features difficult to distinguish.

In the early days of her disappearance, I kept trying to remember her, the dim girl in my English class who had grown up into a blurred and grainy stranger. I seemed to see her sitting at her maple-wood desk beside the radiator, looking down at a book, her arms thin and pale, her brown hair falling partly behind her shoulder and partly before, a girl in a long skirt and white socks, but I could never be certain I wasn't making her up. One night I dreamed her: a girl with black hair who looked at me gravely. I woke up oddly stirred and relieved, but as I opened my eyes I realized that the girl in my dream was Miriam Blumenthal, a witty and laughing girl with blazing black hair, who in dream-disguise had presented herself to me as the missing Elaine.

One detail that troubled us was that Elaine Coleman's keys were discovered on the kitchen table, beside an open newspaper and a saucer. The key ring with its six keys and its silver kitten, the brown leather pocketbook containing her wallet, the fleece-lined coat on the back of a chair—all this suggested a sudden and disturbing departure, but it was the keys that attracted our particular attention, for they included the key to her apartment. We learned that the door could be locked in two ways: from the inside, by turning a knob that turned a bolt, and from the outside, with a key. If the door was locked and the key inside, then

Elaine Coleman cannot have left by the door—unless there was a second key. It was possible, though no one believed it, that someone with a second key had entered and left through her door, or that Elaine herself, using a second key, had left by the door and locked it from the outside. But a thorough police investigation discovered no record of a duplicate key. It seemed far more likely that she had left by one of the four windows. Two were in the kitchen–living room, facing the back, and two in the bedroom, facing the back and side. In the bathroom, there was a small, fifth window, no more than twelve inches in height and width through which it would have been impossible to enter or exit. Directly below the four main windows grew a row of hydrangea and rhododendron bushes. All four windows were closed, though not locked, and the storm windows were in place. It seemed necessary to imagine that Elaine Coleman had deliberately escaped through a second-floor window, fifteen feet up in the air, when she might far more easily have left by the door, or that an intruder had entered through a window and carried her off, taking care to pull both panes back into place. But the bushes, grass, and leaves below the four windows showed no trace of disturbance, nor was there any evidence in the rooms to suggest a break-in.

The second boarder, Mrs. Helen Ziolkowski, a seventy-year-old widow who had lived in the front apartment for twenty years, described Elaine Coleman as a nice young woman, quiet, very pale, the sort who kept to herself. It was the first we had heard of her pallor, which lent her a certain allure. On the last evening, Mrs. Ziolkowski heard the door close and the bolt turn in the lock. She heard the refrigerator door open and close, light footsteps moving about, a dish rattling, a teapot whistling. It was a quiet house and you could hear a lot. She had heard no unusual sounds, no screams, no voices, nothing at any time that might have suggested a struggle. In fact, it had been absolutely silent in Elaine Coleman's apartment from about seven o'clock on; she had been surprised not to hear the usual sounds of dinner being prepared in the kitchen. She herself had gone to bed at eleven o'clock. She was a light sleeper and was up often at night.

I wasn't the only one who kept trying to remember Elaine Coleman. Others who had gone to high school with me, and who now lived in our town with families of their own, remained puzzled or uncertain about who she was, though no one doubted she had actually been there. One of us thought he recalled her in biology, junior year, bent over a frog fastened to the black wax of a dissecting pan. Another recalled her in English class, senior year, not by the radiator but at the back of the room—a girl who didn't say much, a girl with uninteresting hair. But

358 ·• Steven Millhauser

though he remembered her clearly, or said he did, there at the back of the room, he could not remember anything more about her; he couldn't summon up any details.

One night, about three weeks after the disappearance, I woke from a troubling dream that had nothing to do with Elaine Coleman—I was in a room without windows, there was a greenish light, some frightening force was gathering behind the closed door—and sat up in bed. The dream itself no longer upset me, but it seemed to me that I was on the verge of recalling something. In startling detail, I remembered a party I had gone to when I was fifteen or sixteen. I saw the basement play-room very clearly: the piano with sheet music open on the rack, the shine of the piano lamp on the white pages and on the stockings of a girl sitting in a nearby armchair, the striped couch, some guys in the corner playing a child's game with blocks, the cigarette smoke, the bowl of pretzel sticks—and there on a hassock near the window, leaning forward a little, wearing a white blouse and a long dark skirt, her hands in her lap, Elaine Coleman. Her face was sketchy—dark hair some shade of brown, grainy skin—and not entirely to be trusted, since it showed signs of having been infected by the photograph of the missing Elaine, but I had no doubt that I had remembered her.

I tried to bring her into sharper focus, but it was as if I hadn't looked at her directly. The more I tried to recapture that evening, the more sharply I was able to see details of the basement playroom (my hands on the chipped white piano keys, the green and red and yellow blocks forming a higher and higher tower, someone on the swim team moving his arms out from his chest as he demonstrated the butterfly, the dazzling knees of Lorraine Palermo in sheer stockings), but I could not summon Elaine Coleman's face.

According to the landlady, the bedroom showed no signs of distur-bance. The pillow had been removed from under the bedclothes and placed against the headboard. On the nightstand, a cup half filled with tea rested on a postcard announcing the opening of a new hardware store. The bedspread was slightly rumpled; on it lay a white flannel nightgown printed with tiny pale-blue flowers and a fat paperback rest-ing open against the spread. The lamp on the nightstand was still on.

We tried to imagine the landlady in the bedroom doorway, her first steps into the silent room, the afternoon sunlight streaming in past the closed venetian blinds, the pale, hot bulb in the sun-streaked lamp.

The newspapers reported that Elaine Coleman had gone on from high school to attend a small college in Vermont, where she majored in business and wrote one drama review for the school paper. After grad-uation, she lived for a year in the same college town, waitressing at a seafood restaurant, then she returned to our town, where she lived for a few years in a one-room apartment before moving to the two-room apartment on Willow Street. During her college years, her parents had moved to California, from where the father, an electrician, moved alone to Oregon. "She didn't have a mean bone in her body," her mother was quoted as saying. Elaine worked for a year on the local paper, part-timed in a paint store, worked in the post office and a coffee shop, before getting a job in a business-supply store in a neighboring town. People remembered her as a quiet woman, polite, a good worker. She seemed to have no close friends.

I now recalled catching glimpses of a half-familiar face during summers home from college, and later, when I returned to town and settled down. I had long ago forgotten her name. She would be standing at the far end of a supermarket aisle, or on line in a drugstore, or disappearing into a store on Main Street. I noticed her without looking at her, as one might notice a friend's aunt. If our paths crossed, I would nod and pass by, thinking of other things. After all, we had never been friends, that woman and I—we had never been anything. She was someone I'd gone to high school with, that was all, someone I scarcely knew, though it was also true that I had nothing against her. Was it really the missing Elaine? Only after her disappearance did those fleeting encounters seem pierced by a poignance I knew to be false, though I couldn't help feeling it anyway, for it was as if I ought to have stopped and talked to her, warned her, saved her, done something.

My second vivid memory of Elaine Coleman came to me three days after my memory of the party. It was sometime in high school, and I was out walking with my friend Roger on one of those sunny autumn afternoons when the sky is so blue and clear that it ought to be summer, but the sugar maples have turned red and yellow, and smoke from leaf fires stings your eyes. We had gone for a long walk into an unfamiliar neighborhood on the other side of town. Here the houses were small, with detached garages; on the lawns you saw an occasional plastic yellow sunflower or fake deer. Roger was talking about a girl he was crazy about, who played tennis and lived in a fancy house on Gideon Hill, and I was advising him to disguise himself as a caretaker and apply for a job trimming her rosebushes. "The yard move," I said. "It gets 'em every time." "She would never respect me," Roger answered seriously. We were passing a garage where a girl in jeans and a dark parka was tossing a basketball into a hoop without a net. The garage door was open and you could see old furniture inside, couches with lamps lying on them and tables holding upside-down chairs. The basketball hit the rim and came bouncing down the drive toward us. I caught it and tossed it back to the girl, who had started after it but had stopped upon seeing us. I recognized Elaine Coleman. "Thanks," she said, holding the basketball in two hands and hesitating a moment before she lowered her eyes and turned away.

What struck me, as I remembered that afternoon, was the moment of hesitation. It might have meant a number of things, such as "Do you and Roger want to shoot a few?" or "I'd like to invite you to shoot a basket but I don't want to ask you if you don't really want to" or maybe something else entirely, but, in that moment, which seemed charged with uncertainty, Roger glanced sharply at me and mouthed a silent "No." What troubled my memory was the sense that Elaine had seen that look, that judgment; she must have been skilled at reading dismissive signs. We walked away into the blue afternoon of high autumn, talking about the girl on Gideon Hill, and in the clear air I could hear the sharp, repeated sound of the basketball striking the driveway as Elaine Coleman walked back toward the garage.

Is it true that whatever has once been seen is in the mind forever? After my second memory I expected an eruption of images, as if they had only been waiting to reveal themselves. In senior year of high school, I must have seen her every day in English class and homeroom, must have passed her in the halls and seen her in the cafeteria, to say nothing of the inevitable chance meetings in the streets and stores of a small town, but aside from the party and the garage I could summon no further image, not one. Nor could I see her face. It was as if she had no face, no features. Even the three photographs appeared to be of three different people, or perhaps they were three versions of a single person no one had ever seen. And so I returned to my two memories, as if they contained a secret that only intense scrutiny could bring to light. But though I saw, always more clearly, the chipped yellowish-white keys of the piano, the glittering stockings, the blue autumn sky, the sun glinting into the shadowy garage with its chairs and tables and boxes, though I saw, or seemed to see, the scuffed black loafer and white ribbed sock of a foot near the piano and the sparkling black shingles on the garage roof, I could not see more of Elaine Coleman than I had already remembered: the hands in the lap, at the party; the moment of hesitation, in the driveway.

During the first few weeks, when the story still seemed important, the newspapers located someone named Richard Baxter, who worked in a chemical plant in a nearby town. He had last seen Elaine Coleman three years ago. "We went out a few times," he was quoted as saying. "She was a nice girl, quiet. She didn't really have all that much to say." He didn't remember too much about her, he said.

The bafflement of the police, the lack of clues, the locked door, the closed windows, led me to wonder whether we were formulating the problem properly, whether we were failing to take into account some crucial element. In all discussions of the disappearance, only two possibilities, in all their variations, were ever considered: abduction and escape. The first possibility, although it could never be entirely discounted, had been decisively called into question by the police investigation, which found in the rooms and in the yard no evidence whatever of an intruder. It therefore seemed more reasonable to imagine that Elaine Coleman had left of her own volition. Indeed, it was tempting to believe that by an act of will she had broken from her lonely routine and set forth secretly to start a new life. Alone, friendless, restless, unhappy, and nearing her thirtieth birthday, she had at last overcome some inner constriction and surrendered herself to the lure of adventure. This theory was able to make clever use of the abandoned keys, wallet, coat, and car, which became the very proof of the radical nature of her break from everything familiar in her life. Skeptics pointed out that she wasn't likely to get very far without her credit card, her driver's license, and the twenty-seven dollars and thirty-four cents found in her wallet. But what finally rendered the theory suspect was the conventional and hopelessly romantic nature of the imagined escape, which not only required her to triumph over the quiet habits of a lifetime, but was so much what we might have wished for her that it seemed penetrated by desires not her own. Thus I wondered whether there might not be some other way to account for the disappearance, some bolder way that called for a different, more elusive, more dangerous logic.

The police searched the north woods with dogs, dragged the pond behind the lumberyard. For a while, there were rumors that she had been kidnapped in the parking lot where she worked, but two employees had seen her drive off, Mary Blessington had waved to her in the evening, and Mrs. Zolkowski had heard her closing her refrigerator door, rattling a dish, moving around.

If there was no abduction and no escape, then Elaine Coleman must have climbed the stairs, entered her apartment, locked her door, put the milk in the refrigerator, hung her coat over the back of a chair, and—disappeared. Period. End of discussion. Or to put it another way: the disappearance must have taken place *within the apartment itself*. If one ruled out abduction and escape, then Elaine Coleman ought to have been found somewhere in her rooms—perhaps dead in a closet. But the police investigation had been thorough. She appeared to have vanished from her rooms as completely as she had vanished from my mind, leaving behind only a scattering of clues to suggest she had ever been there.

As the investigation slowly unraveled, as the posters faded and at length disappeared, I tried desperately to remember more of Elaine Coleman, as if I owed her at least the courtesy of recollection. What bothered me wasn't so much the disappearance itself, since I had scarcely known her, or even the possible ugliness of that disappearance, but my own failure of memory. Others recalled her still more dimly. It was as if none of us had ever looked at her; or had looked at her while thinking of something more interesting. I felt that we were guilty of some obscure crime. For it seemed to me that we who had seen her now and then out of the corner of our eyes, we who had seen her without seeing her, who without malice had failed to give her our full attention, were already preparing her for the fate that overtook her, were already, in a sense not yet clear to me, pushing her in the direction of disappearance.

It was during this time of failed recollection that I had what can only be called a pseudo-memory of Elaine Coleman, which haunted me precisely to the extent that I did not know how much of her it contained. The time was two or three years before the disappearance. I remembered that I was at a movie theater with a friend, my friend's wife, and a woman I was seeing then. It was a foreign movie, black-and-white, with subtitles; I remembered my friend's wife laughing wildly at the childish translation of a curse, while the actor on the screen smashed his fist against a door. I recalled a big tub of popcorn that the four us passed back and forth. I recalled the chill of the air-conditioning, which made me long for the heat of the summer night. Slowly the lights came on, the credits continued to roll, and, as the four of us began making our way up the crowded aisle, I noticed a woman in dark clothes rising from a seat near the far aisle. I caught only a glimpse of her before looking irritably away. She reminded me of someone I half knew, maybe the girl from my high school whom I sometimes saw and whose name I had forgotten, and I didn't want to catch her eye, didn't want to be forced to exchange meaningless, awkward words with her, whoever she was. In the bright, jammed lobby, I braced myself for the worthless meeting. But for some reason she never emerged from the theater, and, as I stepped with relief into the heat of the summer night, which already was beginning to seem oppressive, I wondered whether she had hung back on purpose because she had seen me turning irritably away. Then I felt a moment of remorse for my harshness toward the half-seen woman in the theater, the pseudo-Elaine, for after all I had nothing against her, the girl who had once been in my English class.

Like a detective, like a lover, I returned relentlessly to the few images I had of her: the dim girl at the party, the girl with the basketball who lowered her eyes, the turned-away face in the yearbook picture, the blurred police photo, the vague person, older now, whom I nodded to occasionally in town, the woman in the theater. I felt as if I had wronged her in some way, as if I had something to atone for. The paltry images seemed to taunt me, as if they held the secret of her disappearance. The hazy girl, the blurred photo . . . Sometimes I felt an inner shaking or trembling, as if I were on the verge of an overwhelming revelation.

One night I dreamed that I was playing basketball with Elaine Coleman. The driveway was also the beach, the ball kept splashing in shallow water, but Elaine Coleman was laughing, her face was radiant though somehow hidden, and, when I woke, I felt that the great failure in my life was never to have evoked that laughter.

As the weather grew colder, I began to notice that people no longer wanted to talk about Elaine Coleman. She had simply disappeared, that was all, and one day she would be found, or forgotten, and that would be that. Life would go on. Sometimes I had the impression that people were angry at her, as if by disappearing she had complicated our lives.

One sunny afternoon in January, I drove to the house on Willow Street. I knew the street, lined now with bare, twisted maples that threw long shadows across the road and onto the fronts of the houses opposite. A brilliant-blue mailbox stood at one corner, beside a telephone pole with a drum-shaped transformer high up under the cross-arm. I parked across from the house, but not directly across, and looked at it furtively, as if I were breaking a law. It was a house like many on the block, two-storied and wood-shingled, with side gables and a black roof. The shingles were painted light gray and the shutters black. I saw pale curtains in all the windows and the path of red slates leading to the door in the side of the house. The door had two small windows near the top, and they too were curtained. I saw a row of bare bushes and a piece of the backyard, where a bird feeder hung from a branch. I tried to imagine her life there, in the quiet house, but I could imagine nothing, nothing at all. It seemed to me that she had never lived there, never gone to my high school—that she was the town's dream, as it lay napping in the cold sun of a January afternoon.

I drove away from that peaceful, mocking street, which seemed to say, "There's nothing wrong here. We're a respectable street. You've had your look, now give it up," but I was further than ever from letting her go. Helplessly I rummaged through my images, searched for clues, sensed directions that led nowhere. I felt her slipping from me, vanishing, a ghost girl, a blurred photo, a woman without features, a figure in dark clothes rising from her seat and floating away.

I returned to the newspaper reports, which I kept in a folder on my night table. One detail that struck me was that the landlady had not actually seen Elaine Coleman on the final evening before her disappearance. The neighbor, who had waved to her at dusk, had not been able to make her out all that well.

Two nights later, I woke suddenly, startled as if by a dream, though I could recall no dream. A moment later the truth shook me like a blow to the temple.

Elaine Coleman did not disappear suddenly, as the police believed, but gradually, over the course of time. Those years of sitting unnoticed in corners, of not being looked at, must have given her a queasy, unstable sense of herself. Often she must have felt almost invisible. If it is true that we exist by impressing ourselves on other minds, by entering other imaginations, then the quiet, unremarkable girl whom no one noticed must at times have felt herself growing vague, as if she were gradually being erased by the world's inattention. In high school, the process of blurring—begun much earlier—had probably not yet reached a critical stage; her face, with its characteristically lowered and averted eyes, had grown only a little uncertain. By the time she returned from college, the erasure had become more advanced. The woman glimpsed in town without ever being seen, the unimagined person whom no one could recall clearly, was growing dim, fading away, vanishing, like a room at dusk. She was moving irrevocably toward the realm of dream.

On that last evening, when Mary Blessington waved to her in the dusk without really seeing her, Elaine Coleman was scarcely more than a shadow. She climbed the stairs to her room, locked the door as usual, put the milk in the refrigerator, and hung her coat over the back of a chair. Behind her, the secondhand mirror barely reflected her. She heated the kettle and sat at the kitchen table, reading the paper and drinking a cup of tea. Had she been feeling tired lately, or was there a sense of lightness, of anticipation? In the bedroom she set her cup of tea down on a postcard on her nightstand and changed into her heavy white nightgown with its little blue flowers. Later, when she felt rested, she would make dinner. She pulled out the pillow and lay down with a book. Dusk was deepening into early night. In the darkening room, she could see a shadowy nightstand, the sleeve of a sweater hanging on a chair, the faint shape of her body on the bed. She turned on the lamp and tried to read. Her eyes, heavy-lidded, began to close. I imagine a not unpleasant tiredness, a feeling of finality, a sensation of dispersion. The next day there was nothing but a nightgown and a paperback on a bed.

It may have been a little different: one evening, she may have become aware of what was happening to her; she may, in a profound movement of her being, have embraced her fate and joined forces with the powers of dissolution.

She is not alone. On street corners at dusk, in the corridors of dark movie theaters, behind the windows of cars in parking lots at melancholy shopping centers illuminated by pale-orange lamps, you sometimes see them, the Elaine Colemans of this world. They lower their eyes, they turn away, they vanish into shadowy places. Sometimes I seem to see, through their nearly transparent skin, a light or a building behind them. I try to catch their eyes, to penetrate them with my attention, but it's always too late, already they are fading, fixed as they are in the long habit of not being noticed. And perhaps the police, who suspected foul play, were not in the end mistaken. For we are no longer innocent, we who do not see and do not remember, we incurious ones, we conspirators in disappearance. I too murdered Elaine Coleman. Let this account be entered in the record.

TIM LEBBON

❖━━━━━━━━━━━━━━━━━━━━━━━━━━━━━━❖

White

Tim Lebbon's first novel, Mesmer, *was shortlisted for the British Fantasy Award for Best Novel. His second book,* Faith in the Flesh—*a collection of two novellas—was runner-up in the Best Collection category a year later. He's had more than seventy stories published in magazines and anthologies, with more due soon in* Last Days, Cemetery Dance *and* Outside the Cage.

His novel Hush *(written in collaboration with Gavin Williams) will be published in September by Razorblade Press, and* Tales *from the Teeth Park (an anthology co-edited with Williams) is forthcoming from the same publisher. A new novella, "Naming of Parts," has been published by PS Publishing. His second novel* The Nature of Balance *and is working on a new novel,* Face, *along with short stories and novellas.*

According to Lebbon, "White" started out as a science fiction story set on another planet . . . and something strange happened to it on the way back to Earth. MOT Press originally published it as a chapbook.

—E. D.

One
The Color of Blood

We found the first body two days before Christmas.

Charley had been out gathering sticks to dry for tinder. She had worked her way through the wild garden and down toward the cliffs, scooping snow from beneath and around bushes and bagging whatever dead twigs she found there. There were no signs, she said. No disturbances in the virgin surface of the snow; no tracks; no warning. Nothing to prepare her for the scene of bloody devastation she stumbled across.

She had rounded a big boulder and seen the red splash in the snow that was all that remained of a human being. The shock froze her comprehension. The reality of the scene struggled to imprint itself on her mind. Then, slowly, what she was looking at finally registered.

She ran back screaming. She'd only recognized her boyfriend by what was left of his shoes.

We were in the dining room trying to make sense of the last few weeks when Charley came bursting in. We spent a lot of time doing that: talking together in the big living rooms of the manor; in pairs, crying and sharing warmth; or alone, staring into darkening skies and struggling to discern a meaning in the infinite. I was one of those more usually alone. I'd been an only child and contrary to popular belief, my upbringing had been a nightmare. I always thought my parents blamed me for the fact that they could not have any more children, and instead of enjoying and reveling in my own childhood, I spent those years watching my mother and father mourn the ghosts of unborn offspring. It would have been funny if it were not so sad.

Charley opened the door by falling into it. She slumped to the floor, hair plastered across her forehead, her eyes two bright sparks peering between the knotted strands. Caked snow fell from her boots and speckled the timber floor, dirtied into slush. The first thing I noticed was its pinkish tinge.

The second thing I saw was the blood covering Charley's hands.

"Charley!" Hayden jumped to his feet and almost caught the frantic woman before she hit the deck. He went down with her, sprawling in a sudden puddle of dirt and tears. He saw the blood then and backed away automatically. "Charley?"

"Get some towels," Ellie said, always the pragmatist, "and a fucking gun."

I'd seen people screaming—all my life I'd never forgotten Jayne's final hours—but I had never seen someone actually *beyond* the point of screaming. Charley gasped and clawed at her throat, trying to open it up and let out the pain and the shock trapped within. It was not exertion that had stolen her breath; it was whatever she had seen.

She told us what that was.

I went with Ellie and Brand. Ellie had a shotgun cradled in the crook of her arm, a bobble hat hiding her severely short hair, her face all hard. There was no room in her life for compliments, but right now she was the one person in the manor I'd choose to be with. She'd been all for trying to make it out alone on foot; I was so glad that she eventually decided to stay.

Brand muttered all the way. "Oh fuck, oh shit, what are we doing coming out here? Like those crazy girls in slasher movies, you know? Always chasing the bad guys instead of running from them? Asking to get their throats cut? Oh man . . ."

In many ways I agreed with him. According to Charley there was little left of Boris to recover, but she could have been wrong. We owed it to him to find out. However harsh the conditions, whatever the like-lihood of his murderer—animal or human—still being out here, we could not leave Boris lying dead in the snow. Apply whatever levels of civilization, foolish custom, or superiority complex you like, it just wasn't done.

Ellie led the way across the manor's front garden and out onto the coastal road. The whole landscape was hidden beneath snow, like old sheet-covered furniture awaiting the homecoming of long-gone owners. I wondered who would ever make use of this land again—who would be left to bother when the snow did finally melt—but that train of thought led only to depression.

We crossed the flat area of the road, following Charley's earlier footprints in the deep snow; even and distinct on the way out, chaotic on the return journey. As if she'd had something following her.

She had. We all saw what had been chasing her when we slid and clambered down toward the cliffs, veering behind the big rock that sig-nified the beginning of the coastal path. The sight of Boris opened up and spread across the snow had pursued her all the way, and was prob-ably still snapping at her heels now. The smell of his insides slowly cooling under an indifferent sky. The sound of his frozen blood crack-ling under foot.

Ellie hefted the gun, holding it waist-high, ready to fire in an instant. Her breath condensed in the air before her, coming slightly faster than moments before. She glanced at the torn-up Boris, then surveyed our surroundings, looking for whoever had done this. East and west along the coast, down toward the cliff edge, up to the lip of rock above us, east and west again; Ellie never looked back down at Boris.

I did. I couldn't keep my eyes off what was left of him. It looked as though something big and powerful had held him up to the rock, scraped and twisted him there for a while, and then calmly taken him apart across the snow-covered path. Spray patterns of blood stood out brighter than their surroundings. Every speck was visible and there were many specks, thousands of them spread across a ten-meter area. I tried

to find a recognizable part of him, but all that was even vaguely iden-
tifiable as human was a hand, stuck to the rock in a mess of frosty
blood, fingers curled in like the legs of a dead spider. The wrist was
tattered, the bone splintered. It had been snapped, not cut.

Brand pointed out a shoe on its side in the snow. "Fuck, Charley
was right. Just his shoes left. Miserable bastard always wore the same
shoes."

I'd already seen the shoe. It was still mostly full. Boris had not been
a miserable bastard. He was introspective, thoughtful, sensitive, sincere,
qualities which Brand would never recognize as anything other than
sourness. Brand was as thick as shit and twice as unpleasant.

The silence seemed to press in around me. Silence, and cold, and a
raw smell of meat, and the sea chanting from below. I was surrounded
by everything.

"Let's get back," I said. Ellie glanced at me and nodded.

"But what about—" Brand started, but Ellie cut in without even
looking at him.

"You want to make bloody snowballs, go ahead. There's not much
to take back. We'll maybe come again later. Maybe."

"What did this?" I said, feeling reality start to shimmy past the
shock I'd been gripped by for the last couple of minutes. "Just what the
hell?"

Ellie backed up to me and glanced at the rock, then both ways along
the path. "I don't want to find out just yet," she said.

Later, alone in my room, I would think about exactly what Ellie
had meant. *I don't want to find out just yet*, she had said, implying that
the perpetrator of Boris's demise would be revealed to us soon. I'd
hardly known Boris, quiet guy that he was, and his fate was just another
line in the strange composition of death that had overcome the whole
country during the last few weeks.

Charley and I were here in the employment of the Department of
the Environment. Our brief was to keep a check on the radiation levels
in the Atlantic Drift, since things had gone to shit in South America
and the dirty reactors began to melt down in Brazil. It was a bad job
with hardly any pay, but it gave us somewhere to live. The others had
tagged along for different reasons; friends and lovers of friends, all
taking the opportunity to get away from things for a while and chill out
in the wilds of Cornwall.

But then things went to shit here as well. On TV, minutes before it
had ceased broadcasting for good, someone called it the ruin.

Then it had started to snow.

———

Hayden had taken Charley upstairs, still trying to quell her hysteria. We had no medicines other than aspirin and cough mixtures, but there were a hundred bottles of wine in the cellar. It seemed that Hayden had already poured most of a bottle down Charley's throat by the time the three of us arrived back at the manor. Not a good idea, I thought—I could hardly imagine what ghosts a drunken Charley would see, what terrors her alcohol-induced dreams held in store for her once she was finally left on her own—but it was not my place to say.

Brand stormed in and with his usual subtlety painted a picture of what we'd seen. "Boris's guts were just everywhere, hanging on the rock, spread over the snow. Melted in, like they were still hot when he was being cut up. What the fuck would do that? Eh? Just what the fuck?"

"Who did it?" Rosalie, our resident paranoid, asked.

I shrugged. "Can't say."

"Why not?"

"Not won't," I said, "can't. Can't tell. There's not too much left to tell by, as Brand has so eloquently revealed."

Ellie stood before the open fire and held out her hands, palms up, as if asking for something. A touch of emotion, I mused, but then my thoughts were often cruel.

"Ellie?" Rosalie demanded an answer.

Ellie shrugged. "We can rule out suicide." Nobody responded.

I went through to the kitchen and opened the back door. We were keeping our beers on a shelf in the rear conservatory now that the electricity had gone off. There was a generator, but not enough fuel to run it for more than an hour every day. We agreed that hot water was a priority for that meager time, so the fridge was now extinct.

I surveyed my choice: Stella; a few final cans of Caffreys; Boddingtons. That had been Jayne's favorite. She'd drunk it in pints, inevitably doing a bad impression of some moustached actor after the first creamy sip. I could still see her sparkling eyes as she tried to think of someone new. . . . I grabbed a Caffreys and shut the back door, and it was as the latch clicked home that I started to shake.

I'd seen a dead man five minutes ago, a man I'd been talking to the previous evening, drinking with, chatting about what the hell had happened to the world, making inebriated plans of escape, knowing all the time that the snow had us trapped here like chickens surrounded by a fiery moat. Boris had been quiet but thoughtful, the most intelligent person here at the manor. It had been his idea to lock the doors to many of the rooms because we never used them, and any heat we managed to generate should be kept in the rooms we did use. He had suggested a long walk as the snow had begun in earnest and it had been our prevarication and, I admit, our arguing that had kept us here long enough for it to matter. By the time Boris had persuaded us to make a go of it, the snow was three feet deep. Five miles and we'd be dead. Maximum. The nearest village was ten miles away.

He was dead. Something had taken him apart, torn him up, ripped him to pieces. I was certain that there had been no cutting involved as Brand had suggested. And yes, his bits did look melted into the snow. Still hot when they struck the surface, bloodying it in death. Still alive and beating as they were taken out.

I sat at the kitchen table and held my head in my hands. Jayne had said that this would hold all the good thoughts in and let the bad ones seep through your fingers, and sometimes it seemed to work. Now it was just a comfort, like the hands of a lover kneading hope into flaccid muscles, or fear from tense ones.

It could not work this time. I had seen a dead man. And there was nothing we could do about it. We should be telling someone, but over the past few months any sense of "relevant authorities" had fast faded away, just as Jayne had two years before; faded away to agony, then confusion, and then to nothing. Nobody knew what had killed her. Growths on her chest and stomach. Bad blood. Life.

I tried to open the can but my fingers were too cold to slip under the ring-pull. I became frustrated, then angry, and eventually my temper threw the can to the floor. It struck the flagstones and one edge split, sending a fine yellowish spray of beer across the old kitchen cupboards. I cried out at the waste. It was a feeling I was becoming more than used to.

"Hey," Ellie said. She put one hand on my shoulder and removed it before I could shrug her away. "They're saying we should tell someone."

"Who?" I turned to look at her, unashamed of my tears. Ellie was a hard bitch. Maybe they made me more of a person than she.

She raised one eyebrow and pursed her lips. "Brand thinks the army. Rosalie thinks the Fairy Underground."

I scoffed. "Fairy-fucking-Underground. Stupid cow."

"She can't help being like that. You ask me, it makes her more suited to how it's all turning out."

"And how's that, exactly?" I hated Ellie sometimes, all her stronger-than-thou talk and steely eyes. But she was also the person I respected the most in our pathetic little group. Now that Boris had gone.

"Well," she said, "for a start, take a look at how we're all reacting to this. Shocked, maybe. Horrified. But it's almost like it was expected."

"It's all been going to shit . . ." I said, but I did not need to continue. We had all known that we were not immune to the rot settling across society, nature, the world. Eventually it would find us. We just had not known when.

"There is the question of who did it," she said quietly.

"Or what."

She nodded. "Or what."

For now, we left it at that.

"How's Charley?"

"I was just going to see," Ellie said. "Coming?"

I nodded and followed her from the room. The beer had stopped spraying and now fizzled into sticky rivulets where the flags joined. I was still thirsty.

Charley looked bad. She was drunk, that was obvious, and she had been sick down herself, and she had wet herself. Hayden was in the process of trying to mop up the mess when we knocked and entered.

"How is she?" Ellie asked pointlessly.

"How do you think?" He did not even glance at us as he tried to hold onto the babbling, crying, laughing, and puking Charley.

"Maybe you shouldn't have given her so much to drink," Ellie said. Hayden sent her daggers but did not reply.

Charley struggled suddenly in his arms, ranting and shouting at the shaded candles in the corners of the room.

"What's that?" I said. "What's she saying?" For some reason it sounded important, like a solution to a problem encoded by grief.

"She's been saying some stuff," Hayden said loudly, so we could hear above Charley's slurred cries. "Stuff about Boris. Seeing angels in the snow. She says his angels came to get him."

"Some angels," Ellie muttered.

"You go down," Hayden said, "I'll stay here with her." He wanted us gone, that much was obvious, so we did not disappoint him.

Downstairs, Brand and Rosalie were hanging around the mobile phone. It had sat on the mantelpiece for the last three weeks like a gun without bullets, ugly and useless. Every now and then someone would try it, receiving only a crackling nothing in response. Random numbers, recalled numbers, numbers held in the phone's memory, all came to naught. Gradually it was tried less—every unsuccessful attempt had been more depressing.

"What?" I said.

"Trying to call someone," Brand said. "Police. Someone."

"So they can come to take fingerprints?" Ellie flopped into one of the old armchairs and began picking at its upholstery, widening a hole she'd been plucking at for days. "Any replies?"

Brand shook his head.

"We've got to do something," Rosalie said, "we can't just sit here while Boris is lying dead out there."

Ellie said nothing. The telephone hissed its amusement. Rosalie looked to me. "There's nothing we can do," I said. "Really, there's not much to collect up. If we did bring his . . . bits . . . back here, what would we do?"

"Bury . . ." Rosalie began.

"Three feet of snow? Frozen ground?"

"And the things," Brand said. The phone crackled again and he turned it off.

"What things?"

Brand looked around our small group. "The things Boris said he'd seen."

Boris had mentioned nothing to me. In our long, drunken talks, he had never talked of any angels in the snow. Upstairs, I'd thought that it was simply Charley drunk and mad with grief, but now Brand had said it too I had the distinct feeling I was missing out on something. I was irked, and upset at feeling irked.

"Things?" Rosalie said, and I closed my eyes. *Oh fuck, don't tell her,* I willed at Brand. She'd regale us with stories of secret societies and messages in the clouds, disease makers who were wiping out the inept and the crippled, the barren and the intellectually inadequate. Jayne had been sterile, so we'd never had kids. The last thing I needed was another one of Rosalie's mad ravings about how my wife had died, why she'd died, who had killed her.

Luckily, Brand seemed of like mind. Maybe the joint he'd lit up had stewed him into silence at last. He turned to the fire and stared into its dying depths, sitting on the edge of the seat as if wondering whether or not to feed it some more. The stack of logs was running low.

"Things?" Rosalie said again, nothing if not persistent.

"No things," I said. "Nothing." I left the room before it all flared up.

In the kitchen I opened another can, carefully this time, and poured it into a tall glass. I stared into creamy depths as bubbles passed up and down. It took a couple of minutes for the drink to settle, and in that time I had recalled Jayne's face, her body, the best times we'd had together. At my first sip, a tear replenished the glass.

That night I heard doors opening and closing as someone wandered between beds. I was too tired to care who.

The next morning I half expected it to be all better. I had the bitter taste of dread in my mouth when I woke up, but also a vague idea that all the bad stuff could only have happened in nightmares. As I dressed— two shirts, a heavy pullover, a jacket—I wondered what awaited me beyond my bedroom door.

In the kitchen Charley was swigging from a fat mug of tea. It steamed so much, it seemed liable to burn whatever it touched. Her lips were red-raw, as were her eyes. She clutched the cup tightly, knuckles white, thumbs twisted into the handle. She looked as though she wanted to never let it go.

I had a sinking feeling in my stomach when I saw her. I glanced out of the window and saw the landscape of snow, added to yet again the previous night, bloated flakes still fluttering down to reinforce the barricade against our escape. Somewhere out there, Boris's parts were frozen memories hidden under a new layer.

"Okay?" I said quietly.

Charley looked up at me as if I'd farted at her mother's funeral. "Of course I'm not okay," she said, enunciating each word carefully. "And what do you care?"

I sat at the table opposite her, yawning, rubbing hands through my greasy hair, generally trying to disperse the remnants of sleep. There was a pot of tea on the table and I took a spare mug and poured a steaming brew. Charley watched my every move. I was aware of her eyes upon me, but I tried not to let it show. The cup shook, I could barely grab a spoon. I'd seen her boyfriend splashed across the snow, I felt terrible about it, but then I realized that she'd seen the same scene. How bad must she be feeling?

"We have to do something," she said.

"Charley—"

"We can't just sit here. We have to go. Boris needs a funeral. We have to go and find someone, get out of this godforsaken place. There must be someone near, able to help, someone to look after us? I need someone to look after me."

The statement was phrased as a question, but I ventured no answer.

"Look," she said, "we have to get out. Don't you see?" She let go of her mug and clasped my hands; hers were hot and sweaty. "The village, we can get there, I know we can."

"No, Charley," I said, but I did not have a chance to finish my sentence (*there's no way out, we tried, and didn't you see the television reports weeks ago?*) before Ellie marched into the room. She paused when she saw Charley, then went to the cupboard and poured herself a bowl of cereal. She used water. We'd run out of milk a week ago.

"There's no telephone," she said, spooning some soggy corn flakes into her mouth. "No television, save some flickering pictures most of us don't want to see. Or believe. There's no radio, other than the occasional foreign channel. Rosie says she speaks French. She's heard them talking of 'the doom.' That's how she translates it, though I think it sounds more like 'the ruin.' The nearest village is ten miles away. We have no motorized transport that will even get out of the garage. To walk it would be suicide." She crunched her limp breakfast, mixing in more sugar to give it some taste.

Charley did not reply. She knew what Ellie was saying, but tears were her only answer.

"So we're here until the snow melts," I said. Ellie really was a straight bitch. Not a glimmer of concern for Charley, not a word of comfort.

Ellie looked at me and stopped chewing for a moment. "I think until it does melt, we're protected." She had a way of coming out with ideas that both enraged me and scared the living shit out of me at the same time.

Charley could only cry.

Later, three of us decided to try to get out. In moments of stress, panic, and mourning, logic holds no sway.

I said I'd go with Brand and Charley. It was one of the most foolish decisions I've ever made, but seeing Charley's eyes as she sat in the kitchen on her own, thinking about her slaughtered boyfriend, listening to Ellie go on about how hopeless it all was . . . I could not say no. And in truth, I was as desperate to leave as anyone.

It was almost ten in the morning when we set out.

Ellie was right, I knew that even then. Her face as she watched us struggle across the garden should have brought me back straightaway: she thought I was a fool. She was the last person in the world I wanted to appear foolish in front of, but still there was that nagging feeling in my heart that pushed me on—a mixture of desire to help Charley and a hopeless feeling that by staying here, we were simply waiting for death to catch up to us.

It seemed to have laid its shroud over the rest of the world already. Weeks ago the television had shown some dreadful sights: people falling ill and dying in the thousands; food riots in London; a nuclear exchange between Greece and Turkey. More, lots more, all of it bad. We'd known something was coming—things had been falling apart for years—but once it began it was a cumulative effect, speeding from a steady trickle toward decline, to a raging torrent. *We're better off where we are*, Boris had said to me. It was ironic that because of him, we were leaving.

I carried the shotgun. Brand had an air pistol, though I'd barely trust him with a sharpened stick. As well as being loud and brash, he spent most of his time doped to the eyeballs. If there was any trouble, I'd be watching out for him as much as anything else.

Something had killed Boris, and whatever it was, animal or human, it was still out there in the snow. Moved on, hopefully, now it had fed. But then again perhaps not. It did not dissuade us from trying.

The snow in the manor garden was almost a meter deep. The three of us had botched together snowshoes of varying effectiveness. Brand wore two snapped-off lengths of picture frame on each foot, which seemed to act more as knives to slice down through the snow than anything else. He was tenaciously pompous; he struggled with his mistake rather than admitting it. Charley had used two frying pans with their handles snapped off, and she seemed to be making good headway. My own creations consisted of circles of mounted canvas cut from the redundant artwork in the manor. Old owners of the estate stared up at me through the snow as I repeatedly stepped on their faces.

By the time we reached the end of the driveway and turned to see Ellie and Hayden watching us, I was sweating and exhausted. We had traveled about fifty meters.

Across the road lay the cliff path leading to Boris's dismembered corpse. Charley glanced that way, perhaps wishing to look down upon her boyfriend one more time.

"Come on," I said, clasping her elbow and heading away. She offered no resistance.

The road was apparent as a slightly lower, smoother plain of snow between the two hedged banks on either side. Everything was glaring white, and we were all wearing sunglasses to prevent snow-blindness. We could see far along the coast from here as the bay swept around toward the east, the craggy cliffs spotted white where snow had drifted onto ledges, an occasional lonely seabird diving to the sea and returning empty-beaked to sing a mournful song for company. In places the snow was cantilevered out over the edge of the cliff, a deadly trap should any of us stray that way. The sea itself surged against the rocks below, but it broke no spray. The usual roar of the waters crashing into the earth, slowly eroding it away and reclaiming it, had changed. It was now more of a grind as tons of slushy ice replaced the usual white horses, not yet forming a solid barrier over the water but still thick enough to temper the waves. In a way it was sad; a huge beast winding down in old age.

I watched as a cormorant plunged down through the chunky ice and failed to break surface again. It was as if it were committing suicide. Who was I to say it was not?

"How far?" Brand asked yet again.

"Ten miles," I said.

"I'm knackered." He had already lit up a joint and he took long, hard pulls on it. I could hear its tip sizzling in the crisp morning air.

"We've come about three hundred meters," I said, and Brand shut up.

It was difficult to talk; we needed all our breath for the effort of walking. Sometimes the snowshoes worked, especially where the surface of the snow had frozen the previous night. Other times we plunged straight in up to our thighs and we had to hold our arms out for balance as we hauled our leg out, just to let it sink in again a step along. The rucksacks did not help. We each carried food, water, and dry clothing, and Brand especially seemed to be having trouble with his.

The sky was a clear blue. The sun rose ahead of us as if mocking the frozen landscape. Some days it started like this, but the snow never seemed to melt. I had almost forgotten what the ground below it looked like; it seemed that the snow had been here forever. When it began our spirits had soared, like a bunch of school kids waking to find the landscape had changed overnight. Charley and I had still gone down to the sea to take our readings, and when we returned there was a snowman in the garden wearing one of her bras and a pair of my briefs. A snowball fight had ensued, during which Brand became a little too aggressive for his own good. We'd ganged up on him and pelted him with snow compacted to ice until he shouted and yelped. We were cold and wet and bruised, but we did not stop laughing for hours.

We'd all dried out in front of the open fire in the huge living room. Rosalie had stripped to her knickers and danced to music on the radio. She was a bit of a sixties throwback, Rosalie, and she didn't seem to realize what her little display did to cosseted people like me. I watched happily enough.

Later, we sat around the fire and told ghost stories. Boris was still with us then, of course, and he came up with the best one, which had us all cowering behind casual expressions. He told us of a man who could not see, hear, or speak, but who knew of the ghosts around him. His life was silent and senseless save for the day his mother died. Then he cried and shouted and raged at the darkness, before curling up and dying himself. His world opened up then, and he no longer felt alone, but whoever he tried to speak to could only fear or loath him. The living could never make friends with the dead. And death had made him more silent than ever.

None of us would admit it, but we were all scared shiftless as we went to bed that night. As usual, doors opened and footsteps padded along corridors. And, as usual, my door remained shut and I slept alone.

Days later the snow was too thick to be enjoyable. It became risky to go outside, and as the woodpile started to dwindle and the radio and television broadcasts turned more grim, we realized that we were becoming trapped. A few of us had tried to get to the village, but it was a halfhearted attempt and we'd returned once we were tired. We figured we'd traveled about two miles along the coast. We had seen no one.

As the days passed and the snow thickened, the atmosphere did likewise with a palpable sense of panic. A week ago, Boris had pointed out that there were no plane trails anymore.

This, our second attempt to reach the village, felt more like life and death. Before Boris had been killed we'd felt confined, but it also gave a sense of protection from the things going on in the world. Now there was a feeling that if we could not get out, worse things would happen to us where we were.

I remembered Jayne as she lay dying from the unknown disease. I had been useless, helpless, hopeless, praying to a God I had long ignored to grant us a kind fate. I refused to sit back and go the same way. I would not go gentle. Fuck fate.

"What was that?"

Brand stopped and tugged the little pistol from his belt. It was stark black against the pure white snow.

"What?"

He nodded. "Over there." I followed his gaze and looked up the sloping hillside. To our right the sea sighed against the base of the cliffs. To our left—the direction Brand was now facing—snowfields led up a gentle slope toward the moors several miles inland. It was a rocky, craggy landscape, and some rocks had managed to hold off the drifts. They peered out darkly here and there, like the faces of drowning men going under for the final time.

"What?" I said again, exasperated. I'd slipped the shotgun off my shoulder and held it waist-high. My finger twitched on the trigger guard. Images of Boris's remains sharpened my senses. I did not want to end up like that.

"I saw something moving. Something white."

"Some snow, perhaps?" Charley said bitterly.

"Something running across the snow," he said, frowning as he concentrated on the middle-distance. The smoke from his joint mingled with his condensing breath.

We stood that way for a minute or two, steaming sweat like smoke signals of exhaustion. I tried taking off my glasses to look, but the glare was too much. I glanced sideways at Charley. She'd pulled a big old revolver form her rucksack and held it with both hands. Her lips were pulled back from her teeth in a feral grimace. She really wanted to use that gun.

I saw nothing. "Could have been a cat. Or a seagull flying low."

"Could have been." Brand shoved the pistol back into his belt and reached around for his water canteen. He tipped it to his lips and cursed. "Frozen!"

"Give it a shake," I said. I knew it would do no good but it might shut him up for a while. "Charley, what's the time?" I had a watch but I wanted to talk to Charley, keep her involved with the present, keep her here. I had started to realize not only what a stupid idea this was, but what an even more idiotic step it had been letting Charley come along. If she wasn't here for revenge, she was blind with grief. I could not see her eyes behind her sunglasses.

"Nearly midday." She was hoisting her rucksack back onto her shoulders, never taking her eyes from the snowscape sloping slowly up and away from us. "What do you think it was?"

I shrugged. "Brand seeing things. Too much wacky tobaccy."

We set off again. Charley was in the lead, I followed close behind, and Brand stumbled along at the rear. It was eerily silent around us, the snow muffling our gasps and puffs, the constant grumble of the sea soon blending into the background as much as it ever did. There was a sort of white noise in my ears: blood pumping; breath ebbing and flowing; snow crunching underfoot. They merged into one whisper, eschewing all outside noise, almost soporific in rhythm. I coughed to break the spell.

"What the hell do we do when we get to the village?" Brand said.

"Send back help," Charley stated slowly, enunciating each word as if to a naive young child.

"But what if the village is like everywhere else we've seen or heard about on TV?"

Charley was silent for a while. So was I. A collage of images tumbled through my mind, hateful and hurtful and sharper because of that. Hazy scenes from the last day of television broadcasts we had watched: loaded ships leaving docks and sailing off to some nebulous sanctuary abroad; shootings in the streets, bodies in the gutters, dogs sniffing at open wounds; an airship, drifting over the hills in some vague attempt to offer hope.

"Don't be stupid," I said.

"Even if it is, there will be help there," Charley said quietly.

"Like hell." Brand lit up another joint. It was cold, we were risking our lives, there may very well be something in the snow itching to attack us . . . but at that moment I wanted nothing more than to take a long haul on Brand's pot, and let casual oblivion anesthetize my fears.

An hour later we found the car.

By my figuring we had come about three miles. We were all but exhausted. My legs ached, knee joints stiff and hot as if on fire.

The road had started a slow curve to the left, heading inland from the coast toward the distant village. Its path had become less distinct, the hedges having sunk slowly into the ground until there was really nothing to distinguish it from the fields of snow on either side. We had been walking the last half-hour on memory alone.

The car was almost completely buried by snow, only one side of the windscreen and the iced-up antenna still visible. There was no sign of the route it had taken; whatever tracks it had made were long-since obliterated by the blizzards. As we approached the snow started again, fat flakes drifting lazily down and landing on the icy surface of last night's fall.

"Do not drive unless absolutely necessary," Brand said. Charley and I ignored him. We unslung our rucksacks and approached the buried shape, all of us keeping hold of our weapons. I meant to ask Charley where she'd got hold of the revolver—whether she'd had it with her when we both came here to test the sea and write environmental reports which would never be read—but now did not seem the time. I had no wish to seem judgmental or patronizing.

As I reached out to knock some of the frozen snow from the windscreen a flight of seagulls cawed and took off from nearby. They had been all but invisible against the snow, but there were at least thirty of them lifting as one, calling loudly as they twirled over our heads and then headed out to sea.

We all shouted out in shock. Charley stumbled sideways as she tried to bring her gun to bear and fell on her back. Brand screeched like a kid, then let off a pop with his air pistol to hide his embarrassment. The pellet found no target. The birds ignored us after the initial fly-past, and they slowly merged with the hazy distance. The new snow shower brought the horizon in close.

"Shit," Charley muttered.

"Yeah." Brand reloaded his pistol without looking at either of us, then rooted around for the joint he'd dropped when he screamed.

Charley and I went back to knocking the snow away, using our gloved hands to make tracks down the windscreen and across the hood. "I think it's a Ford," I said uselessly. "Maybe an old Mondeo." Jayne and I had owned a Mondeo when we'd been courting. Many was the time we had parked in some shaded woodland or beside units on the local industrial estate, wound down the windows and made love as the cool night air looked on. We'd broken down once while I was driving her home; it had made us two hours late and her father had come close to beating me senseless. It was only the oil on my hands that had convinced him of our story.

I closed my eyes.

"Can't see anything," Charley said, jerking me back to cold reality. "Windscreen's frozen up on the inside."

"Take us ages to clear the doors."

"What do you want to do that for?" Brand said. "Dead car, probably full of dead people."

"Dead people may have guns and food and fuel," I said. "Going to give us a hand?"

Brand glanced at the dark windshield, the contents of the car hidden by ice and shadowed by the weight of snow surrounding it. He sat gently on his rucksack, and when he saw it would take his weight without sinking in the snow, he re-lit his joint and stared out to sea. I wondered whether he'd even notice if we left him there.

"We could uncover the passenger door," Charley said. "Driver's side is stuck fast in the drift, take us hours."

We both set about trying to shift snow away from the car. "Keep your eyes open," I said to Brand. He just nodded and watched the sea lift and drop its thickening ice floes. I used the shotgun as a crutch to lift myself onto the hood, and from there to the covered roof.

"What?" Charley said. I ignored her, turning a slow circle, trying to pick out any movement against the fields of white. To the west lay the manor, a couple of miles away and long since hidden by creases in the landscape. To the north the ground still rose steadily away from the sea, rocks protruding here and there along with an occasional clump of trees hardy enough to survive Atlantic storms. Nothing moved. The shower was turning quickly into a storm and I felt suddenly afraid. The manor was at least three miles behind us; the village seven miles ahead. We were in the middle, three weak humans slowly freezing as nature freaked out and threw weeks of snow and ice at us. And here we were, convinced we could defeat it, certain in our own puny minds that we were the rulers here, we called the shots. However much we polluted and contaminated, I knew, we would never call the shots. Nature may let us live within it, but in the end it would purge and clean itself. And whether there would be room for us in the new world . . .

Perhaps this was the first stage of that cleansing. While civilization slaughtered itself, disease and extremes of weather took advantage of our distraction to pick off the weak.

"We should get back," I said.

"But the village—"

"Charley, it's almost two. It'll start getting dark in two hours, maximum. We can't travel in the dark; we might walk right by the village, or stumble onto one of those ice overhangs at the cliff edge. Brand here may get so doped he thinks we're ghosts and shoot us with his pop-gun."

"Hey!"

"But Boris . . ." Charley said. "He's . . . we need help. To bury him. We need to tell someone."

I climbed carefully down from the car roof and landed in the snow beside her. "We'll take a look in the car. Then we should get back. It'll help no one if we freeze to death out here."

"I'm not cold," she said defiantly.

"That's because you're moving, you're working. When you walk you sweat and you'll stay warm. When we have to stop—and eventually we will—you'll stop moving. Your sweat will freeze, and so will you. We'll all freeze. They'll find us in the thaw, you and me huddled up for warmth, Brand with a frozen reefer still in his gob."

Charley smiled, Brand scowled. Both expressions pleased me.

"The door's frozen shut," she said.

"I'll use my key." I punched at the glass with the butt of the shot-gun. After three attempts the glass shattered and I used my gloved hands to clear it all away. I caught a waft of something foul and stale. Charley stepped back with a slight groan. Brand was oblivious.

We peered inside the car, leaning forward so that the weak light could filter in around us.

There was a dead man in the driver's seat. He was frozen solid, hunched up under several blankets, only his eyes and nose visible. Icicles hung from both. His eyelids were still open. On the dashboard a candle had burnt down to nothing more than a puddle of wax, imitating the ice as it dripped forever toward the floor. The scene was so still it was eerie, like a painting so lifelike that textures and shapes could be felt. I noticed the driver's door handle was jammed open, though the door had not budged against the snowdrift burying that side of the car.

At the end he had obviously attempted to get out. I shuddered as I tried to imagine this man's lonely death. It was the second body I'd seen in two days.

"Well?" Brand called from behind us.

"Your drug supplier," Charley said. "Car's full of snow."

I snorted, pleased to hear the humor, but when I looked at her she seemed as sad and forlorn as ever. "Maybe we should see if he brought us anything useful," she said, and I nodded.

Charley was smaller than me so she said she'd go. I went to protest but she was already wriggling through the shattered window, and a minute later she'd thrown out everything loose she could find. She came back out without looking at me.

There was a rucksack half full of canned foods; a petrol can with a swill of fuel in the bottom; a novel frozen at page ninety; some plastic bottles filled with piss and split by the ice; a rifle, but no ammunition; a smaller rucksack with wallet, some papers, an electronic credit card; a photo wallet frozen shut; a plastic bag full of shit; a screwed-up newspaper as hard as wood.

Everything was frozen.

"Let's go," I said. Brand and Charley took a couple of items each and shouldered their rucksacks. I picked up the rifle. We took everything except the shit and piss.

It took us four hours to get back to the manor. Three times on the way Brand said he'd seen something bounding through the snow—a stag, he said, big and white with sparkling antlers—and we dropped everything and went into a defensive huddle. But nothing ever materialized from the worsening storm, even though our imaginations painted all sorts of horrors behind and beyond the snowflakes. If there was anything out there, it kept itself well hidden.

The light was fast fading as we arrived back. Our tracks had been all but covered, and it was only later that I realized how staggeringly lucky we'd been to even find our way home. Perhaps something was on our side, guiding us, steering us back to the manor. Perhaps it was the change in nature taking us home, preparing us for what was to come next.

It was the last favor we were granted.

Hayden cooked us some soup as the others huddled around the fire, listening to our story and trying so hard not to show their disappointment. Brand kept chiming in about the things he'd seen in the snow. Even Ellie's face held the taint of fading hope.

"Boris's angels?" Rosalie suggested. "He *may* have seen angels, you know. They're not averse to steering things their way, when it suits them." Nobody answered.

Charley was crying again, shivering by the fire. Rosalie had wrapped her in blankets and now hugged her close.

"The gun looks okay," Ellie said. She'd sat at the table and stripped and oiled the rifle, listening to us all as we talked. She illustrated the fact by pointing it at the wall and squeezing the trigger a few times. *Click click click.* There was no ammunition for it.

"What about the body?" Rosalie asked. "Did you see who it was?"

I frowned. "What do you mean?"

"Well, if it was someone coming along the road toward the manor, maybe one of us knew him." We were all motionless save for Ellie, who still rooted through the contents of the car. She'd already put the newspaper on the floor so that it could dry out, in the hope of being able to read at least some of it. We'd made out the date: one week ago. The television had stopped showing pictures two weeks ago. There was a week of history in there, if only we could save it.

"He was frozen stiff," I said. "We didn't get a good look . . . and anyway, who'd be coming here? And why? Maybe it was a good job—"

Ellie gasped. There was a tearing sound as she peeled apart more pages of the photo wallet and gasped again, this time struggling to draw in a breath afterward.

"Ellie?"

She did not answer. The others had turned to her but she seemed not to notice. She saw nothing, other than the photographs in her hand. She stared at them for an endless few seconds, eyes moist yet unreadable in the glittering firelight. Then she scraped the chair back across the polished floor, crumpled the photos into her back pocket, and walked quickly from the room.

I followed, glancing at the others to indicate that they should stay where they were. None of them argued. Ellie was already halfway up the long staircase by the time I entered the hallway, but it was not until the final stair that she stopped, turned, and answered my soft calling.

"My husband," she said, "Jack. I haven't seen him for two years." A tear ran icily down her cheek. "We never really made it, you know?" She looked at the wall beside her, as though she could stare straight through and discern logic and truth in the blanked-out landscape beyond. "He was coming here. For me. To find me."

There was nothing I could say. Ellie seemed to forget I was there and she mumbled the next few words to herself. Then she turned and disappeared from view along the upstairs corridor, shadow dancing in the light of disturbed candles.

Back in the living room I told the others that Ellie was all right, she had gone to bed, she was tired and cold and as human as the rest of us. I did not let on about her dead husband, I figured it was really none of their business. Charley glared at me with bloodshot eyes, and I was sure she'd figured it out. Brand flicked bits of carrot from his soup into the fire and watched them sizzle to nothing.

We went to bed soon after. Alone in my room I sat at the window for a long time, huddled in clothes and blankets, staring out at the moonlit brightness of the snow drifts and the fat flakes still falling. I tried to imagine Ellie's estranged husband struggling to steer the car through deepening snow, the radiator clogging in the drift it had buried its nose in, splitting, gushing boiling water and steaming instantly into an ice trap. Sitting there, perhaps not knowing just how near he was, thinking of his wife and how much he needed to see her. And I tried to imagine what desperate events must have driven him to do such a thing, though I did not think too hard.

A door opened and closed quietly, footsteps, another door slipped open to allow a guest entry. I wondered who was sharing a bed tonight.

I saw Jayne, naked and beautiful in the snow, bearing no sign of the illness that had killed her. She beckoned me, drawing me nearer, and at last a door was opening for me as well, a shape coming into the room, white material floating around its hips, or perhaps they were limbs, membranous and thin . . .

My eyes snapped open and I sat up on the bed. I was still dressed from the night before. Dawn streamed in the window and my candle had burnt down to nothing.

Ellie stood next to the bed. Her eyes were red-rimmed and swollen. I tried to pretend I had not noticed.

"Happy Christmas," she said. "Come on. Brand's dead."

Brand was lying just beyond the smashed conservatory doors behind the kitchen. There was a small courtyard area here, protected somewhat by an overhanging roof so that the snow was only about knee-deep. Most of it was red. A drift had already edged its way into the conservatory, and the beer cans on the shelf had frozen and split. No more beer.

He had been punctured by countless holes, each the width of a thumb, all of them clogged with hardened blood. One eye stared hopefully out to the hidden horizon, the other was absent. His hair was also missing; it looked like he'd been scalped. There were bits of him all around—a finger here, a splash of brain there—but he was less mutilated than Boris had been. At least we could see that this smudge in the snow had once been Brand.

Hayden was standing next to him, posing daintily in an effort to avoid stepping in the blood. It was a lost cause. "What the hell was he doing out here?" he asked in disgust.

"I heard doors opening last night," I said. "Maybe he came for a walk. Or a smoke."

"The door was mine," Rosalie said softly. She had appeared behind us and nudged in between Ellie and me. She wore a long, creased shirt. Brand's shirt, I noticed. "Brand was with me until three o'clock this morning. Then he left to go back to his own room, said he was feeling ill. We thought perhaps you shouldn't know about us." Her eyes were wide in an effort not to cry. "We thought everyone would laugh."

Nobody answered. Nobody laughed. Rosalie looked at Brand with more shock than sadness, and I wondered just how often he'd opened her door in the night. The insane, unfair notion that she may even be relieved flashed across my mind, one of those awful thoughts you try to expunge but which hangs around like a guilty secret.

"Maybe we should go inside," I said to Rosalie, but she gave me such an icy glare that I turned away, looking at Brand's shattered body rather than her piercing eyes.

"I'm a big girl now," she said. I could hear her rapid breathing as she tried to contain the disgust and shock at what she saw. I wondered if she'd ever seen a dead body. Most people had, nowadays.

Charley was nowhere to be seen. "I didn't wake her," Ellie said when I queried. "She had enough to handle yesterday. I thought she shouldn't really see this. No need."

And you? I thought, noticing Ellie's puffy eyes, the gauntness of her face, her hands fisting open and closed at her sides. *Are you all right? Did you have enough to handle yesterday?*

"What the hell do we do with him?" Hayden asked. He was still standing closer to Brand than the rest of us, hugging himself to try to preserve some of the warmth from sleep. "I mean, Boris was all over the place, from what I hear. But Brand . . . we have to do something. Bury him, or something. It's Christmas, for God's sake."

"The ground's like iron," I protested.

"So we take it in turns digging," Rosalie said quietly.

"It'll take us—"

"Then I'll do it myself." She walked out into the blooded snow and shattered glass in bare feet, bent over Brand's body, and grabbed under each armpit as if to lift him. She was naked beneath the shirt. Hayden stared in frank fascination. I turned away, embarrassed for myself more than for Rosalie.

"Wait," Ellie sighed. "Rosalie, wait. Let's all dress properly, then we'll come and bury him. Rosalie." The girl stood and smoothed Brand's shirt down over her thighs, perhaps realizing what she had put on display. She looked up at the sky and caught the morning's first snowflake on her nose.

"Snowing," she said. "Just for a fucking change."

We went inside. Hayden remained in the kitchen with the outside door shut and bolted while the rest of us went upstairs to dress, wake Charley, and tell her the grim Yule tidings. Once Rosalie's door had closed I followed Ellie along to her room. She opened her door for me and invited me in, obviously knowing I needed to talk.

Her place was a mess. Perhaps, I thought, she was so busy being strong and mysterious that she had no time for tidying up. Clothes were strewn across the floor, a false covering like the snow outside. Used plates were piled next to her bed, those at the bottom already blurred with mold, the uppermost still showing the remains of the meal we'd had before Boris had been killed. Spaghetti bolognaise, I recalled, to Hayden's own recipe, rich and tangy with tinned tomatoes, strong with garlic, the helpings massive. Somewhere out there Boris's last meal lay frozen in the snow, half digested, torn from his guts—

I snorted and closed my eyes. Another terrible thought that wouldn't go away.

"Brand really saw things in the snow didn't he?" Ellie asked.

"Yes, he was pretty sure. At least, *a* thing. He said it was like a stag, except white. It was bounding along next to us, he said. We stopped a few times but I'm certain I never saw anything. Don't think Charley did, either." I made space on Ellie's bed and sat down. "Why?"

Ellie walked to the window and opened the curtains. The snowstorm had started in earnest, and although her window faced the Atlantic all we could see was a sea of white. She rested her forehead on the cold glass, her breath misting, fading, misting again. "I've seen something too," she said.

Ellie. Seeing things in the snow. Ellie was the nearest we had to a leader, though none of us had ever wanted one. She was strong, if distant. Intelligent, if a little straight with it. She'd never been much of a laugh, even before things had turned to shit, and her dogged conservatism in someone so young annoyed me no end.

Ellie, seeing things in the snow.

I could not bring myself to believe it. I did not want to. If I did accept it then there really were things out there, because Ellie did not lie, and she was not prone to fanciful journeys of the imagination.

"What something?" I asked at last, fearing it a question I would never wish to be answered. But I could not simply ignore it. I could not sit here and listen to Ellie opening up, then stand and walk away. Not with Boris frozen out there, not with Brand still cooling into the landscape.

She rocked her head against the glass. "Don't know. Something white. So how did I see it?" She turned from the window, stared at me, crossed her arms. "From this window," she said. "Two days ago. Just before Charley found Boris. Something flitting across the snow like a bird, except it left faint tracks. As big as a fox, perhaps, but it had more legs. Certainly not a deer."

"Or one of Boris's angels?"

She shook her head and smiled, but there was no humor there. There rarely was. "Don't tell anyone," she said. "I don't want anyone to know. But! We will have to be careful. Take the guns when we try to bury Brand. A couple of us keep a lookout while the others dig. Though I doubt we'll even get through the snow."

"You and guns," I said perplexed. I didn't know how to work what I was trying to ask.

Ellie smiled wryly. "Me and guns. I hate guns."

I stared at her, saying nothing, using silence to pose the next question.

"I have a history," she said. And that was all.

Later, downstairs in the kitchen, Charley told us what she'd managed to read in the paper from the frozen car. In the week since we'd picked up the last TV signal and the paper was printed, things had gone from bad to worse. The illness that had killed my Jayne was claiming millions across the globe. The USA blamed Iraq. Russia blamed China. Blame continued to waste lives. There was civil unrest and shootings in the streets, mass burials at sea, martial law, air strikes, food shortages . . . the words melded into one another as Rosalie recited the reports.

Hayden was trying to cook mince pies without the mince. He was using stewed apples instead, and the kitchen stank sickeningly sweet. None of us felt particularly festive.

Outside, in the heavy snow that even now was attempting to drift in and cover Brand, we were all twitchy. Whoever or—now more likely—whatever had done this could still be around. Guns were held at the ready.

We wrapped him in an old sheet and enclosed this in torn black plastic bags until there was no white or red showing. Ellie and I dragged him around the corner of the house to where there were some old flower beds. We stared to dig where we remembered them to be, but when we got through the snow the ground was too hard. In the end we left him on the surface of the frozen earth and covered the hole back in with snow, mumbling about burying him when the thaw came. The whole process had an unsettling sense of permanence.

As if the snow would never melt.

Later, staring from the dining room window as Hayden brought in a platter of old vegetables as our Christmas feast, I saw something big and white skimming across the surface of the snow. It moved too quickly for me to make it out properly, but I was certain I saw wings.

I turned away from the window, glanced at Ellie and said nothing.

Two
The Color of Fear

During the final few days of Jayne's life I had felt completely hemmed in. Not only physically trapped within our home—and more often the bedroom where she lay—but also mentally hindered. It was a feeling I hated, felt guilty about, and tried desperately to relieve, but it was always there.

I stayed, holding her hand for hour after terrible hour, our palms fused by sweat, her face pasty and contorted by agonies I could barely imagine. Sometimes she would be conscious and alert, sitting up in bed and listening as I read to her, smiling at the humorous parts, trying to ignore the sad ones. She would ask me questions about how things were in the outside world, and I would lie and tell her they were getting better. There was no need to add to her misery. Other times she would be a shadow of her old self, a gray stain on the bed with liquid limbs and weak bowels, a screaming thing with bloody growths sprouting across her skin and pumping their venom inward with uncontrollable, unstoppable tenacity. At these times I would talk truthfully and tell her the reality of things, that the world was going to shit and she would be much better off when she left it.

Even then I did not tell her the complete truth: that I wished I were going with her. Just in case she could still hear.

Wherever I went during those final few days I was under assault, besieged by images of Jayne, thoughts of her impending death, vague ideas of what would happen after she had gone. I tried to fill the landscape of time laid out before me, but Jayne never figured and so the landscape was bare. She was my whole world; without her I could picture nothing to live for. My mind was never free although sometimes, when a doctor found time to visit our house and *tut* and sigh over Jayne's wasting body, I would go for a walk. Mostly she barely knew the doctor was there, for which I was grateful. There was nothing he could do. I would not be able to bear even the faintest glimmer of hope in her eyes.

I strolled through the park opposite our house, staying to the paths so that I did not risk stepping on discarded needles or stumbling across suicides decaying slowly back to nature. The trees were as beautiful as ever, huge emeralds against the grimly polluted sky. Somehow they bled the taint of humanity from their systems. They adapted, changed, and our arrival had really done little to halt their progress. A few years of poisons and disease, perhaps. A shaping of the landscape upon which we projected an idea of control. But when we were all dead and gone our industrial disease on the planet would be little more than a few twisted, corrupted rings in the lifetime of the oldest trees. I wished we could adapt so well.

When Jayne died there was no sense of release. My grief was as great as if she'd been killed at the height of health, her slow decline doing nothing to prepare me for the dread that enveloped me at the moment of her last strangled sigh. Still I was under siege, this time by death. The certainty of its black fingers rested on my shoulders day and night, long past the hour of Jayne's hurried burial in a local football ground alongside a thousand others. I would turn around sometimes and try to see past it, make out some ray of hope in a stranger's gaze. But there was always the blackness bearing down on me, clouding my vision and the gaze of others, promising doom soon.

It's ironic that it was not death that truly scared me, but living. Without Jayne the world was nothing but an empty, dying place.

Then I had come here, an old manor on the rugged South West coast. I'd thought that solitude—a distance between me and the terrible place the world was slowly becoming—would be a balm to my suffering. In reality it was little more than a placebo and realizing that negated it. I felt more trapped than ever.

The morning after Brand's death and botched burial—Boxing Day— I sat at my bedroom window and watched nature laying siege. The snow hugged the landscape like a funeral shroud in negative. The coast was hidden by the cliffs, but I could see the sea further out. There was something that I thought at first to be an iceberg and it took me a few minutes to figure out what it really was; the upturned hull of a big boat. A ferry, perhaps, or one of the huge cruise liners being used to ship people south, away from blighted Britain to the false promise of Australia. I was glad I could not see any more detail. I wondered what we would find washed up in the rock pools that morning, were Charley and I to venture down to the sea.

If I stared hard at the snowbanks, the fields of virgin white, the humped shadows that were our ruined and hidden cars, I could see no sign of movement. An occasional shadow passed across the snow, though it could have been from a bird flying in front of the sun. But if I relaxed my gaze, tried not to concentrate too hard, lowered my eyelids, then I could see them. Sometimes they skimmed low and fast over the snow, twisting like sea serpents or Chinese dragons and throwing up a fine mist of flakes behind them. At other times they lay still and watchful, fading into the background if I looked directly at them until one shadow looked much like the next, but could be so different.

I wanted to talk about them. I wanted to ask Ellie just what the hell they were, because I knew that she had seen them too. I wanted to know what was happening and why it was happening to us. But I had some mad idea that to mention them would make them real, like ghosts in the cupboard and slithering wet things beneath the bed. Best ignore them and they would go away.

I counted a dozen white shapes that morning.

"Anyone dead today?" Rosalie asked.

The statement shocked me, made me wonder just what sort of relationship she and Brand had had, but we all ignored her. No need to aggravate an argument.

Charley sat close to Rosalie, as if a sharing of grief would halve it. Hayden was cooking up bacon and bagels long past their sell-by date. Ellie had not yet come downstairs. She'd been stalking the manor all night, and now we were up she was washing and changing.

"What do we do today?" Charley asked. "Are we going to try to get away again? Get to the village for help?"

I sighed and went to say something, but the thought of those things out in the snow kept me quiet. Nobody else spoke, and the silence was the only answer required.

We ate our stale breakfast, drank tea clotted with powdered milk, listened to the silence outside. It had snowed again in the night and our tracks from the day before had been obliterated. Standing at the sink to wash up I stared through the window, and it was like looking upon the same day as yesterday, the day before, and the day before that; no signs of our presence existed. All footprints had vanished, all echoes of voices swallowed by the snow, shadows covered with another six inches and frozen like corpses in a glacier. I wondered what patterns and traces the snow would hold this evening, when darkness closed in to wipe us away once more.

"We have to tell someone," Charley said. "Something's happening, we should tell someone. We have to do something, we can't just . . ." She trailed off, staring into a cooling cup of tea, perhaps remembering a time before all this had begun, or imagining she could remember. "This is crazy."

"It's God," Rosalie said.

"Huh?" Hayden was already peeling wrinkled old vegetables ready for lunch, constantly busy, always doing something to keep his mind off everything else. I wondered how much really went on behind his fringed brow, how much theorizing he did while he was boiling, how much nostalgia he wallowed in as familiar cooking smells settled into his clothes.

"It's God, fucking us over one more time. Crazy, as Charley says. God and crazy are synonymous."

"Rosie," I said, knowing she hated the shortened name, "if it's not constructive, don't bother. None of this will bring—"

"Anything is more constructive than sod-all, which is what you lot have to got to say this morning. We wake up one morning without one of us dead, and you're all tongue-tied. Bored? Is that it?"

"Rosalie, why—"

"Shut it, Charley. You more than anyone should be thinking about all this. Wondering why the hell we came here a few weeks ago to escape all the shit, and now we've landed right in the middle of it. Right up to our armpits. Drowning in it. Maybe one of us is a Jonah and it's followed—"

"And you think it's God?" I said. I knew that asking the question would give her open opportunity to rant, but in a way I felt she was right, we did need to talk. Sitting here stewing in our own thoughts could not help anyone.

"Oh yes, it's His Holiness," she nodded, "sitting on his pedestal of lost souls, playing around one day and deciding, hmm, maybe I'll have some fun today, been a year since a decent earthquake, a few months since the last big volcano eruption. Soooo, what can I do?"

Ellie appeared then, sat at the table and poured a cup of cold tea that looked like sewer water. Her appearance did nothing to mar Rosalie's flow.

"I know, he says, I'll nudge things to one side, turn them slightly askew, give the world a gasp before I've cleaned my teeth. Just a little, not so that anyone will notice for a while. Get them paranoid. Get them looking over their shoulders at each other. See how the wrinkly pink bastards deal with that one!"

"Why would He do that?" Hayden said.

Rosalie stood and put on a deep voice. "Forget me, will they? I'll show them. Turn over and open your legs, humanity, for I shall root you up the arse."

"Just shut up!" Charley screeched. The kitchen went ringingly quiet, even Rosalie sitting slowly down. "You're full of this sort of shit, Rosie. Always telling us how we're being controlled, manipulated. Who by? Ever seen anyone? There's a hidden agenda behind everything for you, isn't there? If there's no toilet paper after you've had a crap you'd blame it the global dirty-arse conspiracy!"

Hysteria hung silently in the room. The urge to cry grabbed me, but also a yearning to laugh out loud. The air was heavy with held breaths and barely restrained comments, thick with the potential for violence.

"So," Ellie said at last, her voice little more than a whisper, "let's hear some truths."

"What?" Rosalie obviously expected an extension of her foolish monologue. Ellie, however, cut her down.

"Well, for starters has anyone else seen things in the snow?" Heads shook. My own shook as well. I wondered who else was lying with me. "Anyone seen anything strange out there at all?" she continued. "Maybe not the things Brand and Boris saw, but something else?" Again, shaken heads. An uncomfortable shuffling from Hayden as he stirred something on the gas cooker.

"I saw God looking down on us," Rosalie said quietly, "with blood in his eyes." She did not continue or elaborate, did not go off on one of her rants. I think that's why her strange comment stayed with me.

"Right," said Ellie, "then may I make a suggestion. Firstly, there's no point trying to get to the village. The snow's even deeper than it was yesterday, it's colder and freezing to death for the sake of it will achieve nothing. If we did manage to find help, Boris and Brand are long past it." She paused, waiting for assent.

"Fair enough," Charley said quietly. "Yeah, you're right."

"Secondly, we need to make sure the manor is secure. We need to protect ourselves from whatever got at Brand and Boris. There are a dozen rooms on the ground floor, we only use two or three of them. Check the others. Make sure windows are locked and storm shutters are bolted. Make sure French doors aren't loose or liable to break open at the slightest . . . breeze, or whatever."

"What do you think the things out there are?" Hayden asked. "Lock pickers?"

Ellie glanced at his back, looked at me, shrugged. "No," she said, "I don't think so. But there's no use being complacent. We can't try to make it out, so we should do the most we can here. The snow can't last forever, and when it finally melts we'll go to the village then. Agreed?"

Heads nodded.

"If the village is still there," Rosalie cut in. "If everyone isn't dead. If the disease hasn't wiped out most of the country. If a war doesn't start somewhere in the meantime."

"Yes," Ellie sighed impatiently, "if all those things don't happen." She nodded at me. "We'll do the two rooms at the back. The rest of you check the others. There are some tools in the big cupboard under the stairs, some nails and hammers if you need them, a crowbar too. And if you think you need timber to nail across windows . . . if it'll make you feel any better . . . tear up some floorboards in the dining room. They're hardwood, they're strong."

"Oh, let battle commence!" Rosalie cried. She stood quickly, her chair falling onto its back, and stalked from the room with a swish of her long skirts. Charley followed.

Ellie and I went to the rear of the manor. In the first of the large rooms the snow had drifted up against the windows to cut out any view or light from outside. For an instant it seemed as if nothing existed beyond the glass and I wondered if that was the case, then why were we trying to protect ourselves?

Against nothing.

"What do you think is out there?" I asked.

"Have you seen anything?"

I paused. There was something, but nothing I could easily identify or put a name to. What I had seen had been way beyond my ken, white shadows apparent against whiteness. "No," I said, "nothing."

Ellie turned from the window and looked at me in the half-light, and it was obvious that she knew I was lying. "Well, if you do see something, don't tell."

"Why?"

"Boris and Brand told," she said. She did not say any more. They'd seen angels and stags in the snow and they'd talked about it, and now they were dead.

She pushed at one of the window frames. Although the damp timber fragmented at her touch, the snow drift behind it was as effective as a vault door. We moved on to the next window. The room was noisy with unspoken thoughts, and it was only a matter of time before they made themselves heard.

"You think someone in here has something to do with Brand and Boris," I said.

Ellie sat on one of the wide windowsills and sighed deeply. She ran a hand through her spiky hair and rubbed at her neck. I wondered whether she'd had any sleep at all last night. I wondered whose door had been opening and closing; the prickle of jealousy was crazy under the circumstances. I realized all of a sudden how much Ellie reminded me of Jayne, and I swayed under the sudden barrage of memory.

"Who?" she said. "Rosie? Hayden? Don't be soft."

"But you do, don't you?" I said again.

She nodded. Then shook her head. Shrugged. "I don't bloody know, I'm not Sherlock Holmes. It's just strange that Brand and Boris . . ." She trailed off, avoiding my eyes.

"I have seen something out there," I said to break the awkward silence. "Something in the snow. Can't say what. Shadows. Fleeting glimpses. Like everything I see is from the corner of my eye."

Ellie stared at me for so long that I thought she'd died there on the windowsill, a victim of my admission, another dead person to throw outside and let freeze until the thaw came and we could do our burying.

"You've seen what I've seen," she said eventually, verbalizing the trust between us. It felt good, but it also felt a little dangerous. A trust like that could alienate the others, not consciously but in our mind's eye. By working and thinking closer together, perhaps we would drive them further away.

We moved to the next window.

"I've known there was something since you found Jack in his car," Ellie said. "He'd never have just sat there and waited to die. He'd have tried to get out, to get here, no matter how dangerous. He wouldn't have sat watching the candle burn down, listening to the wind, feeling his eyes freeze over. It's just not like him to give in."

"So why did he? Why didn't he get out?"

"There was something waiting for him outside the car. Something he was trying to keep away from." She rattled a window, stared at the snow pressed up against the glass. "Something that would make him rather freeze to death than face it."

We moved on to the last window, Ellie reached out to touch the rusted clasp and there was a loud crash. Glass broke, wood struck wood, someone screamed, all from a distance.

We spun around and ran from the room, listening to the shrieks.

Two voices now, a man and a woman, the woman's muffled. Somewhere in the manor, someone else was dying.

The reaction to death is sometimes as violent as death itself. Shock throws a cautious coolness over the senses, but your stomach still knots, your skin stings as if the Reaper is glaring at you as well. For a second you live that death, and then shameful relief floods in when you see it's someone else.

Such were my thoughts as we turned a corner into the main hallway of the manor. Hayden was hammering at the library door, crashing his fists into the wood hard enough to draw blood. "Charley!" he shouted, again and again. "Charley!" The door shook under his assault but it did not budge. Tears streaked his face, dribble strung from chin to chest. The dark old wood of the door sucked up the blood from his split knuckles. "Charley!"

Ellie and I arrived just ahead of Rosalie.

"Hayden!" Rosalie shouted.

"Charley! In there! She went in and locked the door, and there was a crash and she was screaming!"

"Why did she—" Rosalie began, but Ellie shushed us all with one wave of her hand.

Silence. "No screaming now," she said.

Then we heard other noises through the door, faint and tremulous as if picked up from a distance along a bad telephone line. They sounded like chewing; bone snapping; flesh ripping. I could not believe what I was hearing, but at the same time I remembered the bodies of Boris and Brand. Suddenly I did not want to open the door. I wanted to defy whatever it was laying siege to us here by ignoring the results of its actions. Forget Charley, continue checking the windows and doors, deny whoever or whatever it was the satisfaction—

"Charley," I said quietly. She was a small woman, fragile, strong but sensitive. She'd told me once, sitting at the base of the cliffs before it had begun to snow, how she loved to sit and watch the sea. It made her feel safe. It made her feel a part of nature. She'd never hurt anyone. "Charley."

Hayden kicked at the door again and I added my weight, shouldering into the tough old wood, jarring my body painfully with each impact. Ellie did the same and soon we were taking it in turns. The noises continued between each impact—increased in volume if anything—and our assault became more frantic to cover them up.

If the manor had not been so old and decrepit we would never have broken in. The door was probably as old as all of us put together, but its surround had been replaced some time in the past. Softwood painted as hardwood had slowly crumbled in the damp atmosphere and after a minute the door burst in, frame splintering into the coldness of the library.

One of the three big windows had been smashed. Shattered glass and snapped mullions hung crazily from the frame. The cold had already made the room its home, laying a fine sheen of frost across the thousands of books, hiding some of their titles from view as if to conceal whatever tumultuous history they contained. Snow flurried in, hung around for a while then chose somewhere to settle. It did not melt. Once on the inside, this room was now a part of the outside.

As was Charley.

The area around the broken window was red and Charley had spread. Bits of her hung on the glass like hellish party streamers. Other parts had melted into the snow outside and turned it pink. Some of her was recognizable—her hair splayed out across the soft whiteness, a hand fisted around a melting clump of ice—other parts had never been seen before, because they'd always been inside.

I leaned over and puked. My vomit cleared a space of frost on the floor so I did it again, moving into the room. My stomach was in agonized spasms but I enjoyed seeing the white sheen vanish, as if I were claiming the room back for a time. Then I went to my knees and tried to forget what I'd seen, shake it from my head, pound it from my temples. I felt hands close around my wrists to stop me from punching myself, but I fell forward and struck my forehead on the cold timber floor. If I could forget, if I could drive the image away, perhaps it would no longer be true.

But there was the smell. And the steam, rising from the open body and misting what glass remained. Charley's last breath.

"Shut the door!" I shouted. "Nail it shut! Quickly!"

Ellie had helped me from the room, and now Hayden was pulling on the broken-in door to try to close it again. Rosalie came back from the dining room with a few splintered floorboards, her face pale, eyes staring somewhere no one else could see.

"Hurry!" I shouted. I felt a distance pressing in around me; the walls receding; the ceiling rising. Voices turned slow and deep, movement became stilted. My stomach heaved again but there was nothing left to bring up. I was the center of everything but it was all leaving me, all sight and sound and scent fleeing my faint. And then, clear and bright, Jayne's laugh broke through. Only once, but I knew it was her.

Something brushed my cheek and gave warmth to my face. My jaw clicked and my head turned to one side, slowly but inexorably. Something white blurred across my vision and my other cheek burst into warmth, and I was glad, the cold was the enemy, the cold brought the snow, which brought the fleeting things I had seen outside, things without a name or, perhaps, things with a million names. Or things with a name I already knew.

The warmth was good.

Ellie's mouth moved slowly and watery rumbles tumbled forth. Her words took shape in my mind, hauling themselves together just as events took on their own speed once more.

"Snap out of it," Ellie said, and slapped me across the face again.

Another sound dragged itself together. I could not identify it, but I knew where it was coming from. The others were staring fearfully at the door, Hayden was still leaning back with both hands around the handle, straining to get as far away as possible without letting go.

Scratching. Sniffing. Something rifling through books, snuffling in long-forgotten corners at dust from long-dead people. A slow regular beat, which could have been footfalls or a heartbeat. I realized it was my own and another sound took its place.

"What . . . ?"

Ellie grabbed the tops of my arms and shook me harshly. "You with us? You back with us now?"

I nodded, closing my eyes at the swimming sensation in my head. Vertical fought with horizontal and won out this time. "Yeah."

"Rosalie," Ellie whispered. "Get more boards. Hayden, keep hold of that handle. Just keep hold." She looked at me. "Hand me the nails as I hold my hand out. Now listen. Once I start banging, it may attract."

"What are you doing?" I said.

"Nailing the bastards in."

I thought of the shapes I had watched from my bedroom window, the shadows flowing through other shadows, the ease with which they moved, the strength and beauty they exuded as they passed from drift to drift without leaving any trace behind. I laughed. "You think you can keep them in?"

Rosalie turned a fearful face my way. Her eyes were wide, her mouth hanging open as if readying for a scream.

"You think a few nails will stop them—"

"Just shut up," Ellie hissed, and she slapped me around the face once more. This time I was all there, and the slap was a burning sting rather than a warm caress. My head whipped around and by the time I looked up again Ellie was heaving a board against the doors, steadying it with one elbow and weighing a hammer in the other hand.

Only Rosalie looked at me. What I'd said was still plain on her face—the chance that whatever had done these foul things would find their way in, take us apart as it had done to Boris, to Brand, and now to Charley. And I could say nothing to comfort her. I shook my head, though I had no idea what message I was trying to convey.

Ellie held out her hand and clicked her fingers. Rosalie passed her a nail.

I stepped forward and pressed the board across the door. We had to tilt it so that each end rested across the frame. There were still secretive sounds from inside, like a fox rummaging through a bin late at night. I tried to imagine the scene in the room now but I could not. My mind would not place what I had seen outside into the library, could not stretch to that feat of imagination. I was glad.

For one terrible second I wanted to see. It would only take a kick at the door, a single heave and the whole room would be open to view, and then I would know whatever was in there for the second before it hit me. Jayne perhaps, a white Jayne from elsewhere, holding out her hands so that I could join her once more, just as she had promised on her deathbed. *I'll be with you again*, she had said, and the words had terrified me and comforted me and kept me going ever since. Sometimes I thought they were all that kept me alive—*I'll be with you again*.

"Jayne . . ."

Ellie brought the hammer down. The sound was explosive and I felt the impact transmitted through the wood and into my arms. I expected another impact a second later from the opposite way, but instead we heard the sound of something scampering through the already shattered window.

Ellie kept hammering until the board held firm, then she started another, and another. She did not stop until most of the door was covered, nails protruding at crazy angles, splinters under her fingernails, sweat running across her face and staining her armpits.

"Has it gone?" Rosalie asked. "Is it still in there?"

"Is what still in there, precisely?" I muttered.

We all stood that way for a while, panting with exertion, adrenaline priming us for the chase.

"I think," Ellie said after a while, "we should make some plans."

"What about Charley?" I asked. They all knew what I meant: *we can't just leave her there; we have to do something; she'd do the same for us.*

"Charley's dead," Ellie said, without looking at anyone. "Come on." She headed for the kitchen.

———

"What happened?" Ellie asked.

Hayden was shaking. "I told you. We were checking the rooms, Charley ran in before me and locked the door, I heard glass breaking and . . ." He trailed off.

"And?"

"Screams. I heard her screaming. I heard her dying."

The kitchen fell silent as we all recalled the cries, as if they were still echoing around the manor. They meant different things to each of us. For me, death always meant Jayne.

"Okay, this is how I see things," Ellie said. "There's a wild animal, or wild animals, out there now."

"What wild animals!" Rosalie scoffed. "Mutant badgers come to eat us up? Hedgehogs gone bad?"

"I don't know, but pray it is animals. If a person has done all this, then they'll be able to get in to us. However fucking goofy crazy, they'll have the intelligence to get in. No way to stop them. Nothing we could do." She patted the shotgun resting across her thighs as if to reassure herself of its presence.

"But what animals—"

"Do you know what's happening everywhere?" Ellie shouted, not just at doubting Rosie but at us all. "Do you realize that the world's changing? Every day we wake up there's a new world facing us. And every day there're fewer of us left. I mean the big us, the worldwide us, us humans." Her voice became quieter. "How long before one morning, no one wakes up?"

"What has what's happening elsewhere got to do with all this?" I asked, although inside I already had an idea of what Ellie meant. I think maybe I'd known for a while, but now my mind was opening up, my beliefs stretching, levering fantastic truths into place. They fitted; that terrified me.

"I mean, it's all changing. A disease is wiping out millions and no one knows where it came from. Unrest everywhere, shootings, bombings. Nuclear bombs in the Med, for Christ's sake. You've heard what people have called it; it's the Ruin. Capital R, people. The world's gone bad. Maybe what's happening here is just not that unusual anymore."

"That doesn't tell us what they are," Rosalie said. "Doesn't explain why they're here, or where they come from. Doesn't tell us why Charley did what she did."

"Maybe she wanted to be with Boris again," Hayden said.

I simply stared at him. "I've seen them," I said, and Ellie sighed. "I saw them outside last night."

The others looked at me, Rosalie's eyes still full of the fear I had planted there and was even now propagating.

"So what were they?" Rosalie asked. "Ninja seabirds?"

"I don't know." I ignored her sarcasm. "They were white, but they hid in shadows. Animals, they must have been. There were no people like that. But they were canny. They moved only when I wasn't looking straight at them, otherwise they stayed still and . . . blended in with the snow." Rosalie, I could see, was terrified. The sarcasm was a front. Everything I said scared her more.

"Camouflaged," Hayden said.

"No. They blended in. As if they melted in, but they didn't. I can't really . . ."

"In China," Rosalie said, "white is the color of death. It's the color of happiness and joy. They wear white at funerals."

Ellie spoke quickly, trying to grab back the conversation. "Right. Let's think of what we're going to do. First, no use trying to get out. Agreed? Good. Second, we limit ourselves to a couple of rooms downstairs, the hallway and staircase area and upstairs. Third, do what we can to block up, nail up, glue up the doors to the other rooms and corridors."

"And then?" Rosalie asked quietly. "Charades?"

Ellie shrugged and smiled. "Why not? It is Christmas time."

I'd never dreamt of a white Christmas. I was cursing Bing-fucking-Crosby with every gasped breath I could spare.

The air sang with echoing hammer blows, dropped boards, and groans as hammers crunched fingernails. I was working with Ellie to board up the rest of the downstairs rooms while Hayden and Rosalie tried to lever up the remaining boards in the dining room. We did the windows first, Ellie standing to one side with the shotgun aiming out while I hammered. It was snowing again and I could see vague shapes hiding behind flakes, dipping in and out of the snow like larking dolphins. I think we all saw them, but none of us ventured to say for sure that they were there. Our imagination was pumped up on what had happened and it had started to paint its own pictures.

We finished one of the living rooms and locked the door behind us. There was an awful sense of finality in the heavy thunk of the tumblers clicking in, a feeling that perhaps we would never go into that room again. I'd lived the last few years telling myself that there was no such thing as never—Jayne was dead and I would certainly see her again, after all—but there was nothing in these rooms that I could ever imagine us needing again. They were mostly designed for luxury, and luxury was a conceit of the contented mind. Over the past few weeks, I had seen contentment vanish forever under the gray cloud of humankind's fall from grace.

None of this seemed to matter now as we closed it all in. I thought I should feel sad, for the symbolism of what we were doing if not for the loss itself. Jayne had told me we would be together again, and then she had died and I had felt trapped ever since by her death and the promise of her final words. If nailing up doors would take me closer to her, then so be it.

In the next room I looked out of the window and saw Jayne striding naked toward me through the snow. Fat flakes landed on her shoulders and did not melt, and by the time she was near enough for me to see the look in her eyes she had collapsed down into a drift, leaving a memory there in her place. Something flitted past the window, sending flakes flying against the wind, bristly fur spiking dead white leaves.

I blinked hard and the snow was just snow once more. I turned and looked at Ellie, but she was concentrating too hard to return my stare. For the first time I could see how scared she was—how her hand clasped so tightly around the shotgun barrel that her knuckles were pearly white, her nails a shiny pink—and I wondered exactly what *she* was seeing out there in the white storm.

By midday we had done what we could. The kitchen, one of the living rooms, and the hall and staircase were left open; every other room downstairs was boarded up from the outside in. We'd also covered the windows in those rooms left open, but we left thin viewing ports like horizontal arrow slits in the walls of an old castle. And like the weary defenders of those ancient citadels, we were under siege.

"So what did you all see?" I said as we sat in the kitchen. Nobody denied anything.

"Badgers," Rosalie said. "Big, white, fast. Sliding over the snow like they were on skis. Demon badgers from hell!" She joked, but it was obvious that she was terrified.

"Not badgers," Ellie cut in. "Deer. But wrong. Deer with scales. Or something. All wrong."

"Hayden, what did you see?"

He remained hunched over the cooker, stirring a weak stew of old vegetables and stringy beef. "I didn't see anything."

I went to argue with him but realized he was probably telling the truth. We had all seen something different, why not see nothing at all? Just as unlikely.

"You know," said Ellie, standing at a viewing slot with the snow reflecting sunlight in a band across her face, "we're all seeing white animals. White animals in the snow. So maybe we're seeing nothing at all. Maybe it's our imaginations. Perhaps Hayden is nearer the truth than all of us."

"Boris and the others had pretty strong imaginations, then," said Rosalie, bitter tears animating her eyes.

We were silent once again, stirring our weak milkless tea, all thinking our own thoughts about what was out in the snow. Nobody had asked me what I had seen and I was glad. Last night they were fleeting white shadows, but today I had seen Jayne as well. A Jayne I had known was not really there, even as I watched her coming at me through the snow. *I'll be with you again.*

"In China, white is the color of death," Ellie said. She spoke at the boarded window, never for an instant glancing away. Her hands held onto the shotgun as if it had become one with her body. I wondered what she had been in the past: *I have a history*, she'd said. "White. Happiness and joy."

"It was also the color of mourning for the Victorians," I added.

"And we're in a Victorian manor." Hayden did not turn around as he spoke, but his words sent our imaginations scurrying.

"We're all seeing white animals," Ellie said quietly. "Like white noise. All tones, all frequencies. We're all seeing different things as one."

"Oh," Rosalie whispered, "well, that explains a lot."

I thought I could see where Ellie was coming from; at least I was looking in the right direction. "White noise is used to mask other sounds," I said.

Ellie only nodded.

"There's something else going on here." I sat back in my chair and stared up, trying to divine the truth in the patchwork mold on the kitchen ceiling. "We're not seeing it all."

Ellie glanced away from the window, just for a second. "I don't think we're seeing anything."

Later we found out some more of what was happening. We went to bed, doors opened in the night, footsteps creaked old floorboards. And through the dark the sound of lovemaking drew us all to another, more terrible death.

Three
The Color of Mourning

I had not made love to anyone since Jayne's death. It was months before she died that we last indulged, a bitter, tearful experience when she held a sheet of polythene between our chests and stomachs to prevent her diseased skin touching my own. It did not make for the most romantic of occasions, and afterward she cried herself to sleep as I sat holding her hand and staring into the dark.

After her death I came to the manor, the others came along to find something or escape from something else, and there were secretive noises in the night. The manor was large enough for us to have a room each, but in the darkness doors would open and close again, and every morning the atmosphere at breakfast was different.

My door had never opened and I had opened no doors. There was a lingering guilt over Jayne's death, a sense that I would be betraying her love if I went with someone else. A greater cause of my loneliness was my inherent lack of confidence, a certainty that no one here would be interested in me: I was quiet, introspective, and uninteresting, a fledgling bird devoid of any hope of taking wing with any particular talent. No one would want me.

But none of this could prevent the sense of isolation, subtle jealousy, and yearning I felt each time I heard footsteps in the dark. I never heard anything else—the walls were too thick for that, the building too solid—but my imagination filled in the missing parts. Usually, Ellie was the star. And there lay another problem—lusting after a woman I did not even like very much.

The night it all changed for us was the first time I heard someone making love in the manor. The voice was androgynous in its ecstasy, a high keening, dropping off into a prolonged sigh before rising again. I sat up in bed, trying to shake off the remnants of dreams that clung like seaweed to a drowned corpse. Jayne had been there, of course, and something in the snow, and another something which was Jayne and the snow combined. I recalled wallowing in the sharp whiteness and feeling my skin sliced by ice edges, watching the snow grow pink around me, then white again as Jayne came and spread her cleansing touch across the devastation.

The cry came once more, wanton and unhindered by any sense of decorum.

Who? I thought. *Obviously Hayden, but who was he with? Rosalie? Cynical, paranoid, terrified Rosalie?*

Or Ellie?

I hoped Rosalie.

I sat back against the headboard, unable to lie down and ignore the sound. The curtains hung open—I had no reason to close them—and the moonlight revealed that it was snowing once again. I wondered what was out there watching the sleeping manor, listening to the crazy sounds of lust emanating from a building still spattered with the blood and memory of those who had died so recently. I wondered whether the things out there had any understanding of human emotion—the highs, the lows, the tenacious spirit that could sometimes survive even the most downheartening, devastating events—and what they made of the sound they could hear now. Perhaps they thought they were screams of pain. Ecstasy and thoughtless agony often sounded the same.

The sound continued, rising and falling. Added to it now the noise of something thumping rhythmically against a wall.

I thought of the times before Jayne had been ill, before the great decline had really begun, when most of the population still thought humankind could clean up what it had dirtied and repair what it had torn asunder. We'd been married for several years, our love as deep as ever, our lust still refreshing and invigorating. Car seats, cinemas, woodland, even a telephone box, all had been visited by us at some stage, laughing like adolescents, moaning and sighing together, content in familiarity.

And as I sat there remembering my dead wife, something strange happened. I could not identify exactly when the realization hit me, but I was suddenly sure of one thing: the voice I was listening to was Jayne's. She was moaning as someone else in the house made love to her. She had come in from outside, that cold unreal Jayne I had seen so recently, and she had gone to Hayden's room, and now I was being betrayed by someone I had never betrayed, ever.

I shook my head, knowing it was nonsense but certain also that the voice was hers. I was so sure that I stood, dressed, and opened my bedroom door without considering the impossibility of what was happening. Reality was controlled by the darkness, not by whatever light I could attempt to throw upon it. I may as well have had my eyes closed.

The landing was lit by several shaded candles in wall brackets, their soft light barely reaching the floor, flickering as breezes came from nowhere. Where the light did touch it showed old carpet, worn by time and faded by countless unknown footfalls. The walls hung with shredded paper, damp and torn like dead skin, the lath and plaster beneath pitted and crumbled. The air was thick with age, heavy with must, redolent with faint hints of hauntings. Where my feet fell I could sense the floor dipping slightly beneath me, though whether this was actuality or a runover from my dream I was unsure.

I could have been walking on snow.

I moved toward Hayden's room and the volume of the sighing and crying increased. I paused one door away, my heart thumping not with exertion but with the thought that Jayne was a dozen steps from me, making love with Hayden, a man I hardly really knew.

Jayne's dead, I told myself, and she cried out once, loud, as she came. Another voice then, sighing and straining, and this one was Jayne as well.

Someone touched my elbow. I gasped and spun around, too shocked to scream. Ellie was there in her nightshirt, bare legs hidden in shadow. She had a strange look in her eye. It may have been the subdued lighting. I went to ask her what she was doing here, but then I realized it was probably the same as me. She'd stayed downstairs last night, unwilling to share a watch duty, insistent that we should all sleep.

I went to tell her that Jayne was in there with Hayden, then I realized how stupid this would sound, how foolish it actually *was*.

At least, I thought, *it's not Ellie in there. Rosalie, it must be. At least not Ellie. Certainly not Jayne.*

And Jayne cried out again.

Goosebumps speckled my skin and brought it to life. The hairs on my neck stood to attention, my spine tingled.

"Hayden having a nice time?" someone whispered, and Rosalie stepped up behind Ellie.

I closed my eyes, listening to Jayne's cries. She had once screamed like that in a park, and the keeper had chased us out with his waving torch and throaty shout, the light splaying across our nakedness as we laughed and struggled to gather our clothes around us as we ran.

"Doesn't sound like Hayden to me," Ellie said.

The three of us stood outside Hayden's door for a while, listening to the sounds of lovemaking from within—the cries, the moving bed, the thud of wood against the wall. I felt like an intruder, however much I realized something was very wrong with all of this. Hayden was on his own in there. As we each tried to figure out what we were really hearing, the sounds from within changed. There was not one cry, not two, but many, overlying each other, increasing and expanding until the voice became that of a crowd. The light in the corridor seemed to dim as the crying increased, though it may have been my imagination.

I struggled to make out Jayne's voice and there was a hint of something familiar, a whisper in the cacophony that was so slight as to be little more than an echo of a memory. But still, to me, it was real.

Ellie knelt and peered through the keyhole, and I noticed for the first time that she was carrying her shotgun. She stood quickly and backed away from the door, her mouth opening, eyes widening. "It's Hayden," she said aghast, and then she fired at the door handle and lock.

The explosion tore through the sounds of ecstasy and left them in shreds. They echoed away like streamers in the wind, to be replaced by the lonely moan of a man's voice, pleading not to stop, it was so wonderful so pure so alive . . .

The door swung open. None of us entered the room. We could not move.

Hayden was on his back on the bed, surrounded by the whites from outside. I had seen them as shadows against the snow, little more than pale phantoms, but here in the room they stood out bright and definite. There were several of them; I could not make out an exact number because they squirmed and twisted against each other, and against Hayden. Diaphanous limbs stretched out and wavered in the air, arms or wings or tentacles, tapping at the bed and the wall and the ceiling, leaving spots of ice like ink on blotting paper wherever they touched.

I could see no real faces but I knew that the things were looking at me.

Their crying and sighing had ceased, but Hayden's continued. He moved quickly and violently, thrusting into the malleable shape that still straddled him, not yet noticing our intrusion even though the shotgun blast still rang in my ears. He continued his penetration, but slowly the white lifted itself away until Hayden's cock flopped back wetly onto his stomach.

He raised his head and looked straight at us between his knees, looked *through* one of the things where it flipped itself easily across the bed. The air stank of sex and something else, something cold and old and rotten, frozen forever and only now experiencing a hint of thaw.

"Oh please . . ." he said, though whether he spoke to us or the constantly shifting shapes I could not tell.

I tried to focus, but the whites were minutely out of phase with my vision, shifting to and fro too quickly for me to concentrate. I thought I saw a face, but it may have been a false splay of shadows thrown as a shape turned and sprang to the floor. I searched for something I knew—an arm kinked slightly from an old break; a breast with a mole near the nipple; a smile turned wryly down at the edges—and I realized I was looking for Jayne. Even in all this mess, I thought she may be here. *I'll be with you again*, she had said.

I almost called her name, but Ellie lifted the shotgun and shattered the moment once more. It barked out once, loud, and everything happened so quickly. One instant the white things were there, smothering Hayden and touching him with their fluid limbs. The next, the room was empty of all but us humans, moth-eaten curtains fluttering slightly, window invitingly open. And Hayden's face had disappeared into a red mist.

After the shotgun blast there was only the wet sound of Hayden's brains and skull fragments pattering down onto the bedding. His hard-on still glinted in the weak candlelight. His hands each clasped a fistful of blanket. One leg tipped and rested on the sheets clumped around him. His skin was pale, almost white.

Almost.

Rosalie leaned against the wall, dry heaving. Her dress was wet and heavy with puke and the stink of it had found a home in my nostrils. Ellie was busy reloading the shotgun, mumbling and cursing, trying to look anywhere but at the carnage of Hayden's body.

I could not tear my eyes away. I'd never seen anything like this. Brand and Boris and Charley, yes, their torn and tattered corpses had been terrible to behold, but here . . . I had seen the instant a rounded, functional person had turned into a shattered lump of meat. I'd seen the red splash of Hayden's head as it came apart and hit the wall, big bits ricocheting, the smaller, wetter pieces sticking to the old wallpaper and drawing their dreadful art for all to see. Every detail stood out and demanded my attention, as if the shot had cleared the air and brought light. It seemed red-tinged, the atmosphere itself stained with violence.

Hayden's right hand clasped onto the blanket, opening and closing very slightly, very slowly.

Doesn't feel so cold. Maybe there's a thaw on the way. I thought distractedly, trying perhaps to withdraw somewhere banal and comfortable and familiar . . .

There was a splash of sperm across his stomach. Blood from his ruined head was running down his neck and chest and mixing with it, dribbling soft and pink onto the bed.

Ten seconds ago he was alive. Now he was dead. Extinguished, just like that.

Where is he? I thought. *Where has he gone?*

"Hayden?" I said.

"He's dead!" Ellie hissed, a little too harshly.

"I can see that." But his hand still moved. Slowly. Slightly.

Something was happening at the window. The curtains were still now, but there was a definite sense of movement in the darkness beyond. I caught it from the corner of my eye as I stared at Hayden.

"Rosalie, go get some boards," Ellie whispered.

"You killed Hayden!" Rosalie spat. She coughed up the remnants of her last meal, and they hung on her chin like wet boils. "You blew his head off! You shot him! What the hell, what's going on, what's happening here. I don't know, I don't know . . ."

"The things are coming back in," Ellie said. She shouldered the gun, leaned through the door, and fired at the window. Stray shot plucked at the curtains. There was a cessation of noise from outside, then a rustling, slipping, sliding. It sounded like something flopping around in snow. "Go and get the boards, you two."

Rosalie stumbled noisily along the corridor toward the staircase.

"You killed him," I said lamely.

"He was fucking them," Ellie shouted. Then, quieter: "I didn't mean to . . ." She looked at the body on the bed, only briefly but long enough for me to see her eyes narrow and her lips squeeze tight. "He was fucking them. His fault."

"What were they? What the hell, I've never seen any animals like them."

Ellie grabbed my bicep and squeezed hard, eliciting an unconscious yelp. She had fingers like steel nails. "They aren't animals," she said. "They aren't people. Help me with the door."

Her tone invited no response. She aimed the gun at the open window for as long as she could while I pulled the door shut. The shotgun blast had blown the handle away, and I could not see how we would be able to keep it shut should the whites return. We stood that way for a while, me hunkered down with two fingers through a jagged hole in the door to try to keep it closed, Ellie standing slightly back, aiming the gun at the pocked wood. I wondered whether I'd end up getting shot if the whites chose this moment to climb back into the room and launch themselves at the door . . .

Banging and cursing marked Rosalie's return. She carried several snapped floor boards, the hammer, and nails. I held the boards up, Rosalie nailed, both of us now in Ellie's line of fire. Again I wondered about Ellie and guns, about her history. I was glad when the job was done.

We stepped back from the door and stood there silently, three relative strangers trying to understand and come to terms with what we had seen. But without understanding, coming to terms was impossible. I felt a tear run down my cheek, then another. A sense of breathless panic settled around me, clasping me in cool hands and sending my heart racing.

"What do we do?" I said. "How do we keep those things out?"

"They won't get through the boarded windows," Rosalie said confidently, doubt so evident in her voice.

I remembered how quickly they had moved, how lithe and alert they had been to virtually dodge the blast from Ellie's shotgun.

I held my breath; the others were doing the same.

Noises. Clambering and a soft whistling at first, then light thuds as something ran around the walls of the room, across the ceiling, bounding from the floor and the furniture. Then tearing, slurping, cracking, as the whites fed on what was left of Hayden.

"Let's go down." Ellie suggested. We were already backing away.

Jayne may be in danger, I thought, recalling her waving to me as she walked naked through the snow. If she was out there, and these things were out there as well, she would be at risk. She may not know, she may be too trusting, she may let them take advantage of her, abuse and molest her—

Hayden had been enjoying it. He was not being raped; if anything, he was doing the raping. Even as he died he'd been spurting ignorant bliss across his stomach.

And Jayne was dead. I repeated this over and over, whispering it, not caring if the others heard, certain that they would take no notice. Jayne was dead. Jayne was dead.

I suddenly knew for certain that the whites could smash in at any time, dodge Ellie's clumsy shooting and tear us to shreds in seconds. They could do it, but they did not. They scratched and tapped at windows, clambered around the house, but they did not break in. Not yet.

They were playing with us. Whether they needed us for food, fun, or revenge, it was nothing but a game.

Ellie was smashing up the kitchen.

She kicked open cupboard doors, swept the contents of shelves onto the floor with the barrel of the shotgun, sifted through them with her feet, then did the same to the next cupboard. At first I thought it was blind rage, fear, dread; then I saw that she was searching for something.

"What?" I asked. "What are you doing?"

"Just a hunch."

"What sort of hunch? Ellie, we should be watching out—"

"There's something moving out there," Rosalie said. She was looking through the slit in the boarded window. There was a band of moonlight across her eyes.

"Here!" Ellie said triumphantly. She knelt and rooted around in the mess on the floor, shoving jars and cans aside, delving into a splash of spilled rice a small bottle. "Bastard. The bastard. Oh God, the bastard's been doing it all along."

"There's something out there in the snow," Rosalie said again, louder this time. "It's coming to the manor. It's . . ." Her voice trailed off and I saw her stiffen, her mouth slightly open.

"Rosalie?" I moved toward her, but she glanced at me and waved me away.

"It's okay," she said. "It's nothing."

"Look." Ellie slammed a bottle down on the table and stood back for us to see.

"A bottle."

Ellie nodded. She looked at me and tilted her head. Waiting for me to see, expecting me to realize what she was trying to say.

"A bottle from Hayden's food cupboard," I said.

She nodded again.

I looked at Rosalie. She was still frozen at the window, hands pressed flat to her thighs, eyes wide and full of the moon. "Rosie?" She only shook her head. Nothing wrong, the gesture said, but it did not look like that. It looked like everything was wrong but she was too afraid to tell us. I went to move her out of the way, look for myself, see what had stolen her tongue.

"Poison," Ellie revealed. I paused, glanced at the bottle on the table. Ellie picked it up and held it in front of a candle, shook it, turned it this way and that. "Poison. Hayden's been cooking for us ever since we've been here. And he's always had this bottle. And a couple of times lately, he's added a little extra to certain meals."

"Brand," I nodded, aghast. "And Boris. But why? They were outside, they were killed by those things—"

"Torn up by those things," Ellie corrected. "Killed in here. Then dragged out."

"By Hayden?"

She shrugged. "Why not? He was fucking the whites."

"But why would he want to . . . Why did he have something against Boris and Brand? And Charley? An accident, like he said?"

"I guess he gave her a helping hand," Ellie mused, sitting at the table and rubbing her temples. "They both saw something outside. Boris and Brand, they'd both seen things in the snow. They made it known, they told us all about it, and Hayden heard as well. Maybe he felt threatened. Maybe he thought we'd steal his little sex mates." She stared down at the table, at the rings burnt there over the years by hot mugs, the scratches made by endless cutlery. "Maybe they told him to do it."

"Oh, come on!" I felt my eyes go wide like those of a rabbit caught in car headlights.

Ellie shrugged, stood and rested the gun on her shoulder. "Whatever, we've got to protect ourselves. They may be in soon, you saw them up there. They're intelligent. They're—"

"Animals!" I shouted. "They're animals! How could they tell Hayden anything? How could they get in?"

Ellie looked at me, weighing her reply.

"They're white animals, like you said!"

Ellie shook her head. "They're new. They're unique. They're a part of the change."

New. Unique. The words instilled very little hope in me, and Ellie's next comment did more to scare me than anything that had happened up to now.

"They were using Hayden to get rid of us. Now he's gone . . . well, they've no reason not to do it themselves."

As if on cue, something started to brush up against the outside wall of the house.

"Rosalie!" I shouted. "Step back!"

"It's alright," she said dreamily, "it's only the wind. Nothing there. Nothing to worry about." The sound continued, like soap on sandpaper. It came from beyond the boarded windows but it also seemed to filter through from elsewhere, surrounding us like an audio enemy.

"Ellie," I said, "what can we do?" She seemed to have taken charge so easily that I deferred to her without thinking, assuming she would have a plan with a certainty which was painfully cut down.

"I have no idea." She nursed the shotgun in the crook of her elbow like a baby substitute, and I realized I didn't know her half as well as I thought. Did she have children? I wondered. Where were her family? Where had this level of self-control come from?

"Rosalie," I said carefully, "what are you looking at?" Rosalie was staring through the slit at a moonlit scene none of us could see. Her expression had dropped from scared to melancholy, and I saw a tear trickle down her cheek. She was no longer her old cynical, bitter self. It was as if all her fears had come true and she was content with the fact. "Rosie!" I called again, quietly but firmly.

Rosalie turned to look at us. Reality hit her, but it could not hide the tears. "But he's dead," she said, half question, half statement. Before I could ask whom she was talking about, something hit the house.

The sound of smashing glass came from everywhere: behind the boards across the kitchen windows; out in the corridor; muffled crashes from elsewhere in the dark manor. Rosalie stepped back from the slit just as a long, shimmering white limb came in, glassy nails scratching for her face but ripping the air instead.

Ellie stepped forward, thrust the shotgun through the slit and pulled the trigger. There was no cry of pain, no scream, but the limb withdrew.

Something began to batter against the ruined kitchen window, the vibration traveling through the hastily nailed boards, nail heads emerging slowly from the gouged wood after each impact. Ellie fired again, though I could not see what she was shooting at. As she turned to reload she avoided my questioning glance.

"They're coming in!" I shouted.

"Can it!" Ellie said bitterly. She stepped back as a sliver of timber broke away from the edge of one of the boards, clattering to the floor stained with frost. She shouldered the gun and fired twice through the widening gap. White things began to worm their way between the boards, fingers perhaps, but long and thin and more flexible than any I had ever seen. They twisted and felt blindly across the wood . . . and then wrapped themselves around the exposed nails.

They began to pull.

The nails squealed as they were withdrawn from the wood, one by one.

I hefted the hammer and went at the nails, hitting each of them only once, aiming for those surrounded by cool white digits. As each nail went back in the things around them drew back and squirmed out of sight behind the boards, only to reappear elsewhere. I hammered until my arm ached, resting my left hand against the vibrating timber. Not once did I catch a white digit beneath the hammer, even when I aimed for them specifically. I began to giggle and the sound frightened me. It was the voice of a madman, the utterance of someone looking for his lost mind, and I found that funnier than ever. Every time I hit another nail it reminded me more and more of an old fairground game. Pop the gophers on the head. I wondered what the prize would be tonight.

"What the hell do we do?" I shouted.

Rosalie had stepped away from the windows and now leaned against the kitchen worktop, eyes wide, mouth working slowly in some unknown mantra. I glanced at her between hammer blows and saw her chest rising and falling at an almost impossible speed. She was slipping into shock.

"Where?" I shouted to Ellie over my shoulder.

"The hallway."

"Why?"

"Why not?"

I had no real answer, so I nodded and indicated with a jerk of my head that the other two should go first. Ellie shoved Rosalie ahead of her and stood waiting for me.

I continued bashing with the hammer, but now I had fresh targets. Not only were the slim white limbs nudging aside the boards and working at the nails, but they were also coming through the ventilation bricks at skirting level in the kitchen. They would gain no hold there, I knew; they could never pull their whole body through there. But still I found their presence abhorrent and terrifying, and every third hammer strike was directed at these white monstrosities trying to twist around my ankles.

And at the third missed strike, I knew what they were doing. It was then, also, that I had some true inkling of their intelligence and wiliness. Two digits trapped my leg between them—they were cold and hard, even through my jeans—and they jerked so hard that I felt my skin tearing in their grasp.

I went down and the hammer skittered across the kitchen floor. At the same instant a twisting forest of the things appeared between the boards above me, and in seconds the timber had started to snap and splinter as the onslaught intensified, the attackers now seemingly aware of my predicament. Shards of wood and glass and ice showered down on me, all of them sharp and cutting. And then, looking up, I saw one of the whites appear in the gap above me, framed by broken wood, its own limbs joined by others in their efforts to widen the gap and come in to tear me apart.

Jayne stared down at me. Her face was there but the thing was not her; it was as if her image were projected there, cast onto the pure whiteness of my attacker by memory or circumstance, put there because it knew what the sight would do to me.

I went weak, not because I thought Jayne was there—I knew that I was being fooled—but because her false visage inspired a flood of warm memories through my stunned bones, hitting cold muscles and sending me into a white-hot agony of paused circulation, blood pooling at my extremities, consciousness retreating into the warmer parts of my brain, all thought of escape and salvation and the other two survivors erased by the plain whiteness that invaded from outside, sweeping in through the rent in the wall and promising me a quick, painful death, but only if I no longer struggled, only if I submitted—

The explosion blew away everything but the pain. The thing above me had been so intent upon its imminent kill that it must have missed Ellie, leaning in the kitchen door and shouldering the shotgun.

The thing blew apart. I closed my eyes as I saw it fold up before me, and when I opened them again there was nothing there, not even a shower of dust in the air, no sprinkle of blood, no splash of insides. Whatever it had been it left nothing behind in death.

"Come on!" Ellie hissed, grabbing me under one arm and hauling me across the kitchen floor. I kicked with my feet to help her then finally managed to stand, albeit shakily.

There was now a gaping hole in the boards across the kitchen windows. Weak candlelight bled out and illuminated the falling snow and the shadows behind it. I expected the hole to be filled again in seconds and this time they would pour in, each of them a mimic of Jayne in some terrifying fashion.

"Shut the door," Ellie said calmly. I did so and Rosalie was there with a hammer and nails. We'd run out of broken floorboards, so we simply nailed the door into the frame. It was clumsy and would no doubt prove ineffectual, but it may give us a few more seconds.

But for what? What good would time do us now, other than to extend our agony?

"Now where?" I asked hopelessly. "Now what?" There were sounds all around us; soft thuds from behind the kitchen door, and louder noises from further away. Breaking glass; cracking wood; a gentle rustling, more horrible because they could not be identified. As far as I could see, we really had nowhere to go.

"Upstairs," Ellie said. "The attic. The hatch is outside my room, its got a loft ladder, as far as I know it's the only way up. Maybe we could hold them off until . . ."

"Until they go home for tea," Rosalie whispered. I said nothing. There was no use in verbalizing the hopelessness we felt at the moment, because we could see it in each other's eyes. The snow had been here for weeks and maybe now it would be here forever. Along with whatever strangeness it contained.

Ellie checked the bag of cartridges and handed them to me. "Hand these to me," she said. "Six shots left. Then we have to beat them up."

It was dark inside the manor, even though dawn must now be breaking outside. I thanked God that at least we had some candles left . . . but that got me thinking about God and how He would let this happen, launch these things against us, torture us with the promise of certain death and yet give us these false splashes of hope. I'd spent most of my life thinking that God was indifferent, a passive force holding the big picture together while we acted out our own foolish little plays within it. Now, if He did exist, He could only be a cruel God indeed.

And I'd rather there be nothing than a God who found pleasure or entertainment in the discomfort of His creations.

Maybe Rosalie had been right. She had seen God staring down with blood in his eyes.

As we stumbled out into the main hallway I began to cry, gasping out my fears and my grief, and Ellie held me up and whispered into my ear. "Prove Him wrong if you have to. Prove Him wrong. Help me to survive, and prove Him wrong."

I heard Jayne beyond the main front doors, calling my name into the snowbanks, her voice muffled and bland. I paused, confused, and then I even smelled her, apple-blossom shampoo; the sweet scent of her breath. For a few seconds Jayne was there with me and I could all but hold her hand. None of the last few weeks had happened. We were here on a holiday, but there was something wrong and she was in danger outside. I went to open the doors to her, ask her in and help her, assuage whatever fears she had.

I would have reached the doors and opened them if it were not for Ellie striking me on the shoulder with the stock of the shotgun.

"There's nothing out there but those things!" she shouted. I blinked rapidly as reality settled down around me but it was like wrapping paper, only disguising the truth I thought I knew, not dismissing it completely.

The onslaught increased.

Ellie ran up the stairs, shotgun held out before her. I glanced around once, listening to the sounds coming from near and far, all of them noises of siege, each of them promising pain at any second. Rosalie stood at the foot of the stairs doing likewise. Her face was pale and drawn and corpselike.

"I can't believe Hayden," she said. "He was doing it with them. I can't believe . . . does Ellie really think he . . . ?"

"I can't believe a second of any of this," I said. "I hear my dead wife." As if ashamed of the admission I lowered my eyes as I walked by Rosalie. "Come on," I said. "We can hold out in the attic."

"I don't think so." Her voice was so sure, so full of conviction, that I thought she was all right. Ironic that a statement of doom should inspire such a feeling, but it was as close to the truth as anything.

I thought Rosalie was all right.

It was only as I reached the top of the stairs that I realized she had not followed me.

I looked out over the ornate old banister, down into the hallway where shadows played and cast false impressions on eyes I could barely trust anyway. At first I thought I was seeing things because Rosalie was not stupid; Rosalie was cynical and bitter, but never stupid. She would not do such a thing.

She stood by the open front doors. How I had not heard her unbolting and opening them I do not know, but there she was, a stark shadow against white fluttering snow, dim daylight parting around her and pouring in. Other things came in too, the whites, slinking across the floor and leaving paw prints of frost wherever they came. Rosalie stood with arms held wide in a welcoming embrace.

She said something as the whites launched at her. I could not hear the individual words but I sensed the tone; she was happy. As if she were greeting someone she had not seen for a very long time.

And then they hit her and took her apart in seconds.

"Run!" I shouted, sprinting along the corridor, chasing Ellie's shadow. In seconds I was right behind her, pushing at her shoulders as if this would make her move faster. "Run! Run! Run!"

She glanced back as she ran. "Where's Rosalie?"

"She opened the door." It was all I needed to say. Ellie turned away and concentrated on negotiating a corner in the corridor.

From behind me I heard the things bursting in all around. Those that had slunk past Rosalie must had broken into rooms from the inside even as others came in from outside, helping each other, crashing through our pathetic barricades by force of cooperation.

I noticed how cold it had become. Frost clung to the walls and the old carpet beneath our feet crunched with each footfall. Candles threw erratic shadows at icicle-encrusted ceilings. I felt ice under my fingernails.

Jayne's voice called out behind me and I slowed, but then I ran on once more, desperate to fight what I so wanted to believe. She'd said we would be together again and now she was calling me . . . but she was dead, she was dead. Still she called. Still I ran. And then she started to cry because I was not going to her, and I imagined her naked out there in the snow with white things everywhere. I stopped and turned around.

Ellie grabbed my shoulder, spun me and slapped me across the face. It brought tears to my eyes, but it also brought me back to shady reality. "We're here," she said. "Stay with us." Then she looked over my shoulder. Her eyes widened. She brought the gun up so quickly that it smacked into my ribs, and the explosion in the confined corridor felt like a hammer pummeling my ears.

I turned and saw what she had seen. It was like a drift of snow moving down the corridor toward us, rolling across the walls and ceiling, pouring along the floor. Ellie's shot had blown a hole through it, but the whites quickly regrouped and moved forward once more. Long, fine tendrils felt out before them, freezing the corridor seconds before the things passed by. There were no faces or eyes or mouths, but if I looked long enough I could see Jayne rolling naked in there with them, her mouth wide, arms holding whites to her, into her. If I really listened I was sure I would hear her sighs as she fucked them. They had passed from luring to mocking now that we were trapped, but still . . .

They stopped. The silence was a withheld chuckle.

"Why don't they rush us?" I whispered. Ellie had already pulled down the loft ladder and was waiting to climb up. She reached out and pulled me back, indicating with a nod of her head that I should go first. I reached out for the gun, wanting to give her a chance, but she elbowed me away without taking her eyes off the advancing white mass. "Why don't they . . . ?"

She fired again. The shot tore a hole, but another thing soon filled that hole and stretched out toward us. "I'll shoot you if you stand in my way any more," she said.

I believed her. I handed her two cartridges and scurried up the ladder, trying not to see Jayne where she rolled and writhed, trying not to hear her sighs of ecstasy as the whites did things to her that only I knew she liked.

The instant I made it through the hatch the sounds changed. I heard Ellie squeal as the things rushed, the metallic clack as she slammed the gun shut again, two explosions in quick succession, a wet sound as whites ripped apart. Their charge sounded like a steam train: wood cracked and split; the floorboards were smashed up beneath icy feet; ceilings collapsed. I could not see, but I felt the corridor shattering as they came at Ellie, as if it were suddenly too small to house them all and they were plowing their own way through the manor.

Ellie came up the ladder fast, throwing the shotgun through before hauling herself up after it. I saw a flash of white before she slammed the hatch down and locked it behind her.

"There's no way they can't get up here," I said. "They'll be here in seconds."

Ellie struck a match and lit a pathetic stub of candle. "Last one."

She was panting. In the weak light she looked pale and worn out.

"Let's see what they decide,"she said.

We were in one of four attics in the manor roof. This one was boarded but bare, empty of everything except spiders and dust. Ellie shivered and cried, mumbling about her dead husband Jack frozen in the car. Maybe she heard him. Maybe she'd seen him down there. I found with a twinge of guilt that I could not care less.

"They herded us, didn't they?" I said. I was breathless and aching, but it was similar to the feeling after a good workout; energized, not exhausted.

Ellie shrugged, then nodded. She moved over to me and took the last couple of cartridges from the bag on my belt. As she broke the gun and removed the spent shells her shoulders hitched. She gasped and dropped the gun.

"What? Ellie?" But she was not hearing me. She stared into old shadows which had not been bathed in light for years, seeing some unknown truths there, her mouth falling open into an expression so unfamiliar on her face that it took me some seconds to place it—a smile. Whatever she saw, whatever she heard, it was something she was happy with.

I almost let her go. In the space of a second, all possibilities flashed across my mind. We were going to die, there was no escape, they would take us singly or all in one go, they would starve us out, the snow would never melt, the whites would change and grow and evolve beneath us, we could do nothing, whatever they were they had won already, they had won when humankind brought the ruin down upon itself . . .

Then I leaned over and slapped Ellie across the face. Her head snapped around and she lost her balance, falling onto all fours over the gun.

I heard Jayne's footsteps as she prowled the corridors searching for me, calling my name with increasing exasperation. Her voice was changing from sing-song, to monotone, to panicked. The whites were down there with her, the white animals, all animals, searching and stalking her tender naked body through the freezing manor. I had to help her. I knew what it would mean but at least then we would be together, at least then her last promise to me would have been fulfilled.

Ellie's moan brought me back and for a second I hated her for that. I had been with Jayne and now I was here in some dark, filthy attic with a hundred creatures below trying to find a way to tear me apart. I hated her and I could not help it one little bit.

I moved to one of the sloping rooflights and stared out. I looked for Jayne across the snowscape, but the whites now had other things on their mind. Fooling me was not a priority.

"What do we do?" I asked Ellie, sure even now that she would have an idea, a plan. "How many shots have you got left?"

She looked at me. The candle was too weak to light up her eyes. "Enough." Before I even realized what she was doing she had flipped the shotgun over, wrapped her mouth around the twin barrels, reached down, curved her thumb through the trigger guard, and blasted her brains into the air.

It's been over an hour since Ellie killed herself and left me on my own.

In that time snow has been blown into the attic to cover her body from view. Elsewhere it's merely a sprinkling, but Ellie is little more than a white hump on the floor now, the mess of her head a pink splash across the ever-whitening boards.

At first the noise from downstairs was terrific. The whites raged and ran and screamed, and I curled into a ball and tried to prepare myself for them to smash through the hatch and take me apart. I even considered the shotgun . . . there's one shot left . . . but Ellie was brave, Ellie was strong. I don't have that strength.

Besides, there's Jayne to think of. She's down there now, I know, because I have not heard a sound for ten minutes. Outside it is snowing heavier than I've ever seen, it must be ten feet deep, and there is no movement whatsoever. Inside, below the hatch and throughout the manor, in rooms sealed and broken open, the whites must be waiting. Here and there, Jayne will be waiting with them. For me. So that I can be with her again.

Soon I will open the hatch, make my way downstairs and out through the front doors. I hope, Jayne, that you will meet me there.

JAMES SALLIS

Dear Floods of Her Hair

James Sallis has published more than twenty books, including A Few
Last Words *and* Difficult Lives. *He's been gaining a following with his
Lew Griffin mystery series. He writes a review column for* The Magazine
of Fantasy & Science Fiction *and regularly contributes reviews to
publications such as* The Review of Contemporary Literature, Boston
Review, *and* The Washington Post. *Forthcoming projects include a
biography of Chester Himes, a new novel, collections of poems and
essays, and a two-volume* Collected Stories.

*Although he was a prolific short story writer in the 1970s, Sallis's
short fiction output has trickled to a handful since the early 1980s. So
it is with great pleasure that we reprint "Dear Floods of Her Hair"
here. It was originally published in the May issue of* The Magazine of
Fantasy & Science Fiction.

—E. D.

Muriel left me, left us, I should say, on Monday. The tap in
the kitchen sink sprang a leak, spewing a mist of cold water
onto sheets I spread on the floor, and a hummingbird, furious
that she'd forgotten to refill its feeder just outside, beat at the
window again and again. By the time friends, family, and mourners
began arriving, Thursday around noon, preparations were almost complete.

First thing I did was draw up a schedule. Muriel would have been
proud of me, I thought as I sat at the kitchen table with pen and a pad
of her notepaper, water from the spewing tap slowly soaking into the
corduroy slippers she'd given me last Christmas. Here I'd always been

the improvizer, treading water, swimming reflexively for whatever shore showed itself, while Muriel weighed out options like an assayer, made lists and kept files, saw that laundry got done *before* the last sock fell, shoehorned order into our lives. And now it was all up to me.

Somewhere between sixteen and twenty on my list, the humming-bird gave up its strafing runs and simply hovered an inch from the glass, glaring in at me. They could be remarkably aggressive. Seventeen species of them where we lived. Anna's hummers, Costa's and black-chinned around all year, Rufous, calliope and the rest migrating in from Mexico or various mountain ranges. In that way birds have, males are the colorful ones, mating rituals often spectacular. Some will dive ninety feet straight up, making sure sunlight strikes them in such a way that their metallic colors flare dramatically for females watching from below. These females are dull so as to be inconspicuous on nests the size of walnuts.

Muriel loved this place of cactus and endless sky, mountains looming like the world's own jagged edge, loved the cholla, prickly pear, palo verde, geckos with feet spurred into the back of our window screens at night.

Most of all, though, she loved hummingbirds. Even drew a tiny, stylized hummer for stationery, envelopes, and cards and had it silk-screened onto the sweatshirts she often wore as she sat in front of the computer, daily attending to details of the business (cottage industries, they used to call them) that kept us comfortable here.

That same hummer hovered silently in the upper left corner of the notepad as I inscribed "24."

I gave it a pointed beard and round glasses.

Favorite bird. Hummingbird. Favorite music. *Wozzeck*, Arvo Pärt's *Litany*. Favorite color. Emerald green. Favorite poem. One by Dylan Thomas.

> *The tombstone told when she died.*
> *Her two surnames stopped me still.*
> *A virgin married at rest.*

Memories of my father were also in mind, of course. The one who taught me. I was ten years old when it began, sitting on the floor in a safe corner with knees drawn up reading H. G. Wells, a favorite still. Suddenly I felt *watched*, and when I glanced up, Father's eyes were on me. Good book? he asked. At that point I couldn't imagine a bad one. Just that some were better than others. I lit the next one off the smoldering butt of the last. They all are, I told him. No, he said. A lot of them just make up things.

Mrs. Abneg spoke then. Charles: he's too young, she said. Father looked at her. No. He's ready. Earlier than most, I agree, but this is *our* son. He's not like the rest. Mrs. Abneg ducked her head. The female must be dull so as to be inconspicuous on the nest.

And so I was allowed for the first time into my father's basement workshop. I could barely see over the tops of the sinks, benches, the tilted stainless-steel table with its runnels and drains. Shelves filled with magical jars and pegboards hung with marvelous tools loomed above like promises I would someday keep.

That first session went on for perhaps an hour. I understood little of what my father said then, though whenever he asked was something or another clear I always nodded dutifully yes. Knowledge is a kind of osmosis. And soon enough, of course, our time together in the basement workroom fulfilled itself. Others found themselves shut out. For a time I wondered what Mrs. Abneg or my younger brother might be doing there up above, but not for long. Procedures and practicums, the rigors of my apprenticeship, soon occupied my full attention and all free time. I had far too much to do to squander myself on idle thoughts.

Just as now, I thought.

I set to work.

As I worked, I sang *Wozzeck*.

Drudgery goes best when attention's directed elsewhere—not that pain and loss don't nibble away at us then. Stopping only to feed or rest myself when I could go on no longer, shedding gloves like old skin, I performed as my father taught me. Handsaws, augers and tongs, tools for which there were no names, came into use. I tipped fluids from bright-colored decanters, changed gloves, went on.

> *She cried her white-dressed limbs were bare*
> *And her red lips were kissed black*

Wozzeck was the piece Muriel and I had decided on; with tutorials twice a week and daily practice, I'd got it down as well as might be expected. Not a professional job, certainly, but competent. I sang the parts in rotation, altering pitch and range as required, hearing my own transformed voice roll back from the cellar's recesses.

I'd never really understood painting, poetry, old music, things like that—opera least of all. Whatever I couldn't weigh, quantify, plot on a chart, I had to wonder if it existed at all. I knew how important all this was to Muriel, of course. I'd sit beside her through that aria she loved from *Turandot*, "Nessun dorma," or the second movement of Mozart's Clarinet Quintet watching tears course down her face. I'd see her put down a book and for a moment there'd be this blank look, this stillness, as though she were lost between worlds: deciding.

Often Muriel and I would discuss how we'd come together, the chance and circumspectness of it, other times the many ways in which, jigsawslike, our curves and turnings had become a whole. Then, teasing relentlessly, she would argue that, as an anthropologist, I was not truly a scientist. But I was. And who more alert to the place of ritual in lives?

> *I died before bedtime came*
> *But my womb was bellowing*
> *And I felt with my bare fall*
> *A blazing red harsh head tear up*
> *And the dear floods of his hair.*

My father trained me well. I had not expected ever to bring my skills into practice so soon, of course. How could we have known? Officers had one day appeared at the door just past noon. One was young, perhaps twenty, undergrowth of beard, single discreet earring, the other middle-aged, hair folded over to cover balding scalp. I was twelve. Answered the door wearing shorts and a T-shirt that read *Stress? What Stress?!* Mr. Abneg? the officers addressed me—so I knew. The older one confirmed it: Father was gone, he'd stepped unaware into one of the city's many sinkholes. And so Mrs. Abneg became my responsibility. I had taken care of her, just as Father taught me. Fine workmanship. He would have been proud.

The skull must be boiled (Father taught, all those years ago) until it becomes smooth as stone, then reattached.

This I accomplished with a battery-driven drill and eighteen silver pins from the cloisonnéd box my father passed on to me, his father's before him. Singing Berg the whole while. I'd learned *all* my lessons well.

Legs must fall just so on the chair.

One arm at rest. The other upraised. Each finger arranged according to intricate plan.

Exacting, demanding work.

Fine music, though.

By Thursday Muriel looked more beautiful than ever before—I know this is hard to believe. That afternoon I lifted the wig from its case and placed it on her. Draped the blue veil across the preserved flesh of her chest.

(I, too, can be practical, my dear, see? I can make plans, follow through, take charge. Do what needs be done. And finally have become an artist of sorts in my own right, I suppose.)

The doorbell rang.

Thank you all for coming.

Glasses clink. Steaming cups are raised. There is enough food here to feed the city's teeming poor. I circulate among our guests, Uncle Van, Mrs. Abneg's sister, cousins and nephews, close friends. Some, I can no longer speak to, of course. To others I present small boxes wrapped in bright paper: a toenail or fingernail perhaps, silver of bone, divot of pickled flesh.

Yes. She looks beautiful, doesn't she?

Outside, whispering, night arrives. No whispers in here, as family, friends, and mourners move from lit space to lit space. They manipulate Muriel's limbs into various symbolic patterns. Group about her. Pictures are taken.

It's time, Muriel's brother says, stepping beside me.

And *I* say, Please—as instantly the room falls quiet.

I want to tell you all how much I love her.

I want to tell you we'll be happy now. Everything is in place.

I want to tell you how much we will miss you all.

Listen . . .

One day you'll walk out, a day like any other, to fetch laundry, pick up coffee at the store, drop off mail. You'll take the same route you always do, turn corners as familiar to you as the back of your hand, thinking of nothing in particular. And that's when it will happen. The beauty of this world will fall upon you, push the very words and breath from your lungs. Suddenly, irrevocably, the beauty of this world will break your heart; and lifting hand to face, you will find tears there.

Those tears will be the same as mine, now.

APRIL SELLEY

Mrs. Santa Decides to Move to Florida

April Selley has published poetry in Slipstream, Palo Alto Review, XY Files, Womanpsalms, *and numerous other journals and anthologies. She is also the author of a nonfiction manuscript,* Women of Balconies: Letters from Portugal, Spain, Morocco, and Germany. *She lives in Albany, New York.*

The following poem, a wistful look at the wife of Santa Claus, comes from the Summer 1999 edition of CALYX: A Journal of Art and Literature by Women.

—T. W.

She doesn't remember a time when
she was anywhere except the North Pole
and believes that she truly did
spring from the head of legend.
There was no girlhood among grasses,
no dainty summer dresses.
She has always been married to a man over sixty
and wonders what it would be like
to put her arms around a boy
with no soft flesh.

She bakes—sweet things—
but no food is needed by immortals.
No one gets sick here or loses
a finger to a bandsaw.
The reindeer do not need litter boxes
or their coats brushed.
There will be no children.

The androgynous elves craft a few toys,
but mostly get in shipments from Hong Kong.
Their laughter resonates for miles over the snow.
She hears it whenever she walks away.
She wonders,
if she walks far enough,
if time will begin for her,
if her eyelashes will freeze,
her eyeballs hurt in the −100° cold.
She wonders what the others would do
if they suddenly found her,
like a pillar of salt,
immobilized against the packed white.

She will tell her husband tonight:
she must go
where summer pulsates,
where children play in the streets,
where there is pain.
She wonders what she'll feel
upon seeing her first ocean—
water unfrozen,
the tide going in and out,
the shells and marine bones on the shore,
proclaiming,
"This is mortality.
This is death.
You are real."

JAN HODGMAN

Tanuki

Jan Hodgman spent eight years in monastic training at Zen temples in Japan before turning to fiction writing. She currently lives on Fidalgo Island in Washington, and "Tanuki" is her first published work. It is reprinted here from the Summer 1999 edition of CALYX: A Journal of Art and Literature by Women.

The tanuki—a small, badgerlike animal—is a trickster figure in Japanese folklore. Hodgman drew upon old tanuki tales to create the following gentle, magical story.

—T. W.

The Buddhist nun had lived on Black Bamboo Mountain for over twenty years. She shaved her head after leaving a marriage she could only describe as tasteless. The priest who ordained her thought it might be convenient to have a live-in disciple for various chores and delights, but Koen had other aspirations. After a few wranglings and gropings through morning and evening sutra services, she convinced her ordination master to find a position for her in a remote village temple. And so she had come to Black Bamboo Mountain to live alone and perform the occasional funeral and memorial rites needed by the villagers at the foot of the mountain. In return they brought yen notes in red-bordered envelopes and wheelbarrows full of vegetables and sacks of rice eked out from a life on rocky soil. When Koen was off in the mountains gathering wild herbs or meditating up in the stone hut next to the temple graveyard, they would leave their offerings just inside the entryway.

The temple had been abandoned for more than forty years. The villagers held Black Bamboo Mountain in awe. They found some solace now in having their own village priestess living there, consecrating by her presence a haunted, ominous place full of poisonous *mamushi* snakes and damp clinging spirits. They sensed that the physical placement of the temple buildings, a stone and wood enclave nestled up against a cliff face where a spring charged from underground, somehow gripped unhealthy vapors and unresolved spirits close to earth, a dank torpor invading the grounds. Tales of the exceptional fervor of long-past abbots had been passed down and embellished through generations; village mythology had transformed ardent misanthropes into revered ascetics. The village could only offer meager subsistence to the temple priest, and before Koen there had been no one willing to give up the more lucrative congregations farther down the valley, where the rocky soil eroded into broad fertile rice paddies and lush vegetable gardens.

Every morning at four Koen rose from her bedding on the straw-matted floor, dressed in her black monk's robes, lit a stick of incense in front of the memorial plaque dedicated to her aborted baby (her husband had convinced her that the threat of deformity was great since she had contracted mumps during her pregnancy), whispered a short sutra, and climbed the rocky path to the meditation hut. Her feet knew the bumps and turns of the trail even on the darkest of nights, though others found the leaf-and moss-covered rocks treacherous.

At the top of the path, the meditation hut nestled at the southern end of a small well-tended graveyard. Lofty cedars cast perpetual shadows on the five monuments marking the remains of the temple's previous abbots. Koen tended the graves with care, sweeping the leaves daily, changing the water in the bamboo vases every other day, and replacing the *shikimi* greenery and flowers of the season weekly. She gathered the greenery herself from the surrounding woods and grew some of the flowers—chrysanthemums, godetia, peonies—in pots in the few spots of the temple yard that received sufficient sunlight.

Koen lit a candle and a stick of incense in front of the serene Buddha carved of wood on the tiny hut's altar, then bowed and seated herself in lotus position on her meditation cushion. She gazed out of the screen door at the neatly swept moss carpet of the graveyard before beginning her rounds of meditation. A sense of profound settledness engulfed her, a feeling of place and connectedness, roots reaching deep into the moss-covered soil and branches reaching high up toward the sunlight and beyond. She struck a brass bell three times to invite the beginning of a period of meditation, each ring of the bell fading into the soulful silence of Black Bamboo Mountain at dawn or mingling with a restless breeze in the evening.

After dinner throughout the harsh winter months Koen gathered up leftover rice and vegetables stewed in soy sauce and scooped them into a tin pan. She pushed open the kitchen door with her elbow and with a loud rising and falling whistle and a clicking of her tongue called to the tanuki and other needy creatures. Setting the pan at the base of a cliff of red soil, she walked back to the kitchen, slipped her wooden geta off outside the door, and took up her post over a sink doing dishes and watching for evening visitors.

Sometimes a greedy gargling and oily flapping of wings would signal that the ravens had caught the scent, their inky shapes almost indiscernible in the waning light. But most often a pair of tanuki, badgerlike animals, would cautiously wend their way toward the pan, one of them making a nervous pass at the food before the smaller tanuki would steal from the shadows and join her mate. Any unexpected noise or disturbance would send the two of them skittering back into the blackness, sometimes attempting to drag the pan with them.

Japanese folklore is full of tales about tanuki. The animal is depicted as a trickster, a fool, a grateful friend, or a malicious nuisance, often modeled in pottery clutching a jug of sake and wearing a hat fashioned from a lotus leaf. Dressed in Buddhist priest's robes, the tanuki is sometimes pictured as the essence of gratitude. The tanuki of Black Bamboo Mountain lacked the distended stomachs of the pottery versions—in fact, in the depths of winter, though their rust and chestnut brown coats grew thick and fluffy, their earnestness in gulping down the treats Koen left betrayed their inability to gather sufficient food on their own.

Koen knew that most villagers considered tanuki to be troublesome or even malevolent. Farmers cited examples of raided chicken coops and dug-up sweet potatoes as evidence of their wayward ways. Koen was careful to wait until dark to set out her offerings, knowing that the villagers' uneasiness with the spirits of Black Bamboo Mountain increased with deepening nightfall. Only when there was an unexpected death among the parishioners was it customary for anyone to ascend the darkened steps of the temple gate.

One evening as Koen turned back toward the house after placing a pan of treats in the usual place, she caught the sound of someone walking on the gravel path leading from the temple gate. As she debated whether to hide the pan of food, old widow Kinoshita with the toothless grin waved and called out, "Abbess! Good evening! I've just finished my pickled turnips for New Year's and here's a jar for you!"

Kinoshita-san's husband had been a hard-working farmer, with an unquenchable thirst for sake. He had died in a fiery car accident and left a widow of forty-two and two sons, and there were many good-natured jokes about widow Kinoshita's husband hunting, even in her present toothless state. She was one of the more frequent visitors to Black Bamboo Mountain, bringing bunches of long white radishes from her garden or a freshly cooked delicacy like the pickled turnips. On her way back down to the village, she'd encounter other women, shake her head, and say with a mixture of satisfaction and perplexity, "Such a lonely life in such a desolate place. A little hair, and she'd still have a chance."

Koen usually enjoyed these visits, but this night she was concerned about what widow Kinoshita would say when she saw her feeding the tanuki. "Pardon me, I had some scraps and thought I'd leave them for the 'hungry ghosts,' " Koen said, using the Buddhist term for offerings to departed spirits.

Widow Kinoshita clucked disapprovingly and said, "Everyone knows you feed those damn tanuki. If you ever saw what they can do to a field of sweet potatoes, you'd think twice, but I guess I can't blame you for wanting some company. They're a little furry for my taste, but Lord Buddha knows I wouldn't mind a pal of my own. Eeeee-heeeee!" Widow Kinoshita gave a wide-mouthed cackle and bent over in two with her own joke. Koen enjoyed a laugh too, and the matter was forgotten.

When the winter winds abated and there was no longer a threat of snow, Koen ceased the nightly ritual, fearful that the animals would become completely dependent on her offerings and forget how to fend for themselves. For the first couple nights that she left off feeding them, she thought she caught a glimpse of the larger tanuki hanging around her kitchen door, and once at dawn she had seen him again scrambling up the path to the hut behind her, but now it had been several weeks since she had seen a sign of any tanuki.

On a moonlit dawn in April Koen rose and threw open the shutters to her sleeping room window. For a moment she thought it had snowed during the night, the flash of white on the ground dazzling her eyes. Then she remembered a stiff breeze insinuating itself into her dreams, rattling the shutters, and realized she was gazing on a carpet of freshly fallen cherry blossoms. The dark silhouette of the immense branching cherry tree stood in stark contrast to its blossom-illuminated splendor just the day before. Koen put on her black meditation robes, tied the cording around her waist and, upon lighting the stick of incense in front of the memorial plaque for her lost baby, was filled with a perplexity of anguish and gratitude, a deep recognition of the evanescence of life.

The moon was sinking into the pine-topped hill as she ascended the stone path. The hut seemed to embrace her in her state of deep sensitivity, and lighting another stick of incense before the simple altar, the wafting smoke again spoke to her of impermanence. She thought of a great Japanese Zen master who reportedly made the vow to become a monk upon seeing the curl of incense smoke at his mother's funeral. As she bowed toward her black cushion, she glanced outside and noticed that even in this season there were needles and leaves and a few twigs scattered over the graveyard moss. She sensed her meditation practice as just this—sweeping, sweeping, sweeping. She sat and breathed deeply, inhaling the smoke and the smell of the woods.

At the first striking of the bell, she thought she heard an answering squeak, an almost imperceptible animal sound from somewhere that felt like deep inside her. With the second ring, there was most certainly a louder high-pitched whimper, a muffled answer to the bell. Koen deepened her concentration and hesitated before the final strike of the bell. Her hand strained in midmotion over the brass bowl; she drew in a breath scented with cloves and sandalwood and expectation. As she tapped the bell for the final ring, quieter than usual, she felt her breath enveloping the little hut. Immediately a jumble of squeakings and squawkings broke out from somewhere under the hut's floor, and Koen joined the clamor with a tumble of merry laughter.

So that's what her tanuki friends had been up to lately! The tiny voices were silenced with a lower growl, and Koen, too, feeling chastised, returned to the source of her sitting with renewed vigor. She intuited rather than felt the motion beneath her, could sense the huddle of warm bodies settle into a collective calm that she, too, was part of.

After she slid the heavy wooden door to the hut closed a couple hours later, she walked to the far side of the structure and noticed a crude tunnel dug precisely under the spot where her meditation cushion sat. Koen squatted to peer into the dark cave and a low growl issued from the indistinct depth. She gave a sotto voce version of her rising and falling whistle to reassure the mama and again sensed rather than saw a relaxing of the brood. She made a mental note to bring an offering of food the next time she came to the hut, and she started downward toward the temple yard.

Each day of the following week the tanuki under the hut seemed to grow more comfortable with Koen's presence, no longer shushing when she was on her cushion. She followed in her mind's eye the tumblings and cavortings of the little ones beneath her and saw the mama coming and going from the tunnel a few times. One day after an especially deep meditation session, Koen felt a presence over her right shoulder. Upon opening her eyes and turning her head to glance out the screen door, she saw five furry pups crowded around the doorway peering in at the candle on the altar. One of the tanuki shifted its gaze to hers and with two high-pitched squeaks alerted the others, and they stumbled over each other toward their tunnel. Koen laughed aloud and clapped her hands in joy, delighted with her new friends.

When she left the hut that morning, she saw a few furry faces peeping out of their hole, and she bowed respectfully toward them and said in a quiet voice, "Tanuki-sama! Welcome to the celebration!" She reached the bottom of the stairs and looked back up to see a pile of fur rollicking about in the graveyard with squeaks and squawks, like little kittens. The thought came to her that these were the previous abbots revisiting Black Bamboo Mountain in tanuki guise, expressing their gratitude toward the mountain's sanctuary for lives well lived.

That evening as Koen was finishing up the dishes, the bell announcing a visitor in the entryway jangled. She wondered if widow Kinoshita could have died. She had complained of a bad cough around New Year's and each successive report indicated that she hadn't recovered. Just as she thought this, Koen heard the dry hacking of the woman, and for a moment she thought she might be perceiving her from the other side. This kind of event wasn't unusual for Koen, who experienced the boundaries between life and death as permeable. As the coughing subsided, Koen dried her hands and removed her apron, and when she came into the hall to see the old woman standing in the entryway, she blinked hard and then gave a laugh of relief.

"Abbess," the widow addressed Koen, "the villagers are having a meeting at the village hall and asked me to come invite you."

"Maaaaaa, such trouble for an aged woman. I'm sorry to put you out," Koen replied in a formal manner, wondering what the meeting could be about, requiring her presence at this hour.

"No, no, no, no trouble. Please, come as you are and we'll walk together," said the widow.

Koen took her priest's vestment off a hook near the hallway and draped it around her neck, tossed a shawl around her shoulders, and slipped on her outdoor shoes, still wondering what this meeting could be. She hoped the old woman would clue her in along the way since she didn't feel she could inquire directly. But the old woman chattered on about the moon that morning, the state of her garden, how the village kids were growing up so quickly, and Koen couldn't catch any sign of what this was about.

When they arrived at the village hall, the widow pushed Koen through the door ahead of her, and Koen took in most of the village elders kneeling around the glossy lacquer table, chatting amiably while the women scurried about filling sake and beer glasses. Koen bowed formally with her palms together, and in one voice the villagers cried, "Abbess, welcome!"

The men scooted together making a place of honor for Koen, and she said, "Maaaaaa, such trouble you go to! Don't let me interrupt your fun!"

Upon being seated, the village head placed an empty glass in Koen's hand and gestured for a bottle of beer. "Just a sip among friends," he said, as he poured the glass halfway full. Koen was swept along with the scene and forgot to protest as she nodded in greeting to several of the villagers.

Putting the beer bottle down, the village head shouted, "*Kampai!* Cheers! To our illustrious abbess, guardian of Black Bamboo Mountain!" and all the villagers shouted, "*Kampai!*" while several of the women rushed to pour themselves a swallow to join in the toast. Koen felt the flush immediately as she sipped the beer, a physical reaction to the concentration of attention fixed on her. The village head cleared his voice in the manner of beginning a formal, memorized speech and said, "Koen-sama. Indeed we are all indebted to you for your years of service as abbess and protector of Black Bamboo Mountain."

Koen shifted uneasily on her heels, sensing there was something more than just gratitude motivating this meeting and speech.

"For twenty years you have faithfully served as our spiritual mentor, performing our memorial rites and funerals in a worthy Buddhist manner, helping our ancestors cross over to the other shore. You have tended Black Bamboo Mountain impeccably, serving the spirits of our departed abbots in an exemplary way and, indeed, provided us all with a model of Buddhist virtue." The grizzled man lowered his voice to a conspiratorial tone and continued, "I might say I was one of those who was somewhat skeptical of having a woman assume the position of abbot, but I have nothing but words of praise and gratitude to offer you after your fine service."

"After" my service? Koen thought. So there is some dissatisfaction, some desire to replace me? This thought came to her not with panic or anger, but with a deep sadness. Black Bamboo Mountain was indeed a part of her, and she a part of it. She sensed how the contentment she had striven for in her earlier days had indeed settled upon her in her solitary life on the mountain. But how could she think of leaving? Above the boom of the village head's voice and the hush of the assembly, Koen strained her ears to catch a curious scratching sound from underneath the floor. No one else seemed to notice.

"We of the village have conferred and, knowing what a great

amount of work it is to keep the grounds of the temple to the extent that you have, we feel that at your stage of life it is only right that you be provided with relief from such an onerous task. We therefore have drawn up a design for a small cottage for your retirement, and Tanaka-san," at this point he nodded with an ingratiating grin toward one of the village elders, a wealthy widower retired from his sake and wine delivery business, "has graciously offered a building site at the corner of his property." Again the curious scrabbling of claws on wood focused Koen's attention, a noise that she alone could readily interpret.

"Maaaaaa, it has been my duty and, I may say, delight to be a part of Black Bamboo Mountain these twenty years, and I most certainly am not complaining about the work involved—" Many of the villagers present also saw through the village head's words immediately, knowing how Koen still roamed the forests each spring digging bamboo shoots and continued to rise earlier than most of the farmers. "But if it is the village's will to have me step down, well—I don't know what to say. It's certainly a most generous offer, and I will consider it carefully." Her voice became more distant, as if even now she was moving away from the village. The scratching on the floor had ceased, and Koen strained to follow the actions of her invisible companions. What were they up to?

At this point, the broad-shouldered president of the farmer's alliance stood and said, "As a matter of fact, we've consulted with the temple authorities, and it's been arranged for my son, Kazuhiro, to obtain his priest's papers and succeed you as our next abbot. As you may know, the abbot of Tachitani, the next village, plans to step down from his position, and Kazuhiro will be taking over the duties of that congregation also."

Koen knew she should be concerned, even alarmed, at this turn of events, but her attention was concentrated more closely on her five furry companions outside than on the unexpected proceedings unfolding before her. The widow Kinoshita who had escorted her to the meeting gave her a nudge, and she realized the villagers were awaiting her response.

"Well, I thank all of you for giving me the opportunity to—" and at this, a great clatter of glasses shattering on the kitchen floor diverted everyone, and the village head's wife appeared in the doorway brandishing a broom.

"Tanuki!" she shouted, and everyone laughed and poked each other, some of the farmers vociferously shaking their heads and launching into tales of other furry encounters. Koen, taking advantage of the pandemonium, stood and excused herself, mumbling something about "her children" and the women nearby giggled and made way for her to leave the hall.

Outside in the chilly evening, Koen gave her whistle then clapped her hands in annoyance, shooing the tanuki on home ahead of her. She was joined by widow Kinoshita, who said, "Abbess, I know it's a surprise, but the cottage will really be quite fine. Any one of us would be proud of it. You can do your gardening there, join us for our tea times—" she left off in mid-sentence as she watched Koen hurry toward the temple steps, realizing that though she may have taken her vows out of necessity, the abbess had really been quite content with her life on the mountain. This came as a shock, for it had been Kinoshita who had suggested the plan to the farmers' alliance president when his son, who had earlier refused to take up his share of the family's farm, lost his job in the nearby town.

"Good night, grandmother," Koen called down from the gate of the temple. "Take care in the dark."

"Good night, Abbess. Think about it. Tomorrow you will see it's a good plan," said the old widow, though she knew now her words were false.

The following day when widow Kinoshita returned to the temple to confess her role in the plan, carrying an offering of bamboo shoots dug by her grandchildren, the abbess was nowhere about. The widow pushed open the door to the entryway, calling, "Abbess? Koen-sama?" She noticed the place was tidied up even more than usual, and in the corner of the entryway was a bundle tied up in a purple scarf with the temple's insignia on it. Resting on top were Koen's vestments. The smell of incense suffused the air and Kinoshita-san, rather than feeling a sense of unease, became aware of a supreme serenity. It was not a new feeling. It was just that her preconceived dread of Black Bamboo Mountain fell away, and for once she could appreciate the soulful stillness of the place.

Placing the bamboo shoots next to the bundle clad in purple, widow Kinoshita turned to contemplate ascending the dilapidated steps leading to the meditation hut. Somehow she knew there would be no answer to her calls, and as she closed the door of the entryway and glanced up toward the temple graveyard, she saw amidst the gravestones six tanuki pups peering down at her.

JEFFREY FORD

At Reparata

Jeffrey Ford won a well-deserved World Fantasy Award for his novel
The Physiognomy, *an interstitial work that encompasses fantasy,
mystery, allegory, and science fiction. Last year he published an equally
compelling sequel,* Memoranda. *He is currently at work on the third
and final volume of the series,* The Beyond. *Ford lives in New Jersey,
with his wife and two sons.*

*"At Reparata" is a highly original tour de force of "imaginary
world" fiction, reprinted from the February 1999 edition of the* Event
Horizon *web site, www.eventhorizon.com.*

—*T. W.*

Everyone remembers where they were when they first heard that
Queen Josette had died. I was standing in twilight on that cliff
known as the Cold Shoulder, fly-fishing for bats. Beneath me, the
lights of the palace shone with a soft glow that dissolved decrep-
itude into beauty, and a breeze was blowing in from the south, carrying
with it the remnants of a storm at sea. I had just caught a glimpse of a
star, streaking down behind the distant mountains, when there was a tug
at my line followed hard by a cry that came, like the shout of the earth,
up from the palace. I heard it first in my chest. Words would have failed
to convince me of the fact, but that desperate scream told me plainly
she was dead.

Josette had been an orphan left at the palace gates by a troupe of
wandering actors. She arrived at a point in her life between childhood
and maturity, wondrously lithe and athletic with green eyes and her dark
hair cut like a boy's. I suspect she had been abandoned in hopes that

her beauty and intelligence might work to make her a better life than one found on the road. This was back in the days when Ingess had just begun to build his new court from society's castaways. Upon seeing her, he pronounced she was to be the Lady of the Mirrors, but we all knew that she would some day lose the title to that of Queen. The drama that brought her to this conclusion was ever the court's favorite spectacle and topic of conversation.

Her hair grew long and entangled us all in her charm and innocence. Ingess married her on a cool day in late summer five years after her arrival, and the Overseer of Situations released a thousand butterflies upon the signal of their kiss. We all loved her as a daughter, and the younger ones among us as a mother. She never put on airs or forced the power of her elevated position, understanding better than anyone the equanimity that was the soul of the Palace Reparata. Her kindness was the perfect match for Ingess's comic generosity.

With her passing, His Royal, as he had insisted on being called, came apart like light in a prism. I sat four nights in succession with him in the gardens, smoking my pipe and listening to him weep into sunrise. The quantity of tears drained him of his good looks and left him a haggard wreck, like some old crone, albeit with shining, blonde hair.

"See here, Ingess," I told him but could go no further, the logic of his grief too persuasive.

He'd wave his hand at me and turn his face away.

And so the world he had managed to create with his pirate ancestor's gold, his kingdom, suddenly lost its meaning. Before Josette had succumbed to the poison of a spider bite, Reparata was a place where a wandering beggar might be taken in at any time and made a Court Accountant or Thursday's High Astronomer. Every member of the palace had a title bestowed upon them by His Royal. There was no want at Reparata, and this made it an oasis amidst the sea of disappointment and cruelty that we, each in his or her own way, had found the world to be.

Never before had a royal retinue been comprised of so many lowly worms. The Countess Frouch had been a prostitute known as Yams in the nearby seaside town of Gile. His Royal welcomed her warmly, without judgment, as he did Tendon Durst, a round, bespectacled lunatic who believed beyond a doubt that he was joined at a shared eye with a phantom twin. In a single day's errant wandering, Durst had set out as a confirmed madman and ended the evening at the palace with a room of his own and a title of Philosopher General. We had never before seen someone speak simultaneously from both sides of the mouth, but that night he walked in his sleep and told us twice at once that he would never leave Reparata. We all shared his sentiment.

Even Ringlat the highwayman, hiding from the law, performed his role of Bishop to the Crown righteously. Our lives were transformed by a position in society and whatever bizarre duties His Royal might dream up at his first encounter with us, standing before him at the palace gates, begging for a heel of bread or the eyes from that morning's marsupial dish. Times were bad everywhere, but Ingess was so wealthy, and Reparata was so far removed from the rest of the world, no one who wandered there and had the courage to ask for something was sent away. We lived long bright days as in a book and then, with a fit of narcolepsy, the reader closed his eyes and fell asleep.

If we ever had intentions of fleecing His Royal, the time of his mourning was the perfect opportunity. Instead, we went about our jobs and titles with even greater dedication, taking turns keeping an eye on our melancholic leader. My full title was High and Mighty of Next Week. Ingess, beneath his eccentric sense of humor, must have known that it was the only position vague enough to tame my impulses. On my own, I, who had never done an honest day's work in my life, created and performed a series of ritual tasks that gave definition to my importance at court. Gathering bats in order to exterminate the garden's mosquitos was only one of them. Another was dusting the items in the palace attic.

On Mondays I would usually spend the mornings making proclamations, and on the Monday following the death of Josette, I proclaimed that we should seek some medical help for His Royal. He had begun to see his young wife's spirit floating everywhere and was trying to do himself in with strong drink, insomnia, and grief.

"I see her next to the Fountain of the Dolphins as we speak, Flam," he said to me one night in the gardens.

I looked over at the fountain and saw nothing, but, still, the frantic aspect of his gaze sent a shiver through me.

It turned out to be the first proclamation of mine that was ever acted upon. I got high and mighty on the subject and wasn't waiting until the following week. Carrier pigeons were sent out to all of the surrounding kingdoms, inquiring if there was anyone who could cure the melancholy of loss. A small fortune in gold was the reward. I changed my own title to Conscience of the King and set about to do all in my power to cure Ingess, if not for his own good, then for the good of the state.

While we waited for a reply, His Royal raved and stared, only stopping occasionally to caress the empty air. His mourning reached such a state of hysteria that made me wonder if it was natural. I had the Regal Ascendiary, Chin Mokes, a five-time convicted forger, take over the task of signing the royal notes of purchase in order to keep the Palace running smoothly. A plan was hatched in which one of the women, well powdered and bewigged, would dress up like Josette and, standing in the shadows of the gardens, tell Ingess to stop grieving. After the Countess Frouch laughed at us in that tone that could wither a forest, though, we saw the emptiness of our scheme.

Two harrowing months of sodden depression slithered by at a snail's pace before word finally came that a man from a distant land, a traveling practitioner of medicine, had recently arrived by ship in Gile. Frouch and I went in search of him, traveling through the night in the Royal carriage, driven by none other than Tendon Durst. Though I was wary of the Philosopher's sense of direction, his invisible brother was usually trustworthy. We arrived at daybreak by the sea and witnessed the gulls swarming as the fishing boats set out. "Do you think it is a good idea that you came back?" I asked her as we left the carriage.

"It's a test," she said as she adjusted the position of her tiara atop her spiraling platitudes of hair and stamped out her cigarette. Heels were not the best footwear for the planks and cobblestones of Gile, but she wore them anyway. I thought the mink stole a little much, but who was I to say? To look the Conscience of the King, I wore one of his finer suits, a silk affair with a winged collar and matching cape. In addition, I borrowed a large signet ring encrusted with diamonds. We left the Philosopher General in deep meditation and went forth as Royalty, past the heap of fish skeletons, toward the boardwalk that led to the tavern.

The tavern keeper had known the Countess in her earlier life and was pleased to see her doing so well. We asked if he had beheld the foreign healer and he told us he had.

"A short fellow," he said, "with a long beard. All he wears is a robe and a pair of boots." The tavern keeper laughed. "He comes in every day a little after sunrise and has me make him a drink he taught me called Princess Jang's Tears. It ends with a cloud of froth at the top and a constant green rain falling in a clear sky of gin toward the bottom of the glass. I'd say he knows a thing or two."

I ordered two of them for us, using gold coin as payment. The tavern keeper was ecstatic. We sat by the large front window of the place that looked out across harbor and bay. Neither of us spoke. I was contemplating my transformation over the past years from unwanted vagrant to the executor of a kingdom, and I am sure by the look in Frouch's eyes, she was thinking something similar. The strange drink was bittersweet, cool citrus beneath a cloud of sorrow. Then the doorbell rang and our healer entered.

The tavern keeper introduced us, and the healer bowed so low as to show us his star-shaped bald spot. He told us his name was unimportant but that his reputation was legendary even on the remote Island of the Barking Children.

"You are far flung," the countess said to him, "but can you cure loss?"

"I can cure anything, Countess," was his reply.

"Death?" I asked.

"Death is not a disease," he said.

He agreed to accompany us back to the palace if we would have a drink with him. The tavern keeper created a round of Princess Jang's Tears on the house, and we sat again at the table near the window.

"I feel you have a strong connection to this place, Countess," said the healer.

"You're as sharp as a stick of butter," she said and lit a cigarette.

"Do you regret your days here?" he asked her.

"If I did, I would have to regret life," she said, turning her face to the window. Princess Jang's tears were not the only ones to fall that morning.

The healer nodded and took his drink in a way that showed me he might have a regret or two himself. My hope was that these disappointments did not stem from the health of his patients.

We rode back to the palace in perfect silence. The healer sat next to Frouch, and I was across from them. As the carriage bounced over the poorly maintained road from Gile, I studied the man we had hired. His face, though half hidden by a gray beard, showed its age yet still shone with a placid vitality. I knew he was smiling, though his lips did not move. On the palms of each of his hands were tattoos of coiled snakes. The robe he wore did not appear to be some form of foreign dress but in all reality a cheap flannel bathrobe that might be worn by a fisherman's wife. Around his neck hung an amulet on a piece of string—an outlandish fake ruby orbited by glass diamonds set in a star of tin painted gold. His small burlap sack of belongings squirmed at my feet.

"The young man's grief will consume him if I don't take drastic measures," the healer said to me after he had spent a day studying His Royal. We sat in the dining hall at the western end of that table that was so long and large, we at court called it the island. It was late and most of the palace was asleep. I sipped at coffee and the healer crunched away viciously at a bowl of locusts in wild honey that the palace chef, the Exalted Culinarity, Grenis Saint-Geedon, once a famous assassin, had been so kind as to leave his bed to prepare.

"What do you mean?" I asked.

"Do you see what I am doing with this bowl of holy sustenance?" said the healer, a locust leg sticking out of the right corner of his mouth. "It will eat out his soul."

"Will he die?" I asked.

"That's not the worst part of it," said the old man.

"What are these drastic measures?"

"Let me just say, once I have begun, you will wish you hadn't requested I do so," he said.

"Can you cure him?" I asked.

"That," he said, lifting the bowl to lick it, "is a certainty that has roots in the very first instant of creation."

Either this man was an idiot or so great a physician that his method and bearing were informed by some highly advanced foreign culture. His dress and the manner in which he ate did not suggest the latter, but my most recent glimpse of Ingess trudging like a somnambulist along the great hall was enough to convince me that the healer's diagnosis was correct. His Royal had shriveled miserably and was totally despondent. Even that blonde hair was now disintegrating into salt and floating away in his lethargic wake.

I feared the Countess would lash me with her laughter when she heard of my decision, but I told the healer right then, as he set his bowl back on the table, "Do what you must."

Then the old man's lips moved into a wide grin to reveal a shattered set of teeth. He lifted the amulet from his chest and kissed the audacious ruby at its center. "You'll live to regret this," he told me.

"I already have," I said.

The next morning I had to address the assembled royalty of the court of Reparata on the subject of Ingess and his treatment. We met in the palace theater, all fifty-two of us. I took the stage, again dressed in the fine clothes of His Royal as a way of adding authority to my words. Miraculously, Frouch spared me as I apprised them of my decision, but the others were very skeptical. How could they not be—they had seen and met the healer.

"He's a fake," Chin Mokes cried out, and this got the others going because who better to know a forgery than the Regal Ascendiary?

"Eats insects," said the Exalted Culinarity, spitting as the stories told he had once done on the foreheads of each of his victims.

The Chancellor of Waste went right for the jugular. "He's no physician, he's Grandfather Mess. He couldn't cure a pain in the ass unless he left the room."

"He is legendary even on the remote Island of the Barking Children," I told them.

"Probably for keeping the sidewalks clean," someone shouted.

All of the jewelry of the assembled members of the court dazzled my eyes, and my head began to swim. Perspiration formed along my brow, and for the first time since coming to Reparata, I had that feeling of abandonment that had haunted my wandering for so many years.

Then the Countess stood up and the others instantly quieted down. "You've all had a chance to pass wind. Now its time to get on with the necessity of saving His Royal. Unless another of you has a better plan, we will all follow the healer's advice and see his treatment through."

The Chancellor of Waste opened his mouth wide to speak, but Frouch, without even turning to look at him said, "If you don't want me to laugh at you, you'd better reserve that part of your title that is about to issue from your tongue."

The Chancellor relented and sunk down in his seat as if to duck a derisive giggle.

Before sunrise the next morning, the treatment was begun.

His Royal lay completely naked on a bare table in the palace infirmary, rocking slightly side to side and muttering all manner of weirdness. Frouch and I were present to represent the court during the medical procedure. Beside the healer, the young lad Pester, Prince of the Horse Stalls, was in attendance, sitting on a stool in the corner, ever ready to do the physician's bidding. We also called for Durst, the Philosopher General, to see if he could decipher what might be Ingess's last message to us. It was a generally held belief in those days that one madman could easily interpret the ravings of another. The healer was anxious to begin, but we forestalled him, explaining how important a message from Ingess might be to his loyal subjects.

Durst came in dragging the invisible weight of his twin, and performing the impossible feat of discussing two different subjects simultaneously from either side of his mouth.

"My dear Philosopher," said the Countess. "You give sanity a bad name."

He bowed as far as his stomach would allow, and then stood and listened with something verging on attention to our request. It was heartwarming to see how proud he was to have been of some use in the crisis. He strode with an official bearing over to the table where Ingess lay and leaned down to listen to the feverish stream of words.

While the Philosopher General was performing his duties, Frouch poked me in the side with her elbow and we both had difficulty holding back our laughter at the sight of him. The healer, witnessing the whole thing, merely shook his head and sighed impatiently.

When Durst finally turned around, we asked him what Ingess was saying.

He looked puzzled and told us, "It all sounds like gibberish to me."

The Countess and I broke out laughing.

"But," he continued, holding up his right index finger, "my brother says that His Royal is concerned with a stream running under a bridge."

"Fascinating," said the healer as he ushered Durst out of the infirmary.

Upon his return, the old man lifted his burlap sack onto the table next to Ingess's head. From within it, he retrieved a pair of spectacles whose lenses were long black cylinders capped with metal. He fit the arms of these over His Royal's ears and adjusted the tunnels so that they completely covered the eyes. The moment this strange contraption was in place, Ingess let loose a massive sigh and went completely limp.

"What's this?" I asked.

The healer undid his bathrobe tie, wrapped the flaps around him more completely and retied it securely. "At the ends of those two tunnels there is a picture that appears, because of the way our sight overlaps, to have a third dimension. It is so endlessly fascinating to behold that the viewer thinks of nothing else. Time, pain, regret, are pushed out of the mind by the intricate beauty of the scene."

"What does it show?" asked Frouch.

"I can't explain," said the healer, "it is too complex."

"Why is it necessary?" I asked.

"Because," said the healer, "what I am about to do to your liege would otherwise be so painful that his screams would threaten the sanity of everyone within the confines of the palace." With this, he reached into that bag of his and pulled forth a wriggling green creature the size of a man's index finger.

The Countess and I stepped closer to see exactly what it was he was holding. It was a segmented, jade green, centipedelike thing with a lavender head and tiny black horns.

"Sirimon," he said with a foreign inflection in his voice.

"It looks like a caterpillar," said Frouch.

"Yes, it does," said the old man, "but make no mistake, this is Sirimon."

"He's not going to eat that, is he?" I asked, swallowing hard the memory of the healer's midnight snack.

"Perish the thought," he said, and with great care, he brought his hand down to Ingess's left ear. He gave a high, piercing whistle, and the diminutive creature marched forward across his palm and into the opening in His Royal's head.

Frouch laughed at the sight of it in an attempt to control her horror. I turned away feeling as though I would be sick.

"Now we wait," I heard the healer say. He pulled up a chair and sat down.

Somewhere into our fourth hour of silent waiting, the old man jotted down the ingredients to Princess Jang's Tears and gave it to Pester.

"Tell the barkeep not to forget the bitters," he said.

The boy nodded, and before he could leave the room, I called out, "Make that two."

"Just tell him to keep them coming," called Frouch.

Pester returned, carrying a tray with three glasses and the largest pitcher in the palace, which contained a veritable monsoon of liquid sorrow. Frouch lit a cigarette and the healer poured. We made small talk, and, in the course of our conversation, the healer regaled us with a tale of his most recent patient, a man who, through the obsessive reading of religious texts, had become so simple and crude that he had begun to revert back into the form of an ape.

"His wife had to coax him down from the trees each evening with a trail of bananas."

"Did you change his reading habits?" asked the Countess.

"No, I shaved his body and then prescribed three moderate taps on the head with a mallet at breakfast, lunch, and dinner."

I was about to ask if the poor fellow had come around, but before I could speak, I noticed an irritating, disconcerting little sound that momentarily confused me.

"What is that?" I asked, standing unsteadily.

"Yes, I hear it," said Frouch. "Like the constant crumpling of paper."

"That is Sirimon," said the healer.

I walked over to Ingess and listened. The diminutive noise seemed to be coming from inside his head. Leaning over, I put my ear to his ear. It was with dread that I realized the sound was identical, though quieter because muffled by flesh and skull, to that of the healer working away at his bowl of locust.

"What's the meaning of this?" I yelled.

The old man smiled. "Sirimon is rearranging, creating new pathways, digesting the melancholy."

———

I had fallen asleep and was wrapped in a nightmare memory of childhood when a hand came out of the shadows and smacked me on the back of the head. Coming to, I rubbed my eyes, and standing before me was the healer holding forth his infernal green worm, now bloated and writhing in its obesity.

"Sirimon has finished," he said.

Frouch was over by the table that held Ingess. Her powdered hair had deflated and now hung to the middle of her back. She stared blankly down at His Royal and was laughing as though she was weeping. The healer's optical contraption was gone and Ingess's eyes were rolled back to show only white. His mouth was stretched wide as if trying to release a scream that was too large to fit through the opening.

"Quickly," said the healer, "to the kitchen."

Just then Pester came in leading a group of men—Chin Mokes, Grenis Saint-Geedon, Ringlat, and Durst. There was a whirl of frantic activity, in which we were told to lift His Royal and carry him to the kitchen. Once there, we were instructed to tie him to the huge rotisserie spit on which the Exalted Culinarity would turn whole hogs at feast time. When His Royal was lashed securely to the long metal rod, the healer told Grenis to turn the handle and set it so that the patient's left ear was toward the floor. Then the old man called for Pester to bring a large pot and set it down in the ashes where the fire usually burned.

A moment after the boy set the pot down, a dollop of viscous white fluid dripped from His Royal's ear and splattered inside it. The assembled company all took a step back at the sight of this. Then a steady stream of the goo began to fall, like beer from an open tap, filling the pot.

"He said we must let no harm come to this substance, no matter what happens to it," said Frouch, who had just arrived in the kitchen.

"What in the devil's name is it?" asked Ringlat.

I turned to ask the healer the very same question, but he was no longer in the room.

"Nice work, Flam," said Chin Mokes, "you've turned the King into a flagon of goo."

"Where is that physician?" said Grenis Saint-Geedon, pulling a butcher knife from his rack. He left the room with a murderous look on his face.

Over the course of the next two hours, the pot filled nearly to the brim, and the healer was searched for everywhere but never found. At daybreak, Ingess opened his eyes and yawned.

The palace Reparata rejoiced at the fact that His Royal had been returned to full health. It had been necessary to help him see to his needs for a week or so, but as soon as this period of convalescence had passed, he was up on his feet and performing his royal duties. Much of the hair he had lost had already begun to grow back, and he regained nearly all of his muscular vitality. The deep melancholy was gone, but it had taken some small part of him with it, for now, in his face, there was a series of subtle lines that made him look more mature. No longer did he weep for hours on end. In fact, I did not witness one tear after the ordeal. Neither did he laugh, though, and this small formality was like a pebble in my shoe.

I went one night to the gardens to release the bats and found him, sitting on the bench across from the fountain of the dolphins, staring up at the moon.

"Durst gave a lecture today on the nature of the universe. His belief is that it began with a giant explosion," I said and laughed too hard, trying to get him to join me.

Ingess merely shook his head. "Poor Durst," he said. "I never told you, but I once sent for some word about him to the asylum that he wandered away from. It seems he had a twin brother who drowned when he was ten. He might have saved him but he was too afraid of the water."

"His Royal," I said, exasperated with his response, "why do you stare at the moon?"

"Don't call me that anymore, Flam. I'm not a king. Just a pirate's grandson who was left far too much gold."

"As you wish," I said.

He turned then and forced a smile for me. "I want you to have Saint-Geedon prepare a feast. I need to thank everyone for their efforts to save my life."

I nodded and left him.

Later that night, I sought out Frouch and found her on the terrace that overlooks the reflecting pond. She was sitting in the shadow of a potted mimosa, feeding breadcrumbs to the peacocks.

I pulled up a chair and told her about the feast that would be held in another two days. She brightened at the prospect of this.

"I have a gown I've been waiting to wear," she said.

"How do you feel now that everything is back to normal?" I asked.

"You were brilliant as the Conscience of the King," she said.

"I'd rather put that entire affair behind me," I said. "But there is one thing that I still wonder about."

"The picture at the end of the healer's strange spectacles?" she said.

I shook my head. "What became of that muddle that dripped from Ingess's ear?"

She clapped her hands to send the birds scurrying away and sat forward. "You mean you haven't seen it?" she asked.

"No."

"Come now," she said and stood. "You've got to see this."

She actually took my hand as we walked through hallways, and it made me somewhat nervous to find myself behind the protective field of her dangerous laughter.

We ended our journey in the small chapel at the northern end of the palace. The Ministress of Sleep, old Mrs. Kofnep, was just lighting a last votive candle as we entered. Beyond her, resting on the altar atop a satin pillow of considerable size was a huge ball with fine white hair growing all over it.

"There it is," said Frouch.

"That thing?" I asked, pointing.

Mrs. Kofnep greeted us and then turned her own gaze on the strange object. "I haven't decided if it's an egg or a testicle or a replica of the world," she said with a self-mocking smile.

"It took that form of a perfect sphere the day after it came from His Royal's head," said the Countess.

"The white hair wasn't there two nights ago," said Mrs. Kofnep.

"I had it moved here to protect it," said Frouch.

We stared at it for some time, and then the Ministress of Sleep left us with the usual complaint about her insomnia.

The next day I was busy with preparations for the feast, but before turning in, I went back to the chapel to have another look at the oddity. Changes had obviously taken place, for now it was stretched out and tapered at either end with a large bulge in the middle. The white hair had grown profusely, and wrapped itself around to swaddle whatever was there gently undulating at its core.

The feast was held in the grand ballroom and the Exalted Culinarity had outdone himself with the exotic nature of the dishes served. Crow liver paté on paper-thin slices of candied amber was the appetizer. For the main course there was fowl, hog, beef, and even crocodile done up with fruit and vegetables to appear as tropical islands floating in calm seas of gravy. On each table was placed a punch bowl of Princess Jang's Tears, the drink that had of late become all the rage at Reparata.

Ringlat gave a benediction in which he likened the loss of Josette to highway robbery and our combined efforts to revive Ingess as the true power of the Law. With the exception of Mrs. Kofnep, none of us was overly religious. I looked around as Ringlat finished to see bowed heads and all manner of halfhearted religiously symbolic hand-gesturing. When Durst stood, I was relieved, knowing his drivel would cast out the seriousness of the Bishop's sermon. He did not disappoint. His gift to Ingess, as he put it, was the discovery of the meaning of Time. To represent his tangled ball of musings in a nutshell, he surmised from one side of his mouth that it existed to make eternity pass more quickly, and from the other side that it served to make it pass more slowly. We gave him a standing ovation and then started drinking.

Through the entire gala, His Royal sat on the dais, neither eating nor drinking, but nodding with a mechanical smile to one and all. By my third serving of the Tears, I forgot about my concern for him and stepped out on the dance floor with the Countess. For that evening, she had applied a false beauty mark to her upper lip, and I found it remarkably alluring. At some point in her life, she had been beautiful, and on that evening, dressed in a cream-colored gown, her hair done up in two conical horns and decorated with mimosa blossoms, she approached her former radiance like a clock frozen at only a minute to midnight.

"Flam, your dancing leads me to believe I will have to guide you to your room later with a trail of bananas," she said and whisper-giggled into my left ear. The sound of that laughter did not frighten me, but instead made my head spin as though it were Sirimon opening a new pathway to that portion of the brain that houses desire.

Chin Mokes walked on his hands. Pester spun like a dervish. The Illustrious Shepherd of Dust sang an aria about the unrequited love of a giant. The Majestic Seventh did impressions of farm animals until she passed out beneath the table that held the island of roasted hog. The ballroom was a swirling storm of goodwill and high spirits, while at its center sat Ingess as though asleep with his eyes open. Not once did his smile disappear, not once did he miss a chance to shake hands or give a thank-you kiss, not once did he laugh.

Then, sometime well after the dessert of chocolate balloons, there was a shrill cry of distress and the room went absolutely silent. I looked up from my drink to see what had hushed the crowd and saw the Ministress of Sleep, Mrs. Kofnep, standing just inside the northern entrance to the ballroom, working madly to catch her breath.

"Come quickly," she cried, "something is happening in the chapel." She turned and left in great haste and we all followed.

The small chapel was just large enough to accommodate all of us as long as Pester sat atop Durst's shoulders. We crowded in, panting and perspiring from our dash through the Hall of Light and Shadow, across the rotunda of the Royal Museum, and then down the steps just past the observatory. Up on the altar the white entity, which I now knew was a cocoon, was rippling wildly, rocking and emitting sharp cries high and thin enough to pass through the eye of a needle.

There was an awed silence among the members of the court, and only Ingess had the wherewithal to draw his long dagger in case the expectant birth came forth a terror. People clutched each other as the white fabric of the thing began to tear with a sound like a fat man splitting his trousers. Ingess audibly groaned and his sword clanked to the floor as the thing began to unfurl itself. An explosion of fine white powder was released at the moment of birth and then immediately blown away by some phantom breeze. When that cleared, I saw it above the altar, hovering in the air, a huge, diaphanous moth with wings as big as bedsheets. It looked only a hair more substantial than a ghost, glimmering in the light from the flickering votives.

The crowd became a chorus and voiced a gasp and then a sigh as the thing flapped its huge wings and flew above our heads toward the entrance. Pester, his face a mask of wonder, reached up toward it from where he sat on Durst's shoulders. His index finger ran along its underside as it passed into the hallway, and then his finger, like a flame going out, disappeared from his hand. The boy's mask of wonder became one of horror and he screamed. We meant to help him but by then the powder that had fallen from the moth reached our eyes. It caused in me a feeling of sorrow more deep than the one I experienced upon my mother's death when I was five. The entire court was reduced to tears. Only Ingess had not been affected. I saw him retrieve his dagger from the floor with the same stoic look he had worn at the feast.

When the effects of the moth's powder had worn off, we gathered round Pester to inspect his hand.

"There was no pain," he said. "Only inside, a sadness."

Some touched the spot where the digit had been, still unable to believe it was gone. Ringlat, knowing that as the Bishop he should do something profound at this point but having no clue as to what, took the boy's hand in his and kissed the nub. Mokes actually turned to Tendon Durst for an explanation, and the Philosopher General mumbled something about insect fear and the ringed planet. Chin nodded as if he understood. The strange powder that had fallen now covered Frouch's beauty mark and somewhat disintegrated her power of enchantment. All jabbered like magpies, and the one thing that was finally decided upon was that strong drink was required. Before we left the chapel, Ingess apologized to us, especially Pester, since it had been his royal mind that had been responsible for the moth.

The evening ended with everyone, including the King, drinking themselves into oblivion. We wondered where the creature had wafted off to, but no one wanted to go in search of it. Sometime near daybreak, I and the others trudged like the walking dead to our sleeping chambers to feast on bad dreams. My last thought as I dozed off was of Frouch and her fleeting beauty.

Three days passed without a sign of the moth, and the court began to breathe easier, thinking that it was now time to put aside the tragic saga of Josette's death. I know that Ingess was approached by Saint-Geedon and some of the others about perhaps starting a project that might recapture the old spirit of Reparata, but His Royal very kindly put them off with promises that he would consider the suggestions.

On the night of the third day, I was sitting in the garden with my cage of bats when I spotted the moth. It lifted slowly up like a dispossessed thought of ingenious proportion from behind a row of hedges, causing me to drop my pipe into my lap. I considered running, but its fluid grace as it moved along the wall of green hypnotized me. When I finally adjusted to the shock of its arrival, I noticed that same sound Sirimon had made when cavorting in Ingess's head. In less than a minute it had left a good span of hedge completely devoid of vegetation. What remained was a mere skeleton of branches. I nervously lifted the latch on the bat cage, thinking that their presence might frighten it away. As always they swarmed frantically out and around the garden, but none of them would dare go near the moth. Before I moved from my seat, I saw it consume an entire rose bush, a veritable mile of trailing vine, all of Josette's tiger lilies, and the foliage of an immense weeping willow.

The next morning, the moth having disappeared again, the court gathered in the garden, or I should say where the garden had been. Its destruction was so complete that I could count on my hands the number of leaves still clinging to their branches. There was a certain sadness about the destruction of that special place, but for the time being it was blanketed by a stronger sense of amazement at the enormity of the thing's appetite and its efficiency in satisfying it.

"Do we have a large net?" asked the Chancellor of Waste.

"Why, do you want to be the one to wrestle with it?" asked Pester, holding up his hand for all to see.

"It must be destroyed," said Ringlat, "it's far too dangerous."

"But it is beautiful," said the Illustrious Seventh.

"The garden was beautiful," countered the Bishop. "This thing is evil."

Ingess stepped into the middle of the crowd and turned to look at each of us. "The moth is not to be harmed," he said.

"But it is not righteous," said Ringlat.

"The moth is not to be harmed on pain of death," said Ingess without anger and then turned and strode away toward the palace.

The members of the court said nothing, but each looked at his or her shoes like scolded children. A death threat from Ingess was like an arrow through the heart of Reparata. In that moment, we felt its spirit dissolve.

"Death?" said Chin Mokes when His Royal was out of earshot. He shook his head sadly. The others did the same as they wandered aimlessly away from the missing garden.

I called to Frouch to wait up for me, but to my surprise, she turned and continued on toward the palace.

As we soon learned, the garden was only the beginning. On the next evening it invaded the closets of the southern wing and, moving from room to room, devoured all of the linens and finery of those who resided there. All that remained by way of clothing was the outfits those court members had arrived at Reparata in, which had long ago been stored away in trunks. The next day, I met the Chancellor of Waste at breakfast, and he was wearing the clown outfit that, in his previous life, had been his uniform. The shoes were enormous, the tie too short, the jacket striped and the pants checkered. In a loud voice, he desperately tried to explain and his embarrassment was contagious. It was a disarming sight to see half the royalty of court traipsing about in threadbare attire.

Ingess assigned the royal Accountant to bring gold so that new fashions could be sent for immediately, but when the doors of the counting house were opened, allowing the sunlight access, the moth was startled into flight and brushed past the Accountant. When he was finally able to clear his eyes of the insect's powder and his mind of its resultant depression, he discovered that the creature had a taste for more than just leaves and clothing. A good half of all of that immense trove of gold was gone.

All were skeptical of the story the Accountant told, suspecting him of theft, since he had actually been a pickpocket earlier in his life. A few nights later, though, when the moth returned, more than one witnessed its consumption of jewelry, and Saint-Geedon vouched that it had, in minutes, done away with every place setting of the royal silverware. Ingess had even lost his crown to it, but still, in the face of strident requests that it be exterminated, he refused to relent on his command that it not be harmed.

I went to visit Frouch in her rooms the morning after it dined in our quadrant of the Palace. My own wardrobe had vanished through the night along with just about everything else I owned. When I knocked on the Countess's door I was wearing my old jacket missing an arm and the trousers I had wandered a thousand miles in, whose gaping knee holes made the bottom half of each leg almost superfluous. Putting these things on again was very difficult, and for a moment I considered simply going about in my bathrobe as the healer had.

There was no answer from the Countess, and I was about to leave when I heard something from beyond the door that I at first mistook for the sound of Sirimon. I listened more closely and it came to me that it was Frouch, weeping. In a moment of madness, I opened the door and entered anyway.

"Countess," I called.

"Go away, Flam," she said.

"What's wrong?" I asked, though I already had a good idea. I proceeded down the hallway.

"Don't come in here," she said, but I had to make sure she was all right.

She stood in the middle of her room, wearing the short, revealing dress she had worn ten years earlier when walking the streets of Gile. Her hair was down and unpowdered to show its true mousy brown and gray.

"The dream is finished, Flam," she said, looking up at me with a face that showed every hard moment she had ever lived.

I wanted to comfort her, but I did not know how.

"Countess," I said and took a step forward.

"Countess," she said and laughed in a way that drilled my heart more thoroughly than Sirimon could have.

"Come walk with me," I said. "Let's get some air."

"Get away from me," she said.

Her response angered me greatly. I left her there and went to walk the corridors, talking to myself as if I were Durst. Passing the large oval mirror outside of the library, I caught a glimpse of a fool, jawing away, dressed in my old rags, his hair undone and wild. I knew now what I had looked like years earlier to the inhabitants of those towns I had visited and been evicted from. I needed to get a hold on reality, and so decided to go to the Palace attic and do some dusting. I trudged up the long flight of steps, assuring myself that work was the cure for my woes.

I threw back the door of that hidden sanctuary, and saw instantly that the moth had visited. The creature had cleaned the place out completely, leaving not one candelabra, not the slightest feather from the eagle decoration that had been made for the holidays five years earlier. All of the old objects I had so scrupulously cared for over the years were gone.

"No," I said, and the word echoed out to the far reaches of the empty expanse. Then it struck me that the moth had devoured my very title. The gardens no longer needed bats, the things in the attic did not require dusting, and as for my Monday proclamations, I had been making them long before I ever came to Reparata. At least when I was the High and Mighty of Next Week, the promise of the future always loomed ahead, calling me on. Now, all that was left was the past.

When the moth began devouring the very marble structure of the palace, Ringlat, Chin Mokes and the Chancellor of Waste hatched a conspiracy to do away with it. Many of the others had agreed to help them. As it was put to me when they attempted to conscript me into their plot, "Ingess is not in his right mind. We have to save him again." I was told that Saint-Geedon had been chosen, because of his skills as an assassin, to form a plan to strike the insect down. What was I to do but agree?

I had often wondered what the link was between the professions of hired killer and chef, because Grenis had made the transition from one to the other almost overnight when he chose Reparata as his home. After I watched him create the bomb, though, I no longer had any questions. The outer casing of the device was made from a thick-crusted peasant bread called Latcha, which was a main staple of the farmers in the surrounding countryside. Through a small hole he cut in the top of the loaf, he dug out the dough, leaving it as hollow as a jack-o-lantern. Next came a strange mixture of chemicals and cooking powders, each of which he measured out in exact amounts. To this, he added boxes of nails and pieces of sharp metal. For the finishing touch, he asked Pester to bring him the vanilla.

"What does that do?" I asked.

"For sweetness," he said.

To create the fuse, he pan-fried over a low fire a long piece of string in some of the same ingredients that were used in the main course. When the string had cooled, he inserted the end into the bread, replaced the cap of crust he had cut and then garnished the outside with radishes cut into florets. We gave him a round of applause to which he clicked his heels and nodded sharply.

The moon couldn't have been brighter the night we put our plan into action. It had been decided that we would lay the trap outside the walls of the palace so as not to chance destroying any more of the quickly diminishing structure. Just beyond the gates, there was a deep moat that ran the circumference of Reparata. We crept cautiously out across the drawbridge, which, since there was little threat of invasion in those times, was always left down.

Ten yards off the bridge, and twenty yards to the surrounding tree line, we heaped up a pile of whatever belongings still remained to us. Those who had nothing to give removed curtains from the few rooms that had not been visited yet by the moth. Within this hill of things, we planted the bomb, and then ran the long fuse over to the tree line where we took up positions, hiding in the shadows at the edge of the woods.

There were more than twenty of us in the group. Because I was nervous that Ingess might discover our treachery or that we might fail, I didn't notice that the Countess was among the conspirators until we stood beneath the trees. She had somewhere gotten a set of men's clothing and her hair was tied back.

"Frouch," I whispered, "I didn't know you were part of this."

"I hope that bomb blows the damned bug to tatters, the same way it did to my life," she said. There was an edge to her voice I had never heard before.

I reached out and put my hand on her shoulder, but she shrugged it off and lit a cigarette. I meant to ask her what I had done to make her cross with me, but just then the Philosopher General whispered a duet of, "Behold, the floating hunger."

It flew slowly out past the open gates of Reparata, its wings quietly beating the air. The powder it threw off caught the moonlight and created a misty aura around it. Its antennas twitched at the scent of curtain silk, gown muslin, old shoes, strings of pearls, and the deadly loaf at their center. When it landed with the lightness of a dream feather and began to dine, Saint-Geedon turned to Frouch and nodded. She flicked the ash off her cigarette, puffed it hard three times, and then put the burning end to the tip of the fuse. The tiny spark was away in an instant, eating the treated string faster than even the creature could.

Frouch licked her lips, Ringlat rubbed his hands together, and the Chancellor of Waste wheezed excitedly as that dot of fizzling orange raced toward explosion. When it was exactly halfway to the heap where the moth was busy vanishing an old topcoat, who should appear at the palace gates but Ingess dressed in full battle armor and mounted on Drith, his nag of a war horse. The moment we saw him there, it was obvious he had finally come to his senses and decided to slay the creature as his subjects had begged him. He drew his long sword, pointed it at the moth and then spurred the old horse in the flanks.

As His Royal reached the middle of the drawbridge, the spark reached the loaf. We braced ourselves for apocalypse but all that followed was a miserable little pop, weaker than a champagne cork, and the issuance of a slight stream of smoke. The moth flapped upward in a panic, unharmed, but this sudden motion frightened Drith and he reared to his hind legs, throwing Ingess from his back and into the deep waters of the moat.

The ridiculous course of events left me standing with my mouth open wide. Everyone was stunned by the misadventure.

Then Frouch yelled, "He'll drown in that armor."

She took two steps past me, but I saw that someone else had already begun sprinting toward the moat. It was Durst, and I had never seen his lumpen form move with such speed in all the years I had known him. He did not hesitate at the edge, but awkwardly formed his hands together into an arrowhead in front of him, kicked up his heels in the back, and dove into the water. At the sight of this, we all started running.

I don't know how he found him in the dark at the bottom of that moat, nor do I know how he lifted him to the surface and brought him to the bank. Ringlat and I reached down and pulled His Royal up onto dry land. Pester and Chin Mokes did the same with Durst. In seconds we had Ingess's helmet off, and much to my relief found that he was still faintly breathing.

"He's alive," yelled Ringlat and the assembled company shouted.

Frouch helped us remove the rest of the armor as the others gathered round Durst, patting his head and slapping him on the back. I stole a look at him in the middle of my work and saw that he had lost his spectacles. When I noticed he was no longer bent by the weight of his twin, I had a feeling he would not be needing them.

Whereas the night had brought a miraculous opportunity to the Philosopher General, His Royal had not fared half so well. We freed him of his armor, but no manner of nudging, tapping, or massage could wake him from unconsciousness. My fear that he had been too long underwater without air seemed now to be a fact. Still, we gathered him up and brought him back inside the palace. The structures of the buildings were no longer sound because of the work of the moth, so we carried one of the last remaining beds out into the courtyard and laid him on that. Then we gathered around him like dwarfs around a poisoned princess in a fairy tale and waited with far too much hope than could reasonably be expected.

The other members of the court who were not part of our ill-fated plot now came out of the palace to join us, bringing reports of what little remained in the wake of the moth. Ingess's fortune was now completely gone, the food stores, with the exception of an old pot of moldy cremat, were thoroughly decimated.

"The place is as empty as my heart," said the Illustrious Seventh, who in her ripped tunic from yesteryear was looking none too illustrious.

We stayed in that courtyard through the remainder of the night and the following day, standing around, watching His Royal's every faint breath. From off in the distance came the occasional sounds of some piece of the architecture crumbling and falling with a thunderous crash, having been undermined by the moth's earlier dining. I witnessed with my own eyes the fall of the eastern parapet. It slouched and fell, tons of marble, like a sand castle in the surf.

When the young ones began to complain of hunger there was nothing to give them. None of us had been at Reparata long enough to forget that feeling of utter need. Frouch and some of the others discussed possibilities of where to find food, but nothing came readily to mind. Then Ringlat removed his Bishop's robe, throwing it to the ground. Beneath, he was dressed in the black costume of the highwayman. He borrowed a scarf from one of the ladies and tied it around his face just beneath his eyes.

"Flam," he said. "If I'm not back by nightfall, you will have to think of something else." We watched him run across the courtyard to where Drith stood drinking from a small fountain. With one leap, he went up over the back of the horse and landed in its saddle. Grabbing the reins, he spun the mount to the left, whipped it and gave it his heels. The old nag responded and together they were off like a shot through the gates of Reparata.

The day was as long as any I have ever witnessed. The afternoon dragged on as our expectations of His Royal's recovery grew more faint than his breathing. When things become almost intolerable and some of the very young had begun to cry, the Chancellor of Waste gathered them all together and, borrowing some small objects from the crowd (my pipe, a pocket watch, a knife), he began juggling. Occasionally, he would allow one of the things to hit him on the head before he caught it and sent it back into the cycle. This drew some laughter from the children. For we who were older, the transformation of the Chancellor, himself, from fatuous ass to merry buffoon was marvelous enough to bring a smile in spite of the predicament our king was in. He juggled, acted idiotic, and performed pratfalls for hours, until he finally slumped down onto the ground in exhaustion. The children ran to him and, climbing on his back, used him as a boat while he slept.

"What are we going to do?" Frouch asked as we stood together at twilight, staring down at Ingess, whose condition hadn't changed all day.

I shook my head. "I'm lost," I said.

"We can't stay here any longer," she told me and I wasn't sure by the tone of her voice if she was talking about the entire court or just she and I.

There was no time to question her about this, because just then, Ringlat came charging across the drawbridge on Drith. With one hand he clutched the horse's reins and with the other he held tightly to a bulging cloth gathered up at one end and thrown over his shoulder.

"Dinner," he called as he leaped down from his mount. When he spread the cloth out at our feet, we saw it was filled with all manner of food.

"It seems the lord provides, Bishop," I said to him as everyone crowded around to take something.

"In this case, the lord taketh away. Righteous robbery, Flam," he said. "That road to Enginstan always was a favorite of mine."

"In broad daylight?" I said.

He shrugged, "I wouldn't make a habit of it, but it seems my reputation still lives. When all I demanded was food, they were more than happy to comply. How many do you know who can claim to have been robbed by Ringlat and lived to tell of it? Something to pass down to their grandchildren."

"You're a generous man," I told him as he searched around for where he had dropped his bishop's robe.

There was just enough to eat in that sack to quiet the children and calm the adults. The last crumb of the last loaf was finished just as night settled in. We knew the moth was about, because as soon as it got dark we could hear pieces of the palace coming down. I called for everyone to gather in close to Ingess in case any of the surrounding facade might give way. It was cold and we huddled together on the ground there, a human knot around His Royal. The answer to the question I never got to ask Frouch earlier was answered when she took a place beside me and leaned against my shoulder. I put my arm around her and she closed her eyes.

Some slept but I stared numbly into the dark and listened to the destruction of Reparata. It was just after I was sure I heard the southern colonnade drop into the reflecting pond that Pester stood up.

"It's coming for us," he screamed in a shrill voice, pointing up above with his missing finger.

I looked up at what I at first mistook for the moon, but soon saw was the moth, slowly descending from a great height. The powder was falling toward us, and I roused everyone as quickly as possible so as to have them escape its ill effects. Groggy and scared the company moved quickly back away from Ingess, since it appeared precisely there that the moth would land.

"Will it eat him?" asked Frouch as we looked on in horror, totally powerless to stop it.

"It took Pester's finger with no problem; it devoured solid marble," I said.

The others around us started to yell and wave their arms in an attempt to frighten it away, but the moth, as lovely as a delicate blossom on the breeze, continued in its descent, showering him with its powder. Frouch turned away as it came to rest, laying its body upon the length of Ingess's. A groan went up from the assembled court as it wrapped its wings around him like a pale winding sheet. I watched through tears, expecting at any moment to see the huge insect lift off and leave behind an empty bed. Instead, it gave a long mournful cry and before our eyes, like magic, dissipated into a light fog that continued to hang about the body. Then Ingess roused, filling his lungs with an enormous gasp, and the airy remains of the moth entered him through his mouth and nostrils. He opened his eyes and sat up, and when he finally exhaled, it came as a blast of laughter.

As I approached him, he held his hand out to me, and I could see in his eyes that mischievous look from before the tragedy. He told us that while he was unconscious, he had been with Josette in the garden. She told him to stop grieving or she would never be happy. "We must slough off the cocoon of Reparata," he said.

"That won't be difficult," said Chin Mokes, "there's nothing left."

At this, Ingess laughed again as he had on the day when he bestowed upon me the title of High and Mighty of Next Week. We gathered around him for the last time, penniless, homeless, facing an uncertain future.

The next day, after tearful goodbyes, we left the broken shell of Reparata and scattered out across the countryside like a brood of newborn insects. Without a word between us, Frouch and I decided to travel together. Life on the road was hard, but we had each other to rely on. For no good reason, we made our way to the coast and ended our journey in, of all places, Gile. I became a fisherman on one of the boats and Frouch took a job serving drinks in the tavern. It was a funny thing, but no one ever recognized her from her earlier days. The only one who remembered was the tavern keeper, and he told the customers who asked that she was royalty in disguise.

I had heard that Ingess eventually married again and took up farming. He became famous far and wide for the prodigious nature of his crops and the generous prices at which he sold them. It became known by all of those who might have fallen on hard times that his home was a place of refuge. Although I think of them often, I can not say what became of the rest of the royal court of Reparata. All I know is that years later, when an evil tyrant arose in the north and threatened war on the entire territory, he was found one morning with his throat slit, a gob of spit on his forehead, and smelling strangely of vanilla.

As for that healer, Frouch overheard, at the tavern one evening, a visiting merchant speak of an old man in a bathrobe he had encountered in a drinking establishment in the distant port of Mekshalan. "It seems the old man had arrived with a flea circus that he was sure would cure the Great Pasha's crippling disease of exquisite boredom," said the merchant. "He showed me the circus and I saw nothing but meagre black specks hopping about. When I asked him if he thought they were so entertaining they would lift the great one out of his boredom, he shook his head and said, 'Of course not, but when they get loose in his beard and turban, he'll have plenty to do.' "

In the evenings when I come in off the bay, Frouch is waiting for me at the table by the window of the tavern with plates of food and two glasses of Princess Jang's Tears. As night falls, we head home to our little shack in the dunes, light a fire and lay together, conversing and watching the play of shadows on the ceiling. In those shifting projections, I have had glimpses of Reparata, and Ingess and Josette. An image of the moth also frequently appears there, but the persistent beating of its wings no longer frightens me now that I have learned there are some things in this world that can never be devoured.

WENDY WHEELER

Skin So Green and Fine

Wendy Wheeler teaches fiction writing at the University of Texas. She has published short stories in a variety of anthologies and magazines, including Analog, Aboriginal SF, The Crafters *(Vols. I and II), and* Snow White, Blood Red. *This is the author's first appearance in* The Year's Best Fantasy and Horror.

"Skin So Green and Fine" *takes a classic European fairy tale and transplants it to a sensual New World setting, giving full scope to the erotic tensions inherent in the old story. Wheeler's lush, memorable adult fairy tale is reprinted from* Silver Birch, Blood Moon, *published by Avon Books.*

—T. W.

The day of her wedding to the Snake Man, Bonita made *pastelitos* to be sold on the streets of Santo Domingo just as if it were any other day. But because she was leaving her beloved Papi and the family bakery on Calle El Conde, she made these turnovers very special, with the chicken spicy the way her father liked it, extra raisins, nuts, and peas.

Bonita still had the grit on her fingers from scrubbing the last iron pot when her father got back from sending the boy off with the *pastelito* cart. Papi's curly black hair shone with pomade and many combings. Bonita thought her father in his rented tuxedo was more handsome than ever.

"A joyous day, daughter." Papi's smile was bright, but he wiped the sweat from his lip with a handkerchief that Bonita had laundered, pressed, and scented with citrus cologne the night before.

Who would do for her Papi after she left? wondered Bonita, suddenly a little dizzy now that her adventure had begun. "A lucky marriage indeed," she said dutifully. Now was not the time to be selfish. Her bridegroom's wealth had saved them—the bakery's debts melted like spun sugar, even the business with the Cuban laid to rest. Her Papi was too trusting to deal with men of that nature.

"And who has your heart?" her father said, an old game with them. "Where is your heart, little one?"

Bonita peered into one of his tuxedo pockets. "Is this my heart, Papi?"

He gave a gasp of surprise. "Oh, there is the heart of my favorite daughter!" He hugged Bonita to him. Her cheek rubbed against stiff gabardine. "Had not the rich man asked me for you, I would not have believed you old enough," he said. "Your sisters could not wait to paint their faces and go to the clubs."

As if on cue, Bonita's two older sisters came through the bakery door.

"What are you doing in this kitchen?" scolded Raquella. "Take off that apron, *chica,* and show us the gown your rich bridegroom sent you!" Raquella and Ysabel had themselves only recently married, their father's new prosperity allowing them to find husbands in the *mercado.* Now they were grand señoras, with tall, lacquered hair and shining red nails.

Bonita took one last look at the tiny kitchen. "Remember when Papi bought this place? The funny name painted across the front window? Happily-God-Loves-Me-Bakery-Messenger-of-Happiness."

"A crazy thing, using the name of Our Father like that," said Ysabel. "Just like a Haitian."

There was silence. Raquella narrowed her eyes at Ysabel, who ducked her head and wiped at the countertop.

Bonita's bridegroom was a Haitian, albeit one with a sugarcane plantation somewhere in the Cibao Valley. Although the two races, brown and black, shared the island of Hispaniola, they rarely mixed. This marriage was something of a scandal.

Bonita merely smiled. "But soon you'll have a Haitian for your brother-in-law."

"Yes," Raquella said. "And soon little babies running around! Of whatever color!"

Bonita felt her smile stiffen. "Babies?"

She had resolved to be happy in this marriage. Indeed, the part of her that spent hours gazing out the window of the bakery, wishing for the life of an adventurous woman, that part was happy.

But she had seen her future husband only once, had never touched him. How was she to make babies with this man when she was only a baby herself? For, despite being known as the most beautiful girl on El Conde Street, Bonita had done no more than hold hands with a boy. She had a face like a saint, her sisters told her. Everybody wanted to admire it, but no boys would ever want to kiss it.

As she followed them upstairs, Bonita studied the backsides of her sisters, resplendent in their snug bridesmaid dresses. They waggled before her like two heavy blooms on a fuchsia bush, one red satin and one pink. Raquella and Ysabel were married women now. Did they walk differently? With more . . . experience?

"Raquella, Ysabel," Bonita began. "About the wedding night . . ."

"Ah, the young virgin!" squealed Ysabel. "Wondering about the mysteries of the bedroom, Bonita?"

"Well, I had hoped . . ." said Bonita. "Mama, God bless her soul, is not here to tell me." All three sisters crossed themselves. "The good Father Cristos counsels me to honor my husband's needs. But when I try to imagine it . . ." She made a face.

At the top of the stairs, Ysabel turned to grab Bonita, her neck flushed red. "Your heart is beating, beating faster just thinking about it? *This* is the best part. Afterward you will realize how lucky you are to be innocent!"

Raquella tugged Bonita gently away. "You are right to shudder, little sister," she said. "The bedroom is where the woman's burden weighs the heaviest. When you see for yourself the animal nature of men . . . well, it is a secret all wives share." She looked pointedly in Bonita's bedroom, with its small bed, plain walls, and altar to Saint Theresa. "How like a little nun you have been living."

Ysabel snorted. "That will change!"

"Mother of God, it is one of those places," said Bonita's father when his old sedan creaked to a stop. The cars holding Bonita's sisters and three brothers pulled up alongside them. "This changes everything! No, not for my daughter!"

They had parked before her bridegroom's church, a large building tucked away amidst yucca plants in the Barrio Menor, the Haitian quarter. Colorful images writhed and twined across the stucco walls: candles, crosses, saints, and snakes—snakes wrapped around tree branches, snakes entwined and facing each other, snakes swallowing fruit—all had been painted with more enthusiasm than skill. To the right of the front doors, a cross festooned with plastic flowers stood in what appeared to be a child-sized grave.

"Papi, don't be so quick!" Bonita said, heart sinking despite her resolve. "Surely this can't be a temple of the devil's religion!" All her life, Bonita had heard stories of the Haitian religion—frightening, terrible stories. She pulled again at the gaudy red dress her future husband had sent her. It squeezed her breasts and hips and made her constantly aware of the curves of her body. The white ruffles of the plunging neckline frothed around her face like meringue on a cherry tart.

"Why didn't I ask?" her Papi rubbed at his face, looking years older. "I want a happy marriage for you, not this heathen voodoo. We can break our promise to the rich man, give him back his money. And your sisters' dowries, well, I can fix that, given time."

Through the open car windows, the muffled rhythm of drums flowed across the warm air. God knew what wickedness those people did inside, in the dark.

Bonita closed her eyes and heard Father Cristos's voice telling her again that her pure heart was proof against whatever might come. She'd wondered what he meant; now it made more sense to her.

Then Bonita imagined her father, her family, with all their debts back and new debts added. What did she actually know of voodoo, anyway? Only stories told to frighten children.

"We mustn't be silly, Papi," she said. "This will be a matter for me and my husband. Let us gather my brothers and sisters and go inside."

Two ancient black women in immaculate white cotton dresses led the Arregon family through rooms lit with dozens of candles, heavy with the scent of jasmine and goat and burned feathers. With every step, the music of the drums grew louder. They arrived at a large room swirling with dancing people, more people standing along the walls clapping, all black, many with eyes closed as if in ecstatic prayer. Six drummers bent over brown leather drums. Bonita felt her father's hand tighten on her own. A rope dangled from a hole in the thatch roof to the dusty cement floor.

The floor vibrated with the pounding of the drums, rhythms Bonita could feel deep in her belly. The bodies that whirled around her radiated heat; their blank faces seemed to have no human soul inside them.

A heavyset man appeared before them and waved at the far wall. "Father André has been calling the saints; everything is almost ready." Bonita could see a large shelf crowded with flowers, fruits, bead necklaces, and bottles of rum. Two red wooden chairs sat in front of it. "Please sit before the altar. Your bridegroom, the good monsieur, is preparing himself in the *djévo* and will attend us."

He seemed to notice the apprehension of the Arregon family. "This is your first time at a *houmfor*? We have a very fine temple, and Father

André is a very good *houngan*." He smiled broadly. "He practices only the highest vodoun, only the right-hand magic."

I am the leader in this event, Bonita realized, and led the way to the red chairs and sat in one. Her Papi came to stand behind her, his hand on her shoulder. Father André, a thin, older man in an embroidered cassock, looked over and nodded at them.

Bonita glanced down and saw, touching the toe of her new red shoe, a design in scuffed white-and-black powder. She pulled her foot back and peered closer. Flour and ashes. And beyond, more curls and loops leading right to the altar, where lay the bodies of six headless chickens. Spatters of blood across the floor showed dark as chocolate.

Bonita gulped and looked away, then silently chastised herself. Was she so dainty? How many chickens had she bought at market and plucked herself? Ah, but never in a church, a part of her said.

Then the rhythms of the drums changed. A new group appeared from a side room, carrying several spangled flags. A low moan went up and a path cleared for them through the writhing, shaking dancers.

Another person joined the flag-bearers: a tall man in a brown felt fedora, a long, stylishly cut coat hanging from his broad shoulders, his eyes hidden behind black sunglasses. He followed the marchers with a sinuous grace only slightly marred by the way he dragged his left foot.

The Snake Man. Monsieur Aspic.

Bonita watched her bridegroom approach. He seemed all power and confidence—surely good qualities in a husband. But despite the sweat dripping between her breasts, Bonita shivered.

Monsieur Aspic paused before the other red chair, then turned and sat. Watching him with sidelong glances, Bonita noticed his small ears and almost-bald scalp. The Snake Man's skin was a color between olive and black-brown. And yes, there was a mottled pattern on his cheeks and neck. So the stories were true.

Bonita turned her eyes back to the front.

Monsieur Aspic reached across with a gloved hand to touch her arm. "You honor me with this marriage, *chérie*," he said, leaning close to speak his Haitian-accented Spanish into her ear. "The old ways say to ask the papa. But now, *moi*, I need to ask you. Do you want this thing yourself?" When Bonita hesitated, he added, "Ah, your face is as beautiful and pure as a saint's. *Alors?*"

Blushing from the spicy scent of him, the feel of his breath upon her cheek, Bonita could only say, "Yes."

Father André appeared before them, a white ceramic cup in his hands. Another black man, this one in the dark suit of a civil employee, stood beside him. Father André chanted something in singsong French, then sprinkled scented water on them. Bonita gasped at the cool drops. Father André gave the white cup to an assistant and picked up a lacquered gourd cup. He then took a chicken carcass by its legs and held it upside down over this gourd until blood trickled from the neck hole.

As Father André put the chicken back down, took the gourd cup, and held it high, Bonita began to feel true panic. If he splashed that blood on her, she didn't think she could bear it!

Again the rhythm of the drums changed, faster and more frantic. The priest held the cup out to Monsieur Aspic, who leaned forward and drank a few drops. Another moan went up from the crowd. Horrified, Bonita found herself wondering what the blood tasted like, if it was thick on the tongue. Then the priest held the cup out to Bonita, his old eyes sharp on her face. *She* was to take their sacrament?

A flood of saliva filled Bonita's mouth, and her throat closed. Her soul fluttered in her chest, but Bonita knew her duty. Honor my husband, she told herself. My heart is pure. She leaned forward until the mouth of the cup loomed before her, deep and brown, the blood black inside it with a sour smell of copper. Another smell too—the breath of her husband?

I will be lost, she thought. She jerked her head away.

The old priest just nodded and held the cup up again. Several other worshippers gathered now to sip the blood, many gasping and arching as if in ecstasy. Bonita's eyes stung with tears; then she felt Monsieur Aspic's gloved hand pat her leg comfortingly.

Father André gestured to the government official, who stepped forward. This man spoke to Monsieur Aspic. "I will handle the legalities of this marriage in the eyes of the state and this community. You signify your vows, both legal and spiritual, by the placing of the ring on her finger." Monsieur Aspic took from his breast pocket a gold ring. The official frowned. "Please, sir, remove your gloves for so important a ceremony!"

Monsieur Aspic hesitated, then with a stony expression removed his glove. Over the noise of the drums, Bonita could hear the gasps of her family behind her. She watched, her mind whirling, as Monsieur Aspic reached across her. His hand was large, the fingers long. But the skin . . .

The skin of her bridegroom was covered with dusky green scales.

Monsieur Aspic drove them home himself, the Cadillac sedan heading northwest from the city toward the rich fields of the Cibao Valley. "Why are you wearing that schoolgirl jumper, *jepose?*" he had said to Bonita when she changed for the long trip. "And you a married woman now."

He seemed to be teasing, but he didn't smile much. What am I supposed to wear, she thought, tight red dresses and loose red shoes? "These? These are the clothes of a baker's daughter," she said. He seemed to accept that.

How her father had held her and wept when they left. Bonita watched out the back window as Santo Domingo became nothing more than a distant sprawl of buildings. That is my childhood behind me, she thought. She turned back in her seat and looked at the impassive profile of her husband, still in his hat, glasses, gloves. She tried to think up conversation, but after the early morning at the bakery, the wedding, the food and wine afterward, she couldn't stay awake despite the bumpy road.

Her husband woke her three hours later with a brush of his gloved hand on her cheek.

"It becomes easier each time I drive this journey," he said as she blinked sticky eyes.

"Oh," said Bonita, happy to learn about him. "Because you so rarely go into town?"

Monsieur Aspic stiffened. "*Pas de tout.* I often go into town. Just usually, *moi,* with a chauffeur."

Bonita wondered how she'd offended him. "Then I am impressed with your driving skill," she said. "I never took the lessons to get my license."

He seemed to relax. "Now you can see Bosquet Aspic ahead, which means the 'Aspic Grove.' *Entendu.*" Before them stood a water tower painted blue, many white buildings with orange clay roofs, fences around lush gardens.

"Will someone be there to meet us?" asked Bonita, straining forward.

Monsieur Aspic froze again. "*Non.* My parents, they die many years ago. I have no other family."

Puzzled, Bonita asked, "And no servants either?"

"None." Monsieur Aspic trod harder on the gas pedal, and the sedan jumped quietly forward. "Not anymore." They drove between two gateposts, and the road became smooth and quiet beneath their wheels.

When they pulled up before the huge house, Bonita's heart fell. All over the walls were painted the symbols she'd seen on the temple in the Barrio Menor. And more images: she saw a smiling Saint Patricio, a snake in his hands, and one of Saint Theresa. By far the biggest image was a red-and-orange snake about five meters long with rays of yellow painted around it.

"Such a big snake!" Bonita said.

"That is Lord Djamballah-Wedo, whom we honor in my household," said Monsieur Aspic in a light tone. "His other name is Saint Patricio. He is the lord of fecundity." When Bonita looked quizzical, he added, "The lord of much prosperity and many babies."

"Oh," said Bonita.

Inside, her new home had great expanses of red tile floors and whitewashed stucco walls. Bonita smelled spicy rose perfume and the freshness of well-scrubbed wood. A large tiled fountain stood in the center of the entryway, itself the size of a chapel. Hallways went off to the left and right. Down one of those hallways was her marriage bed.

Quickly, Bonita turned back toward the front door. Two altars were built into the front walls, with jewelry and food laid upon them, fresh flowers, some candies. "Surely someone else tended the house while you were gone?" she asked.

Her husband shook his head. "I honor *Les Invisibles*, so they take care of me. It is the saints I have to thank for my life and sanity." He took off his hat, showing a finely shaped skull. After a moment's hesitation, he took off his gloves also, then his dark glasses, and laid them on a table.

When he turned back to Bonita, she realized she had never seen his eyes before. They were widely set with irises so pale brown as to be gold. Scant lashes, very thin brows, but an intelligent gaze. The snakeskin pattern ended at his jawline.

"I am very tired from the sunlight and the driving, *moi*," Monsieur Aspic told her. "Your rooms are down that hall; mine are down this one. Food and drink are ready for us, and our bathwater is waiting." He stepped close and took her two hands in his. His fingers were hot around hers. "You can stay the night in whichever bed you choose, *ma femme*. I hope it will be mine."

She looked up into those gold eyes, then down at the thin, scaled hands. I should be a wife, she thought, but she imagined those hands touching her. Snake's skin touching her private flesh. She pulled away. "Please, not yet."

"I married you for your generous heart," said the Snake Man, moving away. "And for your saintly beauty. Don't worry, *petite fille*, I won't force you. You must want to be a wife to me. *À bientôt*, then."

Beneath his lids, Bonita thought she saw a glint of pain in the gold eyes.

Though alone, throughout that night Bonita slept fitfully in her huge, luxurious bed. She would awaken, heart beating, sure that someone had caressed her in the dark, but each time it was only the satin sheets and duvet sliding across her skin.

The next morning, she checked the large bedroom closet and found none of her usual cotton jumpers and dresses. Instead, all these clothes were brilliantly colored, silky—and slight. Bonita finally put on a very short green skirt, a tight yellow sweater, and shoes with heels high enough to make her totter.

As she combed and braided her long hair, a strange thing happened. The braids seemed much easier to plait, almost as if other hands helped her. She found it easier to arrange her hair on the crown of her head in a new, elegant style. She looked at herself in the mirror; not the same Bonita at all. Her transformation had already begun.

When she opened her bedroom door, the supper tray with the remains of last night's chicken-and-pea soup was gone. But no note or message from her husband. Had he cleared up? Put her luggage away? Bonita couldn't easily imagine him doing such work.

As she made her way toward what she hoped was the center of the house, she saw a door open onto a back balcony. A table was set with breakfast. With some relief, Bonita went forward to greet Monsieur Aspic. "My husband?" she called, but got no answer. Only one chair here, too. If they indeed had no servants, it was lovely of Monsieur Aspic to cook this meal for her. She soon finished the white cheese omelet and slices of grilled bread.

From her high vantage point, Bonita could see only grazing animals in the nearby pens and the waving cane plants in the distance. No people for miles. So different from the busy shop on Calle El Conde. Then she shook herself. There was a whole plantation to explore! And her husband to find . . .

Bonita wandered throughout the house all that day, never seeing her husband, not even a note to tell her where he was. She thought she found his room—the vodoun drawing on the door looked familiar—but it was locked, and no one answered when she tapped. She tried walking down halls calling the name she'd learned from her marriage license: "Michél? Michél? Are you here?"

She finally gave up the hunt, a little sick at heart. As the youngest of six children, Bonita had never spent a day alone before. If her husband was gone for good, how would she find her way back home? And she had yet to see a telephone. Why, oh, why did such a rich man have no servants?

So Bonita let the large, immaculate house distract her. She could use it to learn about her husband and her circumstance. She avoided the altar with the rum and candies on it because the red, orange, and yellow flowers told her it was for Djamballah-Wedo, the snake god. Once or twice she imagined she heard voices inside a room, only to open the door and find the room empty. Sometimes footsteps seemed to be pacing, just behind her. It felt very lively for an empty house.

And it seemed there was a room here for everything. From the well-stocked pantry and Deepfreeze in the kitchen, Bonita conjectured that she could cook every dish she knew and still have inventory left. She used some rice, beans, and pork to make a *bandera* for lunch. She hoped the smell of cooking food would draw Monsieur Aspic to her, but it was not to be.

Then more investigating. Whenever she came upon them, she studied carefully the many photos of black strangers in prosperous clothes, doing things rich people did. The women in particular seemed sultry, looking at the camera with knowing eyes beneath expensive hats. Was this her future, then?

Finally, as the outdoor light grew dim, Bonita found her way back to the dining room, where a candelabra lit a long walnut table. Savory smells came from a chafing dish, and chopped fresh vegetables filled a large bowl. She walked to the food and stirred the fragrant stew wonderingly. How had Monsieur Aspic managed to cook such a meal without her seeing?

A voice from behind her said, "You've found our dinner, *ma femme*. Shall we sit and eat?"

Monsieur Aspic lounged in a chair, wearing pleated trousers and a pale linen shirt. No sunglasses covered his yellow eyes.

"Where have you been?" Bonita cried before she thought. "You just abandon me all day?" She stopped, aghast. This was not what Father Christos had meant by being a dutiful wife.

Monsieur Aspic merely smiled and shrugged. "I had to sleep extra long, *moi*, to restore my charge. You know this word? It means a special energy. And then I must spend many hours before my altar to feed the saints. They were restless after my time away." He rose and bent down as if to kiss her. Bonita shied away. "I knew that you would be well taken care of," he said. "And you were fine, were you not?"

"Y-yes." Was she being unreasonable? She didn't know how the wife of a rich man filled her days. "But why have you no servants? That's so odd."

Monsieur Aspic turned abruptly to the casserole dish. "They were sent away. You and I can make do by ourselves, with the help of the saints. Ask me no more about it."

"Ask you no more—?" Bonita flopped down on a silk-upholstered dining chair.

"You have too many questions for a new bride, Bonita." He dished up a plate and put it before her. "We must take patience to learn each other. And how did you spend *your* day?"

After a sigh, Bonita picked up her fork. "I—I looked around the house, then found the library and read some, mostly from a collection of essays on science and man." She did not tell him about the book she'd found on vodoun.

"The Montaigne book!" said Monsieur Aspic. He sat to Bonita's left, close enough that she could touch him. "My tutor, Monsieur Henri, had me write my own essays on some of those same subjects."

"Tell me more about your childhood, my husband," said Bonita, half pleased with the married sound of that sentence. And though he wouldn't answer her questions, surely she could glean something from his history.

Monsieur Aspic responded to her efforts, as though her questions were insightful and her comments witty. He became altogether relaxed and engaging, yet smiling seldom. After a while, Bonita almost forgot about his yellow eyes and green scales.

But her husband's eyes traveled often to her smile, to her hands, her shoulders, her chest, her bare legs where the disgraceful skirt didn't cover her properly. A fluttering began in her stomach. "You are very beautiful tonight, *ma femme*," Monsieur Aspic finally said. "It is nice to see you in women's clothing."

"Thank you." Bonita blushed. "These are the clothes you put in my closet for me."

"I did not put them there, but they are for you." Monsieur Aspic put his large hand on her bare knee. His palm was hot. "Bonita, *petite,* you should know. I need you to be a wife to me."

But the wall was up again, at least for Bonita. "If you didn't put the clothes there, then who—?"

"The saints," said her husband. He leaned back in his chair. *"C'est bien,* you need more patience." His voice seemed too casual. "Until tomorrow. Enjoy your dreams." He threw his napkin to the table and left Bonita to find her way to her room alone.

The next morning, Bonita found a tight, aqua-colored dress whose ruffled neckline kept sliding down her shoulders. On the dresser lay silver jewelry inset with turquoise and carnelians. She pulled her hair back and clasped it high, so that waves fell down her back. She chose the lowest heels in her closet because today her quest was outside.

She suspected Monsieur Aspic had a workroom or office in one of the many smaller buildings clustered behind the house. She remembered a set of doors in the west hallway that opened onto a courtyard. After another solitary breakfast and fruitless calling of her husband's name, Bonita hunted for and found the west wing.

She also found an alcove with a beautiful, intricately carved altar as long as her arm. Tiny yellow and pink roses sent up a fresh scent from where they surrounded a graceful statue of Saint Theresa, only half a meter tall. The white marble of her praying hands looked soft as flesh. The marble hair on the statue was pulled back from the face with waves down the shoulders. Bonita's jewelry matched the turquoise beads around the statue's neck.

How charming, thought Bonita, then crossed herself. Saint Theresa was her patron. "Bless me in this marriage," she whispered. "And help me solve its many mysteries."

The courtyard seemed overgrown, with wrought-iron benches and tables. Once through a narrow but tall gate, Bonita turned to look around her. So many buildings, so many twisty paths to take. Where was her husband?

Soon she heard muffled music from behind a fence wall. A short walk brought her to a whitewashed hut with a thatch roof. The walls swarmed with the familiar signs of crosses and snakes, and the blue-painted door stood ajar. From the doorway of the *houmfor* came drumbeats, many rhythms and tones that wove together in a rich texture.

People! Thought Bonita, for surely she heard the work of three dummers at least. Her heart pounding as loudly as the drums, she crept up to the dark doorway. The blackness inside seemed to absorb the light of the candles flickering on the familiar crowded altar. This time she also saw a box of fine Cuban cigars.

But no drummers. The music came from a portable tape player, and the *houmfor* was empty. Then Bonita saw movement on the floor and jumped back, startled. It startled her even more when she recognized him.

It was the Snake Man. His eyes showed only white as he lay belly-down on the dirt floor, flicking his tongue in and out and hissing. He didn't seem to hear Bonita's startled cry. She ran away, shaking, back to the house, ultimately, back to the sensible words in the library.

The book on vodoun, when she finally dared to open it, was a scientific, almost dry, discussion of the Haitian religion. There was indeed a difference, according to the author, between right-hand magic and left-hand magic. Left-hand magic was the stuff of nightmares, those frightening childhood stories she'd heard of curses and zombies. Wasn't the temple in Santo Domingo of the good kind?

To calm herself, Bonita prepared a dinner of spiced chicken in rum that night. At the dinner table, Monsieur Aspic again looked immaculate, even if he did drag his foot a little more. Bonita kept glancing at his face, relieved to see the intelligence that flickered there.

"Wonderful food, *ma femme*," he said. Then, "Bonita," he began in a coaxing voice. "You must learn a little of my religion, of my *société*. Are you still afraid of vodoun?"

"Father Christos says vodoun is wrong," Bonita said shortly. "B-but I will honor your beliefs, for you are my husband."

"Father Christos gives me the sacrament also, and takes my tithes," said Monsieur Aspic. "Has he judged me evil? No, *ma femme*. I honor the saints and ask their help and their good magic in my life. By feeding and calling upon *Les Invisibles*, by letting myself be possessed by the saints, I keep Divine Protection. And another thing." His face looked almost dreamy. "The breath of the saints, when it fills you, it, it—"

"But," Bonita pushed away her plate of chicken. "It's bloody—and blasphemous. And it looks dangerous!"

Monsieur Aspic set his jaw. "It is dangerous. That's why the members of a *société* must be devout, and why the *houngan* leader must be very wise and strong in his spirit."

"Is your *houngan* strong? Is your *société* devout?"

"My *houngan* was my father, and he is dead. My *société* is . . . gone away." Monsieur Aspic bent his head and slumped a little over his meal.

"My husband, I'm sorry." How would she get him to trust her if she challenged him so? "I think maybe I am sharp tonight because I am a little homesick. I—I've never even gone a day before without seeing my Papi. How you must miss your own father."

Monsieur Aspic pushed his chair back. "Maybe my religion can comfort you." He left. Bonita heard a door open and close in a nearby room; then he was back with a small silver pitcher. "This is a *govi*. Because it has held the sacred saints, it has certain power." He filled the *govi* with water and held it out to her.

"Look into it, *ma femme*, and wish to see the face of the person you love most." His golden eyes looked deep into hers.

The silver pitcher felt cool and slick and heavy in her hands. Bonita looked inside it, at the ripples on the surface. Then the water seemed to grow smooth and hard, as if it were a mirror. Bonita saw her father, her beloved Papi, sitting at his place at the yellow kitchen table. He held a cigarette between his thumb and forefinger.

Bonita gasped. "I see him! Papi, oh, Papi!"

The image of her father took a puff of the cigarette, squinted, and gestured toward someone.

"It is your papa's face you see, is it?" asked Monsieur Aspic, back in his chair.

"This is wonderful, my husband. How do you do this?" she said. "No, never mind. I don't want to know." She stood, the *govi* in her arms. "I'm too excited to eat, so please excuse me." Impulsively she leaned toward Monsieur Aspic to hug his neck.

He sat impassively as she put one arm across his broad shoulders. "*Le bon Dieu* give me strength as I wait for a wife to come to me," he said as she left the room.

The next morning, determined to search the other buildings for more clues, Bonita met her husband again. She'd heard a furious bleating and the sound of splashing water. The noise drew her to a cobbled courtyard where Monsieur Aspic, dressed in a damp linen shirt and trousers, wearing a fedora and sunglasses, washed a goat.

The beige nanny gave a twist that almost pulled the rope from Monsieur Aspic's hands. The water hose flopped, soaking his shoulder.

Bonita called out, "Here, my husband, let me help you with her." She took the rope in one hand and with the other began scratching behind the goat's ears.

Monsieur Aspic looked surprised to see Bonita, then picked up a bar of soap and began washing the nanny in earnest. His snakeskin arms showed a sickly olive in the sun. "A good thing you happened by, *ma femme*."

Bonita realized her skirt had ridden up, showing her thigh. "Oh!" she said to distract him. "Now I remember to ask you. What is that beautiful little statue by the courtyard door?"

Monsieur Aspic looked up at her through his dark glasses. "Erzulie. You know her as Saint Theresa. She is the owner of the sweet waters and the teacher of pleasure and happiness."

"Oh. Such a devout saint." Bonita noticed the goat had yellow eyes like her husband's. "What's your pet goat's name?"

"This is not a pet; it has no name."

Bonita ceased the ear scratching. "Then why is it getting bathed?"

"To honor the saints." Monsieur Aspic shook the water from his hands, then walked to the faucet and turned off the hose. "*Merci* for your help. My marshal, he prepared these sacrifices for me. These contrary animals make such a fuss. I hope the saints are pleased with her." Taking the rope from Bonita's hand, he led the goat away. "You may come, too, if you like."

Bonita just looked at him and shook her head. She walked quickly away, but not before she imagined a bleating scream from the direction of the *houmfor*.

That day, Bonita found barns filled with feed and implements. Then she found an odd circle of small, abandoned houses, all with weeds covering their whitewashed foundations and vines overgrowing the orange tile roofs. These mystified her. She knocked on doors and looked in windows to see furniture, books. But no one was home. Why would they just abandon such pleasant, sturdy houses?

Another surprise awaited within the garage. The black sedan they had driven from Santo Domingo was there, along with five other, slightly dusty automobiles. The small red convertible with a black roof seemed to call out to her.

Bonita slid into the driver's seat, a place she'd never before sat at. The red leather upholstery felt warm as human skin. She turned the steering wheel and practiced waving at passersby. "Hello!" she called out. "See my car?"

The garage door in front of her suddenly rumbled up. Monsieur Aspic stood grinning just outside, a set of keys jingling in his hand. He tossed them onto the front seat.

"Drive the car, *petite*," he said.

"I can't drive." Bonita rubbed the wheel and sighed.

"My woman must take care of herself. You'll learn to drive today. *Et voilà*." Monsieur Aspic jumped smoothly over the side of the car, guiding his feet onto the floorboard on the front passenger side. For the first time, Bonita noticed one shoe had a thicker sole.

"I—I don't know," said Bonita. He smelled of soap and cologne.

"Don't fear it. It gets easier once you've started." Monsieur Aspic slid close and reached across her chest, causing Bonita to press back against the seat. "*Tranquilment*, Bonita," he said. "I am just buckling your belt." His muscular thigh pressed against hers. "It will be a wild ride."

At his coaxing, Bonita started the motor, put her feet on two of the three floor pedals, shifted into gear, and they were off, out of the garage and down the driveway. The car jerked and sputtered, but her husband remained calm. A few times he put his green hand over hers to guide the gearshift. Soon they were in fourth gear, speeding down the country road.

"This is fun!" she crowed to the cane fields.

At the dinner that night of fried plantains and pork, Monsieur Aspic promised her the red car for her own once she'd mastered driving. She wanted to ask him about the cluster of abandoned houses, but feared to ruin the happy mood.

After another long look at the neckline of her blouse, her husband finally asked, "Thinking of lessons, *ma femme*, will you come to my room tonight? I want to teach you something else." He smiled a tense smile.

Bonita recalled his strong grip on the wheel, his sturdy thigh next to hers. It gets easier once you've started, she told herself. She opened her mouth to say yes; then his eyes caught the light, reminding her of the golden eyes of the goat. How like the Devil's eyes they looked.

"Can we wait just a little longer, husband?"

"*D'accord.* You must be ready in your heart." His tone was patient, but Bonita saw him look down at his scaly hands as if he hated them.

Monsieur Aspic helped with her lunch preparations the next day, quickly tearing apart a head of cabbage with his clever fingers, attending her instructions closely on how to trim the beef and tenderize it with the edge of a plate.

"*Très bon!*" she called, which made him laugh aloud.

When he began to dice the onions thin at her direction, he stopped, wiping his eyes with his sleeves. "Oh, *ma femme*! What have you done to magic these tears from me?"

"It's just the onions." She laughed. "Everybody knows about onions."

"What about them?" Monsieur Aspic had the stony look again on his face.

"That they, that they—" Now Bonita paused, flour on her hands from breading the meat. "Oh, come. You cooked them in many of the breakfasts you left for me."

Monsieur Aspic sighed. "Once, this room was full of noisy women making delicious things. *Moi*, they chased me off, though sometimes with a treat in my hand." His face looked so lonely as he turned to her. "I tell you, I have not been in this kitchen since we returned. When will you believe what I tell you about the saints, about my religion?"

Bonita ducked her head, unsure. "I—I doubt most boys in the *mercado* know much about kitchens either, what with their mothers and sisters and sweethearts to cook for them. It is a special husband who will learn such skills."

Monsieur Aspic blinked, then grinned. "And a special sweetheart who can teach so well."

Bonita's heart warmed, but she knew she could ask him no more questions that day.

———

In her solitary bath, Bonita would rub soaps and lotions on her body and wonder what it felt like for other hands to touch her all over. Here, maybe. And here. She'd taken to going to bed in her panties, the better for the satin sheets to stroke her. She saw daily in the mirror what fine clothes and leisure hours did to make her look rested and wealthy. And older—almost a woman.

But when it came time each night to say, "Yes, I will be a wife to you," Bonita couldn't do it. Monsieur Aspic had not answered her question about the abandoned houses. He evaded other questions about the fresh flowers in the vases each day, the floors that seemed to sweep themselves, the dust that never gathered.

If he would just show her a little trust, a little faith, maybe she could find the strength to take that long walk to his bedroom. But he didn't. So she put him off for weeks, then a month. With each refusal he grew a little more tense, a little more icily polite.

Then one morning, Bonita was astonished when, breakfasting on her balcony, she saw her husband hacking plants out in the cane fields. She put on the sturdiest of her clothes and went to meet him. He was angry at her offer to help, but finally accepted. "It shames me to do this, for my father raised no field worker," he said. "But this is not a matter the saints can help us with. If we don't bring it in, the cane will rot in the fields. *Entendu*, I thought my life would be different by now."

They traveled the cane fields with massive machetes, hacking off the brown stalks of sugarcane near the ground so new shoots would grow. Monsieur Aspic did this, sweeping from side to side with the knife, his dusty green skin streaked with sweat. Bonita trimmed each stalk of its fronds and stacked them in a flatbed truck. At night they had barely enough energy to bathe and eat.

After three days of this, Bonita surveyed the acres of uncut cane. "How can the two of us finish this in time, husband? Why can't we call in some workers?"

"We cannot," Monsieur Aspic said. "If you had my pride, if you knew the situation, you would know that is impossible."

"Well." This time Bonita didn't accept his evasion. "Pride can kill you if you let it. And if I don't know the situation, it's because you never told me." She turned her back on him and hacked clean another cane stalk. Each leaf she visualized as his forked snake tongue that never told her the truth. That night her exhaustion was even greater.

The next morning, Bonita went to her *govi* and filled it with water. At the image inside, she gasped and almost dropped the pitcher.

Her Papi lay thin and still in a strange bed in a very white room. Lines of pain marked his forehead.

Bonita burst into tears and went to find Monsieur Aspic.

"I cannot see what you see," he told her when she held the *govi* up. "You must tell me why you are crying, *ma femme*. What has happened?"

"My—my Papi," she sobbed. "He is ill, and all I can think of is how much I miss him. How much I miss the bakery. How much—" She put a hand to her face, words gone.

Monsieur Aspic, in work clothes, was headed to the cane fields. "Do you wish to visit them, then?"

She looked at him through wet lashes. "Will you take me?"

Monsieur Aspic shook his head, his jaw set. "I cannot. But if you wish to go so badly, you can drive yourself."

"In the red car? Drive myself?" Bonita's heart jumped into her throat at the thought. But . . . it was for her Papi. "I suppose I could, with a map and many stops to rest."

The next day, Bonita set two leather suitcases and a well-marked map on the front seat of the red car. She smoothed the jacket of her stylish dress. "See you in a week, husband," she said to Monsieur Aspic. They had agreed a week was long enough. When he bent his head to hers, she wrapped her arms around his chest and gave him a hug instead.

"You must come back," he said over the top of her head. "You promised to come back and be my wife."

Three hours was not so long a trip after all. Bonita found a spot to park right in front of the Happiness Bakery, and was gratified to see Esteban loading a cart with *pastelitos*. He raised his eyebrows at the car, then recognized Bonita.

"Bonita? Little *chica*, is that you? My God, girl." He flung open the door of the bakery and shouted, "It's Bonita! The Snake Man has let her come back—and in such a car!"

Between kisses, Bonita inquired, "Where's Papi? Is he sick?"

"He's upstairs, supposed to be resting from the grippe," said Raquella. "Scared us when the doctors put him in the hospital to get fluids into his veins. But he thinks he must run the business or it will fall into ruin."

Ysabel interrupted. "Did you hear about our catering contracts, *chica*? Now we do all the food for weddings, for christenings—"

"Later for that! Papi will be so happy to see her," said Esteban.

When Señor Arregon saw Bonita, tears sprang to his eyes. "Oh, my darling girl!" He hugged her hard. "Are you here for a visit? Is the marriage a happy one?"

"Yes, Papi. But now I am here to make you well and happy. Monsieur Aspic sends his good wishes too."

"Monsieur Aspic?" Raquella laughed. "Don't you call your husband by his Christian name?"

"Christian?" snorted Ysabel. "Not after what we saw in that wedding."

"Your servants must groom you well," said Raquella. "You're looking so sleek and fit."

"Oh, we have no servants," said Bonita shortly, aware for the first time that her sisters envied her.

It turned out her sisters' husbands were too lazy or too arrogant to do any work themselves. The new catering business was for extra income. Bonita was glad to help them make a success of it. She rose early in the morning to cook, stayed up late discussing food presentation. Her father accepted her back as if she'd never left. A flash of her memory stopped her one day: was it Tuesday she was supposed to return? Oh, surely not seven days yet. Her sisters needed her so badly.

But she grew to resent their improper questions. "Does he kiss you with a forked tongue, Bonita?" Ysabel asked one evening as the three of them trimmed sugar roses in the upstairs apartment.

She'd ignored all the other taunts, but today she felt tired. "Monsieur Aspic does not. He respects my wishes."

"Ah, Raquella, this *chica* is still a virgin!" cried Ysabel.

"Oh, you poor girl," cried Raquella. "Six weeks, and he's not forced you or seduced you?"

Ysabel put a hand to her mouth. "Bonita, this one must not like girls. I know! Papi can have the marriage annulled, and we will make this rich man pay us to keep his shameful secret."

"No, we won't," said Bonita. "My husband is kind and wise, and knows magical things."

The sisters exchanged glances. "What kind of magic?" Raquella asked.

Bonita retrieved the *govi* she had packed in her suitcase. Raquella reached out and stroked the metal pitcher. "This is solid silver, I'll bet."

"Whenever I filled this with water, I could see Papi whenever I wanted. Look." Bonita got water from the kitchen tap. As she handed it to Raquella, she looked inside, expecting to see her Papi reading in his bedroom. Instead, the water stiffened, and she saw Monsieur Aspic. "Oh, I see Michél," she cried. There was something terribly wrong, though.

"Let me," said Ysabel. She snatched the *govi*. "I don't see anything in here except my own reflection!"

"Give it back, sister," Bonita said, her voice fierce. "Now."

Ogling her baby sister, Ysabel returned the pitcher. Bonita hugged the *govi* and looked inside.

Monsieur Aspic was dead!

He must be dead; she had never seen him look so thin and still. He lay alone in a large bed, sheets up to his bare chest.

Leaving her sisters to the confectionary, Bonita ran back to her room and began frantically folding and packing her clothes. Her father came upstairs, still in his baker's apron. "Are you leaving tomorrow, Bonita? It seems too early."

"I'm leaving today, Papi." She kept packing. "My husband needs me."

"You know that I will miss you too, don't you?" Her father hugged her shoulders. "And who has your heart? Where is your heart, little one?"

Bonita stopped dead still. "Why, I believe my heart is in a sugarcane plantation in the Cibao Valley," she said. "And pray God it's not too late."

Driving alone for hours in the dark could have frightened Bonita. But she didn't let it. She was more afraid of what she'd find when she returned home. And finally, an hour or two past midnight, she was there. When she opened the heavy door, the house smelled musty and stale. Dirt had blown under the front door, and colored centipedes floated in the entryway fountain.

"Monsieur Aspic?" she called. "My husband? I'm back."

No answer.

Bonita went down the hall to Monsieur Aspic's room and knocked at his door. Did she hear a moan? "Michél? Are you there?" She threw open the doors to a large bedroom with many shuttered windows. Crosses and vodoun paintings filled the walls. Several large designs in flour and ash covered the floor. In a wrought-iron bed against the far wall lay her husband.

She ran to him, aghast.

He was bone-thin and unshaven, his body a field of gray-green scales amidst tangled sheets. "Oh, Michél." She dropped to her knees by the bed. "Your skin is so dry."

"Bonita," Monsieur Aspic said weakly. His eyes opened. "You're back. I thought you had finally had enough of me."

"I'm sorry I'm late," Bonita said, her voice trembling. "I broke my promise to you . . ."

"How could you keep such a promise?" He spoke low. "I wished for too much. Too much . . ."

"Not at all. You are my husband." Bonita stood up and looked around for a water jug. "Any food? What has become of the house and all the helpful spirits?"

"I grew too sad to call on the saints, and they will come only when I honor them." Monsieur Aspic reached out his hand. "Can you bring me water? I drank the last this morning." Bonita found the empty jug and filled it from the bathroom faucet. Her husband gulped down two glassfuls.

"Rest now, husband," she said, "and I will make you soup."

With braised onions and vegetables simmering in the kitchen, Bonita felt the immense emptiness of the house weigh down on her. "Come back, you saints," she called out. "He needs you here."

Her voice just echoed on the air.

She had never believed him before when he talked of magic, of the invisible saints. But now she compared this empty house with the one she had seen ten days ago. Someone, something, was missing now. If she believed that, then what of the rest? The sacrifices. The possession. The . . . ecstasy?

A good wife honored the beliefs of her new household.

Bonita took a haunch of rabbit with her and went out into the dark night to find the *houmfor*. She passed Saint Theresa on the way and shivered at the dry, dead roses.

The paintings on the *houmfor* walls seemed to dance in the candlelight. The open doorway yawned like a dark mouth. Bonita stood on the threshold and felt her skin crawl. "I can't speak French to make you hear me," she said aloud to the darkness within. "But I am here to honor you with this good rabbit—ah, *lapin*—which you can feed on, as is your way." She stepped inside and could smell old candle wax, rum, burned feathers, the scent of washed goat. She lit the candles that still had wicks. "I make this sacrifice in place of my beloved husband." She found a spot on the crowded altar to put the meat. "My husband is ill and needs your help. Please come back. And in return, I will learn to perform the rituals that are permitted an initiate."

The soup was ready when she returned to the kitchen. She filled a bowl, found some fruit and bread, and carried a tray to Monsieur Aspic's room. He sat up so she could feed him. "It is healing food," he said, his voice already stronger. Tears stood in his eyes. "If you wait a moment, I will cover myself to shield your sensibilities."

"Hush and eat," she said. "You're not shocking me." He seemed so frail and young without any clothes. Bonita was able to sit right next to him without trembling.

He ate the rest of the soup himself, and a handful of grapes.

"I can imagine how sticky and uncomfortable you are," said Bonita. She found a basin and some towels and soap. "Pull this down." She tugged at the sheet drawn up to his chest. Beneath, he wore silk briefs. The snakeskin pattern covered all his torso. "Much better," said Bonita. "Who better to tend you than your own wife?"

Monsieur Aspic just set his teeth and avoided her eyes.

She began to sponge him, first on his face and neck, then down to his chest. She held his arms up, the better to wash the curly hair in his armpits. The curve of his biceps struck her as so beautiful she stopped the bathing just to observe him. How long and lean! How fine-boned his face, how full his lips! She began to wash his chest, paying close attention to the flat dark nipples in their nests of hair.

But Monsieur Aspic lay beneath her hands tense and shivering.

"What is it, my husband?" she asked. "Am I hurting you?"

"Only with your kindness," he muttered. Then louder, "You think I don't know what you're thinking? What everybody thinks?"

"And what is that?" Bonita said gently.

"That ugliness is the sign of a diseased soul. You, with your saint's face and generous heart, are proof that beauty inside and beauty outside go together. That is why I hide my skin and my deformity from other people's eyes."

"Deformity?" Bonita then noticed how one bare foot was turned in a little with curled toes. She took the foot in one hand. "This is nothing. And you should meet all the pretty women and handsome men I know who are not worth a *phffft*. *You* have a good soul, Michél. A little too proud, but honorable and generous and willing to sacrifice."

"Hmmm," said Monsieur Aspic, but now finally he began to relax.

"And your skin, my husband, is so fascinating close up." It had a pattern like tiny overlapping feathers, each flake of skin marked with a fine dark edge. It gave the effects of scales. "It is different, but beautiful," Bonita said. Skin so green and fine. She began to kiss it as she washed up the leg now, past the muscular calf with its fine, thick hair, to the knee, the thigh. The skin was warm and soft beneath her lips. Her husband caught his breath and sighed.

Her eyes traveled to that other place at the juncture of his legs, which swelled so round and full beneath the silk. Was this it, then? Was this the secret that married women shared?

At the edge of the mystery, Bonita stopped, trembling, until her husband reached down with surprisingly strong hands, and drew her across his chest. Her face was level with his. His hands were warm against her back.

"Will you stay with me tonight, *ma femme?*" he asked. "Will you be a wife to me?"

As he spoke, his breath filled her mouth, a flavor new yet familiar too. She felt passion ripple through her, possess her thoughts, her heart. She put her lips on his.

The next morning, Bonita awakened to voices and music. She drew the sheet up against the cool morning air on her naked skin. The soreness in her groin made her smile with memories of the night before. Then she heard laughing outside, the slamming of car doors.

The saints had never sounded like this.

Now wide awake, Bonita sat up and looked around. Her husband was gone, but a note on the bedside table said simply, "To work! Love, M."

A chorus of voices sounded just outside the window. Bonita recovered her dress from the floor and opened the shutters. She blinked at the sun, and then again at the sight.

A full dozen cars and trucks were parked around the house. Groups of plainly and cleanly dressed people, most black or mulatto, unloaded boxes, groceries, and suitcases. Six small children ran down the driveway. When her shutters opened, the children called out something in French and waved.

Still wondering, Bonita waved back and closed the shutters.

The bedroom door opened and her husband came in smiling like a bright angel. "*Ma femme,*" he said, enveloping her in an embrace. "You have slept long, and my *société* is already here! Imagine it! Léon, my marshal, says an orange snake spoke from their fire and told them to return. It must have been He. I am so honored."

"Your *société?*" said Bonita. "The other members of your temple?"

"More than that," said her husband, rubbing her arms. "My father's people, and now mine, for I am their *houngan.* I think they grew impatient over my pride." At her quizzical look, he added, "Yes, I was raised and trained as a priest in the right-hand magic. Only I didn't think I was worthy. I became so obsessed with my own ugliness, I didn't have the faith that I could lead these people. They finally left me one day."

"And they abandoned those homes I saw, while you had to do by yourself the work of many?" Now it made sense.

"Pride can kill you if you let it, someone said to me. But I thought if I waited for your heart to tell you to be a wife to me, that would prove my worth." He kissed her again, and she turned in his arms to face him, breast against breast, so that their hearts thudded against each other's chests.

When they left the bedroom an hour later, Bonita made Monsieur Aspic stop at the altar of Saint Theresa. "There were moments in last night's ecstasy when I think I felt her spirit overshadow me. What did you say her other name was?"

Her husband whispered it in her ear, his hand warm on the skin above her heart. "She is Erzulie, the energy of love and the teacher of fulfillment."

Bonita dropped jasmine blooms around the statue, its small marble face so expressive of its full heart. "Send me another lesson tonight, sweet Erzulie," she whispered.

JANE YOLEN

Old Merlin Dancing on the Sands of Time

Jane Yolen has published more than two hundred books of children's fiction, adult fiction, nonfiction, and poetry. She has edited award-winning folklore collections and is the premier writer of modern fairy tales in America today. Her magical novels for adults include Briar Rose; Sister Light, Sister Dark; White Jenna; *and* The One-Armed Queen. *Her most recent poetry collection was* Among Angels, *in collaboration with Nancy Willard. She and her husband have homes in western Massachusetts (where she teaches at Smith College) and St. Andrews, Scotland.*

Yolen portrayed the youth of King Arthur's famous wizard in her "Young Merlin" series of books for children. Now she looks at a different stage of his life in the following poem, written for the Merlin *anthology, edited by Martin H. Greenberg.*

—T. W.

Here on the sands of time, slapping
waters overlapping, his foot
tapping to the waves' length,
strengthening the bonds,
boundaries, sounding boards,
but bored with magic, that tragic
moment of change, he alone remains
unchanged.

Chance was once his favorite game,
gambling with life's odds;
yet oddly counting no cards,
cardinal sins being his suit,
sweet temptations, like hearts,
a heartier hunger than a virgin
verging on her first inter-
course.

He remembers a girl in a tree;
tremendous power surging;
surgeonlike cutting through rock,
then rocketing hanging stones over sea;
seeing a sword slice stone—
astonishing—as if butter
were bettered by the slicing. He
curses

recall, that fall, that autumn,
that tumble of wintry verbs, nouns,
annunciation of endings. Never again
can he gain access to a first wish, a first
wisdom, a first sweetly opening girl,
girdle loosening to let him in,
let him enter that cave he will never
leave.

DENISE LEE

Sailing the Painted Ocean

Denise Lee graduated from the Clarion Writers' Workshop and writes fiction when she isn't working as a technical writer. "Sailing the Painted Ocean" is her fourth published short story. She's sold one novel and is working on a second. Lee is a former editor of Speculations, *a Hugo Award–nominated magazine for science fiction and fantasy writers. She lives in Sunnyvale, California, with two cats and a pair of flamingos named Johnny and Delores.*

Lee says, "When I began writing this story, all I knew was that it would be a 'controlled nightmare' about a ship. That knowledge, and a lifelong fascination with the Titanic *and period costuming, congealed and somehow turned into 'Sailing the Painted Ocean.' The story still surprises me."*

"Sailing the Painted Ocean" was originally published in the June issue of Realms of Fantasy.

—*E. D*

Diastole

I stand on the first-class promenade staring out into the red velvet darkness that surrounds us, the crimson waters that lick, foaming tongues, at our hull.

The stars, all gone.

The sun, no more.

The sky, black-red and faintly luminescent, a horizon forever on the cusp of a dawn that never comes.

And the heat, the stifling, humid heat. The thermometer upon the promenade reads 99 degrees. My navy blue uniform clings like a suit of leeches, and if I close my eyes I can no longer tell where my body begins and ends. I am disembodied, bloated and rising, dissipating like smoke into the sultry air.

We have been lost at sea for nearly three days now.

I am ship's surgeon. Our ship, the R.M.S. *Journey's End*, left London for New York five days ago. On the third day, the frigid Atlantic vanished we know not where; gone, replaced by this nightmare seascape. Not one crewman noted the passing of the normal, the usual, the sane. The skies did not bubble and burn with explosions. German submarines did not threaten us with their torpedoes. A great hurricane did not blow us a thousand leagues off course.

Merely, the sky grew overcast, night fell, and morning never came again.

As if we had sailed, preoccupied, over the edge of the world.

The captain, a taciturn fellow with a drooping, melancholy mustache, informs me that the telegraphist in the Marconi shack has heard nothing for days. His clicks and clatters meet with the profoundest of silences.

By compass, and at our current rate of speed, around twenty knots, we should have reached America by now. With no land in sight, and no stars by which to fix our position, we steam blindly on, fearful that some horrible calamity has struck the world, that some new doomsday weapon has turned the Earth dark and the waters red, as in the time of the Pharaohs.

A plague, born of this present war.

The more religious of the passengers have gathered amidships in the chapel, praying and singing continually, certain that the end has come at last: "And I saw, when he opened the sixth seal, and there was a great earthquake, and the sun became black as sackcloth of hair; and the whole moon became as blood. And the stars of heaven fell upon the earth . . ."

Perhaps they are right. Perhaps it is the Apocalypse come knocking at our door.

Many of the six-hundred-odd passengers not given to prayer, the Lords and Ladies, the ladies and gentlemen, spend their time in the ballroom, stiffly sipping champagne, dancing as though the sun had never left the sky. Bach, Beethoven, the irreverent new Ragtime, the popular tunes of that Cohan fellow can be heard at all hours. The band plays in shifts, by order of the captain.

The passengers of more humble means locked down in steerage either sit wailing in the halls or brawl drunkenly through the common areas, driven half-mad by their fear. Guards have been posted with orders to shoot any rioters attempting passage to the upper decks.

Here on the promenade, no wind tousles my sticky hair. The sea is calm, volcanic glass.

Dark shapes pass beneath us, huge and silent. Smooth. Headless, faceless, tailless. What manner of creature might they be?

They trail us everywhere, hell's version of dolphins. We seem to be in the midst of a great school of them: Krakens, Poseidon's hounds, Jules Verne's fancies, Jonah's imaginations from a bad digestion?

A light tap upon my shoulder. My nurse, a blue-eyed and freckled Irish lass, stands beside me.

"Doctor, we've a new patient in the infirmary, and very sick she is, too." The freckles stand out in dark, huddled clusters upon her paler-than-usual face. The infirmary already overflows with the hysterical and the heat-stricken; we have not slept in nearly forty-eight hours.

"I'll be down presently, Sister." I touch her arm lightly. "You've been a great help." She smiles and is gone.

After a moment, I follow. White-jacketed stewards, aproned stewardesses bearing trays laden with china and gleaming teapots, ladies in feathered hats, men in tail coats and starched shirts swarm around me. "Alexander's Ragtime Band" resonates off the bulwarks. Along the way, in the Grand Salon, I pause in front of a gilt-framed watercolor that I have passed, unnoticed, a thousand times before. Tonight, it becomes distinct, visible. A clipper upon a gray sea, its sails slack, the water still as slate. The eye of a blood-red sun stares dully at the frozen, wakeless ship.

Idle as a painted ship upon a painted ocean . . .

Caught, as we are caught.

My throat gone suddenly dry, I move along.

She lies on a cot in the infirmary, behind a draped white curtain, panting and quite overcome, eyes glittering with fever. She looks to be about twenty years of age. Her companion, a portly matron with a faint scar upon her chin, stands nearby twittering and tightly clasping her hands to her breast. Both wear brown broadcloth travel suits, with high collars buttoned tightly up silver-brooched necks, a style already several years out of fashion.

I crouch beside the girl on the cot. Her golden hair hangs limply to her shoulders. I know what the problem will be before I ask, yet ask anyway. "What seems to be the trouble?"

"Miss Hargrove fainted and had a fit," says the matron. "Oh, you must help her, doctor!"

Hargrove. I know that name, but the Hargrove I recall is a man, a physician.

I listen to Miss Hargrove's chest, hear her heartbeat, strong and regular, metronomic, like a tide.

I stand. "You must get her out of these clothes at once. It's heat prostration."

"Doctor, here? But that's improper!"

"But nothing. If you don't remove her clothing, I will."

The matron gives me a stony stare, but Miss Hargrove laughs, a crystalline, broken, tinkling laugh.

And then in a singsong child's voice, she begins to recite:

> *"The Queen of Hearts*
> *she made some tarts,*
> *all on a summer's day;*
> *the King of Hearts*
> *he stole the tarts,*
> *and took them clean away."*

She smiles at me. "I know where we are."

"She's beside herself! *Do* something at once!" cries the matron.

"It came to me in a dream," continues Miss Hargrove in a conspiratorial, secret-sharing voice, "last night." Something in her eyes holds me to the spot, listening, wondering.

"Here's a riddle, doctor:

> *How many angels on the head of a pin,*
> *how many years in an hour,*
> *how many lives in one heartbeat,*
> *how many fields in one flower?"*

Puzzled, I shake my head slightly.

She smiles again and continues her song. "The Queen of Hearts she made some tarts . . ."

I turn to the matron. "Get those clothes off, then sponge her down. Now!"

Far down the hall, her words follow me like taunting children.

". . . and stole them clean away!"

In my cabin, I lie upon my bunk and try to rest. The porthole is heavily curtained, yet the red-black light invades even the darkest corners of the room. It seeps in, menstrual and suffocating, and stains the cabin walls.

It stains my eyelids; even with closed eyes I cannot block it completely. Red-heavy, the night curls about my face like a cat; I take ragged breaths and strain for sleep. Footfalls and voices, whispering, whispering, echo in the passageway. I rouse myself and creep toward the cabin door, place my ear to the wall.

"That one, she's a loon . . ."

"Such a shame, and what with 'er father being a famous psycho-whatsit, just like that Mr. Fraud . . ."

"I remember 'im—'e was on the last crossin'. 'E's got quite a roving 'and, if you take my meanin' . . ."

Lilting, feminine laughter. The voices fade.

I, too, remember Dr. Hargrove: a habitual smoker of cigars, a dark man, dark as an eclipsed sun. He attracted women like planets, and they orbited him, the wealthy widows, the bored wives, the accommodating stewardesses.

We spoke, on a few occasions, about the weather, the war. He lent me a copy of "Fragments of an Analysis of a Case of Hysteria." And late one evening in the smoking parlor, he applauded Dr. Freud for the abandonment of his latest theory.

"Hysterical Viennese women. They imagine their fathers and uncles in their beds . . . respectable gentlemen, all. Who can believe it?"

"Quite so," I said. "Who, indeed."

The King of Hearts.

And Miss Hargrove, the Queen? Her high-buttoned collar tugs at the edges of my thoughts. Such old-fashioned prudery in one so young.

A trained nurse, if I remember correctly, and her father's assistant.

The corridor is silent.

I return to my bunk. Exhausted, I finally sleep.

And dream, but cannot, when I wake, remember my dream. Something about a child, something I *should* remember.

Out on deck, there is still the heat, the crimson monotony, the silent creatures that follow us through the unending half-night. The only change, a new kind of vegetation that has sprung up in the waters around the *Journey's End*, huge pale leaves that hug the ocean's surface like horizontal sails or a thousand lily pads coalesced into one. They seem harmless enough. Even beautiful: slightly phosphorescent and shape-shifting, flat, otherworldly magnolias afloat upon a red punch sea.

Called by our lack of progress, impotent, yet itching to be of use, the Purser and I lower a big bucket far, far below into the sea. Perhaps, through an analysis of the water, we might discover some new clue as to our whereabouts.

What we pull up fills us with wonder and dread: not red, but slightly golden seawater with one peculiar creature swimming in it, a strange spiral fish half the length of a man's arm. The spiral-fish turns and turns in the bucket, thrashing, corkscrewing about insanely. It has no eyes, no head, no mouth. Turning, turning. Pale as a toadstool.

"What is it?" says the Purser. He pokes it with a finger. The spiral-fish recoils, barely pauses, then resumes its incessant motion.

"One of Carroll's 'slithy toves,' I daresay."

We carry the bucket to the infirmary. I have read of such fauna existing on the floors of the ocean, odd blind things, unearthly and wan, never experiencing the light of the sun. Sea moles. Ocean bats.

But this specimen was discovered near the surface.

I vow to dissect the creature later.

In the infirmary, Miss Alice Hargrove sits quietly upon a cot, clad only in her loosened corset and bloomers; the matron snores on the cot beside her. My Irish nurse's notes indicate that her temperature is now normal. The fever and the heatstroke have passed, but the queerness has not.

She holds a peculiar doll upon her lap. The doll has no head; it wears a blouse, but no petticoats, and is naked from the waist down.

"Hello, doctor," she says, and drops the doll to the floor.

Her small pink tongue flicks out and moves so slowly across parted lips. A finger traces the curve of a breast, while her legs gape wide open. She stares fixedly at my breeches.

My warm face grows warmer, and embarrassment, pity, disgust fill me. I hand her a blanket, looking away.

"Cover yourself, young lady."

"Take off your clothes, cover yourself up . . . Lor', how you carry on."

But she covers herself. And pouts, very prettily. A gentlewoman, with the ways of a common tart. I look at her face, young-old, innocent-used.

An ugly suspicion dawns.

Unthinkable. She is too young.

But I must rule it out, anyway, just to be sure.

With the help of my nurse, I puncture a vein in Miss Hargrove's arm with a shiny hypodermic. Purplish blood spurts into the glass syringe. We release the tourniquet. The deluge ends—

An alarm sounds.

Shouts of "Fire!" and the sound of feet pounding across the decks. But I can smell no smoke.

Outside in the passageway, I catch the arm of a passing crewman, and he stops and flutters there like a kite snagged upon a tree limb.

"What in damnation is happening?"

"Fire, sir, in steerage. I tell you, they've all gone crackers down there. Torched themselves, they have."

I let go his arm, and he gusts off.

Chaos all around, a summer storm of eccentricities. A woman wearing three hats stacked one atop the other skips by, singing softly to herself; a boy with an open trunk beside him throws a pair of stockings, a shirt, a stuffed bear overboard into the sea. Near the rail, an elegantly dressed gentleman calmly scrapes at his hand with a broken champagne glass. Blood oozes from furrows in his palm, soaks into butterfly-and-thundercloud patterns on his once-white cuffs.

"Stop it, man!" I shout.

But he continues engraving his flesh as though he did not hear. I grasp his wrists. He resists, a frown upon his face. We struggle together. Finally I am able to pry the glass from his fingers. He stares at me, surprised, as though he has just wakened from some horrible dream.

"Go to the infirmary now," I say, gently, but with authority. "My nurse will fix you up straight away."

"Yes of course," he mutters, "of course. Thank you." With a befuddled, bovine look in his eye, he makes for the infirmary.

A scream, a woman's scream sounds piercingly along the deck. I whirl. The boy drops a book over the railing. There is no one else in sight. The book hits the water with a tiny splash.

I leave him to his work.

The analysis of Miss Hargrove's blood is complete. As I suspected, the telltale spirochete is there.

The *Treponema pallidum*. The pale turning thread.

An orgy of pale turning threads, a million twisting filaments, a vast infectious web spanning blood, heart, tissues, brain.

They called it lues, "Old Joe," the Pox, "the French Disease."

Tertiary syphilis. A disease of old whores.

Memory loss. Errors in judgment. Seizures.

Madness.

It takes ten to thirty years to bloom, a slow, insidious process.

At first it merely laps at the consciousness, vast and seductive, like a tentative, shy sea. But inevitably the madness comes, a tidal wall of terror, obliterating, annihilating.

Miss Hargrove is only twenty. She exhibits none of the classic symptoms of congenital syphilis: strange, misshapen teeth, blindness, idiocy, among others. She did not, therefore, contract the spirochete during birth.

Beside me, in the bucket on the floor, the spiral-fish turns.

What to do?

Oh, there is the arsenic cure, with its burning fingers, its numbness, its gut-wrenching pains. And its own kind of death.

Wearily, I lay my head upon the table. My heavy eyes close.

And I dream:

A dark man and a bride stand hand in hand at an altar. Mists dance around them. A faint organ pipes sickly music from far, far away.

The bride's small, childish hand trembles. The man grips it tight in his big fist.

Suddenly, I am beside her, in her, looking up into his face, scalded into my memory, a face I've known forever—

Shivering, I open my eyes and am alone in the Grand Salon. I do not remember leaving the infirmary. It is very quiet. For the first time in days, there is no music. The gilt-framed watercolor still hangs on the wall, *but the ship is missing* from its center. A dead, gray-silver sea and a horizon are all that's left, all there is in the entire world.

I wander from deck to deck; no stewards no passengers, no officers, not a soul anywhere. All vanished, perhaps borne away upon the watercolor clipper.

The bridge stands empty, entirely deserted.

Down at the infirmary I search for, but cannot find, my nurse. The patients have disappeared.

Even the matron, gone.

Only Miss Hargrove remains.

I sit at her bedside, her small white hand in mine. Damp gold ringlets, tangled wildly like grapevines, frame her delicate, heart-shaped face. Jade-green eyes, filled with a shimmering, faraway intelligence, stare absently at some mirage that only she can behold.

"Miss Hargrove, what do you see?"

"Why, doctor, don't you know?"

"No, Alice, I don't. Please tell me."

Laughter, untamed and coltlike, ended with a sob. "Me," she whispers, "I see me."

And an odd sensation overtakes me. As if standing between two mirrors, between Alice Hargrove and the mirror of the sea, I feel myself dwindling, repeated to infinity, a man made of glass, dropped suddenly to the floor. Shattered to slivers.

Annihilated.
Other. Alien.
Myself, yet not myself—

The ship lurches, and I nearly lose my footing. My microscope crashes to the deck; a box of glass slides tinkles like wind chimes and shatters into powder beside it.

Shattered, a man made of glass.

And sound, the sound, everywhere, a thrumming louder than a hundred booming cannons. My left ear drips blood down my blue jacket.

Alice Hargrove closes terrified eyes and smiles a tight, small smile.

Through the porthole, a wall of red, a tidal wave higher than the spires of St. Pauls, bears down upon the *Journey's End*. It will reach us any moment.

Miss Hargrove! Is this what we saw in our dreams, the dreams that drove us mad?

We see the face of our father before us. Our throat clots with fear—

Systole

LAURENCE SNYDAL

Grandmother

Laurence Snydal is a retired teacher and practicing musician. He has published thirty-odd poems in such magazines as Blue Unicorn, Caperock, Gulfstream, *and* Columbia. *He is also the author of the advice book for new dads,* The New Father Survival Guide. *He lives in San Jose, California.*

"Grandmother" *is from issue 31 of* Columbia: A Journal of Literature and Art.

—E. D., T. W.

Inside the wolf I touched his liver with my tongue.
I wrapped my fingers all around his heart
And blessed the beat of blood. I lay me down
Between his ribs and let each sighing lung
Massage the ache from these old bones. Apart
From earth, a part of older earth, I'd grown
A snout and such big eyes and teeth so bright
They shone like sunlight. There within the cave
I called my home, I lay within his dream.
I don't remember why she lit the light.
I don't remember who she thought she'd save.
I think about the axe and want to scream.

GARY A. BRAUNBECK

Small Song

Gary A. Braunbeck's stories have appeared in the horror half of this anthology before, but "Small Song" (reprinted from the May issue of The Magazine of Fantasy & Science Fiction) *marks the author's first appearance with a fantasy tale. "Small Song," a meditation on memory and music, was partially inspired by Charles Beaumont's story "Black Country," which, Braunbeck says, "came as close as prose can to capturing music in words."*

Braunbeck was born in Newark, Ohio, in 1960, and currently lives in Columbus. His horror, fantasy, and mystery short stories have appeared in a wide variety of magazines and anthologies, including Twilight Zone, Cemetery Dance, Borderland, Robert Bloch's Psychos, Once Upon a Crime, Danger in D.C., *and* Legends. *His tales have been collected in* Things I Left Behind, *and he has been nominated for the Bram Stoker Award.*

—T. W.

"Whoever is joyous while burning at the stake is not triumphant over pain, but over the fact that there is no pain where he expected it. A parable."   *—FRIEDRICH NIETZSCHE*

M y college roommate once asked, "Do you believe in voices?" It was four-fifteen in the morning and we were both fractured on Jim Beam and joints while cramming for finals. Like so many other bell-bottomed, pot-smoking, self-styled middle-class mystics of the 1970s, we'd read too much Gibran and Sri Chinmoy

Ghose and the Avatar Meher-Baba and enjoyed nothing more than es-
pousing our quasi-quantum rigmarole to prove how clever and enlightened we were.

"What was that again?"

"Do you believe in voices? Then where are they located? Are they
physical things?"

"Wonderful. Three drinks and a couple of tokes and you go Zen on
me."

He leaned back into a cloud of Hawaiian Seedless smoke and
grinned. "C'mon, man, you're the brainiac majoring in physics, you
gotta have some idea where I'm coming from. I mean, you ever think
about this shit for too long? You ask yourself questions, right? Like . . .
okay, here you go: Does Beethoven's Fifth Symphony cease to exist
once the orchestra stops playing, or is it just some fuckin' ink trails on
sheets of parchment paper in a library somewhere? Like, if you destroy
the paper it's written on so no orchestra can ever play it again, does it
still continue to exist?" He shuddered and reached for the bottle. "Questions, man. They'll mess with your head."

He OD'd a few years later and wound up part of the vegetable stew
in some laughing academy but I still think of him the way he used
to be.

I think a lot about the way things used to be.

Do you believe in voices?

Listen to my life.

I did not recognize my daughter when she came back from the dead.

It was the end of spring, I was fighting a losing battle with the
sinus/ear infection that always came round this time of year, and since
it was going to rain soon I decided to take a shortcut through the ersatz-
park behind the Altman Museum in downtown Cedar Hill. I'd forgotten
to bring my decongestants and ear-drops that morning and by ten-thirty
felt as if someone had drilled a hole in my skull and filled it with rubber
cement. I lived only twelve minutes' walk from a crummy $5.25 an-
hour job, which gave me just enough time to stagger home during my
lunch break, hit the drugs, scarf down a sandwich, and get back.

Though I often took this shortcut I made it a point never to linger;
too many memories waited there, ready to jump down my throat. Aside
from the sixty or so seconds it took to sprint through the park, I hadn't
spent any significant amount of time there in over five years, not since
the death of my three-year-old daughter from—unbelievable as it
sounds—mononucleosis.

I was nearing the south exit when I made the first of three mistakes—I noticed the new sculpture that stood near the corner of the plat.

The second mistake immediately followed.

I stopped to look at it.

It stood about seven feet high, ten feet wide, and six feet deep. The figures were made of synthetic stone and fiberglass covered with wire mesh, colored in tones of terracotta and ash. There were fifty female figures in the piece. All of them were naked. Some covered their faces with their hands, some knelt, some stood, a few were lying prone as if draped over a sacrificial altar, while others clutched their stomachs or were folded in a heap. Most of them were screaming. Pain, anger, grief, confusion—all of these were brutally etched on their faces, raw and unspeakably ugly.

But none was more gut-wrenching than the face of the woman in the center. Hers was a look of sadness so total that at first it seemed like disinterest; then I saw the small crescent of tears brimming in one of her eyes and realized the permanence of her heartbreak, that here was a genuinely good and caring woman, full of passion, understanding, and tenderness, who had dreamed in her youthful loneliness of finding her soulmate and then, years later, just when she'd started to believe she would never know the love that poets and singers described, found her One Great True Love and gave her soul completely to him, bore him a child, and in the instant when her husband stood with their daughter cradled in his arms this woman believed with all her delicate heart that everything was going to be just fine.

This had been Karen's favorite spot in the city, and we'd often brought Melissa here; she loved to sit and watch the ducks and swans. Our favorite spot outside the city had been the beach at Buckeye Lake. Karen and Melissa liked to go there and look for sea shells. Of all the shells they had collected over the years, Melissa's favorites were a pair of large, perfect, shiny conch shells. Whenever we took a trip, those shells had to accompany us. Melissa bestowed more affection on those shells than most children did their pets. They had been on the table next to her hospital bed the night she died.

"It is something to see, isn't it?" came a voice.

She was sitting on a bench near the small pond where the ducks and swans lounged in the water. Something about her reminded me of my ex-wife, no big surprise—every woman reminded me of Karen in one way or another.

"Yes," I said, not wanting to look at it again but doing so anyway. "It's very . . . powerful."

I don't know why I made this third mistake, striking up a conversation with this young woman. I'd only wanted to get home. My head was a blister ready to burst and the thought of my medication was a sweet siren's melody.

"Are you feeling all right?"

Startled, I looked away from the sculpture. When had she come up next to me? Why was I down on one knee? Who'd lodged the icepick in my eardrum?

She helped me to my feet and guided me over to the bench. Sitting next to me, she leaned in to take a closer look at my face. "Don't take this the wrong way, but you look like hell."

"Good. I'd hate to feel this lousy and have it be just my little secret."

She laughed, patting my hand. "Great line. Lou Grant on *The Mary Tyler Moore Show*. I'll bet you used to watch it all the time. You seem the type."

"Look, I appreciate your giving me a . . . a h-hand like this but I think I'd better get home and—"

"Shhh," she whispered, placing a finger against my lips. " 'You will say nothing. I will answer not a word / And nothing will be able to shake our accord.' "

"Uh-huh. And that is . . . ?"

"From a poem by Corbiere. 'Rhapsody of the Deaf Man.' You suddenly reminded me of it. A little bitter and angry, a little sad and distant, but also strong and mysterious and sensual in a . . . I don't know, a smoldering, tipsy kind of way. Does that make sense?" She shrugged. "It doesn't have to make sense to you, just to me."

I did not, repeat *not*, want this. I'd spent a lot of time, effort, and liver tissue in order to vanish from my old life and make myself as invisible to the world as a person could be without actually disintegrating into thin air; the last goddamn thing I needed was for someone to say, *Hey, wanna be friends?*

The pain and pressure came howling forward again. I winced, closing my eyes and pulling inward.

She cupped my head in her hands. "Does it hurt that much?"

". . . godyeah . . ." I didn't have the strength to pull away.

Her hands slipped upward, covering my ears and gently tilting back my head. "Better?"

"A little." I opened my eyes. "What are you, a nurse or something?"

"Or something." She reached into the canvas bag next to her and pulled out a small portable compact disc player, along with a set of headphones that she plugged into the player, then tried to put over my ears.

"Whoa," I said. "What . . . what do you think you're doing?"

"You'll see."

"Look, I can't put those on, the pressure's bad enough as it is and if—"

In a series of movements so quick and smooth they might as well have been one motion, she leaned forward, kissed me on the cheek in an intensely affectionate way, and slipped the headphones over my ears.

Listen: I was ten years old when I got my first rock album, a 1971 release from Dunhill Records, *Steppenwolf Live.* I played it to death but no track did I play more than the six-minute version of "Born To Be Wild" that closed side four. (Forget the anemic studio version that FM stations play during Friday rush hour; the '71 live recording kicks ass in a way the studio version can only admire from the cheap seats.) I played that song so much the grooves in the record began to wear down and little scratches, pops, and hisses—noises I came to think of as "echofuzz"—worked their way into the music. Still, I played it, and after a while the echofuzz became part of the song for me. *I'd* put it there, it came from me, and so, to my mind, that made me part of the song, slamming my bad ass onto the seat of a chrome-roaring hog under heavy metal thunder.

And now I was listening to it again. This was not the clean, re-mastered CD version, this was from the record, *my* record, the one I'd lost fifteen, twenty years ago: there was the hiss that almost drowned out John Kay's growling vocals at one point, followed by a series of pops in the middle of an instrumental passage, then, near the end of the song, the scratches that underscored a wailing guitar run, the kind of high-pitched, squealing, uncoiling-barbed-wire run that has to be surgically removed from your brain. I was so amazed to be hearing it again after all these years that it took a few moments to realize the pressure in my ears was gone and my sinuses were clear and open, enabling me to breathe freely.

The song came to its snarling-hurricane conclusion and I removed the headphones. "Where in God's name did you find this?"

"So it did help? You really feel better?"

"Yeah."

Most men could have swum a hundred raging rivers on the memory of the smile she offered to me, which was suddenly so much like Karen's I couldn't look.

"Why did you kiss me?"

She blushed. "I wanted to. I've wanted to for a long time, ever since . . ."

"Since what?"

She handed a small photograph to me. "Since this night."

I looked at the photo. Something pulled tight in my chest, frayed apart, and snaked like tendrils of black, searing smoke into my eyes. I pressed my hand against my mouth as if I could stop the tears through sheer force of will; if I did not allow air to pass into my lungs, I would not cry. I'd rather have had a fatal aneurysm at that moment than allow this particular memory to resurface.

"Who the *fuck* are you?" I said through clenched teeth.

Her face became a placid mask . . . except for a small crescent of tears brimming in one of her eyes. "Don't you recognize me?" She reached over and brushed the back of my hand with her fingertips.

Something like an electric shock snarled up my arm and—

—and there I was on that last night with Karen. She was crying and shaking beside me in bed, just like every night since we'd buried Melissa five weeks ago. I stared at the ceiling, feeling nothing; not for her, myself, not even, it seemed, for the loss of our little girl because all children would eventually be crushed under the weight of a future that was merciless and uncaring if not actively malignant, and when at last I looked at Karen I felt embarrassed at being human because we truly believed we could heal most forms of hurt by telling someone that we loved them, and then Karen was facing me, her eyes empty and furious at the same time: "I dreamed that when we buried Melissa, one of her arms came up out of the dirt holding a rose in its hand. You gave me a shovel and I threw down more dirt but her arm just kept coming up, and every time the rose bloomed a little more. You said, 'We can't let that happen, we can't let it bloom; and the next time her arm came up you beat it with the shovel, then you made me beat it until it slunk down into the dirt and never came up again. We both felt so happy *then, and I hated you for that! I don't want her to be dead, I want her alive so maybe we can pull ourselves out of the open grave our life has been since then—don't look at me like that, you know it's true, but you've done nothing, said nothing, you probably don't even feel anything and I can't stand it, I don't want to hate you so please, please just . . . touch me, even if you don't mean it . . ."*

I yanked back my hand, then shoved myself off the bench and started backing away from her, still clutching the photo.

". . . I don't know how you got this," I croaked, "but you have *no right*, damn you . . . you have no right to . . . to . . . *ohgod* I don't want to think about this . . ."

"You have to," she whispered, slowly rising to her feet and coming toward me.

". . . no . . ."

She stopped moving and held up her hands, palms out. "I won't come any closer, I promise. I didn't mean to throw that at you so soon but I . . . I don't have a lot of time—and neither do you."

"Is that some kind of threat?"

She shook her head. "No. It's just that you've been trying so hard to forget and it's killing you. It will kill you. If you keep going like you have been you won't last another year." She lowered her head, folded her hands, and began tapping the tops of her thumbs together. Karen used to do the same thing whenever she felt anxious. "How many times in the last six months have you thought about suicide? How many times have you looked at your prescriptions and thought about quadrupling the doses? Christ, you have to take three different antidepressants just to get yourself started in the morning!"

"Please don't look at me like that."

"Then get to the punch line."

"Fine. If you go on living—scratch that—if you go on *existing* as you have been, you're going to do it. You'll miss a couple of doses and sink into one of your moods, and then you'll open the door to the cabinet underneath your sink, you'll take out that bottle of Chivas Regal you've got hidden back there—you remember that bottle, the one your AA sponsor doesn't know about—and you'll wash down the rest of your pills with it."

I couldn't think of anything to say.

How in hell did she know about the scotch? I hadn't even broken the seal around the cap yet.

The doctors had made it clear enough—if I started drinking again, I would die. It was that simple. I had no intention of ever starting again; it was just that, for some reason, knowing there was liquor nearby made it easier *not* to drink.

She wiped her eyes, then stood hugging herself. "I was allowed one day, *one day* from the future I never had, to see you again. I used half of that day three years ago—if you think hard enough, you'll remember seeing me. I spent hours looking for you that day. I—" She shook her head angrily, took a deep breath, and looked at her watch. "I've been waiting here since eight this morning, hoping you'd come by. Four hours and fifteen minutes gone."

She was crazy, that had to be it, and I said as much.

"Then explain the picture."

Not daring to look at it again, I held the photograph up to her face and crumpled it into a ball.

"You go to hell, lady." Then I turned and walked quickly away from her.

"I can't follow you!" she cried out. "I can only—please stop! *Please!*" Her cheeks shone with tears. There was not one part of her that wasn't shaking. "I'm sorry, but I can't . . . I've got less than eight hours left."

I decided to play along with her. "Why can't you follow me?"

She held out one of her hands. In it was a small rosebud. "It's going to bloom very soon, you see, probably before the day's over, and when it blooms I'll have to . . . please don't go. I can't follow you because you're going to places I never went. This park is the only place left from your past that you ever go to. Please don't leave. Please. There's so little time left and I want it to count for something. I've mi—"

"Then stay here. Look at the statue, get soaked in the rain and wait for your rose to bloom, I don't care, just leave me alone—which shouldn't be too difficult because I won't be coming back here again."

Something behind her eyes crumbled.

And that's how I left her.

I got back to my apartment, took my decongestants, and ate a little something. I would not think about her or the photograph or anything she said. I would not. Would. Not.

Because of being delayed in the park I didn't have time to make it back to work on foot—but there was just enough time to catch the #19 bus at the corner.

I arrived with a minute or so to spare, just in time to see the Operation Mainstream van drop off one of its handicapped passengers, a young man in an electronic wheelchair who was balancing a small briefcase in his lap.

I watched as he moved his chair onto the hydraulic platform. The van's driver pressed a button on the control board and the platform hissed, then buzzed as it slowly lowered the young man toward the ground. It sounded exactly like the mechanism that had lowered Melissa's coffin into its grave.

Even after the man disembarked and the platform had folded back into place, I could still hear its buzzing. The van pulled away, the young man moved a small lever on the arm of his chair and began rolling in the opposite direction . . . and the buzzing persisted like the white static noise of a snowy television screen. Thinking it was just the infection kicking into a higher gear, I pulled my nose spray from my pocket and pumped a shot up each nostril.

No good.

The static was still in my ears. It quickly rose in pitch and volume to become a physical weight on my skull, and as the #19 arrived I stumbled around, pressing a finger into each ear, trying to create a vacuum to relieve the pressure, but nothing seemed to help. I must have looked absurd or, worse, stoned, because the bus driver took one look at me, closed the doors, and drove away.

I shook my head a few times, violently, then pulled my fingers from my ears—the static was not gone, but the weight of it was.

There were so many sounds—scratch that—there were so many *impressions* of sound. That's the only way I can describe it. And though none of the impressions were those of voices, they were nonetheless talking.

Some of these communicating impressions were so quiet they seemed barely to exist at all. I almost smiled then, thinking of Dr. Seuss's *Horton Hears a Who*—Melissa's favorite story. I'd read it to her every night, even on her last.

One of the impressions called for my attention, even though no actual words were spoken.

I looked toward the man in the wheelchair.

It *couldn't* have been him because his only means of communicating with the world was through the small personal computer—what I had thought to be a briefcase—fitted to his chair. The computer employed a program that allowed him to select words from a series of menus on the screen by pressing a switch near his left thumb. This program could also be controlled by head or eye movement, enabling him to select up to fifteen words a minute, then "speak" by sending those words to a speech synthesizer that had been added to the computer only this morning.

I had never seen this man before.

I knew all of this because the cells in his dying body and the integrated circuitry of the computer were talking to the synthesizer in the same clinical, matter-of-fact tone that a physician might use when dictating notes for a patient's medical records.

I clearly heard them.

But I was hearing the impossible; a conversation between mathematical equations, electronic impulses, and myriad physiological mechanisms, all of whom had agreed to conduct their little mixer at the same specific neuron receptor site.

As the man maneuvered his chair around the corner and the conversation grew fainter, a single thought, irrational though it was, came to me: *Her.*

She did this.

Somehow that girl in the park was responsible.

Sound, I thought. *This is all connected to sound.*

Or the impressions *caused by its absence.*

The Vedic religious traditions believe in the "vibration metaphor": throw a pebble in a pond, and the vibrations ripple outward in concentric circles; strike a bell, and it vibrates in waves of sound; meditate on a thought, and it will echo through the realm of the collective unconscious.

But what pebble, what bell, what thought, was now sending ripples through the world I knew?

The first few spattering drops of rain started coming down. I buttoned my coat and turned up the collar, my hands shaking—

My hand.

I remembered the electric shock I'd felt when she touched me earlier.

That was when she had done it.

I held my hand in front of my face and looked at it.

Something about standing like this, bundled up and shuddering with my hand in front of my face, triggered a memory of another time, two, maybe three years ago . . .

. . . *I was sickeningly drunk, wandering near the Cedar Street bridge. It was snowing heavily, high winds, blowing and drifting, blizzard conditions. I was trying to remember why I had come this way when I suddenly found myself calf-deep in snow. It grew very dark; the darkness the blind know. The cold penetrated to the marrow of my bones. I pulled myself out of the snow and stumbled forward, though I couldn't see a thing. My feet were heavy lumps of ice in my cheap canvas shoes. My body turned numb with cold, making me aware not only of the embodied side of life where everything was black darkness, bitter cold, and churning snow but—so close it seemed I could step right into it—also of the unembodied side of life. Colors that transcended color. Sensations that transcended sentience. Sounds that transcended sound. I was freezing to death.*

I saw beings emerge from the swirling snow and pelting ice. One of them moved toward me. She smiled. She held a cold rose. I thought she was Death and asked her to take me. She gestured to me follow. I groped my way down the snowy embankment and followed her under the bridge. She was gone, but in her place was a large cardboard packing box with wrapping paper inside. Slowly, clumsily, I got into the box and pulled the wrapping paper around me. Then I wept, for something about her had moved me in a way I hadn't known since the days when I'd had a family . . .

Now, standing in the rain near the bus stop, I thought of what the young woman had said.

. . . If you think hard enough, you'll remember seeing me . . .

I shoved my hands into my pockets and started back toward the park.

Along the way I passed several people; some were on foot, others were in cars, but I was aware of the depths of their existence as strongly as I was aware of my own breathing.

And I heard things.

I saw an old woman and heard the first time she had made love to her husband.

I heard a child's fear of its first day at preschool.

A bird's irritation at the rain.

The quenching of a garden's thirst.

I broke into a run. The spattering of rain became a heavy sprinkling. I heard the empty spaces between the raindrops.

She was still there when I arrived. I went up to her and grabbed her by the shoulders. *"What did you do to me?"*

"I had to make you come back."

"Why? What do you want?"

Her lower lip quivered. "I want you to remember." She handed the photograph to me once again. It was smooth and perfect, as if I'd never crumpled it.

"You're dying inside," she said. "I don't want you to hurt anymore. You're not the monster you think you are. People make mistakes. It's time you understood that it's okay to just pay the fine and go home."

"I don't want to think about it," I said, dropping onto the bench. "I don't . . ."

But I couldn't stop the memory coming back, nor could I stop myself from looking down at the face of the man I used to be and thinking: *You stupid fucker.*

There was a time when you had the world by the balls, didn't you? Acing your finals and graduating in the top five percent of your class, snagging a great teaching position at an oh-so-private Ivy League school, then marrying a beautiful woman who loved you and gave you a perfect daughter who thought you were the bestest thing in the whole great big wide world *I love Daddy thiiiiiiiiiiiiiiiiiis much!* You were so safe and smug within the myopic borders of your world, and you never once gave a thought to being undone by an absurdity, did you? Because that's what it was, an absolute, certified, in-goddamn-comprehensible absurdity that in this country, in this age, with so much wondrous medical technology there for the paying, that a happy, radiant, inquisitive little girl with a giggle that brought tears to your eyes could die from a disease you're supposed to get from kissing or burning your candle at both ends. Well, I got a Muppet News Flash for you, pal; it is possible for a three-year-old girl who loves to watch ducks and collect sea shells to feel bad, and then a bit worse, and then a whole helluva lot worse, and finally lousy in a way that requires machines and tubes and pills and catheters and before you know it you're sitting in the front pew at good ol' St. Francis de Sales Church on Granville Street along with your wife and parents and in-laws and X-amount of your balding school-boy chums listening to some second-rate organist eviscerate Bach's "Sheep May Safely Graze" and dreading the moment when two dozen children from your daughter's preschool are going to stand up and sing "Let There Be Peace on Earth" because *that's* when you're going to lose it and lose it bad and wonder how but mostly why something like this could happen. Just forget it, pal, just scratch that "why" business right off the list because there's no making sense of some shit, and your nice manners and fine credit record and good insurance notwithstanding, it is possible—and you have a crisp, clean copy of Autopsy #A72–196 to remind you in case you forget—for a three-year-old girl to contract Epstein-Barr virus and have her immune system degrade so quickly that she acquires, in spite of your fine house and dazzling grin and that award-winning thesis on Heisenberg's Uncertainty Principle, a thing called *acute interstitial pneumonia*, then another thing called *purulent exudate*, which gets lonely in a hurry and so invites *pelvic venous plexis* to come join the party and presto-change-o!—you're looking at a little girl who in less than four weeks curls up into a wheezing skeleton and turns yellow and finally dies in a torturous series of sputtering little agonies, and you can't even get to her bedside to hold her hand because of the tubes and wires and bandages and all the rest of the *Close En-counters of the Third-fucking-Kind* hardware dwarfing this room where all the numbers are zero and all the lines are flat, so when she dies it is without the final benefit of a warm, loving human touch tingling on her skin to let her know that you will always love her and will miss her every second of every hour of every day for the rest of your life.

It is also possible for that little girl's daddy to collapse in on himself and ignore his wife's grief until she can't take the loneliness any-more and leaves him to wallow in the wreckage that was once their marriage, and when he finally lifts his head he finds himself alone, al-coholic, and unemployed. He also discovers that his insurance has been bled dry, so he has to sell his car, then his stocks, and then his house in order to pay off medical and funeral expenses.

It is likewise possible that, having nowhere to go, he will hock his wedding ring, spend the money on liquor, and try to drink himself to death.

He will come very close to succeeding.

Then one morning he awakens in the psych ward of the county hospital where he's been drying out since a couple of cops found him unconscious in a large cardboard box beneath a bridge, lying in a puddle of his own puke and just half a mile from the gates to the graveyard where his little girl is buried. A social worker helps him to find a job and a place to stay so that, if anyone cares to ask, he can say that he's a janitor—give him a mop and a bucket and a bottle of Windex, he's hell on wheels—and that he lives in a two-room apartment just twelve minutes' walk from the office building where he sweeps floors and scrubs toilets for nine hours a day, five days a week.

Lastly, though, and here's the real kicker, it is quite possible that on his way home from his crummy job one day he will meet a young woman who looks too much like his ex-wife, and this woman will show him a picture that in no way, by no stretch of his alcohol-damaged imagination, could possibly exist.

"Do you remember it now, that moment in the picture?"

I nodded my head; a stray tear flung itself down onto the photograph like a suicide plummeting toward the pavement.

"Good," she whispered. "Because that moment is when your small song revealed itself to you."

". . . my what . . . ?"

"The voice of your soul. You *do* believe in voices, don't you? The voice of your soul holds your history, all your memories and hopes and dreams, your baser impulses and higher aspirations; it's what truly defines you. And when it reveals itself to you, as yours did, it will tell you the purpose of your life, the reason why you exist.

"It's different with every person. A dancer's small song might reveal itself to them at the moment a strenuous, complicated piece of choreography they've been struggling with suddenly becomes as effortlessly liquid as cascading water. The man in the wheelchair, his small song is still looking for its voice—that's what you heard; a child trying to learn a new language."

I started to speak but she placed her finger against my lips and shook her head. "Shhh. 'You will say nothing . . . nothing will be able to shake our accord.' " She tilted back her head, caught a few raindrops on her tongue, then said, "Years ago there was a concert on PBS commemorating Aaron Copland's seventy-fifth birthday. Leonard Bernstein conducted and he was really *on* that night. The concert closed with *A Lincoln Portrait* and the second the piece was over, that phenomenal crescendo still ringing in the air, Bernstein dropped his head and wept like a baby. That was when his small song revealed itself to him. He'd hit his pinnacle and everything had fallen into place in a wondrous way that only he and no one else could have brought about—he knew it, you could see it in his face. Later, someone asked him why he'd wept and he said, 'This piece will never again be played as gloriously as it was tonight. I thank God I was the one to conduct.'

"It's that way with all small songs; only one time in a life will conditions be right for it to reveal itself and once that's happened, it never speaks again. Think of the song a swan can sing only at the moment of its death." She touched my cheek, then faced the pond. "I always liked watching the swans more than the ducks."

And I knew. I think it's possible I had known all along.

I looked at the picture in my hand.

An overhead view. A man kneels on a hospital bed amidst the debris of tubes and hoses and electronic monitoring wires. He clutches what looks like an empty white laundry sack to his chest, only the sack has strawberry-blonde hair. On the floor next to the bed is an expensive piece of medical equipment that is sparking and smoldering because he knocked it out of his way in order to climb onto the bed and get to the sack before it was too late.

You know from the look on his face that he didn't make it.

It's hard to tell if he's crying or snarling . . . until you see the shadow of something like love buried deep in the dark wreckage of his face. He has no thought for his wife, who even now lies sleeping on a couch in the nurse's lounge, having been forced by him to rest for a bit.

The photo captures a phenomenon you've heard about many times before from people who claim to have had an out-of-body experience.

This was the last earthly image seen by my three-year-old daughter as her soul left her body at the moment of her death.

"Where are the conch shells?" I said. "They were right here, on the table beside the bed. I remember that they were there but . . . they're not in the picture."

She reached into her canvas bag and pulled them out, setting them between us. They were smooth and shiny and perfect. "I was careful not to break them, just like you used to tell me."

I marveled at her beauty; she had her mother's rose-petal smile and blue sapphire eyes, but also my slightly crooked nose and somewhat weak chin—to keep her humble, I assume. Still, she was even more stunning as an adult than Karen and I had imagined she'd be.

Her eyes regarded me as if I were the bestest thing in the whole great big wide world. "Hi, Daddy," she whispered, then reached over and took hold of my hands. Her touch was a drink of cool, clean water after a lifetime under the scorching desert sun.

"H-hi," I managed to get out. "God, hon, I've missed you so . . . so much . . ." I fumbled for something else to say but there were no words. How could there be?

"I've missed you, too," she said. "Please say you'll stay here with me. We'll have almost seven hours together. You can . . . you can say good-bye this time."

My heart sank. "Why is there so little time? Why were you given only one day?"

"Because that's what you asked for, remember? When you talked to Father Ehwald after the funeral. You said you'd give anything to have me back for just one more day."

Something clogged in my throat. "I didn't think anyone was listening."

She put her hand through my arm and kissed my cheek, then looked out at the pond. "Not to ruin the warm fuzziness of this moment, but did you know they won't let you feed the ducks anymore? Isn't that a bitch? I wanted to give them some popcorn but that vendor doesn't come around here these days."

"He hasn't been around for a long time."

She huffed. "Well, I think that sucks. How're you supposed to have any fun if you can't feed the ducks? I'll bet if enough people complained, they'd change it back to how it used to be."

"You're pouting."

"I am? Sorry."

"No. I used to love it when you were a kid, the way you'd pout like the whole world had conspired to ruin your day."

"*Well*, that's what it felt like. I was trying to learn about the world. How're you supposed to discover anything when all the crabby old adults are breathing their rules down your neck all the time? And you were the worst, don't deny it. Especially that business about your computer."

"You wanted to pour Kool-Aid on the keyboard! I used to think I'd have to hire armed guards to keep you away from it."

"You could have locked your office door."

"And miss catching you in the act? No way."

"That's wicked."

"You were a wicked child sometimes. *Kool-Aid*, for chrissakes!"

"I was three. Sue me." She looked at me and we both burst out laughing. It felt odd. I hadn't laughed in a long, long time.

She hugged me again. "God, Daddy, I really have missed you. And so does Mom. She thinks about us all the time—but mostly she thinks about you."

"Do you . . . do you know where she is? My God, I tried to find her right after I got out of the hospital, but she'd moved away and—"

"Shhh, Dad, please. Just listen, okay? This has to do with Mom, too.

"Every living thing has its small song, but there have been countless things and people who, for whatever reason—a moment of fear or hesitation, weariness or grief, anger or confusion—didn't hear the voice of their soul when it spoke to them. But what it said didn't cease to exist simply because it wasn't heard; a tree that falls in the forest still makes a sound even if there's no one there, radio and television transmissions that'll never be picked up by a receiver still bounce through space; and, just so you know, Beethoven's Fifth Symphony *doesn't* cease to exist just because the orchestra stops playing." She held out the conch shells. "Take them."

"Why?"

"Because you need to hear some of the others."

"How, when I didn't even hear my own? You said that once it reveals itself it never speaks again."

"Yes, I did. But I never said that it doesn't leave an echo.

"And all things left behind can be found if you look hard enough. How do you think I was able to dig up that dumb Steppenwolf song of yours, Mr. Echofuzz?" She shook her head and laughed softly. "Oh boy, if you knew how much mnemonic resonance I had to sift through . . ."

She placed the shells in my hands. "That's why so many people feel empty and spend their lives looking for something they can't quite define. That's why the world is so miserable—all of those lonely, unheard small songs."

I looked at the shells in my hands. "Are these . . . ?"

She shrugged. "They have to go *somewhere*, don't they? What do you think you hear when you hold a sea shell to your ear? 'It sounds like the ocean.' "

"You mean that ocean-sound is—?"

"Well, *duh*. But people never listen well enough, they never get past the first . . . *layer* of sound. Go on, Dad, listen. Hear it for yourself so you'll know that all of that mystical bullshit you talked about in college, that you thought it would be nice to believe in, is true."

Not feeling at all foolish or self-conscious, I held the shells against my ears, listening.

And was aware of every exquisite moment as the sound waves registered as a massive but muted ocean roar—
—becoming the crash of waves scattering on a beach—
—then one wave breaking apart—
—becoming a small pool into which a pebble was dropped—
—and the ripples expanded outward in concentric circles, becoming a rhythm—
—then rhythms.
Rhythms and pulsings.
Rhythms and pulsings and tones.
The rhythms and the pulsings and the tones of the universe.
The rhythm of insects and heartbeats, of whisperings and thunder and bodies locked in sex; the pulsing runs of birdsong and tolling bells and whistling breaths; tones of infant birth-cries, canticle moans of graveside mourners; cicada arpeggios, descants from whales breaking the surface and trillings of single cells in division and in death; the thunderous tympani of gorillas in Africa beating their chests; the chirpings of crickets; the growl of cancer cells devouring delicate tissues; modulated vibrations of a million locusts in migration; the primeval groans from shifting tectonic plates; the *gloriae* of melting polar ice-caps; madrigal dawn; *andante* night; and the brassy, sassy blues from the light of a long-dead star as it staggered like a drunkard toward the Earth: a polythematic assault.

I heard thoughts and sensed dreams and absorbed impressions as they were passed from psyche to psyche with compulsive speed and more sensory layers than my brain, anyone's brain, any*thing*'s brain could possibly absorb. The atmosphere was packed with millions upon millions-squared of swirling, drifting, reeling bits of consciousness.

Attuned to the majestic cacophony I heard the murmur of every cell; the synchronic rustling of blood brushing against arterial walls; the clicking of countless synapses; and I realized that somewhere, under-lying all life, there was a continual music that had been playing since life began, and that its sounds, its rhythms and pulsings and tones, were the refrain of something more, the distant memory of the chorus from an earlier song, a sub-organic score for transposing the inanimate, ran-dom matter of chaos into the enigmatic, lavish, magnificent, improbable, ordered dance of living forms, rearranging matter and consciousness into miraculous symmetry, away from probability, against entropy, lifting everything toward a sublime awareness so acute, so incandescent and encompassing I thought everything within me would burst into flames from the overpowering *wholeness*.

I was hearing the voice of the soul, maybe of all souls.

I felt divided from my body, standing outside my flesh observing all of it, my only companion the delicate echo of a single voice-note, pure and easy and somehow incomplete, that rose above the cacophony and whistled through me like a breeze through an open window. I tried to grasp the echo, to make sure I had understood its meaning, but it was gone too quickly.

I turned toward Melissa. My daughter said nothing, only gestured toward the sculpture.

I rose to my feet as the rain grew more dense and moved toward it.

I couldn't speak. I couldn't breathe.

All fifty figures were still there, and all of them still suffered unimaginable pain—

—but now all of them, their hands grasping synthetic stone roses, had Karen's face.

God pity women who love unselfishly, true souls who offer their hearts and dreams to men who don't deserve them, whose grief must be borne privately so they might be strong for the weaker ones they love, who grow used to being lonely in the company of a husband too self-absorbed to notice their pain, who must sustain themselves on memories of tenderness rather than the promise of it, and who continue to love faithfully even if that love is never returned in equal measure. May whatever joy there is in your life be safe from harm. God pity your selflessness. I once knew such a woman and, for a time, loved her as best I could. But it wasn't enough to protect her from the night. Forgive me.

I climbed onto the base of the sculpture and pulled myself close enough to kiss her wonderful lips if they had been real, to hear her laugh that so often had given me the strength to go on, to remember how she had, for a while, opened me up to feelings and tiny kindnesses that most men never experience; and close enough for all of that, I knew her outrage, her loss, her terrible loneliness and sorrow, this splendid woman who'd needed so much from me but asked for so little and didn't get even that much—

—here, before me, was Karen's hurt made physical, and I could see now in all of the figures' expressions the terrible evolution of what she'd gone through; from the look on her face when I'd told her that Melissa had died to the way she'd forced herself not to cry the day she walked out of my life, I had now before my eyes all the feelings I never heard with my heart.

I fell backward onto the spongy ground. Melissa knelt beside me and took my hands. "I love you, Dad."

She held me in her arms, rocking me like a baby, there under the pounding rain and the perpetually grief-stricken gazes of her mother.

Melissa touched my cheek, then kissed my forehead. "Did you hear it?"

". . . yes . . ."

"So you know?"

". . . godyeah."

She kissed me again, then held me closer. "I wish you hadn't loved me so much."

I grasped one of her hands in mine, brought it to my lips. "Me too, hon. I'm s-sorry, but me too."

And almost added: *Because.*

Because if I hadn't loved her so much, I would have seen that my wife's pain was so much greater than my own, and I would have helped her through it, and we would have gone on together.

It was as simple as that: the purpose of my life had been to share it with her. For better or for worse, as the saying goes.

"You have to find her, Daddy," whispered Melissa. "It's going to be hard, and it might take a long time, but you have to find her. She still hurts so much. She never stopped needing you. Or loving you."

"Oh Christ, honey . . . *how*?"

"Shhh." She placed her finger against my lips and pressed her rose into my palm. "You just have to . . . listen . . ."

For a while we listened together, holding each other on that bench in the rain, until the afternoon faded into twilight and the twilight into night.

I tried to say all of the things I had dreamed of saying to her for so many years but there wasn't enough time. How could there have been?

In her last moments Melissa took my hands in hers and kissed my cheek once again.

"I've wasted so much time," I whispered to her. "We could have had an entire day but I—"

"I love you. And when love is present, no time is ever wasted. I've had my lifetime with you today, and that's enough. It has to be." She wrapped her arms around me. "Good-bye, Daddy. You'll be happy again someday."

I looked down at the rose she had given to me. It was in full bloom. "Good-bye, hon. I wish—"

"Shhh, you mustn't—"

And then she was gone.

I moved back into the cacophony layer by lonely layer. I listened to the old songs, the sad songs, the bitter, misused, and jubilant songs, all so ephemeral, all so small. I listen still. Every moment of every day, wherever I go, they are with me.

The echo of Karen's small song is here, somewhere. If I can find it, it will lead me back to her. So I listen for it. Truly listen. And I prepare for the day when life shall continue by her side.

In the night I hear the poetry of this world; the patience of the darkness, the sighing of the moon, the laughter of dreams.

A pressed rose rests in my breast pocket.

My daughter's kiss still lingers on my cheek.

In my hands are two perfect shells.

I will find my wife, no matter how long it takes.

And I warn the universe: *I will not lose her a second time.*

Do you believe in voices?

Then listen.

Listen.

Listen . . .

GEMMA FILES

The Emperor's Old Bones

Gemma Files has a B.A. in magazine journalism from Toronto's Ryerson University, writes freelance film criticism and independent local movie scene coverage for Toronto's Eye Weekly *magazine, and writes horror short stories for a variety of small-press magazines (including* Palace Corbie, Grue, *and* TransVersions) *and anthologies (*Demon Sex, Seductive Spectres, *and* Northern Frights 2). *She also teaches the Trebas Institute's screenwriting course. She wrote and directed her first short film,* Say Thanks, *in 1998. A number of her short stories have been adapted (two by her) and shown on Showtime's* The Hunger, *a half-hour anthology TV series.*

The author says that the dish in her story really does exist in a more benign form. "The Emperor's Old Bones" was originally published in Northern Frights 5.

—E. D.

Oh, buying and selling . . . you know . . . life.

—TOM STOPPARD, AFTER J. G. BALLARD.

One day in 1941, not long after the fall of Shanghai, my amah (our live-in Chinese maid of all work, who often doubled as my nurse) left me sleeping alone in the abandoned hulk of what had once been my family's home, went out, and never came back . . . a turn of events which didn't actually surprise me all that much, since my parents had done something rather similar only a few brief weeks before. I woke up without light or food, surrounded by useless luxury—the discarded detritus of Empire and family alike. And fifteen more days of boredom and starvation were to pass before I saw another living soul.

I was ten years old.

After the war was over, I learned that my parents had managed to bribe their way as far as the harbor, where they became separated in the crush while trying to board a ship back "home." My mother died of dysentery in a camp outside of Hangkow; the ship went down halfway to Hong Kong, taking my father with it. What happened to my amah, I honestly don't know—though I do feel it only fair to mention that I never really tried to find out, either.

The house and I, meanwhile, stayed right where we were—uncared for, unclaimed—until Ellis Iseland broke in, and took everything she could carry.

Including me.

"So what's your handle, *tai pan?*" She asked, back at the dockside garage she'd been squatting in, as she went through the pockets of my school uniform.

(It would be twenty more years before I realized that her own endlessly evocative name was just another bad joke—one some immigration official had played on her family, perhaps.)

"Timothy Darbersmere," I replied, weakly. Over her shoulder, I could see the frying pan still sitting on the table, steaming slightly, clogged with burnt rice. At that moment in time, I would have gladly drunk my own urine in order to be allowed to lick it out, no matter how badly I might hurt my tongue and fingers in doing so.

Her eyes followed mine—a calm flick of a glance, contemptuously knowing, arched eyebrows barely sketched in cinnamon.

"Not yet, kid," she said.

"I'm really very hungry, Ellis."

"I really believe you, Tim. But not yet." She took a pack of cigarettes from her sleeve, tapped one out, lit it. Sat back. Looked at me again, eyes narrowing contemplatively. The plume of smoke she blew was exactly the same non-color as her slant, level, heavy-lidded gaze.

"Just to save time, by the way, here's the house rules," she said. "Long as you're with me, I eat first. Always."

"That's not fair."

"Probably not. But that's the way it's gonna be, 'cause I'm thinking for two, and I can't afford to be listening to my stomach instead of my gut." She took another drag. "Besides which, I'm bigger than you."

"My father says adults who threaten children are bullies."

"Yeah, well, that's some pretty impressive moralizing, coming from a mook who dumped his own kid to get out of Shanghai alive."

I couldn't say she wasn't right, and she knew it, so I just stared at her. She was exoticism personified—the first full-blown Yank I'd ever met, the first adult (Caucasian) woman I'd ever seen wearing trousers. Her flat, Midwestern accent lent a certain fascination to everything she said, however repulsive.

"People will do exactly whatever they think they can get away with, Tim," she told me, "for as long as they think they can get away with it. That's human nature. So don't get all high-hat about it, use it. Everything's got its uses—everything, and everybody."

"Even you, Ellis?"

"Especially me, Tim. As you will see."

It was Ellis, my diffident ally—the only person I have ever met who seemed capable of flourishing in any given situation—who taught me the basic rules of commerce: to always first assess things at their true value, when gauge exactly how much extra a person in desperate circumstances would be willing to pay for them. And her lessons have stood me in good stead, during all these intervening years. At the age of sixty-six, I remain not only still alive, but a rather rich man, to boot—import/export, antiques, some minor drug smuggling intermittently punctuated (on the more creative side) by the publication of a string of slim, speculative novels. These last items have apparently garnered me some kind of cult following amongst fans of such fiction, most specifically—ironically enough—in the United States of America.

But time is an onion, as my third wife used to say: The more of it you peel away, searching for the hidden connections between action and reaction, the more it gives you something to cry over.

So now, thanks to the established temporal conventions of literature, we all slip fluidly from 1941 to 1999—to St. Louis, Missouri, and the middle leg of my first-ever stateside visit, as part of a tour in support of my recently published childhood memoirs.

The last book signing was at four. Three hours later, I was already firmly ensconced in my comfortable suite at the downtown Four Seasons Hotel. Huang came by around eight, along with my room service trolley. He had a briefcase full of files and a sly, shy grin, which lit up his usually impassive face from somewhere deep inside.

"Racked up a lotta time on this one, Mr. Darbersmere," he said, in his second-generation Cockney growl. "Spent a lotta your money, too."

"Mmm." I uncapped the tray. "Good thing my publisher gave me that advance, then, isn't it?"

"Yeah, good fing. But it don't matter much now."

He threw the files down on the table between us. I opened the top one and leafed delicately through, between mouthfuls. There were schedules, marriage and citizenship certificates, medical records. Police records, going back to 1953, with charges ranging from fraud to trafficking in stolen goods, and listed under several different aliases. Plus a sheaf of photos, all taken from a safe distance.

I tapped one.

"Is this her?"

Huang shrugged. "You tell me—you're the one 'oo knew 'er."

I took another bite, nodding absently. Thinking: *Did I? Really? Ever?*

As much as anyone, I suppose.

To get us out of Shanghai, Ellis traded a can of petrol for a spot on a farmer's truck coming back from the market—then cut our unlucky savior's throat with her straight razor outside the city limits, and sold his truck for a load of cigarettes, lipstick, and nylons. This got us shelter on a floating whorehouse off the banks of the Yangtze, where she eventually hooked us up with a pirate trawler full of U.S. deserters and other assorted scum, whose captain proved to be some slippery variety of old friend.

The trawler took us up and down-river, dodging the Japanese and preying on the weak, then trading the resultant loot to anyone else we came in contact with. We sold opium and penicillin to the warlords, maps and passports to the D.P.s, motor oil and dynamite to the Kuomintang, Allied and Japanese spies to each other. But our most profitable commodity, as ever, remained people—mainly because those we dealt with were always so endlessly eager to help set their own price.

I look at myself in the bathroom mirror now, tall and silver-haired—features still cleanly cut, yet somehow fragile, like Sir Laurence Olivier after the medical bills set in. At this morning's signing, a pale young woman with a bolt through her septum told me: "No offense, Mr. Darbersmere, but you're—like—a real babe. For an old guy."

I smiled, gently. And told her: "You should have seen me when I was twelve, my dear."

That was back in 1943, the year that Ellis sold me for the first time—or rented me out, rather, to the mayor of some tiny port village, who threatened to keep us docked until the next Japanese inspection. Ellis had done her best to convince him that we were just another boatload of Brits fleeing internment, even shucking her habitual male drag to reveal a surprisingly lush female figure and donning one of my mother's old dresses instead, much as it obviously disgusted her to do so. But all to no avail.

"You know I'd do it, Tim," she told me, impatiently pacing the trawler's deck as a passing group of her crewmates whistled appreciatively from shore. "Christ knows I've tried. But the fact is, he doesn't want me. He wants you."

I frowned. "Wants me?"

"To go with him, Tim. You know—grown-up stuff."

"Like you and Ho Tseng, last week, after the dance at Sister Chin's?"

"Yeah, sorta like that."

She plumped herself down on a tarpaulined crate full of dynamite—clearly labeled, in Cantonese, as "dried fruit"—and kicked off one of her borrowed high-heeled shoes, rubbing her foot morosely. Her cinnamon hair hung loose in the stinking wind, back-lit to a fine fever.

I felt her appraising stare play up and down me like a fine gray mist, and shivered.

"If I do this, will you owe me, Ellis?"

"You bet I will, kid."

"Always take me with you?"

There had been some brief talk of replacing me with Brian Thompson-Greenaway, another refugee, after I had mishandled a particularly choice assignment—protecting Ellis's private stash of American currency from fellow scavengers while she recuperated from a beating inflicted by an irate Japanese officer, into whom she'd accidentally bumped while ashore. Though she wisely put up no resistance—one of Ellis's more admirable skills involved her always knowing when it was in her best interest *not* to defend herself—the damage left her pissing blood for a week, and she had not been happy to discover her money gone once she was recovered enough to look for it.

She lit a new cigarette, shading her eyes against the flame of her Ronson.

" 'Course," she said, sucking in smoke.

"Never leave me?"

"Sure, kid. Why not?"

I learned to love duplicity from Ellis, to distrust everyone except those who have no loyalty and play no favorites. Lie to me, however badly, and you are virtually guaranteed my fullest attention.

I don't remember if I really believed her promises, even then. But

I did what she asked anyway, without qualm or regret. She must have understood that I would do anything for her, no matter how morally suspect, if she only asked me politely enough.

In this one way, at least, I was still definitively British.

Afterward, I was ill for a long time—some sort of psychosomatic reaction to the visceral shock of my deflowering, I suppose. I lay in a bath of sweat on Ellis's hammock, under the trawler's one intact mosquito net. Sometimes I felt her sponge me with a rag dipped in rice wine, while singing to me—softly, along with the radio:

A faded postcard from exotic places . . . a cigarette that's marked with lipstick traces . . . oh, how the ghost of you clings . . .

And did I merely dream that once, at the very height of my sickness, she held me on her hip and hugged me close? That she actually slipped her jacket open and offered me her breast, so paradoxically soft and firm, its nipple almost as pale as the rest of her night-dweller's flesh?

That sweet swoon of ecstasy. That first hot stab of infantile desire. That unwitting link between recent childish violation and a desperate longing for adult consummation. I was far too young to know what I was doing, but she did. She had to. And since it served her purposes, she simply chose not to care.

Such complete amorality: It fascinates me. Looking back, I see it always has—like everything else about her, fetishized over the years into an inescapable pattern of hopeless attraction and inevitable abandonment.

My first wife's family fled the former Yugoslavia shortly before the end of the war; she had high cheekbones and pale eyes, set at a Baltic slant. My second wife had a wealth of long, slightly coarse hair, the color of unground cloves. My third wife told stories—ineptly, compulsively. All of them were, on average, at least five years my elder.

And sooner or later, all of them left me.

Oh, Ellis, I sometimes wonder whether anyone else alive remembers you as I do—or remembers you at all, given your well-cultivated talent for blending in, for getting by, for rendering yourself unremarkable. And I really don't know what I'll do if this woman Huang has found for me turns out not to be you. There's not much time left in which to start over, after all.

For either of us.

Last night, I called the number Huang's father gave me before I left London. The man on the other end of the line identified himself as the master chef of the Precious Dragon Shrine restaurant.

"Oh yes, *tai pan* Darbersmere," he said when I mentioned my name. "I was indeed informed, by that respected personage who we both know, that you might honor my unworthiest of businesses with the request for some small service."

"One such as only your estimable self could provide."

"The *tai pan* flatters, as is his right. Which is the dish he wishes to order?"

"The Emperor's Old Bones."

A pause ensued—fairly long, as such things go. I could hear a Cantopop ballad filtering in, perhaps from somewhere in the kitchen, duelling for precedence with the more classical strains of a wailing *erhu*. The Precious Dragon Shrine's master chef drew a single long, low breath.

"*Tai pan,*" he said, finally, "for such a meal . . . one must provide the meat oneself."

"Believe me, Grandfather, I am well aware of such considerations. You may be assured that the meat will be available, whenever you are ready to begin its cooking."

Another breath—shorter, this time. Calmer.

"Realizing that it has probably been a long time since anyone has requested this dish," I continued, "I am, of course, more than willing to raise the price our mutual friend has already set."

"Oh, no, *tai pan.*"

"For your trouble."

"*Tai pan*, please. It is not necessary to insult me."

"I must assure you, Grandfather, that no such insult was intended."

A burst of scolding rose from the kitchen, silencing the ballad in mid-ecstatic lament. The master chef paused again. Then said:

"I will need at least three days' notice to prepare my staff."

I smiled. Replying, with a confidence which—I hoped—at least sounded genuine:

"Three days should be more than sufficient."

The very old woman (eighty-nine, at least) who may or may not have once called herself Ellis Iseland now lives quietly in a genteelly shabby area of St. Louis, officially registered under the far less interesting name of Mrs. Munro. Huang's pictures show a figure held carefully erect, yet helplessly shrunken in on itself—its once-straight spine softened by the onslaught of osteoporosis. Her face has gone loose around the jawline, skin powdery, hair a short, stiff gray crown of marcelled waves.

She dresses drably. Shapeless feminine weeds, widow-black. Her arthritic feet are wedged into Chinese slippers—a small touch of nostalgic irony? Both her snubbed cat's nose and the half-sneering set of her wrinkled mouth seem familiar, but her slanted eyes—the most important giveaway, their original non-color—are kept hidden beneath a thick-lensed pair of bifocal sunglasses, essential protection for someone whose sight may not last the rest of the year.

And though her medical files indicate that she is in the preliminary stages of lung and throat cancer, her trip a day to the local corner store always includes the purchase of at least one pack of cigarettes, the brand apparently unimportant, as long as it contains a sufficient portion of nicotine. She lights one right outside the front door, and has almost finished it by the time she rounds the corner of her block.

Her neighbors seen to think well of her. Their children wave as she goes by, cane in one hand, cigarette in the other. She nods acknowledgment, but does not wave back.

This familiar arrogance, seeping up unchecked through her last, most perfect disguise: the mask of age, which bestows a kind of retroactive innocence on even its most experienced victims. I have recently begun to take advantage of its charms myself, whenever it suits my fancy to do so.

I look at these pictures, again and again. I study her face, searching in vain for even the ruin of that cool, smooth, inventively untrustworthy operator who once held both my fortune and my heart in the palm of her mannishly large hand.

It was Ellis who first told me about the Emperor's Old Bones—and she is still the only person in the world with whom I would ever care to share that terrible meal, no matter what doing so might cost me.

If, indeed, I ever end up eating it at all.

"Yeah, I saw it done down in Hong Kong," Ellis told us, gesturing with her chopsticks. We sat behind a lacquered screen at the back of Sister Chin's, two nights before our scheduled rendezvous with the warlord Wao Ruyen, from whom Ellis had already accepted some mysteriously unspecified commission. I watched her eat—waiting my turn, as ever—while Brian Thompson-Greenaway (also present, much to my annoyance) sat in the corner and watched us both, openly ravenous.

"They take a carp, right—you know, those big fish some rich Chinks keep in fancy pools, out in the garden? Supposed to live hundreds of years, you believe all that 'Confucius says' hooey. So they take this carp and they fillet it, all over, so the flesh is hanging off it in strips. But they do it so well, so carefully, they keep the carp alive through the whole thing. It's sittin' there on a plate, twitching, eyes rollin' around. Get close enough, you can look right in through the ribcage and see the heart still beating."

She popped another piece of Mu Shu pork in her mouth, and smiled down at Brian, who gulped—apparently suddenly too queasy to either resent or envy her proximity to the food.

"Then they bring out this big pot full of boiling oil," she continued, "and they run hooks through the fish's gills and tail. So they can pick it up at both ends. And while it's floppin' around, tryin' to get free, they dip all those hangin' pieces of flesh in the oil—one side first, then the other, all nice and neat. Fish is probably in so much pain already it doesn't even notice. So it's still alive when they put it back down . . . alive, and cooked, and ready to eat."

"And then—they eat it."

"Sure do, Tim."

"*Alive*, I mean."

Brian now looked distinctly green. Ellis shot him another glance, openly amused by his lack of stamina, then turned back to me.

"Well yeah, that's kinda the whole point of the exercise. You keep the carp alive until you've eaten it, and all that long life just sorta transfers over to you."

"Like magic," I said. She nodded.

"Exactly. 'Cause that's exactly what it is."

I considered her statement for a moment.

"My father," I commented, at last, "always told us that magic was a load of bunk."

Ellis snorted. "And why does this not surprise me?" She asked, of nobody in particular. Then: "Fine, I'll bite. What do you think?"

"I think . . ." I said slowly, ". . . that if it works . . . then who cares?"

She looked at me. Snorted again. And then she actually laughed, an infectious, unmalicious laugh that seemed to belong to someone far younger, far less complicated. It made me gape to hear it. Using her chopsticks, she plucked the last piece of pork deftly from her plate and popped it into my open mouth.

"Tim," she said, "for a spoiled Limey brat, sometimes you're okay."

I swallowed the pork, without really tasting it. Before I could stop myself, I had already blurted out:

"I wish we were the same age, Ellis."

This time she stared. I felt a sudden blush turn my whole face crimson. Now it was Brian's turn to gape, amazed by my idiotic effrontery.

"Yeah, well, not me," she said. "I like it just fine with you bein' the kid, and me not."

"Why?"

She looked at me again. I blushed even more deeply, heat prickling at my hairline. Amazingly, however, no explosion followed. Ellis simply took another sip of her tea, and replied:

" 'Cause the fact is, Tim, if you were my age—good-lookin' like you are, smart like you're gonna be—I could probably do some pretty stupid things over you."

Magic. Some might say it's become my stock in trade—as a writer, at least. Though the humble craft of buying and selling also involves a kind of legerdemain, as Ellis knew so well; sleight of hand, or price, depending on your product . . . and your clientele.

But true magic? Here, now, at the end of the twentieth century, in this brave new world of one-hundred-slot CD players and incessant afternoon talk shows?

I have seen so many things in my long life, most of which I would have thought impossible had they not taken place right in front of me. From the bank of the Yangtze river, I saw the bright white smoke of an atomic bomb go up over Nagasaki, like a tear in the fabric of the horizon. In Chungking harbor, I saw two grown men stab each other to death over the corpse of a dog because one wanted to bury it, while the other wanted to eat it. And just beyond the Shanghai city limits, I saw Ellis cut that farmer's throat with one quick twist of her wrist, so close to me that the spurt of his severed jugular misted my cheek with red.

But as I grow ever closer to my own personal twilight, the thing I remember most vividly is watching—through the window of a Franco-Vietnamese arms-dealer's car, on my way to a cool white house in Saigon, where I would wait out the final days of the war in relative comfort and safety—as a pair of barefoot coolies pulled the denuded skeleton of Brian Thompson-Greenway from a culvert full of malaria-laden water. I knew it was him, because even after Wao Ruyen's court had consumed the rest of his pathetic little body, they had left his face nearly untouched—there not being quite enough flesh on a child's skull, apparently, to be worth the extra effort of filleting . . . let alone of cooking.

And I remember, with almost comparable vividness, when—just a year ago—I saw the former warlord Wao, Huang's most respected father, sitting in a Limehouse nightclub with his Number One and Number Two wife at either elbow. Looking half the age he did when I first met him, in that endless last July of 1945, before black science altered our world forever. Before Ellis sold him Brian instead of me, and then fled for the Manchurian border, leaving me to fend for myself in the wake of her departure.

After all this, should the idea of true magic seem so very difficult to swallow? I think not.

No stranger than the empty shell of Hiroshima, cupped around Ground Zero, its citizenry reduced to shadows in the wake of the blast's last terrible glare. And certainly no stranger than the fact that I should think a woman so palpably incapable of loving anyone might nevertheless be capable of loving me, simply because—at the last moment—she suddenly decided not to let a rich criminal regain his youth and prolong his days by eating me alive, in accordance with the ancient and terrible ritual of the Emperor's Old Bones.

This morning, I told my publicist that I was far too ill to sign any books today—a particularly swift and virulent touch of the twenty-four-hour flu, no doubt. She said she understood completely. An hour later, I sat in Huang's car across the street from the corner store, watching "Mrs. Munro" make her slow way down the street to pick up her daily dose of slow, coughing death.

On her way back, I rolled down the car window and yelled: *"Lai gen wo ma, wai guai!"*

(Come with me, white ghost! An insulting little Mandarin phrase, occasionally used by passing Kuomintang jeep drivers to alert certain long-nosed Barbarian smugglers to the possibility that their dealings might soon be interrupted by an approaching group of Japanese soldiers.)

Huang glanced up from his copy of *Rolling Stone's* Hot List, impressed. "Pretty good accent," he commented.

But my eyes were on "Mrs. Munro," who had also heard—and stopped in mid-step, swinging her half-blind gray head toward the sound, more as though scenting than scanning. I saw my own face leering back at me in miniature from the lenses of her prescription sunglasses, doubled and distorted by the distance between us. I saw her raise one palm to shade her eyes even further against the sun, the wrinkles across her nose contracting as she squinted her hidden eyes.

And then I saw her slip her glasses off to reveal those eyes: still slant, still gray. Still empty.

I turned to Huang.

"It's her," I told him.

Huang nodded. "Thought so. When you want me to do it?"

"Tonight?"

"Whatever you say, Mr. D."

Very early on the morning before Ellis left me behind, I woke to find her sitting next to me in the red half-darkness of the ship's hold.

"Kid," she said, "I got a little job lined up for you today."

I felt so cold. "What kind of job, Ellis?" I asked, faintly—though I already had a fairly good idea. Quietly, she replied:

"The grown-up kind."

"Who?"

"French guy, up from Saigon, with enough jade and rifles to buy us over the border. He's rich, educated; not bad company, either. For a fruit."

"That's reassuring," I muttered, and turned on my side, studying the wall. Behind me, I heard her lighter click open, then catch and spark—felt the faint lick of her breath as she exhaled, transmuting nicotine into smoke and ash. The steady pressure of her attention itched like an insect crawling on my skin: fiercely concentrated, alien almost to the point of vague disgust, infinitely patient.

"War's on its last legs," she told me. "That's what I keep hearing. You got the Communists comin' up on one side, with maybe the Russians slipping in behind 'em, and the good old U.S. of A. everywhere else. Phillippines are already down for the count, now Tokyo's in bombing range. Pretty soon, our little outfit is gonna be so long gone, we won't even remember what it looked like. My educated opinion? It's sink or swim, and we need all the life jackets that money can buy." She paused. "You listening to me? Kid?"

I shut my eyes again, marshaling my heart rate.

"Kid?" Ellis repeated.

Still without answering—or opening my eyes—I pulled the mosquito net aside, and let gravity roll me free of the hammock's sweaty clasp. I was fourteen years old now, white-blonde and deeply tanned from the river-reflected sun; almost her height, even in my permanently bare feet. Looking up, I found I could finally meet her gray gaze head-on.

" 'Us'," I said. " 'We.' As in you and I?"

"Yeah, sure. You and me."

I nodded at Brian, who lay nearby, deep asleep and snoring. "And what about him?"

Ellis shrugged.

"I don't know, Tim," she said. "What *about* him?"

I looked back down at Brian, who hadn't shifted position, not even when my shadow fell over his face. Idly, I inquired:

"You'll still be there when I get back, won't you, Ellis?"

Outside, through the porthole, I could see that the rising sun had just cracked the horizon; she turned, haloed against it. Blew some more smoke. Asking:

"Why the hell wouldn't I be?"

"I don't know. But you wouldn't use my being away on this job as a good excuse to leave me behind, though—would you?"

She looked at me. Exhaled again. And said, evenly:

"You know, Tim, I'm gettin' pretty goddamn sick of you asking me that question. So gimme one good reason not to, or let it lie."

Lightly, quickly—too quickly even for my own well-honed sense of self-preservation to prevent me—I laid my hands on either side of her face and pulled her to me, hard. Our breath met, mingled, in sudden intimacy; hers tasted of equal parts tobacco and surprise. My daring had brought me just close enough to smell her own personal scent, under the shell of everyday decay we all stank of: a cool, intoxicating rush of non-fragrance, firm and acrid as an unearthed tuber. It burned my nose.

"We should always stay together," I said, "because I *love* you, Ellis."

I crushed my mouth down on hers, forcing it open. I stuck my tongue inside her mouth as far as it would go and ran it around, just like the mayor of that first tiny port village had once done with me. I fastened my teeth deep into the inner flesh of her lower lip, and bit down until I felt her knees give way with the shock of it. Felt myself rear up, hard and jerking, against her soft underbelly. Felt *her* feel it.

It was the first and only time I ever saw her eyes widen in anything but anger.

With barely a moment's pause, she punched me right in the face, so hard I felt my jaw crack. I fell at her feet, coughing blood.

"Eh—!" I began, amazed. But her eyes froze me in mid-syllable— so gray, so cold.

"Get it straight, *tai pan*," she said, " 'cause I'm only gonna say it once. I don't buy. I *sell*."

Then she kicked me in the stomach with one steel-toed army boot, and leaned over me as I lay there, gasping and hugging myself tight— my chest contracting, eyes dimming. Her eyes pouring over me like liquid ice. Like sleet. Swelling her voice like some great Arctic river, as she spoke the last words I ever heard her say:

"So don't you even *try* to play me like a trick, and think I'll let you get away with it."

Was Ellis evil? Am I? I've never thought so, though earlier this week I did give one of those legendary American Welfare mothers $25,000

in cash to sell me her least-loved child. He's in the next room right
now, playing Nintendo. Huang is watching him. I think he likes Huang.
He probably likes me, for that matter. We are the first English people
he has ever met, and our accents fascinate him. Last night, we ordered
in pizza; he ate until he was sick, then ate more, and fell asleep in front
of an HBO basketball game. If I let him stay with me another week, he
might become sated enough to convince himself he loves me.

The master chef at the Precious Dragon Shrine tells me that the
Emperor's Old Bones bestows upon its consumer as much life force as
its consumee would have eventually gone through had he or she been
permitted to live out the rest of their days unchecked—and since the
child I bought claims to be roughly ten years old (a highly significant
age, in retrospect), this translates to perhaps an additional sixty years of
life for every person who participates, whether the dish is eaten alone
or shared. Which only makes sense, really. It's an act of magic, after
all.

And this is good news for me, since the relative experiential gap
between a man in his upper twenties and a woman in her upper thirties—especially compared to that between a boy of fourteen and a
woman of twenty-eight—is almost insignificant.

Looking back, I don't know if I've ever loved anyone but Ellis—
if I'm even capable of loving anyone else. But finally, after all these
wasted years, I do know what I want. And who.

And how to get them both.

It's a terrible thing I'm doing, and an even worse thing I'm going
to do. But when it's done, I'll have what I want, and everything else—
all doubts, all fears, all piddling, queasy little notions of goodness, and
decency, and basic human kinship—all that useless lot can just go hang,
and twist and rot in the wind while they're at it. I've lived much too
long with my own unsatisfied desire to simply hold my aching parts—
whatever best applies, be it stomach or otherwise—and congratulate
myself on my forbearance anymore. I'm not mad, or sick, or even yearning after a long-lost love that I can never regain and never really had
in the first place. I'm just hungry, and I want to *eat*.

And morality . . . has nothing to do with it.

Because if there's one single thing you taught me, Ellis—one lesson
I've retained throughout every twist and turn of this snaky thing I call
my life—it's that hunger has no moral structure.

Huang came back late this morning, limping and cursing, after a brief
detour to the office of an understanding doctor who his father keeps on
international retainer. I am obscurely pleased to discover that Ellis can

still defend herself; even after Huang's first roundhouse put her on the pavement, she still somehow managed to slip her razor open without him noticing, then slide it shallowly across the back of his Achilles tendon. More painful than debilitating, but rather well done nevertheless, for a woman who can no longer wear shoes that require her to tie her own laces.

I am almost as pleased, however, to hear that nothing Ellis may have done actually succeeded in preventing Huang from completing his mission—and beating her, with methodical skill, to within an inch of her corrupt and dreadful old life.

I have already told my publicist that I witnessed the whole awful scene, and asked her to find out which hospital poor Mrs. Munro has been taken to. I myself, meanwhile, will drive the boy to the kitchen of the Precious Dragon Shrine restaurant, where I am sure the master chef and his staff will do their best to keep him entertained until later tonight. Huang has lent him his pocket Gameboy, which should help.

Ah. That must be the phone now, ringing.

The woman in bed thirty-seven of the Morleigh Memorial Hospital's charity wing, one of the few left operating in St. Louis—in America, possibly—opens her swollen left eye a crack, just far enough to reveal a slit of red-tinged white and a wandering, dilated pupil, barely rimmed in gray.

"Hello, Ellis," I say.

I sit by her bedside, as I have done for the last six hours. The screens enshrouding us from the rest of the ward, with its rustlings and moans, reduce all movement outside this tiny area to a play of flickering shadows—much like the visions one might glimpse in passing through a double haze of fever and mosquito net, after suffering a violent shock to one's fragile sense of physical and moral integrity.

. . . and oh, how the ghost of you clings . . .

She clears her throat, wetly. Tells me, without even a flicker of hesitation:

"Nuh . . . Ellis. Muh num iss . . . Munro."

She peers up at me, straining to lift her bruise-stung lids. I wait, patiently.

"Tuh—"

"That's a good start."

I see her bare broken teeth at my patronizing tone, perhaps reflexively. Pause. And then, after a long moment:

"Tim."

"Good show, Ellis. Got it in one."

Movement at the bottom of the bed: Huang, stepping through the gap between the screens. Ellis sees him, and stiffens. I nod in his direction, without turning.

"I believe you and Mr. Huang have already met," I say. "Mr. Wao Huang, that is; you'll remember his father, the former warlord Wao Ruyen. He certainly remembers you—and with some gratitude, or so he told me."

Huang takes his customary place at my elbow. Ellis's eyes move with him, helplessly—and I recall how my own eyes used to follow her about in a similarly fascinated manner, breathless and attentive on her briefest word, her smallest motion.

"I see you can still take quite a beating, Ellis," I observe, lightly. "Unfortunately for you, however, it's not going to be quite so easy to recover from this particular melee as it once was, is it? Old age, and all that." To Huang: "Have the doctors reached any conclusion yet, as regards Mrs. Munro's long-term prognosis?"

"Wouldn't say as 'ow there was one, *tai pan*."

"Well, yes. Quite."

I glance back, only to find that Ellis' eyes have turned to me at last. And I can read them so clearly, now—like clean, black text through gray rice paper, lit from behind by a cold and colorless flame. No distance. No mystery at all.

When her mouth opens again, I know exactly what word she's struggling to shape.

"Duh . . . deal?"

Oh, yes.

I rise, slowly, as Huang pulls the chair back for me. Some statements, I find, need room in which to be delivered properly—or perhaps I'm simply being facetious. My writer's overdeveloped sense of the dramatic, working double-time.

I wrote this speech out last night and rehearsed it several times in front of the bathroom mirror. I wonder if it sounds rehearsed. Does calculated artifice fall into the same general category as outright deception? If so, Ellis ought to be able to hear it in my voice. But I don't suppose she's really apt to be listening for such fine distinctions, given the stress of this mutually culminative moment.

"I won't say you've nothing I want, Ellis, even now. But what I really want—what I've always wanted—is to be the seller, for once, and not the sold. To be the only one who has what you want desperately, and to set my price wherever I think it fair."

Adding, with the arch of a significant brow: "—or know it to be unfair."

I study her battered face. The bruises form a new mask, impenetrable as any of the others she's worn. The irony is palpable: Just as Ellis's nature abhors emotional accessibility, so nature—seemingly—reshapes itself at will to keep her motivations securely hidden.

"I've arranged for a meal," I tell her. "The menu consists of a single dish, one with which I believe we're both equally familiar. The name of that dish is the Emperor's Old Bones, and my staff will begin to cook it whenever I give the word. Now, you and I may share this meal, or we may not. We may regain our youth, and double our lives, and be together for at least as long as we've been apart—or we may not. But I promise you this, Ellis: No matter what I eventually end up doing, the extent of your participation in the matter will be exactly defined by how much you are willing to pay me for the privilege."

I gesture to Huang, who slips a pack of cigarettes from his coat pocket. I tap one out. I light it, take a drag. Savor the sensation.

Ellis just watches.

"So here's the deal, then: If you promise to be very, very nice to me—and never, ever leave me again—for the rest of our extremely long partnership—"

I pause. Blow out the smoke. Wait.

And conclude, finally:

"—then you can eat first."

I offer Ellis the cigarette, slowly. Slowly, she takes it from me, holding it delicately between two splinted fingers. She raises it to her torn and grimacing mouth. Inhales. Exhales those familiar twin plumes of smoke, expertly, through her crushed and broken nose. Is that a tear at the corner of her eye, or an upwelling of rheum? Or neither?

"Juss like . . . ahways," she says.

And gives me an awful parody of my own smile. Which I—return. With interest.

Later, as Huang helps Ellis out of bed and into the hospital's service elevator, I sit in the car, waiting. I take out my cellular phone. The master chef of the Precious Dragon Shrine restaurant answers on the first ring.

"How is . . . the boy?" I ask him.

"Fine, *tai pan*."

There is a pause, during which I once more hear music filtering in from the other end of the line—the tinny little song of a video game in progress, intermittently punctuated by the clatter of kitchen implement. Laughter, both adult and child.

"Do you wish to cancel your order, *tai pan* Darbersmere?" The master chef asks me, delicately.

Through the hospital's back doors, I can see the service elevator's lights crawling steadily downward—the floors reeling themselves off, numeral by numeral. Fifth. Fourth. Third.

"Tai pan?"

Second. First.

"No. I do not."

The elevator doors are opening. I can see Huang guiding Ellis out, puppeting her deftly along with her own crutches. Those miraculously trained hands of his, able to open or salve wounds with equal expertise.

"Then I may begin cooking," the master chef says. Not really meaning it as a question.

Huang holds the door open. Ellis steps through. I listen to the Gameboy's idiot song, and know that I have spent every minute of every day of my life preparing to make this decision, ever since that last morning on the Yangtze. That I have made it so many times already, in fact, that nothing I do or say now can ever stop it from being made. Any more than I can bring back the child Brian Thompson-Greenaway was, before he went up the hill to Wao Ruyen's fortress, hand in stupidly trusting hand with Ellis—or the child I was, before Ellis broke into my parents' house and saved me from one particular fate worse than death, only to show me how many, many others there were to choose from.

Or the child that Ellis must have been, once upon a very distant time, before whatever happened to make her as she now is—then set her loose to move at will through an unsuspecting world, preying on other lost children.

. . . these foolish things . . . remind me of you.

"Yes," I say. "You may."

SUSANNA CLARKE

The Duke of Wellington Misplaces His Horse

Susanna Clarke has only been publishing fiction since 1996, and yet this tale marks her third appearance in The Year's Best Fantasy *and* Horror. *Specializing in historical fantasy (reminiscent of the classic tales of Sylvia Townsend Warner), Clarke has written short stories for* Starlight I; Starlight II; Black Swan, White Raven; *and* The Sandman: Book of Dreams. *She lives in Cambridge, England, where she is working on her first novel.*

"The Duke of Wellington Misplaces His Horse" is set in the woodland village of Wall, a English town on the border of Faerieland. Wall is the creation of writer Neil Gaiman and artist Charles Vess, from their Mythopoeic Award–winning graphic novel, Stardust. *As in the original publication by Gaiman and Vess, Clarke tips her hat to such early fantasists as Lawrence Housman and Hope Mirrlees in the following sprightly tale. She wrote the story for* A Fall of Stardust, *a limited-edition portfolio of prints by thirty artists, published by Charles Vess's Green Man Press.*

—T. W.

The people of the village of Wall in——shire are celebrated for their independent spirit. It is not their way to bow down before great men. An aristocratic title makes no impression upon them, and anything in the nature of pride and haughtiness they detest. In 1819 the proudest man in all of England was, without a doubt, the Duke of Wellington. This was not particularly surprising; when a man has twice defeated the armies of the wicked French Emperor, Napoleon Bonaparte, it is only natural that he should have a rather high opinion of himself.

In late September of that year the Duke happened to spend one night at the Seventh Magpie in Wall and, though it was only one night, Duke and village soon quarreled. It began with a general dissatisfaction on both sides at the other side's insolent behavior, but it soon resolved itself into a skirmish over Mrs. Pumphrey's embroidery scissors.

The Duke's visit occurred when Mr. Bromios was away from Wall. He had gone somewhere to buy wine, as he did from time to time. Some people said that when he came back from one of these expeditions he smelt faintly of the sea, but other people said it was more like aniseed. Mr. Bromios had left the Seventh Magpie in the care of Mr. and Mrs. Pumphrey.

Mrs. Pumphrey sent her husband to fetch her scissors from the upstairs parlor where the Duke was at dinner, but the Duke sent Mr. Pumphrey away again because he did not like to be disturbed while he was eating. Consequently when Mrs. Pumphrey took in the roast pork she banged it upon the table and gave the Duke a look to show him what she thought of him. This so enraged the Duke that he hid her scissors in his breeches pocket (though he fully intended to return them in the morning when he left).

That night a poor clergyman called Duzamour arrived at the inn. At first Mr. Pumphrey told him that they had no room but, on discovering that Mr. Duzamour had a horse, Mr. Pumphrey changed his mind, for he thought he saw a way to vent some of his anger against the Duke. He told John Cockcroft, the stable man, to remove the Duke's noble chestnut stallion from the warm, comfortable stable and install Mr. Duzamour's ancient gray mare in his place.

"But what shall I do with the Duke's horse?" asked John.

"Oh!" said Mr. Pumphrey spitefully, "there is a perfectly good meadow over the road with not so much as a goat grazing in it. Put it there!"

The next morning the Duke rose and looked out of the window. He saw his favorite horse, Copenhagen, contentedly eating grass in a large green meadow. After breakfast the Duke took a stroll in that direction to give Copenhagen a bit of white bread. For some reason two men with cudgels stood, one upon either side of the entrance to the meadow. One of them spoke to the Duke, but the Duke had no attention to spare for whatever the fellow might be saying (it was something about a bull), because at that precise moment he saw Copenhagen walk between the trees on the far side of the meadow and disappear from view. The Duke looked round and discovered that one of the men had raised his staff as though intending to strike him!

The Duke stared at him in amazement.

The man hesitated, as though asking himself if he really intended to strike the Duke, who was, after all, Europe's Defender and the Nation's Hero. It was only a moment's hesitation, but it was enough: the Duke strode forward into Faerie in pursuit of Copenhagen.

Beyond the trees the Duke found himself upon a little white path in a pleasant country of round, plump hills. Scattered among the hills were ancient woods of oak and ash that were so overgrown with ivy, dog-roses, and honeysuckle that each wood was a solid mass of greenery.

The Duke had only gone a mile or so when he came to a stone house surrounded by a dark moat. The moat was spanned by a bridge so thick with moss that it appeared to have been built out of green velvet cushions. The stone-tiled roof of the house was supported by crumbling stone giants who were bowed and bent by its weight.

Thinking that one of the inhabitants of the house might have seen Copenhagen, the Duke went up to the door and knocked. He waited a while and then began to look in at all the windows. The rooms were bare. The sunlight made golden stripes upon the dusty floors. One room contained a battered pewter goblet, but that seemed to be the full stretch of the house's furnishings until, that is, the Duke came to the last window.

In the last room a young woman in a gown of deepest garnet red was seated upon a wooden stool with her back to the window. She was sewing. Spread out around her was a vast and magnificent piece of embroidery. Reflections of its rich hues danced upon the walls and ceiling. If she had held a molten stained-glass window in her lap the effect could not have been more wonderful.

The room contained only one other thing: a shabby birdcage that hung from the ceiling with a sad-looking bird inside it.

"I wonder, my dear," said the Duke leaning in through the open window, "if you might have seen my charger?"

"No," said the young lady, continuing to sew.

"A pity," said the Duke. "Poor Copenhagen. He was with me at Waterloo and I shall be sorry to lose him. I hope whoever finds him is kind to him. Poor fellow."

There was a silence while the Duke contemplated the elegant curve of the young lady's white neck.

"My dear," he said, "Might I come in and have a few moments' conversation with you?"

"As you wish," said the young lady.

Inside, the Duke was pleased to find that the young lady was every bit as good-looking as his first glimpse of her had suggested. "This is a remarkably pretty spot, my dear," he said, "although it seems a little lonely. If you have no objection I shall keep you company for an hour or two."

"I have no objection," said the lady, "but you must promise not disturb me at my work."

"And for whom are you doing such a monstrous quantity of embroidery, my dear?"

The lady smiled ever so slightly. "Why, for you, of course!" she said.

The Duke was surprised to hear this. "And might I be permitted to look?" he asked.

"Certainly," said the lady.

The Duke went round and peered over her shoulder at her work. It consisted of thousands upon thousands of the most exquisite embroidered pictures, some of which seemed very odd and some of which seemed quite familiar.

Three in particular struck the Duke as extraordinary. Here was a chestnut horse, remarkably like Copenhagen, running in a meadow with the village of Wall behind him; then came a picture of the Duke himself walking along a little white path among round green hills; and then came a picture of the Duke here in this very room, looking down over the lady's shoulder at the embroidery! It was complete in every detail— even the sad-looking bird in the cage was there.

At that moment a large brindled rat ran out a hole in the wainscotting and began to gnaw on a corner of the embroidery. It happened to be the part which depicted the birdcage. But what was most extraordinary was that the instant the stitches were broken, the cage in the room disappeared. With a joyous burst of song the bird flew out of the window.

Well, that is very odd to be sure! thought the Duke. But now that I come to think of it, she could not possibly have worked those pictures since I arrived. She must have embroidered those scenes before the events happened! It seems that whatever this lady sews into her pictures is sure to come to pass. What comes next, I wonder?

He looked again.

The next picture was of a knight in silver armor arriving at the house. The one after that showed the Duke and the knight engaged in a violent quarrel, and the last picture (which the lady was just finishing) showed the knight plunging his sword into the Duke.

"But this is most unfair!" he cried indignantly. "This fellow has a sword, a spear, a dagger, and a what-you-may-call-it with a spiked ball on the end of a chain! Whereas I have no weapon whatsoever!"

The lady shrugged as if that were no concern of hers.

"But could you not embroider me a little sword? Or a pistol perhaps?" asked the Duke.

"No," said the lady. She finished her sewing and, securing the last thread with a stout knot, she rose and left the room.

The Duke looked out of the window and saw upon the brow of the hill a sparkle, such as might be produced by sunlight striking silver armor, and a dancing speck of brilliant color, which might have been a scarlet feather on top of a helmet.

The Duke made a rapid search through the house for some sort of weapon, but found nothing but the battered pewter cup. He returned to the room which contained the embroidery.

"I have it!" He was suddenly struck with a most original idea. "I will not quarrel with him! Then he will not kill me!" He looked down at the embroidery. "Oh, but he has such a conceited expression! Who could help but quarrel with such a ninny!"

Gloomily the Duke plunged his hands into his breeches pocket and found something cold and metallic: Mrs. Pumphrey's needlework scissors.

"A weapon at last, by God! Oh! But what is the use? I doubt very much that he will be so obliging as to stand still while I poke these little blades through the chinks in his armor."

The knight in silver armor was crossing the moss-covered bridge. The clatter of his horse's hooves and the clank-clank-clank of his armor sounded throughout the house. His scarlet plume passed by the window.

"Wait!" cried the Duke. "I do believe that this is not a military problem at all. It is a problem of needlework!"

He took Mrs. Pumphrey's scissors and snipped all the threads in the pictures which showed the knight arriving at the house; their quarrel; and his own death. When he had finished he looked out of the window; the knight was nowhere to be seen.

"Excellent!" he cried. "Now, for the rest!"

With a great deal of concentration, muttering, and pricking of his fingers he added some pictures of his own to the lady's embroidery, all in the largest, ugliest stitches imaginable. The Duke's first picture showed a stick figure (himself) leaving the house, the next was of his joyful reunion with a stick horse (Copenhagen), and the third and last showed their safe return through the gap in the wall.

He would have liked to embroider some horrible disaster befalling the village of Wall. Indeed he did go so far as to pick out some violent-colored red and orange silks for the purpose, but in the end he was obliged to give it up, his skills in embroidery being in no way equal to the task.

He picked up his hat and walked out of the ancient stone house. Outside he found Copenhagen waiting for him—precisely where his large stitches had shown the horse would be—and great was their rejoicing at the sight of one another. Then the Duke of Wellington mounted upon his horse's back and rode back to Wall.

The Duke believed that he had suffered no ill effects from his short sojourn in the moated house. In later life he was at different times a diplomat, a statesman, and Prime Minister of Great Britain, but he came more and more to believe that all his exertions were in vain. He told Mrs. Arbuthnot (a close friend) that "on the battlefields of Europe I was master of my own destiny, but as a politician there are so many other people I must please, so many compromises I must make, that I am at best a stick figure."

Mrs. Arbuthnot wondered why the Duke suddenly looked so alarmed and turned pale.

STEVE RASNIC TEM

Halloween Street

"Halloween Street" is part of a story cycle Tem is writing about Halloween and will be the title piece in his first German-language collection. The story was originally published in the July issue of The Magazine of Fantasy & Science Fiction.

—*E. D.*

Halloween street. No one could remember who had first given it that name. It had no other. There was no street sign, had never been a street sign. Halloween Street bordered the creek, and there was only one way to get there—over a rickety bridge of rotting wood. Gray timbers had worn partway through the vague red stain. The city had declared it safe only for foot or bike traffic.

The street had only eight houses, and no one could remember more than three of those being occupied at any one time. Renters never lasted long.

It was a perfect place to take other kids—the smaller ones, or the ones a little more nervous than yourself—on Halloween night. Just to give them a little scare. Just to get them to wet their pants.

Most of the time all the houses stayed empty. An old lady had supposedly lived in one of the houses for years, but no one knew anything more about her, except that they thought she'd died there several years before. Elderly twin brothers had once owned the two center houses, each with twin high-peaked gables on the second story like skeptical eyebrows, narrow front doors, and small windows that froze over every winter. The brothers had lived there only six months, fighting loudly with each other the entire time.

The houses at the end of the street were in the worst shape, missing most of their roof shingles and sloughing off paint chips the way a tree sheds leaves. Both houses leaned toward the center of the block, as if two great hands had attempted to squeeze the block from either side. Another three houses had suffered outside fire damage. The blackened boards looked like permanent, arbitrary shadows.

But it was the eighth house that bothered the kids most. There was nothing wrong with it.

It was the kind of house any of them would have liked to live in. Painted bright white like a dairy so that it glowed even at night, with wide friendly windows and a bright blue roof.

And flowers that grew naturally and a lawn seemingly immune to weeds.

Who took care of it? It just didn't make any sense. Even when the kids guided newcomers over to Halloween Street they stayed away from the white house.

The little girl's name was Laura, and she lived across the creek from Halloween Street. From her bedroom window she could see all the houses. She could see who went there and she could see everything they did. She didn't stop to analyze, or pass judgments. She merely witnessed, and now and then spoke an almost inaudible "Hi" to her window and to those visiting on the other side. An occasional "Hi" to the houses of Halloween Street.

Laura should have been pretty. She had wispy blonde hair so pale it appeared white in most light, worn long down her back. She had small lips and hands that were like gauges to her health: soft and pink when she was feeling good, pale and dry when she was doing poorly.

But Laura was not pretty. There was nothing really wrong about her face: it was just vague. A cruel aunt with a drinking problem used to say that "it lacked character." Her mother once took her to a lady who cut silhouette portraits out of crisp black paper at a shopping mall. Her mother paid the lady five dollars to do one of Laura. The lady had finally given up in exasperation, exclaiming "The child has no profile!"

Laura overheard her mother and father talking about it one time. "I see things in her face," her mother had said.

"What do you mean?" Her father always sounded impatient with her mother.

"I don't *know* what I mean! I see things in her face and I can never remember exactly what I saw! Shadows and . . . white, something so white I feel like she's going to disappear into it. Like clouds . . . or a snowbank."

Her father had laughed in astonishment. "You're crazy!"

"You know what I mean!" her mother shouted back. "You don't even look at her directly anymore because you *know* what I mean! It's not exactly sadness in her face, not exactly. Just something born with her, something out of place. She was born out of place. My God! She's eleven years old! She's been like this since she was a baby!"

"She's a pretty little girl." Laura could tell her father didn't really mean that.

"What about her eyes? Tell me about her eyes, Dick!"

"What *about* her eyes? She has nice eyes . . ."

"*Describe* them for me, then! Can you *describe* them? What color are they? What shape?"

Her father didn't say anything. Soon after the argument he'd stomped out of the house. Laura knew he couldn't describe her eyes. Nobody could.

Laura didn't make judgments when other people talked about her. She just listened. And watched with eyes no one could describe. Eyes no one could remember.

No, it wasn't that she was sad, Laura thought. It wasn't that her parents were mean to her or that she had a terrible life. Her parents weren't ever mean to her and although she didn't know exactly what kind of life she had, she knew it wasn't terrible.

She didn't enjoy things like other kids did. She didn't enjoy playing or watching television or talking to the other kids. She didn't *enjoy*, really. She had quiet thoughts, instead. She had quiet thoughts when she pretended to be asleep but was really listening to all her parents' conversations, all their arguments. She had quiet thoughts when she watched people. She had quiet thoughts when people could not describe her eyes. She had quiet thoughts while gazing at Halloween Street, the glowing white house, and all the things that happened there.

She had quiet thoughts pretending that she hadn't been born out of place, that she hadn't been born anyplace at all.

Laura could have been popular, living so close to Halloween Street, seeing it out of her bedroom window. No other kid lived so close or had such a good view. But of course she wasn't popular. She didn't share Halloween Street. She sat at her desk at school all day and didn't talk about Halloween Street at all.

That last Halloween Laura got dressed to go out. That made her mother happy—Laura had never gone trick-or-treating before. Her mother had always encouraged her to go, had made or bought her costumes, taken her to parties at church or school, parties the other kids dressed up for:

ghosts and vampires and princesses, giggling and running around with their masks like grotesquely swollen heads. But Laura wouldn't wear a costume. She'd sit solemn-faced, unmoving, until her mother finally gave up and took her home. And she'd never go trick-or-treating, never wear a costume.

After she'd told her mother that she wanted to go out that night her mother had driven her around town desperately trying to find a costume for her. Laura sat impassively on the passenger side, dutifully got out at each store her mother took her to, and each time shook her head when asked if she liked each of the few remaining costumes.

"I don't know where else we can try, Laura," her mother said, sorting through a pile of mismatched costume pieces at a drugstore in a mall. "It'll be dark in a couple of hours, and so far you haven't liked a *thing* I've shown you."

Laura reached into the pile and pulled out a cheap face mask. The face was that of a middle-aged woman, or a young man, cheeks and lips rouged a bright red, eye shadow dark as a bruise, eyebrows a heavy and coarse dark line.

"But, honey. Isn't that a little . . ." Laura shoved the mask into her mother's hand. "Well, all right." She picked up a bundle of bright blue cloth from the table. "How about this pretty robe to go with it?" Laura didn't look at the robe. She just nodded and headed for the door, her face already a mask itself.

Laura left the house that night after most of the other trick-or-treaters had come and gone. Her interest in Halloween actually seemed less than ever this year; she stayed in her bedroom as goblins and witches and all manner of stunted, warped creatures came to the front door singly and in groups, giggling and dancing and playing tricks on each other. She could see a few of them over on Halloween Street, not going up to any of the houses but rather running up and down the short street close to the houses in I-dare-you races. But not near as many as in years past.

Now and then her mother would come up and open her door. "Honey, don't you want to leave yet? I swear everybody'll be all out of the goodies if you don't go soon." And each time Laura shook her head, still staring out the window, still watching Halloween Street.

Finally, after most of the other kids had returned to their homes, Laura came down the stairs wearing her best dress and the cheap mask her mother had bought for her.

Her father and mother were in the living room, her mother having retrieved the blue robe from the hall closet.

"She's wearing her best dress, Ann. Besides, it's damned late for her to be going out now."

Her mother eyed her nervously. "I could drive you, honey." Laura shook her head.

"Well, okay, just let me cover your nice dress with the robe. Don't want to get it dirty."

"She's just a *kid*, for chrissake! We can't let her decide!" Her father had dropped his newspaper on the floor. He turned his back on Laura so she wouldn't see his face, wouldn't know how angry he was with both of them. But Laura *knew*. "And that *mask*! Looks like a *whore's* face! Hell, how can she even see? Can't even see her eyes under that." But Laura could see his. All red and sad-looking.

"She's doing something normal for a change," her mother whispered harshly. "Can't you see that? That's more important."

Without a word Laura walked over and pulled the robe out of her mother's arms. After some hesitation, after Laura's father had stomped out of the room, her mother helped her get it on. It was much too large, but her mother gasped "How beautiful!" in exaggerated fashion. Laura walked toward the door. Her mother ran to the door and opened it ahead of her. "Have a good time!" she said in a mock-cheery voice. Laura could see the near panic in the eyes above the distorted grin, and she left without saying goodbye.

A few houses down the sidewalk she pulled the robe off and threw it behind a hedge. She walked on, her head held stiff and erect, the mask's rouge shining bright red in the streetlights, her best dress a soft cream color in the dimness, stirred lightly by the breeze. She walked on to Halloween Street.

She stopped on the bridge and looked down into the creek. A young man's face, a middle-aged woman's face gazed back at her out of dark water and yellow reflections. The mouth seemed to be bleeding.

She walked on to Halloween Street. She was the only one there. The only one to see.

She walked on in her best dress and her shiny mask with eyes no one could see.

The houses on Halloween Street looked the way they always did, empty and dark. Except for the one that glowed the color of clouds, or snow.

The houses on Halloween Street looked their own way, sounded their own way, moved their own way. Lost in their own quiet thoughts. Born out of place.

You could not see their eyes.

Laura went up to the white house with the neatly trimmed yard and the flowers that grew without care. Its color like blowing snow. Its color like heaven. She went inside.

The old woman gazed out her window as goblins and spooks, pirates and ballerinas crossed the bridge to enter Halloween Street. She bit her lip to make it redder. She rubbed at her ancient, blind eyes, rubbing the dark eyeshadow up into the coarse line of brow. She was not beautiful, but she was not hideous either. Not yet. In any case no one ever remembered her face.

Her fine, snow-white hair was beautiful, and long down her back.

She had the most wonderful house on the street, the only one with flowers, the only one that glowed. It was her home, the place where she belonged. All the children, all the children who dared, came to her house every Halloween for treats.

"Come along," she said to the window, staring out at Halloween Street. "Come along," she said, as the treat bags rustled and shifted around her. "You don't remember, do you?" as the first of the giggling goblins knocked at her door. "You've quite forgotten," as the door began to shake from eager goblin fists, eager goblin laughs. "Now scratch your swollen little head, scratch your head. You forgot that first and last, Halloween is for the dead."

TIA V. TRAVIS

The Kiss

Tia V. Travis is from western Canada. She plays guitar for the southwestern-influenced band, the Franklin Slaughter Ranch, and played bass with the country-punk band, Curse of Horseflesh. Travis has a forthcoming chapbook from Subterranean Press and is at work on a magic realist retelling of Hans Christian Andersen's "The Snow Queen." She recently moved to Northern California, where she lives with husband, writer Norman Partridge, and their cat, Minou.

I asked Travis what inspired her story. Her response: "Partly, it was my first summer in the United States, not far from the town of Martinez in Northern California, where the story is set. It was my hottest summer ever! I wrote in the afternoon; every night I played guitar, listened to lounge music, and swam in the pool (not mine, of course!). Frank Sinatra had just cashed in his chips at the Big Casino in the Sky in May; I wanted to record the passing of an era in some small way. I remember seeing the sign where the Sands Hotel used to be: 'Thanks, Las Vegas, for 51 years.' The 's' was falling out. 'S' for So Long? And thanks for what? Just a black, gaping hole."

"The Kiss" was first published in Subterranean Gallery, *edited by Richard T. Chizmar and William K. Schafer.*

—E. D.

> 'Twas on the Isle of Capri that I found her
> Beneath the shade of an old walnut tree
> I can still see the flow'rs blooming round her
> Where we met on the Isle of Capri
> —*"THE ISLE OF CAPRI," JIMMY KENNEDY, 1934*

The angel's heart was torn from its chest.

The stained glass box that had held it was smashed; ruby tears scattered the fountain. The ruins of the valentine lay amidst splinters of red glass and oak leaves mottled with rot. Soaked through, it had been half-devoured by birds. I didn't know whether it had been ripped away strip by ragged strip, or swallowed mouthful by mouthful, a bloody red delicacy fought over by many. Either way, it came as no shock that there was nothing left but as a few anemic tatters. This was a cemetery, after all, and in the land of the dead the birds were reigning lords.

They perched everywhere: on the crypts, on the cypress and oak, on the eavestroughs where the rain ran rivers into the sodden earth. At the funeral forty years ago their ancestors had screamed obscenities from the trees as the preacher droned on and on about love and eternity. Furious screeches and feathered rage. I clutched Sister Constance-Evangeline's black habit in a hailstorm of birds and terror, covering my ears until all I could hear was the rushing of blood . . . the beating of wings.

But the birds didn't frighten me now as they did then. I slogged through the mud toward the fountain.

The heart was in ruins, but a sinewy strand of scarlet crepe still twisted around the rusted wire frame. Bleached by sun and leeched by rain, the crepe was white as aged scar tissue. When I touched it, it collapsed into stringy fibers. The last damp mouthful of air trapped within the empty chamber expired on a breath of wind. Gently, I replaced what was left of the heart in the fountain bowl. Stained amber with the sap of cypress needles, it seemed more like a Canopic jar, and my heart, my heart lay dead within.

I tried to remember the day when they buried my mother, but I felt as empty as that dead husk. Forty years will do that to you. It wasn't that I didn't understand the pain; I just couldn't feel it anymore.

For stone angels and dead whores there is no pain, I reminded myself. A crepe heart does not beat. A lifeless body does not suffer the ravages of nature's savage little ways, nor does it endure the gut wrenching of scavengers as they tear it to shreds. For the dead there are no haunting regrets, no aching remorses, no taunting dreams to torment deep into the night. There is no laughter, no music, no dancing. No dream of an Isle of Capri . . .

Mixed blessings.

The blessings of heartless angels.

The workings of the human heart have always been a mystery to me.

The heart of my mother, Lana Lake, has been the greatest mystery of all. Nothing remains of that heart now but a dry, empty chamber, a mummified fist wrapped around a hardened clot where once had been caged a wild and fiercely beating thing, scarlet and raw as ripped silk.

In the autumn of 1958 when I was eleven years old, my mother, Lana Lake, was bombed out of her mind in the back garden on a bed of crushed birds-of-paradise. She shouted to the sky that spun overhead like a blue top that I could mix an Angel's Kiss so coo-coo crazy Frank Sinatra himself would have married me on the spot for one sip of that utterly endsville elixir.

He was between mistresses, Lana said with a wicked wink that blushed me down to my bare toes. At the wedding, she storied her enraptured audience of one, Francis Albert would stare into my eyes with his cause-for-swooning baby blues. He would hold me tenderly in his arms and croon "The Isle of Capri" until it was my bedtime and Mrs. Sinatra arrived to take him home.

I laughed in sheer delight at the possibilities, licking fingers sticky with pomegranate juice. Careless crimson fingerprints decorated the front of my virgin-white Catholic school blouse. The long black woolen stockings and sensible shoes had long since been kicked off in favor of squirming bare toes.

It had been Daddy's idea for me to attend Our Lady of Perpetual Sorrow Convent School for Girls. I hated his surprisingly stubborn old world ways, making me go just because his own mother had, God rest her soul. I couldn't wait to run home to my sinning mother, who would lightheartedly endure my tortured reading of catechisms as she painted my toenails an unrepentant shade of Mary Magdalene red.

"So, should I call him?" Lana said in her leading way.

"Frank *Sinatra*?"

She snatched my pomegranate and sucked the bitten part. She sang: *"Call the one who loves you only, I can be so warm and tender . . ."*

"No no no!" I rolled on the grass, shrieking with embarrassed laughter.

"He owes me a favor," Lana added in a low, theatrical voice.

I sat up in a tumble of fallen leaves. "He does?"

"What do you think?" On the tip of her tongue, a bright red jewel glittered. Pomegranate seed, like the one she wore in her navel when she did her routine. It disappeared into her mouth, a red spark on that dancing tongue. *"Call me, don't be afraid, you can caaalll me, baby it's late . . ."*

Skip and a jump. That's what my heart did. Mother really *had* met

Sinatra, and every night after that I practically expected The Man with the Golden Charm to magically appear on my doorstep in a black tuxedo, with a handkerchief as orange as birds-of-paradise tucked sharp-as-you-please in the breastpocket.

Now that was style, Lana said. Ring-a-ding-ding.

For an aperitif I would serve him an Angel's Kiss: equal parts white creme de cacao, creme de violette, prunelle, and sweet cream.

That was the Angel's Kiss.

Too candy-sweet for anyone else, Mother downed them like after-dinner mints after dancing all night at the Cocoa Club.

The Cocoa Club: there was a swinging spot. Peter Lawford, one of Sinatra's fellow rat-packers, had bought the prohibition clip joint for a song in 1952 and fixed it up. Pink neon martini glasses and twin palm trees with beckoning fronds out front. It was the place where you went to see and be seen if you were *anybody at all* in the San Francisco Bay area. Tuxedos were a way of life for the men; the women wore black satin strapless evening dresses and shoulder-length gloves and elaborate jewelry from exclusive shops. Every table had little silver deco lights that lit up the room like diamonds. The waiters with their pencil-thin mustachios swept the tables over their heads like party hats, gliding down the grand staircase to the backlit stage. Best seat in the house, when you slipped them a little something extra. *Duke 'em good!* in Sinatra's slangbook, but he was way too slick to flaunt a bill.

Daddy pounded the pads at the Cocoa Club every night. *Ba da da!* The hottest drummer in town, Joe Caiola would dish it up any way you liked it: slow and swinging or fast and hopping. He'd learned to bang the bongos from the master, Chano Pozo himself, when he and Daddy palled around with Dizzy Gillespie.

Sometimes for a few extra bucks he'd fly down to Los Angeles or to New York or Chicago and sit in with Sam Butera or Artie Shaw's band or some other swingers who were hip to the beat. Or maybe Sinatra would hire him for a private party at the Tonga Room at the Fairmont and then word would get out about this real gone cat who could really lick those skins, and then everyone else would want him for their parties, too.

Bongos were big back then, and Daddy would get top dollar for those gigs. Sometimes he'd even team up with Tito Contreros or Jack Costanza and then the money would roll in on a cloud of fine Cuban cigar smoke because Sinatra and his pallies were outrageous tippers and they partied every night when they were in town. But as hot as Daddy was, my mother was the main attraction.

Lana Lake was a "class act," Daddy said, even when she stripped down to the bare canvas. She was a work of art, a living painting with a beating heart and eyes outlined in fiery yellow like the birds-of-paradise she loved.

Once when they were doing the bossa nova and thought I was asleep on a stack of records, I saw her slip her tongue into the heart of a bird-of-paradise and I thought I'd die. They danced like they were built for each other, Mother and Daddy: not just the bossa nova, but the mambo, the samba, the tango. Lana cocked her hips for Perez Prado and swung to Count Basie and jumped to Louis Prima. There was Sinatra, of course, the Ultimate Big Spender. "Isle of Capri" was Lana's favorite, though she liked others: "Three Coins in the Fountain" and "Love is the Tender Trap," and the melancholy "Don't Cry, Joe" that was like a dance hall after closing.

Daddy would hold Mother close, his dark head buried in her shoulder. "Amorino, amorino . . ." he whispered over and over, like a man lost at sea and found.

Don't cry, Joe
Let her go, let her go, let her go
Lana's voice warm and dark as espresso at midnight.
You've gotta realize this is the windup
Things will be much better when you make your mind up . . .
Dancing slow and easy, her hands wrapped in his hair, pulling, pulling . . .

Daddy could sing, too, but mostly he liked to play the drums with a subtle, expert flick of his wrists. A true musician, Joe Caiola would lose himself in the rhythm, the ghost of a cigarette in the ashtray, a cylinder of burned ash.

Sometimes it would be jazz drums with lots of metal brushes, with his eyes half-closed like window shades. The fringe of the brushes was like the fringe of his eyelashes as they swept his cheekbone. It was an angular face with too many planes and corners. It sliced shadows in the lamplight and made a chiaroscuro of his features.

"A face you could get cut on," I'd heard my mother say more than once.

"Or a face you could cut," Daddy teased back with a mischievous swat of brushes.

Tino laughed, ice clinking in his glass with a little *cha cha cha.* Jack Daniel's and ice. That's how he liked it. "Maybe a face *Cassie* could cut, eh, Joe?"

Daddy icepicked a look at him while Mother, poured into a jade silk sheath, slipped out from behind the Chinese screen. The needle swung across Martin Denny's *Exotica* on the hi-fi. Screeching birds with jeweled plumes, grinning monkeys and purring leopards, growling wild things on the prowl in the heart of the jungle where claws could cut to the quick.

"You hear what I said, Lana?" Tino lazily tipped back his J.D.

"Don't tempt me, Tino," Lana said, waving a finger at him. Polished fingernails the shade of dragonfly wings. "Don't . . ."

She smiled at them both with an upturned curve of her lips, and most times it would be fine, but sometimes there'd be something there behind the smile, a sheet-lightning flash of temper that raised the hairs on my neck.

Sometimes Daddy called Mother his Scarlet Tornado. Sometimes, his Red Flame.

White ice melting red flame, burning the glass, the two as one.

I was alone in the cemetery. The air was wet with the late winter rain that had already soaked both me and my shredded heart through the skin. A brisk wind shook a shimmering wash of icy drops from the shadow-dark cypresses. It rattled the twisted branches of the black oaks that grew behind the crypt, shedding their leaves in the angel's fountain. All around me stormed a cyclone of cypress needles, of torn black oak leaves. They whipped around the worn crevices of the headstones with leafy tongues. They clung like leeches to my shivering body. God, I was cold.

I stared at the graveyard birds lined up in the trees like snipers. They watched my every movement. Talons raked straight to the heart, deep enough to draw blood. What was I doing here?

Chasing the ghost of a song.

My hands started to shake, but I couldn't leave.

"I *can't* leave," I whispered. To the birds, to myself, I wasn't sure. The wind carried my voice through the branches of the black oaks, rustled through the wings of a thousand birds whose eyes never left me, not once in forty years. *I have to hear that song again. I have to know.*

In the early 1940s, before I was born, my mother had some throwaway bit parts in crime movies. She was invariably cast as the seductive siren for whom they dragged the rivers while the opening credits ran: *Murder on the Rocks. The Sweet Kill. Venus Under Glass. Sonata for a Night Angel.* No big studios, no contracts, no options. It was all strictly B-league. Still, Lana's not inconsiderable onscreen charms had attracted her share of attention, almost all of it male. And while Lana Lake might have been a minor starlet in the Tinseltown constellation, she shone bright as Polaris in her hometown of Martinez after she'd decided that dancing and drinking, not moviemaking, were more in tune with her natural nocturnal rhythms.

Location turned out to be everything of course. Martinez, a shot-glass toss away from San Francisco's infamous Cocoa Club, was not only home to Lana Lake, but to the equally infamous martini. Mother's martini of choice was, naturally, Dean Martin's choice. *The Flame of Love: swirl three drops expensive sherry in an iced stem glass, then pour out. Squeeze one strip of orange peel into the glass and flambe. Throw away the peel. Fill the glass with ice to chill it. Toss out ice. Add very expensive vodka, then flambe another strip of orange peel around the rim. Throw away the peel. Stir very gently.*

"*I like a new Lincoln with all of its class,*" Mother sang to Daddy while sitting in his lap. "*I like a martini and burn on the glass!*"

That was Lana Lake: burn on the glass all the way.

Myself, I'd never experienced the forbidden and fermented fruits of the Cocoa Club. And liberal as Lana was, she still couldn't slip me under the velvet ropes and into the back door of the smoky nightspot.

To make up for it, she rehearsed her act for us in the living room, for Daddy and me, and maybe some of the boys in the band who always seemed to be lounging around there, smoking and joking, or tinkling "Street Scene '58" on the piano, because sooner or later, everyone ended up at our house.

Including Daddy.

Lana's little trick started like this: first she would disappear behind the Chinese screen—*Chinoise, en Francais*, she explained in a crazy put-on accent, not quite French, not quite anything. Then she would slink out from behind the screen with a seductive wink of an emerald eye.

And then she would dance.

The lights played with the curves of her silhouette on rice paper as satiny-smooth as the head of Daddy's snare drum. He kept time with the jive of her hips. His shirt sleeves would be rolled up, the collar unbuttoned, his deeply tanned skin dark against his white undershirt. Cigarette half-forgotten in the corner of his mouth as he stared at her. As we all stared at her.

Luis Ramirez whistled. "Now that's what I call a sweet little cookie," he said, shaking his head.

"A *fortune* cookie. All wrapped up in Chinese silk," Daddy said with a proud swish of cymbals. He wasn't the only one who loved Mother. We all loved her: the boys in the band, and Daddy, and me. Burn on the glass, all the way.

Lana had hundreds of costumes jammed in her closet like pinatas:

Spanish bullfighter bolero jacket and a snorting black bull painted above her breast. Caravan gypsy with bright scarves and an evil silver blade licking the tip of her rouged nipple. Queen of the Nile in a sleek leopard pelt and a painted python with a gleaming amber eye that wound around her narrow waist.

Daddy's wife, Cassandra (she liked to be called Mrs. Joe Caiola), had called Mother a common whore. Right to her face, once when we ran into her in town. With all those people standing there like a church choir. Nervous titters and uneasy glances all around. Lana Lake was Lana Lake, after all, and there was no telling what she'd do for a slight like that. To everyone's shock, Mother only smiled, and we kept walking. Still, there was an angry tightness to her steps. Red dress. Red high heels. Red hair bouncing down her back, burning like her cheeks.

I never understood, then, how it was possible to hate something so unabashedly beautiful. I was transfixed by an unrestrained female beauty that only a girl of eleven, uninitiated to the mysteries that awaited the thrust into adulthood, could be. God, how I wanted that life for myself: a hundred handsome boyfriends to drive me anywhere I wanted in a shiny new limousine. And a private jet to fly me to the Isle of Capri.

They should burn that damn club down, I heard Mrs. Caiola say. She was arguing with Daddy in the house next door. It was a scorching summer morning; all the windows were open. You couldn't help but hear her.

Burn it down . . .

Instantly my nostrils singed with blazing palm fronds, scorched maitre d's, bandstands showering sparks, highball glasses exploding like a string of firecrackers behind the bar. I envisioned incinerated skeletons locked in charred embraces, teeth clattering on the dancefloor like smoky pearls from a scattered necklace with every step. Would they really burn it down?

But the Cocoa Club remained open in spite of Cassandra Caiola, a glorification of all things sinful, a palace of pleasure, a den of desire.

Sometimes Lana would wear a G-string of tiny pagodas and the spangled pasties of Imperial China. On those formal occasions Mother, with an artist's steady hand and a little silver mirror, would paint an oriental dragon that began at her left breast and licked the nape of her neck with a forked tongue. When Lana breathed, the dragon breathed, and my heart pounded with excitement. When she danced . . . it was like watching the unfolding of an origami bird. The Emperor's Nightingale with nipples like ripe red raspberries. Her arms moved like vines, slim as the necks of Ming vases. The dragon sank its claws into her creamy

as she clattered open the screen door and ran, barefoot, into the heart of a nightmare. But after forty years, the song had stuck in my throat.

My eyes ached from the blinding white of the marble, the blinding white of the sky. I stared at the heart in the fountain, drained and pale. It became for me another heart: my mother's heart, pumping wet and red and hard through the splinters of a rib cage that gleamed white as the wings of the painted angel gracing her left breast.

The angel had bled a halo of red.

The red was everywhere, a flutter of red smears on Mother's hands and face, like the frantic sweep of butterfly wings.

The red was on Daddy's face, too. Mother bent over him on the floor in a widening pool of blood, her mouth pressed tightly to the third finger of his left hand in the rich, wet kiss of one who loves deeply.

It was not her own ring she kissed.

A bubble of blood escaped her lips.

It burst, like the world, around us all.

Mother and Daddy and Cassandra and me. The four of us, together. As we always would be.

Red flame and thieving birds, the two burned into one. Blood and aches.

My shoulders heaved as I held the statue. I started to cry, but no tears came.

"What's a whore?" I asked Mother the afternoon after Mrs. Caiola had called her that in the street. Instantly, I chewed my tongue in regret. Mother's lips tightened, quivered a little. Without a word she drew me into arms as cool as a Tom Collins. The breeze rustled musically through the leaves of the eucalyptus trees in the backyard. The sound of a thousand chopsticks, swish swish . . .

We listened, Mother and I. I closed my eyes and leaned back in her arms. After a moment she started to hum softly. Snapped her fingers. Staring across the garden at the white picket fence next door, she sang in a low, deliberate voice: *"She gets too hungry for dinner at eight . . ."*

The bedroom window was open. The pane refracted a dazzle of green light. Someone stirred behind the stiff muslin curtain, ever so slightly.

Singing louder, now: *"She loves the theater, but never comes late!"* She tumbled me to my feet. Eucalyptus seed shells sprayed from my skirt as she swept me across the garden.

I grinned at Mother, but she wasn't looking at me. Not at me.

"Sing it with me, baby!" she cried. *"She loves the theater, but never comes late!"*

Thoughts of mysterious whores vanished. I sang the only words I could remember, sang them, off-key, at the top of my lungs: *"SHE'D NEVER BOTHER WITH PEOPLE SHE'D HATE!"*

Lana wasn't dancing now. A smile twisted her lips as she stared straight at the window.

Big finale, now, lots of brass. I did a cartwheel and belted it out: *"THAT'S WHY THE LADY IS A TRAMP!"*

The curtains in the house next door snapped shut.

Mother blew her a kiss.

I collapsed in the grass, sweaty and breathless and gassed to be alive.

In the Whispering Pines Cemetery, the wind stole the kiss I blew and carried it back to the curtain of trees, the peering eyes in the branches. Red hair lashed my eyes and I turned away from the trees. Instead, I gazed up at the stone angel, at the gaping cavity in its chest where its life had gushed, at the wings that hooked a silver awning of sky. In the corner of one eye balanced a single black teardrop: spider. A delicate leg caught in a shred of web, quivered in the wind like a trembling eyelash. Eternally poised, I knew the arachnid teardrop would never fall. The spider itself was long-dead, and its hollow shell had, over time, become little more than a crust of sleep in the angel's eye.

The angel's dry eye.

God weeps no tears for whores.

A roosting magpie, thief of hearts, cawed from the cypress with bony branch-wings dark as dusk. Soon night would roll in on the back of a rumbling black thunderhead. I grit my teeth hard, knuckles white on marble ankles.

Why had she done it? God, I didn't know—how could I? All I knew was that the angel's heart had not been torn out, then. Not yet. The heart still beat, if only for a few moments more. It felt everything. Knew everything. Told everything. It whispered a single word: a wet red kiss blown to me from across a kitchen floor, from the lips of the dying to the heart of the living.

One kiss, one word.

Summertime was nearly over
Blue Italian sky above

One kiss, one word.

I said, "Lady, I'm a rover
Can you spare a sweet word of love?"

One word was enough. I never forgot what Mother had whispered as she lay, her life seeping away from her, from me, in the burnished brass light of that autumn afternoon. But I had misunderstood what she meant by it. Until this moment. Maybe, until this moment. It was this remembering that had carried me back to the angel's arms.

Remembering and time, and dreams and hearts, and forgotten songs and dying angels. The kiss of angels, painted and real and dancing and drunk, with lips wide open and hearts torn out, as sweet as creme de cacao.

Mrs. Caiola never did leave Daddy. She threatened to a thousand times but there was no way in hell she'd give him his freedom so he could be with *her*. That's how Daddy told it, anyhow, when he and Mother stayed up late talking and I caught snatches of their heated discussions in the other room.

Then there were the angry accusations and counteraccusations pitched back and forth through the night like hardballs from the house next door. Begging on both sides. *Cassandra, this is crazy. You know it isn't any good. Why don't you let me go? Not on your life, Joe. Not on your GODDAMNED life.*

Then she'd turn on the waterworks. That's what Mother called them, with a fed-up snort.

I knew about waterworks.

"What does the water in the convent fountain taste like, Capri?" she asked me once, squeezing my hands. "Jesus' tears?"

"Creme de cacao," I answered, giggling.

An angel's kiss . . .

Sunday afternoons, after the Cocoa Club shakedown, I poured and mixed the Angel's Kisses carefully. I set them on a tray inlaid with opal dragons that wound round it like the painted twin on Lana's neck. Then I took them on tiptoe to her boudoir. Stolen sips of Angel's Kisses. I used to think in sweet rapture: she's like that. An Angel's Kiss, as pure as bliss . . .

Mother, lying in bed with a sleeping mask strewn on the sheets like a leftover from a masquerade, sipped her drink. "Mmm. Just the thing for that Mood Indigo," she confided.

"The mood indigo?"

Shadow of a smile. "Mood Indigo, baby."

Through Mother's bedroom window I watched Cassandra Caiola click-click-click down the sunny front walk in high heels and a Christian Dior suit. Her hair was pulled tightly back from her carefully made-up face, not a strand out of place. She paused, frowning, fastening the little pearl buttons on her gloves. I'd never seen her go anywhere without those gloves. Perfect and pristine and white as ice. She called Daddy's name sharply as she unlocked the door to her Cadillac, so shiny you could see your reflection in it. White, just like her gloves.

White ice melting red flame, burning the glass, the two as one.

Mother and Cassandra: fire and ice.

I watched Daddy amble out of the house and toss his cigarette on the sidewalk. Slouch his hat forward. Slam.

"You know that wasn't our arrangement, Joe." Backing out. "*You* said you wanted a child. And far be it for *me* to stand in your way, especially since you'd already knocked her up. Though God only knows what *that* one will turn—" squeal of rubber "—with a mother like that." Angry lips in a rearview mirror.

Not looking at her. Tapping a rhythm on the dash.

"You *know* what an understanding woman I am, Joe. You *know* I am. But I've had just about enough of living right next door to that— that—"

Sigh. "Why don't you just let me go, then, Cassandra."

We never heard the reply as the Cadillac peeled down the driveway.

Lana lay languidly in bed. She lifted her glass. "Here's to sweethearts and wives," she said wryly. "May they never meet."

The Angel's Kiss.

Full on the lips.

It was time that had carried me to Whispering Pines, to the place where my Mother lay wrapped in her past like a skein of stars. It was time, chased by the ghost of a song I couldn't quite remember, and couldn't quite forget. And now I stood with the iron door swung open wide behind me.

A wet northern California wind blew at my back, bringing with it a smattering of soaked black oak leaves. Inside the crypt it was dim, but there was still a little dying afternoon light. I knew I'd be able to see what I needed to see.

I had to see Mother's rich red lips while Sinatra sang the word and Lana spoke it with that terrible hurt, that desperate pleading in her eyes. One word.

One sweet word of love

For a moment I wasn't sure if the little suitcase record player I'd left for her would still be there. Somehow, I'd always imagined ghostly hands spiriting Lana away at last to that elusive Mediterranean isle. But there it was as it had waited in the vault the last four decades. Beside it, under a thick layer of dust, lay the brilliant laminated cover of Frank Sinatra's "Come Fly with Me." Old Blue Eyes, now dust himself, his voice echoing in a tomb.

I picked up the record. It smelled of damp, of decay, of shut-in places. But in my mind, a song rang out that was gay and swinging, a song that was really going somewhere. A song brimming with sparkling vino and Italian palazzis and illicit romance. It was the song that once had carried me away to a beautiful villa on the Isle of Capri, an isle of tangerine sunsets and whispered words of love.

I stood with my eyes closed, unconsciously swaying to a song I heard only in memory. And, swaying, I remembered, at last, the song I had forgotten.

The weeklies sizzled with stories of Mother splashing full glasses of champagne in men's faces. Stories of hard stinging slaps that rang through the room. Her fits of temper were legendary, as was her childish pouting, her brooding silences and black depressions when she'd scratch the needle across "The Isle of Capri" again and again. Sometimes Daddy would walk in whistling some tune kicking around in his head, unsuspecting with his hands in his pockets, and she'd spring like a striking cobra. Back him into a corner. He'd grin at her and throw up his hands in surrender, and she'd spit out, "Joe, you really are a sonofabitch." Then she'd kiss him hard and bite his lip until it bled.

It was a savage dance, that give and take of love they had, stronger and wilder than any act the Cocoa Club had ever witnessed. No one was particularly surprised when Lana Lake and Joe Caiola turned up dead in a pool of red on her kitchen floor. A man between two houses, between two worlds—ice-cold wife in one, red-hot mistress and child in the other. Maybe Mrs. Joe Caiola could put up with an "arrangement" like that, but not a wildcat like Lana Lake. People like Lana, their passions boiled over like a pot of sauce on the stove.

I remember everything about that moment: Lana's chili pepper red toreador pants . . . the spicy smell of Daddy's favorite Napoli spaghetti sauce bubbling like Mount Vesuvius before a blast . . . the ripe odor of fresh garlic and pungent garden oregano and ripe roma tomatoes the color of arterial blood . . . the heavy gun on the floor by Lana's bare feet. Red lacquer, chipped on the pinkie.

I remember the pain and horror in Mother's eyes, the desperate pleading, the grasping fingers, the little choking sound she made as she tried to speak. . . .

I tried to picture that kitchen now: blood that had pooled and seeped into linoleum that was now badly discolored. Knife on a butcher block where decades-old onions had shriveled up like blackened flies. An apron stained with tomato sauce the color of blood, and an ice box filled with dried-out spaghetti, a forty year old menu that never changed.

Old Blue Eyes hit it on the head: *She wore a lovely meatball on her finger.*

It turned out Daddy had been shot through the heart with a bullet from the same .22 automatic Tino Alvarez gave Lana to protect herself from the crazy nuts who were always hitting on her at the club. She'd even used it once, shot a man in the crotch without an ounce of remorse. Clutching the bloody mess in his pants he'd stumbled to the bar on the corner, where he soused what was left of his manhood in a glass of scotch because a guy there told him he'd heard somewhere it made a pretty good disinfectant. The screams were heard clear to the next county.

So the story ran, anyhow. . . . The tabloids had a parade with it. Mother was acquitted, and after that, everyone in town knew about the .22 locked in the nightstand. Everyone. And men knew better than to tangle with Lana Lake.

Everyone also knew how Mother wanted Joe Caiola all to herself for years, and how things would never, ever be the way she wanted them, not while Cassandra Caiola was kicking up her little white Christian Dior pumps in protest.

It was the standard story: one too many nights, one too many fights. And it wasn't too hard for people to picture Lana storming off to the bedroom in tears, banging open the nightstand, fumbling around for the gun. . . .

Maybe she'd even meant to go after Cassandra, but it never got as far as that. Somehow the gun went off. Lana herself was probably as surprised as hell. And what was left now with Joe lying dead on the floor? Snake eyes, no matter which way you rolled it, and nothing left to do but squeeze the trigger one more time.

Don't cry Joe. Let her go, let her go, let her go . . .

God, let him go.

What do you say, baby . . . you and me on the Isle of Capri . . .

Don't joke, Joe.

I thought about the gun. About Cassandra Caiola. About how Cassandra had bought our house the day after the funerals. It stood there for the next forty years. Boarded up, falling into disrepair, a sprawling little bungalow choked in a stranglehold of climbing vines as thick as a dragon's body. The vines bled green in the rain, and the rain seeped into the ground.

Over the years I'd often wondered how the sunlight would look as it filtered through the windowpanes in the house where once upon a time, I'd danced in a dream. Heavy, still green light that made everything look as though you were seeing it through a glass-bottomed boat, a sleepy lagoon.

It was a haunted house in every sense, wrapped in its secrets, and its faded Chinese screens, and its undrunk bottles of creme de cacao, now crystallized sugar. All those unmixed Angel's Kisses. Sweetcream dreams, sour-curdled by time.

I don't know how long I stood there like that in the tomb, but when I opened my eyes it was almost dark and Sinatra's smile was a white spark in the moonlight. I put the record down. Touched the casket wrapped in its sensuous cloak of dust. I held my breath as I lifted the lid—carefully, carefully—and the dust fell from it in sparkles, the spent lanterns of weary fireflies.

There were those who said that Lana Lake was buried naked in the sapphire-blue mink stole Joe Caiola had once draped over her milk-white shoulders. *Confession* magazine reported, with more than a hint of smug morality, that they had buried her in her G-string.

I tried to imagine that G-string, swinging across the cavern of my mother's caved-in pelvis, a glittering rope bridge over a dead sea of peacock feathers now powdered to iridescent dust.

I didn't know for certain what I would find in that box.

But my breath caught in my throat when I saw her red hair. Still red as blood. Dried blood. I thought of the heart I had made all those years ago, that childish cathedral of paper and wire, now rusted away. My eyes drifted down to the bird-of-paradise I had twisted between her fingers, pale entwined swan necks. A ghost of fragrance still lingered in the withered blooms. I blinked back the tears that balanced on my lower lashes.

God weeps no tears for dead whores, Capri.

I made myself look.

Down.

There, there.

I couldn't help it: my eyes misted as I stared at the beaded vertebra that shone in the faint light like a strand of luminescent pearls, pearl upon shimmering pearl. Concentric layers of secrets. God in heaven, she was so beautiful, even now.

She whispered softly, "It's best not to linger,"
Then as I kissed her hand I could see

And now I *did* see. There. There. Beneath the delicate spinal column. Shaking, I slipped a hand through the gentle curve of bone.

She wore a plain golden ring on her finger
Twas goodbye on the Isle of Capri

There. On the satin lining.

A plain golden ring, sucked off the hand of a dead man and trapped for forty years in the throat of the woman who loved him.

A plain golden ring.

It was the last verse of the song. The verse I couldn't remember. Until now.

And now I remembered everything. The pain and horror in Mother's eyes, the desperate pleading, the grasping fingers, the little choking sound she made as she tried to speak. . . .

It wasn't horror in her eyes, but fear. Fear that even her own daughter would misunderstand the deaths that had come too soon. And now I knew what my mother had been trying to tell me that copper autumn afternoon so long ago. One word:

"Capri," she had said. *Capri* . . .

But it wasn't my name she whispered with those lush red lips. Not a beg for forgiveness, a desperate cry for understanding. It was the name of the song: "The Isle of Capri."

And then—standing there at my mother's casket—I knew what it was she'd tried to tell me but couldn't. Couldn't—because a wedding ring engraved with the name of a murderess had lodged in her windpipe like a piece of candy and stolen her voice.

Forever Cassandra.

And that plain golden ring had never been found.

The police, and the courts, and the press, and the people, had all believed Cassandra Caiola. And why shouldn't they? She was beautiful, an ice goddess sitting there in the witness stand in her black Christian Dior and veiled hat, wringing her white-gloved hands with just the appropriate touch of widow's wetness in her eyes.

Not the same set of gloves she'd had on when she shot first her husband, then his mistress, before spinning smartly on her high heels and click-click-clicking out of the kitchen. Always the perfect lady, that particular pair of gloves had been neatly disposed of. One, two, three. As easy as that.

Except the mistress hadn't died quite as quickly as the husband. The mistress had time for one last kiss, a kiss that would name her murderess.

Forty years later.

Dabbing her eyes, careful not to smudge her makeup, Cassandra explained to the court that she and Joe had reconciled, that he had gone over to Lana Lake's to tell her once and for all he wanted nothing more to do with her, that he was suing for custody of his daughter Capri on the grounds that Lana was an unfit mother, and that Cassandra, waiting for his return, had heard the gunshots all the way across the garden. It was Cassandra who had called the police.

Everyone pitied the little girl sitting there in her black woollen school uniform beside Sister Constance-Evangeline of Our Lady of Perpetual Sorrow. Capri Lake, the daughter of the whore, with her downcast eyes and burning red cheeks and hands locked tightly in her lap like a heart without a key.

And what a kind and generous woman was Cassandra Caiola to welcome into her own home, with open arms, the illegitimate child of her husband's mistress.

It was how Joe would have wanted it, Mrs. Caiola explained. She had never been able to have children of her own. He would have wanted her to raise the child as her own flesh and blood to be a respectable and decent young lady. And everyone's head nodded in sympathetic agreement, and Cassandra smiled secretly to herself, and in that moment, the course of my life changed forever.

Forever Cassandra.

A hand clad in an ice-white glove that smelled of Chanel No. 5 closed around a wrist braceleted with ruby tears. I was led numbly down the courtroom steps through a mill of people and reporters and photographers with flashbulbs. There was a controlled yet agonizing wrench of my arm socket as I ducked my head into the shining white Cadillac, and Cassandra Caiola drove us silently back to a house without dancing, without song, without love.

It took time to learn the music of silence.

It took my life.

But little by little, Cassandra Caiola became Mother to me. For I had always lived in the house without music.

God weeps no tears for dead whores, Capri. God weeps no tears.

Little by little, with Sister Constance-Evangeline's compassionate guidance.

God weeps no tears, Capri. God weeps no tears.

And eventually, I too, wept no more, and Cassandra Caiola at last heard me whisper the word she wanted so desperately to hear—

one sweet word of love

And truly, there was no sweeter revenge for Cassandra Caiola than to hear the word *whore* on the lips of Lana Lake's daughter. She made me say it again and again, a record without end, until she laughed and laughed out loud and tears sprang to her eyes, because this was music to her ears like no other music could be. It was the only music I ever heard again.

At least, it seemed that way for a very long time. But in the end it was the song that drew me back. The song that gave me my name and flowed in my veins, the song that drew me back to what I had lost. Back to the house of dancing, and singing, and life.

Back to the Isle of Capri.

Thunder shattered a sky as dark as wet satin. The moon was a weeping eye.

"Is that you?"

Not once had I heard her say it with her own lips. *Capri.* She couldn't stand to say it.

"Where have you been all this time? Close the door, it's cold."

I said nothing as I shook the rain from my hair. My hair was a light strawberry blond that had never darkened to the luxurious auburn of my mother's. I hadn't inherited her beautiful hair, or her talent for dance, or her brazen love of exhibition.

Her fiery temper was, in me, a slow, burning ember.

Red flame melting white ice.

Cassandra Caiola sat stiffly in the straight-backed chair that looked down on Lana Lake's bungalow. Living her life through the window-pane as she had for forty years.

Rain sluiced through the leaves of the towering eucalyptus trees. Decades of dead leaves and blue gum mulched into the ground with mounds of peeling silver bark. The house seemed like it was slowly sinking. Dissolving into nothing.

Some nights, the moonlight danced on the minty leaves like silver drops of water, and the breeze swished through them like Daddy's brushes, and we'd listen to them, Cassandra and I, in our chairs by the window, in the house without music.

And on other nights, like tonight, the wind rattled through the trees and a litter of hard-shelled fruit clattered on the tiled roof like an iron drum, and we'd listen, *ba da da*, in the house without music.

Cassandra's head nodded in memory. Her eyes were almost closed. The sky was clear now, and I stared at her profile in bas relief, white as marble in the moonlight.

I thought of the angel and its features of stone, and I wondered what was in Cassandra's heart. But for stone angels and dead whores there are no haunting regrets, no aching remorses, no taunting dreams to torment deep into the night. There is no laughter, no music, no dancing. No dream of an Isle of Capri . . .

In this light, Cassandra's eyes had no color of their own. They were the color of eucalyptus leaves reflected in Lana's bedroom window.

"What's that on your lips?" she demanded.

Crushed red beetles, the juice of wild pomegranates, a whore's lipstick, Napoli spaghetti sauce, something else, something red—

In my mind I heard a shot ring out as if it were yesterday. I saw Lana run into the kitchen screaming, a half-tied apron on her hips, slipping on blood and chili peppers in a grotesque dance, a balance of life. I saw the spreading crimson stain on the floor as she cradled Daddy's head in her lap.

I saw her lips, full and red.

I saw the rich, wet kiss of one who had loved deeply.

I had never kissed nor been kissed.

Now I kissed the woman who had been my mother for forty years.

I kissed her with Lana Lake's fierce burning passion.

I bit her lip until it bled, and then I shoved the plain golden ring hard into her mouth, snaking it around her tongue.

She started to choke. Her hands flew up like twin birds, raking me with the fingers of a murderess, but I didn't feel a thing. The daughters of dead whores never do.

I kissed her again until she stopped breathing, and her last breath amounted to less than the mouthful of air in my ruined paper heart.

Afterward I stood at the window and stared at my reflection.

I stood there for a long time thinking of nothing, nothing at all.

Then I threw the window open wide and breathed in the exotic, peppery perfume of the dripping eucalyptus. I listened to the primal music of the rain tap-tapping on the tiled roof of the bungalow like a set of coo-coo crazy drumsticks. The wet wind blew branches against the pane and threw dark shadows against the Chinese screen like the sinuous curves of a dragon, and the shadows danced with the moon.

BILL LEWIS

The Beast
The Hedge

Bill Lewis is an English poet, storyteller, performance artist, and visual artist. His books include Rage Without Anger, The Wine of Connecting, An Intellect of the Heart, Shattered English, *and* Leaving the Autoroute. *He has traveled extensively, giving readings and performances in England, Europe, the United States, and South America. He currently lives in Chatham, Kent, where he is a founding member of the Medway Poets Group, and teaches courses on writing and film at adult education centers, schools, and prisons. Having come from a rural working-class background, Lewis is committed to bringing poetry and art to people from all walks of life. The following fairy tale poems are reprinted from his most recent collection,* Beauty Is the Beast.

—T. W

The Beast

The Beast sits by the telephone
Beauty does not call anymore.

Outside across the lawn a peacock
cries out like a woman being murdered.

The Beast sits inside, curtains block
the gardens where stone animals crowd.

The Beast wears a black eye patch.
Beauty stabbed him in the eye

with the slim blade of her body.
Her smile is a Stanley knife.

The delicate lines around her mouth
cut deep into his sight. His vision hurts.

She is not cruel but her face is
a loaded gun that he presses against
the temple of his memory.

He is caught in a pincer movement,
his bad body image on one side
Beauty on the other.

He reads Angela Carter novels, fairy tales
and Mother Goose and hopes that wisdom

does not go stale over the centuries.
In those stories she always returns.

To be honest he fears that a little.
He has, after all, only one eye left.

He plays records. It is the nature of
the Beast to own vinyl, not a CD collection.

Julie London *cries him a river* Frank Sinatra
sings, *it can happen to you/*
      fairy tales can come true

He does not know that sentimentality
is an act of violence.

In the dark bedroom his good eye waters.

The Hedge

The Old English and German
words *Hag* and *Hex* come
from the same word as Hedge.

A Wise woman, a Witch is
literally a *Hedge Woman.*

Living close to the borderlands.
She told me to look over the

hedge and asked, what can you see?

The dormant part of me, surrounded
by thorns that the waking me hacks

at with a sword. Entering the palace
I pass several sleeping personalities

I enter a bedroom, a bridal suite.
I kiss the mirror. The kiss is a

lip shaped circle of condensation.

A misty ghost of a mouth.

The glass turns to water and I fall
into myself. I can't swim.

I'm drowning.
Beauty wakes up in me.

CHARLES DE LINT

Pixel Pixies

*Canadian author Charles de Lint is one of the most acclaimed writers
of mythic fiction today, specializing in works that bring folkloric themes
into modern urban settings. Most of his fiction in the last decade has
been set in the imaginary city of Newford, a place where Native myths
collide with the tales, beliefs, and spirits brought to North America by
immigrant groups.* Works in this vein include the novels Memory and
Dream, Trader, *and* Someplace to Be Flying, *and the story collections*
Dreams Underfoot, The Ivory and the Horn, *and* Moonlight and Vines.
His most recent novel is Forests of the Heart, *which takes place in
Newford and in the Arizona desert. De Lint is also a Celtic folk
musician, a folklore scholar, and a book reviewer. He lives in Ottawa,
Ontario, with his wife MaryAnn, a musician and artist.*

*"Pixel Pixies" is a whimsical story about a hobgoblin who lives in
a Newford bookstore. It is part of a series of limited-edition chapbooks
published each Christmas by Triskell Press and distributed to the
author's friends and colleagues. It is a pleasure to include the tale here.*

—T. W.

Only when Mistress Holly had retired to her apartment above the
store would Dick Bobbins peep out from behind the furnace
where he'd spent the day dreaming and drowsing and reading
the books he borrowed from the shelves upstairs. He would
carefully check the basement for unexpected visitors and listen for a
telltale floorboard to creak from above. Only when he was very very
sure that the mistress, and especially her little dog, had both, indeed,
gone upstairs, would he creep all the way out of his hidden hobhole.

Every night, he followed the same routine.

Standing on the cement floor, he brushed the sleeves of his drab little jacket and combed his curly brown hair with his fingers. Rubbing his palms briskly together, he plucked last night's borrowed book from his hidey-hole and made his way up the steep basement steps to the store. Standing only two feet high, this might have been an arduous process all on its own, but he was quick and agile, as a hob should be, and in no time at all he'd be standing in amongst the books, considering where to begin the night's work.

There was dusting and sweeping to do, books to be put away. Lovely books. It didn't matter to Dick if they were serious leather-bound tomes or paperbacks with garish covers. He loved them all, for they were filled with words, and words were magic to this hob. Wise and clever humans had used some marvelous spell to imbue each book with every kind of story and character you could imagine, and many you couldn't. If you knew the key to unlock the words, you could experience them all.

Sometimes Dick would remember a time when he hadn't been able to read. All he could do then was riffle the pages and try to smell the stories out of them. But now, oh now, he was a magician, too, for he could unearth the hidden enchantment in the books any time he wanted to. They were his nourishment and his joy, weren't they just.

So first he worked, earning his keep. Then he would choose a new book from those that had come into the store while he was in his hob-hole, drowsing away the day. Sitting on top of one of the bookcases, he'd read until it got light outside and it was time to return to his hiding place behind the furnace, the book under his arm in case he woke early and wanted to finish the story while he waited for the mistress to go to bed once more.

I hate computers.

Not when they do what they're supposed to. Not even when I'm the one who's made some stupid mistake, like deleting a file I didn't intend to, or exiting one without saving it. I've still got a few of those old warhorse programs on my machine that don't pop up a reminder asking if I want to save the file I was working on.

No, it's when they seem to have a mind of their own. The keyboard freezing for no apparent reason. Getting an error message that you're out of disc space when you know you've got at least a couple of gigs free. Passwords becoming temporarily, and certainly arbitrarily, obsolete. Those and a hundred other, usually minor, but always annoying, irritations.

Sometimes it's enough to make you want to pick up the nearest component of the machine and fling it against the wall.

For all the effort they save, the little tasks that they automate and their wonderful storage capacity, at times like this—when everything's going as wrong as it can go—their benefits can't come close to outweighing their annoyances.

My present situation was partly my own fault. I'd been updating my inventory all afternoon and before saving the file and backing it up, I'd decided to go on the Internet to check some of my competitors' prices. The used-book business, which is what I'm in, has probably the most arbitrary pricing in the world. Though I suppose that can be expanded to include any business specializing in collectibles.

I logged on without any trouble and went merrily browsing through listings on the various book search pages, making notes on the particularly interesting items, a few of which I actually had in stock. It wasn't until I tried to exit my browser that the trouble started. My browser wouldn't close and I couldn't switch to another window. Nor could I log off the Internet.

Deciding it had something to do with the page I was on—I know that doesn't make much sense, but I make no pretense to being more than vaguely competent when it comes to knowing how the software actually interfaces with the hardware—I called up the drop-down menu of "My Favorites" and clicked on my own home page. What I got was a fan shrine to pro wrestling star Steve Austin.

I tried again and ended up at a commercial software site.

The third time I was taken to the site of someone named Cindy Margolis—the most downloaded woman on the Internet, according to the *Guinness Book of World Records*. Not on this computer, my dear.

I made another attempt to get off-line, then tried to access my home page again. Each time I found myself in some new outlandish and unrelated site.

Finally I tried one of the links on the last page I'd reached. It was supposed to bring me to Netscape's home page. Instead I found myself on the Web site of a real estate company in Santa Fe, looking at a cluster of pictures of the vaguely Spanish-styled houses that they were selling.

I sighed, tried to break my Internet connection for what felt like the hundredth time, but the "Connect to" window still wouldn't come up.

I could have rebooted, of course. That would have gotten me off-line. But it would also mean that I'd lose the whole afternoon's work because, being the stupid woman I was, I hadn't had the foresight to save the stupid file before I went gadding about on the stupid Internet.

"Oh, you stupid machine," I muttered.

From the front window display where she was napping, I heard Snippet, my Jack Russell terrier, stir. I turned to reassure her that, no, she was still my perfect little dog. When I swiveled my chair to face the computer again, I realized that there was a woman standing on the other side of the counter.

I'd seen her come into the store earlier, but I'd lost track of everything in my one-sided battle of wits with the computer—it having the wits, of course. She was a very striking woman, her dark brown hair falling in Pre-Raphaelite curls that were streaked with green, her eyes both warm and distant, like an odd mix of a perfect summer's day and the mystery you can feel swell up inside you when you look up into the stars on a crisp, clear autumn night. There was something familiar about her, but I couldn't quite place it. She wasn't one of my regulars.

She gave me a sympathetic smile.

"I suppose it was only a matter of time before they got into the computers," she said.

I blinked. "What?"

"Try putting your sweater on inside-out."

My face had to be registering the confusion I was feeling, but she simply continued to smile.

"I know it sounds silly," she said. "But humor me. Give it a try."

Anyone in retail knows, you get all kinds. And the secondhand market gets more than its fair share, trust me on that. If there's a loopy person anywhere within a hundred blocks of my store, you can bet they'll eventually find their way inside. The woman standing on the other side of my counter looked harmless enough, if somewhat exotic, but you just never know anymore, do you?

"What have you got to lose?" she asked.

I was about to lose an afternoon's work as things stood, so what was a little pride on top of that.

I stood up and took my sweater off, turned it inside out, and put it back on again.

"Now give it a try," the woman said.

I called up the "Connect to" window and this time it came up. When I put the cursor on the "Disconnect" button and clicked, I was logged off. I quickly shut down my browser and saved the file I'd been working on all afternoon.

"You're a life-saver," I told the woman. "How did you know that would work?" I paused, thought about what I'd just said, what had just happened. "*Why* would that work?"

"I've had some experience with pixies and their like," she said.

"Pixies," I repeated. "You think there are pixies in my computer?"

"Hopefully, not. If you're lucky, they're still on the Internet and didn't follow you home."

I gave her a curious look. "You're serious, aren't you?"

"At times," she said, smiling again. "And this is one of them."

I thought about one of my friends, an electronic pen pal in Arizona, who had this theory that the first atom bomb detonation forever changed the way that magic would appear in the world. According to him, the spirits live in the wires now instead of the trees. They travel through phone and modem lines, take up residence in computers and appliances where they live on electricity and lord knows what else.

It looked like Richard wasn't alone in his theories, not that I pooh-poohed them myself. I'm part of a collective that originated this electronic database called the Wordwood. After it took on a life of its own, I pretty much keep an open mind about things that most people would consider preposterous.

"I'd like to buy this," the woman went on.

She held up a trade paperback copy of *The Beggars' Shore* by Zak Mucha.

"Good choice," I said.

It never surprises me how many truly excellent books end up in the secondary market. Not that I'm complaining—it's what keeps me in business.

"Please take it as thanks for your advice," I added.

"You're sure?"

I looked down at my computer, where my afternoon's work was now safely saved in its file.

"Oh, yes," I told her.

"Thank you," she said. Reaching into her pocket, she took out a business card and gave it to me. "Call me if you ever need any other advice along the same lines."

The business card simply said "The Kelledys" in a large script. Under it were the names "Meran and Cerin" and a phone number. Now I knew why, earlier, she'd seemed familiar. It had just been seeing her here in the store, out of context, that had thrown me.

"I love your music," I told her. "I've seen you and your husband play several times."

She gave me another of those kind smiles of hers.

"You can probably turn your sweater around again now," she said as she left.

Snippet and I watched her walk by the window. I took off my sweater and put it back on properly.

"Time for your walk," I told Snippet. "But first let me back up this file to a zip disk."

That night, after the mistress and her little dog had gone upstairs, Dick Bobbins crept out of his hobhole and made his nightly journey up to the store. He replaced the copy of *The Woods Colt* that he'd been reading, putting it neatly back on the fiction shelf under "W" for Williamson, fetched the duster, and started his work. He finished the "History" and "Local Interest" sections, dusting and straightening the books, and was climbing up onto the "Poetry" shelves near the back of the store when he paused, hearing something from the front of the store.

Reflected in the front window, he could see the glow of the computer's monitor and realized that the machine had turned on by itself. That couldn't be good. A faint giggle spilled out of the computer's speakers, quickly followed by a chorus of other voices, tittering and snickering. That was even less good.

A male face appeared on the screen, looking for all the world as though it could see out of the machine. Behind him other faces appeared, a whole gaggle of little men in green clothes, good-naturedly pushing and shoving each other, whispering and giggling. They were red-haired like the mistress, but there the resemblance ended. Where she was pretty, they were ugly, with short faces, turned-up noses, squinting eyes and pointed ears.

This wasn't good at all, Dick thought, recognizing the pixies for what they were. Everybody knew how you spelled "trouble." It was "P-I-X-Y."

And then they started to clamber out of the screen, which shouldn't have been possible at all, but Dick was a hob and he understood that just because something shouldn't be able to happen, didn't mean it couldn't. Or wouldn't.

"Oh, this is bad," he said mournfully. "Bad bad bad."

He gave a quick look up to the ceiling. He had to warn the mistress. But it was already too late. Between one thought and the next, a dozen or more pixies had climbed out of the computer onto her desk, not the one of them taller than his own waist. They began riffling through her papers, using her pens and ruler as swords to poke at each other. Two of them started a pushing match that resulted in a small stack of books falling off the side of the desk. They landed with a bang on the floor.

The sound was so loud that Dick was sure the mistress would come down to investigate, she and her fierce little dog. The pixies all stood like little statutes until first one, then another, started to giggle again.

When they began to all shove at a bigger stack of books, Dick couldn't wait any longer.

Quick as a monkey, he scurried down to the floor.

"Stop!" he shouted as he ran to the front of the store.

And, "Here, you!"

And, "Don't!"

The pixies turned at the sound of his voice and Dick skidded to a stop.

"Oh, oh," he said.

The little men were still giggling and elbowing each other, but there was a wicked light in their eyes now, and they were all looking at him with those dark, considering gazes. Poor Dick realized that he hadn't thought any of this through in the least bit properly, for now that he had their attention, he had no idea what to do with it. They might only be a third his size, individually, but there were at least twenty of them and everybody knew just how mean a pixy could be, did he set his mind to it.

"Well, will you look at that," one of the pixies said. "It's a little hobberdy man." He looked at his companions. "What shall we do with him?"

"Smash him!"

"Whack him!"

"Find a puddle and drown him!"

Dick turned and fled, back the way he'd come. The pixies streamed from the top of Mistress Holly's desk, laughing wickedly and shouting threats as they chased him. Up the "Poetry" shelves Dick went, all the way to the very top. When he looked back down, he saw that the pixies weren't following the route he'd taken.

He allowed himself a moment's relief. Perhaps he was safe. Perhaps they couldn't climb. Perhaps they were afraid of heights.

Or, he realized with dismay, perhaps they meant to bring the whole bookcase crashing down, and him with it.

For the little men had gathered at the bottom of the bookcase and were putting their shoulders to its base. They might be small, but they were strong, and soon the tall stand of shelves was tottering unsteadily, swaying back and forth. A loose book fell out. Then another.

"No, no! You mustn't!" Dick cried down to them.

But he was too late.

With cries of "Hooray!" from the little men below, the bookcase came tumbling down, spraying books all around it. It smashed into its neighbor, bringing that stand of shelves down as well. By the time Dick hit the floor, hundreds of books were scattered all over the carpet and he was sitting on top of a tall, unsteady mountain of poetry, clutching his head, awaiting the worst.

The pixies came clambering up its slopes, the wicked lights in their eyes shining fierce and bright. He was, Dick realized, about to become an ex-hob. Except then he heard the door to Mistress Holly's apartment open at the top of the back stairs.

Rescued, he thought. And not a moment too soon. She would chase them off.

All the little men froze and Dick looked for a place to hide from the mistress's gaze.

But the pixies seemed unconcerned. Another soft round of giggles arose from them as, one by one, they transformed into soft, glittering lights no bigger than the mouth of a shot glass. The lights rose up from the floor where they'd been standing and went sailing toward the front of the store. When the mistress appeared at the foot of the stairs, her dog at her heels, she didn't even look at the fallen bookshelves. She saw only the lights, her eyes widening with happy delight.

Oh, no, Dick thought. They're pixy-leading her.

The little dog began to growl and bark and tug at the hem of her long flannel nightgown, but she paid no attention to it. Smiling a dreamy smile, she lifted her arms above her head like a ballerina and began to follow the dancing lights to the front of the store. Dick watched as pixy magic made the door pop open and a gust of chilly air burst in. Goosebumps popped up on the mistress's forearms but she never seemed to notice the cold. Her gaze was locked on the lights as they swooped, around and around in a gallitrap circle, then went shimmering out onto the street beyond. In moments she would follow them, out into the night and who knew what terrible danger.

Her little dog let go of her hem and ran ahead, barking at the lights. But it was no use. The pixies weren't frightened and the mistress wasn't roused.

It was up to him, Dick realized.

He ran up behind her and grabbed her ankle, bracing himself. Like the pixies, he was much stronger than his size might give him to appear. He held firm as the mistress tried to raise her foot. She lost her balance and down she went, down and down, toppling like some enormous tree. Dick jumped back, hands to his mouth, appalled at what he'd had to do. She banged her shoulder against a display at the front of the store, sending yet another mass of books cascading onto the floor.

Landing heavily on her arms, she stayed bent over for a long time before she finally looked up. She shook her head as though to clear it.

The pixy lights had returned to the store, buzzing angrily about, but it was no use. The spell had been broken. One by one, they zoomed out of the store, down the street and were quickly lost from sight. The mistress's little dog ran back out onto the sidewalk and continued to bark at them, long after they were gone.

"Please let me be dreaming . . ." the mistress said.

Dick stooped quickly out of sight as she looked about at the sudden ruin of the store. He peeked at her from his hiding place, watched her rub at her face, then slowly stand up and massage her shoulder where it had hit the display. She called the dog back in, but stood in the doorway herself for a long time, staring out at the street, before she finally shut and locked the door behind her.

Oh, it was all such a horrible, terrible, awful mess.

"I'm sorry, I'm sorry, I'm sorry," Dick murmured, his voice barely a whisper, tears blurring his eyes.

The mistress couldn't hear him. She gave the store another survey, then shook her head.

"Come on, Snippet," she said to the dog. "We're going back to bed. Because this is just a dream."

She picked her way through the fallen books and shelves as she spoke.

"And when we wake up tomorrow everything will be back to normal."

But it wouldn't be. Dick knew. This was more of a mess than even the most industrious of hobs could clear up in just one night. But he did what he could until the morning came, one eye on the task at hand, the other on the windows in case the horrible pixies decided to return. Though what he'd do if they did, probably only the moon knew, and she wasn't telling.

Did you ever wake up from the weirdest, most unpleasant dream, only to find that it wasn't a dream at all?

When I came down to the store that morning, I literally had to lean against the wall at the foot of the stairs and catch my breath. I felt all faint and woozy. Snippet walked daintily ahead of me, sniffing the fallen books and whining softly.

An earthquake, I told myself. That's what it had been. I must have woken up right after the main shock, come down half-asleep and seen the mess, and just gone right back to bed again, thinking I was dreaming.

Except there'd been those dancing lights. Like a dozen or more Tinkerbells. Or fireflies. Calling me to follow, follow, follow, out into the night, until I'd tripped and fallen . . .

I shook my head slowly, trying to clear it. My shoulder was still sore and I massaged it as I took in the damage.

Actually, the mess wasn't as bad as it had looked at first. Many of the books appeared to have toppled from the shelves and landed in relatively alphabetical order.

Snippet whined again, but this time it was her "I really have to go" whine, so I grabbed her leash and a plastic bag from behind the desk and out we went for her morning constitutional.

It was brisk outside, but warm for early December, and there still wasn't any snow. At first glance, the damage from the quake appeared to be fairly marginal, considering it had managed to topple a couple of the bookcases in my store. The worst I could see were that all garbage canisters on the block had been overturned, the wind picking up the paper litter and carrying it in eddying pools up and down the street. Other than that, everything seemed pretty much normal. At least it did until I stopped into Café Joe's down the street to get my morning latte.

Joe Lapegna had originally operated a sandwich bar at the same location, but with the coming of Starbucks to town, he'd quickly seen which way the wind was blowing and renovated his place into a café. He'd done a good job with the décor. His café was every bit as contemporary and urban as any of the other high-end coffee bars in the city, the only real difference being that, instead of young college kids with rings through their noses, you got Joe serving the lattes and espressos. Joe with his broad shoulders and meaty, tattooed forearms, a fat caterpillar of a black moustache perched on his upper lip.

Before I could mention the quake, Joe started to tell me how he'd opened up this morning to find every porcelain mug in the store broken. None of the other breakables, not the plates or coffeemakers. Nothing else was even out of place.

"What a weird quake it was," I said.

"Quake?" Joe said. "What quake?"

I waved a hand at the broken china he was sweeping up.

"This was vandals," he said. "Some little bastards broke in and had themselves a laugh."

So I told him about the bookcases in my shop, but he only shook his head.

"You hear anything about a quake on the radio?" he asked.

"I wasn't listening to it."

"I was. There was nothing. And what kind of a quake only breaks mugs and knocks over a couple of bookcases?"

Now that I thought of it, it was odd that there hadn't been any other disruption in my own store. If those bookcases had come down, why hadn't the front window display? I'd noticed a few books had fallen off my desk, but that was about it.

"It's so weird," I repeated.

Joe shook his head. "Nothing weird about it. Just some punks out having their idea of fun."

By the time I got back to my own store, I didn't know what to think. Snippet and I stopped in at a few other places along the strip and while everyone had damage to report, none of it was what could be put down to a quake. In the bakery, all the pies had been thrown against the front windows. In the hardware store, each and every electrical bulb was smashed—though they looked as though they'd simply exploded. All the rolls of paper towels and toilet paper from the grocery store had been tossed up into the trees behind their shipping and receiving bays, turning the bare-branched oaks and elms into bizarre mummy-like versions of themselves. And on it went.

The police arrived not long after I returned to the store. I felt like such a fool when one of the detectives came by to interview me. Yes, I'd heard the crash and come down to investigate. No, I hadn't seen anything.

I couldn't bring myself to mention the dancing lights.

No, I hadn't thought to phone it in.

"I thought I was dreaming," I told him. "I was half-asleep when I came downstairs and didn't think it had really happened. It wasn't until I came back down in the morning . . ."

The detective was of the opinion that it had been gang-related, kids out on the prowl, egging each other on until it had gotten out of control.

I thought about it when he left and knew he had to be right. The damage we'd sustained was all on the level of pranks—mean-spirited, to be sure, but pranks nonetheless. I didn't like the idea of our little area being the sudden target of vandals, but there really wasn't any other logical explanation. At least none occurred to me until I stepped back into the store and glanced at my computer. That's when I remembered Meran Kelledy, how she'd gotten me to turn my sweater inside out and the odd things she'd been saying about pixies on the Web.

If you're lucky, they're still on the Internet and didn't follow you home.

Of course that wasn't even remotely logical. But it made me think. After all, if the Wordwood database could take on a life of its own, who was to say that pixies on the Internet was any more improbable? As my friend Richard likes to point out, everyone has odd problems with their computers that could as easily be attributed to mischievous spirits as to software glitches. At least they could be if your mind was inclined to think along those lines, and mine certainly was.

I stood for a long moment, staring at the screen of my computer. I don't know exactly at what point I realized that the machine was on. I'd turned it off last night before Snippet and I went up to the apartment. And I hadn't stopped to turn it on this morning before we'd gone out. So either I was getting monumentally forgetful, or I'd turned it on while sleepwalking last night, or . . .

I glanced over at Snippet, who was once again sniffing everything as though she'd never been in the store before. Or as if someone or something interesting and strange *had*.

"This is silly," I said.

But I dug out Meran's card and called the number on it all the same, staring at the computer screen as I did. I just hoped nobody had been tinkering with my files.

Bookstore hobs are a relatively recent phenomenon, dating back only a couple of hundred years. Dick knew hobs back home in the old country who'd lived in the same household for three times that length of time. He'd been a farm hob himself, once, living on a Devon steading for two hundred and twelve years until a new family moved in and began to take his services for granted. When one year they actually dared to complain about how poorly the harvest had been put away, he'd thrown every bit of it down into a nearby ravine and set off to find new habitation.

A cousin who lived in a shop had suggested to Dick that he try the same, but there were fewer commercial establishments in those days and they all had their own hob by the time he went looking, first up into Somerset, then back down through Devon, finally moving west to Cornwall. In the end, he made his home in a small cubbyhole of a bookstore he found in Penzance. He lived there for years until the place went out of business, the owner setting sail for North America with plans to open another shop in the new land once he arrived.

Dick had followed, taking up residence in the new store when it was established. That was where he'd taught himself to read.

But he soon discovered that stores didn't have the longevity of a farm. They opened and closed up business seemingly on nothing more than a whim, which made it a hard life for a hob, always looking for a new place to live. By the latter part of this century, he had moved twelve times in the space of five years before finally settling into the place he now called home, the bookstore of his present mistress with its simple sign out front:

Holly Rue—Used Books

He'd discovered that a quality used book store was always the best. Libraries were good, too, but they were usually home to displaced gargoyles and the ghosts of writers and had no room for a hob as well. He'd tried new book stores, but the smaller ones couldn't keep him busy enough and the large ones were too bright, their hours of business too long. And he loved the wide and eclectic range of old and new books to be explored in a shop such as Mistress Holly's, titles that wandered far from the beaten path, or worthy books no longer in print, but nonetheless inspired. The stories he found in them sustained him in a way that nothing else could, for they fed the heart and the spirit.

But this morning, sitting behind the furnace, he only felt old and tired. There'd been no time to read at all last night, and he hadn't thought to bring a book down with him when he finally had to leave the store.

"I hate pixies," he said, his voice soft and lonely in the darkness. "I really really do."

Faeries and pixies had never gotten along, especially not since the last pitched battle between them in the old country when the faeries had been driven back across the River Parrett, leaving everything west of the Parrett as pixyland. For years, hobs such as Dick had lived a clandestine existence in their little steadings, avoiding the attention of pixies whenever they could.

Dick hadn't needed last night's experience to tell him why.

After a while he heard the mistress and her dog leave the store, so he crept out from behind the furnace to stand guard in case the pixies returned while the pair of them were gone. Though what he would do if the pixies did come back, he had no idea. He was an absolute failure when it came to protecting anything, that had been made all too clear last night.

Luckily the question never arose. Mistress Holly and the dog returned and he slipped back behind the furnace, morosely clutching his knees and rocking back and forth, waiting for the night to come. He could hear life go on upstairs. Someone came by to help the mistress right the fallen bookcases. Customers arrived and left with much discussion of the vandalism on the street. Most of the time he could hear only the mistress, replacing the books on their shelves.

"I should be doing that," Dick said. "That's my job."

But he was only an incompetent hob, concealed in his hidey-hole, of no use to anyone until they all went to bed and he could go about his business. And even then, any ruffian could come along and bully him and what could he do to stop them?

Dick's mood went from bad to worse, from sad to sadder still. It might have lasted all the day, growing unhappier with each passing hour, except at mid-morning he suddenly sat up, ears and nose quivering. A presence had come into the store above. A piece of an old mystery, walking about as plain as could be.

He realized that he'd sensed it yesterday as well, while he was dozing. Then he'd put it down to the dream he was wandering in, forgetting all about it when he woke. But today, wide awake, he couldn't ignore it. There was an oak king's daughter upstairs, an old and powerful spirit walking far from her woods. He began to shiver. Important faerie such as she wouldn't be out and about unless the need was great. His shiver deepened. Perhaps she'd come to reprimand him for the job so poorly done. She might turn him into a stick or a mouse.

Oh, this was very bad. First pixies, now this.

Whatever was he going to do? However could he even begin to explain that he'd meant to chase the pixies away, truly he had, but he simply wasn't big enough, nor strong enough. Perhaps not even brave enough.

He rocked back and forth, harder now, his face burrowed against his knees.

After I'd made my call to Meran, David, who works at the deli down the street, came by and helped me stand the bookcases upright once more. The deli hadn't been spared a visit from the vandals either. He told me that they'd taken all the sausages out of the freezer and used them to spell out rude words on the floor.

"Remember when all we had to worry about was some graffiti on the walls outside?" he asked when he was leaving.

I was still replacing books on the shelves when Meran arrived. She looked around the store while I expanded on what I'd told her over the phone. Her brow furrowed thoughtfully and I was wondering if she was going to tell me to put my sweater on backwards again.

"You must have a hob in here," she said.

"A what?"

It was the last thing I expected her to say.

"A hobgoblin," she said. "A brownie. A little faerie man who dusts and tidies and keeps things neat."

"I just thought it didn't get all that dirty," I said, realizing as I spoke how ridiculous that sounded.

Because, when I thought about it, a helpful brownie living in the store explained a lot. While I certainly ran the vacuum cleaner over the carpets every other morning or so, and dusted when I could, the place never seemed to need much cleaning. My apartment upstairs required more and it didn't get a fraction of the traffic.

And it wasn't just the cleaning. The store, for all its clutter, was organized, though half the time I didn't know how. But I always seemed to be able to lay my hand on whatever I needed to find without having to root about too much. Books often got put away without my remembering I'd done it. Others mysteriously vanished, then reappeared a day or so later, properly filed in their appropriate section—even if they had originally disappeared from the top of my desk. I rarely needed to alphabetize my sections while my colleagues in other stores were constantly complaining of the mess their customers left behind.

"But aren't you supposed to leave cakes and cream out for them?" I found myself asking.

"You never leave a specific gift," Meran said. "Not unless you want him to leave. It's better to simply 'forget' a cake or a sweet treat on one of the shelves when you leave for the night."

"I haven't even done that. What could he be living on?"

Meran smiled as she looked around the store. "Maybe the books nourish him. Stranger things have been known to happen in Faerie."

"Faerie," I repeated slowly.

Bad enough I'd helped create a database on the Internet that had taken on a life of its own. Now my store was in Faerie. Or at least straddling the border, I supposed. Maybe the one had come about because of the other.

"Your hob will know what happened here last night," Meran said.

"But how would we even go about asking him?"

It seemed a logical question, since I'd never known I had one living with me in the first place. But Meran only smiled.

"Oh, I can usually get their attention," she told me.

She called out something in a foreign language, a handful of words that rang with great strength and appeared to linger and echo longer than they should. The poor little man who came sidling up from the basement in response looked absolutely terrified. He was all curly hair and raggedy clothes with a broad face that, I assumed from the laugh lines, normally didn't look so miserable. He was carrying a battered little leather carpetbag and held a brown cloth cap in his hand. He couldn't have been more than two feet tall.

All I could do was stare at him, though I did have the foresight to pick up Snippet before she could lunge in his direction. I could feel the growl rumbling in her chest more than hear it. I think she was as surprised as me to find that he'd been living in our basement all this time.

Meran sat on her haunches, bringing her head down to the general level of the hob's. To put him at ease, I supposed, so I did the same myself. The little man didn't appear to lose any of his nervousness. I could see his knees knocking against each other, his cheek twitching.

"B-begging your pardon, your ladyship," he said to Meran. His gaze slid to me and I gave him a quick smile. He blinked, swallowed hard, and returned his attention to my companion. "Dick Bobbins," he added, giving a quick nod of his head. "At your service, as it were. I'll just be on my way, then, no harm done."

"Why are you so frightened of me?" Meran asked.

He looked at the floor. "Well, you're a king's daughter, aren't you just, and I'm only me."

A king's daughter? I thought.

Meran smiled. "We're all only who we are, no one of more importance than the other."

"Easy for you to say," he began. Then his eyes grew wide and he put a hand to his mouth. "Oh, that was a bad thing to say to such a great and wise lady such as yourself."

Meran glanced at me. "They think we're like movie stars," she explained. "Just because we were born in a court instead of a hobhole."

I was getting a bit of a case of the celebrity nerves myself. Court? King's daughter? Who exactly *was* this woman?

"But you know," she went on, returning her attention to the little man, "my father's court was only a glade, our palace no more than a tree."

He nodded quickly, giving her a thin smile that never reached his eyes.

"Well, wonderful to meet you," he said. "Must be on my way now."

He picked up his carpetbag and started to sidle toward the other aisle that wasn't blocked by what he must see as two great big hulking women and a dog.

"But we need your help," Meran told him.

Whereupon he burst into tears.

The mothering instinct that makes me such a sap for Snippet kicked into gear and I wanted to hold him in my arms and comfort him. But I had Snippet to consider, straining in my grip, the growl in her chest quite audible now. And I wasn't sure how the little man would have taken my sympathies. After all, he might be child-sized, but for all his tears, he was obviously an adult, not a child. And if the stories were anything to go by, he was probably older than me—by a few hundred years.

Meran had no such compunction. She slipped up to him and put her arms around him, cradling his face against the crook of her shoulder.

It took a while before we coaxed the story out of him. I locked the front door and we went upstairs to my kitchen where I made tea for us all. Sitting at the table, raised up to the proper height by a stack of books, Dick told us about the pixies coming out of the computer screen, how they'd knocked down the bookcases and finally disappeared into the night. The small mug I'd given him looked enormous in his hands. He fell silent when he was done and stared glumly down at the steam rising from his tea.

"But none of what they did was your fault," I told him.

"Kind of you to say," he managed. He had to stop and sniff, wipe his nose on his sleeve. "But if I'd b-been braver—"

"They *would* have drowned you in a puddle," Meran said. "And I think you were brave, shouting at them the way you did and then rescuing your mistress from being pixy-led."

I remembered those dancing lights and shivered. I knew those stories as well. There weren't any swamps or marshes to be led into around here, but there were eighteen-wheelers out on the highway only a few blocks away. Entranced as I'd been, the pixies could easily have walked me right out in front of any one of them. I was lucky to only have a sore shoulder.

"Do you . . . really think so?" he asked, sitting up a little straighter. We both nodded.

Snippet was lying under my chair, her curiosity having been satisfied that Dick was only one more visitor and therefore out-of-bounds in terms of biting and barking at. There'd been a nervous moment while she'd sniffed at his trembling hand and he'd looked as though he was ready to scurry up one of the bookcases, but they quickly made their peace. Now Snippet was only bored and had fallen asleep.

"Well," Meran said. "It's time we put our heads together and consider how we can put our unwanted visitors back where they came from and keep them there."

"Back onto the Internet?" I asked. "Do you really think we should?"

"Well, we could try to kill them . . ."

I shook my head. That seemed too extreme. I started to protest only to see that she'd been teasing me.

"We could take a thousand of them out of the Web," Meran said, "and still not have them all. Once tricksy folk like pixies have their foot in a place, you can't ever be completely rid of them." She smiled. "But if we can get them to go back in, there are measures we can take to stop them from troubling you again."

"And what about everybody else on-line?" I asked.

Meran shrugged. "They'll have to take their chances—just like they do when they go for a walk in the woods. The little people are every-where."

I glanced across my kitchen table to where the hob was sitting and thought, no kidding.

"The trick, if you'll pardon my speaking out of turn," Dick said, "is to play on their curiosity."

Meran gave him an encouraging smile. "We want your help," she said. "Go on."

The little man sat up straighter still and put his shoulders back.

"We could use a book that's never been read," he said. "We could put it in the middle of the road, in front of the store. That would certainly make me curious."

"An excellent idea," Meran told him.

"And then we could use the old spell of bell, book, and candle. The churchmen stole that one from us."

Even I'd heard of it. Bell, book, and candle had once been another way of saying excommunication in the Catholic Church. After pro-nouncing the sentence, the officiating cleric would close his book, ex-tinguish the candle, and toll the bell as if for someone who had died. The book symbolized the book of life, the candle a man's soul, removed from the sight of God as the candle had been from the sight of men.

But I didn't get the unread book bit.

"Do you mean a brand new book?" I asked. "A particular copy that nobody might have opened yet, or one that's so bad that no one's ac-tually made their way all the way through it?"

"Though someone would have had to," Dick said, "for it to have been published in the first place. I meant the way books were made in the old days, with the pages still sealed. You had to cut them apart as you read them."

"Oh, I remember those," Meran said.

Like she was there. I took another look at her and sighed. Maybe she had been.

"Do you have any like that?" she asked.

"Yes," I said slowly, unable to hide my reluctance.

I didn't particularly like the idea of putting a collector's item like that out in the middle of the road.

But in the end, that's what we did.

The only book I had that passed Dick's inspection was *The Trembling of the Veil* by William Butler Yeats, number seventy-one of a thousand-copy edition privately printed by T. Werner Laurie, Ltd. in 1922. All the pages were still sealed at the top. It was currently listing on the

Internet in the $450 to $500 range and I kept it safely stowed away in the glass-doored bookcase that held my first editions.

The other two items were easier to deal with. I had a lovely brass bell that my friend Tatiana had given me for Christmas last year and a whole box of fat white candles just because I liked to burn them. But it broke my heart to go out onto the street around two A.M., and place the Yeats on the pavement.

We left the front door to the store ajar, the computer on. I wasn't entirely sure how we were supposed to lure the pixies back into the store and then onto the Internet once more, but Meran took a flute out of her bag and fit the wooden pieces of it together. She spoke of a calling-on music and Dick nodded sagely, so I simply went along with their better experience. Mind you, I also wasn't all that sure that my Yeats would actually draw the pixies back in the first place, but what did I know?

We all hid in the alleyway running between my store and the futon shop, except for Snippet, who was locked up in my apartment. She hadn't been very pleased by that. After an hour of crouching in the cold in the alley, I wasn't feeling very pleased myself. What if the pixies didn't come? What if they did, but they approached from the fields behind the store and came traipsing up this very alleyway?

By three-thirty we all had a terrible chill. Looking up at my apartment, I could see Snippet lying in the window of the dining room, looking down at us. She didn't appear to have forgiven me yet and I would happily have changed places with her.

"Maybe we should just—"

I didn't get to finish with "call it a night." Meran put a finger to her lips and hugged the wall. I looked past her to the street.

At first I didn't see anything. There was just my Yeats, lying there on the pavement, waiting for a car to come and run over it. But then I saw the little man, not even half the size of Dick, come creeping up from the sewer grating. He was followed by two more. Another pair came down the brick wall of the temporary office help building across the street. Small dancing lights that I remembered too clearly from last night dipped and wove their way from the other end of the block, descending to the pavement and becoming more of the little men when they drew near to the book. One of them poked at it with his foot and I had visions of them tearing it apart.

Meran glanced at Dick and he nodded, mouthing the words, "That's the lot of them."

She nodded back and took her flute out from under her coat where she'd been keeping it warm.

At this point I wasn't really thinking of how the calling music would work. I'm sure my mouth hung agape as I stared at the pixies. I felt light-headed, a big grin tugging at my lips. Yes, they were pranksters, and mean-spirited ones at that. But they were also magical. The way they'd changed from little lights to little men . . . I'd never seen anything like it before. The hob who lived in my bookstore was magical, too, of course, but somehow it wasn't the same thing. He was already familiar, so down-to-earth. Sitting around during the afternoon and evening while we waited, I'd had a delightful time talking books with him, as though he were an old friend. I'd completely forgotten that he was a little magic man himself.

The pixies were truly puzzled by the book. I suppose it would be odd from any perspective, a book that old, never once having been opened or read. It defeated the whole purpose of why it had been made.

I'm not sure when Meran began to play her flute. The soft breathy sound of it seemed to come from nowhere and everywhere, all at once, a resonant wave of slow, stately notes, one falling after the other, rolling into a melody that was at once hauntingly strange and heartachingly familiar.

The pixies lifted their heads at the sound. I wasn't sure what I'd expected, but when they began to dance, I almost clapped my hands. They were so funny. Their bodies kept perfect time to the music, but their little eyes glared at Meran as she stepped out of the alley and Pied Pipered them into the store.

Dick fetched the Yeats and then he and I followed after, arriving in time to see the music make the little men dance up onto my chair, onto the desk, until they began to vanish, one by one, into the screen of my monitor, a fat candle sitting on top of it, its flame flickering with their movement. Dick opened the book and I took the bell out of my pocket.

Meran took the flute from her lips.

"Now," she said.

Dick slapped the book closed, she leaned forward and blew out the candle while I began to chime the bell, the clear brass notes ringing in the silence left behind by the flute. We saw a horde of little faces staring out at us from the screen, eyes glaring. One of the little men actually popped back through, but Dick caught him by the leg and tossed him back into the screen.

Meran laid her flute down on the desk and brought out a garland she'd made earlier of rowan twigs, green leaves and red berry sprigs still attached in places. When she laid it on top of the monitor, we heard the modem dial up my Internet service. When the connection was made, the little men vanished from the screen. The last turned his bum toward us and let out a loud fart before he, too, was gone.

The three of us couldn't help it. We all broke up.

"That went rather well," Meran said when we finally caught our breath. "My husband Cerin is usually the one to handle this sort of thing, but it's nice to know I haven't forgotten how to deal with such rascals myself. And that it's probably best he didn't come along this evening. He can seem rather fierce and I don't doubt poor Dick here would thought him far too menacing."

I looked around the store.

"Where *is* Dick?" I asked.

But the little man was gone. I couldn't believe it. Surely he hadn't just up and left us like in the stories.

"Hobs and brownies," Meran said when I asked, her voice gentle, "they tend to take their leave rather abruptly when the tale is done."

"I thought you had to leave them a suit of clothes or something."

Meran shrugged. "Sometimes simply being identified is enough to make them go."

"Why does it have to be like that?"

"I'm not really sure. I suppose it's a rule or something, or a geas—a thing that has to happen. Or perhaps it's no more than a simple habit they've handed down from one generation to the next."

"But I *loved* the idea of him living here," I said. "I thought it would be so much fun. With all the work he's been doing, I'd have been happy to make him a partner."

Meran smiled. "Faerie and commerce don't usually go hand in hand."

"But you and your husband play music for money."

Her smile grew wider, her eyes enigmatic, but also amused.

"What makes you think we're faerie?" she asked.

"Well, you . . . that is . . ."

"I'll tell you a secret," she said, relenting. "We're something else again, but what exactly that might be, even we have no idea anymore. Mostly we're the same as you. Where we differ is that Cerin and I always live with half a foot in the otherworld that you've only visited these past few days."

"And only the borders of it, I'm sure."

She shrugged. "Faerie is everywhere. It just *seems* closer at certain times, in certain places."

She began to take her flute apart and stow the wooden pieces away in the instrument's carrying case.

"Your hob will be fine," she said. "The kindly ones such as he always find a good household to live in."

"I hope so," I said. "But all the same, I was really looking forward to getting to know him better."

Dick Bobbins got an odd feeling listening to the two of them talk, his mistress and the oak king's daughter. Neither was quite what he'd expected. Mistress Holly was far kinder and not at all the brusque, rather self-centered human that figured in so many old hob fireside tales. And her ladyship . . . well, who would have thought that one of the highborn would treat a simple hob as though they stood on equal footing? It was all very unexpected.

But it was time for him to go. He could feel it in his blood and in his bones.

He waited while they said their goodbyes. Waited while Mistress Holly took the dog out for a last quick pee before the pair of them retired to their apartment. Then he had the store completely to himself, with no chance of unexpected company. He fetched his little leather carpetbag from his hobhole behind the furnace and came back upstairs to say goodbye to the books, to the store, to his home.

Finally all there was left to do was to spell the door open, step outside and go. He hesitated on the welcoming carpet, thinking of what Mistress Holly had asked, what her ladyship had answered. Was the leaving song that ran in his blood and rumbled in his bones truly a geas, or only habit? How was a poor hob to know? If it was a rule, then who had made it and what would happen if he broke it?

He took a step away from the door, back into the store and paused, waiting for he didn't know what. Some force to propel him out the door. A flash of light to burn down from the sky and strike him where he stood. Instead all he felt was the heaviness in his heart and the funny tingling warmth he'd known when he'd heard the mistress say how she'd been looking forward to getting to know him. That she wanted him to be a partner in her store. Him. Dick Bobbins, of all things.

He looked at the stairs leading up to her apartment.

Just as an experiment, he made his way over to them, then up the risers, one by one, until he stood at her door.

Oh, did he dare, did he dare?

He took a deep breath and squared his shoulders. Then setting down his carpetbag, he twisted his cloth cap in his hands for a long moment before he finally lifted an arm and rapped a knuckle against the wood panel of Mistress Holly's door.

ELIZABETH BIRMINGHAM

Falling Away

*Elizabeth Birmingham is a doctoral candidate in rhetoric at Iowa State
University, where she is writing her dissertation on disciplinary
discourse in architectural studies. She has had work published in* The
River Oak Review, Discourse, The Briar Cliff Review, *and* Prairie
Schooner. *She lives in Fargo, North Dakota, with her partner and
children.*

*"Falling Away" is a tale of ghosts, spirits (in both senses of the
word), and transformation. This deeply moving story, my personal
favorite of the year, comes from the Spring 1999 edition of* Prairie
Schooner, *published in Nebraska.*

—*T. W.*

When I drank, I preferred tequila, double-shots, straight, lime
not lemon, salt on the side. But when it came right down to
it, and it often did, I drank anything. Anything within reason:
I never took a shot of rubbing alcohol, or my grandmother's
favorite, vanilla extract. I'll admit to half a bottle of Cepacol, once,
when I was in the hospital at Cherokee, the second time, and I had some
ugly DTs. Later, I made a deal with this Indian kid in the laundry and
he brought me pints of peppermint Schnapps when he changed the
sheets. Let me recommend the mouthwash. It goes down smoother.

I'm on the wagon because of Jimmy, who got sober and does AA
and all that. He's a great kid, so I do what I can for him, like pour away
the half-gallon tequila I kept under the sink. My not drinking is for
Jimmy, not for me, but I do know one AA thing I believe in. One day
at a time. That's my advice on life: don't look forward and don't look

back because either way you'll realize you're in this endless tunnel, too far in for even a pinprick of light from either side. Only today's gray is worth thinking about, and if it's bland and colorless, it's still nothing like stepping into the void of yesterday or tomorrow. Maybe there's color there, but I think it's all red.

Too bad I give advice better than I take it. I had this slip on my birthday. I looked back. Big mistake, that, pause to look back and they'll catch up, whoever's chasing. The ghosts followed Jimmy, his mother and grandmother, lonely for him, he said. He heard their whistling at night, calling him to the river. He thinks he won't follow again, and I believe him. An angel follows me, grinning, through my life; I turn my face away, but feel him there. I hide, but he finds me, always when I think I've forgotten. On my birthday, he found me again.

My birthday, thirty years old, but keep that quiet. Jimmy thinks I'm twenty-eight, and that makes him jumpy enough. He kicked the shit out of this white guy outside the Copper Dollar who called me as his old lady. A figure of speech, Jimbo, I told him, and dragged his skinny Omaha ass away from there quick. Not even drunk, he's just twenty and looking for a fight sometimes. Wish he wouldn't go after the biggest redneck he can find, though. I like him—liked him ever since I fished him out of the Missouri, a year ago February, downstream of IBP, floating face down in five feet of stinking river water. Looking for his mother.

On May Day, I was born, so they named me Mary Grace, oldest girl, Irish Catholic; there's an inevitability there, to my life, and if I look back squinting, I see the patterns, turn really fast and they stretch out ahead of me, too, all the same, before and after, until I can't distinguish sooner from later, now from then. I remember so little clearly, the future follows hazy, too; I'd never muddle my way out, fighting it. Like falling disoriented into deep water, you move and you aren't necessarily swimming to the surface: stay where you are and go where you float. Advice, that is.

I was up in Sioux City on May Day doing Thursday stuff, library, groceries, supplies for my work—I make rosaries, hand-blown glass beads and cast sterling silver, for women who want to contemplate the mysteries and sorrows on a work of art. There are more of them than you'd think. Women, and mysteries and sorrows, all.

Because I was there, and because it was May Day, I walked into church, my childhood church, to light a candle for my mother who gave birth to me on this day, before. My mother, who had seven children by the time she was twenty-eight and died at thirty: drank a few shots of rubbing alcohol in a hot bath. She was pregnant; I never believed she was trying to kill herself. I see the patterns. Lighting a candle for her on my birthday seemed harmless, but it was looking back. I'd forgotten I couldn't hide from him.

I learned all the things I would know about my religion by the time I was five; enough to make me fall away, though I do have these slips, candle lighting, rosaries. I can deny it, but I can't escape it; it's there like a cultural unconscious, dragging at my ankles. I walked into church on my thirtieth birthday, smelled spring flowers and incense, and saw all the Sundays of all my childhood, telescoped down, like my grandmother's traveling medicine cup, to a flat single day-memory like bright magic, I'm there:

Five years old, my birthday, maybe. My church is IC. Immaculate Conception. I'd prefer a Saint church. I don't know what Immaculate Conception means, in fact, it means nothing. A mystery, my mother told me, but all is mystery. Holding my grandmother's hand, I walk down the center aisle toward the flower-strewn altar. Spring flowers, daffodils, tulips, crocuses. I smell the hyacinths, even over the heady sandalwood incense. May Day is a feast day, for the Virgin. I genuflect, for reasons unknown. All is unknown, and I'm forced to guess at meanings. I slide into the pew inhabited already by an abandoned seed corn cap and crushed Cheerios left by babies at 7:30 mass. I move toward the cap, but my grandmother pokes her index nail into my thigh. Long, horny nails, nicotine-yellowed and filed sharp. I say nothing, but look up at her. "You don't know whose that is," she hisses, low.

My mother stays in the cry room, hugely pregnant and deserted with her three other babies. I'm the only one big enough to sit at mass with Grandma. I kneel beside Grandma while she says the rosary. They pray the rosary aloud, all these old women, and they're almost all women, almost all old. All the young women kneel in the mind-numbing din of the cry room, with their babies. The men, I think, sit in their cars listening to the radio. I'm not sure what men do. Another mystery, the things of men. They're not here, though, and they come in long after the rosary, sit in the back, and leave after communion. My own father goes to mass at 5:00 on Saturday night, so he can sleep late on Sunday. He comes home, silent and angry, smelling of beer. My mother says communion wine.

I kneel until my knees ache and then I keep kneeling. Mass won't begin for twenty more minutes. I watch how the morning light glitters through the stained glass; I watch the red and blue and green flicker across my grandmother's mumbling lips, moving fingers. "Hail Mary, full of Grace," the old women drone. I turn to see which window, which saint, falls across my grandmother's face, but I turn too far, looking behind, and she pinches my arm, the tender part, just above the elbow, in the back. I make no sound and stare forward, hold myself straight.

We finish the rosary, and my grandmother sits back. Her back doesn't lean against the pew; she holds herself rigidly away. I want to know why she does this, but won't ask now and know I'll forget later. I try to sit like her, but it hurts, aches deep. I study the statue of the Annunciation, Mary and the archangel Gabriel, to the left of the altar. Mary's hand pushes him away, her face turns toward me, afraid. I see my mother in her eyes. I can't help you, I whisper silently. I pray for a sign, squinting my eyes tight until I see map-lines inside my eyeballs. The angel winks at me, but he nearly always does, so this isn't my sign. I fear him as Mary does; I fear he'll follow me home.

The memory came strong, overwhelming and dizzying, like the smell of hyacinths in the spring-warm church, on May Day. I hoard those bright memories; color comes rare for me. On my thirtieth birthday I prayed for a memory of my mother. I have only one: her beautiful face, now bluish and swollen, just under water in the tub, in our black-and-white tiled bathroom. I'm eleven. I know she's dead. I hold her cold hand and don't call my father for many moments, because he will be so angry with her. Even dead, she needs me to protect her from his anger. I touch her hair floating dark on the water's surface, so very long, unpinned and wet. I think of Ophelia. There's rosemary, that's for remembrance. I don't remember where I learned of Hamlet, though, at eleven. I made up a memory, once, to explain this odd association, a memory of my mother and I seeing the Olivier movie together at the neighborhood theater in Morningside. I knew this couldn't have happened, though; it was too late for Olivier, too soon for Mel Gibson. But even so, I kept the manufactured memory, and like the many others, it works, when I don't question too deeply.

I knelt until my knees hurt, there in the church of my childhood, before the marble Annunciation, the flickering ten-cent candles. I dropped a quarter in the metal box and took three candles, stuck them in the red pressed-glass votives. I wrote my mother's name in the book of those to receive prayers, there at the church where she was once refused burial. When I saw the angel recognized me I lit my candles and left. But I knew I invited him by turning back. He followed me home; he was my grandmother's pinch, now, for looking behind.

Jimmy met me at the Hy-Vee, driving his ancient El Camino. Drying concrete caked his clothes, his hair grayed with dust but for the black lines where his bandana and OSHA ear protectors had been. He helped me get the groceries out to the car. We drove back to Nebraska, down the dusty roads to the lone trailer near the river. Not my trailer

or even Jimmy's—we're squatters there. I'd lived there once with Leon
Wintercamp, who worked down at IBP until the spring he tried to get
some of the Mexicans organized to get a little medical. One night he
didn't come home. For a long time I figured someday he'd float up from
the river bottom, but he never did. Three years ago. Nobody told me to
leave, and down on the Res I'm still Leon's crazy water-ghost woman.
I've pulled three men from the river, but Leon was the first. The second
guy was already dead, but I thought he might be Leon and pulled him
out. I can walk on the water, the old timers say. The river tasted me
once, spit me back out, so I'm not afraid of her. I'll go in. The worst
that could happen isn't all that bad.

Jimmy didn't talk much; he just drove. No radio, so we listened to
the sounds of the highway, low and humming, voices nearly, just on
the other side of this world, calling up through the bald tires of the El
Camino. I didn't need to say this to Jimmy, he heard them, too, their
seductive calls and whistles. We didn't talk to cover them. He's Omaha,
and he says that's how they are. At least when he says something I
know it's important. Most men aim silence like a weapon, control with
the weight of it, but Jimmy's not talking is only quiet: transparent and
reverent, letting the road have its say. He just smiled at me, and reached
over to squeeze my leg above the knee every now and then while he
drove along, eyes on the road. I'd scream and jump and he'd laugh,
every time. I like that kid.

The wild cats scattered as we drove up to Leon's trailer. The corrugated aluminum skirting hung loose and they lived underneath. Jimmy
helped me unload the groceries, then I heard him in the bathroom, running a bath. Every night he takes a bubble bath while I cook us dinner.
One night, a year ago, not long after the river: I walk in on him, as he
lies all bent in the trailer-sized tub, knees up, black hair floating like
water-weeds, covered with glistening soap bubbles. Breathing through
a drinking straw, taking in air in tiny sips. I never asked. He told me
once how warm the river embraced before I pulled him out and how he
remembered then, before he was born, when he was still in his mother.
How she wanted him back. He doesn't resent me, though. I told him I
wanted him more than the river did, and that was enough; it made sense
then. With the walk into the river, he walked his hableceya, vision
seeking. He saw both worlds, and he chose mine.

Jimmy came out, clean, as I sliced potatoes into the bacon grease
for fires. He wore the black silk kimono Leon had bought me up in the
Cities. He hadn't done much to dry his hair, so it dripped. "What should
I do?"

"You're OK," I told him. "Just sit. You want me to get you a glass of Kool-aid?" He nodded. "Ice?"

"No, that's OK. No ice." He sat at the table and I finished the potatoes and poured him a glass of Kool-aid. He drinks it by the gallon—any red flavor: strawberry, raspberry, black cherry. I buy the sugar for it by the ten-pound bag. He can't believe I don't like it, and thinks I practice some amazing form of self-denial. I handed him the glass, then took the dish towel from my shoulder and squeezed out the ends of his hair.

"How many eggs?"

"Three." He stood and stepped to the door and poured a little of his Kool-aid onto the stoop. Ok'u wanagi, sharing with the ghosts he said, like he used to share his whiskey.

"I bet your mother wishes you weren't AA," I said.

I was joking, but he thought about it. "She's pretty happy lately. She likes you. She calls you Mni-wascasca wanagi." Move-water ghost. River ghost, he told me. I don't always trust his Lakota, I think he's making it up as he goes. But we all do that, don't we? He paused for a while, but I knew he wasn't done talking, so I waited. "I asked, at AA, if I needed to keep around whiskey for the ghosts, and they said no way. Ghosts like Kool-aid or Coke. Just so they're remembered."

"I'm glad she likes me." I thought about the nearly full half-gallon of tequila I poured out onto the steps before I picked up Jimmy out of detox. No wonder she liked me.

Before we ate, Jimmy took a pie tin of bacon, eggs, and potatoes out under the box elder tree. I watched him trot out there, black robe flapping, followed by three cats: the yellow tom, the pregnant three-colored kitten, and the other female, gray, and now tailless from an encounter with the El Camino's fan belt last winter. He put the plate down, said his offering to call the ghosts, even as the cats ate. He stood a long moment gazing at the river, still high and muddy from spring thaw and rains. Don't be thinking about that river, I told him with my mind, and he turned and smiled at me where I stood in the window.

After dinner, Jimmy washed and I dried. He had two more glasses of Kool-aid and I had a cigarette. I got out the six Louis L' Amour books I'd picked up for him at the library. He'd already read one, but it was a good one, one he'd like to read again, he said. He settled onto the sofa to read and I began carving the wax I used to design the crucifixes and decade beads for my rosaries. I do lost wax silversmithing, so every one, every cross, every bead is different. I usually carve forty before I make the plaster molds and bring them up to Sioux City to use the centrifuge at the Art Center to inject the molten silver. I've done it without, all by hand, but air bubbles and such ruin about half, making all the carving time a waste. Besides, this way the Art Center markets a lot of the rosaries for me, to places all over the country—and gets me huge mark-ups, near $400 each. I need to sell two a month to stay alive and stay in business. Lately, I've been selling five or six.

He woke in the night; I felt him jerk and knew he dreamed of falling. "Jimmy?" He jumped again, at my whisper.

"Gracie," he turned to me, breathing fast. "Somebody's out there."

"The cats."

"No. I gotta go look." But he didn't move to get up.

"Stay. You were dreaming."

"He's looking for you."

"Oh," I said. "It's OK. I know him. He followed me out of church today. He can't get in. Go back to sleep." I held him until he relaxed back to sleep, but I listened in the dark for the angel:

I'm eighteen again, restrained, my wrists held down by wide, Velcroed bands. I'm unsure what is real, now, and what is in my mind. "Do you know where you are?" the nurse asks me every time she wanders through. If I know the right answer, when I say Cherokee, she gives me a shot. "Hell," I answer finally. She smiles, her teeth sharp, and I know I'm right. She leaves me be. The angel stands near my bed sometimes, watching me with pale eyes, touching my hair. He found me at my sister's funeral. Or my mother's funeral. Or maybe my funeral. The faces in the coffin are indistinguishable, all river-bloated. The hands clutch ugly plastic rosaries to the chests. Funerals are a time of looking back, and he found me. Annie cut her wrists in the bathtub at the Thrifty Scot motel, pregnant. Sixteen. I can't help her. I didn't know. Even dead, they don't let her in the church where she was baptized, confirmed, and had her first Holy Communion. The church where she first confessed her seven-year-old sins to Fr. Kelley and had to say five rosaries as penance.

The doctor is tall and blondish, neither young nor old, his face hard and smooth, like marble. He holds a clipboard and pen, but he writes nothing down. "Why were you in the river, Mary?"

"I was looking for my sister."

"Why did you think she would be in the river?"

"That's where I would go."

"That's where you did go." He grins at me, his pale eyes crinkle.

At night, he touches my face, his fingers, slender and cool and dry, unbraid my hair. I turn away, afraid, but I can't turn far. "No." I fight the strength of the Velcro, but I'm no match. "Don't be afraid," he whispers. Fear not, I hear my angel say. He lies beside me in the metal hospital bed, in the ward that goes on forever on both sides of me. I can't see the end of the women, Velcroed into their beds. No one can help me. They've made us helpless. Not the hospital only, but long before. The blackness begins as a pinprick, right before my eyes, and grows in concentric rings until the light falls away entirely. I believe, when they tell me I'm crazy.

I pray for proof of my visions, and God answers my prayers. I remember this: My father sits by my bed, holds my hand, tied down, because I have suicidal tendencies. I'm a danger to myself and others. Others. He looks bad under fluorescent lighting, in the sterile white of the ward. He's drunk and crying. They've told him, and for a moment I think someone will help me. I think my father will help me, because I'm still so young, and in spite of what I know about him, I wish and hope he is stronger than he is. "Gracie," he says, and he's crying, his nose is running. I can't look at him and instead I watch the gray shadows of the metal ceiling fan. "The boy who did this to you is gone. You're safe here now. He's gone."

"No." I whisper it. I'm not certain if the bed is turning or if the fan is on. "No."

My father nods. "Yes. The doctor told me. They've sent him away. He's gone." I don't even cry. Not worth it. I've been powerless for so long I can't even cry at it. "You need to have an operation."

"No." I think I know what he means, and know he could not say the word. An operation.

"It wasn't your fault, baby." He tries to touch my face, but I turn away. He cries. "They've paid us money, damages." He holds up a check, for $1,000. How little I'm worth, what little value my future has. "I'll save it for you. For college, when you come home."

"No." I see who is crazy. I'm drugged and tied down and powerless, but I'm not crazy.

I decided to sleep. I preferred gray dreams to those memories. I turned away from Jimmy, who slept like a corpse, flat on his back, breathing soundlessly, and unmoving.

The archangel Gabriel cornered me in the shower. I rinsed the shampoo out of my hair, I opened my eyes, and there he stood. Wet and skinny and blonde with huge wings that didn't have feathers, but iridescent scales. A little reptilian, but pitiful and puny in spite of that. He squinted against the water, shielded his eyes with his left hand. "Blessed art thou among women," he said, but it came out nearly a question. A man tries a line like that he should at least say it like he means it. Otherwise it's a little insulting, I think. Am I blessed? Am I not blessed? Is this angel in my shower being sarcastic?

"Don't you have a better line?" I asked him.

His pale eyes widened, and he stepped back, crushing his wings against the blue molded shower stall. I heard it pop, as his weight pushed the hollow plastic. He was afraid of me. The shower was too small for me, and him and those wings. Scales rained down and washed toward my feet; they were sharp, like glass, but his feet were cut, not mine. "I've not needed one," he said.

"You do now. I'm not tied up." I held my arms up to him, but that's not all I meant. He winced. "I've had DTs more real than you." I squeezed past him, stepped out of the shower, slid the door back closed, shutting him in with the water. I woke up. Jimmy lay beside me, still, and it was very early. I marveled at it, my power in my dream, thought about it. He's nothing, my angel, but a weak and foolish man.

Even in the gray of pre-dawn Jimmy looked too young, asleep and unguarded. "Jimmy?" He woke instantly, without sound or movement, no transition, asleep to wide awake when I touched him. I told him my dream. I told him, then, of walking into the river to find Annie, and waking tied up in Cherokee. I told him of electric shock, as my punishment for not going crazy, and never remembering time again, of never knowing the order of my life, before or after, yesterday, today or tomorrow. My memories stolen: names and faces and lives and all their depth and color. He lay on his back, one arm bent behind his head, watching the ceiling while I told, and then he said nothing until I turned to look at him.

"I wondered why they called you ghost. Your people are all gone," he said, then, "Your dream. What do you think it means?"

I shook my head. "I don't know."

"He was afraid of you."

"Yeah." The second time I stayed at Cherokee, in detox: I'm twenty-three, older than I ever thought I would be. I drink the Schnapps only a little, to keep me steady, and I'm straighter than I've been in two years. I play around in art therapy, with silver and glass. I make rosaries and crucifixes and talismans, which I hang at the head of the bed, twine around the bars in the window, to protect me. Light shines through the colored glass beads, making a multicolored quilt across the white cotton blanket. The beauty protects me, makes my blanket heavy with magic. Death, to the uninvited. He knows I know him, and he stays far, though I see him watch me sometimes, tapping his slender fingers against the tabletop when I walk into the cafeteria. Once, he speaks to me. "Mary. I thought that was you. You've cut off your hair."

"Shaved. Growing back, now." The Schnapps makes me brave,

reckless. "Don't even think about it," I say, and I show him my hands, mime a shove, even though he stands with another doctor.

"He was afraid of me," I told Jimmy.

"Go after him," Jimmy said. "Walk your hableceya, go after him. He took your people, go take them back. Or stay wanagiwinya."

"I don't know how." Then I admitted, "I'm afraid."

"He's running, now. I walked to ask my mother about my people, who I am. I found you." He shrugged, a little embarrassed. "You found me. I see why, now. You need your people back, or you'll always be a ghost." I watched the light come into the room, and waited. When he ended the sentence like a question, I knew he had more to say. He told me the story of the lost boy who goes on his vision quest, knowing he might be a great man, if he can find himself in his people: He goes after his vision like a hunter stalking a deer. He chooses the vision he wants and he hunts it down. It leads him to the pathway to the otherworld. He is sure of his strength, his vision, and he steps into the otherworld. This is not his vision, the one he wants, though. He follows the vision the spirits want him to have, and he knows this too late, tries to step back across, but the arms of the dead are so warm, he hasn't the will to step away from his people, once found. Death's daughter loves him, and returns him to the world of the living, but she must step back across to return him. Here she is mortal, but she steps back across.

"You think I'm Death's daughter?"

He turned to me and laughed. Really laughed, loud, like I've rarely heard him laugh. "No. You missed the point." I so often do with his stories.

"Which is?"

"Find your people. I'm Death's daughter." He left me, walked outside to watch the sun rise over the river mist. I watched him from the window, in his blue boxers, standing in the dusty yard, the cats leaning into his thin boy's legs.

I heard him call his job-boss, the man who was Sioux, Ogalala maybe, but raised in the Cities and whiter than white. Jimmy had told me the man didn't like his Indians to act Indiany. I heard Jimmy saying, "Four days. Today and Monday. She gotta wakan kuwa. I'm staying." He glanced down the hall at me, then grinned, rolled his eyes, and held out the phone receiver. He called because he's working his program, acting responsible. When I first met him he'd get bored with a job and that was that. He'd quit going. I heard his boss complain, loudly. "You don't get no time 'cause your girlfriend's doing Winnebago magic for spirit chasing. Even the union don't give you that. Hell, even the ACLU don't give you that."

"OK," Jimmy said to him. "I work good for you. I show up, on white time, work hard. I want two days. Don't matter, though. There's other jobs." Jimmy thinks there are, and I realized that's why I like him so much. Not many started at $16.90, especially for a long-haired Indian tenth-grade-dropout. I shook my head, but he nodded, still grinning at me. "Yeah," he said, curling the phone cord around his little finger. "Tuesday, early. Yeah, yeah. I owe you overtime. Yeah." He hung up the phone. "Four days," he said to me. Then he nodded to the phone. "He hopes you catch your vision."

"Right."

"Really. He said that. He don't know his people either, you know?"

Jimmy got me ready for my walk. I couldn't eat or drink. He left me in the yard to pray. To keep praying. I knelt in the dirt and prayed my rosary. Around noon I was hot, so I went into the trailer. Jimmy sat on the sofa, drinking a Kool-Aid, watching *Donahue*. "You gotta keep praying, Gracie." He didn't look up at me.

"It's hot."

"Save it up. It'll be cold, later."

"There's no vision, Jimmy."

"You won't see nothing for two, three days."

"So why'd you stay home from work today?"

He sat up and turned around to look at me. "So you wouldn't come in and have a glass of milk and a sandwich. Get outside and pray."

"Jesus Christ. Can I have a cigarette?"

He thought about it for a long time, eyes closed, like he was consulting. "Yeah. The smoke carries your prayers up." I picked up my cigarettes and matches, and I know I sort of sighed and stomped around for a minute because Jimmy laughed at me. "Get your ass outside. You don't get no vision in the trailer. Save up the sun, for when you're cold tonight."

"You can't make me sleep outside."

He shrugged. "I can't make you do nothing. You do what you want. Get your ass outside." I did. I smoked and prayed the rosary on my knees. I got dizzy and prayed the rosary sitting.

About five I went inside to pee, but I didn't even ask for a drink. Jimmy stood over the stove, stirring up macaroni and cheese. "How you doing?"

"OK," I told him.

"I'll come out later. You aren't supposed to go to sleep, you know."

I sat in the driveway again, clutching the rosary, a cigarette in my mouth, when he brought out a plate of orange macaroni and cheese. "My mother likes your cooking better."

"The cats'll eat anything, though." Four of them swarmed around the plate today. Jimmy turned back to the house. "Bring in the pie plate," I said. He did. I hate it when I have to go out under the box elder tree before I can cook or serve dinner. Eventually, the ghosts would have all the plates.

He came out after sunset, wrapped in a blanket from the bed, and sat on the stoop, behind me. "How much sun you store up, Gracie?"

"Not enough."

"Good. The cold'll keep you awake." He didn't talk to me anymore, but I felt him sitting back there. I quit praying and watched the stars, listened to the river. Late, I heard a coyote call. The cold didn't keep me awake for long, but it wasn't good sleep, sitting cross-legged in the driveway, so I didn't think it mattered much that I drifted off a few times. I didn't think I dreamed.

I watched the sun rise and heard the screen door slam as Jimmy went in. I followed him, went to the bathroom. I wanted a drink. Water, but I didn't. He came in and looked me over. "You're doing good," he said. "When I said three days, I wasn't thinking about how little you are. You won't need to come in again."

"Can't I come in to pee?"

"I don't think you'll need to. You sweat everything out, when you don't drink." I just nodded. "Don't want to talk?"

I shook my head. "Not really."

"You're getting there, then. You want to talk with the spirits, now. Sit," he told me, and dropped the toilet lid. I sat. He dug in the drawer and found his tube of zinc, covered my nose and cheeks and lips. "You got burned yesterday, wasichu." I hadn't noticed. I'd been storing the sun, for night. "OK. Out."

I prayed some, but my prayers were just words, meaningless. I recited nursery rhymes, finding a different one for each bead of my rosary. I tried to remember all the words and music to every song on "Truckin'." Then the words to every other Dead song I could think of. I made up words. All words, though, and no meanings. I stored the hot sun into me, not just for tonight, but for winter. If I saved some sun every day, I'd be warm all winter. I closed my eyes. Don't look ahead.

Jimmy brought the food, for the cats. The ghosts. He didn't speak to me, but took away the melamine plate from last night, held it up to me so I could see he remembered. I nodded. I saw the ghosts after the sunset. A man and a woman. The woman was Jimmy's mother, I knew; she looked like him, but shorter and not as pretty. They sat under the box elder tree and watched me. Finally the man said, "He don't know nothing about chasing visions. He don't speak Lakota good either. You know that, don't you, wasichu? That's Indian bullshit. He's feeding you bullshit."

"He knows Lakota better than Winnebago," Jimmy's mother said.

"You don't teach him nothing, woman, that's why. He has to go to the Indian Center in Sioux City to learn who he is, then make up the rest."

"Maybe you shouldn't run off like coyote when I show you your son. Maybe then he'd know who he is."

The man shrugged. "Maybe." They were quiet, there, watching the stars. "You want a vision?" the man asked me. I nodded. "You got smokes?" I nodded again. My throat hurt, so I didn't much want to talk. He came over and sat beside me, sat close. "You share a smoke with me?"

"Sure." I fumbled with the matches, lit a cigarette, took a drag and held it for him. He took a drag, inhaling deeply, eyes closed.

"She's a good cook. She gave me a whole bottle, to drink, once." The woman came over and sat close, too. I shared my cigarette with them.

"Smoke another," the man said. I did. "Now ask for your vision. Ask in these words: Waniyetu wikcemna ma yamni. Miye kuwa wow-icake. Miye kinica wicaka kuwa." I didn't know Lakota, but for the words Jimmy tells me, and this still sounded like Jimmy's bullshit Lakota. I knew those words, though, in my mind: I am thirty. I seek for truth. I try to speak the truth I follow after. I repeated his Lakota, truth or not: it was my truth. Jimmy's father was Sioux. I didn't know if Jimmy knew this or not. He told me he had no father. I told him I didn't, either.

I leave my cigarettes for them and walk to the river, chasing my vision. It's just ahead, a shimmer in the moonlight. I want to find my mother, before she bloats and turns blue. I want to tell my father he sold me for too little. I want to call him weak, and tell him his anger taught me fear. I want to give my angel a shove into the river, and stand above him, watch him as the blackness closes around. "Don't be afraid," I'll say, as the swift water carries him away. I want to name him once and finally, before all those who say he's a good man. I want to find Annie, to say she could tell me anything. I would try to help. I hold my rosary tight in my fist. These are the sorrows, these and many more. They walk behind me, propelling me to the river, but they're not my vision. I pray for my vision, follow its pale glow.

The half-moon throws a silver trail onto moving black water, a path. I step out onto it, feel the wet on the bottoms of my bare feet. The river runs wide here, and I follow the path, sloshing out past the middle, like

I'm walking in rain puddles, until I'm closer to Iowa, and Nebraska lies far behind. My vision stops, just ahead, so I stop. I look down into the water, see a face there, and give Leon my hand. He steps out beside me, pretty dead, with a tire around his waist. "I thought you might be in here."

"Yeah. I know you looked for me. You were good to me, Gracie. I don't want you walking on the water no more."

"Just tonight," I tell him.

"OK. Don't be giving me no more Kool-aid, either." I nod, wait for him. "The kid's OK. He'll do. The cats like him." I liked Leon. I feel the loss of him for the first time, hard in the back of my throat. "I'm a mystery. Don't be sad." He smiles. The power of his quiet smile isn't diminished by death. I kiss him, though he's river-cold and three years dead, he's still Leon, under that, and I always liked him fine. He teases me, "Don't make me want to take you with me. Choose your world. There's your vision." He fades even as I turn to look. The silvery light coalesces to form someone I don't know. A girl, very pretty, like Annie, a little, but without the sad eyes. She's naked, and washed pale by the moonlight, but for her dark eyes and hair.

"Who are you?"

"Nitawa cuwitku," she smiles wide as she speaks.

"I have no daughter."

She raises an eyebrow and shrugs, speaks shy, Indiany English, then. "I speak your truth."

"You aren't my vision. I won't look back," I say. "I couldn't help you."

She nods, "I've brought you something." She holds to me a fragrant, spiny-leafed sprig, which I accept, touching her warm hand. She says, "There's rosemary, that's for remembrance." It hurts to look at her, never born. It hurts in my shoulders, and my back, from the general anesthetic, and aches deep in the low, empty place where my womb was. I nod, wait for her words. "That's all." She smiles, eyes down. "But this is from me."

She touches my hand, and I remember: I'm sitting on our flowered sofa, cuddled near my mother. I think I'm nine. She opens a library book of paintings by Pre-Raphaelites. Each picture is magic, and color. We turn the pages together, gasping our delight at each new offering. We turn to Ophelia, lying in the crystal river, strewn with flowers, momentarily buoyed to the water's surface by her lace dress. Her hair floats loose around her, and I reach out to touch one of my mother's long curls, escaped from her tight pinning. She tells me a story of Ophelia, a loose interpretation of Hamlet, maybe, in which Ophelia is the central tragedy. The tragedy is love and trust betrayed. She says to me, "There's rosemary, that's for remembrance." And there is rosemary in the picture, we find it. Pansies, too. We look longer, read until some child cries, and my mother kisses me and hurries off, leaving me with the book. I turn back to Ophelia, and try to memorize the tapestry of color there.

I look up at my spirit daughter. "Remember," she says to me, before she falls away, dissolving into light alone.

Not the vision I chased, but the vision the spirits granted. I turn back to Nebraska, and see all my people there, standing around me, alive and dead both, vibrant and glowing in spite of the silver moon and black water. As I pass them, my life pours by in a shining rainbow of light and I begin spewing out the names, vomiting the memories that pour in from outside myself. All the names, and I know so many, and they spill away, naming with color the unnamed darkness that had surrounded me for so long. When Death's daughter touches my hair, I turn to him and accept a drink of water. "Small drinks," Jimmy says. "Just a little at first."

Honorable Mentions: 1999

Adams, Benjamin and Bonansinga, Jay, "Butcher Moon," *Play It Again Sam.*

Adams, Margaret, "Angels" (poem), *The Louisville Review*, Winter.

Allende, Isabel, "Evangelina," translated from the Spanish by Margaret Sayers Penden, *The American Voice* 50.

Anderson, Poul, "The Shrine for Lost Children," *The Magazine of Fantasy & Science Fiction*, Oct./Nov.

Aniolowski, Scott David, "The Idol," *Tales Out of Innsmouth.*

Antoni, Robert, "My Grandmother's Tale of How Crab-o Lost His Head," *The Paris Review* 152.

Arnzen, Michael, "Wasp Sting Makes Barber Slash Man's Throat," *Bedtime Stories to Darken Your Dreams.*

Asher, Neal L., "The Gurnard," *Kimota* 10.

———, "Sucker," *Sackcloth & Ashes* 4.

Atkins, Peter, "Dr. Arcadia," *The Wishmaster.*

———, "Faithfulness," Ibid.

Barker, Trey R., "Boom Boom, Wallis Simpson," *A Midsummer's Night's Terror.*

Bassham, Gayla D., "Harold," *Cemetery Sonata.*

Baumer, Jennifer Rachel, "Savannah's Room," *Not One of Us* 21.

Beai, Steve, "In Lopez Canyon," *Indigenous Fiction* 3.

Becker, Lisa, "The Roots of Evil," *Cemetery Sonata.*

Bell, M. Shayne, "And All Our Banners Flying," *F&SF*, Apr.

Benbow, Margaret, "Vampire Meets Maiden" (poem), *Wisconsin Academy Review*, Fall.

Bennett, Nancy, "Silent Dreams: (A Ghost's Lament)" (poem), *Flesh & Blood* 4.

Berman, Judith, "The Window," *Asimov's Science Fiction*, Aug.

Bestwick, Simon, "Going Under, Flying High," *Sackcloth & Ashes* 3.

———, "I'm Telling You Why," *Sackcloth & Ashes* 4.

———, "Thrice Seen," *Enigmatic Tales*, Summer.

————, "Welcome to Mengele's," *Nasty Piece of Work* 11.

Betancourt, John Gregory, "Sympathy for Zombies," *Weird Tales* 315.

Bishop, Kirsten, "The Love of Beauty," *Aurealis* 24.

Bisson, Terry, "macs," *F&SF*, Oct./Nov.

Black, Sharon, "Soul," *Penny Dreadful* 9.

Block, Lawrence, "In for a Penny," *Ellery Queen's Mystery Magazine*, Dec.

Bobes, Merlinda, "Before the Moon Rises," *Southerly*, Autumn.

Bocock, Maclin, "The Baker's Daughter," *Citizen of the World*.

Bowes, Richard, "A Huntsman Passing By," *F&SF*, June.

Boyczuk, Robert, "The Back Shed," *On Spec*, Spring.

Bradfield, Scott, "Dazzle Redux," *F&SF*, Dec.

Bradshaw, Paul, "The Lonely Ones," *Alternate Lives Enigmatic Novellas No. 5*.

————, "The Vanishers," Ibid.

Braunbeck, Gary A., "All the Unlived Moments," *Future Crimes*.

————, "I'll Play the Blues for You," *Subterranean Gallery*.

————, "In Hollow Houses," *Whitley Strieber's Aliens*.

————, "One Brown Mouse," *Alien Abductions*.

Braunbeck, Gary A. and Snyder, Lucy A., "Still Life Drama," *Bedtime Stories to Darken Your Dreams*.

Bray, Marian Flandrick, "City Magic," *Marion Zimmer Bradley's Fantasy Magazine*, Winter.

Brennert, Alan, "The White City," *Future Crimes*.

Bretnor, Reginald, "The Haunting of H. M. S. Dryad," *Weird Tales* 314.

Bricker, Calvin K., "Summer House," *Cemetery Sonata*.

Brockman, Jeffery M., "A Misery of Shoes," *Chelsea* 66.

Bryant, Edward, "The Clock That Counts the Dead," *White of the Moon: New Tales of Madness and Dread*.

————, "Shuttlecock," *The Crow: Shattered Lives & Broken Dreams*.

————, "Styx and Bones," *999*.

Bryant, Edward and Barker, Trey R., "The Flicker Man," *Whitley Strieber's Aliens*.

Burgess, Donna Taylor, "Night" (poem), *Weird Tales* 314.

Burt, Steven E., "Lighthouse Moths," *Lincoln County Weekly*, October, 28 and *Threshold*, Winter.

Cacek, P. D., "Fireflies," *Whitley Strieber's Aliens*.

————, "The Grave," *999*.

Cadnum, Michael, "Ella and the Canary Prince," chapbook.

Calder, Richard, "Impakto," *Interzone* 150.

Campbell, Bonnie Jo, "Gorilla Girl," *Women & Other Animals*.

Campbell, Ramsey, "Agatha's Ghost," *White of the Moon*.

————, "Becoming Visible," *Neonlit*.

————, "The Entertainment," *999*.

Cannon, Peter, "Bride of Azathoth," *Forever Azathoth*.

————, "The Hound of the Partridgevilles," Ibid.

————, "Son of Azathoth," Ibid.

Cañón, James, "The Two Miracles of the Gringos' Virgin," *Bésame Mucho.*

Capewell, Laura, "Bring out Your Dead," *Cemetery Sonata.*

Card, Orson Scott, "Vessel," *F&SF*, Dec.

Cardosa, Onelio Jorge, "The Storyteller," *Dream with No Name: Contemporary Fiction from Cuba.*

Carroll, Jonathan, "Fish in a Barrel," *F&SF*, Oct./Nov.

Carruth, Jim, "Harvest Moon" (poem), *Nasty Piece of Work* 12.

Case, David, "Anachrona," *Brotherly Love & Other Tales of Faith and Knowledge.*

————, "Brotherly Love" (novella), Ibid.

————, "The Ogre of the Cleft," Ibid.

Casil, Amy Sterling, "My Son, My Self," *Writers of the Future, Volume XV.*

Cave, Hugh B., "A Voice in the Wild," *Northern Frights 5.*

Chadbourn, Mark, "Love and Death at the End of the World," *The Last Continent: New Tales of Zotnique.*

————, "Wan Light," *Sackcloth & Ashes* 5.

————, "Where the Black Dog Runs," *Peeping Tom* 33.

Chapman, Stepan, "Buzzy Motions" (poem), *Not One of Us* 22.

Christian, M., "Needle Taste," *Errata* (web site), June.

————, "Orphans," *Talebones* 17.

Christiansen, Gitte, "Voyage to Abydos," *Aurealis* 24.

Clark, Alan M. and Bauman, Jill, "Mousenight," *Bedtime Stories to Darken Your Dreams.*

Clark, Simon "The Pass," *Houses at the Borderland.*

————, "Two Dead Detectives," *Crime Time* 2.3.

Clark, Simon and Ford, John B., "The Derelict of Death," chapbook.

Clegg, Douglas, "Becoming Men," *Subterranean Gallery.*

————, "The Joss House," *Deadbolt Magazine*, Autumn.

————, "The Little Mermaid," *Palace Corbie Eight.*

————, "The Machinery of the Night," *The Asylum, Volume 1: The Psycho Ward.*

Clink, Carolyn, "Franklin Expedition, 1848" (poem), *Tesseracts #7.*

Collins, Nancy A., "Catfish Gal Blues," *999.*

————, "Lynch" (novella), CD Publications.

Collins, Ron, "A Gathering of Bones," *Flights of Fantasy.*

Comtois, Pierre, "The Old Ones' Signs," *Tales Out of Innsmouth.*

Constantine, Storm, "Curse of the Snake," *The Oracle Lips.*

————, "Panquilia in the Ruins," Ibid.

Coover, Robert, "The Photographer," *Fence*, Fall/Winter.

Copper, Basil, "The Grass," *Whispers in the Night.*

————, "In a Darkling Wood" (novella), Ibid.

————, "The Obelisk," Ibid.

————, "One for the Pot," Ibid.

———, "Riding the Chariot," Ibid.

———, "The Summerhouse," Ibid.

Couzens, Gary, "Amber," *Roadworks* 5.

———, "The Day of the Outing," *Roadworks* 6.

Coville, Bruce, "The Giant's Tooth," *Realms of Fantasy*, Dec.

———, "The Golden Sail," *Odder Than Ever.*

———, "The Stinky Princess," Ibid.

Coward, Mat, "We Have Fed You All for a Thousand Years," *The Third Alternative* 20.

Cox, Cardinal, "The Tower," *Enigmatic Tales*, Spring.

Critchley, Ian, "A New New Forest," *Neonlit*, Volume 2.

Crow, Christine, "If Pigs Could Fly," *The Mammoth Book of Lesbian Short Stories.*

Crowther, Peter, "Cleaning Up," *Dark Regions and Horror Magazine*, Winter.

———, "Dark Times," *Subterranean Gallery.*

———, "Gallagher's Arm," *The Longest Single Note and Other Strange Compositions.*

———, "Late Night Pick-Up," *Alien Abductions.*

Crowther, Peter and Lovegrove, James, "The Hand that Feeds" (novella), chapbook.

Cutter, Leah R., "Gulkhanam," *Talebones* 16.

D'Ammassa, Don, "Wormdance," *Asimov's SF*, May.

Daniels, Keith Allen, "Angels of the Half-Spans" (poem), *Talebones* 16.

Davis, John, "The Miracle," *Bedtime Stories to Darken Your Dreams.*

de Kruyff, Nicholas, "Burger's Head," *F&SF*, May.

de Lint, Charles, "The Buffalo Man," Subterranean Press chapbook.

———, "Forest of Stone," *Merlin.*

———, "If I Close My Eyes Forever," *Moonlight and Vines.*

———, "In the Land of the Unforgiven," Ibid.

de Winter, Corinne, "Dream of Cities" (poem), *Edgar: Digested Verse* 3.

Dean, Elizabeth, "Yankee Winter," *Dead Promises.*

DeChancie, John, "Slow Dance for a Dead Princess," *Dangerous Magic.*

Dedman, Stephen, "A Single Shadow," *Weird Tales* 316.

———, "The Vision of a Vanished Good," *The Lady of Situations.*

Deja, Thomas, "The Smoking Glass Grin," *Not One of Us* 22.

Diago, Evelio Rosero, "Brides by Night," translated from the Spanish by Jennifer Gabrielle Edwards, *Michigan Quarterly Review*, Spring.

DiChario, Nicholas A., "Movin' On," *Weird Tales* 315.

———, "Sarajevo," *F&SF*, Mar.

Dietrich, Bryan, "The Secret Diaries of Lois Lane" (poem), *Prairie Schooner*, Spring.

Disch, Thomas M., "The Owl and the Pussycat," *999.*

Dixit, Shikhar, "Calamity in Repose," *MindMares Magazine*, Winter.

———, "Kidnap Cantata with Accompanying Dial Tone," *Nasty Snips.*

Dixon, Scott, "Chilling," *Night Terrors* 8.

Doig, James, "Mathrafal," *Ghosts & Scholars* 29.

———, "The Wild Hunt," *Ghosts & Scholars* 28.

Domecq, Alcina Lubitch, "La Llorana," translated from the Spanish by Ilan Stavans, *The Literary Review*, Fall.

Donaldson, Stephen R., "The Killing Stroke," *Reave the Just and Other Tales*.

——, "Penance," Ibid.

D'Onofrio, Deborah Therese, "Rozsa-Neni and Farkas Asszony," *Realms of Fantasy*, Aug.

Dorr, James S., "The Calm," *New Mythos Legends*.

——, "The Great Man," *The Strand Magazine* 2.

Duncan, Andy, "The Executioners' Guild" (novella), *Asimov's SF*, Aug.

East, Christopher, "Gallery of the Eighth Day," *The Third Alternative* 21.

Edghill, India, "The Courtesan Who Loved Cats," *Catfantastic V*.

Eklund, Gordon R., "The Cross Road Blues," *F&SF*, Feb.

Eller, Steve, "Bodily Fluids," *Not One of Us* 21.

Ellison, Harlan, "Objects of Desire in the Mirror Are Closer than They Appear," *Fantasy and Science Fiction*, Oct/Nov.

Emshwiller, Carol, "Acceptance Speech," *F&FS*, Oct/Nov.

Engstrom, Elizabeth, "The Shyanne Letters," *The Alchemy of Love*.

——, "Vargas County," *Bedtime Stories to Darken Your Dreams*.

Etchemendy, Nancy, "Werewife," *F&SF*, June.

Files, Gemma, "Blood Makes Noise," *TransVersions* 11.

Finch, Paul, "The Dandy Dogs," *The Dark Satanic . . . Enigmatic Novellas No. 2*.

——, "The Gaff," *Enigmatic Tales*, Autumn.

——, "The Hotel on the Borderland," *Houses at the Borderland* (CD-ROM).

——, "The Magic Lantern Show," *The Dark Satanic . . . Enigmatic Novellas No. 2*.

Fisher, Dennis and Fisher, Joe, "Jazz Funeral," *Dark Regions and Horror Magazine*, Summer.

Fishler, Barry, "Heartstrings," *The Third Alternative* 19.

Fletcher, Kay, "The Peewold Amphisbaena," *Ghosts & Scholars* 29.

Fletcher, Nigel, "The Eye of the Beholder," *Albedo One* 18.

Ford, Jeffrey, "Pansolapia," *Event Horizon* (web site), July.

Fowler, Christopher, "The Human Element," *Uncut*.

——, "Living Proof," *The Edge*.

——, "Thirteen Places of Interest in Kentish Town," *Uncut*.

——, "Two Murders," Ibid.

Fox, Chris, "Condensation," *Enigmatic Tales*, Summer.

Frackelton, Alan, "The Book of Dreams," *Roadworks* 5.

Friesner, Esther M., "Chanoyu," *Asimov's SF*, Mar.

——, "How to Make Unicorn Pie," *F&SF*, Jan.

——, "Jolene's Motel," *Whitley Strieber's Aliens*.

Fritch, Charles, "Different," *California Sorcery*.

Frost, Gregory, "Collecting Dust," *White of the Moon*.

Gaiman, Neil, "The Facts in the Case of the Departure of Miss Finch," *Tales of the Unanticipated* 20.

————, "Goliath," *whatisthematrix.com* (web site).

Garcia y Robertson, R., "Strongbow," *F&SF*, Aug.

Gardner, C. A. "For David, with Love" (poem), *Not One of Us* 22.

Gifune, Greg F., "Chasing Moonlight," *MindMares Magazine*, Fall.

Giron, Sephera, "Release," *The Asylum, Volume 1: The Psycho Ward.*

Glass, Alexander, "The Mirror Repair'd," *Interzone* 139.

Glassco, Bruce, "Wailer," *Realms of Fantasy*, Aug.

Godfrey, Owen D., "The Dinner," *The Rhizome Factor*, Mar.

Goldstein, Lisa, "The Witch's Child," *Realms of Fantasy*, Dec.

Gonzales, J. F., "Love Hurts," *The Asylum, Volume 1: The Psycho Ward.*

Gorman, Ed, "Angie," *999.*

————, "The Last Sunset," *Alien Abductions.*

————, "Such a Good Girl," *Subterranean Gallery.*

Gould, Jason, "A Breach of Tissue," *The Third Alternative* 19.

————, "Menace to Society," *Nasty Piece of Work* 12.

Green, Scott E., "Cairn on the Shore of the Gulf of Finland" (poem), *Dreams and Nightmares* 53.

Greenwood, Gary, "Feather," *Sackcloth & Ashes* 4.

Grey, John, "Scream 6" (poem), *Dreams and Nightmares* 53.

Griffith, Clay and Griffith, Susan, "The Taste," *A Fistful of Dead Guys.*

Gunther, Clare, "The Artificial Vagina Bottle" (poem), *Nasty Piece of Work* 11.

Hall, James W., "Crack," *Murder and Obsession.*

Hauser, Erik, "The Intruder," *All Hallows* 22.

Henderson, C. J., "Fleas of the Dragon," *Tales Out of Innsmouth.*

————, "To Cast Out Fear," *New Mythos Legends.*

Hennessy, John, "Urban and His Daughter" (poem), *The Sewanee Review*, Fall.

Hoffman, Nina Kiriki, "Toobychubbies," *Alien Abductions.*

Hood, Robert, "Ground Underfoot," *Aurealis* 23.

Hopkins, Brian A., "Five Days in April," *Chiaroscuro* (web site), July.

Hopkinson, Nalo, "Slow Cold Chick," *Northern Frights* 5.

Howard, Terpsichore, "Lalin Bonheur," *Flyway*, Winter 1998/1999.

Hughes, Rhys, "Nothing More Common," *Enigmatic Tales*, Winter.

————, "A Rape of Knots," *Nasty Piece of Work* 13.

Humphries, Dwight E., "Dead Takes Forever" (poem), *Dreams and Nightmares* 53.

————, "Harvest Home" (poem), *Penny Dreadful* 11.

Hunter, Ian, "The View," *Enigmatic Tales*, Summer.

Jackson, Roger, "My Family and Other Vampires," *Sackcloth & Ashes* 3.

Jacob, Charlee, "Through Venetian Blinds," *Dread in the Beast.*

Jacobs, Harvey, "The Vanishing Virgin," *Silver Birch, Blood Moon.*

Jakeman, Jane, "The Barzakh," *All Hallows* 21.

Jamieson, Trent, "Whispers in Darkness" (poem), *Masque Noir* 1.

Janks, Gregory, "The One-Eyed Man," *Writers of the Future XV.*

Johnson, George Clayton, "The Man Who Was Slugger Malone," *California Sorcery.*

Johnson, Kij, "Chenting, In the Land of the Dead," *Realms of Fantasy*, Oct.

Johnson, Melissa, "Guinevere" (poem), *The Connecticut Review*, Fall.

Joyce, Graham, "Leningrad Nights" (novella), PS Publishing.

Kalfus, Ken, "Salt," *PU-239 and Other Russian Fantasies.*

Kallio, Koka Li, "In Chains of Song," *Altair* 4.

Kasturi, Sandra, "Sea Wrack" (poem), *On Spec*, Spring.

Keene, Brian, "The Burn Barrel," *Houses at the Borderland* (CD-ROM).

Kennett, Rick and Stevens, Bryce, "Rookwood," *Aurealis* 24.

Kenworthy, Christopher, "The Rot," *Interzone* 147.

Ketchum, Jack, "Right to Life" (novella), chapbook.

Kewley, Jodie, "Bare Walls," *Eidolon* 28.

Kiernan, Caitlín R., "Rats Live on No Evil Star," *White of the Moon.*

Kilpatrick, Nancy, "A Fishy Tale," *Tails from the Pet Shop.*

Kilworth, Garry, "The Frog Chauffeur," *Silver Birch, Blood Moon.*

King, Stephen, "The Road Virus Heads North," *999.*

Knez, Dora, "The One Forbidden Thing," *Lady Churchill's Rosebud Wristlet*, Vol. 3, No. 1.

Kollar, Sybil, "Skirting the Demons" (poem), *Columbia: A Journal of Literature and Art* 31.

Kress, Nancy, "Clad in Gossamer," *Silver Birch, Blood Moon.*

Kriseova, Eda, "A Whirl of Witches," translated from the Czech by Andree Collier, *Partisan Review*, Fall.

Kulpa, Kathryn, "Jenny," *Indigenous Fiction* 2.

Lahain, Carrieann, "After the Hurricane," *Peeping Tom* 33.

———, "Penelope," *Prisoners of the Night* 11.

Lamsley, Terry, "The Stunted House," *Subterranean Gallery.*

Lane, Joel, "Another Frame," *White of the Moon.*

———, "The Gardner" (poem), *Nasty Piece of Work* 11.

———, "His Master's Voice," *Kimota* 10.

Lane, Joel and Morgan, Chris, "Feels Like Underground," *F&SF*, Apr.

Lange, Mike, "The Dead of Winter," *Weird Tales* 316.

Lannes, Roberta, "Feng Shui," *White of the Moon.*

Lansdale, Joe R., "Mad Dog Summer" (novella), *999.*

Lebbon, Tim, "Bomber's Moon," *Bonetree* (web site), June.

———, "Pelts," *Sackcloth & Ashes* 5.

Lebbon, Tim and Lewis, D. F., "Dirty Pipes," *Peeping Tom* 34.

Lee, Edward, "ICU," *999.*

———, "Operator 'B' " (novella), CD Publications.

———, "The Ushers," *The Ushers.*

Lee, Edward and Pelan, John, "The Scarlet Succubus," *The Last Continent.*

Lee, Tanith, "An Iron Bride," *Weird Tales* 318.

————, "Kiss Kiss," *Silver Birch, Blood Moon.*

————, "Unlocking the Golden Cage," *Weird Tales* 315.

Leever, Carol E., "Moonlight on Water," *Sword & Sorceress XVI.*

Lehane, Dennis, "Running Out of Dog," *Murder and Obsession.*

Levin, Dana, "Eyeless Baby" (poem), *In the Surgical Theatre.*

————, "Hive" (poem), Ibid.

————, "Magpie" (poem), Ibid.

————, "Paul, Roosevelt Island" (poem), Ibid.

————, "Wing" (poem), Ibid.

Levine, Jeffrey, "Goddesses in the Vieux Carre" (poem), *Quarterly West*, Autumn/Winter.

Levy, Debra, "Museum Pieces," *Columbia: A Journal of Literature and Art* 31.

Lieberman, Kim-An, "Wings" (poem), *Prairie Schooner*, Winter.

Lieberman, Laurence, "Wolf of the Skies" (poem), *The Hudson Review*, Summer.

Ligotti, Thomas, "The Shadow, The Darkness," *999.*

Link, Kelly, "The Dictator's Wife," *Lady Churchill's Rosebud Wristlet*, Vol. 3, No. 2.

————, "Survivor's Ball (or, The Donner Party)" *Dark Planet* (web site).

Linzer, Anna, "Ghost Dancing," *Ghost Dancing.*

Little, Bentley, "The Theater," *999.*

Lockley, Steve, "The Angel's Kiss," *Kimota* 11.

Lovegrove, James, "How the Other Half Lives" (novella), PS Publishing.

Luce, Gregory, "The Deep End," *Tales out of Innsmouth.*

Lustbader, Eric Van, "Slow Burn," *Murder and Obsession.*

MacAllister, Carol, "Night Voices" (poem), *Edgar: Digested Verse* 3.

MacGregor, Susan, "Oyster Love," *Northern Frights 5.*

Maclay, John, "The Final Order," *Grue Magazine* 19.

————, "A Place by the Sea," *Noirotica 3/Night Tales.*

————, "Stakeout," *Night Tales.*

Malito, John, "Resurrection" (poem), *The Antioch Review*, Winter.

Marano, Michael, "Burden," *Gothic.net* (web site), Mar.

Markus, Deborah, "Bitter Pills," *Cemetery Sonata.*

Marshall, Paul, "The Big Questions," *Unhinged* 2.

Masterton, Graham, "Friend in Need," *White of the Moon.*

Matheson, Richard, "Always Before Your Voice," *California Sorcery.*

Maycock, Brian, "Maiden," *The Dream Zone* 3.

Maynard, L. H. and Sims, M. P. N., "An English Country Garden," *graveworm.com* (web site).

————, "An Office in the Grays Inn Road," *Enigmatic Tales*, Summer.

Mayo, Wendell, "B. Horror," *B. Horror and Other Stories.*

McAuley, Paul J., "I Spy," *White of the Moon.*

McBain, Ed, "Barking at Butterflies," *Murder and Obsession.*

McBride, Sally, "Doing Drugs," *Northern Frights 5.*

McCann, Janet, "The Home of the Radioactive Cats" (poem), *The Midwest Quarterly*, Summer.

McCartney, R. G., "The Spider," *Aurealis* 24.

McComas, Steve, "anybody home?" (poem), *Weird Tales* 316.

McKiernan, Dennis L., "Darkness," *999*.

McKinley, Robin, "Marsh-Magic," *Silver Birch, Blood Moon*.

McLaughlin, Mark, "The Vainglorious Simulacrum of Mungha Sorcyllamia," *The Last Continent*.

———, "Zom Bee Moo Vee," *Zom Bee Moo Vee*.

McNaughton, Brian, "The Benevolent Emperor," *The Last Continent*.

———, "The Doom That Came to Innsmouth," *Tales Out of Innsmouth*.

Meddor, Michael, "The Wizard Retires," *F&SF*, Sep.

Mooney, Brian, "Vultures Gather," *Dark Detectives*.

Morlan, A. R., "The Gemutlichkeit Escape," *Challenging Destiny*.

———, "White Comma" (poem), *TransVersions* 10.

Morrell, David, "Rio Grande Gothic" (novella), *999*.

Morris, Anthony, "The Chair," *Candlelight Ghost Stories . . . Enigmatic Novellas No. 3*.

———, "The Squire's Walk," Ibid.

Morton, Lisa, "A New Force of Nature," *White of the Moon*.

Mundt, Martin, "Wet with Me," *When the Bough Breaks*.

Navarro, Yvonne, "Deadtimes 1961–Reprisal," *Palace Corbie Eight*.

Newman, Kim, "Amerikanski Dead at the Moscow Morgue," *999*.

——— "Andy Warhol's Dracula" (novella), *Event Horizon* (web site), June.

———, "Angel Down, Sussex" (novella), *Interzone* 149.

———, "The Biafran Bank Manager," *Dark Detectives*.

———, "The Duel of Seven Stars," Ibid.

———, "Une etrange aventure de Richard Blaine," *The Time Out Book of Paris Short Stories*.

———, "Further Developments in the Strange Case of Dr. Jekyll & Mr. Hyde," *Past Poisons* 2.

———, "The Mummy's Heart," *Dark Detectives*.

———, "The Trouble with Barrymore," Ibid.

———, "A Victorian Ghost Story," *Interzone* 139.

Newton, Kurt, "Bloom" (poem), *Five Spots on the Newt*.

———, "The Street Urchin" (poem), Ibid.

Nicholls, Mark, "In Eastern Waters," *All Hallows* 22.

———, "The Way That All Things End," *Enigmatic Tales*, Winter.

Nichols, Catherine, "Family Reunion," *Cemetery Sonata*.

Nicholson, Scott, "Three-Dollar Corpse," *Dead Promises*.

Nickels, Tim, "The Hungry Shine," *Timeout: Net Books*.

Nickle, David, "Ground-Bound," *On Spec*, Spring.

————, "Night of the Tar Baby," *Northern Frights 5*.

Oates, Joyce Carol, "The Ruins of Contracoeur" (novella), *999*.

————, "The Vampire," *Murder and Obsession*.

Ochse, Weston, "Family Man," *At the Brink of Madness* 1.

————, "Holy Ghost Hit Parade," *Darkness Within* 1.

O'Connor, John, "Antibodies," *Palace Corbie Eight*.

O'Driscoll, Mike, "Hello Darkness," *The Third Alternative* 21.

————, "A One-way Ticket to Palookaville," *Indigenous Fiction* 3.

Oldknow, Anthony, "Quintinshill," *Ghosts & Scholars* 28.

Ong, Alistair, "The Artist," *Aurealis* 23.

Owton, Martin, "The Grass Is Always Greener," *Kimota* 11.

Partridge, Norman, "Carne Muerta," *Cemetery Dance* 30.

————, "The Mojave Two-Step," *Future Crimes*.

Patrice, Helen, "Shaping Up," *Interzone* 149.

Pauloma, Sari, "Slow Snow," *The Dream Zone* 2.

Pelan, John, "Old Songs Waken," *The Urbanite* 11.

Pelevin, Viktor, "The Greek Version," *AGNI* 13.

Pendragon, Michael, "The Curiosity Piece," *Nightscapes*.

Penha, James, "Stone and Dust," *Columbia: A Journal of Literature and Art*, Winter.

Piccirilli, Tom, "Mount of the Oath" (novella), *Deep into that Darkness Peering*.

————, "Of Darkness I Acknowledge Mine," *New Mythos Legends*.

————, "The Serpent Was More Subtle," *Future Crimes*.

————, "Tracking the Death Angel," *The Best of the American West II*.

————, "Water Music for the Tillers of Soil," *Deep into that Darkness Peering*.

————, "Where the Martyred Flesh Knows Serenity," Ibid.

Piché, J. Marc, "In Your Place of Power (Transmogrifications)" (poem), *Tesseracts 7*.

Pillsworth, Anne M., "Geldman's Pharmacy," *Night Terrors* 8.

Powell, James, "Jane's Head," *Northern Frights 5*.

————, "Jerrold's Meat," *EQMM*, Apr.

Raffo, Susan, "Apértif," *Night Shade*.

Rainey, Stephen Mark, "The Fire Dogs of Balustrade," *New Mythos Legends*.

Ratcliffe, David, "The Pebble-Dash Genie," *Peeping Tom* 33.

Rath, Tina, "A Study in Black and White," *Ghosts & Scholars* 29.

Rathbone, Wendy, "The Shadow-Garden" (poem), *Dreams and Nightmares* 52.

Ray, Jean, "Gold Teeth," *My Own Private Spectres*.

————, "The Hand of Götz von Berlichingen," Ibid.

————, "House of Storks," Ibid.

————, "The Marlywick Cemetery," Ibid.

————, "My Own Private Spectres," Ibid.

————, "The Pink Terror," Ibid.

————, "Saint Judas of the Night," Ibid.

————, "Spider Master," Ibid.

———, "Streets (A Document)," Ibid.

Redding, Judith M., "Mud," *Night Shade.*

Redwood, Steve, "Sarcophagus," *Enigmatic Tales,* Winter.

Reed, Robert, "Mac and Me," *Asimov's SF,* Feb.

Reisman, Jessica Wynne, "Raney's Hounds," *Realms of Fantasy,* Oct.

Reisz, Kristopher, "Teddy Bear," *Bloodsongs* 11.

Resnick, Mike, "Hunting the Snark" (novella), *Asimov's SF,* Dec.

Reynolds, Alastair, "Viper," Ibid.

Rich, Mark, "Think of the Dead Monkey in the Sky," *Palace Corbie Eight.*

———, "Zothique Mi Amor," *Talebones* 15.

Richards, James, "Adams's Song" (poem), *BYU Studies,* Vol. 38, No. 3.

Rickert, M., "The Girl Who Ate Butterflies," *F&SF,* Aug.

Riedel, Kate, "Mausturm," *Realms of Fantasy,* June.

Rings, Eve, "The Cannibal's Daughter," *Chiaroscuro* (web site) 1.

Roberts, Michele, "Fluency," *The Time Out Book of Paris Short Stories.*

Rosen, Barbara, "Box of Light," *Sepulchre,* Summer.

———, "The People Next Door," *Night Terrors* 8.

Rowe, Christopher, "Sally Harpe," *Realms of Fantasy,* Oct.

Royle, Nicholas, "The Roundabout," *White of the Moon.*

Rucker, Lynda E., "Different Angels," *The Third Alternative* 19.

Ruckley, Brian, "Gibbons," *The Third Alternative* 20.

Rusch, Kristine Kathryn, "The Women of Whale Rock," *F&SF,* Mar.

Russell, Doug, "Singin' Man," *Space and Time* 90.

Russell, Jay, "Down," *Waltzes and Whispers.*

———, "Dracula's Eyes," Ibid.

———, "Revenge of the Zombie Studpuppies," Ibid.

———, "What Ever Happened to Baby June," *White of the Moon.*

Russo, Patricia, "Dog Lover," *Not One of Us* 21.

———, "La Lattaia," *Tales of the Unanticipated* 20.

Rutherford, Derek, "The Making of Mark," *All Hallows* 20.

Sallee, Wayne Allen, "Orient Are," *Grue Magazine* 19.

Samman, Ghada, "The Metallic Crocodile," *The Square Moon.*

Sanders, Joe, "When the Sun Rises," *Limestone* (University of Kentucky), Spring.

Sandner, David, "The Cry of Those Waiting Under the Bridge" (poem), *Weird Tales* 318.

Savile, Steve, "Icarus Descending," chapbook.

———, "The Last Picture of Summer," *Sackcloth & Ashes* 5.

———, "Remember Me Yesterday," Ibid.

———, "Send Me Dead Flowers," *Sci-Fright* 1.

Schow, David J., "Unhasped," *White of the Moon.*

Schroeder, Karl, "Dawn," *Tesseracts* 7.

Schweitzer, Darrel, "Bitter Chivalry," *Realms of Fantasy,* Feb.

Searles, Vera, "The Man in the Rain," *Fantastique,* Summer.

Seitz, Hunter, "The Last Child of the Day," *All Hallows* 21.

Shawl, Nisi, "The Pragmatical Princess," *Asimov's SF*, Jan.

Sheers, Owen, "The Cab Driver's Story," *Neonlit.*

Shepard, Lucius, "Crocodile Rock" (novella), *F&SF*, Oct./Nov.

Shepherd, D., "Theseus" (poem), *The Literary Review*, Feb.

Sherwood, Frances, "Basil the Dog," *Atlantic Monthly*, Sep.

Shimkus, James, "The Noonday Devil," *New Mythos Legends.*

Shiner, Lewis, "Lizard Men of Los Angeles," *F&SF*, July.

Shirley, John, "Brittany? Oh: She's in Translucent Blue," *Really Really Really Really Weird Stories.*

Silva, David B., "The Last Full Measure of Devotion," *Subterranean Gallery.*

———, "Nothing as It Seems," *Whitley Strieber's Aliens.*

———, "Placenta in Black," *Deadbolt Magazine*, Spring.

Silverberg, Robert, "A Hero of the Empire," *F&SF*, Oct./Nov.

Sinclair, Lisa, "The Hanging Tree" (poem), *Edgar: Digested Verse* 3.

Singleton, Sarah, "In the Mirror," *Enigmatic Novellas No. 4.*

———, "The Red Bottle," *Enigmatic Tales*, Summer.

Sivier, David, "Black Harlequinade," *Zest* 7.

Slavin, Julia, "Covered," *The Woman Who Cut Off Her Leg at the Maidstone Club.*

Sloan, Kay, "Rolling Buddha," *Pleiades*, Summer.

Smith, Douglas, "Spirit Dance," *The Third Alternative* 22.

———, "State of Disorder," *Amazing Stories*, Winter.

Smith, James Robert, "A Last, Longing Look," *Whitley Strieber's Aliens.*

Smith, Michael Marshall, "The Book of Irrational Numbers," *999.*

———, "A Convenient Arrangement," *Cemetery Dance* 31.

———, "Everybody Goes," *The Third Alternative* 19.

———, "The Vaccinator" (novella), chapbook.

Snyder, Jena, "Love Knot," *On Spec*, Spring.

Somtow, S. P., "The Hero's Celluloid Journey" (novella), *Weird Tales* 314.

Stableford, Brian, "The Gateway of Eternity" (novella), *Interzone* 139 and 140.

———, "Rent," *Weird Tales* 314.

———, "Rose, Crowned with Thorns," *White of the Moon.*

Stirling, Jan, "Ill Met by Moonlight," *Dead Promises.*

Stone, Del, Jr., "Feeders," *New Mythos Legends.*

Storm, Sue, "The Secret Garden," *Palace Corbie Eight.*

Stuart, Pamela, "Grandma's Box," *Enigmatic Tales*, Autumn.

Sturgis, Susanna J., "The Blizzard's Daughter," *Stars Inside Her.*

Sykes, Jerry, "Roots," *Mean Time.*

———, "Sleep that Burns," *Future Crimes.*

Taylor, Keith, "Daggers and a Serpent," *Weird Tales* 316.

———, "Emissaries of Doom," *Weird Tales* 318.

Taylor, Lucy, "Ashes of Longing, Ashes of Lust," *The Last Continent.*

Taylor, Peggy J., "Brigit" (poem), *CALYX: A Journal of Art and Literature by Women*, Summer.

Tem, Melanie, "The Willful Child, the Black Dog, and the Beanstalk," *Silver Birch, Blood Moon*.

Tem, Steve Rasnic, "In His Image," *Crime Wave 2: Deepest Red*.

———, "The Mouse's Bedtime Story," *Bedtime Stories to Darken Your Dreams*.

———, "Tricks & Treats: One Night on Halloween Street," *F&SF*, Dec.

Tennant, Peter, "Letting Go," *Sackcloth & Ashes* 6.

———, "The Threshing Floor," *Nasty Piece of Work* 12.

Tessier, Thomas, "Lulu," *Lulu and One Other*.

———, "Nightsuite," *Ibid*.

Thatcher, Franklin, "By Other Windings," *Writers of the Future, Volume XV*.

Thees, Lester, "Flash," *MindMares Magazine*, Spring.

Thomas, G. W., "Waking Dream," *Flesh & Blood* 4.

Thomas, Jeffrey, "The Cellar Gods," *New Mythos Legends*.

———, "Corpse Candles," *Cthulhu Codex* 15.

———, "Through Obscure Glass," *Avatars of the Old Ones*.

Thomas, Scott, "Ellette," *Penny Dreadful* 11.

Thurlow, Clifford, "An Irresistible Artifice," *Psychotrope* 7.

Tiedemann, Mark W., "Gallo," *Asimov's SF*, Mar.

Tilton, Lois, "The Scientific Community," *Asimov's SF*, Sep.

Tucker, James A., "Picture His Horror," *Kimota* 10.

Urban, Scott H., "Household Goods," *The Edge* 5.

Valentine, Mark, "The Craft of Arioch," *In Violet Veils*.

———, "In Violet Veils," *Ibid*.

VanderMeer, Jeff, "The Strange Case of X," *White of the Moon*.

———, "The Transformation of Martin Lake," *Palace Corbie Eight*.

Van Pelt, James, "Shark Attack: A Love Story," *Weird Tales* 317.

Vaughn, Carrie, "The Girl with the Pre-Raphaelite Hair," *Talebones* 17.

Vu, Tran, "The Dragon Hunt," *The Dragon Hunt*.

Wade, Susan, "Ivory Bones," *Silver Birch, Blood Moon*.

Wagner, Erica, "The Taste of Apricots," *The Time Out Book of Paris Short Stories*.

Walker, Dale L., "In the Meadow," *The Best of the American West II*.

Walsh, Pat, "Midwinter Mass," *All Hallows* 21.

Walther, Paul, "The Gandy Dancer," *Enigmatic Tales*, Autumn.

Wandrei, Donald, "A Stranger Passes," *Colossus*.

Ward, Gregory, "Time Flies," *Northern Frights 5*.

Ward, Kyla, "The Feast," *Aurealis* 24.

Webb, Don, "Afterward," *Not One of Us* 21.

———, "The Jest of Yig," *Interzone* 143.

———, "Others to Act as Our Claws," *Dread* 6.

———, "Serenade at the End of Time," *The Last Continent*.

Weiner, Andrew, "Crossing," *Northern Frights 5.*

Wentworth, K. D., "The Girl Who Loved Fire," *Realms of Fantasy*, Aug.

West, Michelle, "Sunrise," *A Dangerous Magic.*

Westgard, Sten, "A Brother Grimm," *Realms of Fantasy*, Aug.

———, "The Marriage Doll," *Lady Churchill's Rosebud Wristlet*, Vol. 3, No. 1.

———, "The Numbers of the Dead," *The Third Alternative* 22.

———, "Twilight at Djemaa el Fna," *The Third Alternative* 21.

What, Leslie, "The Cost of Doing Business," *Amazing Stories*, Winter.

Wheeler, Susan, "Benny the Beaver: My Father's Tale" (poem), *Colorado Review*, Fall/ Winter.

Whitbourn, John, "But After This, the Judgement," *More Binscombe Tales.*

———, "Canterbury's Dilemma," Ibid.

———, "It'll All Be Over by Christmas," Ibid.

———, "Up from the Cellar, or England Expects!" Ibid.

Whitman, David, "A Momentary Thing," *The Edge* 5.

Williams, Liz, "Nightside," *The Third Alternative* 20.

———, "Outremer," *Unhinged* 2.

Williams, Walter Jon, "Argonautica," *Asimov's SF*, Oct./Nov.

Willis, Connie, "Epiphany," *Miracle and Other Christmas Stories.*

———, "The Winds of Marble Arch" (novella), *Asimov's SF*, Oct./Nov.

Wilson, Colin, "The Tomb of the Old Ones" (novella), *The Antarktos Cycle.*

Wilson, F. Paul, "Aftershock," *Realms of Fantasy*, Dec.

———, "Night Dive," *Cemetery Dance* 32.

Wilson, L. A., Jr., "The Cold Room," *Alfred Hitchcock's Mystery Magazine*, Apr.

Wilson, Mehitobel, "Cutglass," *Chiaroscuro* (web site) 1.

———, "Strays," *Gothic.net* (web site), Apr.

Wilson, Robert Charles, "Plato's Mirror," *Northern Frights 5.*

Winter, Laurel, "Sky Eyes," *F&SF*, Mar.

Winterson, Jeanette, "The Three Friends," *Columbia*, Winter.

Wisman, Ken, "The Voice of the Turtle," *Dark Regions and Horror Magazine*, Winter.

Wolfe, Gene, "A Fish Story," *F&SF*, Oct./Nov.

———, "A Traveler in Desert Lands," *The Last Continent.*

Woodworth, Stephen, "Her," *F&SF*, Feb.

Wuori, G. K., "Glory," *Nude in a Tub.*

Wurster, Michael, "Last Reunion," *Penny Dreadful* 9.

Yasgur, Batya Swift, "Against the Grace of Fire," *Weird Tales* 314.

York, Pat, "You Wandered Off Like a Foolish Child to Break Your Heart and Mine," *Silver Birch, Blood Moon.*

Yourgrau, Barry, "Money," *Haunted Traveller.*

———, "Monsters," Ibid.

———, "Pouches," Ibid.

———, "Upriver," Ibid.

Zucker, Rachel, "Eating in the Underworld" (poem), *Pleiades*, Summer.

The People Behind the Book

Horror editor ELLEN DATLOW was the fiction editor for *Omni Magazine* and *Omni Online* for seventeen years, after which she edited the online magazine *Event Horizon*. She is currently the fiction editor for *SCIFI.COM* (www. scifi.com). She has edited numerous anthologies, including *Alien Sex; Little Deaths; Lethal Kisses; Off Limits; Sirens and other Daemon Lovers; Black Heart, Ivory Bones*; and *A Wolf at the Door* (the last three with Terri Windling). Her most recent anthology is *Vanishing Acts*. She has won five World Fantasy Awards for her editing. She lives in New York City.

Fantasy editor TERRI WINDLING has been an editor of fantasy literature for almost two decades, winning five World Fantasy Awards for her work. She has published more than twenty-five anthologies. As a fiction writer, her books include *The Wood Wife* (winner of the Mythopoeic Award), *A Midsummer Night's Faery Tale*, and *The Raven Queen* (with Ellen Steiber). She also writes a regular column on folklore for *Realms of Fantasy* magazine. As a painter, she has exhibited in a number of museums across the United States and abroad. She divides her time between homes in Devon, England, and Tucson, Arizona.

Packager JAMES FRENKEL edited Dell Books' science fiction and fantasy in the late 1970s and early 1980s, was the publisher of Bluejay Books in the 1980s, and has been a consulting editor for Tor Books for more than ten years. Along with KRISTOPHER O'HIGGINS, assistant extraordinaire and supermodel, and a legion of student interns, Frenkel edits, packages, and agents books in Madison, Wisconsin.

Media critic ED BRYANT is an award-winning writer of science fiction, fantasy, and horror. He has had short fiction published in numerous magazines and anthologies. He has won the Nebula Award for his fiction. His work also includes writing for television. He lives in Denver, Colorado.

Comics critic SETH JOHNSON is a freelance writer whose work ranges from copywriting, writing software manuals and book reviews, to developing the adventure game *Sketch!* He lives in Madison, Wisconsin.

Artist THOMAS CANTY has won the World Fantasy Award for Best Artist. He has painted illustrations for innumerable books, ranging from fantasy and horror to suspense and thrillers. He is also an art director, and has designed many books and book jackets during a career that spans over twenty years. He has painted and designed the covers for every volume of *The Year's Best Fantasy and Horror*. He lives in New England.